P9-CEC-232

BRANDYWINE HUNDRED
BRANCH LIBRARY
1300 FOULK ROAD
WILMINGTON, DE 19803

DYNASTY 34

The Winding Road

Also in the Dynasty series:

DYNASTY

34

The Winding Road

Cynthia Harrod-Eagles

sphere

SPHERE

First published in Great Britain in 2011 by Sphere

Copyright © Cynthia Harrod-Eagles 2011

The moral right of the author has been asserted.

*All characters and events in this publication, other
than those clearly in the public domain, are fictitious
and any resemblance to real persons,
living or dead, is purely coincidental.*

All rights reserved.
No part of this publication may be reproduced,
stored in a retrieval system, or transmitted, in any
form or by any means, without the prior
permission in writing of the publisher, nor be
otherwise circulated in any form of binding or
cover other than that in which it is published and
without a similar condition including this
condition being imposed on the subsequent purchaser.

A CIP catalogue record for this book
is available from the British Library.

ISBN 978-1-84744-143-0

Typeset in Plantin by
Palimpsest Book Production Limited, Falkirk, Stirlingshire
Printed and bound in Great Britain by Clays Ltd, St Ives plc

Papers used by Sphere are from well-managed forests
and other responsible sources.

MIX
Paper from
responsible sources
FSC
www.fsc.org   FSC® C104740

Sphere
An imprint of
Little, Brown Book Group
100 Victoria Embankment
London EC4Y 0DY

An Hachette UK Company
www.hachette.co.uk

www.littlebrown.co.uk

For my readers,
faithful followers of the Morland story,
who always wanted to know
What Happened Next

THE MORLANDS OF MORLAND PLACE

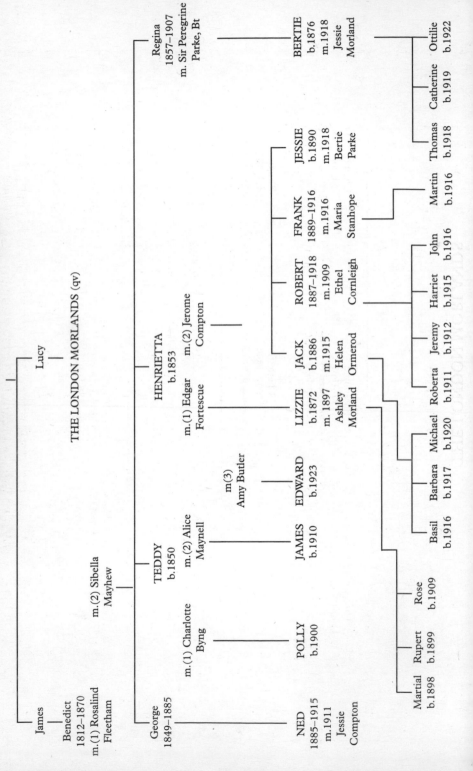

THE LONDON MORLANDS

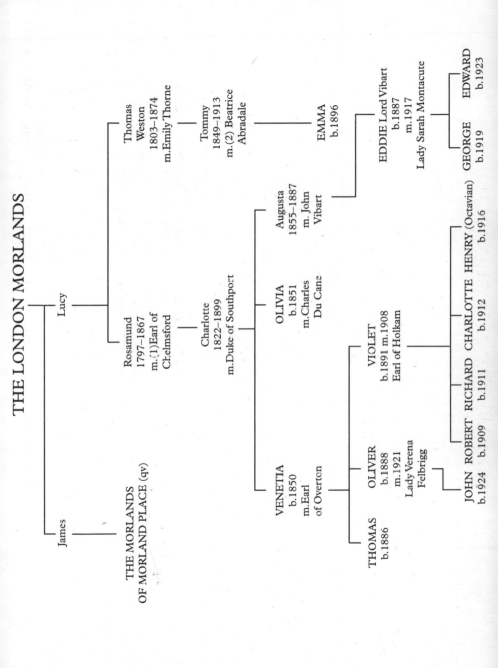

James — Lucy

THE MORLANDS
OF MORLAND PLACE (qv)

Rosamund
1797–1867
m.(1)Earl of
Chelmsford

Thomas
Weston
1803–1874
m.Emily Thorne

Charlotte
1822–1899
m.Duke of Southport

Tommy
1849–1913
m.(2) Beatrice
Abradale

VENETIA
b.1850
m.Earl
of Overton

OLIVIA
b.1851
m.Charles
Du Cane

Augusta
1855–1887
m.John
Vibart

EMMA
b.1896

EDDIE Lord Vibart
b.1887
m.1917
Lady Sarah Montacute

THOMAS
b.1886

OLIVER
b.1888
m.1921
Lady Verena
Felbrigg

VIOLET
b.1891 m.1908
Earl of Holkam

GEORGE
b.1919

EDWARD
b.1923

JOHN
b.1924

ROBERT
b.1909

RICHARD
b.1911

CHARLOTTE
b.1912

HENRY (Octavian)
b.1916

BOOK ONE

New Directions

'Thank you, whatever comes.' And then she turned
And, as the ray of sun on hanging flowers
Fades when the wind hath lifted them aside,
Went swiftly from me. Nay, whatever comes,
One hour was sunlit and the most high gods
May not make boast of any better thing
Than to have watched that hour as it passed.

Ezra Pound: Erat Hora

CHAPTER ONE

January 1925

Was there anything nicer, Polly wondered, than to lie in your warm bed daydreaming while a bitter New York winter morning faded from black to grey outside? She was thinking about the night before, when she had gone to the opening of the Palm Beach Club, a glittering affair of top society people and celebrities, including two movie stars, a congressman and his wife. The band had been good: the Washingtonians – borrowed from the Hollywood Club, which was closed for refurbishment – featuring a 'hot' trumpeter, Bubber Miley, and an up-and-coming jazz pianist, Edward 'Duke' Ellington. There were crowds of onlookers outside, and dozens of press photographers, and as she had walked from the kerb to the door, the flashes had gone off on all sides to record the fact that, Polly Morgan, of Maison Polly, New York's newest, most exciting fashion house, was there.

There had been another photographer inside, and when she had shed her wrap she paused for him, turning to make sure he got the best view of her gown. It was peacock blue and gold, gracefully draped and gathered at the hip, the skirt ending four inches above the ankle to show off the peacock silk stockings and gold shoes. She had painted her eyes in Egyptian style, and wore a close-fitting cap made of overlapping petals of gold foil. Being tall and svelte and beautiful,

3

she was her own best advertisement, and made sure to be seen at every important social event wearing one of her own outfits.

It helped, of course, to enter on the arm of one of New York's most recognisable men, Renfrew Hawthorne Alexander. He was rich, possessed of business acumen that the wealthiest in New York admired – and it didn't hurt, Polly thought, that he was also very handsome. In his mid-thirties, a giant of a man but lithe as a panther, he was whispered, because of his vital dark looks and thick black hair, to be part Apache Indian. A trace of Indian blood conferred a hint of raffishness, which could spell social disaster, but the mamas didn't mind because of his wealth, beautiful clothes and impeccable manners, while it simply made their daughters squirm deliciously.

Polly had met him last fall at a party given by her friend Julie Gilbert Margesson, the mayonnaise heiress – there was a pot of Gilbert's ready-made in every kitchen and delicatessen. She had married Franklin D. Margesson, the beef baron, and was an enthusiastic patron of the arts and a noted hostess. Polly had found Ren's height and looks exciting and almost intimidating, spurring her to be at her sparkling best, and he had plainly taken a shine to her and asked to see her again. They had been photographed together at the opening of the Met season in September, and now, four months later, he had become one of her regular escorts.

The social columns had wondered, in tones varying from the mildly interested to the downright bitchy, whether Ren Alexander would fare any better with the aloof Miss Morland than her previous 'romances', such as Jay Van Plesset, Max Schneider and, most recently, Chase Hazard. Chase was an outstandingly handsome young man and, as well as rejoicing in a splendid name, was a Whitney cousin and very rich. He had been in love with the cool Miss Morland for months. The fact that these liaisons had come to nothing added to

4

her reputation as unattainable. She didn't mind. It was good for business: women wanted to emulate her, have lots of suitors and the confidence to turn them down.

Ren Alexander was older than the others, which Polly liked. He was sophisticated, at ease with the world, and handled things, like helping her with her coat, securing taxis, paying waiters and tipping doormen, expertly and without fuss. He was never at a loss for conversation and, best of all, he never tried to make love to her. She was tired of red-faced, tongue-tied moon-calves who became tiresomely spoony, or stammered that she was the most b-beautiful g-girl they had ever met and wanted to take her home to meet their mothers. Ren looked at her sometimes with a glow in his green-gold eyes that told her he admired her, but that was all. Polly enjoyed being admired, but she wanted no romance.

At the Palm Beach opening, she, Ren Alexander and the Margessons had shared a table with the Roderick Towers – *he* was a stockbroker and son of a diplomat, and *she* had been Flora Whitney, daughter of the racehorse breeder Harry Payne Whitney. Ren was a business adviser to both Tower and Harry Whitney, and Polly suspected she had him to thank that Flora had recently come to her for a gown. It had given her a foothold on a whole new stratum of New York society. The Whitneys were unimaginably rich: Harry had inherited something like fifty million dollars, and then had married a Vanderbilt heiress with a score of millions of her own. They moved in a small circle of the super-rich, who were as far above the merely wealthy as the wealthy were above the ordinary citizen. To gain them as customers would be the most fabulous good fortune.

So it was important for her business that Polly was seen at the opening with these people, but otherwise she had found much of the evening dull. Flora Tower had been moody and withdrawn, Julie unusually preoccupied, and the three men had talked politics. There were times when she had looked across at other tables, where the Bright Young People were chatting about bands, movies, fashions and gossip, and wished herself over there. That had been her set until Ren had entered her life – still was, when she was not with him.

She had never cared about politics at home in England, and the American sort was a mystery. She could barely yet tell the Democrats from the Republicans, and the word 'caucus' always put her in mind of *Alice in Wonderland*. But politics was Ren's greatest passion, besides business and finance. He had many acquaintances in the political world, and was not unknown at the White House, through his business connections with Herbert C. Hoover, the Secretary of Commerce (and wryly dubbed Under-secretary of Everything Else because of his wide influence). When Polly did not see Ren for a few days, she could be fairly sure he was in Washington, talking to important people. It added to his glamour.

The election of Calvin Coolidge over John W. Davis in November 1924 had been a matter of supreme indifference to her, but she gathered that people did not know quite what to make of the new President, which inclined her towards him: she liked enigmas. He was cool, withdrawn and aloof, as people said she was; so she would say, if anyone asked, that she liked him. Having an opinion on the subject went down well with Ren, so she tried to cultivate a few more. But it was hard to concentrate when the swing music called to her so strongly.

She loved to dance for the same reason that she loved hunting at home – because for a time she could be taken over by sheer physical sensation and cease to think about anything. Ren was a good dancer, and he didn't talk much while they danced, for which she was grateful. It was another of the things she liked about him. She was obliged out of politeness to dance with the other men at the table, and they talked, dragging her from her mindless ecstasy to answer them. Rod Tower danced well, but she didn't like him much: he smelt strongly of drink and held her too close. Frank Margesson was a nice man, but dull, and no dancer.

At midnight Rod Tower was for going on somewhere, but no-one else was keen and the party broke up. Ren had seen her home in a taxi through the brilliant, frozen canyons of Manhattan. He had parted with her at the street door of the hotel with his usual proper handshake – except that this time he did not release her hand at once.

'Thank you,' he said. 'Your presence made the evening perfect.' He stood for a moment, looking at her intently, still holding her hand. Then he bowed over it and kissed it. 'May I call you later?'

'Of course,' Polly said, managing to sound cool and unmoved though inwardly she was flustered. He had never kissed her hand before, and she was suddenly and intensely aware of his powerful body and coiled strength so close to her. What if he were to sweep her off her feet – literally? He was big and strong enough to pick her up and make nothing of it, and she would not have been able to stop him. For a split second she had seen herself pinioned helpless in his arms as he kissed her passionately, and something inside her had clenched and shuddered in anticipation.

The next instant he had released her hand and stepped back, and she turned away and walked in, past the porter holding the door for her, feeling faintly ashamed of herself.

Now, in the morning, the image of that moment last night came to her again, and it was disturbing. *He* was disturbing. His big, dark, slightly farouche maleness was almost frightening, but in a strangely delicious way. She forced her mind away from the dangerous Mr Alexander and thought instead of what she had to do at work that morning.

Her cousin Lennie had helped her set up the business and his grandmother Ruth had put up most of the money, a vote of confidence in her that she appreciated. Maison Polly was on 34th, just off Fifth Avenue, and in a little more than a year it had carved out a place for itself in the intensely competitive fashion world. It was tremendously hard work, and she was proud of what she had achieved. Little Polly Morland of Morland Place, who had been nothing but her father's daughter, had taken New York by the scruff of the neck and made it notice her. That was a matter for pride.

She had only to look around her to see the results: her apartment in the Delft was in one of the best parts of the fashionable Upper West Side. Her bedroom was a bower of peach, cream and *café-au-lait*, silk curtains over voile at the windows, close-fitted cream carpet on the floor, dainty mock-nineteenth-century-French furniture with gilded legs, mirror glass everywhere. She thought of the bedroom she had left behind in Morland Place: heavy, dark and oak-panelled, full of dull objects and ugly furniture that had been in the family for centuries; nothing new, nothing chosen by her or for her. And no central heating! In winter there had been ice on the *inside* of the windows until a housemaid came creeping up mouselike to light the fire.

She had come a long way; and most of the time she was too busy to be lonely, or to regret what she had left behind.

The door opened, and her maid, Plummer, came in. 'Your tray, madam.'

Polly sat up, and Plummer placed it across her knees. Tea and toast – Plummer thought it very refined that she took tea rather than coffee. She went to draw the curtains. 'Very sharp out,' she advised. 'Shall I put out the smoke-blue tweed?' Polly nodded, inspecting the jam dish. Imported cherry jam – she had had great difficulty in weaning Plummer off dull grape jelly.

'And Mr Manning is in the parlour with the newspapers, madam,' Plummer went on. 'He said he could wait half an hour if you wanted to take your bath.'

'Oh, no, he can come in,' Polly said. 'Just hand me that bed-jacket.' It was quilted peach satin trimmed with marabou and, with its high neck and long sleeves, ought to cover her enough to satisfy even old sobersides Lennie. 'Have you given him coffee?'

'I was just about to, madam.'

'Bring it to him here.'

Cousin Lennie was a cousin at some removes, but she had known him for so many years – he had first come to stay at Morland Place when she was only fourteen – that she looked on him as a brother.

He, however, did not wish to see Polly as a sister but as something much dearer, which made being received in her bedroom not entirely comfortable for him. He came in hesitantly and, for a moment, avoided looking at her directly as she sat up in bed.

'I could have waited,' he said.

'I'm perfectly decent,' she said, with a shade of impatience. 'I thought you'd have been gone by now. Weren't you leaving first thing this morning?'

Lennie took a chair from beside the window and brought it closer. He was tall, and handsome in an unemphatic way – in fact, what you noticed most about his face was its *niceness* rather than good looks. He had also proved an adroit businessman. He had built up a radio business just at the time radio was becoming popular, so that now he had shops all over New York and up and down the east coast, and was in the process of building a factory in New Jersey to replace the muddle of workshops from which he had started. Nice, ordinary, kind Lennie was on his way to becoming very rich.

'That was the plan,' he said, sitting down, 'but something came up last night at the factory, and as I was the only one who could sort it out, I was there all night.'

She eyed him over her teacup. 'You look very good for someone who hasn't been to bed.'

9

'Oh, I went home and bathed and changed, but I'd missed my train. I'll have to go tomorrow instead.'

Polly was impressed by the equanimity with which he was taking it. Crossing America, rather than travelling up and down the coast, was a big undertaking. It took four days and three nights, and involved a Pullman train, the Century, to Chicago, a bus or taxi from one Chicago station to the other, and then the Chief to the west coast. In summer it was too hot, in winter it was too cold, and it was rarely safe to open the windows. It was a crowded, reasonably uncomfortable five days lost from your life, and the only good thing to say about it was that it was better than doing the same journey by covered wagon.

Plummer came in with his coffee; when she had gone again, he went on, 'Wouldn't it be grand if one could fly? I wonder no-one's thought of starting up an airship service. It would have to go a long way round to avoid the mountains, but with comfortable accommodation on board that wouldn't matter.'

'All the way to California?' Polly said, spreading cherry jam thickly on a slice of toast. She offered him the slice, and he took it absently, so she spread herself another. 'What exactly are you going there for, anyway?'

'To see if conditions are right to start a string of stores along the west coast, the way I have over this side. A lot of rich people live in Los Angeles.'

'Beverly Hills?' she said. 'That's where all the cinema stars live, isn't it?'

'So they say. Think what a good advertisement it would be if one of my radiograms was photographed at Pickfair.'

'I've read Douglas Fairbanks and Mary Pickford give fabulous dinners,' Polly said. 'Everyone important goes, not just film actors – though they say Charlie Chaplin lives right next door. Do you think you'll get invited?'

'I will be one day, when everyone who is anyone has a

Manning's radio. The west coast is ripe for picking: radios, radiograms – and for those beach parties, I'm designing a new portable gramophone.' He smiled. 'I thought Pola Negri might like one in lizardskin, with her initials picked out in diamonds, so she can dance on the sand for Rudolph Valentino.'

'Oh, you have it all worked out!' Polly laughed. 'Hollywood will eat you up. You'll have your head turned by some sultry star and never come back to us.'

'I'll always come back,' he said seriously.

She turned her eyes away. She didn't want him to think she was encouraging him.

He saw this with resignation. He knew she was nursing a broken heart – some man she had loved who had been killed during the war – but he was willing to wait, his whole life if need be. She had said she could never love anyone else – well, neither could he. 'You won't get yourself into any trouble while I'm away, will you?' he said lightly.

She looked at him again, and decided he was joking. 'No, what trouble could I get into?' she said.

'I'm afraid last night's triumph might have turned your head.'

'After last night's triumph, as you call it, all the new orders will keep me too busy for mischief.'

'Then I'm surprised you're idling in bed, and not in your office already.'

'I shall get up as soon as you've gone. But I'm glad you called in.'

'I couldn't go without saying goodbye. And to tell you you looked extremely beautiful last night in your Egyptian costume.'

'How do you know?' she asked suspiciously.

'I've seen the papers,' he said. 'A very nice photo of you in the lobby.' He looked at her humorously. 'Why? Did you think I was hanging around outside the Palm Beach to catch a glimpse of you, like some poor hopeless swain?'

11

She had the grace to blush. 'The headdress wasn't actually Egyptian, but nobody noticed. I copied it from a Phrygian cap in the museum. It was too hot for dancing in, really,' she admitted.

'It looked good, though. No sign of the Tut-Ankh-Amun craze fading?'

'It had better not, before my spring collection, or I'll be ruined.'

He looked down at the half-eaten toast in his hand to avoid her eyes as he said diffidently, 'You and Alexander looked handsome side by side in the paper. He's a striking fellow.'

'I suppose so,' she said cautiously.

'Rich, too. I wonder how come he's not married by now.'

'Perhaps he prefers being single,' Polly said. 'Some people do, you know.'

She didn't say, 'Like me, for instance,' but he heard the thought anyway. He looked up, and smiled, lighting his face in a way that made him seem very attractive. Polly felt kind towards him, and sorry. She knew why *he* was still single, and it made her sad.

'Well, I'd better get going,' he said. 'Much as I'd like to sit and chat with you all day . . .'

She saw him staring absently at his piece of toast and said, 'Give that to me. You don't want to get jam on your suit.'

'Jam,' he said. 'How English. One day, I must introduce you to the delights of peanut butter and jelly.'

'Sounds revolting,' she said cheerfully.

'You mustn't belittle the very heart of American cuisine.'

He borrowed her napkin to wipe his fingers, and stooped to kiss her cheek. 'Be good,' he said. And then he was gone.

She had a long-standing appointment for luncheon with Lennie's Granny Ruth. With her late start she would have been glad to cancel, but one didn't 'chuck' a grand Southern lady like her, so she took herself along at the due time to Brevoort's Hotel. Granny Ruth was devoted to the Café there, saying it was the only place in New York where you could get real French food. Since she had never been out of America, Polly wondered how she knew; but it was not a thing to say to her, unless you wanted to feel the sharp side of her tongue.

Ruth had virtually brought Lennie up, after his mother died when he was a baby. She lived with him and Lennie's father, Patrick, an architect, in a big old-fashioned apartment off Sixth. Lennie said there was plenty of room for all of them, and until he was married there was no point in his having a separate establishment. Polly had been around them all long enough now to know the real reason: Ruth would have been heartbroken if he went. She would never have shown it, though: she was seventy-nine and had lived through the Civil War in the South and the even more terrible Reconstruction after it. Grit and pride were bone-deep in her. A lady doesn't complain, she had been told every day as a rebellious child; and in old age such rules now sustained her. She never complained – and her back never touched the chair she sat in.

She was glad to see Polly, and rose to greet her with a kiss as if she had never known what stiffness was.

'I brought you this,' Polly said. 'I got an extra pot when I ordered it.'

Ruth took the little pot and looked at the label. '*Confiture de Cerises*,' she read. She had a hint of Southern to her accent even yet, and the French sounded pleasant in her soft, slow voice. 'How nice. Thank you, honey. You know how I like Cont'nental jelly. Sit down, dear, and tell me what you've been doing. How was the opening last night? Was your costume a success?'

Polly told her everything – Ruth liked details. 'There was

13

a very good photograph of the gown in the paper this morning, and I think there'll be more in the Sundays,' she concluded.

'Lennie saw it this morning,' Ruth said. 'He said you and Alexander make a handsome couple.'

'We're not a couple,' Polly said, sensing disapproval.

'*Are* you not?' Ruth gave her a penetrating look. 'You seem to be spending an awful lot of time with him lately.'

'He's just one of my escorts,' Polly said, trying to sound indifferent; but his big, male image was in her mind again, making her self-conscious.

Ruth noticed the blush. 'How much do you know about him?' she demanded.

'Hardly anything, but what does it matter? I enjoy his company, and he's a good dancer,' Polly said. 'What more do I need to know?'

'Nothing, dear, not a thing, as long as you don't mean to marry him.'

'Well, I don't,' Polly said, annoyed and trying not to show it.

Ruth tapped her hand. 'Hoity-toity. I'm allowed to ask you tricksy questions. What's the good of being old as Methuselah if you can't be cussed and annoy people? Now Ren Alexander's mighty rich, that I *do* know, and he's good-looking, if you like that sort of thing. Better than that washed-out Hazard boy who's been making a fool of himself over you this half-year, anyway. But he has no family that I've heard of, and he seems to have come from nowhere. And I never can make out what *is* his line of business.'

Polly didn't really know either. 'The business of making money, I guess.'

'Is he a stockbroker?' Ruth suggested.

'I don't think so. I know what one of *those* is. I think he just invests money and makes a profit and invests the profit in something else.'

'A speculator,' Ruth said, with a hint of disdain.

14

'Maybe. But some very rich people seek his advice, so he must know what he's doing.'

'Hmph,' said Ruth, unconvinced. She liked there to be something tangible behind money. It should come from building railroads or ranching cattle or digging up diamonds. 'Be that as it may, a man with no family's not to be trusted. Money comes easy and goes easy when it's not family money, and doesn't have its feet under some good, solid table. So if he makes you an offer, you mind and take advice before you give him an answer.'

'There won't *be* an offer,' Polly said, 'because he isn't sweet on me. And if there was, I wouldn't accept it. I never intend to marry.'

Ruth eyed her sternly. 'Don't you know what makes God laugh? It's girls saying, "I never intend to marry"! Someone will come for you one day, and pick you right off the tree like a ripe big peach. Just 'cause some fellow you fancied got killed in the war don't mean you can waste yourself away.'

'I don't know what you—' Polly began, and bit her lip, disconcerted that Ruth knew so much.

Ruth's scolding tone softened. 'I know, honey, I know. I loved my husband Pick so much it hurt, and when he got killed at Manassas I thought I'd die. But people like you and me don't die. God has better things for us to do.' Her scowl reappeared. 'Just don't you go marrying any old person because you think your heart's in the ice-box. It'll thaw one day, and when it does, you don't want to be stuck married to someone you don't give a rap about.'

'I don't need to marry *anyone*,' Polly said, annoyed again. Why did everyone feel they could tell her what to do? Lennie did it all the time – and Cousin Ashley, who had charge of her money, and his wife Lizzie, who seemed to feel she ought to be a mother to Polly. *I'm twenty-five years old, almost,* she thought. *When do I get to say what I do?*

'Need and want are different things. Besides, a woman's

15

not complete without a man, any more'n the other way round.' Ruth saw the line of stubbornness appear between Polly's brows. 'You can make mule faces at me all you want,' she said, 'but *someone's* got to look out for you. You think you're up to snuff, but you're still wet behind the ears, 'specially when it comes to men. It's a dam' disgrace that your father lets you live in an apartment all on your own.'

'The Morgan twins did,' Polly said, her frown disappearing now they were on a familiar circuit. 'They had a town house on Fifth together *and* they were only sixteen.'

'And look how *that* turned out,' Ruth said with triumph. 'Both married at seventeen to shocking unsuitable men – Thelma to that Converse divorcé, and that won't last, and Mercedes, or Gloria as she calls herself now—'

'You can't say she didn't marry well,' Polly interrupted.

'If you think money is the only thing that matters. Reggie Vanderbilt's more than twice her age, and—' She remembered too late the reason Polly had made her home in New York and refused to go home: that her father had remarried, a woman thirty years his junior. She changed tack quickly: 'And that's enough of talking about other people's business. I wonder how far Lennie's got. What do you think of his plan to open up on the west coast?'

Polly gladly accepted the new topic, and the conversation continued on more comfortable lines.

The winter day had ended by the time she left the office, stepping out into the bustle of Fifth Avenue, dark and brilliant, full of streetlamps and headlamps, lit shop windows, slow-moving traffic and brisk pedestrians heading for the bus stops and subway stations. It had turned even colder, biting at her nose and ears, so cold it even hurt her eyeballs. Paper-sellers had the evening editions out, their breath smoking up on the frozen air as they shouted the headlines;

16

street vendors were bobbing about beside their little carts, blowing on their fingers, and there was a smell of pretzels and hot nuts on the air. Polly felt a sense of exhilaration. Manhattan lay before her, promising her that, whatever she chose to do, she would have an exciting evening. The sense of freedom the place gave her filled her with energy. The possibilities seemed endless to a bright, healthy young woman with money of her own.

She took a cab home. Plummer was waiting for her. 'Some flowers arrived for you, madam,' she said, her voice more impressed than such a normal event warranted.

They'd be from Lennie, Polly thought – it was like him to send her flowers because he was going to be out of town for a while. Or possibly Chase, still pursuing the impossible.

When she saw them, she saw why Plummer was impressed. January was a difficult month for flowers, with nothing but rather strained-looking hothouse blooms. But when Polly drew apart the waxed paper, she saw white roses – a dozen of them – and from the scent that arose she knew they had been grown outside. Definitely not Chase. But where would Lennie get real roses in January?

'They must have cost the earth,' she murmured. And *white* roses, so unusual, where a lesser man would have sent yellow (safe) or pink (sentimental). What a foolish gesture! She was touched and just a little exasperated, for she had made her feelings known to him so often. She took up the card that lay on top.

Nothing less than white roses would do for the most beautiful woman in New York. In admiration, R.H. Alexander.

Polly felt her cheeks warm at the words. She looked up and saw from Plummer's expression that she had read the

17

card before Polly came in. It was annoying, but there was nothing one could do. Any servant would do the same – the difference was that an English servant would have been better at concealing it. 'Put them in water, will you?' she said shortly.

She had hardly got to her room when the house telephone rang, and a moment later Plummer appeared, taut with excitement, and said, 'Mr Alexander is downstairs, madam. Shall I have them send him up?'

This was unexpected. He had asked if he could call her, which meant the telephone. Or had she misunderstood him? Had he said, 'May I call *on* you'? She glanced quickly at her reflection in the nearest mirror and saw that she was tidy and that her smoke-blue tweed two-piece was becoming. And it was not yet time to dress for the evening. 'Very well. I'll see him for a few minutes.'

Plummer went away and she took the chance to wash her hands, pat her face with cold water and brush her hair. Looking in the mirror dispassionately she saw that she was beautiful, but her habitual control of her feelings made her expression remote, as if she had been carved out of alabaster, and her short-cropped hair added to the image of a young Greek hero, carved in stone. For an instant the reflection didn't seem like her: it was like looking at a separate person, and she felt a frisson of fear and loneliness. Where was Miss Polly Morland, the belle of Yorkshire, who had given and taken love so readily? She had run from the Old World when Erich was killed – Erich, her only love, whom no-one must ever know about, because he was a German, and to love him was the worst sin she could ever commit. But it seemed so long ago, now, like a story from another age. What was she doing here, all alone, so far from home?

She shook the thoughts away, turned from the mirror and wondered what Alexander wanted. Perhaps to secure her for some occasion coming up. But he could have done that by

18

telephone. She heard the apartment doorbell and the sounds of arrival, and went out.

He looked even bigger and darker in her parlour – as the drawing-room was called at the Delft – like some large, anomalous animal the room was not designed for. *Too wild for polite spaces*, she thought. *The buffalo in the parlour.* The absurdity of the thought told her she was nervous. Plummer had his hat in her hand and was helping him off with his overcoat, spotted with damp on the shoulders. He had dark shadows under his eyes, as though he had not slept last night – she imagined him going straight on to do business when he left her at the door.

She needed to speak before she lost nerve. 'Thank you for the flowers. They're beautiful.' He bowed his head in acknowledgement; his bright eyes never wavered from her face. 'But wherever did you get white roses at this time of year? And with such a lovely scent?'

'Florida,' he said. 'They bloom all year there. I had them flown up.'

The concept struck her dumb for a moment. Florida was a thousand miles away. What on earth would it cost to send an aeroplane all that way and back? That he should go to so much trouble and vast expense merely to give her flowers was extraordinary, and somehow horrible. It was out of all proportion. It gave her no pleasure. 'I didn't know you had an aeroplane,' she said falteringly.

He saw he had made a misjudgement, and smoothly covered it. 'I don't – not yet, anyhow. But there are regular mail flights between Miami and New York. It was a matter of a telephone call or two to have them put on board.'

'Oh,' she said, and felt only partly relieved. It was still too much. 'Thank you.'

'I wanted you to have the best. Nothing less would satisfy me.'

Ah, she thought, it was his pride, not my worth, that

prompted it. The idea made her more comfortable. 'Won't you sit down?' she invited.

'Thank you,' he said. 'I won't stay long, but there is something I want to say to you. I meant to make an appointment, but I happened to be passing, and the doorman said you had just come in, so I thought I'd take a chance. Is it convenient?'

'Yes, quite,' Polly said, bewildered. It sounded as if he had some business proposition to put to her. Was he going to invite her to invest in something? Or did he want to invest in her fashion house? Or perhaps some pet charity . . . 'Do go on.'

He seemed to take a moment to order his thoughts, sitting square and upright in the chair he had chosen – which, being imitation French Empire like the rest of the furniture, hardly seemed up to the job. *The buffalo in the— No, stop thinking that!* She had taken the seat opposite, and felt strangely exposed to his gaze. She had never been alone with him in a private room before. Of course he would behave himself *– but what if he didn't?*

'Miss Morland,' he began, 'we have known each other for some months now, but I have never spoken to you about my plans for the future. When I came east, ten years ago, I came to conquer new worlds. I have always been ambitious. I believe ambition, drive and determination are important qualities in a man. In fact, in my view, a man is hardly a man without them.'

'Indeed,' Polly murmured, since he seemed to want something from her at that point.

He went on: 'I had a little capital, and in those ten years I have put it to good use. You have heard me spoken of, I'm sure, as a wealthy man. I'm respected in the world of finance and of business. And I dine with the best families in New York. In short, I have a social position as well as a comfortable fortune. So you may ask yourself, what fresh worlds are there to conquer? Should I not be satisfied and rest on my laurels?'

Polly looked at him, bemused but intrigued. Why was he telling her all this? But she saw that a truly ambitious man could never reach the end of his ambitions. He must always go on. 'No,' she said. 'I don't think you would be able to do that.'

He seemed pleased by her answer. 'I should have known *you* would understand. No, I cannot stand still. Money is nothing without power, and power lies in the world of politics. I have laid the groundwork, developed the contacts. You have heard me speak, I dare say, of Mr Herbert Hoover. When he was appointed Secretary of Commerce, it was looked upon as a minor cabinet post, but he had his own ideas. Commerce is the backbone of the country, and the foundation for everything Americans care about.'

'Yes,' said Polly.

'Now that Mr Coolidge has won a second term, on Hoover's recommendation he has asked me to join him. I am to be financial adviser to the government. It is a salaried position, and I shall have my own office in Wall Street and, more importantly, the President's ear.'

Polly thought it appropriate at that point to murmur congratulations, though the finer points of the American governmental system were a blank to her.

Alexander went on: 'But that's only the beginning. Hoover is on the up, and he's apt to be president one day – if not next time, the time after. And when he is, I shall have my pick of secretaryships. And when he's done his two terms, Miss Morland, with his backing I shall secure the Republican nomination, and stand for election. And I shall win.' His eyes glowed.

Polly was gazing at him, mesmerised. 'I'm sure of it,' she said.

'I shall be President of the United States. Maybe as early

as 1937 – twelve years from now. I shall be forty-seven then, only a year older than Ulysses S. Grant, the youngest president ever to take office.'

She could see it in her mind's eye. She had seen photographs of other presidents taking the oath of office, and it was easy to transpose Ren's impressive, mighty form, to see him in the White House, making speeches, hosting banquets for foreign leaders, reviewing troops. He would be the most important man in the world. It was a dazzling prospect. 'You will make a fine president,' she said, captured by the image.

He looked at her intently for a long moment. 'You don't ask why I tell you all this.'

She was silent. She didn't know. *He can't be here asking for a donation to his campaign funds, not from me, with all his wealth.*

'I will tell you what you will not ask,' he said, leaning forward and clasping his hands on his knees. 'A man in the public eye must have a wife. Above all, the President needs a consort. She must be the right woman. A woman of beauty, poise, intelligence and conduct. A woman fitted for the highest rank. This great country deserves nothing less. Miss Morland, you are that woman. You are fitted by nature and accomplishment to be the First Lady of the land. And I have come to admire you very deeply. Will you accept your destiny? Will you marry me?'

He thrust out his hand, palm upwards, as though intending to run off with her there and then to Washington.

Polly was too astonished to speak. It had all happened so suddenly, and the prospect was dizzying. Her usual smooth refusal of *I never mean to marry* did not enter her mind. This was a proposal of a completely different order. Ren Alexander was no rich society brat. He was a man of power and consequence, so different from her other escorts that she had never viewed him as a possible suitor. She had not seen this

22

coming. He *loved* her? He wanted to *marry* her? She had no answer ready.

She heard herself say, 'I was not expecting this.'

He smiled. 'And yet you remain so composed. One of the many things I admire about you is the way you are never at a loss. You will bring great distinction to the White House.'

Ah! He had introduced a new figure into her imaginings. There, at the top of a noble staircase, stood the tall, striking figure of President Alexander, immaculate in evening dress, welcoming distinguished guests from all over the world; and now, at his side, she could see the First Lady, exquisitely gowned as always, glittering with jewels, receiving, with her famed poise, princes and presidents and prime ministers – perhaps even the King of England himself. It was a prospect too glorious to turn away from. Her ambition was piqued. Was this astonishing dream really possible? *First Lady of the land.* It was flattering, intoxicating – it was irresistible.

He spoke again, his hand still outstretched. 'Miss Morland, I am a passionate man. What I want I *will* have. I know I should give you time to think about this, but I *must* have an answer. At least tell me what you are thinking. Is the idea completely abhorrent to you?'

'Oh, no!' she said, and her voice sounded faint to her and almost wild. 'Not that – not at all.'

He stood up abruptly, and she stood too, automatically. He was very close to her: she could feel the heat of his body, smell the scent of him, and it made her tremble. 'Miss Morland,' he said softly, but with no less force. 'Polly. You are beautiful and desirable and I have never met a woman I admired more.' She looked up into his green-gold eyes. There seemed so much of him, he blanked out the rest of the world, even thought itself. She felt his breath on her face as he said insistently, 'Will you marry me? Say yes, and I will bring you the whole world and lay it at your feet.'

It was not possible to go back. 'Yes,' she said.

She saw his look of triumph. Then he put his arms round her. They were hard as iron with muscle, and the heat of him was tremendous. The furnace of him engulfed her. He bent his head, his lips were against hers, he was kissing her. It was as well he was holding her, for her legs seemed boneless. He was lifting her slightly off her feet. It was something like her imagining of the night before, only far more intense, and she felt the same clenching sensation deep inside her. His great presence and strength, the potency of his sexual being, the inner flame that was his drive and spirit and self-hood, were almost too much for her. She was excited – and afraid.

He removed his mouth from hers to say, 'My beautiful Polly. My wife. You will be all mine.'

And, helpless as a mouse in a hawk's grasp, she said, again, 'Yes.'

CHAPTER TWO

The moment the official announcement appeared in the press, the newsmen gathered outside the Delft and Maison Polly. Polly dressed extra carefully that day, and went out to pose artfully, first at the one door and then at the other. She smiled, and responded to the requests to remove her glove and show the ring, but answered no questions. That evening, Alexander was seen arriving at her building in evening dress with red roses (hothouse, no scent, but they were for public consumption), then escorting her into the Ritz-Carlton for dinner (their famed *crème vichyssoise glacée* and lobster, said the society columns) and later into a Broadway theatre showing the latest O'Neill play.

The photographs the following day showed the big dark man with the sylph-like golden girl on his arm, and the columns became rapturous about the couple and the match. They described her midnight blue pleated silk evening gown, and talked about her fashion house, and by the end of the week there had been big spreads in two magazines, and speculation had begun about the wedding gown the lovely designer would create for herself.

Polly was well satisfied with the publicity so far. She was not so pleased to be summoned – there was no other word for it – by Ruth on the Sunday evening. She had sent the old lady a letter announcing the engagement but had not been in person to see her, and had refused two invitations

25

to visit her since then. But there was no getting out of it. She would have to face her sooner or later.

Ruth received her in her drawing-room where she was sitting alone – Lennie was still in California and Patrick was at a meeting. She did not rise to greet her, as she usually did, and when Polly approached to kiss her, she drew her head back and gestured to a chair. 'No kissing! I don't know if I'm ready for that. Sit down there. Is that your engagement ring? Flashy, ain't it?' From the ring she looked up into Polly's face, and studied it for a moment, unsmiling. Polly at first held her gaze defiantly, but at last had to look down, and felt herself blushing – though some of it was annoyance.

'So you're engaged,' Ruth said. 'What are you up to, miss?'

'Up to?' Polly said feebly.

'Don't play with me. Not a fortnight since, you told me that Alexander man wasn't sweet on you.'

'I didn't know he was.'

'Nor you on him.'

This was harder to answer. But why should she have to? Polly closed her lips. Ruth stared at her, her eyes hard and bright. 'He asked me to marry him, and I said yes,' Polly said at last. 'Why is that so hard to understand?'

'Don't sass me.'

'I'm over twenty-one,' Polly said, with rising annoyance. 'I can marry who I like. And what's wrong with Ren, anyway?'

'Oh, it's *Ren*, now, is it?'

'He's handsome, rich, smart, and anyone would think him a good match. I just don't know what you've got against him.'

'I don't know either, honey. It's just you're rushing into it hard and fast, like as if you feel guilty about something. And I don't hear you mention love. Marriage is more than a pretty dress and a bunch of flowers, you know.'

Polly felt cold all down her spine. For a moment the

26

onrush of events since Ren had proposed was checked and held motionless, so that her thoughts and feelings, shaken free of the momentum, were able to form fully. Marry Ren Alexander? The idea was suddenly frightening, and so strange to her that it was as if it must have been someone else who had said 'yes' – the Polly in the newspapers, not the real one who lived inside Polly's head. Why was she marrying him? She knew nothing about him. He was so alien, so much outside her, that he might have come from another planet. Was that what marriage should be?

And yet – and yet . . . He was exciting. *It* was exciting. It was an adventure, and she would be poor-spirited to turn it down. How could she go back now to the familiar routines of her old life, and never know what would have happened? She couldn't go back. It was too late, anyway. It was in the newspapers. It was in the public realm. It *would* happen, whatever she felt, because everyone now expected it. And she did want it. She remembered the heat of his body and that inexplicable convulsion deep inside her when he had kissed her. She wanted him; she must have him.

'Of course I know that,' she answered Ruth at last. 'You mustn't worry.'

Ruth looked at her carefully, and when she spoke, she sounded tired. 'Did you find out what he did?'

Polly answered indirectly: 'He's been offered a government position by Mr Coolidge. Financial adviser to the government. It's just the first step – he's going to be president one day.'

'Oh, is that so?' Ruth said. 'Well, that makes all the difference. And you'll be the President's wife. How nice.'

It was plainly sarcasm. Polly narrowed her eyes. 'I *will* marry him.'

Ruth sighed. 'Well, if that's the way it is, all I can do is try to make things easier for you. In case you want to run away some day.'

'I won't—' Polly began, but Ruth held up her hand.

'Oh, hush up,' she said, but quite kindly. 'I'm too tired now for argufying. Just listen. Can you do that?' Polly was silent. 'You know that I own all but a little piece of your business. I always meant to leave you my share when I died, but I was going to hold on to it till then, in case it hit a rocky patch. Well, I'm still going to give it to you, but I'll make it my wedding gift. I'll make the whole thing over to you. I want you to have something to fall back on, case it all goes wrong.'

Polly was touched. 'Thank you. You're very kind. It won't all go wrong – but thank you,' she said hastily, as Ruth looked about to get cross again. 'I don't know why you're so good to me.'

''Cause I see a little bit of me in you,' Ruth said. She leaned forward and cupped her hand round Polly's cheek. 'Course, I was never so beautiful as you – and that's your burden, honey. You'll find that out one day. It's hard for a man to see you, past all that beauty. But the man who loves you in spite of it, not because of it – that's the man you'll find happiness with. Whether that's Ren Alexander or not, I don't know, but you heed my words. You think I'm a mad old woman and talking hogwash, but you'll know one day I was right.'

Polly put her hand over Ruth's, then drew it from her cheek and kissed it. 'I don't think you're mad, or old, and you never talk hogwash.'

Ruth snatched her hand away, and scowled ferociously. 'Oh, don't I? But you never heed me, all the same! Go on and leave me now. I'm getting mad again, and getting mad ain't good for my heart. Go on!' Polly rose, looked at Ruth uncertainly, and turned away.

But when she got to the door, the old lady called out, 'Mind I get an invitation to the wedding! The best seat, right down the front where I can see and hear everything. And all the parties, too.'

28

'You wouldn't like to come on the honeymoon?' Polly enquired.

'Sassy! Don't think I wouldn't!' They smiled at each other for a moment, and then Ruth recollected herself and scowled again. 'Might as well get what I can out of a sorry situation,' she muttered. 'Go 'way, missy. I've not finished being cross with you. Go on, now. I need to rest.'

In North Yorkshire the snow was down. For three weeks a bitter, flaying wind had been blowing straight from the north; then one night it had veered north-easterly, gathering moisture over the sea, bringing the snow, thick, relentless masses of it, to settle onto the already frozen ground. Wise stockmen had smelt it coming and got their beasts in, to fold-yard, close and barn, and just as well. The snow fell so heavily, obliterating the world in a whirling dance of white death, that for three days it was impossible to get out.

After three days the food and water they had left with the animals would be running out; after five days they would start to die. But on the fourth day the wind dropped and backed northerly, the snow stopped, and the freeze set in again under still air and a cruel, empty sky. The Riding lay paralysed under a shroud of snow, as far as the eye could see: rolling billows of white, pierced here and there by the black etching of hedge tops and naked trees. Poets and artists might be moved by the sight, but it was a silent and terrible beauty, bringing death to small creatures, birds, livestock, old folk.

At Twelvetrees House, Jessie and Bertie, their servants and three children were snug and comfortable. Their new house was solidly built of stone, with thick walls and a tight roof, and Jessie had learned prudent housekeeping from her mother Henrietta at Morland Place, so the larder and store-rooms were full and there was an ample stock of coal and wood.

The older children, Thomas, who was six, and Catherine, five, found the novelty exciting at first, were thrilled by the blizzards and not being able to go to school, but grew restless as the confinement continued, and had to be found things to do. Two-year-old Ottilie's routines were hardly changed, except that her daily walk was cancelled, but having her brother and sister home more than compensated for that: they were gods to her.

Jessie and Bertie were concerned about the horses, and as soon as the blizzards stopped they set out, with every available hand, to dig a path through to the stables. The daily workers had not been able to get in, so the resident staff were struggling with the feeding, grooming and mucking-out, and were relieved to see help arriving. As soon as the yard had been cleared and a straw ring laid down, there was led exercise to provide for all the horses. Jessie even brought down Thomas and Catherine, well bundled up, to help with that. They could walk round and round leading a horse as well as anyone.

Bertie was worried about his cattle – a herd of pedigreed dairy Shorthorns – out at Bishop Winthorpe, but the roads were impassable and there was nothing he could do about it. The stockman was not, of course, on the telephone, so there was no way of getting a report on what was going on. He just had to trust his man and hope for the best.

The telephone line to Morland Place had gone out on the first day of the blizzard, but Jessie was not worried about their safety. Morland Place had withstood the weather for five hundred years: only Cromwell's cannon – the Morlands had been Royalists – had ever breached the walls. It was a secure haven for her mother, Henrietta, her uncle Teddy and his wife Amy, the servants and the eight assorted children. Five of them were the children of Henrietta's two sons who had died in the war. One, Laura, was the daughter of their former chaplain: invalided out of the army with shell-shock, he had suffered a relapse when his wife died, and was now living with the brothers at Ampleforth. Of Teddy's two sons, James, who was fourteen, had gone back to Eton after the Christmas recess before the snow started; his half-brother, Edward, almost two, was the 'baby' of the nurseries.

When Bertie finally judged it possible to get through from Twelvetrees to Morland Place, Jessie insisted on going with him. 'It will be very rough going,' he warned.

'I just want to get out,' Jessie said.

'You want to make sure your mother's all right,' he countered.

'Well, baby Edward had a cold, and if she caught it from him, you know what she's like – she won't go to bed unless someone makes her.'

They wrapped up in their warmest clothes and stoutest boots, and resisted the wails of Thomas, who wanted to go too. 'I want to see Grandma,' he cried. 'I want to play with John and Martin.'

'It's too hard a walk for you,' said his heartless mother. 'We're not even taking the dogs, and they have four legs each.'

The going was harder than she had anticipated. Sometimes the frozen crust would bear her weight, but too often she found herself struggling through knee-deep, even waist-deep drifts. It was exhausting. 'Do you want to go back?' Bertie asked, noticing she was flagging.

'No,' she said shortly. She needed all her breath. 'Come too far now.'

But at last they came in sight of Morland Place, sitting square and solid, as permanent as if it had grown up out of the ground, with the chimneys showing above the outer walls, sending comfortable wreaths of smoke up into the still air.

Now the going was easier, and when they reached the home stables, the path was clear, worn by the traffic back and forth from the house. A bundled-up figure came hurrying out as they passed the entrance to the yard. It was Eddoes, the head man, who had been a stable boy up at the house years ago and had come back to them after the war, knowing no other home. He drew himself up before Bertie in a soldierly way, and snatched off his cap, showing the bald area on the side of his head where there was a piece of shrapnel in his brain that the doctors did not dare remove. The scarf wrapped round his lower face was crusted with ice where his breath had frozen on it.

He had come out to tell them that the postman had got through that morning for the first time since the snow started.

'We haven't had anything yet,' Jessie said.

'Yours is there too, sir, m'lady. T'postie didn't reckon he could make it out to Twelvetrees, the idle beggar. Master said one of us s'd take it oop later, on'y you're here now, m'lady. But there's sad news.'

'What is it?' Jessie asked, with a feeling of apprehension. The world around seemed too still; two crows in the big oak across the track set up a raucous yarking, call and answer, with another far off in a tall elm. She was glad of Bertie's solid arm under her gloved hand.

'It's very sad and shocking, Miss Jessie,' Eddoes said, forgetting himself for a moment. 'It's that poor Father Palgrave – though Mr Sawry says master said it was no blame t' th' holy brothers, no neglect or owt like that.'

'What happened to Father Palgrave?' Jessie asked. Servants always liked to drag out bad news in this lugubrious way.

'Dead, miss – m'lady,' Eddoes said impressively. 'T' poor gentleman walked out into t' snow one day and no-one missed him until it was ower late. They searched for him, but by the time they found him he were dead – starved o' cold like a winter bird, Miss Jessie, all curled up in a snowdrift.' This poetic flight moved him so much he had to blow his nose.

'But how dreadful,' Jessie said, exchanging a look with Bertie. 'The poor man must have been terribly disturbed.'

'Aye, miss – m'lady – out of his mind wit' t' shell-shock, poor gentleman. He wouldn'ta knew what he was doing.'

'I'm sure that's right,' Bertie said. 'Thank you for warning us, Eddoes.'

'Yes, sir,' Eddoes said. He looked at Jessie. 'They say it's a kindly death, Miss Jessie. You come over all warm at the end and go to sleep. So they say.'

They walked on, sobered by the news. 'It's perhaps for the best, as far as Palgrave's concerned,' Bertie said after a moment. 'He was in torment all the time.'

'But I thought he was getting better, with the brothers,' Jessie said. Bertie heard the tone of her voice and stopped, looking down to see the tears on her cheeks. She was remembering all the good things about Denis Palgrave – his gaiety, his intelligence, his courage in the face of his illness, his love for his wife Maria, his devotion to the children in his charge.

He pulled out a handkerchief and handed it to her. 'No-one can know what goes on in a fractured mind,' he said. 'We can heal so much of the body, but not that – never that.'

'Mother's going to be so upset,' she said. 'And Uncle Teddy – he felt responsible for him.'

'He did everything he could.'

'And – oh dear – that poor child!' Jessie exclaimed. 'Poor little Laura! Now she's lost her father as well as her mother.'

But Laura had never known her mother, Bertie thought, and Palgrave had left while she was still a tiny baby. She had been brought up by Henrietta and the nursery-maids at Morland Place. 'I don't think she's any more of an orphan now than she was before,' he said.

The freeze was followed by a sudden thaw that melted the snow so quickly there were floods. Cellars in York filled up, the river overflowed its banks above the town, fields were turned into lakes, sheep and cattle were hastily moved to higher ground, horses just let out were brought in again, and from trudging through the snow, folk were reduced to toiling through the mud – a change no-one thought for the better.

But two weeks more saw the floods fall back and a drying wind firmed the wet land. When things were back to normal, Jessie went up to Morland Place one morning to find another commotion, this time brought about by the news from America. Letters had arrived, from Ashley, with a sheet inside from Lizzie, and a formal declaration from Renfrew Alexander.

Teddy was beside himself. 'This, from a complete stranger! And nothing from her! Not a word! My little girl, to be marrying this – this *man*,' he invested the word with a powerful outrage, 'and she doesn't write a single word to me.'

'Lizzie says she's still angry,' Henrietta murmured to Jessie, 'about – you know.' Amy was not in the room, having gone to fetch her work basket and check on Edward, who was still poorly, but she didn't want to upset Teddy any more than he already was.

'That's so foolish,' Jessie said. 'She ought to have got over it by now. She's not a child any more.'

'Lizzie says that Polly said she'd write *after* she was married, because that's what her father did.'

'But who is this man?' Jessie asked. 'He must be respectable, surely. I mean, Polly wouldn't . . .' She wasn't sure how to finish that sentence.

Teddy intercepted the question, waving Ashley's letter. 'Ashley says he's rich. He's checked it all for me – a good man, that Ashley. The money is quite pukka. And he's well known to the top society of New York.'

'Well, that's good, isn't it?' Jessie said.

'But no-one knows anything about his family,' Henrietta said.

'I don't suppose that sort of thing matters so much in America,' Jessie hazarded.

'That's what Lizzie says.'

'Well, it matters to me,' Teddy cried. 'It must be stopped!'

'But, Ted, she's of age. No-one can stop her, only advise,' Henrietta said. 'And Lizzie's met him and thinks he's a decent man.' She looked at Lizzie's sheet, which she held in her hand. 'Clever, she says, and ambitious. Handsome, too – for what that matters.'

'Ambitious?' Jessie queried, watching her uncle out of the corner of her eye. He was reading Mr Alexander's letter again and grinding his teeth.

'Going into politics,' Henrietta said. 'The man he's *protégé* to is someone we know over here – Mr Hoover. You remember, Cousin Venetia knew him quite well in the war. And his wife – they did wonderful work for the Belgian refugees.' She looked at Teddy anxiously. 'Venetia used to dine with them, so you know *they*'re respectable.'

'If everything's above board, why is it being done in such a hurry?' Teddy demanded. 'An April wedding, when he only proposed in January?'

Amy came back into the room, holding her work basket, and looked from person to person to gauge the temperature of the emotions. 'He's asleep,' she said. 'What were you talking about?'

'And this fellow Alexander,' Teddy went on, shaking the letter as if it were Alexander's neck.

'My dear,' Amy said sensibly, 'you know you would never have thought anyone good enough for her. Don't get into a rage. It isn't good for you.'

Teddy subsided, sliding easily from anger into mourning. 'To think I used to plan how she would marry the Prince of Wales one day.' He looked from face to face in appeal. 'What am I to do?'

Amy would not answer – she was too aware that the whole problem began with her. Henrietta and Jessie exchanged a look, and at last Henrietta said gently, 'Write Polly a kind letter, saying how pleased you are with the news, and wishing her every happiness. Mend some bridges.'

'It wasn't me who broke them in the first place,' he said plaintively.

'All the more reason to be magnanimous,' Henrietta said. 'You're her father – it's the letter you *ought* to write.'

Duty always played well with Teddy. Henrietta could see he was thinking about it. She pressed home her advantage. 'Marriage will settle her, make her grow up, and she'll see how silly she's been. If you make the first move, it leaves the door open. But if you let it go too far without extending the olive branch . . .' she shrugged '. . . you may never see her again.'

Teddy nodded, though rather glumly. 'I suppose you're right,' he said, and took another wrathful glance at Alexander's letter. 'Renfrew Alexander! What sort of a name is that? Is the fellow Scotch?'

'He's Polly's choice,' Jessie said. 'That's all that matters now.'

'"Write her a kind letter",' he said, looking at Jessie with a sarcasm that just failed to mask the pain underneath. 'I suppose you want me to write *him* a kind letter, too?'

'Yes,' said Jessie. 'His to you is very polite.'

'Hmph! Anything else you want me to do, while I'm at it? Don't hesitate to mention it, you know.'

Jessie thought a moment, and then smiled. 'Yes,' she said. 'Send a wedding present.'

The taxi cab stopped, and Lennie leaned across and looked out of the window at a run-down street with rubbish blowing in the gutters, and a tall, shabby building with soot-stained brickwork and dirty windows. 'Is this it?' he asked doubtfully.

'This is it, bud. No mistake,' the driver said cheerfully. He laid his arm along the back of his seat and looked over his shoulder, gauging the quality of his passenger's overcoat and hat. 'Want me to wait?' he suggested.

'Yes, perhaps that would be a good idea,' Lennie said. He felt nervous and slightly guilty, and the cabbie seemed like the last friendly face in an unknown world.

'You're the boss.' The cabbie stuck his arm out of the window and hooked round to open the door for him. Lennie stepped out and looked up at the building.

'Private dick, huh?' the cabbie suggested.

'I beg your pardon?'

'Private detective. Don't look like you're goin' to the top floor. Divorce case? Tryna catch the little woman out?'

Lennie gave him a dampening look. 'Wait here, please,' he said. He pulled his muffler tight to his neck against the sharp cold, crossed the sidewalk and went up the steps to the front door.

'You're the boss,' the cabbie said, behind him, relit his short, noxious cigar and settled back in the stuffy warmth.

Inside the narrow, dark hall there was a legend on the wall. The top floor was occupied by 'Madame Hortense – French Lessons'. Lennie smiled to himself. Now he understood the cab driver's remark. The first floor housed a tax attorney – he wondered what that was a euphemism for, since all the tax attorneys he had ever met were rich men.

The second floor was 'Anson Detective Agency – Please Walk Up'. Lennie obeyed, up stairs that were uncovered wood and made his steps echo. The dull green paint was coming off the walls in flaky patches, like some unfortunate skin disease, and a very inadequate bare bulb hung from the ceiling on each landing, the better to view the dust and discarded cigarette ends in the corners.

He had got the recommendation from the doorman of a hotel, and wondered now if he had been wise to trust the source. But when he reached his destination and pushed open the door, he found himself in a small but bright office, with carpet on the floor, and a lampshade on the light, and a smart-looking aluminium blonde with an aggressive marcel wave clattering away at a typewriter – somehow managing not to shatter fingernails that were not only painted bright red but were very long and pointed. Lennie watched them in fascination to the end of the line, when the girl lashed the carriage-return over, looked up at him and smiled with a brightness and fixity that seemed to have nothing to do with him. 'Kin I hep yew?' she asked, in a nasal New York twang.

'I've come to see Mr Delaney. I have an appointment.'

'Sure! Go right on in,' the girl said, without asking his name. She reached out an arm and rapped loudly on the door behind and to the side of her desk. 'Go on in – he's expecting you,' she urged.

Lennie opened the door, and found himself in a small square room that had the dirty window on to the street. There was just room in it for a desk with a chair in front of it and a row of metal filing cabinets. The desk was covered with papers, and the man on the far side was scribbling busily in pencil, referring all the while to a black-bound notebook in front of him. But as soon as Lennie closed the door behind him he sprang to his feet, shoved out his hand, and said, 'Mick Delaney. How can I help you?'

He was a big man, and it was a big hand. Despite his eager movements and the thick, rather overlong brown hair, he was not as young as he appeared. Closer inspection revealed the lines in the boyish face that made him nearer to forty than twenty, and his eyes were shrewd, level and noticing. Lennie felt somewhat reassured.

'Delaney?' he said, shaking the hand. 'I thought the name was Anson.'

'Bought the name with the business,' Delaney said. 'Anson retired to Florida – wife wanted sunshine for her chest complaint. I've been here ten years. Ex New York Police

Department, same as Anson. I was invalided out – took one in the leg.' He slapped his thigh, as one might encourage a weary horse. 'Sit down, tell me how I can help, Mr . . . ?'

'Manning,' Lennie said, a little surprised since he had given his name when he made the appointment.

He began to reach for a card, and Delaney held up a hand, rather in the manner of a policeman stopping traffic, and said, 'Sometimes our clients don't want to use their own name. That's fine by me. Discretion is everything in this game. The less I know about my clients, often the better.'

'Discretion,' Lennie said, and felt the little warmth of shame again. But Polly's happiness was at stake. He braced himself. 'Yes, I must have an assurance of your discretion. The subject of my enquiries must never know anyone has been asking questions.'

Delaney nodded as though that were the norm. 'You want someone followed? Divorce case, is it?'

'No,' Lennie said, 'nothing like that. I want you to find out everything you can about a certain person – where he came from, what his background is, where his money comes from. He's apparently a rich businessman, well connected in society, but nobody knows anything about his origins.'

Delaney had been making jottings in another black-bound notebook. 'And what's the party's name?'

Lennie swallowed. This was the point of no return. 'Renfrew Hawthorne Alexander.'

Delaney wrote it down. 'I've heard of him, of course. Seen his picture in the papers a time or two. He's engaged to marry that fashion-house lady, am I right?'

'She's my cousin,' Lennie said.

Delaney looked up. 'Beautiful girl,' he commented, in a neutral voice, but his eyes were cop's eyes again, appraising.

Lennie's mouth was dry. 'I want to be sure that – that she's wise to marry him.'

Delaney nodded again. 'Find the skeletons in the cupboard.'

He leaned back in his chair and seesawed his pencil between his first and second fingers, thinking. 'How far d'you want to go back? Where he was born, who his parents were, brothers and sisters – that sort of thing?'

'Yes. Everyone knows what he's been doing for the last ten years, but before that – nothing.'

'Could be difficult,' Delaney said. 'If a man wants to cover his tracks, this is the country to do it. *Un*covering what he doesn't want known could work out expensive.'

'If you don't want the job . . .'

'Got to be honest with you. It's your money. But you've come to the right place. I've got contacts in police departments and city halls all over the country, and my colleague – who does the footwork – is the best in the business. If anyone can find out what you want to know, it's me and Tony Torino. But it'll mean a lot of travelling for Tony, and it won't come cheap. Especially as you don't want anyone to know we're asking. That's all I'm saying. Don't want you to get into something without understanding what it means.'

But Lennie had already faced what it meant: that he was spying on Polly's intended behind her back, which was underhand and dishonourable and which, if she ever found out, would probably make her hate him. But he had been horrified when he got back from California and found her deeply involved in wedding plans. He had hidden his feelings when he spoke to her: she was already peeved that Granny Ruth had cast doubt on the engagement, and he didn't want to alienate her. So he had pretended to be pleased, and his reward had been her relief and gratitude. Now she saw him as her ally, and he wouldn't have given up that position as her confidant, no matter how much pain it gave him.

But he couldn't stand by and do nothing. He was sure there was something odd about Alexander, and he wanted to find out what it was *before* the wedding, rather than after.

Delaney had been watching him. Now he said, 'So, do you want us to go ahead?'

'Yes,' said Lennie. 'Can you start at once? There isn't much time. The wedding is in April.'

Delaney smiled. 'Luckily it's quiet at the moment. I can put our full resources on to it, starting right now. I'd better explain our charging system to you. And there is the matter of a deposit – working money up front. All payments in cash. No cheques. You won't want anyone to be able to trace it back to you.'

'I understand,' said Lennie. He had anticipated this. Inside his jacket, under his voluminous overcoat, his wallet was fat and heavy.

'Okay, so I'd better get some details from you. Betty!' he yelled suddenly.

The door to the outer office opened, and the girl stuck her blonde head in. 'Yeah?'

'Coffee,' he said.

'Sure,' she said, and the head disappeared.

'Now,' said Delaney, turning to a clean page.

In consequence of a new collar, which gave both him and Cooper a great deal of trouble in getting the studs in, Bertie was down to breakfast well after his wife. She had obviously passed the time by taking a look at the paper, for it was lying on the table beside her place, but she was not looking at it now: she was staring into space in a strangely rigid way.

The dogs – her Morland hound Bran and his pointer bitch Ellie – got up politely and came to greet him, but he patted them absently, sensing something was wrong.

'Good morning, my love,' he said. Then he saw with concern that she could not speak because she was trying not to cry. 'What is it?' he asked.

She gave a sort of gasp. 'It's – nothing. It's—' She got up hastily from the table and hurried out, with Bran at her

41

heels, passing Cooper in the doorway. Cooper doubled as Bertie's valet and butler, and had grown into the position since they had lived at Twelvetrees, so that Bertie no longer felt there was anything odd in the appointment, made originally out of affection for his former soldier-servant.

Bertie made to follow Jessie, but Cooper stood in his way. 'Beg pardon, sir – better not.'

'What?' Bertie said, distracted. His wife was upset – he must go to her.

'Her ladyship was crying, sir,' Cooper said. He had even developed a stately, butlery way of speaking. 'In my experience, sir, the ladies is best left for five minutes to cry the worst off.' He gave a slight bow of the head and disappeared towards the kitchen. Bertie did not know what experience Cooper pretended to have of 'the ladies' – he had never been married. He didn't agree, anyway, when it was his own darling Jessie in question, but he did pause to look at the paper to see if there was anything that might have caused her distress. It was open at the obituaries page, but a rapid scan did not reveal any name that was familiar. So he put the paper down and hurried after her, and Ellie, pleased by any change to the routine, bounced after him.

Jessie was in the bedroom, standing by the window, her hand on Bran's head, which had been placed thoughtfully within reach. She did not turn, and he came up behind her, rested one hand on her shoulder and with the other offered his handkerchief. She took it, wiped her eyes and blew her nose.

He laid his lips gently against the back of her neck, and said, 'What is it, darling? Tell me.'

She didn't speak for a moment, still applying the handkerchief. Then she turned and looked up at him, pink of eye and nose, and said, 'It's not – it's so – it's difficult.'

He waited for more, then raised an eyebrow. 'Heartfelt, but not enlightening. Was it the obituaries page? Has someone died?'

She nodded. 'I was relieved. I felt relief. Then I was ashamed of feeling it.' Tears rose again. She used the handkerchief, wiping her eyes carefully, then took a shaky breath and said, 'It's something I've kept from you, Bertie. Perhaps I shouldn't have, but I did it for the best.'

'I'm sure you did,' he said, mystified. 'Do you want to tell me about it now?' She nodded dolefully. He sat on the window-seat and drew her down beside him. Across the room the door opened almost soundlessly, then closed again – Jessie's maid Podmore looking in and hastily retreating. 'Who was it who died?' he prompted gently. 'I didn't see any name I recognised.'

'You didn't know him. A man called John Smith,' she said. 'That wasn't his real name. Or, at least, I suppose not. No-one knew what his name really was.'

'And what was this John Smith to you?' Bertie asked. Her hands rested, warm and trusting in his. Outside, the winds of March lashed the bare trees back and forth against the grey sky and rattled the windows with a brief impatience.

Jessie drew a deep breath, and said, 'I'll tell you from the beginning – though there's not much to tell. I was in London visiting Violet. It was in 1919 – you were still in Cologne. One day she was at a fitting, and I was looking at the shops on my own. I was just passing the Ritz when a woman crossed in front of me, pushing a man in a wheelchair. I could see she'd been a nurse. And he—' A breath. 'Just for a moment, I thought it was Ned.'

Bertie knew better than to speak. Ned, her first husband, had been lost at Neuve Chapelle, his body never found. The army had declared him dead in due course, and Bertie and Jessie had married. All the implications were instantly clear to him.

She went on, 'I followed them in. They'd disappeared, but I asked a waiter, who knew them. He said the man had lost both legs and his memory during the war. No-one knew who he was. The Germans had put him down as John Smith. They didn't even know if he was an officer. After the Armistice he was dumped in a Belgian hospital and the woman had nursed him. When the war ended, she married him – her fiancé had been killed early on.'

'It happened a lot,' Bertie said neutrally.

Jessie looked at him in distress. 'You and I were married – after waiting so long. I was pregnant with Catherine. And he – he'd found comfort, the woman had someone to love – what was I to do? I wasn't even sure it *was* him. It didn't look much like him. It was only a sort of feeling I had, just for a moment.' She looked at him with terrible appeal. 'It would have caused so much hurt to everyone. You, me, our children. Uncle Teddy. Suppose it wasn't Ned after all? It would have broken his heart to give him hope and then dash it. I couldn't see who would benefit.'

'No, I see that,' Bertie said.

'So I kept it secret.'

'Even from me.'

'If I'd told you, you might have felt you had to make enquiries. And then – suppose it was him? I couldn't have gone back to him. And he wouldn't have wanted me. But our marriage would have been made bigamous and the children—'

'Yes,' said Bertie. The children would have been illegitimate. Divorce and remarriage could have sorted out the problem for Jessie and Bertie, but the children would have stayed illegitimate.

'And if it wasn't him, I'd have upset everyone for nothing – John Smith, too, and his wife. They might never have felt secure again.'

Bertie drew her against him again. 'My poor darling,' he said. 'To have carried this all alone for so long. It must have been dreadful for you.'

'You're not angry?'

'No, only sad. I wish I could have shared the burden with you. But you're right – I probably *would* have felt something had to be done.'

Jessie interlaced her fingers with his. 'But that's not the worst thing. I've been afraid, all these years, that, if it was Ned, he might suddenly regain his memory. People do sometimes. So when I saw he was dead – God forgive me, I was glad.'

'It was a natural reaction,' he said steadily.

'No, no, it was wrong! I'm ashamed. His health must have been so damaged, all that time in German prison hospitals, with such terrible wounds – and they say they starved them at the end.'

'They didn't have enough food for their own soldiers, let alone prisoners,' Bertie said.

'Poor man. One can only imagine his sufferings. But all I could feel was relief that he was dead and it need never come out. Can you forgive me?'

'Oh my darling,' was all he said, but it was enough. There was silence between them for a while, and then Jessie looked at him with a new anxiety.

'You don't think – you won't want to do anything now?'

He had been thinking of that, of course. If John Smith had been Ned, the fact that he was now dead did not make their marriage any less bigamous. And suppose someone at some time uncovered the secret? Suppose some old colleague from the war or the hospital turned up and gave out the news? It was too horrible to contemplate. Bigamy in such cases would not be punished by the law – they need not fear prison – but the shame, the social consequences, and the consequences to the children were appalling. If they did nothing, they would have to live with the uncertainty for the rest of their lives, and the risk – slight though it might be – that their carefully constructed house would be brought tumbling down.

But if John Smith had not been Ned, or there was no way to prove it one way or the other, a hornets' nest would have been stirred up for nothing. God, what a dilemma!

She was looking at him, fearful, hopeful, and still ashamed. No, he could not do that to her – to his family.

'It wasn't him,' he said. 'Ned was killed at Neuve Chapelle.'

'The body was never found.'

'Half of the dead in the war were never found.'

'John Smith had lost both legs. Ned's servant said Ned had wounds to both legs and his head.'

'So did thousands of others. Why *did* you think it was him? Just because of that?'

'I don't know. It was a fleeting thing, a sort of – jolt, when I saw him. But he looked right at me without recognition. And he looked older than Ned would have been. And – not really very like him, after all.'

Bertie tried a careful smile. 'There you are, then. There's really no reason to think it was Ned, no reason at all. And poor John Smith is dead now – God rest his soul – so we can put this behind us and forget it, never speak of it again.'

Not speak of it, no, Jessie thought, but forget it? She looked down at their linked hands. She loved Bertie more than life; he and the children were everything to her. 'What about . . .' she began, in a small voice. She couldn't get the words right. 'Are we really married?'

His arm tightened round her shoulders, but she didn't see, because her head was down, the expression of pain that passed over his face. 'We are married,' he said. 'By the law of the land, and by God's law. Everything's all right now, my darling. No-one can take you from me.'

Behind her closed eyes, Jessie thought that there would always be the seed of doubt in the back of the mind, but she would have to live with that. She had lived with it long enough already. At least John Smith's death had put it into the furthest realms of the unlikely.

46

She freed herself and stood up. 'You must be starving,' she said. 'We'd better go down to breakfast. The eggs will be hard.'

'Let's throw economy to the winds and order fresh,' Bertie said magnificently. She would never talk about it again, he knew, but would she stop thinking about it? There would always be the seed of doubt in the back of the mind, but he would have to live with that. He hoped life would keep her busy enough for it to stay at the back.

On the way downstairs she said, 'Father Palgrave, John Smith. I wonder who will be the third?'

'You don't believe that nonsense, do you?' he said robustly.

'Of course not,' she said. 'Just making conversation.'

CHAPTER THREE

Henrietta returned from the kitchen, where she had been discussing with Mrs Stark whether the pheasants hanging in the game room were ready for that night's dinner, and found her brother just coming in from estate business in a swirl of dogs.

'Dear me, that wind is sharp,' he said, as Sawry helped him out of his overcoat. The dogs hurried straight to the Great Hall fire. 'Still from the north – no rain in it. I don't remember a March as dry as this.' He drew out a handkerchief to dry his watering eyes. 'Where's Amy?' It was generally his first question when he came in.

'She's in the nursery,' Henrietta responded. 'I think Edward's a bit better today. She took up some gruel, and he ate most of it.'

'I'll go up and see,' Teddy said, starting in that direction.

'Teddy – wait a minute,' said Henrietta. 'I've been meaning to ask you: you were holding Father Palgrave's position for him, but now he's gone, poor man, couldn't we find another chaplain?'

Teddy frowned. 'Do we really need one? I know we've always had a chaplain-tutor, but all the children are at school now, except Edward, and he's too young for tutoring.'

'But I do so miss having the chapel served,' Henrietta said. 'If we had a chaplain, he could take over some of the

48

correspondence – I'm sure Miss Husthwaite has more than enough to do. And there are lots of papers in the archive that ought to be sorted and catalogued.'

He patted her shoulder. 'I'll think about it,' he said, and seeing her disappointment, he added, 'Oh, very well, I'll speak to the dean. How would that be?'

'Thank you,' Henrietta said. 'Pheasants tonight,' she added, knowing it would please him.

The dean came up with an elegant solution. 'What you need is a scholar, someone looking for light pastoral duties to leave time to do his own research.'

'Is there such a person?' Teddy asked.

'Indeed, that's what made me think of it. Have you come across John Julian?'

'I don't know the name,' Teddy said.

'He's on the Bishop of Ripon's staff, but I know he isn't happy there. He came from an Oxford college – used to lecture on Tudor domestic economy and the role of the chaplain in fifteenth- and sixteenth-century households. He had to leave when he got married. His wife died, sad to say, and I know he'd be glad to get back to academe, but there's no vacancy for him. Those college places are snapped up as soon as they fall vacant. He's been working on the most tremendous treatise for years and years, and I suspect he'd jump at the chance of a post where he had time for his writing.'

'Wouldn't the Bishop mind?'

'Bishops always have a queue of young favourites waiting for preferment, and never enough places for them,' the dean said. 'I imagine the Bishop would be glad to be rid of him.'

'Rid of him?' Teddy queried, alarmed.

The dean raised his hands. 'Oh, don't worry, he's a perfectly decent chap, just a touch vague at times. Not fitted for the hurly-burly of the cathedral. Frightfully brainy fellow.

But he's good company. I've dined with him at the Bishop's table several times. Plays a good game of chess, I'm told.'

So it was decided that Teddy should meet him and, if he liked him, have him to Morland Place to be interviewed by Henrietta. Julian turned out to be a tall, lean man in his fifties, slightly stooped, with bushy grey hair and spectacles that were always slipping to the end of his nose.

Teddy's doubts were eased by the fact that his pointer Bess went straight to Julian, tail swinging. He admired and stroked her, and said, 'It's a while since I've taken out a gun.'

'You shoot?' Teddy said, brightening.

'Fairly useful at one time. I enjoy getting out of doors when I can, as an antidote to too much reading. A man owes a duty to his physical body as well as his mind.'

This accorded with Teddy's views. *'Mens sana in corpore sano,'* he murmured.

'Just so,' said Julian. 'Sadly, in my present position there seems little time for fresh air. Diocesan duties never cease.' He patted Bess again. 'How old is this lovely little lady? Have you bred from her?'

Bess was standing with her nose jammed devotedly to Julian's knee, and from a happy discussion of her breeding history, it was a short step to Morland Place in general and an invitation to come and visit. It was all Teddy could do not to offer the position there and then; but in fairness, it was important that Henrietta took to the fellow.

She was rather nervous about meeting an academic, but his age and quiet demeanour reassured her. The details were ironed out, letters written, and John Julian was to join them at the end of the month. The only point of difference was that he did not care to be called 'Father' Julian, which he said would make him uncomfortable. Henrietta let it go. She knew most of the staff would call him 'Father' anyway, out of habit. She supposed he would get used to it in time.

★　★　★

On the day Mr Julian was to arrive, Miss Husthwaite did not appear at her usual time. This was so unusual as to cause immediate concern. Teddy, who was going into York later on business, said he would find time to call round to the Stonebow, where she lived with her father in a flat above a shop.

But while they were still at breakfast a message arrived. Henrietta went out into the hall to see an undersized boy, scab-kneed and stockingless in worn boots, with a spectacularly dirty face.

He handed over a grubby and creased envelope. 'Leddy give me a penny to bring it,' he said, unabashed by his surroundings. 'She said you'd give me another when Ah got here.'

'We'll see,' Henrietta said quellingly. 'What *is* that on your face?'

He rubbed at it vaguely with his sleeve. 'Lick'rish,' he said with reminiscent pleasure. 'A whole penn'orth.'

Henrietta opened the note. It was from Miss Husthwaite, apologising profusely for her absence. Her father had died in the night and there were arrangements to be taken care of. She hoped to be forgiven for taking the day off, and would be back tomorrow.

Henrietta said to the boy, 'Wait and take back a reply, and you shall have a penny.' And to Sawry, who was hovering, itching to throw the malodorous urchin out, 'I shall only be a minute.'

In the drawing-room she penned a quick note, expressing her sympathy, urging Miss Husthwaite not to think of coming back until she felt able to, and asking if there was anything she could do to help. Back in the hall, where the boy and the butler were silently ignoring each other, finely balanced for cheek on the one side and disapprobation on the other, she gave the boy the note and twopence – it was a long walk for someone so small – and a stern admonishment to deliver the letter *before* he spent the money this time.

Teddy, already missing his secretary – he didn't know where anything was without her – called at her house when he went into York, but she was not in – presumably she was seeing the registrar or a funeral director. He called again after his meeting, and found her at home, composed but pale and red-eyed.

She insisted on preparing a tray of tea for her visitor and apologised for the modesty of her home. Teddy looked round, with interest politely concealed. Everything was as neat as wax, like Miss Husthwaite herself, but very spare. There were few ornaments or pictures, the carpet had been carefully mended, and the wallpaper was rubbed almost white in several places.

'It was quite sudden,' she told him, when she had poured. 'I heard him call in the night, but when I went into his room, he was already past speech. He died half an hour later. I'm glad I was able to be there with him.'

'Perhaps it's a blessing that it was so quick,' Teddy said.

'That's what I tell myself,' she said. 'He'd have hated to be bedridden. But it's hard to think of life without him. He and I have been very close since my mother died.'

He asked her about the funeral arrangements, and told her that the servants wanted to send a wreath, which touched her. 'So very kind, when they did not know him. I had not thought—' She brought out a large man's handkerchief and blew briskly.

'You are very much missed, you know,' Teddy told her. 'By everyone.'

She emerged from the handkerchief. 'I'm so sorry, Mr Morland. It must be very inconvenient for you. Perhaps if you would be so good as to open the mail yourself today, I will deal with everything tomorrow. I hope there will be

52

nothing urgent in it. I can't think of anything that was imminent, apart from the new master for St Edward's, but that can surely wait one day. And the outstanding order for cattle nuts – oh, and the . . .'

'It can all wait. You are not to think of coming back until you are ready,' Teddy said. 'We'll manage until then. The new chaplain comes today, so he can help if need be.'

'Oh, goodness, yes, the chaplain. I had forgotten. But he won't know where anything is kept. My filing system – as an academic, he might be used to something different.'

'You're not to worry.' Teddy reached out and patted her arm. 'Now, is there anything I can help with, or Mrs Compton? If there's anything at all, you must promise to let us know. And,' he continued, delicately, 'I don't know if there are any financial considerations – sometimes a sudden event can leave one temporarily embarrassed . . .'

'Oh, no,' Miss Husthwaite said, deeply moved. 'Thank you so much for enquiring, but I always have a little put aside for emergencies. I shall manage beautifully.'

Teddy looked around at the bare room, and thought that was probably an exaggeration. And funerals, even the plainest of them, did not come cheap. On the other hand, Miss Husthwaite's salary would only have to keep one rather than two in future; and Mr Husthwaite might have left some small legacy for his daughter. In any case, he could not hurt her pride, so he said nothing more.

Teddy was back at Morland Place in time to welcome John Julian, who arrived with a large trunk full of books and papers and a small suitcase full of clothes. A crate containing the rest of his belongings had been delivered during the day.

Tea was served in the drawing-room, and Jessie and Bertie came over to join the party and meet the new chaplain. The tea was lavish, and Julian seemed to enjoy it very much, praising the Morland Place muffins (which he said took him back to his Oxford days) and Mrs Stark's Eccles cakes. He seemed very happy to be surrounded by dogs, which Henrietta took to be a good sign. He chatted to Bertie about army life – he had served as an army chaplain for two years after being called up in 1917 – and listened with interest when Jessie talked about polo ponies and her new plan to breed heavy horses for the railway trade. And when tea was finished, he expressed more interest in seeing the chapel and the library than his own quarters.

By the time he withdrew to unpack his belongings in the priest's room, he had created such a favourable opinion that the women were agreeing it felt as though he had been among them much longer than a few hours.

'I just hope Miss Husthwaite likes him when she gets back,' Henrietta said. 'Oh dear, poor Miss Husthwaite. Do you think I ought to send her a basket? She won't want to bother with cooking at a time like this. And I presume she'll have people back after the funeral.'

Jessie looked at Bertie with a struck expression. 'I've just realised – that's the third death,' she said.

Miss Husthwaite was away for four days, and came back at the end of the week, on the day after the funeral, looking worn but otherwise her same old self, neat and brisk. The gleam of fun in her blue eyes might be quenched for the time being, but she was ready to get down to the heap of work that had accumulated in her absence.

Henrietta was sure she had come back too soon, and plied her with dishes at luncheon in the hope of building up her strength. When six o'clock came and she was still toiling among the papers, Henrietta went into the steward's room and said that it was too late for her to go home, and she must stay to dinner and for the night.

'I'll have Mrs Tapworth make up one of the bachelor rooms for you,' she said firmly, to show she would brook no argument. 'We are only family to dine tonight, so you mustn't think you need to dress.'

'But I haven't any things with me,' Miss Husthwaite protested.

'I always have spare things for unexpected guests,' Henrietta said. 'Please do stay. Your fire won't be lit at home. It's too horrid at this time of year to be going home to a cold house.'

And Miss Husthwaite, who felt tired to death anyway, thought of that bicycle ride over the dark, bumpy tracks back to York, and the empty flat awaiting her, and was brought almost to tears. There was nothing to go home for now. Her father had always had the place warm and welcoming for her, and they had chatted about their separate days over supper and the fire. It was a windy night, and moonless. The thought of staying was irresistible.

'Thank you, you're very kind. If it's no trouble, I'd be grateful to stay.'

She went home on Saturday afternoon, and during Sunday Henrietta brooded about her, and finally spoke to Teddy and Amy.

'It does seem silly, now she doesn't have to go back to take care of her father. It's a long bicycle ride when the weather's bad, and we have plenty of rooms.'

Teddy thought of the monk-like flat, and going home to no fire lit, night after night. 'She should live in,' he decreed. 'What do you think, my love?'

Amy, remembering how overwhelming her own change from solitary lodgings to big household had seemed at first, said, 'It must be for her to decide. She might like her independence.'

Miss Husthwaite hardly needed to think. Her father had left her nothing – no debts, but no inheritance either – and she had no great attachment to the flat, which he had moved into when medical expenses incurred on behalf of

55

his wife had forced a change to smaller quarters. She had few possessions, had made few friends, and the journey back and forth could only grow more onerous. She was fond of Morland Place, and its inhabitants, to whom over the years she had become a source of sensible advice and practical help. It was, indeed, all the family she had. And she was by nature a sociable creature, not meant for solitude. So she accepted the invitation to 'live in' with gratitude.

She kept to herself the final thing that had weighted her decision: the hope that, living there, she might be able to have a small dog. She had always wanted a dog, ever since she was a child, but it had never been possible because she had worked in offices all her life. But, she reasoned, what difference would one more small dog make to Morland Place? A little mongrel or terrier that would sleep in the steward's room while she was working, which she could take out for walks at lunchtime and after work. She would wait until she had settled in before broaching it with Mr Morland, but she thought – she was sure, really – he wouldn't mind.

On the 4th of March 1925, the incoming President Coolidge had had his inaugural speech broadcast on radio. Lennie had not been slow in realising what a boost to radio ownership this might prove, so he had been busy organising advertising for his stores, and creating displays in their windows on the subject of the White House, the presidency, and eminent radio enthusiasts in general. Radio was one of the new industries Coolidge was known to favour government support for; in return, Lennie was quite willing to favour Mr Coolidge.

A month had passed since he had placed his enquiry with the Anson Detective Agency. In the mean time he had met Alexander in Polly's company, and studied him. He found it disconcerting not to be able to come to any conclusion about him. The man was evidently intelligent and sharp about business; he had good manners, and a certain charm. But there was something closed off, almost watchful about him. It was impossible to feel one knew him, or to guess what he was thinking. He plainly admired Polly, but did he love her?

Of course, Polly was like that herself – cool, withdrawn, not given to showing her feelings. Perhaps that was what had attracted them to each other. Lennie had to acknowledge that they might behave differently when they were alone together. But oh! Imagining them alone together was not something he wanted to do. He was torn by conflicting feelings – wanting Polly to be happy, but not wanting her to marry anyone but him; being glad that she had found someone to love, wondering if she *did* love him, fearing that Alexander was not worthy of her.

With that last thought in mind, he was glad to receive a message at last from the agency asking him to come in for a progress report. He entered the office to find the aluminium blonde absent, and Delaney himself sitting in her chair, leaning back with his hands behind his head and his feet on the desk, displaying a thin place in the sole of his right shoe that would soon become a hole. He was talking to another man, small and slight in an overcoat and brown fedora with the front brim bent down. At Lennie's entrance they both stopped talking abruptly, and the small man quickly turned his face away, hunching his shoulders and pulling his hat further down.

Delaney said, 'It's all right, this is Mr Manning.' The small man gave Lennie a quick, appraising glance under the brim. Delaney said to Lennie, 'Don't mind Tony. He depends on not being recognised. Tony Torino. Won't you sit down? It's Betty's lunch break, so I'm manning the phone. Tony, stop fidgeting and get a chair from my office.'

Torino did as he was bade, fetched a chair and sat on it, while Lennie took the visitor's ·chair, and Delaney courteously removed his feet from the desk and offered cigarettes. Torino did not take off his hat, but pushed it back a little, revealing a narrow and very swarthy face, clean-shaven but blue with rampant beard growth. He had dark eyes, a forelock of black curly hair, and looked to be in his forties.

'So, your enquiry,' Delaney said. 'We found in a newspaper article the target stated that he comes from Akron, Ohio, so that's where we looked first. Fastest growing city in America, Akron – they make every damn thing there, from kids' toy marbles to Zeppelins. Population's quadrupled in ten years, which makes it a hard goddam place to find someone in. Talk about your needle in the haystack. But I told you Tony's the best. He tracked him down in the end.'

'And?' Lennie asked, unwilling to waste time admiring Delaney's hound.

Delaney looked at the notebook on the desk in front of him. 'Father, Jacob Alexander, no middle name. He had a hardware store. Mother, Doris Renfrew Hawthorne, helped behind the counter. Target went to public school, helped in the shop evenings and weekends. All very normal. We found a neighbour who told us Doris died when target was eighteen – cancer. He took over running the shop instead of going on to college, with his dad doing the accounts. Apparently the old man was a whizz at math. Target turned the place from a mom-and-pop store to a modern, go-ahead business, increased turnover, got a neighbourhood name for being smart. Then when he was twenty-three the old man died of pneumonia – it's Christawful cold and wet in Ohio in the winter – and target sold the business, took the money and lit out for the bright lights.'

'That's it?' Lennie said, when he stopped. Delaney shrugged. 'No brothers or sisters?'

'Nope. Just the boy and old mom and dad making an honest living with a little family business in small-town America. Heartwarming story, isn't it?'

58

Tony Torino snorted.

Lennie stared. 'All right, what are you holding back? You've got something else.'

'Yeah.' Delaney grinned with satisfaction. He tipped the chair back on its hind legs and put his hands behind his head again, enjoying himself. 'I told you we had contacts in all the police departments in the country. Turns out the Alexanders were known to our boys in blue.'

'He has a police record?' Lennie asked, aghast.

'No, not like that. See, there was a big influx of people into Akron all at once, and when that happens there can be tensions between the different groups. And came a time when the Alexanders, among others, were having their windows broken, and nasty notes through the door. See, Jacob Alexander might sound Scotch, but he'd changed his name from Jacob Arkady. He was a Latvian Jew, came over here looking for a better life – apparently it couldn't get much worse than it was in Latvia, wherever that is.'

'Alexander was a Jew?' Lennie said in surprise, trying to fit that with Ren's appearance and physique.

'Pop was, but not the religious sort. Guess he wanted to leave all that behind with Russky oppression. Mom Doris was just the ordinary home-grown kind-of-Christian-if-anything American girl. Anyway, there was a bunch of some other kinda Russian types in the neighbourhood, who didn't like Latvians and particularly not Jews, so there was trouble, and the cops had to look out for them. But here's the thing – when all this was happening, they were new in Akron. They moved there when our target was fourteen.'

'Where from?'

'We don't know. See, Tony didn't know how far you wanted to go back. We'd found his father and mother, respectable home life et cetera. You might be happy with that. But here's something else.' He righted the chair with a crash and planked his arms on the desk, leaning forward to fix Lennie with a gaze. 'We got photos of the Alexanders from that time and – well, you look.'

He pushed them across the table. One was obviously a police mugshot of a small, worried man, decidedly Jewish-looking, with full lips and rather bulbous, sad brown eyes below a ragged cut on his forehead. Lennie could see no resemblance between him and Ren at all. The other was a newspaper photograph of a street scene – some kind of parade going on, to judge by the hand-held flags – and the shot was of the crowd lining the sidewalk. Three figures standing together in front of a shop had been ringed in ink. One was the same small man, the middle figure was a tall, dark-haired youth Lennie had no difficulty in identifying as Ren, and on his other side was a small, thin woman with a very white face and what looked like fair hair, straight and drawn back in a bun. The boy between them was a giant bracketed by elves.

Lennie looked from the photograph to Delaney, who was waiting for him with a broad smile. 'Nice, huh? And here's the last little touch that makes it perfect. Doris was fifty-eight when she died and the old man was sixty-two, making her forty when Renfrew was born and Dad forty-four. No other kids, as I said. Talk about your cuckoo in the nest.'

'He wasn't their son?' Lennie said.

'Can't say that for sure, but it doesn't look likely, does it? So here's our mystery. They turn up in Akron with a nearly full-grown cuckoo, who turns the family biz around, then when Pop croaks, pockets the money and disappears.'

'Disappears?' Lennie frowned. 'But he came to New York.'

'He came to New York in 1915. He left Akron – and who can blame him? – in 1913. Two missing years. Plus the fourteen before Akron, and what looks like a set of missing parents.' He sat up, folded his arms, and smiled. 'Now it's up to you.'

Lennie was frowning in thought. 'Huh?' he said.

'All nice as apple pie as far as it goes. You can leave it there if you want. We've no evidence that there was ever anything shady about the target. And I have to tell you this – Akron was the easy bit. If you want Tony to go on, it's gonna get expensive. And who knows if he'll find anything anyway?'

Lennie shook his head. He felt bad enough about having started this, and to go on would be giving in to suspicion he had no right to harbour. But he couldn't help being piqued. Cuckoo in the nest was right. If he wasn't the son of Jacob and Doris Alexander, who the heck was he? It wasn't just that Polly was going to marry him, but presumably they would have children, and who knew what blood he was going to bring into the family? A man could make his own life regardless of his background, but what was in his blood would get passed down to his children, whether it was good or bad. Didn't he owe it to Polly to follow the story to its conclusion? Ren Alexander might be the best man on the planet, but Lennie needed to *know* that before he could rest.

'I want you to go ahead,' he said. He was committing himself not just to expense – that hardly mattered – but to he did not know what pain. For if there was something shady about Ren, and he tried to tell Polly, the most likely outcome was that she would turn against him, not Ren. Still, man was born asking questions. And maybe it would all turn out all right, and nobody need ever know.

April came in cold and wet in Yorkshire. By the time Easter arrived the temperature was stuck in the forties, and mental images of sunshine, bouncing lambs, primroses and violets failed before the constantly grey skies, and the teeming rain masking the sodden fields in veils of mist. Twelvetrees stables had cracked heels and mud fever to contend with, and Teddy was worried about the sheep, which can stand the cold but are susceptible to damp.

61

But the children were all off school for the Easter holiday, and their influx of noise and movement cheered everyone up. James came home from Eton. Henrietta's daughter-in-law Ethel came with her second husband from Knaresborough, where they now lived, to stay, so that Ethel could have time with her children. Jessie and Bertie and their children were in and out every day. Teddy loved nothing more than to have the family gathered under his roof. To add to his satisfaction, Edward seemed to have got over his cold at last and, though too pale and thin, was as lively as a cricket and enjoying the visitors as much as anyone.

After the quiet reflectiveness of Good Friday, Easter Saturday was a waiting day. Teddy saw to the killing of the geese for Sunday's feast and went out to look at the sheep. Ethel and Donald went visiting in York. Jessie took James and the older children out on a long ride, despite the rain. Henrietta and Amy devised the floral decorations for the house and chapel for the following day, and Miss Husthwaite and Mr Julian had a long and vigorous theological debate, which entirely prevented them finishing the game of chess they had started.

In the middle of the morning a carrier arrived with a large parcel, accompanied by a letter addressed to Teddy in a rather delicate, spidery hand that no-one recognised.

Soon afterwards Teddy came in from talking to the shepherd – 'Two more ewes lambed this morning, two lots of twins. I'm thinking we'll have to set up some kind of shelter out there if it keeps on raining' – and, looking at the letter, said, 'It's from the brothers. Look, the postmark is Ampleforth.'

'What can they have to say, after all this time?' Henrietta said, coming close.

Teddy opened the letter. 'If they want a donation, I shall send one. They were very good to poor Father Palgrave.'

It was from the Father Abbot, stating that the accompanying parcel contained the late Denis Palgrave's effects, and explaining that his room had been cleared immediately after his death to accommodate a new arrival, and the objects had been mistakenly put into storage, where they had only just been found.

> I believe the brother responsible did not know that Father Palgrave had any family, and I apologise for the delay in sending them back to you. I hope they may prove of some comfort to his unfortunate child. The manuscript is something he had been working on most diligently for many months. I have not read it, so cannot say what the subject matter is. I leave it to you to determine whether it is something suitable for his daughter to see in the fullness of time.

'If he was so disturbed he wandered out into the snow to die, it's not likely that anything he wrote would even make sense,' Teddy said, when he had read out the letter.

Amy said, 'Laura's only four. Whatever it is, there's no need to bother her with it now.'

'But one day she may be glad to have something that belonged to her father,' Julian said. 'As I understand, she never really knew either parent, poor child.'

Teddy put the parcel on the hall table, and untied the string. Inside was a thick pile of handwritten sheets, and lying on the top was a battered, leather-bound prayer book, and a crucifix, about eight inches tall, ebony bound in silver, with an ivory figure of the Christ.

'I remember that,' Henrietta said. 'He used to have it in his room here.'

'It's rather beautiful,' Amy said. 'I expect Laura will be glad to have it.'

Teddy handed it to her, and the prayer book, and picked up the top sheet of the manuscript. '"*Mémoires* of a Chaplain in the Trenches",' he read the title. 'Well, that's sane enough.'

He began to read the first page, and when he got to the bottom, automatically turned to the next, before stopping himself and looking up at the others, patiently waiting for a comment. 'It certainly reads all right,' he said. 'If it goes on as it begins . . .'

'May I?' said Julian, took the first page and read it rapidly. 'I see what you mean. If I might suggest – would you allow me to take charge of the manuscript and read it for you?'

'Oh, by all means,' Teddy said, passing it over with relief. 'It's much more your sort of thing than mine. I've never been a great reader. You'll be able to say if there's any merit in it.'

'I shall be honoured to undertake the job. As I was an army chaplain myself, I can bring a certain perspective to it.' He flicked through a few pages. 'The handwriting is rather poor in places. I expect the poor man was agitated – or perhaps writing by candlelight.'

'May I help?' Miss Husthwaite said. 'Though I shouldn't boast, I'm rather good at deciphering bad handwriting. I came across a lot of terrible "fists" in my office life.'

'I should welcome your collaboration – if it's agreeable to all?'

'Oh yes, yes,' Teddy said comfortably. 'Brain work to the brainboxes, that's what I say. Go to it – and let's not say anything to little Laura until we know what we have, eh?'

'Of course not,' said Julian.

'We can work in the steward's room in the evenings,' said Miss Husthwaite, 'so as not to disturb anyone.'

'It will mean giving up our battles over the chess board.'

'Oh, chess is just a game,' she said dismissively.

Teddy laughed. 'You'll be saying bridge is just a game next!'

'So it is. Whereas this,' touching the manuscript, 'is real life. Oh, I *do* hope it's good, for Laura's sake.'

★   ★   ★

64

Easter Day came with all its solemn, glad, triumphant celebration. The chapel was a bower of greenery and flowers – yellow, white and purple, the colours of Easter – when John Julian held the service for the whole household, including Jessie and Bertie and their children, and the favourite carols rang to the rafters. The waiting was over. Christ had risen, and hope had come back to the world.

The dining-table was extended and all the children, right down to baby Edward in his high chair, joined the adults for breakfast. They had spent the previous afternoon painting patterns on eggs, a different one for each person. For a wonder, the rain had actually stopped, and though the sky was still cloudy, there was the odd patch of cold blue and the occasional gleam of pale sunshine, sparkling on the raindrops in the hedges. Everyone except Edward and Ottilie went for a walk after breakfast, and the dogs rushed out with them, delighted to be out of doors and in company.

Among them ran Miss Husthwaite's little white terrier-mongrel, which she had called Rusty because of a reddish patch over one eye. She sighed when she looked at him. Kind Mr Morland had said at once she should have a dog if she wished, and she had got Rusty on recommendation from one of the estate farmers, as a one-year-old failed ratter – she thought it better not to have to train a puppy. She had brought him home in triumph, but far from lying at her feet and gazing at her devotedly while she worked, he had abandoned her almost immediately to join the pack of house-dogs, and rarely, it seemed, gave her a thought.

She would not give up lightly, and insisted every day on attaching a lead to his collar and taking him for a walk at lunchtime and after work, but though Rusty went along with her, he did not seem to see her in the light of a beloved mistress, even though she had saved him from being knocked on the head. He liked nothing better than to dash about with the other dogs, investigate smells – the riper the better – roll in cow dung, and lie with his new friends in a living carpet in front of the Great Hall fire. The Morland pack had corrupted him, she thought sadly, watching his white rear end disappear under a hedge far ahead of her.

After the walk there was the grand Easter Sunday dinner: three roast geese, their breasts golden and crisp, brought in on vast salvers, set around with gilded apples. Outside, the brief respite was over, the clouds had drawn together, and the rain returned, splattering against the windows. But the drawing-room after dinner was cosy, with the fire built up, and everyone played silly games with the children, except for Julian and Miss Husthwaite, who sat at the table at the far end, reading the manuscript. As it grew dark, Henrietta and Amy went out to the kitchen to make the tea – the servants had the afternoon off – and then Jessie sat at the piano and played all the songs she could think of for everyone to sing. As she played, she looked around at the faces, and remembered those that were missing. Family, she thought: family was everything. And those who were gone had given their lives so that those who survived could enjoy this – this perfect peace.

Peace at last, though it had taken all these years since the war ended. The country was quiet, England had no more enemies, the national debt and unemployment were down, and the old divisions seemed to be worn away. Perhaps in the turbulence of modern history it might only be a hiatus – time would tell – but for now she would enjoy it for what it was.

Jack and Helen had been invited to Morland Place, but preferred to celebrate Easter at home, for Jack, who was a pilot with Imperial Airways, on the Continental run, did not want to spend his precious free time travelling. He had an extra day off in the middle of the week after Easter, and since the children were still off school, they went up to Town on the electric railway to see the demonstration at Selfridges, which had been in all the papers. A Scottish engineer called John Logie Baird was showing moving pictures said to be transmitted by radio technology, and Jack, always interested in new science, was eager to see for himself.

They took their two elder children, Basil and Barbara, nine and eight years old; Michael, only four, had been left with a neighbour. He had also taken charge of Stalky, the black half-Bedlington, which had taken the place of Rug, Jack's old mongrel that had died the year before. Being left in the company of Stalky was a consolation to Michael for missing the outing, and as the neighbour owned two jolly little terriers, Michael was talking about organising races.

'I just hope he doesn't cause chaos,' Helen had said, when they dropped Michael off.

'Michael can cause chaos sitting still doing nothing,' Jack had said, which hadn't reassured her.

The moving pictures, which Mr Baird was calling 'television' – Jack said the word was an abomination, as 'tele' was from the Greek and 'vision' from the Latin – turned out to be less exciting than they sounded, being merely silhouettes of people moving about in a grey soup background. You needed to understand the achievement to experience the thrill, but the science was beyond the children and they were soon bored by it. But the train journey and coming up to London were a treat anyway, and the shops were a wonder to them. And then, after a walk in the park to see the ducks (and to remove some of their excess energy), they were brought to a peak of bliss by luncheon at the Lyons Corner House on Tottenham Court Road. They rarely ate anywhere but at home, and the novelty and wonder of it reduced them temporarily to silence.

Their aunt Molly, always a favourite with them, met them there by arrangement.

'I have to be quick, I'm afraid,' she said, as she was shown to their table. 'There are *looks* if one is late back from lunch and, if one is very late, *things said*.' Molly, ten years younger than Helen – she'd been a late baby and had come as a great surprise to her mother – was a civil servant and worked in the Department of Health. 'So what was it like?' she asked.

'What was what like?' Jack asked innocently.

'Ass! The wonder of the age, the moving pictures. The tele-whatyoumaycall.'

Jack pursed his lips judiciously. 'I couldn't possibly describe it. You would have to see it for yourself.'

Molly looked at him with narrowed eyes. 'I'll talk to someone sensible. Basil, what did you think of the tele-movies?'

'They weren't proper pictures,' Basil dismissed them. There were more important things on his mind. 'Mummy says I can have anything I like. I'm having two puddings.'

Molly leaned forward confidentially. 'I wouldn't do that, old chap. I hear they have baked beans here, and you'd never have room for them.'

'Thank you for the thought, Molly dear, but that's frying pan and fire as far as I'm concerned,' Helen said.

'Oh, but I've heard they're terribly nourishing.'

The waitress came and they ordered. The sisters both opted for the mutton chops, with boiled potatoes, cabbage and carrots. 'How I long for spring and some different vegetables,' Helen said. 'One gets so tired of cabbage.'

'Think of cauliflower,' Molly said wistfully. 'And new peas, and greens . . .'

'Asparagus,' Jack joined in.

'Oh, don't!' said Helen. 'I can't bear it. And they say spring's going to be late this year.'

'Now I know what to bring you back from France,' Jack laughed. 'Not French perfume but French *légumes*.'

'So how are things in the wonderful world of aviation?' Molly asked, when the waitress had gone away. 'Been doing any pioneering?'

It was rather a tease, because Jack had been one of the earliest fliers (his Royal Aero Club aviator's certificate was number twenty-three) and he had always hoped he would go down in history as the first to do something – fly across the Atlantic, break a speed or height record – but somehow he had always missed out. He had ended up flying a passenger route from Croydon to Le Bourget. But he enjoyed his job, and he had a sense of humour, so he gave her a solemn look and said, 'As a matter of fact, I have.'

'Really?' she said suspiciously.

'It's true,' said Jack. 'On my last schedule to Paris, we showed the passengers a cinema film during the journey. I think you'll find that was the first time air passengers ever watched a movie in flight.'

Molly laughed. 'I hope they put that in the encyclopaedias! What film was it, by the way?'

'Something called *The Lost World*. I didn't get to see it myself, but I believe it had to do with dinosaurs.'

'It's from Sir Arthur Conan Doyle's book, ignoramus,' Helen said. 'An explorer finds a remote plateau in South America where prehistoric animals have survived.'

'I wish I could see it,' Basil said.

'You'll have to save up and buy a seat on your daddy's aeroplane,' Molly said.

'Well, I *will*,' Basil said stoutly, 'because when I'm ten, Daddy says I'm to have pocket money.'

'Good for you,' Molly said. 'Doesn't anyone want to know if I have news?'

'Do you have news, Molly dear?' Helen asked obediently.

'Lots,' said Molly. 'To begin with, I'm moving house. I've taken a little flat in Mecklenburgh Square. It isn't much, just a sitting-room with a gas stove and sink in the corner and a tiny bedroom, but I shall have my own latch-key and be perfectly private.'

'What brought that on?' Jack asked.

'Oh, I'm just sick of landladies and communal eating.'

'I don't blame you,' Jack said. He had had his time living in lodgings. Helen never had, going straight from the parental to the marital home.

'I'm going to be a modern bachelor girl, and fry sausages and make cocoa, and have friends in when I want to – which is the most important thing.'

'Mecklenburgh Square? That's near the British Museum, isn't it?'

'Not far. It's just off Gray's Inn Road, at the back of the Foundling Hospital – or where the Foundling Hospital used to be before they moved it. It's a nice square with a garden and trees, and lots of artists live there – painters and writers and musicians and so on – so I shall have interesting people to make friends with.'

'No friends among the civil servants?' Jack asked. He had always hoped Molly would meet an agreeable under-secretary and get married.

'Women are invisible in the civil service,' she said. 'You could spend your whole life there and still you'd never get above a certain grade. And the men above you would still call you "Miss Er". That's why I'm leaving.'

'Leaving?' Helen said in shock.

'That's the other part of my news.'

'But is it wise? To give up such a good, secure job?'

Molly smiled. 'Helen, dear, security is all very well, but you only have one life and I've wasted enough of mine doing dull things. Don't you want to know what the new job is, before you condemn me?'

'I wasn't condemning,' Helen said hastily. 'I only want what's best for you.'

'The excuse of the tyrant through the ages,' Molly said, but she grinned to show she was joking.

'What *is* the new job?' Jack asked.

'I'm going to work for a newspaper. I shall only be a junior copywriter, and the pay isn't as good, but at least there I can advance by my own efforts. And I shall be doing something I like, something I'm good at.'

'Well, I think that's tremendous,' Jack said. 'It will be exciting being in the know and getting to hear everything first.'

'I know you always did like writing,' Helen said.

'I've been trying my hand at some stories for a while now. I've had one in the *Pall Mall Magazine*, and one in *Hutchinson's Adventure Stories*.'

'Actually published? But why didn't you say? I'd have loved to see your name in print,' Helen said.

'Oh, they weren't anything very wonderful,' Molly said. 'I'm learning my trade. And anyway, I had to do them under a pen name – I'm D. H. Montagu. The Department would have had a fit if I'd used my own. That's another good reason for leaving the civil service. I want to be a writer – not just short stories, but novels.'

'What sort of books will you write, Aunty Molly?' Basil asked, proving he had been listening, despite the cigarette cards he had been playing with under the table.

'Detective stories,' she said promptly. 'I love reading them – Agatha Christie, Freeman Wills Crofts, R. Austin Freeman. And I can't help thinking I could do as well myself, if not better.'

'I'm sure you could,' Jack said. 'But no more modesty – I want to read everything you have published from now on. I like a rattling good yarn, especially during those long, dull waits between flights.'

'The long, dull waits between flights are what the rest of us call real life,' said Helen.

'You know I didn't mean that.'

'I don't expect they're dull for Helen, anyway,' Molly said. 'More a sort of stretching on the rack. How do you bear it, Nel?'

Helen shrugged. 'You'd have thought one would get used to it, after the war, but one never does.'

Jack looked concerned. 'You don't sit at home worrying about me every time?'

'Of course I do.'

'But it isn't really dangerous.'

'Last Christmas Eve,' Helen reminded him.

'Oh,' Jack said. 'Well, let's not go into that again.'

'Oh, yes,' Molly said. 'I remember.' An Imperial aeroplane had crashed while taking off from Croydon. The pilot and seven passengers had all been killed. 'You hear about aeroplane crashes all the time,' she said reasonably.

'You hear about automobile crashes too, but it doesn't stop you getting into one,' Jack said. 'Anyway, let's change the subject. *Pas devant les enfants*.'

'I know what that means,' Basil said. 'It means something you don't want me to hear.'

'Which includes practically everything, you intolerable little bubble-pipe,' Helen said.

He eyed his mother, wondering whether she was serious. In case she was, he turned his full charm on his aunt, an easier target. 'What were your stories about, Aunty?' he said. 'Can you tell us one?'

'Blatant,' Jack muttered. 'He doesn't get it from me.'

'Well,' Molly began obligingly, 'I can tell you a new one I've just thought of. There was a junior civil servant who came home one day to find a fabulous diamond in his coat pocket, obviously slipped in there by someone while he was on the omnibus . . .'

CHAPTER FOUR

Polly was lunching with Julie Margesson and her friend Freda Holland, an older and extremely elegant woman, who was an enthusiastic patron of the arts. She was always 'discovering' painters and launching them on to the social high seas of New York, and since she was very rich and stinted nothing, her launches were always worth attending.

They talked at first about an exhibition Freda was getting up to promote one of her new young artists. She wanted Julie to help fund it, and in return Julie wanted Freda to help a young violinist of her acquaintance, so there was some delicate horse-trading. Polly was happy just to listen, enjoying not being the centre of attention for once.

It was not to last, for they were interrupted by a harsh and insistent call, like that of a large bird. 'Girls, there you are! *What* a little tête-à-tête! Mm-mm! Julie, dear, Freda my love, and the delicious little Miss Polly Morland, looking as if butter wouldn't melt. I bet I can guess what the subject is! My dears, no-one in the whole of New York is talking about anything else!'

She clicked her fingers at a waiter to bring a chair and, without asking, placed herself at their table, and told the waiter to bring her a martini. She was Olga Graham, a very thin, smart, restless woman who smoked constantly and had – perhaps in consequence – a strikingly deep and husky voice. She had black, rather greasy-looking hair drawn back in a bun, and she always dressed in black, wore scarlet lipstick and had long, scarlet talons. She tapped them on the table while she looked around, even as she talked, as though constantly hoping for something more amusing to come along. Polly didn't much like Olga: there was something sly and sharp about her, and Polly found her intimidating. She had a suspicion that Julie didn't like her much, either, but she was a fashionable person to be seen with – she seemed to know everyone in New York – and she went to every opening night, gala concert and gallery launch.

'We were talking about Nikolai Petrovich, my pet violinist,' Julie said mildly.

'Don't tell *me*!' said Olga. 'It was the Wedding, I know, the Wedding! I can see it on your faces. I can't open a newspaper without reading about the "fairytale couple" and being told to admire a certain person's "English beauty" and "modesty".'

She said it sharply, with a sour look at Polly, so that for an instant Polly felt she ought to apologise. She had got used to the press following her around, and the battery of flashes that met her every time she stepped through a door, but it didn't follow that she liked it.

'I can't help what the newspapers say,' she said, in her own defence.

Olga wasn't listening. 'I can't get over it,' she said, thrusting a cigarette into her amber holder and lighting it. Sometimes in the evening she smoked short, thin cigars. 'Every woman in New York's been mad for Ren Alexander since he first appeared on the scene – and I mean *women*, dear, not just girls. And then *you* snaffle him right from under our noses, Miss Pure as the Driven Snow!'

'I don't know what you mean,' Polly said, a little offended.

'Oh, don't take a miff at me, I mean it as a compliment. You look like a china doll, dear. You look as if you haven't the sense to come in out of the rain, but you've the brains

74

to run that fashion house of yours, and if you've actually persuaded the divine Mr Alexander to propose to you, you must have something the rest of us haven't got. So spill the beans, dearie. Ren being what he is – and we all know what he is – what did you do to snare him? Tell us your secret. Share your little tricks.'

'Olga,' Julie said warningly.

Olga waved her cigarette dismissingly, and then drew on it. 'Oh, I know. We're all pretending like mad it's simply Cupid and his little darts. I won't say a word. But strictly *entre nous*, Polly dear, is he *absolute heaven*? You know what I mean.'

'I'm afraid I don't,' Polly said.

'Where it counts, darling. He's so dark and dangerous-looking, he makes me shiver. Those big hands. That mouth. I just know he could give me a thrill.'

'Olga!' Julie said again, more forcefully.

'A thrill?' Polly asked, puzzled.

'These days a woman is just as entitled to her thrill as a man. We all believe that, don't we, girls? It's not all one-way traffic any more.' She gave Polly a sly look. 'The men who can make it happen are thin on the ground, God knows. But with that corsair for a husband – well, I guarantee I'm not the only girl who'll be longing to be you on your wedding night.' She laughed huskily.

Freda said calmly, 'Olga, I believe we're making Polly uncomfortable. Remember, she's English.'

'Oh, sure, sure. Don't want to turn the English rose into a blushing rose!' She winked, and changed the subject. 'Tell me, dear, what are you doing about bridesmaids? I heard from Baby Wenzler you aren't having any – surely that can't be right.'

'I had intended just to have one,' Polly admitted. 'My cousin Lizzie's daughter Rose.'

'That delicious girl I see at Maison Polly sometimes? *Such* an air she has – as if she expects everyone to be looking at her.'

'She wants to be an actress. She's persuaded her mother to let her go to stage school this fall instead of finishing school.'

'That should knock the nonsense out of her,' Olga said. 'Girls in stage school get all kinds of hell thrown at them. Toughens them up for the real world. I know. My first had enough little actresses in tow, and I heard all the sob-stories. But tell about the bridesmaids. You changed your mind?'

'Ren said it was a terrible waste of an opportunity only to have one. Lots of the people he needs to further his career have daughters or granddaughters of the right age, and asking them would – I'm not sure how to put it – make them grateful, I suppose.'

Freda and Julie exchanged a glance. 'No need to explain, dear,' Freda said. 'We understand.'

Olga took a suck at her cigarette and muttered, 'God, that's cold!'

'I beg your pardon?' said Polly, not sure she had heard right.

'I said that's smart thinking. How many are you going to have?'

'Eight. Ren said the church is big enough to take it. He's given me a list.' When she said it aloud, it sounded odd; but the fact was that Polly had no female friends in New York who were not married women. If the bridesmaids were important to Ren's career, it made sense for him to choose them. 'I'm sure they're all nice girls,' she concluded. 'And I'll still have Rose.'

'I suppose you'll be designing their dresses,' Olga said. 'What are they like?'

'They're to be very simple, because the girls are all different sizes and have different colouring. I've gone for layers of cream chiffon to just below the knee, with a dropped waist and a broad sash, and chaplets of white flowers on their heads.' She sighed. 'I must say it gave me an awful lot of extra work, just when I had so much to do anyway.'

'Never mind,' Olga said. 'It will all be worth it when you find yourself in bed with big Ren Alexander.'

'Didn't I see in the papers you and Ren were at the Guild Theater last week?' Freda said quickly, managing to cover the end of Olga's sentence.

'Oh, yes – it was the première of *Caesar and Cleopatra*,' Polly said, grateful to get away from the wedding. 'I wasn't looking forward to it – I thought it was going to be Shakespeare.'

'That's *Antony and Cleopatra*,' Julie said.

'I know that now,' Polly said humbly. 'George Bernard Shaw turns out to be *much* easier going.'

'Oh, you peach!' Olga laughed, but in a different, more pleasant way from before. 'Aren't you just delicious? I'm going to have to take you in hand when you're married and educate you about the theatre. Julie only cares for ballet and opera, and Freda her blessed painters. I'm going to make sure you know all the important plays – at least well enough to talk about them at dinner parties. All those senators' and congressmen's wives don't know any better, and I won't have them looking down their noses at you, pet that you are. We'll make her our project, won't we, girls?'

Freda said, 'Polly has her own way of coping, I've noticed. In company, when she has nothing to say, she keeps her mouth shut.'

'Ouch!' said Olga. 'Well, I guess I deserved that. But you know I don't mean any harm, don't you, Polly?'

Polly made a noncommittal noise rather than tell a lie.

Being betrothed to Ren sounded more glamorous in the papers than it was in real life. Since he had proposed to her, they had hardly ever been alone. His business life was even busier than hers, and their evenings together were spent being sociable with important people, and being seen in public places. He was introducing her to a whole new section of society: politicians, businessmen, diplomats and the super-rich. She thought of them as the Washington Set, because it seemed that the foothills of government was where they all camped, and the heights of the White House what they yearned to scale.

They were older than her – most of them were older than Ren – and very sober, serious people. The men talked politics and money on a level beyond her comprehension, and barely noticed her. It was their wives Polly had to get on with: women devoted to furthering their husbands' careers, busy with committees, charities, functions, entertaining. They were very proper, careful of their reputations, determined to secure the exact degree of respect they felt due to them. They were brusque with servants, waiters and porters. They played bridge and golf. Polly found them desperately dull.

For their part, they were interested in but suspicious of her. She was too young, too beautiful; she was English; she had her own business, created from nothing; they did not know what to make of her. Polly always felt they were waiting for her to make a mistake so they could pounce on it. It made her even more silent in company; and then they thought her aloof.

Though Olga's directness embarrassed her, of course she *had* thought about that side of marriage – the bedroom business. Growing up with animals, she was not ignorant of sex and reproduction; and she had overheard bits of muttered conversations. It seemed to get very mixed reviews among women, though there was those like Olga who talked of it as something desirable, especially 'the thrill'. Polly didn't know exactly what that was, but she wondered if it was something to do with the sensation she had when Ren kissed her.

78

She had always been glad that he didn't get spoony with her, but now she was committed to spending the rest of her life with him, she wished he would make love to her just a bit, just now and then, to show how he felt about her. But apart from the occasional kiss – and he would always end it much too soon for her wishes – he treated her as he always had, respectfully and with admiration, but no intimacy.

Meanwhile, what with running her business, working on the wedding, being pursued by the press, and wondering about, longing for and fearing the wedding night, her emotions were being wound up tighter than a watch-spring. She was a person who had long kept her feelings hidden from the world, and she had no outlet to lessen the pressure.

Lennie was also feeling the tension. The day was drawing closer, and he still had no definitive information about Alexander. Whenever he pressed him, Delaney simply shrugged and said these things took time. 'You have to be patient. I warned you this would be the hard part. If you want us to stop, say so, but it can't be done quicker.'

Lennie hesitated, gave him more money and told him to keep on. He wasn't sure whether it would be worse to find something out about Alexander *after* he had married Polly – what would he do with the information then? – or never to know one way or the other. But always he came to the conclusion that he needed to know, so that he could watch out for Polly's best interests.

Meanwhile, he tried to see in Polly the euphoric bloom that brides were supposed to exhibit as their nuptials approached, and saw only that she looked much the same as always, except a little worn and shadowed round the eyes.

He called one day when she had just got home from the office and saw at once from the tension in her face that something had happened. 'You look tired,' he said. 'You're trying to do too much. Fixing up the wedding—'

'Oh, it's not so bad,' Polly said. 'I have lots of help. Lizzie is arranging everything at the church, and the Ansonia is doing the wedding breakfast – I only had to choose the menu. I do find it hard being followed around by the press. I don't mind them looking, but they *will* ask me questions, the same ones over and over. It's very wearing.'

'And I see Alexander has you gadding about night after night.'

'It doesn't feel much like gadding,' she said unwarily, 'more like hard work.'

'Poor Polly. Are his friends very dull?'

'I didn't mean that. Important people *are* hard work. I don't know if you'd even call them his friends. It's business, really.'

Before Lennie could ask an imprudent question, Plummer came in with a tray of tea. It was the time in the day Polly most felt she needed it, when she was back from work and about to start a different sort of work, the evening round. Plummer had brought an extra cup, and a plate of bread-and-butter – Polly had had to train her, but she now took great pride in how thinly she could cut it.

Polly poured, and Lennie studied the set of her mouth. When she had handed him cup and plate, he said, 'Something's wrong, Polly. I can tell. What is it?'

She looked up, paused, and gave in. 'Nothing's wrong. But I had something from my father today. A letter and a package. Look.' She took a small box from the sofa-table and held it out to him, open. 'Diamond earrings to go with my diamond necklace.'

'They're beautiful,' Lennie said. He was enough of a man of the world to know at a glance that, while not vulgarly large, they were superb stones, and must have cost a lot.

'It's his wedding present to me,' she said. Her mouth was set hard. 'Trying to buy my favour.'

'You know that's not it,' Lennie said.

80

'What is it, then?'

'He's your father. He loves you. I bet he'd love to have been here to give you away.'

'He "gave me away" when he married that woman. He made it very clear then that he had no more use for me.'

'The love a man feels for a wife is different from the love he feels for his child. They don't cancel each other out. You *know* that, except when you're being childish. And selfish.'

'Selfish?' The word angered her.

'Why should you want to prevent him having the happiness a wife can bring him? That's selfish – and cruel. He's an old man—'

'And he's married a girl not much older than me!'

'If they don't mind the age difference, what business is it of yours?'

She was shocked by the directness, as he had meant her to be. 'But—' she began, and could not go on. Tears welled up in her eyes, and for once she couldn't force them back down.

Lennie went and sat beside her on the sofa. He took her hand. 'What is it, Polly darling? Tell me. What's really hurting you?'

'He sent me a letter,' she said with difficulty. Her throat ached. 'He said – he wished he could be here. Hoped I'd be always happy. No hard words. Just – kind. And I was so m-mean to him!'

And then she was in his arms, her head on his shoulder, and the pain was staggering out of her in choking half-sentences. He held her quietly, and reflected that it was really the same wound they were all carrying, more or less: the war. The long strain of it; her cousins Ned, Frank and Robbie falling; so many childhood friends lost. There had been years of anxiety about Jack, the shock of his going missing and then turning up as a prisoner. And most of all, of course,

81

the man: the man she had loved, whose name she still would not say; the man who had taken her heart, and then had been killed. Wearied and worn by so much loss and anxiety, grieving for her lost love, she had fled a devastated land to America, to try to find some wholeness.

But then her father, the one person in whose eyes she had always come first, whose love for her had always been unconditional – the rock and foundation of her life – had knocked the ground out from under her feet. She *had* reacted like a child, he thought, but who could blame her? She thought she had lost everything. It was the last straw.

He held her without speaking until she had cried herself out. Then he went on holding her while she rested quietly against his shoulder.

At last she stirred and began to sit up. He provided her with his handkerchief.

'I'm sorry,' she said at last, in a small, exhausted voice. 'I must look awful.'

Despite the weeping, the pallor of tears, the red eyes and pink nose, she was still unbearably beautiful to him. 'You don't,' he said.

She regarded him for a long moment, taking something from him, he didn't know what. Then she said humbly, 'Do you really think Daddy still loves me?'

'Of course,' he said. 'I *know* he does.'

She sighed shakily, and was quiet for a while, thinking. Then she said, 'I still hate her. I can't help it. I know it's wrong, but – but she's taken part of him away from me.'

'What she has is a part you could never have had,' Lennie said. 'The part he gave your mother, and then Aunt Alice. You mustn't begrudge him, Polly. If you love someone, you have to want them to be happy, even if it isn't – with you.'

She was scalded. 'Oh, Lennie! I'm sorry. I'm so sorry. I wish I could love you that way – I really, really do.'

'I know. But you don't, and I have to live with it. All

I want for now is that you should be happy. Will you be happy with Alexander?'

'Yes,' she said, but still looking troubled.

'Do you love him?' It was the question he had never asked, for fear of the answer.

'Yes,' she said. And his punishment was that he did not know what she meant by that. He did not know if she was in love with Ren, and that he must therefore give her up; or that she was not, and that he must therefore prepare to witness her suffering. Either way was bad.

He thought that 'yes' was her whole answer, but before he could come to the end of his reasoning and speak again, she said, 'He excites me, and intrigues me. He offers me a new and different life. For the rest – well, you can never know until you're married, can you? It has to be chance. But he will be someone of my own, someone who is completely for me, and I want that so much. So you can be happy for *me*, Lennie, dear.'

Lennie turned his mind resolutely away from all the problems her words stirred up. He must help her, that was all. Always help her. 'What will you do about your father?'

'What should I do?'

'You know that. Write to him. Thank him for the gift, and his good wishes. Apologise for ignoring him for so long.' She sighed. 'I know it will be hard for you. But it's the right thing to do. Will you?'

'Yes,' she said. 'I'll write to him.'

'A kind letter? A warm letter?'

'Yes.'

'Good girl. And now, how about washing your face, and letting me take you out to Horn & Hardart's for pie?'

She smiled. 'You're so foolish!'

'I'm serious. Cherry pie – I know that's your favourite. With ice cream on top if you like.'

'Now you've done it,' Polly smiled. 'You know I can't resist ice cream. Wait while I tidy myself up.'

In ten minutes they were out and walking down towards Broadway arm in arm, through a grey-blue, gusty dusk.

'Why is pie called "*à la mode*" when you have ice cream on it?' she asked.

Oliver and his mother were having luncheon together at home. He had had an unexpected gap in his normally busy day, and his wife Verena was lunching out with the ladies of one of her committees. He had been intending to go to his club, but then had reflected that his mother would certainly like the company, and that the food was better at home.

Venetia had retired from surgery, and now had only her medical researches to keep her amused. Oliver was the busy one, building up his practice, performing plastic surgery at the Winchmore, where he took both private and free patients, and, increasingly, at various nursing homes and small hospitals in and around London. He had specialised in plastics during the war, working on burned and disfigured airmen at the Sidcup unit under Harold Gillies. Once the war ended, the unit had closed down, and since none of the big hospitals had a plastics department, he had had to start from scratch. It was tremendously hard work.

'I had an interesting case yesterday,' he told his mother, over the cutlets. 'Didn't have a chance to tell you about it last night.'

'No, you were too busy fiddling with that infernal wireless of yours for conversation,' Venetia said. 'What was that cater-wauling that so fascinated you?'

'I was trying to get Layton and Johnstone. Don't look so disapproving. They're very well thought of in cabaret circles. They were singing "Strut, Miss Lizzie",' he added mischievously.

84

Venetia shuddered. 'I wish I hadn't asked. Tell me about your interesting case.'

'It was a boy referred to me from Fawcett, the urologist at the Southport. Closer examination showed the boy to be, in fact, a girl. The underdeveloped penis was really an over-developed clitoris, and the scrotum was undivided labia majora, behind which were the labia minora, hymen and vagina, all present and correct. The mother said the boy's father had always worried about him being a bit of a cissy, not good at games, more interested in reading stories than climbing trees. It's a good job we got the case before puberty – imagine his perplexity if his "son" had started growing breasts instead of a beard.'

'Poor child. It will be quite an adjustment for the parents to make. Are they uneducated people?'

'I'm afraid so. The father's a porter at Covent Garden market. But he'll be happier with a proper daughter than a son he despises. I tidied it all up there, divided the labia, reduced the clitoris – fortunately the urethra was in the right place.' He went into some professional details, which his mother absorbed with interest. 'I'm thinking of writing it up for the *Lancet*.'

'If you do that, you'll have all sorts of crusty old fossils howling at you for tampering with God's work. Anything to do with the sexual organs brings out the beast in our older members. They'll say changing males into females is the devil's work.'

'She was already a female.'

'That won't stop them saying it.'

Oliver sighed. He knew it was true. 'They're already down on me every time I do anything outside burns and recon-struction, like that rhinoplasty last month. They sneer and tell me I'm better suited to the beauty parlour than a hospital.'

'But you wouldn't want to perform surgery just because of an individual's vanity?' Venetia asked.

'You can't deny there are people whose lives are made a hell by disfiguring birthmarks, for instance, or ugly moles. And grossly oversized mammaries can cause a woman real pain and inconvenience, as well as making her miserable. I had a burn case at the Winchmore – you remember, I mentioned it at the time – where the protrusion of her breasts had caused her clothing to catch fire from the stove, with horrible results.'

'Hmm,' said Venetia. 'But where do you draw the line between a woman reduced to a miserable hermit because of her appearance, and a woman who merely wishes she were more beautiful?'

'I use my judgement, of course, Mother, dear. Don't we practitioners do that all the time?' He put down his fork. 'You would want to *ban* purely cosmetic surgery?'

She looked startled. 'Ban it? Certainly not. Can't have the law interfering with medical decisions. Besides, banning something just makes people want it more, and creates an illegal market.'

'Like alcohol in the United States.'

'Precisely. From what we read, the place is crawling with dreadful gangsters. No, it's pointless to ban the things people want. Much better to give it to 'em and tax it.'

Oliver laughed. 'Sound economics! They ought to have consulted you over the budget.' Comment on it was filling the papers.

'I'm sure I could have made a better fist of it,' Venetia grumbled. 'Death duties sky high. And supertax – what a notion!'

'But income tax is coming down to four shillings. That's good news. What about this new old age pension? They say it will double the income of the poorest old folk.'

'Charity saps a man's spirit,' she said.

'You can't object to the return to the Gold Standard?' he tried.

'It's nothing but a gesture,' she said. 'Heaven help us if we have to rely on Winston Churchill for fiscal policy! He knows no more about finance than the kitchen cat.'

Oliver was always amused by her strictures. She and Churchill had clashed in the suffragette years and she had never forgiven him.

'Besides, I can't see the point of returning to the Gold Standard if we aren't to have gold coinage again,' she went on. 'This wretched paper money seems to be here to stay. Do you remember, when you were young, your father used to give you a sovereign on your birthday?'

He nodded. 'It was such a special thing – far nicer than silver or banknotes. Still, we must be modern, eh, Mum?'

'Hm,' she said, her mind evidently off on another track. 'Modern – you young people think that excuses everything.'

'Mother, darling, I'm hardly "you young people" any more. I'm thirty-seven, and a respectable married man.' He eyed her frown and said gently, 'You're thinking about Violet?'

'I can't like this business between her and the Prince of Wales,' she confessed. 'And I can't like that young man, either. He's rackety and spoilt and thinks of nothing but his own pleasure.'

'What else is there is for a Prince of Wales to do? Look at your own particular one – Bertie. Scandal after scandal, but he made a perfectly good king.'

'He was a shrewd and clever man,' Venetia said. 'I can't see anything in this "David" but self-indulgence. What *does* Violet see in him?'

'Well, he's good-looking, lively – and she hasn't had much liveliness in her life so far. She chose the wrong husband for that.'

'Holkam *is* rather a stick,' Venetia admitted.

'And Wales is terribly devoted, you know.'

'For the time being. I'm just afraid it will ruin Violet. If it became public . . .'

'It never will, not in this country. No-one outside the inner circle ever heard of Freda Dudley Ward.'

'True.' She was the previous favourite, who had been dropped when the Prince of Wales took a fancy to Violet – though he had remained friendly with her, and was fond of her children.

'And it isn't doing Holkam any harm, you know. As the man whose wife has the ear of the future king, he can hope for all sorts of advancement. It's not a bad start, PPS to the Colonial Secretary, and I hear he's seen around the corridors all the time with Churchill and the Home Secretary.'

'I don't care a fig for Holkam's career – if that's what it is.'

'You may not care about him, but anything he achieves will benefit his children – who are your grandchildren, don't forget. It will do Robert and Richard good at Eton to have a father close to the cabinet, and open up possibilities for them after university. And Charlotte will need a good husband in seven or eight years' time.'

'And little Henry, what of him?' Venetia said. Henry – or Octavian, as Violet called him – was the child of Violet's *affaire* with the painter Octavian Laidislaw, who had died at the Somme. Holkam had acknowledged the child as the price of avoiding scandal, but it had been a horribly worrying time.

'Oh, I think he'll do all right,' Oliver said cheerfully. 'Nice little chap. Quite a hand at drawing, you know – I suppose that's his father coming out in him.'

'Violet encourages him. I wish she wouldn't. It would be fatal to annoy Holkam.'

'I shouldn't worry. Oddly enough, I have a notion that secretly, Holkam likes little Henry the best of the bunch.'

'Even if that's true, he's not likely to be so accommodating if Violet presents him with another brat from an illicit liaison.'

'I wouldn't worry,' he told his mother. 'I don't think that will happen. Anyway, she's getting a nice rest from the prince this year, with this African tour of his, and then South America in September.'

The Morland–Alexander wedding was to take place in the Cathedral Church of St John the Divine on Amsterdam Avenue. When the cornerstone had been laid in 1892, it had been intended when finished to rival, and indeed far surpass, the glamorous St Patrick's in Fifth Avenue; to be not only the biggest church in New York, but the biggest in the world. Work had been going on steadily for three decades but it was still nowhere near finished. Even in its unfinished state, however, it was impressive, a grand and noble edifice of stone, originally Romanesque but now (since the architect had been changed halfway through) mostly Gothic. As a bishop's seat, it had a magnificent interior that would seat ten thousand. Polly had seen it once, and found the idea of being married there rather daunting.

The wedding breakfast was to take place in the Assembly Room at the Ansonia, the apartment-hotel on Broadway between 73rd and 74th: a gigantic building in the French *beaux-arts* style, with a mansard roof and unusual round corner turrets topped with lantern-like copper finials. It had a central open stairwell that swept up all eighteen floors to a vast domed skylight, and public rooms of unparalleled magnificence. Originally, it had even had a pasture on the roof supporting cows, chickens, ducks and goats, to provide fresh milk and eggs to the tenants and guests, the surplus being sold off daily to the public in the basement shopping arcade; but the city authorities had closed down the 'farm in the sky' in 1907.

It was, quite simply, the grandest hotel in New York, and Ren had taken an apartment there for him and Polly to occupy until their house was ready.

All the arrangements were in hand. At the church, the hymns had been chosen, the flowers ordered, the seating plan finalised. At the Ansonia, the menu had been agreed, and the band was booked for the dancing afterwards. The invitation cards had been ordered from a large department store, which had not only sent them out but was keeping the list of acceptances, and receiving and displaying the wedding presents. New York understood about busy people, and knew how to make life easier for them.

Patrick was to stand in for Polly's father and give her away; and Ruth had insisted that Polly must spend the night before the wedding at their apartment. Despite the Morgan twins, or perhaps even because of them, Ruth felt it was wrong for unmarried girls to live alone; and for Polly to be married from her own apartment would only emphasise the shameful situation.

The last few days before the wedding flew past. She and Ren managed one last dinner alone together, and it was like an oasis of calm in the frantic activity. Instead of the Waldorf-Astoria, or any of the expensive restaurants where they met the Washington Set, Ren took her to an out-of-the-way Italian speakeasy called the Palermo Club, a Sicilian family-run restaurant, with Mamma and the daughters doing the cooking and Papa making wine in the basement. Ren tipped the taxi-driver to outrun the press, and then tipped the maître d' to give them the most secluded table and tell no-one they were there. Consequently, they had the first peace and quiet together for weeks.

Polly had never had Italian food before, and loved the rich, simple tastes of meat, tomatoes, cheese and wine. 'This is so nice,' she said. The restaurant was dimly lit with candles, and there were checked tablecloths, and a trio playing smooth jazz.

'I thought you might like it for a change.'

'The staff seem to know you.'

'It's been one of my favourite haunts for years. With speak-easies, the food is usually poor, but here you can get good things to eat and drink, and no fear of a raid.'

'Why not?'

'Oh, the Italians generally come to an arrangement with the cops,' he said. 'There are a lot of them in the police department. Some precincts are practically family affairs.'

Polly smiled. 'I love the things you know.'

'You're looking tired,' Ren said, examining her by the candlelight. 'You've been working too hard. Not long to go now.'

'There's a lot of nonsense in the papers about the wedding,' Polly said. 'Did you see the piece that talked about my father being "an English lord"?'

Ren shrugged. 'A lot of people think all English gentlemen are lords.'

'It's so sad you don't have any family.'

He put his hand over hers where it rested on the table, and she felt that indefinable quake inside. 'You and I will be our own family.'

'You and I – and our children?' she said, greatly daring.

He paused. 'I want for us to have children, of course,' he said, 'but I don't think we should start right in. It will take up too much of your time, and we need to get ourselves established first. You don't mind?' His eyes were watchful on her face.

'No – I mean – whatever you think best. But I don't know how—' She had heard about preventing babies, but had no idea how it was done.

'I wouldn't expect you to. You must leave that to me. I'll take care of everything.'

He released her hand, and she was glad to concentrate on her meatballs and spaghetti for a few moments to hide her shyness. He ate, too, and having swallowed a mouthful, said, 'Which brings us neatly to the subject of the honeymoon. I haven't had a chance to speak to you about it before now. We're going to have a week on Long Island – it will give us a chance to look for a suitable summer house at the same time – and then have a week or so in Washington. I want to show you off there, and introduce you to some people who won't be at the wedding.'

'So we're only going to be away for two weeks?'

'Two or three weeks at the most. It's better at the moment if I'm not away for too long – there's a great deal to be done in my new office, and it would be foolish to waste the momentum the wedding has given me. People soon forget you if you are not right under their noses.'

'That's all right,' Polly said, trying to be brisk. Hadn't she always told herself she liked him for not being romantic with her? 'I have so many new orders coming in, it would be inconvenient to be away a long time. And then there's the fall show to start work on.'

'In April?'

'Of course. People want their fall outfits all ready and waiting when they come back to town. You have to work ahead.'

'Well, that won't be your problem, anyway. You'll be putting in a manager to run everything.'

Polly felt an odd shiver of foreboding. 'What do you mean?'

He raised an eyebrow. 'You won't be able to go on running the thing yourself once we're married.'

'I thought you were proud of me for setting up my own business,' Polly said carefully.

'Of course I am,' he said. 'And the experience will be useful to you. But you'll have a house to run – two houses, because we'll have to spend a lot of time in Washington. You'll have all our entertaining to arrange, and any number of people to keep up with. You simply won't have time to run Maison Polly as well.'

Polly swallowed hurt, and tried to be practical. 'It isn't as easy as you think. Madame Renée can run the salon and the girls, but she can't run the business and make decisions.'

'That's what you'll have a manager for.'

'A manager can't design the clothes.'

'You'll find a designer,' he said serenely. 'Some talented kid wanting a leg up. They're everywhere. And there's no reason you shouldn't do the odd bit of designing, and keep an overall eye on things. But you won't be going in there every day as you do now. You'll have a more important job to do. As a married woman, your first duty will be to me.'

'Of course,' she said, but her voice sounded light and unreal to her.

'We'll find the right person to take over, don't worry. The rag business is no different from any other. Management is a skill in itself, you know – ask your cousin Lennie. Now, regarding our New York house,' he went on, 'I've heard of a property coming on to the market on Fifth Avenue, facing the Park, near the Seventy-second Street gate.'

He went on to describe it, and other thoughts fell away as she listened and grew excited. A house of her own!

Out of the corner of her eye she saw someone approach their table – a fashionably dressed woman, perhaps wanting to congratulate Polly on the upcoming wedding. The maître d' intercepted her and turned her away. That was the sort of power Ren had; and it was only the beginning.

CHAPTER FIVE

Polly was dreaming of Erich. It was so long now since she had last seen him that generally in her dreams he was just a shape, his features indistinguishable. But this time it was unusually vivid and she could see him clearly. It was the same old dream. He was in a long, slow queue of prisoners of war, shuffling along the quayside and mounting the gangplank of the steamer. What she could see, and they could not, was that at the top an armed guard was shooting each man as he reached him. She tried to cry out a warning, but she could not make a sound. She tried to run to him, but her feet would not move. She could only watch helplessly as he moved patiently step by step away from her and towards his doom . . .

She woke with a choked cry, and found herself staring at an unrecognised ceiling. For a moment she did not know where she was, or how far through her life she had got. The dread of the dream clung to her like cobwebs. *Erich? Was he in danger?*

Then she woke fully, and the sickening realisation came to her with all the force of the first time. He was dead. He had been killed by an anti-German mob at the dockyard as he was being sent home. She would never see him again.

Finally, like a radio tuning in, the understanding came of where she was. The ceiling belonged to the bedroom she had been given at Patrick's apartment for her wedding eve, which meant that this was her wedding day. Today she was going marry Ren Alexander, and her whole life would change completely. No dream, this: she would have a real husband by this day's end, flesh and blood and mind and passion. She was afraid, but hopeful. She wanted this, though she had no idea how it would turn out.

Plummer came in with her tea, put the tray down to open the curtains, and said, 'It's a lovely day, miss. Not too hot and not too cold. Just right.' She looked as taut as a piano string, half excited, half nervous.

She put the tray across Polly's knees, and said, 'The brides-maids have started arriving, miss. Would you rather have breakfast in here? No-one will think it strange, and Mrs Morland is out there to take care of them.'

The bridesmaids had all been invited to breakfast and to dress – Ruth had said if you didn't get them all together well beforehand they'd be arriving at the church in dribs and drabs, and some of them might not arrive at all – and Lizzie, who was bringing Rose anyway, had offered to super-vise them, and protect them from Ruth's tongue.

'Yes, I'd rather,' Polly said. Already through the door she could hear the sound of excited chatter, and the thought of going out there and being shrieked at made her feel slightly sick. 'I don't want any breakfast, though,' she said. 'I couldn't eat it.'

It was the wrong thing to say, for in a short time it brought Ruth herself, driving the housemaid Ellen, carrying a tray, before her. 'No nonsense about not eating. I won't have to do with niminy-piminy girls who put on die-away airs to be interesting. You've a long day before you. Eat your breakfast and let's have no more monkey-shines.'

It was as bracing as smelling-salts, and under the gimlet eye Polly had to make a start on the breakfast – and found, of course, that she felt better at once. The next interruption was Ruth's elderly lady's-maid, Stanford, who was being lent to help her dress because Plummer was by now in a state of excitement that almost neutralised her usefulness.

All the dresses had been delivered from the workshop the day before, and were hanging from various picture rails in their muslin bags, like so many ghosts. Stanford brought Polly's, divested it of its wrapping and hung it on the wardrobe door. It had taken up so much of the efforts of her seamstresses and cost a fortune in overtime, but one look told Polly it had been worth it.

Hems this year were just below the knee, but Polly had felt that was not dignified, so she had compromised with a muddled hemline: the overskirt hem was three inches below the knee, and the cream silk underskirt had handkerchief points reaching almost to her ankle.

The overdress was of the finest lawn, embroidered all over in white silk in a swirling pattern of roses and leaves. It was edged with delicate needle lace, which had been made for her by an old French *émigrée* who lived on East Thirty-fifth Street. The embroidery had been done by two of her own women and had taken weeks. The skirt was ruched down the left side, the gathers held by silk roses, with tiny crystal beads sewn on them like dewdrops.

There was little to do with her hair, which was at its shortest, and after brushing it, Plummer and Stanford lifted on the headdress. It was low across the forehead in the cloche style, white silk sewn all over with white flowers made of layers of stiffened lawn and net and decorated with seed pearls. From the headdress hung the eight-foot veil of antique Valenciennes lace. This fabulously valuable piece of material came from the warehouse of a cloth merchant with whom she had done a great deal of business, and who hoped she would do a great deal more in future. She had bought the lawn and the silk from him, and he had lent her the lace on condition that any description of the dress she gave to a magazine would mention his business.

Plummer was just clasping the double strand of pearls, lent by Lizzie, around her neck when there was a knock at the door and Ellen came in with the bouquet, which had just arrived. It was simple, of white roses and gardenias set against ferns.

'Oh, miss,' Ellen said fervently, 'you look lovely, miss.'

Polly turned to the mirror, seeing herself properly for the first time. Until now, the gown had been business, something designed to impress the world. Now she saw herself: the white of the overdress softened by the cream of underskirt and veil, the richness and simplicity. It was a magical figure made of clouds, every girl's dream of a wedding. But the figure in the mirror had Polly's face. *It was really happening.*

By the time she stepped out into the drawing-room of the flat, the eight bridesmaids were ready – anonymous sylphides whose murmurs of admiration were like the cooing of doves. Only Rose separated herself from the mass to dart forward and kiss Polly, becoming an individual as she whispered, 'You're *beautiful*!'

And then, finally, they were all gone, and there was just her and Patrick. Ellen came to say the car was ready, and carried the end of her veil downstairs for her, helped her across the sidewalk and into the car. There was quite a crowd gathered, and there were cries of admiration and good-luck wishes as well as the flash of cameras. Patrick entered the car and settled himself beside her. She felt his large calmness, and was glad of it. From childhood upward, all girls imagined their wedding day; but that was play, and this was real. Today she was going to be married irrevocably to big Ren Alexander. She swallowed. *What was she doing?*

As if he had heard her thought, Patrick reached across and laid a kindly hand over hers. 'Nervous?' he said. 'It's natural. You'll be fine when the moment comes.'

He was very like Lennie, she thought, accepting the comfort numbly. Or perhaps she should say Lennie was like him.

Lennie had been banished by Ruth to spend the wedding eve at Lizzie's house – he supposed from some rigid sense of Southern propriety on Ruth's part – and went to the church with Ashley, in a car that picked up Ashley's son Martial and his wife Mimi and their children on the way.

Lennie had volunteered early to be one of the ushers, because he had known he would need to keep himself busy. At the church he greeted people, directed them or showed them to their seats, dealt with a minor crisis regarding a flower arrangement and a guest with chronic hay-fever, fraternised with the policemen keeping the crowds back, and ejected a pressman trying to sneak in with the guests.

All went well until Alexander arrived with his best man, Tosh Whitney Loomis, heir to a chemical fortune and related to so many of the top families his middle names should have been legion. Alexander – tall, handsome, exquisitely dressed – smiled to left and right for the crowds and the cameras, but there was a flicker of a muscle twitching in his left cheek, which Lennie was close enough to observe. *He was nervous.* It was enough to change him from a blank thing, a draper's mannequin, into real flesh and blood, and it seared Lennie to the heart, because this warm incarnate man was going to marry Polly and take her away from him for ever.

Ren spotted him and took a step out of his way to shake Lennie's hand and flash a smile at him – like a politician already, Lennie managed to think sourly, though the smile seemed so genuine he had to fight against its charm. Then he was gone, into the church to take up his position by the altar to wait for Polly. *Oh, God, to wait for Polly!*

And still he knew nothing about him. Delaney's last report was that Jacob Arkady had gone to California after passing through Immigration, and it was there that he had met and married Doris Hawthorne. But there was no sign of young Renfrew in their lives, and it seemed it was not from California that they had gone to Ohio. There was a gap in between. Did Mr Manning want them to continue with the search? Because more money would be needed if he did. Half determined, half ashamed, Lennie had parted with some more greenbacks. *Where had Alexander come from?* He had to know.

The bridesmaids arrived, spilling out from the two cars, like milk from a tumbled pitcher. A chatter of bridesmaids, a flutter of bridesmaids, brushing down their skirts and straightening each other's chaplets. Only one was distinguishable, the one with Rose's face, very solemn and taking her duty seriously, until she caught Lennie's eye and gave a huge, schoolgirl grin of delight. He should go inside now. His part was ended until the ceremony was over. He did not want to see Polly arrive. Yet he could not make himself leave.

He retreated into the shadow of the porch, but then his feet nailed themselves to the ground. *Don't do this to yourself!* Here was the car. Still time to run. But he stayed put. The body of bridesmaids swayed with eagerness, the car drew up, his father climbed out like a monument of calm. And then *she* stepped out.

His vision was blurred. He saw only the white shape of a bride. The dress was elegant, rich but understated, as he could have guessed it would be. Her long veil trailed out after her, and the breeze caught it and billowed it a little. The bridesmaids hurried forward, the leading two – Rose and a senator's daughter – to carry the end of it. Polly was tall, so the veil did not make a very long train. The bride came past him, a ghostly figure, a paradigm. She would not see him. He had drawn back as far as he could into the shadows.

But as if she had known he was there, she turned her face to him just as she passed. It was a white, tense face. If he had been called to name the emotion he would have had to say apprehension. For the split second she seemed not to recognise him. Then she smiled and tilted her head to him – rueful, apologetic, the smile seemed – and then she was gone.

A better man, a quicker-witted man, he told himself afterwards, as he made his way to his seat, would have grabbed her hand in that instant and run away with her. But, no, that was foolish. She was not on her way to the guillotine. She had chosen her husband for herself, without even the breath of familial pressure. And she had had years of opportunity to choose Lennie if she had wanted him. He had to accept she didn't love him, and never would. This was the day when he must finally put her out of his mind and get on with his life.

The idea was bleak. And he still did not trust Alexander. She was his cousin, and he would always have to keep an eye on her, be there if anything happened. *That* idea was a lot more comfortable, and he decided to keep hold of it.

Polly came out of the church on Ren's arm as Mrs Alexander to a barrage of flashes and huge cheering from the crowd. Who *were* all those people, and why did they care? None of it seemed real at all. She turned this way and that at the camera's bidding. The clouds moved across the high, pale-blue sky and she lost track of time. She half expected the sun to be going down because the day had seemed so long already.

Ren, the gigantic figure beside her, was the least real of all. She hadn't looked at his face, even when saying her piece at the altar. She hadn't looked at the priest's, either, or Patrick's, or any of the bridesmaids'. The only face she had seen since she left the apartment was Lennie's, in that brief moment when she passed him in the porch – poor Lennie looking as though he was on the way to the guillotine, but smiling, smiling in adversity.

Finally the cars came up to take everyone the short distance to the Ansonia. The wedding breakfast was magnificent: iced anchovy creams, salmon mayonnaise, chicken *à la* Maryland, cheese puffs, peaches in chartreuse jelly, meringues and ice cream. Polly couldn't eat. She tried a mouthful or two, but had difficulty swallowing. She drank champagne instead, because it was cold and felt refreshing, but it was an illusion, for it did not refresh. Her sense of distance from everything increased.

It went on for a very long time, and there were speeches and toasts, and the reading out of telegrams. Polly drifted on a sea of words and heard none of them. At some point dancing began. Polly draped her veil over her arm and danced with Ren, who still had no face. Then it seemed she had to dance with every other man at the wedding. The pins holding her headdress in place were hurting her scalp, the veil was heavy and she was terrified of getting it torn. It made no sense to her, in her bemused state, to be dancing in her wedding-dress and veil. Dancing was what you did in restaurants and clubs.

At last the cake was wheeled in (the Ansonia had done them proud) and she and Ren had to cut it. His hand resting over hers on the knife was damp – it was very warm in here. The knife was ceremonial and silver, not sharp enough, and Ren had to press hard enough to hurt her to get through the icing. But once the first cut was made, the staff did the rest, and distributed the pieces, and there was more champagne, and more speeches.

After the last speech they walked through the applauding, congratulating throng to the door of the Assembly Room. There the awkwardness of the fact that they were not going away suddenly struck Polly. There was no seeing them off to the station – they only had to go upstairs. There was a strained pause. Then Ren, who must have felt it too, cried, 'To the elevator!' and scooped her up in his arms.

He was strong enough to do it neatly, though she was unprepared, and the veil was an entanglement. Amid cheers he carried her rapidly across the foyer to the elevators. Fortunately there was one there, ready – it would have been a dreadful anticlimax if they had had to wait with everyone watching. As soon as the door closed, he set her on her feet and then, despite the presence of the elevator boy, he kissed her. It took her by surprise, and she felt nothing at first; but as he went on kissing her, she began to feel again that loosening pang in her stomach.

He released her lips at last, straightening up. 'That's on account,' he said softly. Out of the corner of her eye she saw the elevator boy smirking. 'Expect full payment later.'

Later. Well, yes, she was coming to it, now – the act, the revelation, the knowledge. She was afraid, but excited. She knew now that she wanted it, though she had no idea what *it* was. But she wanted *him*, to possess and be possessed, to be close, to be one. And that was what love gave, wasn't it – oneness?

Across the hall from the elevator to the door of the apartment, and Plummer was there to greet them, and Ren's valet Stevens, a short, swarthy, taciturn man, whom Plummer eyed with considerable reserve. They stood back to allow the bridal couple to step over the threshold. Polly turned enquiringly to Ren, unsure of how the business was to proceed. But he was taking the gardenia from his buttonhole and dropping it onto the vestibule table. He stooped and kissed her on the cheek, and said, 'You must excuse me, my love, if I go downstairs again for a while.'

'Downstairs?' she faltered. She had braced herself for what was to come. This was not how it was meant to go. Now, if ever, was the time for Ren to be romantic. She'd have forgiven him any degree of spoonyness at that point.

'I'm sorry,' he said, 'but there are people I must see. The wedding was a wonderful excuse to get certain people together who aren't usually in the same place at the same time, and I can't waste the opportunity. I know you understand. Why don't you make yourself comfortable, and I'll see you later?'

And with that, he was gone.

Polly had only seen the apartment briefly, when Ren took her around it after signing the lease. It was large and grand in the Ansonia style, with high ceilings and moulded cornices, chandeliers and Persian carpets. It had a huge parlour, with a grand piano and a bay window giving sweeping views north and south along Broadway; a handsome oval dining-room, a library, two bedrooms with a dressing-room in between, a vast bathroom, and a kitchen with servants' bedrooms beyond.

Plummer had put Polly's things into one of the bedrooms, and now led her to it. She couldn't help noticing that Ren's things were not there. Stevens must have unpacked him into the other bedroom. She did not know how these things were arranged in America. At home, her father had slept in the same room with his wife, but she knew that among the upper classes, like Violet and Lord Holkam, separate rooms were the norm.

She stood in the middle of the room, foolish in her wedding finery all alone, and felt lost. In the wardrobe mirror she caught Plummer's eye, and her maid hurried to her with a look of motherly concern she had never seen before. 'Let me help you out of that dress, madam. It'd be a shame if it was to get spoilt, let alone that lace. And then I'll run you a nice, deep bath. Your poor feet must be worn out with all the standing and dancing you've done today.'

It was a new departure for Plummer, but Polly let herself be cosseted. The bath was a great comfort. She lingered in it for nearly an hour, topping up the hot water whenever it cooled, her tired mind drifting, unfocused. Everything was too strange to be thought about. Instead, she visited the past.

She remembered baths at home, in England, in the big enamelled tub drawn up before the bedroom fire, with towels warming in the rosy glow, and a housemaid to bring you more water, and scrub your back for you. And always a dog, nose on paws, waiting for you, or growing impatient and trying to drink the bathwater.

Her fingers grew pruny, and she dragged herself out, dried herself and put on the eau-de-Nil silk and lace négligée set Plummer had left for her. There being no sign of her husband, she got into bed, meaning to read until he came up to – to do whatever he would do. But it had been a long day, which itself had been the culmination of a time of great exertion, and she was very tired. She had hardly read two sentences before she was asleep.

She woke, confused, not knowing where she was for a moment. The apartments in the Ansonia had very thick walls, and there was no sound anywhere. Someone – she supposed it was Plummer – had taken the book from her hand and turned out the lights, all but the reading lamp on the far side of the bed. What had wakened her?

Then she saw the door to the dressing-room was open, and she heard the sound of a drawer being closed in there. At once she was fully awake, her heart bumping. It must be Ren, come up to bed at last. She reached across to the bedside table for her watch – it was almost twelve. His form, in a dark red silk dressing-gown, filled the doorway, then he was in, closing the door behind him, and the vast bedroom seemed suddenly too small to hold him. He came and sat down on the edge of the bed, and took her hand. His big dark face bent towards her, and she smelt Colgate dental cream not quite masking the fine brandy behind it.

'Well?' he said.

She wanted to say something, but somehow couldn't catch her breath.

104

'Don't be afraid,' he said. 'I should think the worse of myself if I couldn't make you happy.' He was studying her face intently, and she now, perforce, looked into his. She couldn't make anything of it. It was a collection of features she knew tolerably well, but she could not make them turn into a coherent whole. Who *was* Ren? He was a stranger to her, and yet she had married him, and they were now, she presumed, to become lovers. Her body felt tight and hard, rejecting the idea of being broached. She didn't know what to do. She didn't want to know. *I want to go home*, she thought. But that was silly – this was home now.

He said, 'You've never done this before.'

She wanted to say, of course not, but her mouth was dry and she could only shake her head. But he knew the answer, anyway.

He bent and kissed her on the forehead. Then his warm lips drifted down, kissed her eyelids, the tip of her nose, and settled on her mouth. After a moment the tingling began, and when she started to respond, his hand came up and stroked her head, cupped her cheek, then slid down her neck to her breast. She stiffened, but he did not remove the hand. His fingers explored her and, with a mixture of shame and excitement, she felt the nipple grow hard and erect under his touch.

As if this had been a sign, he stopped kissing her, stood up, and said, 'We'd better have the light off.' Her eyes followed him round the bed. She was aware, now, that under the red silk dressing-gown he was naked, and she half wished he was not so considerate as to provide her with darkness. Terrifying though the idea was, she wanted to see him. But he switched off the light. She heard a rustle of silk, then felt the jerk of the covers and the bending of the mattress as he got into bed.

Now she could feel his searing heat beside her; his hand was on her breast, he was kissing her, and she felt something like a thump in the pit of her stomach, the arrival of desire. She was kissing him back with greedy eagerness. Whatever he would do, she wanted it. She had waited years for this, to know what it was that lovers did. She felt as though she were teetering on the edge of an abyss, but she *wanted* to fall. The plummet would be exciting; and she had a notion that she would find she was able to fly.

Wandering around the British Museum one Saturday afternoon in May, Molly saw a woman in a very smart dress and jacket of linen, in the new shade of beige called Sand Dune, and was amused with herself that she knew such a thing as the name of a colour. Working on a newspaper had introduced her to many new areas of knowledge, some more welcome than others.

Perhaps feeling she was being stared at, the woman turned, and Molly saw under the shade of the cloche hat (the style was universal now) a face she knew.

'Emma! Fancy meeting you here.'

Emma Weston had been frowning, though perhaps it was in thought rather than dislike of being accosted, because the frown dissolved instantly, and she came towards Molly with a warm smile.

'How nice to see you. It's been an age. What are you doing here?'

'Enjoying free entertainment. I live not too far away.'

'You were in lodgings in Marylebone last time I saw you.'

'Yes – I changed jobs and house. I have a little flat off the Gray's Inn Road. I'm more surprised to see you here, though.'

'Why should it surprise you?'

'Too fusty for one of the Bright Young Things, I'd have thought. Whenever I see you mentioned in the press, it's in the pursuit of pleasure. There was a picture of you last week dressed in a sort of Chinese costume – very fetching.'

'Japanese, actually. That was Fritz Pennington's Madame

Butterfly party. All the girls came as Madame Butterfly, and all the men as Lieutenant Pinkerton. Except for Elizabeth Ponsonby, who came as Lieutenant Pinkerton, and Kit who came as Madame Butterfly. Too funny! But it's not all parties, you know. I have my own business now,' Emma concluded.

'Yes, I know. Decorating houses. You did Mrs Oglander's Eastern Fantasia, and now everyone wants one.'

Emma laughed. 'That flat was an abomination, but it was what she wanted. Don't judge me by it. I come here quite often, looking for new ideas. How do you know so much about it, anyway?'

'I work for a newspaper,' Molly said. 'I don't get to do the serious stories yet, but I do have to read everything that comes in, in the interests of learning the trade.'

'Is that what I am, a story?' Emma said.

'Dear Emma, you always have been, from the moment you became a rich and beautiful heiress. There's a terrific morgue file on you at the newspaper.'

Emma wrinkled her lovely nose. 'What's a morgue file?'

'A file where we keep all the cuttings and information on someone, in case we suddenly have to do a story about them. One of the jobs I *am* allowed to do – as the lowest of the juniors on the staff – is filing the cuttings. There's everything in yours, from your heroism in the war to appearing at the Ritz with cropped hair.' She became suddenly serious. 'And Peter Gresham's accident. I'm so sorry. It must have been terrible for you. I did write to you, but I don't know if you got my letter.'

Emma looked away. 'I don't really remember much from that time. It's rather a blur.' It hadn't been an accident, that was the worst thing. Her fiancé had shot himself – another casualty of the war, one of those men whose courage had been tested beyond the ability of their minds to heal. That had been four years ago. She tried never to think about him now – or of the two previous men she had loved, who had both been killed in action. To turn the attention away from herself, she asked, 'What about you? Is there a man in your life?'

'Not me,' Molly said cheerfully, as she always did. 'I expect the person I was meant to marry was killed in the war.' It was a commonplace; but realising what she had said, she put her hand to her mouth. 'Oh, damn, I've put my foot in it again. I'm sorry, Emma. I always was a clumsy fool.'

'It's all right,' Emma said. 'Look here, what are you doing now? Let's go and have tea somewhere.'

Molly was glad to be forgiven. 'I'd like that. But come and have tea in my flat – do! Then we can talk as long as we like without having waitresses clearing up around us.'

'If it's no trouble. I'd like to see where you live,' Emma said. She wanted to make amends. During the war, when she and Molly had been close, they had talked of living together when the war was over, but their lives had gone different ways. She had never even seen the inside of Molly's previous lodgings, nor invited Molly to her luxurious apartment in Queen's Walk.

'It's no trouble at all. We'll stop on the way and get some cakes.'

They walked together towards the exit, and Molly said, 'Where's Benson?'

'They don't allow dogs in the British Museum. I left him at home.'

'Poor boy.'

'He doesn't mind. It's hard to get him interested in antiquities.'

Outside, Emma automatically waved down a taxi, which dashed to her side with a readiness they never showed for Molly on the few occasions she indulged in one. Emma had a diamond arrow in her cloche, pearls round her neck, her skirt was fashionably just below the knee, and she had a light fur tippet hanging over one shoulder. No cab driver could fail to spot the difference between her, and Molly in her ready-made, with the safe mid-calf hem and last year's hat. Inwardly Molly shrugged. Things were what they were: Emma was one of the richest women in the country, and Molly's wages just went round if she didn't have any extra expenses. She was only glad that Emma seemed to want to be friends again. She told the taxi driver to stop at the little bakery on the corner of Guilford Street and dashed in to buy a dozen mixed cakes, and tried to remember if she had left her home tidy that morning.

Emma did look rather like a peacock in a chicken run as she trod up the drab stairs; but when Molly let them into her flat with the Yale key that still gave her an absurd thrill of ownership, she paused at the door and said, 'Oh, this is nice.'

Molly saw that she meant it, and was pleased. The room had been the drawing-room of the original house, so it had a high ceiling with elaborate cornices, a marble fireplace and wonderful tall windows looking onto the square with its private garden and magnificent plane trees. 'It's light and sunny,' she said. 'And I do like the view.'

'Yes, but I meant I like what you've done with it,' Emma said, casting what had become a professional eye around. 'The way you've covered the chairs, for instance.'

'The flat came furnished,' Molly said. 'Everything was pretty horrid, except for the chiffonier, so I had to do something.'

She couldn't have afforded furniture of her own, but she had bought some bright red coarse cotton and covered the chairs and sofa, removed the nasty curtains and made blinds in the same material. She had painted the walls – which had been wallpapered in a tobacco-coloured floral pattern – plain white. She had made a curtain of drab to conceal the kitchen corner, removed and stored in a box the various knick-knacks the landlady had scattered about the place, and made garlands of ivy and dried hops to hang along the picture rails and across the top of the windows.

'You really have a talent, you know. The plain white walls are so daring, and the dark green of the ivy goes wonderfully against the scarlet,' Emma said. 'I think I could make use of that idea somewhere. And the big vase standing in the hearth filled with bulrushes. What made you think of that?'

Molly laughed. 'Anything that doesn't cost much gets thought of. As it is, I've run myself close to Micawberdom moving here – you never realise until you have a place of your own how many things you have to buy. There's lots more I'd like to do, when my wages catch up with me. I've discovered a wonderful street market in North Kensington where they have all sorts of things terribly cheap that only want cleaning up and putting in the right place – like that vase, which I got for sixpence because the man said it was too big for modern taste. Likewise the bust over there.' It stood in the darkest corner on a tall plant stand, gleaming white – a head of Michelangelo's *David*, with a chipped nose. 'It isn't alabaster, of course, only plaster. Some art student's apprentice piece, I dare say. But he gives the place an air, don't you think?'

'Certainly. And the paintings – so modern. Interesting how much better they look against a white wall. Where did you get those?'

'There are a brace of painters, Megs and Ida, living in the basement. They donated the pictures they felt didn't work, but I'm happy with them.' She grinned. 'Frankly, I can't tell one oblong of pure colour from another, and multi-coloured splashes all look the same to me. Modern art is such frightful bosh, don't you think?'

'I hope you don't tell them that.'

'I'm not quite such a barbarian,' Molly said. 'We're a very artistic community in this house. The artists share the basement with a potter, Ingrid, who makes sporty figurines – she

110

has a kiln down the garden. At the back on this floor are two architecture students, Felix and Pooley, very nice boys. Next floor up is a music teacher, Popovka, and Nina Simonova, a ballet mistress who used to dance with the Maryinsky, and in the attic there's an out-of-work actor, Simon Baron, who teaches voice training and mime.'

'How exciting,' Emma said.

'Mecklenburgh Square is rather like that: a little Bohemia, out of the world. They stretch a point and allow journalism to be a form of art – and allow me to be a journalist, which is even more of a stretch. It's very nice,' she went on, 'to have people to invite in – and a place to invite them into. Now, make yourself comfortable while I put the kettle on.'

She went over to the kitchen corner and drew back the curtain.

'That's a clever thought,' Emma said. 'And where's the bathroom? I should like to powder my nose.'

'Out of the door, along the passage, and the last door on the left,' Molly said, filling the kettle at the tap.

When Emma came back, the tea was ready, and she took off her hat and threw it with her fur onto the sofa. She had her hair shingle-cut, the new style that had come in the year before: a bob with the hair at the back cut very short with a razor in a V-shape on the neck. Molly envied Emma her naturally curly hair. Her own she had to wave at home with tongs heated over the gas ring and the consequent danger of scorching. A permanent wave at a hairdresser's cost three or four guineas – and the word 'permanent' in any case was somewhat exaggerated.

'Now, tell me all about your new job,' Emma said.

Molly obliged – 'Not that there's much to tell yet. I'm still learning the trade' – and then asked Emma about her business.

'I'm awash with customers,' Emma said. 'I've actually had to put up my prices to discourage them. It amazes me how little imagination people have about their own houses. Except for one woman who wanted to cover her bedroom, in a beautiful Georgian house, entirely with aluminium sheeting.' She shuddered. 'That was a case of too *much* imagination. I managed to put her off but it was a close-run thing.'

'Well, you should be proud of yourself,' Molly said. 'You make things more beautiful, and that adds to the joy of the world. All I do is rewrite court reports no-one will ever read, and file cuttings in a dusty basement. I suppose one day someone will discover the scientific reason that newspaper offices are so much more dusty than anywhere else on earth.'

At that moment there was a knock at Molly's door. She dashed to answer it, and ushered in a man saying, 'Emma, do let me introduce to you one of my neighbours. Mr Popovka lives upstairs. He's the music teacher I mentioned.'

He was an elderly man, not particularly tall, but so thin he appeared taller than he was. His face was pale, his eyes large, dark and melancholy. He wore a plum velvet jacket, a black scarf round his neck, and his grey hair was longer than the usual fashion for men, which Emma supposed was another sign of his being 'an artist'.

'I would not wish to disturb you,' he said, in a beautifully modulated, liquid voice, with an accent and a rolling r that would have given Emma the clue, had she not got it already from his name.

'No disturbance. Come and have some tea,' Molly said. 'I bought too many cakes and someone must help us eat them.'

Emma liked the look of him, and stood up, offering her hand. 'I'm Emma Weston, an old friend of Molly's.'

He took the hand as though it were something fragile and precious, and bowed over it, not quite touching it with his lips. It was done in a manner no Englishman could emulate. 'Miss Emma Weston, I am delighted to make your acquaintance. I know you by sight very well, but I never thought I would have the honour of being in the same room with you.'

112

'Pop is a terrible flirt,' Molly said. 'He used to play in the ballet orchestra with the Maryinsky in Petersburg, and sucked up romance and drama from an early age. He had all the ballerinas running about after him. Now he only has Nina – the ballet mistress upstairs. Once a week they drink vodka and talk in Russian until they're both in floods of tears.'

'Miss Molly is irreverent. She takes nothing seriously,' Popovka said. 'Whereas *you*,' he went on, studying Emma intently, 'have great tragedy in your eyes. You should have been an actress. You have a face for the stage. Or the opera – can you sing? As Dido, as Tosca, you would have them weeping like little children from the stalls to the balcony.'

'Now, Pop, do stop. Sit down and talk sensibly – he can, Emma, when he wants – and I'll give you tea. You shall drink it in the English style, however. He and Nina have Russian tea upstairs. Nina has a samovar. They put jam in it – you can't think how disgusting!'

Popovka gave Emma a twinkling look as he sat beside her. 'Whereas the English take a delicate, aromatic herbal drink, and put into it a fluid squeezed from the mammary glands of cattle.'

Emma now felt completely relaxed and, as Molly handed her another cup of tea, began to enjoy herself more than she had for a long time. Her usual recreations were going to restaurants, nightclubs and other rich people's houses, to dinners, dances and parties, and at weekends and in the summer to various sporting events. But none of the people she met, in endlessly recycled combinations, were like Mr Popovka.

Soon she had heard his entire life history, and had managed to tell her own without feeling in the least that he was prying, or even sounding very sad about it. 'So,' he said, when she had come to the end, 'now you make beautiful the homes of others, a noble task, for we all need beauty around us to remind us of God. And you go in the company of the handsome Lord Westhoven, I know. Are you going to marry him?'

Somehow the question did not offend when it came from a man whose deep, dark eyes embraced her with equal amounts of sorrow, merriment and admiration.

'I don't know. Perhaps, one day. But he hasn't asked me.'

'Better you don't wait for that. Men do not know their own best interest. And we are very shy, you know, much more shy than women. Yes, yes, you should marry the lord earl. Is he rich?'

'Not as rich as me, but rich enough. Don't you think that would be a waste – money marrying money?'

'Not at all. Good things should not be spread too thinly, lest they evaporate. Let beauty marry beauty and intelligence wed intelligence. I mean to find a very clever man for Molly.'

'Because I'm not beautiful, you see,' Molly interrupted.

He frowned at her. 'You are as beautiful as you need to be, when you have such a good brain. But you must be sure to take the right man. Bring to me any man you are considering, and I shall tell you whether he will do or not.'

'I promise I'll do that,' Molly laughed.

He looked at Emma. 'She thinks I am not serious. With a face like mine, she thinks me a clown. But who does she talk to, I ask you, about the things she learns in her new job?'

'You?' Emma guessed.

'Pop likes to have deep intellectual and political conversations with me,' Molly said. 'He thinks I'm too frivolous, and has it on his conscience to "bring me up right".'

Popovka waved her to silence. 'She tells me what she learns, and I tell her what to think about it. The world is a dangerous place, Miss Emma Weston. More dangerous now than when you drove an ambulance with shells bursting around you. Ideas kill more men than bombs, many, many times more, and you cannot hear them coming.

114

How many did Bolshevism kill in my own dear country? And socialism in Germany?'

'But Germany is harmless now, surely,' Emma said. 'They've had a terrible time since the war. It's knocked the stuffing out of them.'

'The currency has settled down, since Stresemann brought in the Rentenmark,' Molly said, 'and you don't hear so much about civil unrest.'

'It is a dangerous place,' Popovka said. 'Don't be fooled. In difficult times, men crave strong leaders, to bring order out of chaos; but strong leaders always go bad, and the price of order is too high, always too high. You see what happened in my country. It will happen in Germany.'

'And England?' Emma asked.

Popovka smiled. 'Not in England, because here you do not fear chaos, you embrace it. The Englishman instinctively prefers the amateur to the professional. He is suspicious of efficiency. He dislikes to be told what to do. Here you have muddle – benign muddle – and it will always save you. Think, Miss Weston: your soldiers in the Great War did not march to songs of glory and the fatherland and the flag. They sang songs of bully beef and jam, trousers and boots, and the sergeant stealing the rum.'

'Yes,' said Emma. She had been there. She had heard them. 'Still, they fought like devils.'

'They fought like devils,' he agreed, 'for the right to make fun of everything they held dear. Shall I tell you the great curse of Bolshevists and socialists – the Reds, the Leftists, whatever you wish to call them?' He leaned forward. '*They don't make jokes.*'

Molly said, 'But there's trouble coming here, too, you know. There's bound to be a coal strike sooner or later. With cheap coal coming in from Germany and Poland again, the mines are running at a loss, and all the owners can do is cut wages or make the hours longer. The miners won't stand for that.'

Emma looked at Molly, impressed that she knew so much. Molly caught her eye and shrugged.

Popovka nodded. 'Yes, there will be trouble. But not revolution. Revolution is a serious business, and the English enjoy jokes too much to give them up.'

The conversation ranged over other topics – *The Constant Nymph*, whether wireless broadcasting would kill concert-going, the Bloomsbury Group, whether Priscilla Wimbush in *Crome Yellow* was really meant to be Lady Ottoline Morrell, whether Rudolph Valentino's attractiveness to women was a sort of femininity in his appearance, whether monkey glands could prolong human life, whether dogs made better pets than cats, whether golf was a sport or a game. By the time Mr Popovka stood up to take his leave, Emma felt as though her mind had gone through a satisfying session of Swedish PT.

'It has been a great pleasure to meet you, Miss Emma Weston,' Popovka said, bowing over her hand again. 'I shall read of your activities with even keener interest now.'

When he had gone, taking with him the remaining cakes 'for Nina – she loves sweet things, and she is too thin', Emma said, 'I must go too. I have to get back and change.'

'It's been good to see you again,' Molly said.

'I've enjoyed it very much,' Emma said, with enough enthusiasm for Molly to take a chance.

'Will you have supper with me one day? I know a jolly little place in Soho where they do real French rustic cooking. Not as swish as the places you usually go, of course—'

Emma laughed. 'You may find I already know it. Kit is devoted to obscure little restaurants in Soho – he searches them out. But I'd love to meet you one evening. I'm so glad we bumped into each other. Let's not lose touch again.'

And as Molly said afterwards to Helen, when she next met her, you couldn't ask for a more positive response than that. 'I think age is mellowing her.'

'What nonsense you talk,' Helen said. 'Age indeed!'

'Well, she's older than me. She must be nearly thirty.'

'You forget that when you drifted apart she had gone through the war and a terrible bereavement. If anything has mellowed her, it's time's well-known healing powers.'

CHAPTER SIX

Working on Father Palgrave's manuscript was keeping Julian and Miss Husthwaite pleasantly busy outside their official duties. Miss Husthwaite used her skill in deciphering bad handwriting, and transposed the manuscript into type. Julian then went through the pages and made little marks where he felt something could be better expressed or needed 'tidying up'. Then he and Miss Husthwaite read the script together and agreed – or quite frequently disagreed – on any corrections. Julian came down on the side of not changing anything unless it were *absolutely* necessary. 'They're not our words to change,' he said. 'We owe a duty to that poor man to allow his own voice to speak without interference.'

And Miss Husthwaite said, 'He was not himself a great deal of the time. And I don't believe we do him justice by leaving confused and repetitive passages untouched. We ought to be making sure the book says what he wanted it to say.'

'But are we justified in assuming that we know what he wanted to say?'

'I think we can make very good assumptions most of the time.'

'But the rest of the time?'

'We have to use our judgement. Surely any editor of any book must do that.'

'But who set us up as editors?'

'My dear sir, we set *ourselves* up. Don't be so self-effacing. If poor Father Palgrave is to communicate at all from beyond the grave, he needs us to mediate for him. Otherwise, all he has left the world is a pile of scribbled sheets, and no-one, not even his daughter, will ever read them.'

The arguments were vigorous and extremely enjoyable, and as they were mature and intelligent adults – or, more importantly, because they had very similar tastes – they always came to an amicable agreement.

She arrived one Saturday afternoon at the priest's room with the latest pages she had been transposing, and knocked at the door. Julian opened it, revealing behind him a room that he had made cosy. The chimney alcoves were lined with books – the estate carpenter had made and fitted shelves for him – and on the mantelpiece were some cups from his university sporting days and one or two interesting *objets trouvés*. There were paintings on the walls, four small landscape oils, and a collection of miniatures, including one of his late wife. He had rearranged the furniture, and imported pieces of his own. A small table stood between one armchair and the chimney wall on which was a silver tray bearing decanters and glasses, and lamps arranged round the room lit it pleasantly but not glaringly. It was a room that invited one to come in and be comfortable.

The latest addition stood on a table over in the corner, a wooden box, about sixteen inches square, with elongated glass globes sticking out of the top: Julian's wireless receiver. A pair of earphones lay beside it, and a small chair was placed up against it. Here, when he could get the tuning just right, Julian could sit and listen to classical music broadcast from station 2L0 in London via the newly opened high-power transmitter at Daventry. He called it a wonder of the age.

Miss Husthwaite, offered a turn at listening-in, declined to put anything connected to the electricity over her ears.

An electric shock so close to the brain would probably be fatal, she reasoned, and she worried so much about it that he had ceased to discuss what he listened to with her, and allowed her to think the apparatus stood idle most evenings.

Today Miss Husthwaite's eyes were not drawn to the evil genie in the corner. Though it was early July, it had not been hot, and this room, on the cold side of the house, could feel clammy even in the middle of summer. Julian had had a fire lit. It crackled cheerfully under the chimney, sending a flickering light glancing along the gilt on the spines of his books, sparkling on the cut glass of his decanters, and glowing in the amber heart of the sherry within. And before the fire, on his hearth rug, lay a small terrier mongrel, his white coat rosy in the fireglow, sprawled out on his side with his eyes closed in bliss.

Miss Husthwaite sighed. 'So that's where he got to. I thought he must be out with the other dogs.'

'He came scratching at my door an hour ago,' Julian said. Rusty cocked one ear to the voices, but did not open his eyes. 'I'm sorry. I thought perhaps you'd gone out somewhere. It's the fire he came for,' he added consolingly. 'That dog has a cat's instinct for a warm place. I expect he could smell it all through the house.'

'It's nice of you to put it like that,' Miss Husthwaite said, 'but the plain fact of the matter is that he doesn't like me. He'd sooner be anywhere than with me.'

'No, no, that's not true,' Julian said. 'He owes his life to you.'

She gave him a stern look. 'He's just a dog. He doesn't know that. You needn't humour me.'

'Very well. I think the truth is that he was brought up by men, and he's more of a man's dog than a woman's. But there's no reason he shouldn't change.'

Miss Husthwaite looked at her pet, and saw the small barrel of his body lift and fall in a deep, contented sigh. 'It's no use. Since he seems to have chosen you, you might as well have him.'

'I couldn't agree to that,' Julian said. 'He's your dog. But perhaps I might share him. We might take him out for walks together.'

'I should like that very much,' Miss Husthwaite said. There was a moment of possibility in the room that seemed on the brink of unfurling, like a rose, in the warmth; but then her self-consciousness made her shrink in embarrassment like a salted snail.

Julian saw it and politely turned away. 'Do sit down – and may I offer you sherry? Or would you prefer tea?'

'I think it's too early for sherry,' Miss Husthwaite said, taking her usual seat on the sofa – they always sat next to each other at these sessions so they could both look at the manuscript. 'We have a great deal of work to do.'

'Then I shall ring for tea. It's about the right time.'

A housemaid brought up tea – she brought enough for two, alerted by the mysterious backstairs network that Miss Husthwaite was with Mr Julian, 'workin' on that pile o' papers t' poor Father left' – and they got down to wrangling over the latest changes.

'You know,' Julian said, when a natural pause occurred, 'this book is really going to be very good. The power of the writing, the clarity of the vision . . .'

'The terrible poignancy of the story,' Miss Husthwaite agreed. 'I think when it's done, it ought to be properly published, not just typed out for Laura.'

'I concur completely. When we're done, we ought to suggest to Mr Morland that he submit it to some suitable London publisher. But it does occur to me that there's something missing.'

'A context?'

'Exactly. You feel the same?'

'I feel, as someone who was not there, that I would like

to know more about the background to the experiences Mr Palgrave was describing. The history.'

'Perhaps even a map or two, or a diagram of the situation.'

Miss Husthwaite nodded. 'But how to do it? Would it not sully the purity of the book? You, who are so reluctant to change anything . . .'

'It can – indeed it must – be done with the utmost sensitivity; and it must be clear to the reader what has been added and what is the voice of the original—'

'Without making it too fragmented, or it will be unreadable.' Miss Husthwaite's eyes were shining. 'It would be a *fascinating* task. I could do the research, verify the facts from the best sources. I should enjoy that *very* much.'

'And I could do the writing – it's just the sort of thing I like – with you to keep a check on me, of course.'

'We must ask Mr Morland what he thinks.'

They looked at each other for a moment, each absorbed with imagining the challenge and satisfaction of such a task, and the pleasure of working together on something original and so worthwhile.

'It would take a long time,' Julian said. 'It would delay completing the book, perhaps for years.'

'Laura's only four. She won't be interested in reading her papa's words for a long time yet. I think it would be respectful to his memory to do the best job we can, and make a book she can be proud of.'

'Then we are in agreement,' Julian said, with satisfaction. He smiled at his companion. Rusty groaned in his sleep and rolled over to toast the other side. The prospect for all three looked very inviting. 'Won't you have the last piece of parkin, Miss Husthwaite? And another cup of tea? I think there's still something in the pot.'

'Let me pour,' she said.

* * *

Lennie went back to town on business in August, found a note waiting for him from the agency and went round there at once.

The outer office was stifling, and the secretary's desk was empty and clear: she was on vacation. In Delaney's room the window onto the street was open, but there was not a breath of air, only the sound of the traffic as it rumbled back and forth, with the occasional hot and fretful outburst of horns. A fruit vendor somewhere below called out monotonously, 'Awnges, fifty cents a dozen!' and a fly, unable to find the open bottom half of the window, bothered about at the top and beat its head on the glass.

Lennie mopped his neck with his handkerchief. 'Don't you ever go away?' he asked.

'Nope,' said Delaney, swinging back on to his chair's hind legs. 'Can't afford to. I take the old lady and the kid to Coney Island for the day – that's my vacation.' Lennie had somehow not associated Delaney with a wife and child.

'It's hot,' he said unoriginally.

'Never notice it myself,' said Delaney. 'Take a pew. Coffee?'

'God, no! You've some information on Alexander?' Lennie prompted him. 'About time, too.'

'I told you it'd be a long job,' Delaney said. 'I reckon Tony's done well to get on the line as fast as he did.'

But she's married, Lennie thought. Whatever you've found out, it's too late. He hadn't seen her to speak to since the wedding, but she and Alexander had given some dazzling parties, well reported in the gossip columns, had been seen everywhere it was important to be seen, had spent some time in Washington, and now had disappeared, like everyone else, to Long Island for the summer months.

'Well, carry on,' he said, sitting down and loosening his tie a little. In front of Delaney it hardly mattered. 'What have you found out?'

'Arizona,' said Delaney. 'From Los Angeles, the Alexanders

moved to Tucson. Ran a hardware store on the south side – old Jacob seems to've been a born shopkeeper. They were respectable and reasonably prosperous. Just the two of 'em – no kids.'

'I wonder why they chose Tucson,' Lennie said.

'Desert climate, clean dry air. Lotta gas victims have settled there since the war. Maybe Jacob had chest problems, coming from Latvia. Sounds like a foggy place to me. His death certificate in Akron said he died of bronchitis. Speculation,' he added, in fairness. 'Just my guess.'

Lennie accepted it with a wave of the hand. 'So when did Ren come on the scene?'

'Interesting story. Tony got it from an old guy used to be their neighbour. It seems old man Alexander got himself a little automobile. Loved it like a child, polished it, drove the missus to church on a Sunday, giving people he knew a toot and a lift of his hat as he went past like the Emperor of Everywhere. Get the picture?'

'Clearly,' said Lennie.

'So one day he takes Doris out for a drive, on the road towards Nogales. Just about to turn back when Doris says, "What's that beside the road up ahead?" Jacob says, "Looks like someone in trouble." So they go and see. Turns out to be an Indian woman, sitting beside the road, with a kid about eight. She's just slumped there in the dust like a pile of washing, completely done in, end of her tether. The kid's in better shape, but both of them are thin, barefoot and their clothes are ragged. Well, Jacob's a bit nervous – Tucson hadn't forgotten the Apache raids and attacks by any means, and he's taken in all the stories. What if the woman's bait, and they're going to be ambushed? But there's no-one else in sight, and Doris says, "We can't leave 'em here. The woman's sick – she may die." So they get 'em into the automobile, and off they go back to Tucson.'

They took them into their house, and called out their own

doctor to the woman. He shook his head over her. She died a couple of days later, leaving them with the child on their hands.

'They had to pay the doctor's bill, and pay for a funeral for the woman. Then there was the kid to take care of. Cost 'em quite a bit one way and another, but if ever Jacob got to sounding doubtful, Doris would give him a sharp look and say it was their Christian duty. Well, Jacob wasn't a Christian, but there it was. Fact was that Doris had never had a kid, was never going to have a kid, and she wanted this one. So they kept him.'

'But – who *were* they?' Lennie demanded.

'The woman was an Apache, but she spoke English all right, and she talked to them a bit before she died. Seemed she'd gone off the rails with a white man, had a child. He walked out on her, when the boy was about two, and she went back to her people. Her father was the chief, and he was fond of her, her being his only child, so he took her in and protected her against the rest of the tribe, who were not happy about it. She'd shamed herself and the whole Indian nation, you see. As soon as he died, the new chief sent her packing. Since then she'd been wandering about, keeping herself and the boy by doing whatever odd jobs she could get for money or food. But it was all downhill, and she was on the last lap when the Alexanders found her.'

'So Ren Alexander is half Apache?' Lennie said. He had only admitted to being part-Indian – a small part, far back, he had said. And no wonder. A little dash of Indian blood, as long as it was vague and in the distant past, was romantic; but so much, and so specific, would not go down well in social circles. The attitude of 'the only good Indian is a dead Indian' was still widespread. 'And the Alexanders adopted him?'

'Sure. Gave him an English name. Renfrew was Doris's mother's maiden name, and Hawthorne was hers. She doted

125

on the boy. He was handsome, but sullen – naturally enough in the circumstances. The neighbours were not pleased about having an Indian kid around, and the Alexanders suffered for it. Some people boycotted the store, and no-one would sit next to them in church. Everything that got broken or stolen was blamed on Ren, and when he went to school he was always getting into fights in the playground, and in trouble with the teachers. In the end he learned to hold his own. Our informant said he was a real tough kid – tall, lean as a whip, with hard little fists that shot out so fast you wouldn't see 'em. And he'd never cry, no matter how much he was hurt – which he was, plenty.'

Lennie was silent. His sympathies were engaged, and he didn't want them to be. At last he said, 'Why did they move again?'

'I guess it was too hard. They needed a fresh start, some-where no-one knew them, and no-one need ever know the kid wasn't theirs. But there was one last bit of trouble in Tucson, which might have tipped the balance. The school principal came round one day to say young Alexander had gone into business on his own account, lending his pocket money to boys who'd run short, and charging interest. From what we know of him since, that probably was true. Anyhow, the principal said it had to stop right then and there, and demanded the boy give the money back. So, of course, there was a line out the door of kids claiming he'd diddled them, and old man Alexander had no alternative but to pay up, even though the kid denied most of them. One or two of the parents hinted they were thinking of complaining to the cops. A few weeks later, the Alexanders had a going-out-of-business sale and were gone in a cloud of dust, leaving no forwarding address.'

'And they turned up in Akron?'

'Yeah. The dates fit all right. From then on, no hint was ever given that the boy wasn't their own flesh and blood, and he seems to have kept his nose clean, so it appears lessons were learned.' Delaney put his hands behind his head and regarded Lennie with interest. 'I guess the guy looks enough like his real father to get away with being a genuine white man. I've only seen photographs of him, but as far as I remember he looks okay.'

'He actually says he has a little Apache blood,' Lennie said, 'though he gives the impression it's a long way back.'

Delaney nodded. 'Well, I'll be darned. The old Injun pride, eh? Can't deny his people, though he tries to tread the safe line. There must be a volcano fermenting inside that man – rejected by his mother's people and then his father's, and only allowed to get on in the world if he pretends to be what he's not.'

'He's got his revenge,' Lennie said. 'He's made himself very rich, and worked his way into society at the highest level. And now—'

'He's married your cousin.'

'Yes.'

There was a silence, and then Delaney said encouragingly, 'Well, I can see it's a shock to you, but on the bright side, he's never done anything wrong that we heard of, been in trouble with the cops, anything of that sort. And he's made his own way against big odds, which you got to admire.'

'I don't admire anything about the man,' Lennie said bitterly. The sympathy he had briefly felt had evaporated, because now he was facing the consequences of his own actions. He had done this underhand thing, enquired about Ren behind his back, and now he had to decide what to do with the knowledge. 'Why couldn't you have found all this out sooner?' he demanded.

'Do you *know* how difficult it is to trace a man who doesn't want to be traced? America's a big country, my friend.' Another silence. Delaney glanced at his watch. 'Do you want us to find out any more? There's still ten years to cover from

127

the time he left Akron, and that ought to be easier to get at, because a lot of it's been in the public eye.'

'No,' Lennie said. 'For God's sake, let it be. I wish I'd never started this thing.'

'Yeah,' said Delaney, with sympathy. 'You'd be surprised how many of our clients say that.'

Jessie was lungeing her yearling, Timber – a fine black fellow with one white sock, one of the first offspring of their stallion Flying Colours. Her dear old horse Hotspur had died during the winter at the age of twenty-one. Fortunately she had already, at Bertie's urging, provided herself with a new riding horse, the chestnut Hermes, but though he was good and willing, he was not a top-flight hunter. For that, she was pinning her hopes on Timber, who had superb hocks and a fine eye. He was also full of spirit, and lungeing him rarely turned out to be the bread-and-butter exercise it was meant to be. This morning, for instance, he was telling her he simply *couldn't* circle anti-clockwise, and when she insisted, he fly-bucked and twisted on the other end of the rope like a fish. Two days ago he had circled perfectly anti-clockwise but had refused to go in the other direction.

'Pure naughtiness,' she told him, calling him in to the centre to calm him down. He bowed his head and lipped her palm hopefully. 'No, nothing for you until you do it properly,' she said. 'Work first, reward afterwards.' He snorted, and then rubbed his itchy nose long and luxuriously up and down her front. She caressed his neck and ears affectionately. With his colouring and his elegantly cut head, he had rather a look of dear old Hotspur. She wondered briefly if the souls of beloved animals came back in other bodies to be with you again. 'Enough now,' she said, and sent him out again, and this time, apparently refreshed by the interlude, he circled perfectly anti-clockwise, his head nicely placed and his hocks under him. Suspiciously she tried him on the other rein, and he went perfectly that way as well. Jessie could have sworn there was a smirk on his dark lips.

'Humbug,' she said, when she called him in. She gave him a wrinkled little store apple, which he crunched with pleasure, throwing his head up and down for the sweetness.

She turned him out with the other yearlings and watched him roll, legs flailing ridiculously in the air. He went right over three times. You were supposed to tell the value of a horse by how he rolled – every time right over was a hundred guineas. *But he's worth more than that to me.* Finally he heaved himself to his feet, shook vigorously, gave her a long, thoughtful look, and walked off to find the perfect spot to start grazing.

Jessie remained leaning on the fence, staring at the horses but not really seeing them, her mind far away. She didn't even see Bertie approach, until Bran, who had been lying in the grass at her feet, jumped up to run and meet Ellie and Wolf halfway in an ecstasy of silent greeting. Wolf was the Morland whelp Jessie had given Bertie for his birthday. He was out of Uncle Teddy's promising new breeding bitch, Ismène, sired by his own dog Tiger, and Jessie had had to use considerable charm to extract one of the litter from him.

Bertie came to kiss her and said, 'Why so pensive, my lady?'

'Oh – nothing really,' she said automatically.

'You looked downcast. Is Timber not going well?'

'No – I mean, he *is* going well, but it wasn't that.'

'Thinking about poor little Edward?' he asked.

It was six weeks now since he had died, but it had been so sudden that it was perhaps even more of a shock than a child's death usually was. Though rather small for his age, he had been perfectly lively, until one day he had had a coughing fit while playing in the day-nursery, and shortly afterwards had collapsed and died before Dr Hasty could

129

get there. Hasty had said he thought it might have been a pulmonary embolism, and had hinted about doing a post-mortem examination to be sure, but the suggestion had so enraged Teddy he had sent Hasty from the house and rumbled about changing to another physician for the future.

But the anger was too fleeting for him to act upon it. His grief for his son was terrible to see, but Amy's loss was even greater: Edward was her only child. It was therapeutic for Teddy to have to curb his own sorrow in the interests of taking care of her and trying to comfort her. She suffered, white and silent, and the house was an uncomfortable place to be that summer.

Jessie had been much affected by it, and Bertie had known without telling him that she was thinking, *If Edward could be snatched away like that without warning, what security has any of us got?* Her three children were all rosy and robust when compared with Edward but, as she understood it, an embolism could happen to anyone. In the days after Edward's death Bertie had often found her brooding with an absent look on her face, or looked for her in the evening only to find her in the nursery, staring at the sleeping children.

But now she started at his question, looked faintly guilty, and said, 'No, not that. Actually, I was – I was just thinking about poor Ned.'

'Ah,' said Bertie.

'We were such friends when we were young. He always stood up for me.' She shrugged. 'We should never have married. But even so . . . It was bad enough losing Frank and Robbie, but at least we know how they fell, and where they're buried. Ned just disappeared. It seems all wrong that we'll never know how he died, and he'll never have a proper grave. He was a *good* person.'

Bertie had put his arm round her, and squeezed her shoulder comfortingly. 'So you don't think, then, that John Smith *was* Ned?' he asked carefully.

Jessie frowned. 'No, I don't think it could have been him. Either way, *our* Ned is just as lost.' She looked up at Bertie. 'I never loved him as I love you, but that only makes it worse, really.'

'I know.'

'I feel guilty.'

'I know.'

She was glad he did not try to talk her out of her guilt. Things were what they were.

After a moment he said, 'I feel guilty too. Oh, about many things, but particularly about my friend Pennyfather. He was invalided out, and we wrote back and forth for a while, but then it lapsed. I was still in the war, and there was so much to do. But I should have looked him up after the peace, and I didn't. I feel bad about that.'

Jessie nodded. 'Why don't you do it now?'

He gave her an apologetic smile. 'Actually, I have. I put enquiries in train a couple of weeks ago, and finally got an answer. It wasn't good news. Pennyfather died in 1919. His widow moved, which was why it was hard to find them. But I have an address now.'

'And you'd like to go and see them,' Jessie hazarded.

'Yes. Do you mind?'

'Of course not.'

'I'd like to make sure she and the children are all right. They live down in the West Country. Would you mind if I disappeared for a few days?'

'No, darling. Go with my blessing.'

'And took Cooper with me?'

'By all means.'

'I thought I'd go next week when Violet's here, so you won't be all alone.'

Violet was coming to stay at Shawes, her mother's house just a mile away from Morland Place, with her children. Her eldest,

131

Robert, who was fifteen, was going to visit a schoolfriend, but she was bringing Richard, thirteen, Charlotte, twelve, and Henry Octavian, who had just turned nine. Best of all, from Jessie's point of view, Lord Holkam was going grouse-shooting in Scotland at the invitation of the Farquars, to a house-party that would include the Strathmores, who as parents-in-law to Prince Albert were worth cultivating. The prince and his wife would be at nearby Balmoral and an invitation to the castle for the whole house-party was likely. Holkam was already well placed with the Prince of Wales, through Violet, but closer acquaintance with the prince had led him to join the discreet band of those who doubted he would ever be king, and he felt it was wise to cover all possibilities.

Violet for once had put her foot down and told him he must go *en garçon* to the Farquars: she was going to Shawes. The Prince of Wales was on another of his long overseas trips, this time to South America, and she was eager to take the opportunity of his absence to have a real rest. She didn't know how Freda Dudley Ward had managed – and he still rang Freda at unearthly hours for chats. Even when abroad, he sent her long letters and cables which, if not replied to at once, elicited further hurt and anxious cables.

Holkam was doubtful about how Violet's absence would go down with the Royal Family, but since no definite invitation had been issued, except by the Farquars, he had no strong grounds for objecting to her refusal. And, he reflected, the King must know perfectly well that the prince had been squiring Lady Holkam everywhere for the past three years, and might be quite glad not to be forced to notice her.

There was a week of frantic activity at Shawes, as cleaners, decorators and gardeners made the house and grounds ready. Jessie liked to go past when she could on her rides to see what progress was being made. Finally, Holkam staff arrived and extra servants were engaged – with some difficulty, in August – and at last the station manager rang both Twelvetrees and Morland Place from York station to say the countess and her 'suite', as he put it rather grandly, had descended from the train at twelve fourteen and disappeared into her own motor-car (driven down the day before) and several taxis.

Jessie planned to call the next morning, giving Violet time to make her arrangements, and leave a card if it was still not convenient; but Violet could not have been at Shawes more than an hour before she telephoned Twelvetrees House and asked Jessie to come over to tea.

'Are you sure?' Jessie said. 'I thought you would need to settle in.'

'The servants are doing the settling,' Violet said. 'There's nothing for me to do, and I long to see a friendly face. Do come if you're not busy.'

In the old days, Jessie might have ridden over – she always rode if she had the chance – but Violet was so grand now, or at least moved in such grand circles, that she had no desire to arrive in riding habit and smelling of horse. So she dressed herself in her nicest day dress and drove herself over in the Austin 7 Bertie had bought for her the year before so that she could be independent – and it was lucky that he had, since he and Cooper had taken the big Morris.

She was glad she had made the effort. The maid (Jessie recognised her, a local girl, the daughter of a woman who had worked in the munitions factory during the war) showed her into the drawing-room where Violet was waiting, looking exquisite in a dress of pleated lavender silk, with several rows of pearls of increasing length round her neck, and pearls surrounded with diamonds in her ears. Violet was thirty-four, just six months younger than Jessie, but still marvellously beautiful, with a flawless white skin and those deep blue eyes. The shock to Jessie was that her luxuriant black hair, which she had always refused to cut, was now cropped and marcel-waved at the front.

'Jessie, darling! Thank you for coming! You can't think how bored I was after that journey.'

'It's lovely to see you.' They embraced, and Jessie couldn't help saying, 'But, oh, Vi, your hair!'

Violet put her hand up to the back of it. 'I know,' she said ruefully. 'I hated parting with it. And I still can't quite get used to it. But one can't wear a cloche with long hair, and what other style is there, these days?'

Jessie's unruly curls had been cut long ago. 'It suits you – makes you look younger. And I like mine short. It's so nice just to be able to pull a brush through one's hair and be done. When I remember the agonies we used to go through when we were coming out, sitting there with a maid working away for hours, and our heads stuck full of pins like a hedgehog! I don't think I'd grow it again even if the styles change.'

'Oh, don't say that!' Violet said. 'If long hair comes back, what on earth does one do? It takes years to grow. Come and sit down – tea will be here in a minute – and let me look at you. It's been so long. I don't know why I never see you any more.'

'We don't really move in the same circles now,' Jessie said.

'I don't see why. Lady Parke is fully the equal of Lady Holkam.'

Jessie laughed. 'Polite, but untrue! I'm just a baronet's wife. But in any case, I didn't mean that. I make a very small circle from Twelvetrees to Morland Place to York and back, and my concerns are all domestic. I'm perfectly happy with that. Now I have Bertie and my children around me, I want for nothing more.'

Violet sighed. 'I envy you – no, I really do. I'd swap every-thing to be happy the way you and Bertie are.'

Jessie hesitated delicately, but the way seemed to have been opened. 'I thought you and Holkam were getting on all right, these days.'

'Oh, we are, but we're just good friends. Not like you and Bertie. I don't see very much of him, really. He has his work, and I suppose he has his own friends, because he's not at home a great deal. We go to official functions and big parties together, but otherwise . . .' She left it hanging.

Jessie felt a huge sadness for her lovely cousin, who had married for love but found her husband very different from the handsome beau who had wooed her. She had finally found love in the arms of another man, only to have him snatched away by the war – he had fallen at the Somme. Jessie had suffered too, but at least her story had had a happy ending.

'Well,' she said carefully, 'you have the prince now. David.'

'I do love him, but he tires me out. Clubs, restaurants, dancing – I rarely get home before half past four – and then as soon as he gets back home he rings me up to talk. He rings several times a day, if we're not together.'

'Bertie said he heard he's devoted to you.'

'But he's so unhappy. And he drinks so much – I can't keep up with it. It's as though he has to do everything to excess to make himself forget.'

'What is he unhappy about?' Jessie asked. It was fascinating, this inside view of the man who would be king one day.

'Oh, what he calls the "chronic state" of being Prince of Wales. The official duties, shaking hands with hundreds of strangers, all the ceremony and pomp, which he hates. He complains that he has no real power to change anything, but on the other hand he is never free to be himself. Followed everywhere by newspapermen, surrounded by servants and officials, all inspecting him and telling tales to the King. Well,' she added, seeing Jessie's surprise, 'that's what he believes. The King really is harsh with him. David says he can never get anything right for his father. If he goes to Sandringham, he's criticised for every little thing – like wearing a jacket just the wrong shade, or being a minute late for luncheon. But if he makes an excuse and doesn't go, he's called selfish and ungrateful and told he's breaking his father's heart.'

'Oh dear. I can see that must be difficult.'

'There's always an atmosphere when he goes to Sandringham,' Violet went on. 'He and the King disagree about *everything*. And they're always telling him he must get married, and he doesn't want to a bit. They push all those foreign princesses at him, but he's absolutely determined he will only marry the right person.'

'You?'

Violet looked surprised. '*Me?* Of course not. I'm already married. No, it would have to be someone suitable, someone who was up to the duties, he does see that, but he's determined it must be someone agreeable to him, even if it's not a love match – and he's pretty much resigned himself that it won't be.' She sighed. 'The only way out for him is to actually become king. Then he can rewrite all the rules, and be a modern monarch. But that can't happen until the King dies, and obviously he can't hope for that. So he's just terribly frustrated.'

'Poor Violet,' Jessie said.

'No, it's "poor David", really. And we do have happy times together. He's the greatest fun when we're with a crowd of our friends at the Embassy, dancing. And we play golf, and go to the races. And hunting – of course I can't keep up with him, he takes his own line and rides neck-or-nothing, but I like the meets and hacking to the first draw, and it's lovely afterwards, tea and dinner and everyone so contented and jolly.'

'Yes, I love hunting days, too,' Jessie said, glad to find common ground with her.

They talked about horses a little, and then Violet asked about Jessie's children, and the conversation became more normal and easy than it could ever be when the subject was the heir to the throne. 'Can I come over tomorrow and meet them? And see your new house – I never have, yet. Is it really nice?'

'*I* think so,' Jessie said. 'There's nothing quite so nice as building your own house and having everything just the way you want it.'

'Do you remember when we were little girls we wanted a cottage with a white paling fence and roses round the door?'

'As I remember, it was *you* wanted that. I wanted to be a boy and join the army. I thought boys had all the fun.'

'Until the war came along,' Violet said.

They were silent a moment. Then Jessie said, 'You will come to dinner one evening, while you're here, won't you?'

'Of course. And I expect there'll be invitations to Morland Place as well.'

'Not the least doubt in the world,' Jessie laughed. 'I'm only surprised Uncle Teddy hasn't got a card on your mantel-piece already. And the Morland Place children will want to see yours – where are they, by the way?'

'Having tea upstairs. I wanted you to myself to begin with. But we'll go up in a minute.'

'And next week is race week,' Jessie concluded, 'so there'll be lots going on for that.'

'I hadn't forgotten. Freddie's coming down for it.' Sir Frederick Copthall, Bart, was Violet's long-standing friend and escort, a wealthy bachelor who filled in for Holkam on many an occasion, and was in the address-book of every London hostess: there were always more unattached women than men, particularly easy-going ones with perfect manners.

'I'm glad,' Jessie said. 'I like Freddie.'

'Everyone likes Freddie,' Violet said.

Jessie wondered what Freddie thought of the whole David situation, but it wasn't something she could ask. She supposed it might become obvious next week. At all events, she was glad that, though Violet had a husband she didn't love and a prince who wore her out, at least she had Freddie.

Bertie came back from Somerset in sober mood. 'It makes you realise all over again how lucky we are,' he said, over a late supper.

'Was it really bad?' she asked.

'Oh, they weren't living in penury, but in some ways that makes it worse. There's something about people like that struggling along, never complaining, trying to keep up the appearance of respectability that's terribly depressing.'

'How poor are they?'

'Her father had a little land, but had to sell it. Her mother died during the Spanish flu outbreak, and what with doctor's bills and falling rents and having three more mouths to feed, he had to keep selling off things to keep their heads above water. Now they struggle along on her widow's pension and a tiny annuity of his. He wouldn't have told me himself, of course – too proud – but I managed to coax it out of her during a walk round the garden, just the two of us. They're both terribly thin. I imagine they half starve themselves to make sure the boys are provided for. I remember her as a plump little thing, like a sparrow, but now there's nothing of her.'

'What about the boys?'

'They're the image of their father. It was painful to see them – like two ghosts reproaching me. Not that *they* reproached me, you understand. Fine young fellows with perfect manners. Called me "sir" and treated me with the utmost respect. The elder boy, Simon, is sixteen, and he's got work as a clerk in a bank in Wincanton. There was simply no money for him to carry on at school, let alone university, though he's a bright lad. The younger, William – God, he's got a grin just like old Pennyfather! – he's just turned fifteen.'

'So they have to find a place for him, too, now? Is he going into the bank as well?'

'Wincanton's a tiny place. There aren't two bank billets. They're talking about a large draper's shop in the high street. You can see it would just about kill the grandfather to see the boy serve behind a counter – though William himself makes light of it. He's a nice fellow. The thing is, he's mad about horses.'

'There's racing at Wincanton, isn't there?' Jessie remembered.

'Used to be, and the boy used to hang around it every spare hour of the day. But the lease on the farm where they held the racing ran out this year. The chairman of the company, Lord Stalbridge, put up some money and they're taking on a new place and building a new course with a grandstand and all the facilities, but it won't be open for business for a year or so. Nothing there for William. So I was wondering, do you think we could take him on?' He raised anxious eyes from his plate to Jessie's face.

'Take him on? As a groom, you mean? It's rather humble. Won't the grandfather object to that?'

'Better than a draper's assistant. I know the boy would do anything to get out of working in a shop – he's dreading it. And if we teach him all we know, he could become a trainer himself one day. There's no shame in that. What do you think?'

Jessie saw he still felt guilty about Pennyfather and wanted to do something to help, but she couldn't help feeling the grandfather would be offended at the idea of the boy being a mere groom. 'Perhaps we could call the job something else,' she suggested. 'Apprentice trainer. Assistant stable manager. No, wait – assistant to the *chef d'équipe*!'

Bertie laughed, though his eyes were still anxious. 'Who's the *chef d'équipe*?'

'Well, I suppose I am, at the moment, but when William's trained, he will be.'

'You're serious, then? I thought you were making fun. You mean we can do something for him?'

'Of course, darling. We can always do with another hand, particularly one with intelligence and ambition. He can make himself useful until he's learned the trade and then I can hand over the management to him. I'll enjoy just being able to please myself, and do the jobs I like.'

'You're a wonderful woman,' Bertie said, his heart in his voice.

'Where do you want to put him? There's an empty room over the stables, or I'm sure we can find a room in the village for him.'

'Well,' Bertie said awkwardly, 'the thing is, he *is* a gentleman's son, and I know May Pennyfather will be anxious about his going so far away. She'd want me to keep a fatherly eye on him.'

Jessie concealed her amusement. 'You want him to live here? In Twelvetrees House?'

'Is that completely out of the question?'

'Of course not. We have plenty of room. And Thomas will be thrilled to have a new big brother.'

'Bless you, darling.' Bertie said. 'I'll write to the Pennyfathers at once, and suggest the boy starts in September. They'll want the rest of the summer together.'

CHAPTER SEVEN

At the races, Freddie Copthall offered to escort Jessie to the collecting-ring, as everyone else was busy with the picnic, the children or each other, or just too comfortable to move.

'Take my arm,' he offered. 'Easier to protect you from the crush that way.'

Jessie slipped her hand under it, felt appreciatively the fine cloth of his sleeve and smelt the delicate verbena fragrance of the eau-de-Cologne he used. She glanced up at his face as he steered them both through the crowd, and saw it gravely concentrating. He was such a *nice* man, she thought, and it was good for Violet that she had such a staunch friend; but she suddenly wondered whether it was good for him. Of course, there were men who preferred the bachelor life, and for them, a married woman made a pleasant and safe companion. On the other hand, it would be sad if he had been in love with Violet all these years, knowing he could never have her. He was handsome, she saw, and not yet forty. Did marriage never cross his mind?

Impulsively she said, 'Do you mind if I ask you something?' He looked down at her enquiringly. 'Something rather impertinent.'

Now he looked alarmed. 'I wish you wouldn't,' he said. 'I'm not very good at these *ladies'* questions. Can't we talk about horses? Who do you fancy for the next race?'

'I'll tell you which horse is going to win it, if you like,'

Jessie said, 'if you'll just tell me one thing. About the Prince of Wales and Violet.'

'Oh,' Freddie said. 'That.' He sighed, and said, 'It isn't what you think, you know.'

'What do I think?'

'People talk of her being his mistress, but there's nothing like that, I assure you.' He reddened at having to address such a subject.

'But what is he *like*?' Jessie asked. 'Do you like him? Does Violet really love him? I can't make it out.'

Freddie looked gloomy. 'No-one can. Makin' a devil of a figure of Violet. But what can anyone do? He's the Prince of Wales. Can't say no to him.' He thought a moment. 'That's the problem.'

'Does she love him?'

'Oh, I dare say,' he said rather grumpily. 'He's handsome, charmin'. Looks much younger than he is – comes across as rather pathetic, and women seem to like that. Can't understand it m'self. Suppose they want to mother him. Though why any man should want . . .' He frowned, thinking.

'You don't like him?' Jessie hazarded, not supposing she would have much of an answer, for Freddie never had a bad word for anyone.

It seemed, though, that he was at the end of some tether. 'Like him? He keeps people waitin', chucks at the last minute, keeps the servants up till all hours.' He actually stood still, fists clenched, his face reddening with the effort to hold in all his frustration. 'Good God, the man wears soft collars!' he burst out. 'A dinner jacket instead of tails! It ain't right! He went out huntin' one day last season in ratcatcher. Didn't know where to look.'

This last revelation seemed to vent the last of his steam for suddenly his scowl cleared and he looked guilty. He glanced around him, and bent towards Jessie to say, 'Beg pardon. Shouldn't have said those things. Shockin' bad form, blackguardin' a fellow behind his back. Can't think what came over me. You won't repeat?'

'Of course not,' Jessie said. 'It must be awkward for you, seeing him monopolise Violet, when you and she have been friends for so long.'

'It's the devil,' he admitted. 'That's why I'm makin' myself scarce.'

'What's that?'

'I'm getting married.'

Jessie couldn't remember ever being more astonished. 'Married?'

'Yes. Very nice girl, friend of Sarah Vibart's. Met her at one of Sarah and Eddie's parties. Cordelia Flaxman. Her pater's head of Flaxman's Bank, has a place down in Hampshire. Can't think what she sees in a fool like me, but for some reason she's taken a fancy to me, and I think she's simply spiffing.' He was blushing again. 'Going to make her Lady Copthall in September. Buy a place. Never had an estate until now. Time to settle down.'

'That's wonderful! Congratulations,' Jessie said. 'I had no idea.'

'Haven't told Violet yet,' he said anxiously, 'so mum's the word. Can't find the right moment. Thought I'd do it last night but m' tongue got tied, don't know why. I'll tell her tonight. Think she'll take it all right?'

'She'll be delighted for you,' Jessie assured him.

'Cordelia,' Freddie said, 'well, a chance like that comes along once in a chap's life.'

Jessie had promised not to repeat Freddie's views on the Prince of Wales, but she told Bertie about his engagement that night in bed. Bertie's reaction was pretty much as she had expected: pleasure on Freddie's behalf – 'He deserves a happy settlement. He had a damn good war' – and concern on Violet's. 'It will be a shock to her. She's used to having

143

him at her beck and call, and it will leave quite a hole. Poor Violet. But perhaps it will do her good in the long run. Knock some sense into her.'

'You don't think she has sense?' Jessie said, a little indignant on behalf of her friend.

'She's not like you, my love,' Bertie said succinctly.

'But what does she do that isn't sensible?'

'She should never have got involved with the Prince of Wales. Can't think why Holkam encourages it.'

'He thinks it will be good for them in the long run. Jobs, and positions for the children and so on.'

'He's a fool,' Bertie said tersely. 'I must say, if it was you the prince was running after, I'd knock his block off, heir to the throne or no heir to the throne.'

Curled snugly in his arms, Jessie couldn't help thinking that *that* was the way a husband ought to react.

Freddie married Cordelia Flaxman at St Margaret's in September. Eddie Vibart stood up with him as his best man and Violet's daughter Charlotte was one of the bridesmaids. Violet sat in a pew with Sarah Vibart, Oliver and Verena, Emma and Kit, and her mother, and smiled all the way through the ceremony; and showed every sign of being delighted with the business at the reception afterwards. Everyone said afterwards that it was a charming wedding.

Since it had taken place in September, it was all over before most people came back to Town, and by the time the great houses began to fill up, the happy couple were out of sight on their honeymoon; but still it was the topic of the first week or so. Everyone in the capital liked Freddie, so they were glad he had found a pleasing woman: the Flaxmans were respectable, though being bankers not quite of the *ton*.

The great speculation was how Violet Holkam felt about it. She was famous for decorum and keeping her own counsel, so they weren't likely to get anything out of *her*, but it didn't

144

stop the bolder elements trying. The Prince of Wales was still in South America, so she was rather exposed, feeling very much the lack of her usual escort at her side, until Lord Holkam should come back to Town for the opening of Parliament. She was forced to go down to Brancaster. There she tended her garden and hid from the world, and cried as much as she could without leaving the evidence in her face to feed the servants' gossip. She wanted to be happy for Freddie, but she felt instead as though he had died. She had lost Laidislaw, her great love, and now she had lost her great friend, and she was all alone in the world. It was the first time in many years that she went to Town to meet her husband with gladness.

Holkam's presence protected her from too much impertinence; and there was the return of the prince from his tour to look forward to.

Her mother, when she visited her, said, 'You must feel Freddie's absence, my love.'

'Very much,' Violet agreed dolefully.

'But I believe it was a love match. So you must be happy for him. I hope I didn't bring you up to be selfish, Violet.'

'I *am* happy for him. It's just awkward as things are. Holkam is busy so much, and he doesn't care for the same sort of entertainments.'

'Then you must find yourself another young man to take his place. You must meet plenty of them. Some of the equerries are very nice boys.' She gave Violet a level look. 'You can't depend on being the prince's favourite for ever, you know,' she said, quite kindly. It was the most direct reference she had ever made to Violet about the situation, which she preferred generally to ignore. 'You ought not to neglect your other friends.'

Violet had a sudden desire to fling herself into her mother's lap and cry, 'Oh, Mama, I'm in such a mess! Make it right, please!'

But before she could make any catastrophic confession, the butler, Ardworth, came in, looking rather impressed, and said, 'His Royal Highness the Prince of Wales is on the telephone, my lady, asking for Lady Holkam.'

'He's back,' Violet said.

'His Royal Highness is telephoning from Portsmouth, my lady,' said Ardworth, who would afterwards in the servants' hall confide to Miss Carless, my lady's maid, that the prince had been so eager, he had telephoned around to find where Lady Holkam might be, rather than wait until he got back to London. To which Carless replied with a sniff that, in her opinion, a man might as *well* wait before telephoning another man's wife, even if he was a prince.

Polly was back in New York in September, working on the fall collection, which would be unveiled in October, and Lennie, just back from Boston, had to call in several places before he ran her to earth in the workshop in the Lower East Side 'garment district', where she was debating about some embroidery with her head woman. She was looking, he thought, more beautiful than ever, though heavy-eyed, as though she had not slept much lately. He noticed that she had had her hair cut very recently, and that it was shorter than ever at the back; and that the hem of her skirt was only just covering her knees. It was still a delightful shock to him to see so much of a respectable woman's legs. In their flesh-coloured silk stockings, they looked as though they were naked.

'Lennie!' she said, and gave him a glad smile that warmed his heart. 'What are you doing here?'

'Looking for you. I just blew in from Boston and was trying to find someone to have dinner with tonight. The apartment is all shut up – Pa and Granny are still in Oyster Bay.'

'Oh dear, we have some business people to dinner tonight,' Polly said. 'They never seem to go away. Why don't you

146

come too? You're a business person – you'd probably enjoy them.'

'I can't butt in on your evening just like that,' Lennie said. He didn't want to have to see Polly and Ren together.

'It's no bother,' she said. 'It might brighten up the evening for me. And you can't eat alone in a restaurant. That would be too sad.'

He avoided the issue. 'Is that for your new collection?'

'Yes, and I'm frightfully behind with the designs. My cutters are screaming to know what to do, but I couldn't get Ren to let me come back any sooner, and there's a limit to what you can do by mail.'

'Pretty colours. Like a tapestry.'

'Thank you. Egypt and the east are out at last, thank the Lord,' Polly said. 'We're going with gypsies this season. Rich colours, gold thread, lots of embroidery, and reliefs of plain white muslin. I think it should look very striking. Hems are going shorter again, but embroidered bands or fur along the bottom will help those who don't like to show their knees. You don't know another word for "gypsy", do you? It's the only thing I don't like. It doesn't have quite the right tone. I thought of going with "corsair" but it seems they were pirates, not gypsies.'

Lennie thought. 'How about "Zigeuner"?'

'Oh, I like that. How do you spell it? And it means gypsy, does it?'

'More or less.'

'*Zigeuner*. Make a note for me, Mrs Blake. The Zigeuner Collection. Lennie, you're a gem.'

'Glad to be of help. How about rewarding me by letting me take you out for ice cream?'

'Oh, darling, I can't! I have so much to do. Come to dinner and we can talk then.'

'Can't do that. I've just remembered I promised a chap to meet him at the club later. Spare me half an hour now, for a cup of coffee, and then I'll get myself out of your hair.'

'It will have to be here, then,' Polly said. 'I've a little cubbyhole through there where we can be private. Mrs Blake, do you think you could ask Tina to bring us some coffee?'

In a dusty little room hardly bigger than a cupboard, littered deep with bolts of material, scraps, ends of tape and ribbon, boxes of buttons, ledgers, trays of correspondence, and drawings of long-legged women in dresses of every style and length, Polly and Lennie sat opposite each other across the battered table, which looked as though it had been regularly attacked with a penknife, and finally talked – first about Polly's business and then about Lennie's, about various members of the family, and one or two common friends.

When these topics were exhausted, Lennie said, 'I've barely seen you since the wedding – not to talk to. But married life seems to be suiting you. You look very well.'

'Do I? Thank you. I thought I must be haggard. We've been so busy, I don't seem to have had a moment to sit down since – well, since the beginning of this year. And things aren't getting any quieter. Apart from the collection, there's the house to oversee. Ren's ordered so many alterations, and someone has to look in now and then and get the builders moving. And we have to go to Washington at the end of October, and find a house there. Ren says there's a place called Alexandria where the smart people live.'

'You'll like it,' Lennie said. 'It's very old, so it'll feel more like England to you.'

'Oh, England! That seems so far away. I had a nice letter from my father, though, hoping we'd come and visit one day. I expect we will, but it's hard to see *when*, Ren's so busy.'

'But what about you? Apart from being busy – are you *happy*?'

'Of course I am,' she said.

He put his hand across the table and laid it on hers. 'Don't just give an automatic answer. Not to me, Polly. I need to know if you really *are* happy. Is marriage what you expected?'

She met his eyes, and he could not read their expression. But she seemed to take his question seriously. 'I don't know,' she said. 'I'm not sure I really knew what to expect. Perhaps it *isn't*, quite – but not in a bad way. It's such a whirligig, so much happening all the time, people coming and going, names to remember, meals to plan, and everything seems to be so *important*, as if you daren't get the least thing wrong or the whole world will come crashing down. But it's exciting – like riding a galloping horse, with the air rushing past so fast you can hardly draw breath. And I feel as if I'm going somewhere, not just marking time – somewhere that matters.'

None of which really answered his question. He swallowed, and said, 'And Ren?' He wanted to ask, how does he treat you, is he kind, attentive, does he tell you how beautiful you are, does he make love to you? *Do you love him?* That most of all.

She did not pretend not to understand him. She turned her hand over under his and clasped it around his fingers, warm and affectionate. 'He's an exciting man,' she said. 'He takes my breath away.' He said nothing, and she added, 'Oh, Lennie, don't torture yourself. I'm married now. Forget about me. Find some really nice girl to love.'

'Do you love him?' he asked, the knowledge he had of Alexander like a thorn inside his head.

Polly thought of that tall, dark, enigmatic man she lived with – barely lived with, for he was out so much, so busy, and when he was home there were so often other people there. And when she was alone with him, it was like being shut up with a great and terrifying force like a typhoon that might burst out in any direction. She was exhilarated, dazzled – and a little afraid of him: not that he would hurt her, but that she would disappoint him; or that he would step so far outside her understanding that she would lose him.

And then there was that other side to marriage, unimaginable before the act. His passion filled her equally with fear and excitement, and the physical pleasure, when it came, was almost secondary. She did not understand what it meant to him, and was afraid there were levels and layers below the obvious that she could not comprehend – and almost did not want to. When he hung above her, his great sleek body held from crushing hers by the iron muscles of his arms, and his green-gold eyes gleamed at her, and his white teeth showed between his firm lips, it was like being in bed with a wild animal. *Where had this man come from, to be so different?* Surely no ordinary mortals had been his parents. He must have been forged by the gods out of pure fire.

She said, 'Yes, I love him.'

Lennie looked at her for a long moment, then sighed, and said, 'I'm glad.' And he was, of course. He could not jeopardise that. He would have to keep to himself the information he had paid for so dearly.

On a spring day in 1926, Oliver's last patient of the morning came into his consulting room in Queen Anne Street with his head theatrically high. His air of flamboyance was emphasised by his hat, a Homburg with a rather large brim, and a pair of blue-tinted glasses that hid his eyes. He removed both with a flourish, and stood before Oliver posed like a statue, a tall, svelte man, very handsome, with bright blue eyes, a Grecian profile, and thick, fair wavy hair, worn a little longer than Town fashion dictated, so that it covered the tops of his ears and brushed his collar at the back.

Oliver advanced from behind his desk with his hand extended. 'Mr George Higgins? I don't think we've met?'

The beautifully manicured hand was placed briefly in his, and the blue eyes scanned his face carefully. 'I can see you know who I am really,' he said.

150

Oliver smiled. 'My wife and I go to the cinema now and then. We saw you in *Lord of the Dunes*.'

Raymond Romano seemed pleased rather than otherwise to be recognised, but said, 'George Higgins is actually my real name. I'm from Cambridge originally. But I don't want anyone to know what Raymond Romano has come to see you about. It could ruin me if it got into the papers.'

'Absolute discretion is an important part of the plastic surgeon's profession,' said Oliver. 'Won't you sit down?'

The young man sat with the graceful fluidity of a dancer, crossed his legs, and tweaked the crease of his trousers straight. 'Your receptionist is to be trusted, I hope?'

'Absolutely.'

'Because I think she recognised me, despite the dark glasses.'

'Young women like her go to the cinema a great deal. But she knows better than to breathe a word. I am consulted by many eminent people. So please put away your fears, and tell me what the problem is.'

'This!' said Raymond Romano and, with a dramatic gesture, pushed the hair away from his right ear.

'May I?' Oliver asked, and came round the desk. The cinema star's left ear was normal, and the bottom of the right ear matched it, but the top half was missing entirely. There was no sign of trauma or scarring. 'Congenital?' he asked.

'I beg your pardon?'

'Were you born this way?'

'Yes,' he said bitterly, 'and how I suffered for it at school! It's why I went into acting, really, to get away from horrible people. I've always managed to hide it by growing my hair long – no-one minds that in the film business. And, of course, in *Lord of the Dunes* and *Prince of the Steppes* I wore a sort of turban thing most of the time, and when I took it off I had hair down to my shoulders.' He tossed his head a little. 'Luckily I have wonderfully thick, strong hair. Some actors

151

I could mention simply couldn't have grown so much, but I could have hair down to my waist if the part called for it.'

'How fortunate,' Oliver murmured, sitting on the edge of his desk with an informality he would never have considered with most of his patients. He was enjoying the encounter.

Mr Higgins looked a little put out. 'Fortunate, you call it? To have such a blemish as *this*,' he gestured towards the ear, 'when my looks are so important to my career? And who knows whether I'll be able to have my hair long in my next part? Desert princes are pretty much out now, you know. They're saying that costume drama is out completely, and it will be all modern-day stuff. I *have* to be able to have short hair.'

'Fortunately, I can do something about that for you.'

'You can?' Mr Higgins clasped his hands before his chest and gazed up at Oliver. 'Help me, and I'll be in your debt for *ever*!'

Oliver stopped himself saying that his fees weren't *quite* that ruinous. He had a feeling Mr Higgins was enjoying himself in his present role and would not want it spoiled by jokes.

'It's quite simple. I would take a small sliver of cartilage from one of your ribs to make the basic structure, then the rest would be done with skin grafts. When I've finished, no-one will be able to tell the difference between your two ears. You'll forget yourself which was the incomplete one.'

'Do you really mean it? Oh, the miracle of modern medicine! How long would it take?'

'Six months, more or less.'

'Six months!' He sounded horrified.

'I would have to do it in stages, each stage taking a few days. You would be able to carry on with your normal life in between treatments.'

Higgins clasped his hands again, differently this time, more the anxious mother than the rapturous maiden. 'Would it cost an awful, *awful* lot?'

'It depends on what you regard as the true cost of beauty. My fee would be three hundred guineas, but what is that compared with the value to your career?'

Higgins blinked, and thought for a moment, and Oliver saw him drop briefly out of his role and do some calculations. 'Well,' he sighed in the end, 'I suppose I have no choice. But you really promise me it will work? The new ear will be perfect?'

Oliver permitted himself a stern look. 'I am as much an artist in my way as you, sir, and I would scorn to produce anything but a perfect result. You may place yourself entirely in my hands. I promise you, you will not be disappointed.'

George Higgins had barely departed when Kit came in, unannounced. 'Your girl told me you were alone,' he excused himself. 'And you'll never guess who I met on the stairs!'

Oliver smiled. 'You know perfectly well he came from seeing me. The floor above is empty.'

'Rhetorical device. My dear, *what* is the handsome and famous Raymond Romano consulting you for? If ever there was a piece of perfection in human form, it's him.'

'Perfection?' Oliver said wryly. 'Have you actually seen *Lord of the Dunes*?'

Kit shrugged. 'Film acting is not the same as stage acting. And I wasn't talking about that, anyway. What *can* he have for you to correct?'

'You know I can't discuss my patients. And, as far as I'm concerned, that was Mr George Higgins. I trust you will remember that too.'

'Of course I won't tell a soul he's been consulting you. I wonder what he's in London for. He didn't mention, I suppose?'

'Not a word. You'll just have to guess.'

'Oh, I think I can do better than that. There's a girl I know who works for a theatrical agent. She's bound to know.'

'A girl you know?' Oliver enquired.

'Not like that. She shares a flat with the manicurist I go to in Jermyn Street.'

'Oh. Well, not that I'm not glad to see you . . .' Oliver went on, gesturing towards the papers on his desk.

'I was just passing,' Kit said. 'Dropped in to chat. No ulterior.' He took out his watch and consulted it. 'Good Lord, it's almost one o'clock. Time to toddle along to the club and fold a chop into the system. Can I tempt you?'

Oliver laughed. 'No ulterior, eh? It's just that you are congenitally incapable of eating alone.'

'I might get buttonholed by some bore,' Kit said. 'You don't know what it is to be burdened with irresistible magnetism.'

'You and Raymond Romano would have a lot to talk about. All right, I'll come. I've just time,' Oliver said, standing up and reaching for his hat. 'Your trouble,' he went on, when they were out in the street and looking for a taxi, 'is that you don't have enough to do.'

'Do go on,' said Kit. 'I love people telling me what my trouble is.'

'Idleness doesn't suit you,' Oliver persisted. 'You were a damned good surgeon – better than me when we were both out in France.'

'Not better, just quicker.'

'I hate to see all that talent go to waste. What do you do with yourself all day now?'

'I don't know. See people. Write letters. Advise Emma on fitting out her apartments. I never seem to have a moment to myself, I know that.'

'Except at mealtimes.'

The newspaper-seller on the corner of Harley Street was shouting something, and as they neared they saw the headline on his board: *Girl born to Duchess of York*. Kit darted over to buy a copy and joined Oliver in the taxi he had just secured.

'Well, now, this is good news,' he said, reading the rather meagre report. 'Born in the early hours of this morning. A healthy girl. Mother and child doing well.'

'It would have been better if it had been a boy, of course,' said Oliver.

'But still, it takes the pressure off the Prince of Wales,' said Kit. 'They won't be badgering him to marry quite so much. He'll be delighted. And that will take the pressure off Violet. If he's happy, she's happy. They'll be at Eddie's tonight – Holkam's bringing Violet. Emma and I are dining there. Are you going?'

'Yes, Verena and I have been invited.'

'Oh, good, then we'll all be together. If Wales doesn't chuck. Perfect excuse to be late, for once, with the new baby. I've heard the Yorks are going to be near neighbours,' Kit said. 'They've taken the lease on 145 Piccadilly.' Oliver's cousin Eddie and his wife, Sarah, lived at 143. 'It will need some alterations before they can move in, so it won't be for a few months.'

'It will need a nursery suite, I suppose,' Oliver said.

'Yes, and all the main rooms need redecorating. I'm trying to get Eddie to push for Emma to do it. It would be a feather in her cap if she did some work for the Yorks.'

'I suppose the prince will be around all the more often,' Oliver said, 'with his brother next door to his equerry.'

'Yes, all very cosy, isn't it?' said Kit.

To avoid the traffic on Regent Street, the cabbie had slipped across into Soho and was zigzagging his way down towards St James's. As they turned from Bridle Lane into Brewer Street Kit suddenly sat forward.

'Talking of the devil, isn't that Holkam? Coming out of that door on Sherwood Street?'

'Is it?' Oliver looked back, but couldn't see.

'Looked awfully like him. I'd know that hat of his anywhere. Queer sort of place for him to be, though.'

'You mean that house on the corner?' It was shabby, with peeling paint. 'Couldn't have been him.'

'I'm sure it was,' Kit said. 'I couldn't be more fascinated! He must have been consulting a clairvoyant or a mesmerist or something. All sorts of odd people have rooms in this quarter.'

Oliver laughed. 'The last person in the world to consult a clairvoyant will be Holkam. You can place money on that. Ask him tonight when you see him.'

'What – and risk a diplomatic incident? He doesn't like me anyway.'

'I'm not sure Holkam likes anyone.'

'Oh, everybody likes *someone*,' Kit said lightly. 'Even if it's only *amour propre*. Here we are. I hope they've got the pea soup on. Only decent thing to eat in this place. Can't think why clubs have the worst food in London.'

'To give the members something to talk about,' Oliver said.

Kit looked up at the façade of the finest gentleman's club in the world. 'Wonder where Raymond Romano is staying? Hotels are such soulless places.'

The threats made in the summer of 1925 of a coal strike had been taken seriously, and for the nine months since then, a Royal Commission under Sir Herbert Samuel – the former High Commissioner to Palestine – had been looking into the troubles of the coal mining industry.

The mining industry was doing badly. Heavy demands on coal during the war years had depleted the rich seams, and what coal remained was harder to extract and less profitable. Exports had fallen dramatically in recent years, with Poland and the United States coming into the market, and the Dawes

Plan allowing Germany to pay part of its reparation to France and Italy in 'free' coal. Mine owners, like other exporters, also said the return to the Gold Standard had made the pound too strong and prices too high.

'But the Gold Standard's not to blame,' Jack said, when the subject came up between him and Helen. 'Our only real competitors are Germany and America and our prices are hardly higher than theirs – about two and a half per cent. Not worth worrying about. The real problem is that Polish coal is better. And our cottons can't compete with American for quality. The world has moved on and we haven't. They don't want our old-fashioned goods at any price.'

Faced with falling profits, the mine owners had proposed to reduce wages and lengthen hours. The Miners' Federation response had been 'Not a penny off the pay, not a minute on the day.' During the war, they had formed a Triple Alliance of unions with the railway workers and the dockers, which gave them formidable power. In the summer of 1925 the TUC had backed the miners and threatened to call a general strike if the miners' pay was reduced. The government had stepped in to buy time, and paid a subsidy to keep the miners' wages up while the Samuel Commission was sitting.

The Commission reported on the 10th of March 1926, recommending, among other things, national agreements and radical reorganisation to deal with poor productivity – and a reduction in miners' wages.

'One can't help feeling sorry for them,' Helen said, when the report was published in the newspapers. 'It must be a dreadful job.'

'Yes, especially in the deep and narrow seams,' Jack said. 'One wonders how much longer coal mining can remain viable at all in this country. There are much easier and richer seams abroad.'

'But we must have our own coal,' Helen said, taken aback. 'We can't rely on other countries. They could cut us off and cripple us. What would have happened in the war if we'd got our coal from Germany?'

'I agree. But there are other considerations. There is a lot of Communist infiltration in the miners' union. It may not just be a dispute about wages.'

'Socialist revolution?' Helen said. Since 1917, the thought was never far below the surface. 'You don't really think—'

'No, I don't think, not really. But we have to be vigilant. It happened in Russia and Germany.'

'I read a book a couple of years ago,' Helen said. '*The Battle of London.*'

'Yes, I remember. By Hugh Addison. A general strike paralyses the country, making way for a workers' uprising, bloody revolution, and a knock-out blow from the Germans. Lurid stuff.'

'Yes, that's what I thought at the time. But if the TUC does call a general strike . . . Suppose that's just the beginning?'

When Molly came to visit one Sunday in April the topic arose again. 'It probably won't come to anything,' she said. 'The TUC has threatened general strikes before, and nothing came of it. But if they do want to test the ground, they won't find us unprepared.'

'What do you mean?' Helen asked. 'Do you know something?'

'Oh, it's not a deep secret. It'll be common knowledge soon enough,' Molly said. 'While Samuel has been sitting, the government's been quietly getting on with making arrangements. The Organisation for the Maintenance of Supplies, it's called – the OMS. In the event of a general strike, the country will be divided into ten regions, each under a civil commissioner, charged with maintaining essential services and distributing goods – food and coal and so on. Volunteers and special constables will be signed up. They've even been readying people to drive the trains.' She grinned. 'There's many a man who's realised his childhood dream and had a go at being an engine driver! They teach them at weekends on the private railways belonging to big factories.'

'Don't let Basil hear that,' Helen said. 'He'd run away in an instant.'

'You'll be wanted,' Molly said. 'They'll need anyone who can drive a car.'

'I shall have to stay with the children if the schools close, which I suppose they will.'

'But it won't come to that,' Jack said. 'Good sense will prevail in the end. This is England.'

'I tend to agree with you,' Molly said. 'From what I've heard, the TUC leaders have no stomach for the fight, and Baldwin knows that. There'll be last-minute talks and a deal will be struck.'

'I hope so,' Helen said. 'It would be dreadful to have one section of the country set against another in that way.'

In the wake of the Samuel Report, the mine owners posted notices announcing that employment on current conditions would terminate on the 30th of April. If the miners wanted to work, they would have to accept a new deal: an extra hour on the working day, and a return to the wage of 1921 – a cut of thirteen and a half per cent. On the 1st of May the miners were locked out. The General Council of the TUC took over responsibility for the miners' dispute and contacted the government asking for talks, warning that they were prepared to call out the 'front ranks' in a general strike from midnight on the 3rd of May.

Late in the evening of Sunday, the 2nd, the miners' leaders met with the cabinet, the mine owners and TUC representatives in Downing Street. The union leader Ernest Bevin, to avoid deadlock, suggested there should be an independent wages board, which would oversee the reorganisation of the mining industry, and then adjudicate wage rates. The TUC and the government were broadly in agreement that some wage reduction and much reorganisation was needed; but the mine owners did not want to accept any reorganisation, the miners would not countenance any loss of pay, and the government refused to negotiate at all unless the strike was first called off.

Meanwhile, that Sunday, Baldwin had sent John Davidson, the MP, to meet Lord Burnham, the representative of the Newspaper Proprietors' Association. The TUC had said it was going to call out the print workers and close down all the newspapers. Davidson and Burnham agreed that it was important some kind of news-sheet should be produced. The NPA would recruit the necessary volunteers for a bulletin to be published and distributed to town halls, post offices and other such public buildings, while the government would appoint an official editor to oversee the operation.

In the early hours of Monday, the 3rd of May, the print workers at the *Daily Mail* stopped work, refusing to set the leader article. Entitled 'For King and Country', it included a passage they objected to: 'A General Strike is not an industrial dispute. It is a revolutionary movement which can only succeed by destroying the Government and subverting the right and liberties of the people.'

The Prime Minister issued a note citing 'overt acts including interference with the freedom of the Press' as a reason for ending talks with the TUC. The TUC issued a manifesto disclaiming all responsibility for the 'calamity that now threatens', which lay entirely with the government and the mine owners. The strike had become inevitable, and would begin at 11.59 p.m.

There were lively exchanges in the House of Commons that day. Baldwin stated that he did not believe the TUC leaders were in control of the situation; that despotic power was in the hands of a small group; and that a general strike imperilled the very freedom of the Constitution. Winston

Churchill accused the TUC of trying to overthrow the government. Ramsay MacDonald said he was for peace, and would stand for peace until the very end. J. H. Thomas said that all the workers wanted was justice. Lloyd George said it was not an ordinary dispute but an attempt to force the government's hand, though he thought it was a mistake for the government to say it would not negotiate under duress. Then the Emergency Powers Act was put in place, allowing the government to requisition food, fuel, stores, vehicles and tramways, and prohibit meetings, and allowing the police to act without a warrant.

Molly arrived home early in the afternoon, and had barely pulled off her hat when there was a knock at her door and Popovka appeared. He had Nina Simonova, the ballet teacher, behind him – even more skeletally thin than him, her black hair parted in the centre and dragged into a bun behind, dressed in black to the ankles, with ballet slippers below, and a thick grey shawl round her shoulders, because she felt the cold all the time, even in midsummer.

'I saw you come across the square,' said Popovka. 'I am glad you are home safely. I was worried about you.'

'Why on earth?' Molly said. 'Nothing's happening yet.'

'But the time will come when the streets are not safe. Certain men, who ought always to be kept busy, will be idle, and idle hands do mischief.'

'I did not dare to open the school today,' Nina said. 'Why are you here, *galubchik*?'

'Our newspaper is to be the one to bring out the official bulletin. Our proprietor met John Davidson at noon and the deal was done, so we were sent home. Our printers have been told by their union not to co-operate, and nobody knows who is to do the actual work, so it's all a bit of a muddle at the moment.'

'Ah, yes, the official newspaper,' said Popovka.

'It's to be called the *British Gazette*, and the official editor will be Winston Churchill,' Molly told them. 'My editor, who knows Davidson pretty well, says it was him who pushed Baldwin to put Churchill in charge, just to keep him from getting into even worse trouble. He's afraid Churchill will inflame the situation and we'll end up with an army of Bolsheviks on the streets.'

Nina's large eyes widened even further. 'Oh, do not jest! We have seen such things, Pop and I, in our own dear country.' Emotion overcame her, and she lapsed briefly into Russian.

Popovka said seriously, 'The first thing the Bolsheviks did in the revolution was to seize the newspapers and telephone exchanges. To control the means of communication is to control the truth.'

'Churchill wanted to commandeer the British Broadcasting Company,' Molly admitted, 'and John Reith practically ran all the way to the Admiralty, where Davidson has set up his office, to get his word in first. He persuaded Davidson that it would look better if the BBC remained independent. So he's going to be allowed to run a news service for the first time – five broadcasts a day.'

'And you wait to hear if you will be required to work?' Popovka said.

'Oh, they won't want me. They're expecting trouble from the strikers, and they think it's too dangerous for women. They're going to billet the men who volunteer in the Inland Revenue offices across the road, to save them having to travel to work every day, and there'll be police to guard both buildings in case the strikers try to shut the *Gazette* down. So I'm surplus to requirements,' Molly concluded.

'You sound disappointed,' Nina said. 'But you cannot wish to go into danger?'

At that moment the street door below slammed and there was a sound of pounding feet on the stairs. The two students from the first-floor back appeared, and stopped at the sight of the gathering at Molly's door.

'Oh, is it a public meeting within the meaning of the act?' said Pooley.

'I say, Ormerod's home,' said Felix. 'That means the newspapers really have come out.'

'Not officially until midnight,' Molly said, and told her story again.

'Well, we've been out and about,' Felix said, 'and there's all sorts of preparations going on, notices stuck up on walls and lamp-posts. It's all frightfully exciting – like the war all over again.'

'You were only a child when the war ended,' Molly pointed out.

'Well, the bit of it I remember was exciting.'

'Hyde Park is closed,' Pooley interrupted, 'and they're setting up huts and temporary buildings, like an army camp. Positive hive of activity. A policeman told us they're putting a complete telephone system in there. I couldn't be more interested, could you?'

'But the best bit is they're registering volunteers in the Foreign Office quad,' Felix said excitedly. 'A chap said people are signing on at the rate of five hundred an hour.'

'Four hundred, he said.'

'Either way, we have to get a move on or we'll miss our chance. I say, Ormerod, now you're here, why don't you come with us? It will be the most tremendous go.'

'They won't want women.'

'You don't know until you try,' Pooley said. 'Come on! You don't want to have to tell your grandchildren you missed the whole thing.'

'All right, I'll come,' Molly said, and looked at Popovka. 'What about you?'

'I have a mind to go with you,' he said, his gravity in startling contrast to the student's elation. 'The forces of civilisation are being tested. But I fear to leave Simonova all alone.'

163

Nina clasped his hands and gazed seriously into his face. 'You must not think of that when there is duty to be done. If things get bad, I will go to the basement and wait with the girls there. Go with God, *tovarich*, and put me from your mind.'

They left her standing on the landing, her hands folded on her breast, hugging her shawl around her, and clattered downstairs and out into the dry, cool May day.

CHAPTER EIGHT

Tuesday, May the 4th began with an eerie silence at the railway stations. In London the Underground was effectively at a standstill, only three hundred out of more than four thousand buses were running, mostly driven by volunteers, and a mere nine out of two thousand trams. The roads were choked with slow-moving traffic, and the background sound in every street was the steady tramp of feet as office workers walked to work.

Up and down the country, the unionised workers stayed at home, closing down transport, iron and steel, engineering, printing, chemicals, power stations and the building industries. Towns with non-unionised industries were less affected, except by the universal interruption to transport. The only national newspaper to appear was *The Times*, in a severely malnourished four-page edition. Its chairman, J. J. Astor, contemptuous of the pusillanimity of the other proprietors, had sent his printers home with kind words on Monday evening, telling them that he knew it wasn't their fault, then rolled up his sleeves and spent the night trying to teach middle-aged journalists how to operate the presses and carry the heavy loads of paper needed to feed them.

In London the docks were closed and were heavily picketed – London dockers were the most loyal members of the Triple Alliance – but during the day almost five hundred Cambridge students arrived as volunteers, their first task to unload the tons of newsprint ordered in from Holland by the government, to make sure the *British Gazette* could not be starved out.

There was a violent incident at the Blackwall Tunnel, where a crowd of strikers had stopped cars and made the passengers get out and walk. The police had to make several baton charges before the blockade could be broken up, and there had been casualties, who were taken to Poplar Hospital. And at Canning Town cars were stopped and, in some cases the engines smashed, before the police arrived to disperse the mob. But for the most part, the day passed off quietly, with preparations going ahead in an orderly way, and people seeming more bemused by the novelty of the situation than alarmed or distressed.

In York, Lord Grey had been appointed commissioner, and had at once asked both Bertie and Teddy to serve on his committee. All sorts of motor vehicles had been requisitioned, and food and coal distribution were the primary concerns.

The unions were in something of a muddle over food distribution. On the one hand they did not want to be guilty of starving the population if they hindered it; but on the other they might be accused of strike-breaking and disloyalty if they helped. Often it came down to the detail of which foods were to be moved, and in what quantities. Works committees, which were set up to manage the strike at the local level, settled individually on different degrees of co-operation with the civil commissions; equally, in some districts the commissioner consulted and worked closely with the local works committee, while in others he was overtly hostile to it.

In York, Lord Grey tended to be conciliatory, wanting only to get the job done. As much of the industry in and around York was on a small scale and not unionised, life for most people continued uninterrupted. The schools opened, and there were few absentee teachers; offices and small works functioned normally, and as there was food in the shops, most people did not wonder how it had got there. The main difference was the silence of the railway station and sidings, the absence of buses and trams, and the consequent increase of motor-cars and bicycles.

After food distribution, the maintenance of law and order was the main concern. Police leave had been cancelled, as had the leave of the soldiers at the nearby barracks, who were standing by in case of disturbance, or if help were needed in shifting supplies. Special constables had been signed on, and Bertie, with his long military experience, had been put in charge of that side of things, while Teddy headed the sub-committee for fuel distribution. He decided that, until it was seen how things panned out, coal ought to be rationed. Only a hundredweight at one time could be sold, and none to anyone who had five hundredweight already. The power stations needed to be kept going, though fortunately the demands for heat were lower than if the strike had taken place in winter, and the long May dusk meant lights did not have to be turned on too early.

Henrietta and Amy were busy making sure that the old and sick of the estate and village were taken care of, and Morland Place became an unofficial centre for help and information for those who could not get into York because of the transport strike. They even provided minor medical care – Henrietta was used to administering first aid for the family and servants – and Bertie dubbed it the Forward Aid Station. For Amy, the change of duties came as a welcome distraction from her sorrow over losing her son; to do good works was the best antidote to the selfishness of mourning.

Jessie had volunteered straight away – anyone who could drive was much in demand – and spent her days driving a lorry back and forth from the depot to the outlying villages. Bertie was anxious about her safety, and made sure that all food lorries travelled in convoy with a police escort, and had 'FOOD ONLY' chalked on their sides. He further insisted that female drivers – Jessie was not the only lady volunteer – had a male non-driver sitting beside them. Jessie accepted his strictures comfortably. She knew she was being useful; and she was enjoying the experience, though it was tiring at first turning the wheel of the heavy lorry, and changing the stiff gears. 'I'm developing the most unladylike muscles in my arms,' she confessed.

The person who was enjoying the strike most was probably William Pennyfather. He had settled in at Twelvetrees House and had proved a great asset. Plentiful food and regular work had filled him out, and he had shot up two inches since the autumn; but what was most noticeable was his happy disposition and sense of fun, which had come out of hiding now his anxieties over his future were allayed. Everyone liked him, he kept mealtimes cheerful, and as Jessie had predicted, the children adored him, especially Ottilie. He played with her with an endearing lack of the usual young man's dignity. She would run to him as soon as she saw him with her arms outstretched to be picked up, and even, to her parents' chagrin, preferred 'my William' to read her a bedside story and tuck her in.

Bertie loved William's jokes and his infectious chuckle, and told Jessie that he was growing more like his father all the time. 'Sometimes I look at him and I see dear old Pennyfather looking back at me with the gleam of humour I remember so well.'

'Is it easing the guilt?' she asked.

'I think it is,' he said. 'You've no regrets about taking him in?'

'Goodness, no! He's a delight to have about the house, and he's wonderful at the stables. Not just good with the horses, but really beginning to manage now. He has a knack of handling people, so that even the older grooms don't mind asking him what to do. He's a real asset, darling. You did a good thing.'

When the strike started, William mourned that he was not yet able to drive, as he longed to be useful. On the first day, Jessie drove him into York and left him to find something to do. He discovered that there was a large number of animals at the railway station, their journeys interrupted by the strike, and as no-one seemed to know what to do about them, he took it on himself to organise their care, finding volunteers, buckets for water, and fodder from the stores, which he got the food committee to release. When that was working well, he delegated it to one of the volunteers and went off to see what else he could do.

He met a shopkeeper hanging about disconsolately in front of the station: a fishmonger, who was complaining that, with no trains, he could not get any fish up from Hull port to sell. Another man, who had two charabancs for hire, was sighing that he had no customers. William swiftly put the two together, found a volunteer who could drive among the idlers, and organised a trip to the coast to pick up a load of fish and bring it back, stacking the crates inside the coaches, on the seats and all down the aisles.

Bertie praised his ingenuity, but said, 'Remind me not to hire one of Maltby's charas for a month or two, until the smell has faded.' He mentioned the incident to Lord Grey, who said William was just the sort of young man the country needed, and brought him into the official fold.

So the first two days of the strike passed off relatively smoothly. The strikers, perhaps deciding the populace was adapting *too* well and forgetting what the strike was about, arranged a march through the city each afternoon, carrying their trade banners and accompanied by a brass band. It boosted their morale, drew attention to themselves, and stopped the traffic; and the onlookers waved and sometimes cheered as they passed – though Bertie said to Jessie that

that was probably more because everyone loved a band than from solidarity with the strike.

In London, things were less cheerful on the second day of the strike. For one thing, a thick brown fog had settled over the city around lunchtime. Fog always lowered the spirits, and since there were rumours flying about that the gas was to go off, many people did not turn on the lights but sat in the unnatural gloom, which gave a sense of foreboding. The guards at Buckingham Palace were in khaki instead of ceremonial red for the first time in peacetime history, which made them suddenly noticeable, and reminded Mr Popovka of scenes at the Winter Palace in St Petersburg he had rather forget. There were extra policemen everywhere, and soldiers guarding the docks and other strategic places, which made it feel as if a revolution was imminent.

An article on the front page of the *British Gazette* said that, without the *Gazette*, 'this great nation' would be reduced to the level of African natives dependent on bush rumour – rumour that would 'poison the air, raise panics and disorders, inflame fears and passions together, and carry us all to depths which no sane man of any party or class would care even to contemplate'. With Churchill as official editor, it was to be expected that the paper would emphasise the disadvantages of the strike, but on a dark, foggy afternoon they were not words to engender much cheer.

And there were more violent incidents, mostly around transport. There were reported to be gangs roaming the East End, smashing cars and attacking volunteers and strike-breakers. Attempts to run trams out of Camberwell depot had to be abandoned when an ugly crowd started smashing windows and threatening the drivers. In Hammersmith, Canning Town and Poplar, buses were stopped by violent pickets blockading the depots. Arrests were made, and the few buses that did manage to get out on to the street had to have a policeman sitting up beside the driver, and the windows covered with netting; in Chiswick, each driver was accompanied by a soldier. A warship was brought up the Thames so that the sailors could help with unloading, and the students working on the wharves were being guarded by soldiers.

Perhaps the most alarming incident was the attack on the offices of *The Times* in Printing House Square. Petrol was poured down a shaft normally used for bringing in newsprint from the street, and flaming rags were thrown in after it, causing a huge fireball and a thirty-foot-high wall of flame. Fortunately the area was concreted, and the great rolls of newsprint, being tightly packed, were slow to catch fire. The volunteer workers were able to put out the blaze, but the shock of the incident and its wicked intentions made a great impression on the educated and the law-abiding. It had the perverse effect, in a certain section of society, of increasing support for *The Times* in its current form. It became a badge of honour to be seen carrying a copy, or to have one lying visible in one's drawing-room, and to say that one's son or nephew was taking his turn at guarding the premises or helping out with the printing.

Emma had been a FANY during the war, driving an ambulance in Flanders: years of hard physical work and responsibility, long hours, discomfort, cold and dirt, and real personal danger. She had been shelled and bombed, she had transported horribly wounded soldiers under fire, she had seen sights no-one should ever see; and in addition had lost two men she had loved. She had emerged in 1919 physically and spiritually exhausted; and in the throes of reaction to that intolerable effort, like many others of her generation, she had seen no purpose in anything any more. She had given herself up to the pursuit of meaning-less pleasure, drinking and dancing and parties until the small hours, often with Kit, and always in the company of others of the set known as the Bright Young People. At weekends they went to house-parties and sporting events, moving in a series of small circles of the same faces, the same music, the same jokes, the same gossip.

Into this sameness, the General Strike came like a breath of fresh air. Kit had burst into her apartment on the first day at an unusually early hour for him – it was barely half past ten. She had been awake – she often slept badly – and was lying waiting for Spencer to decide it was time to bring her her tea, too weary to be bothered to ring. She heard Kit's arrival, as did Benson, her little brown mongrel, who slept on the end of her bed. He jumped up, wagging his tail, then sprang off the bed to jam his nose against the door in eagerness, as he always did.

'You're a fool,' she told him. 'You'll get hit by the door again.' He only wagged the more at the sound of her voice, and a moment later the door did open and banged him on the head because he could not jump backwards fast enough. It didn't seem to bother him, though. He shot straight past Spencer, who was making the announcement, and flung himself passionately at Kit, prancing on his hind legs and wagging his whole hindquarters.

'Hello, Benny old fruit,' Kit said. 'Not these trousers – down then. Emma, what are you doing still in bed?'

'What are you doing up?' she countered. It hadn't been a particularly late evening, but it was after two when they had parted at the door of Stretton House.

Kit lifted his hands in exasperation. 'It's the first day of the best adventure since the war! The revolution is upon us! Our country needs us! Tommy Beaufort came all the way back from Paris for it, and here you are, lounging in bed as though nothing is happening.'

'Well, what *is* happening?' Emma asked, pulling on a bed jacket. 'Spencer, I'll have my tea now.'

'Oh, my dear, haven't I just told you? The revolution!

172

Can't you just see it? The Red Flag hanging over the town hall, the post office barricaded, the overturned tram blocking the road. Whispered conversations in alleys, shady-looking coves hanging around a brazier on every street corner. The railway engine that arrives in the dead of night with the charismatic leader standing on the footplate. The prison gates flung open and gangs of drunken criminals roaming the streets. Moscow, Budapest, Berlin – they've all had theirs. We're rather late having ours, but it's here at last.'

'How *can* you be so pleased about it?' Emma asked, but she knew. She had felt a little tingle of reprehensible excitement too. It was something *different*, and they all craved novelty.

'I couldn't think it more thrilling,' Kit said. 'They're signing up people all over the place. Tommy Beaufort has joined Tony Spencer's show – a sort of flying squad to protect the food convoys. You have to swear an oath of loyalty and they give you a truncheon and a tin hat. Too divine! I must have mine.'

'But they won't let women join,' Emma said.

'No, darling, but they'll want all the drivers they can get, and with your war record, you'll be snapped up. So do stop sulking and come along.'

'I'm not sulking,' Emma objected. 'And I can't get up until you leave the room,' she pointed out.

'I'm leaving like a tree, just as fast as I can. I'll wait in the drawing-room with Benson – only *do* hurry!'

Perhaps because the war was such a recent memory, people adapted quickly to the new circumstances, and with the particular attitude that marked them out as British: resigned, tolerant, stoical and wry. Despite the impression the strike made on the country, the vast majority of the employed were not unionised, and were not 'out'. People walked to work, or bicycled, and from the suburbs there was soon a regular and, in the British way, unofficial service, as those with motor-cars gave lifts to those without. Some propped a piece of card in the windscreen showing their destination like a bus; some had a discreet cardboard box for contributions to petrol; some carried a poker or large spanner on the seat in case of trouble.

The schools remained open, and children learned the wartime lessons of 'carrying on' and 'not making a fuss'. Women at home looked to their less fortunate neighbours. Some with a spare room gave accommodation to a commuter from further away. A new kind of social event sprang up overnight: listening-in parties, where those with wireless sets invited those without to come round and hear the official news broadcasts. They took the place of bridge evenings. There were even recipes swapped for suitable refreshments for such occasions; and the *Ladies' Mirror* suggested that wives and mothers should have a cold buffet laid out ready for the hungry workers at whatever time they might manage to struggle home. Corned beef, hard-boiled eggs, cold sausages, ham, sardines, cheese and fruit would make a tempting meal for the weary arrival.

Molly had been disappointed not to get into something more exciting than helping out at a canteen set up at the corner of Hyde Park, but she told herself sternly that it was the helping that mattered. Pooley and Felix had joined some other students loading and unloading goods at Paddington station, where they seemed to feel confident they would 'be in a scrap' sooner or later. Popovka, who had revealed an unexpected ability to understand railway signals – something he had evidently learned during the Russian Revolution, but would not talk about – had been seized with cries of joy by the railway owners and carried away to explain the mysteries of the signal box to some retired army officers, self-consciously wearing their gardening tweeds so as not to get their good clothes dirty.

And Molly tended an urn, filled teapots, and distributed

thick white mugs of tea and large, filling buns to hungry soldiers, policemen and strike-breakers of all degrees. It was fun being close to the park, where there was always something going on, and she got to chat to a variety of people, and to hear many different degrees of sympathy towards the strikers. The most virulently against were the two ladies she shared the daytime duty with: Lady D'Aubeny and Mrs Potter. Both had been very active during the war and evidently regarded that as the high point in their lives. They competed to tell stories about their experiences and triumphs, and only politeness made them take turns, for Molly was sure neither actually listened to the other, only waited for her to stop so she could begin. When they got to the end of their own experiences (without which, Molly began to believe, Germany would certainly have won), they began on the heroism and danger faced by various relatives – husbands, sons, nephews and cousins – and then to the hardships each had selflessly faced, and the appalling behaviour of various servants. This was the background to her days, like the sound of the sea, which she could ignore or listen to as she pleased. When she had stopped being irritated, she found it rather soothing.

But when she went home at night, she had no personal triumphs to recount. It became the custom for everyone to gather in the basement flat and bring their commons with them; sometimes the artists would toast sausages at the fire, or someone would go out for fish and chips; they pooled everything and brought in some quart bottles of beer, so it was like a party every evening. But Molly had only second-hand adventures to relate, things told her by the men she served with tea and buns. Still, it was something: the artists and Nina could only talk about shortages in the shops and convoys they had seen going by.

When she was at her post on the Friday, during a slack moment when she had no customers, she saw an ambulance drive slowly past and, watching it idly, suddenly realised that the driver was Emma, with Benson perched up beside her. She shouted and waved, hardly hoping to be noticed, but Emma had the window down, and perhaps the movement attracted her attention, for Molly saw her turn her face that way in the moment before she had moved past.

So it proved, for later that afternoon, when she was pouring tea for a couple of soldiers, she saw Emma approaching, dressed in a tough brown jacket and skirt, the hem modestly calf-length, and a very plain hat. Despite these precautions, her face was so very pretty that the two soldiers automatically sucked their teeth and said, 'Hello, darling!' But Benson gave a warning bark, and Emma bent a stern but kindly look on them and said, 'Thank you, lads, but would you excuse me?' with such authority that they backed away respectfully with their mugs and gave her place.

'It *was* you,' Emma said to Molly. 'I thought it was, but I only caught a glimpse as I went past so I wasn't sure. Is this your "war work"?'

'Yes, and don't laugh, for I'm afraid it was the best I could get. They don't seem to be very keen on women. How did you get an ambulance?'

'I told them I was in the FANY during the war, and that did it,' Emma said. 'I've seen one or two of my old FANY colleagues, as a matter of fact, and they tell me that the War Office actually *sent* for Boss Franklin and told her they wanted her to provide twenty cars and drivers from Monday morning. A great triumph for the corps.'

'It must have been fun to see your old friends,' Molly said.

Emma assented, but in fact it had been painful, too. It reminded her too much of those war days, the agony of the job itself, but also the warmth of companionship and belonging, which had meant so much to her, an orphan, at the time. The women she had met had greeted her like a long-lost sister, and at once burst into news about other old

176

colleagues: of those who had married, those who had businesses, those who had scattered through the Empire; of good
news and bad; of poor Foxy, dead of appendicitis, Armstrong,
now Mrs Roger Savile, who had two adorable little boys,
Hutchinson running a livery stables in Hampshire, Mac in
Rhodesia and Crockett in Australia, and Waddell, complete
with tin leg, taking over the secretaryship at Headquarters.
'You should go along there,' 'Dusty' Miller had said, with
her bright, guileless gaze fixed on Emma's face. 'It's a shame
you dropped out, Weston.'

'Yes, do go,' Coryton had said, equally trusting. 'We're
needed now like never before, and it will do the old corps
no end of good to have our best people show up. Go and
sign up, Westie, do! Once a FANY, always a FANY, you
know.'

But she had not gone. She felt lost and lonely and somehow
ashamed. During the war she had come to resemble these
bright, confident, practical girls, and been accepted as one
of them, because the situation demanded it; but she was not
like them inside. And behind the innocent phrase 'It's a
shame you dropped out', she read a criticism. FANYs were
supposed to remain loyal to the corps for ever, and she had
abandoned them. She had not been doing worthy things,
or advancing the cause of women. She did not go to the
reunions because she could not face the questions that would
be asked, the disappointment she thought she would see in
their eyes; and she could not have borne the pain of being
reminded that she was not one of them, and never had been,
really.

However, having been a FANY during the war – and a
decorated one at that – meant automatic acceptance as
a driver. The retired major with one arm who had been
dealing with recruitment knew what he had before him and
sent her straight away to take over an ambulance. 'So here
we are again,' she concluded her abbreviated story, 'behind

the wheel, with Benson beside me, just like the old days. I must confess I am enjoying it.'

'Why shouldn't you?' Molly said. 'I wish I was doing something more useful. Has Kit joined up?'

'Oh, yes – he's joined a defence corps. They accompany convoys in case of trouble from strikers, but so far, he says, all that's happened is some name-calling, and once the strikers threw handfuls of mud at the lorries. I think he's aching for a scrap – I can't think why. One of the things I like best about driving this ambulance is that I'm not being shot at, and there isn't a terribly wounded soldier in the back, suffering agonies every time I go over a bump.'

'It's the male nature,' Molly said. 'Felix and Pooley are just the same. They're working at the railway yard. They get jostled a bit every day when they go on shift, and the pickets shout threats and brandish staves of wood and so on, but so far that's all. They're just waiting for an all-out battle where they can bloody some noses.'

'Men are strange,' said Emma. 'I hoped when I volunteered that I might get to drive a bus, because I've always wanted to try it, but they said it was too dangerous for females, and from what I hear they were right. I'm glad no-one's likely to attack an ambulance. Even strikers aren't that bad.'

'I don't think they're bad at all,' Molly said.

Emma looked surprised. 'You don't agree with the strike, surely?'

'No, of course not. Obviously we can't have the government and the people held to ransom like that. It's undemocratic and wrong. But I don't think the strikers are wicked people, only that they don't know what else to do.'

A couple of men came up and, since her colleagues were busy, Molly had to break off and serve them. When she returned, Emma said, 'I shall have to go – I'm back on duty in half an hour. When do you get off?'

'About nine, usually.'

'Well, why don't you join Kit and me for supper tonight? We're going with a few others to the Ritz – it'll be fun. Everyone will be coming straight from strike-breaking, so we won't be dressing. Please do – I'd like to have more time to talk to you.'

Molly didn't see the appeal in Emma's eyes: she only thought of the Ritz, and the staff at the Ritz, and the sort of friends Kit Westhoven was likely to bring along, and was glad to have an excuse. She said, 'I'm sorry, I'd love to, but I'm already engaged. All of us in the house are going out to supper for a change, to a little place in Soho where they do a marvellous half-crown dinner with wine.' She hesitated. 'Why don't *you* come with *us*?'

They looked at each other for a moment, and it was in both their minds that a quiet supper, just the two of them, would be the most fun. But Emma said, 'I can't. I've promised the others. I can't chuck.'

And Molly agreed she couldn't chuck either.

It was a lively gathering at the Ritz that night. The management had relaxed the dress rules for the duration of the strike, which made it feel like wartime all over again. There was a great deal of drinking, a great deal of boasting, a lot of laughter, and Emma danced with everyone, but she felt strangely detached from the whole thing. Everyone was envious of her doing something so important as driving an ambulance, and she tried to make a story of it for them, but she couldn't summon the energy, and ended by being very vague and unsatisfactory.

When she danced with Kit, he said, 'Are you all right? You seem a bit out of sorts. Driving the old blood-wagon wearing you out?'

'Not really. But it made me think about the war, I suppose. You must think about it sometimes?'

'Never give it head-room,' he said, then suddenly dropped

his flippant air and said, 'I try not to think about it, to tell you the truth, and most of the time I manage it. It's like a room full of horrors inside my head that I've locked, and I never want to look in there again. But the strange thing is, no matter how often I throw away the key, somehow it's always there again, a little shiny thing, hanging on a hook, winking at me, saying, "Go on, take a peek. Just a peek." I know exactly how Bluebeard's wife felt.'

'Poor Kit. I never imagined—'

'Didn't you? I don the motley to fool myself, not you,' he said, looking down at her seriously. 'You're the one person I know understands, because you saw what I saw. I don't know how Oliver goes on doing what he does when he doesn't even have to. When the war ended I just wanted to run away as far and as fast as I could, and keep on running.'

'I know,' Emma said. 'But it doesn't work, does it?'

'Not all the time. But we can keep trying.' They were two-stepping and he tightened his grip on her and whirled her round the end of the dance-floor in three rapid turns that made her head spin. 'Dancing helps. Champagne helps. Horse-racing helps, for some unfathomable reason – the sight of all those jolly nags belting along as fast as they can lay hoof to ground takes me right out of myself. And this strike, damn its eyes, helps. Except that it's proving rather tame.'

Emma shook her head. 'How can you want a fight? That's too much like the war.'

'Well,' he said, with an air of wisdom, 'the war wasn't so bad sometimes, when we were in the middle of it. It's thinking about it afterwards that hurts.'

'Don't joke about it,' she pleaded, looking up at him.

'My dear child,' he said grimly, 'what can one do but joke? That was what they did to the world, the wise elders who took us into that mess: they made every bad joke afterwards redundant. Have I mentioned, by the way, how ravishingly beautiful you are tonight? That forbidding suit of yours

180

makes you look like Mary Pickford unconvincingly playing a governess.'

'Idiot,' she said. He was back to frivolity, and she knew it was a relief to both of them. Human beings could not bear too much reality.

They left around midnight to go on to a nightclub. Piccadilly seemed oddly empty without its omnibuses, but there was still traffic about, and an unusual number of pedestrians, as there had been ever since the strike began. Emma and Kit were in the lead as they came down the steps, the others behind arguing about whether to take a taxi or walk, and as they paused on the pavement, Emma found herself hailed by someone walking past, a drably dressed woman with a slight limp.

With a sinking of the heart, she realised it was Vera Polk, the woman who had first persuaded her to join the FANY, and who had harangued her on more than one occasion about her failure to keep up with the corps since the war ended. Vera was looking older, she thought: the hair showing under her hat was grizzled, and there were deep lines in her face, whether of pain or sorrow she didn't know. She had stopped full in Emma's path so it was not possible simply to acknowledge her and move on.

'Hello, Vera,' she said warily.

Vera looked past Emma to her companions, closed her eyes and shook her head briefly as though disgusted but not surprised at the company Emma was keeping. The rest of the group clattered past to the kerb to look for taxis, politely ignoring the encounter on the pavement, but Kit remained at Emma's side, perhaps sensing some kind of threat.

'The Ritz again,' Vera said. 'It must be like a second home to you.'

Emma had unthinkingly invited Vera there for tea once, and Vera had embarrassed her by telling her off very audibly.

'They don't mind us coming in in working clothes,' she

heard herself say, and was immediately cross with herself for justifying anything to her nemesis.

'I heard you were driving an ambulance again,' Vera said. She looked pointedly at Kit. Emma didn't want to introduce them to each other, but there seemed no way out of it.

'My friend Kit Westhoven. Vera Polk, of the FANY.'

Kit bowed blankly, obviously still wondering what it was all about, but Vera's eyes widened a moment as if in recognition. 'Earl Westhoven,' she said, and the fact that she got his title right ought to have warned Emma of something, but she was too irritated by the whole thing to notice.

Vera turned her attention back to Emma. 'Well done for volunteering, and I'm glad they gave you an ambulance, but why didn't you come round to Beauchamp Place?'

'I'm not a member of the corps any more,' Emma said impatiently. 'You know that.'

'You can always rejoin. We've had several other lapsed members come in in the last few days.'

'*Other* lapsed members? I thought *I* was the only traitor,' Emma said bitterly.

'*They* kept in touch,' Vera said. 'Well, it's not too late. Come round tomorrow and we'll sign you back on.'

'I don't want to rejoin. That's all over for me now,' Emma said.

'Once a FANY, always a FANY,' Vera said. Emma had believed it once, long ago, in the mud and potholes of Flanders. 'We need you. This is our golden chance to get some official status with the War Office – Franklin's working like a beaver to get us recognised. Your name would go down well. You might open doors for us.'

'I don't—' Emma began, but Vera rode over her.

'And *you* need *us*,' she said firmly. 'No use denying it. Do you think *this*,' she waved a hand towards the Ritz, 'is a rational way for a grown woman to behave? I *know* why you do it, and *you* know what the remedy is. Come back to us, do some useful work, be with your friends again, your own kind, people who care for you and understand you. You don't think these people,' now she waved the other way, at the crowd by the kerb, 'care two hoots about you?'

'I really can't stand here arguing with you,' Emma said, more angry with herself for feeling near to tears than with Vera, who was what she was and always had been. The others had managed to hail two taxis, which had drawn up to the kerb and were ticking comfortably while destinations were discussed. 'I have to go – my friends are waiting.'

She went past Vera, afraid she would grab her arm, but Vera did not move, though she called out, '*We*'re your friends, Emma. Not them. And I won't give up.'

Emma almost flung herself into the second taxi, and Kit bundled in after her. Ronnie Austin, Flo Vanderbeek and Padua Worseley climbed in too. Ronnie took the drop seat and the two girls squeezed in beside Emma.

'Who was that *extraordinary* woman?' Ronnie asked. 'I couldn't be more intrigued.'

'Someone from Emma's dark past,' Padua said. 'She looked so earnest – too chilling!'

'She's a spy, that's all,' said Flo. 'A Mata Hari.'

'She looked like a cit,' Ronnie said. 'How do you know someone like that, Emma? I smell a mystery!'

'Is it a murder mystery?' Padua giggled. 'Did you kill someone years ago and she's come to blackmail you about it?'

'Oh, do stop yapping about it,' Kit said, in his most world-weary voice. 'Too yawn-making, Paddy. Has anyone decided where we're going? We seem to be following the other cab. Ten to one but they're following someone else, and we'll end up at the Hammersmith Palais or the Paddington Baths.'

In the darkness, Emma squeezed Kit's hand in thanks for changing the subject.

Padua was instantly diverted. She had the tenacity, Emma

thought, of a butterfly. 'But how thrilling,' she said. 'I'd love to go to the Palais, and see how the real people go on.'

'They're not animals at the zoo, to be stared at,' Emma said.

Padua opened her eyes wide. 'Goodness, you do sound strict. Like one's governess. I couldn't be more quelled.'

'God, I hope so,' Ronnie said. 'You really are the most intolerable little bagpipe, Padsy.'

'That's what my mother says,' Padua giggled. 'She says my sisters are so sensible I must be a changeling. She says someone must have left me on the doorstep.'

'And for your information, Emma,' Ronnie went on, 'we're going to the Embassy. The Prince of Wales came back from Biarritz specially for the strike, and Billy Grasmere said he'd be at the Embassy tonight with Violet Holkam and a big crowd.'

'Oh, *good*,' said Flo.

'Oh, God,' Kit groaned theatrically.

Emma stayed silent, feeling bruised by the encounter with Vera, after Molly and on top of her other experiences that day. The taxi trundled through the familiar streets, and after a moment she discovered that her hand was still in Kit's. It felt so comfortable she let it stay there.

Friday, the 7th of May, the fourth day of the strike, was the strikers' first Friday without a pay-packet, and a nervousness spread through both sides of the dispute, the unions worrying that the strike would crumble, and the government afraid of escalating violence. Few unions had the resources to distribute strike pay. Some levied those still in work to pay a dole to the strikers. Thousands had to rely on what little was available through Poor Law relief.

In Glasgow there had been a night of violence, triggered by a rumour that students were being brought in to run the trams. Stone-throwing turned to window-smashing, shops were looted, and as liquor was stolen, the rioting spread. In Hull a mob attacked trains, and sailors were landed from a navy ship to help police break it up. There was rioting in Liverpool and Ipswich.

The union problem over food distribution did not improve. Rumours were going about that goods of all sorts were being 'smuggled' in lorries marked 'FOOD ONLY'. The TUC argued about what constituted food and what didn't, and the transport and railway unions called for a total ban on all food movement. Conflicting orders flew back and forth. In York the distribution workers went on strike, then went back to work, then were told to distribute milk and bread only, and only to their own members. There was a sense that the strike was approaching a watershed, and in the afternoon Sir Herbert Samuel met TUC representatives in Bryanston Square for negotiations but failed to reach any common ground.

But on the whole the nation was 'carrying on carrying on'. Food was getting through, people were getting in to work, and this was both a good and a bad thing. For the most part, the country felt detached from the conflict, only waited, like spectators at a football match, to see which side would win, government or trade unions. But at any moment a link in the chain could break, and supplies and vital services could be catastrophically interrupted. Then it would be a different matter entirely.

In the early hours of Saturday morning, while it was still dark, a convoy of lorries two miles long, escorted by armoured cars, brought soldiers to the encampment in Hyde Park: Guardsmen in steel helmets, with Tank Corps drivers at the wheels. And as dawn broke the new force moved eastwards to Victoria Docks to open the dockside warehouses and release the sacks of flour being denied movement by the pickets. Rumour said the home secretary, Joynson-Hicks, had told them to use whatever force was necessary. It was a display of strength largely wasted on the half-empty Saturday-morning streets (many shops had not opened). As the convoy returned to Hyde Park fully laden, there was no attempt made to interfere with it, and the rather thin crowds cheered and waved mildly as though it were a fancy-dress parade.

When Molly went on duty, more rumours were circulating. It was said that the idea had come from Winston Churchill, who had wanted to have hidden machine-gun emplacements along the route as well as tanks in the convoy. Another said that as the convoy was leaving the dock gates, through a very hostile crowd, one old lady ran alongside a tank shouting abuse at it. When she shouted, 'Bastard!' a small iron window in the tank opened, and a Tommy poked his head out and said, ''Ello, Muvver, fancy meeting you 'ere.'

One rumour that did appear to be true was that Joynson-Hicks – or Jix, as he was almost universally called – had announced a new full-time volunteer police force for the capital, called the Civil Constabulary Reserve, to be drawn from Territorial regiments, reserves and public schoolboys in OTC. There was an instant and eager response from the many young men who had longed for a scrap, and the drill halls all over London, turned into recruiting offices, did a brisk trade.

And in Bryanston Square Samuel met the negotiating committee again, and got nowhere. The government would not negotiate under duress, and the TUC would not give up the strike without first securing some concessions.

CHAPTER NINE

By Monday, shortage of supplies was affecting industries outside the strike, and factories were closing or laying off. In York, three thousand were laid off; Teddy had to put his factories in Manchester on short time, and takings in his Makepeace's stores in Manchester and Leeds were down so much he had closed them all on Saturday afternoon and was contemplating a full day closing instead of the mid-week half-day.

More trains were running, but it was still only a fraction of the usual number, and because of their irregularity they mostly ran empty. This was fortunate as there was a sharp increase in accidents. It was not possible to train the enthusiastic volunteers properly in the time available, and where trains did run, often the signals were not working. Near Edinburgh a passenger train ran into a goods train, and in the south-west, a volunteer driver, unable to stop, drove his train straight through Bristol Temple Meads and only managed to stop eventually at Bath by emptying the fire-box. It was commonplace for trains to smash through level-crossing gates and pass signals at danger; and the damage done to locomotives by inexperienced volunteers was said to run into thousands of pounds.

There was widespread concern about the railway horses, the thousands of them that transported goods to and from the yards and took part in shunting and other sidings work. At

Paddington, the staff from Tattersalls went in to feed, water and exercise them; at other depots, local hunting ladies organised rotas for their care. Sometimes their usual handlers were exempted from the strike by their union for the purpose. Pitmen were also exempted from the strike to the extent of caring for the ponies stranded down the mines.

On Monday afternoon, Molly was at her usual post by the tea urn when a man came up. It was cool and raining lightly and he was wearing a smart light tweed coat and a brown trilby. She had noticed him before, but it had always been one of the others who served him – deliberately, she supposed, for Lady D'Aubeny and Mrs Potter were quick to seize on any gentleman customers while leaving the rougher elements strictly to Molly. But this time they were both busy being fascinated by a Guards officer, and the man came to Molly, lifted his hat, and said, 'Can I trouble you for a cup of tea?'

He had an educated voice and a pleasant face, with quick, humorous eyes. She liked the look of him at once. She poured the tea and said, 'I've seen you here before.'

'I've been a few times. I find the park interesting, and I hear a great deal more just by listening to conversations than by asking questions or reading the *Gazette.*'

'Oh, the *Gazette* is full of propaganda,' Molly said. 'The *Herald,* too.' That was the TUC's daily news-sheet.

'Do you read both?' he said. 'I'm impressed.'

'Why so?'

'Most people like their propaganda to be uniform.'

'I wasn't always a tea lady, you know.'

He laughed. Molly thought she had never seen such beautiful teeth. 'I'm perfectly sure of it. My name's Blake, by the way – Vivian Blake.'

'Molly Ormerod.' She extended her hand. He shook it, and held onto it a moment longer than was strictly necessary, while looking into her face with an interest that she could not have found offensive, even if she had wanted to.

'What were you before the siren call of the urn dragged you into this Charybdis?' he asked. 'I hope that's not an impertinent question.'

'I work for a newspaper,' she said. 'I was – or I suppose I still will be when the strike's ended – a junior copywriter. But Mr Churchill commandeered my newspaper's offices, and they didn't want women. They said it was too dangerous, but I'm pretty sure it's more a case of "Don't let the girls play, they spoil everything."'

'I'm sure you're right,' he said. 'I'm in the printed-word business, too – at the other end. My uncle is chairman of a publishing house – Dorcas Overstreet.'

Her eyebrows went up. It was a very famous imprint. 'That must be interesting.'

'It is,' he said. 'I went in at the bottom while I was still at university, and I've worked my way up to managing editor. The old man has been very good to me. He hasn't any children so I suppose I'm being groomed to assume the purple at some distant point. I'm very fond of him, so I hope it *will* be distant.'

'How is the strike affecting you?' Molly asked.

'We're short of paper, of course, but it isn't so critical for us – we can delay publication by a few days or weeks without the world collapsing around us. The *Gazette* sucks in everything – as you know.'

'Yes, you'd think Mr Churchill would have enough to do being Chancellor of the Exchequer, without having to expand his empire that way.'

'I think he relishes being a press baron and top-notch editor. You know that within thirty-six hours of the start of the strike, he'd taken over not just your newspaper's offices, but the Argus Press, the Northfleet paper works, Somerset House, the W. H. Smith despatch warehouse, and Phoenix Wharf to store all the newsprint he's commandeered. Everyone else has the dickens of a job to get hold of paper, but of course he can call on jolly Jack Tars to unload his ships, and he has a fleet of official cars lined up to carry off bundles of the *Gazette* and distribute them round the country.'

'You do know a lot about it,' Molly said.

'I speak from bitter experience,' he said, but his smile was anything but bitter. He seemed so full of energy, and Molly guessed he was enjoying the strike. Perhaps his way up the ladder at Dorcas Overstreet had been a little lacking in challenge for him. 'I'm rather underemployed at the moment, so when I heard about the attempt to burn down *The Times*, I went along and volunteered my services.'

'Oh, how exciting. Are you helping to write it?' Molly asked. It was something she'd have liked to do, if only they'd allowed women.

'No, there were plenty of volunteers for that end of it, and they've got far less butter-fingered chaps than me to man the presses. I pop along there at the end of the night and help with the distribution. It's rather awkward, you see. They only have a tiny courtyard, and to reach it you have to go down a narrow alley where two cars can't pass. So it all has to be carefully planned and run like a military operation, each car backing down to the yard at exactly the right moment to load up. I've borrowed my uncle's Daimler – much roomier than my little runabout.'

'Are you having trouble with pickets?'

'We did at first. Because of the narrow alley it's easy for the strikers to blockade. But the chairman got together a defence squad of his own – a group of fit young rowing and rugger Blues with plenty of muscles and enthusiasm. We call them the Jazz Band because they all come to work in Fair Isle pullovers – a sort of unofficial uniform. It would take a brave – or, rather, foolish – picket to stand up to them. After one short, sharp episode of fisticuffs on Thursday, they've given us no trouble.'

Molly smiled. 'I don't suppose that pleases the Jazz Band. If they're anything like my friends, they'll be just longing for a scrap.'

'Well, yes, I'm afraid it is a bit of an anticlimax. They're more or less redundant now. To tell you the truth, I don't think the pickets' hearts are really in it. It's a very dull job – cold, too, in the middle of the night. They're really only a token force now, and they don't even bother to shout abuse at us. In fact, this morning one of them asked me for an early copy of the paper, and if I had any racing tips. And I'm told they always salute Major Astor when he goes in or out.'

'You'll be taking them mugs of tea before long,' Molly said. 'Poor things, it must be hard to have every man's hand against you.'

'They can end it in a minute by calling off the strike.'

'The union leaders could call off the strike. The ordinary man can't do much about it.'

'Well, of course, one does have some sympathy with them, but mainly because they haven't a hope of winning. If they were likely to succeed, it would be a very different matter.'

'Do you really think they haven't a hope?'

'Certainly. Everything's going on pretty much as usual. People are getting to work and food is getting to the shops, while the strikers will just get weaker. If they were going to have an effect, it would have shown itself by now. And, you know, even if the claims are true and there are three million out on strike, that's only three million out of a work force of nearly twenty. The effect is exaggerated because they've managed to stop so much of the transport system.'

Some soldiers came up for tea and she had to break off to serve them. She thought he might leave in the interim, but when she had poured the tea, dispensed buns and taken the money, she saw he was still there, leaning against the far corner of the stand, looking at the passing traffic. A lone bus went past, with barbed wire wound round its engine, and a uniformed policeman sitting beside what was obviously a middle-class volunteer driver – he looked like an ex-RAF flyer. The afternoon was chilly and slightly misty: he had a striped muffler tucked inside the neck of his greatcoat and looked as though he was enjoying himself mightily. Behind came a van with 'Hancocks' painted on its side. It was full of working girls, all in overcoats and cloche hats, the last row of four sitting with their legs dangling over the tailboard. They smiled and waved to the soldiers as they passed. And behind that again was an open lorry with eight of the Civil Constabulary Reserve standing in the flatbed, holding onto the sides, looking self-conscious in their tin hats, being driven off to some duty or other.

'You know,' he said, without turning, as though aware she had just come up behind him, 'none of this seems real. Those young men – do they really look like the representatives of the will of the people, facing down a vicious minority bent on Red revolution?'

'No, it's more like *opera buffa*,' Molly said. 'You know that all the electricity to the docks went off this afternoon? A power station was shut down, and the refrigerated stores full of frozen meat were in danger. The navy solved the problem by linking the batteries of four submarines together and running the stores off them.'

'I hadn't heard that,' Blake said.

'I hear all sorts of things from the officers,' she said, gesturing towards the army camp. 'The point is, the power was only out for twenty minutes. The electricians had consulted with the navy beforehand about when would be a good time for them to walk out. You're right, it isn't reality, it's a play, and everyone knows his part.'

'It will end in tears, but only for the few,' he said. He turned away from the road to look at Molly. 'I've so enjoyed talking to you. I think it's the most sensible conversation I've had in months.'

'I've enjoyed it too,' she said.

'Look here,' said Blake, 'I can see your two attendant Gorgons glaring at you for chatting to me when you should be working. But I'd love to go on talking to you. Do you think we might meet up later, perhaps, when you've finished for the day? I hope you don't think me awfully forward for asking.'

'Not at all,' Molly said, thinking briefly of Popovka's rule, that she should not entrust herself to anyone she could not imagine introducing to him. But she could imagine them getting on with each other very well.

'What about this evening? Would you care to take supper with me? I know a rather jolly little restaurant in Bloomsbury – on the corner of Coptic Street, near the British Museum.'

'I know where that is. I live in Mecklenburgh Square.'

'Really? I've always thought that looked an interesting place. So, this evening, then?'

'This evening,' said Molly.

Emma was just about to go off duty when one of the despatchers, Buckley – an earnest young man in Oxford bags with hair that started the day oiled back but flopped over his forehead by the end of it – hurried up and said, 'I say, I'm awf'ly sorry to have to ask, when I know you've had a hard day and so forth, but there's a bit of a to-do in the Commercial Road, several people hurt, and they're calling for a second ambulance. Could you possibly toddle down?' He looked anxious, and caressed Benson, who was sitting on the front seat staring out through the open door.

'Of course I'll go,' Emma said, with an inward sigh. But duty was duty.

'Couldn't feel worse about asking, but everyone else is out already. They're sending over a couple of Defence Corps chaps to go with you, just in case, though I'm sure there won't really be any danger,' said Buckley, but with a look that feared the opposite. He was too chivalrous to bear lightly the idea of sending any woman, even a former FANY, into a war zone.

'Don't worry,' she said. 'No-one attacks ambulances. I don't need an escort.'

'Oh, but they're coming anyway,' Buckley said. 'They'll be here any minute. Do wait for them. I couldn't bear to think of you going alone.'

'I've been shelled and bombed and shot at by real experts, back in the war,' Emma said. She mounted into her cab, closed the door and, with a jaunty wave, drove off. But as she reached the gates of the yard, her way was blocked by two Defence Corps men, with armbands, tin hats and truncheons. She braked perforce, then Benson began to bark and she saw one of them was Kit.

He touched his tin hat. 'Are you the intrepid ambulance gal we are to have the pleasure of escorting into battle?' he asked.

'Quite unnecessary, and there'll be no battle, but I'll enjoy the company, I suppose,' she said. 'Hop in.'

Kit opened the door. 'Budge up, Benson. May I have the honour of presenting my comrade in arms? This is Johnny Fitzgerald. Fitz, Miss Emma Weston, the fastest gun in the Ambulance Corps.'

'How de do,' Fitzgerald said laconically, getting in beside Kit, and that was all he did say. While Emma drove, Kit sat with Benson on his lap and told her his day's news, which didn't amount to a great deal. 'Where there really are dangerous crowds they send the police in, or the army. Such a bore. We've hardly had a bloody nose between us. What about you?'

'I got sent to a train crash at Royal Oak this afternoon. Two hurt. The points were set the wrong way and the train went into a siding instead of along the main line and ran into the back of some goods wagons. Fortunately it wasn't going fast. The driver concussed himself and his fireman fell off the footplate and broke his arm.'

'What was the fireman doing on the footplate?' Kit asked.

'I believe he was shouting, "Look out for that goods train."'

Kit snorted laughter. 'I say, I think this whole strike thing is rather bogus, don't you? Are you off after this call? What about a spot of supper somewhere? Just the two of us for a change.'

'I must go home and wash first. Dining in my working clothes has lost the appeal of novelty.'

'All right, I'll pick you up at nine, and we'll go and find somewhere with a decent band.'

It was easy enough to find the right place. At a place where the road was narrow, a steel hawser had been stretched across between two lamp-posts, and this had apparently been driven into at some speed by a lorry, which had slewed round sideways and crashed into one of the lamp-posts, bending it at an obeisant angle. Behind the wire, a further temporary barrier had been built out of crates, old tyres and a couple of handcarts, and behind this there was a large group of young, strong-looking and hostile dock workers.

On the near side another crowd, which parted to let the ambulance through, was shouting and jeering at the dockers, but keeping at a safe distance; and the lorry driver was sitting on the pavement, clearly dazed, with blood running down his face from a head injury. Between the hawser and the second barricade were two policemen, who presumably had come to the lorry driver's aid, but were now battling with half a dozen burly men in shabby caps and jackets.

The report to the ambulance depot had clearly been muddled, for there was no other ambulance and only the one casualty visible. Emma halted, and Fitzgerald flung open his door, leaped down and ran to the policemen's aid. 'Can you see to the driver chap?' Kit asked. 'I've got to get over there, or Fitz will go down as well.'

He didn't seem to anticipate any trouble for Emma, and she didn't either. She grabbed her bag and jumped down, with Benson behind her, causing an excited upsurge of cries from the onlookers, who were intrigued by the novelty of a woman in these circumstances. She knelt down by the injured man, and pulled out some wadding to clean the blood from the wound to see how bad it was.

'What happened to you?' she asked, mainly to see if he was rational.

'Drove into that bloody wire,' he muttered. 'Didn't see the bastard. Used that trick in the war meself. Took a Jerry clean orf 'is motorbike a time or two. Who're you, miss? You didn't orter be 'ere.'

'Trooper Weston, First Aid Nursing Yeomanry,' she said. 'You might have a bit of a fracture here. Hit your head on the windscreen? Keep quite still, now.'

'FANY, are you?' he mumbled dazedly. 'First Anywhere, that's what we useter say. Bloody Jerries put a wire acrorse the road. Could be an ambush. Watch out for Jerries. Lorst me tin 'at. Start shelling any minute. Where's me tin 'at? Where's Billy? Billy Sutton, me mate. Where's Billy? He copped a packet when the shell blew us up.'

She was bandaging his head wound carefully, but was worried at his rambling, afraid he was becoming agitated. It was only when she had secured the end of the bandage and looked round to see if anyone could help her move him to the ambulance that she realised the situation had changed. The onlookers, perhaps encouraged by Emma's presence, had advanced, and were shouting abuse at the dockers, and the boldest of them had gone to the relief of Kit and Fitzgerald and the policemen, both of whom had lost their helmets, in their battle with the strikers. The strikers were returning the abuse with interest, and some people in the buildings to either side of the road were leaning out of their windows adding to the audible battle, though on which side it wasn't clear.

Now, as Emma looked around, she saw a woman lean out of a window opposite and drop a large pot containing an aspidistra, which struck one of the combatants and felled him.

At once the onlookers surged forward, bent on revenge, and the dockers were climbing over their barricade to join the fray. Missiles started to be thrown from both sides. Emma crouched over the driver, hoping not to be hit, wondering how she could get him to safety. She ought to go and attend to the man who had been hit by the pot, before the battle overtook him, too.

The situation was beginning to look nasty. There was a mass of struggling bodies now in the area between the two barriers, and the air was briny with increased hostility. Kit was in there somewhere – she couldn't see him any more – and she realised that Benson had left her side, and assumed he had gone back to the ambulance.

Then there was the welcome sound of a police whistle, and a lorry full of Civil Constabulary Reserve careered round the corner and came up at speed. It screeched to a halt, and the men jumped down, yelling, and flung themselves into the fray with gusto. There was a lot of shouting, grunts and oaths, and Emma heard one high-pitched cry, as though a woman or child had been mixed up in the middle of it. The onlooker mob rapidly melted away before the Reserve, who already had a reputation for hitting out first and asking questions later; and in a very few minutes the dockers also broke and ran, scattering to disappear down side-streets and alleys, with the Reserve hunting them, giving tongue in their excitement.

To her relief, Emma saw Kit, seemingly unhurt, bending over one of the policemen, who appeared to have been laid out. Fitzgerald had disappeared with the hunters. The man who had been hit by the pot was sitting up, with a woman from the onlookers kneeling beside him; the other policeman had a bloody nose and his tunic was torn down one breast.

She propped her first patient against the wall and told him not to move, then hurried over. The man hit by the pot seemed to have been struck on the shoulder; the woman tending him was his wife. She was weeping and abusing the strikers in very graphic terms, but Emma thought he was not badly hurt and could be safely left to her. The policeman had a ragged gash on his forehead, a cut and swollen lip, and a black eye that was already swelling. 'Some bugger chucked a brick at him,' the other policeman said. 'You a nurse, miss?'

'Thank God you're all right,' Kit said, looking up at her. 'Should never have sent you into this. Damned stupid.'

'I'm all right,' Emma said. 'I'm worried about the lorry driver, though. I think he's concussed. Could have a fractured skull, too. Can you help me get him into the ambulance?'

'I'll help you, miss,' said the policeman.

'How's your colleague?'

'He's not concussed,' Kit said. 'Got a shiner to beat the band. Lost a tooth, too, so he can't speak very well. Take it easy, old chap. We'll get you to the hospital.'

The wounded man said something incomprehensible through swollen lips, and spat blood onto the ground.

Some of the onlookers were drifting back, now the fighting was over, and a couple of them helped to get the lorry driver and the policeman into the ambulance. Some others were taking down the barrier, but Emma got the impression they were more interested in securing the materials than in opening the road. She realised for the first time how poorly dressed they were. Some children had come out of the houses to stare. Those who had boots had no stockings to them; their clothes seemed to have been cut down from adult garments. And while she was helping the policeman to his feet, she looked beyond him to an open door of a tenement, and had a glimpse beyond it of a squalid room, furnished only with a wooden table, a single kitchen chair, and an iron bedstead pushed into the corner. The smell coming from that room made her nose wrinkle.

When they had got the two injured men into the ambulance – the pot man had disappeared with his wife – Emma climbed up into the cab and was about to put the engine into gear when an absence beside her called to her as insistently as any voice.

'Where's Benson?' she said. She looked over her shoulder into the back but he was not with the injured.

'Wasn't he with you?' Kit asked.

'He followed me down, but I didn't see him after the fight started. I thought he'd come back here.' She climbed back down, calling. Kit jumped down from his side, looking round and whistling.

Just before where the barricade had been, there was a small brown heap that might have been a discarded piece of clothing, but wasn't. Emma was on her knees, flinching hands reaching for him, but she could see that he was dead. His eyes were open and staring, and a trickle of blood had run from his mouth. A lump of concrete lying nearby had blood on it, and there was a wound to the back of his skull. She remembered the high-pitched cry. Had someone deliberately hit him, or had he been the victim of a random missile?

There was a ringing in her ears, like the rushing sound of the sea, and she felt strangely detached, as though living at arm's length from herself. Out of the sea-noise she heard Kit saying, 'Emma, Emma, I'm so sorry. Poor little chap. I'm so sorry.'

She slid her hands under and lifted the soft, limp body, and cradling it against her, got to her feet. 'I must get the wounded back.' Was that her voice? Apparently. At the ambulance, she had nowhere to put Benson. In the back, the uninjured policeman took off his ripped tunic. 'Here, miss,' he said. 'Let me.' She handed him over, and the policeman wrapped him in his tunic and laid him gently down. Emma dragged her eyes away, got into her seat and put the ambulance into reverse.

'Are you all right?' came Kit's tender voice from beside her.

'Of course,' she said briskly. 'Must get the injured to hospital. I'm worried about that lorry driver.'

Emma's eerie calm lasted all the way home, into and out of the bath, and while dressing herself – it was Spencer's night off. She came out from her bedroom fixing her earrings, to find the faithful Kit still waiting for her, ready to take her out to supper or apply whatever other comfort he could. 'You don't need to look at me like that,' she said. 'I'm perfectly all right.'

He stood up. 'I know you went through the war and everything, but I don't think you are.'

'Oh, Kit,' she said, in an exasperated tone, 'just help me on with my coat. I'm starving.' And, in that moment, she looked around automatically for Benson. The space where he ought to have been was empty. Her chest ached, her eyes burned, and suddenly great, tearing sobs began to force their way up her throat. She held out her hands in helpless appeal, and Kit was there, Kit caught her and drew her into his arms.

'He was – he was – just – a dog,' she gasped, but had no more chance of stopping the tears now than of turning back the tide. Benson was the last. Now she had lost everyone. 'There's – nothing – left!' she managed to cry, and her voice was ugly with grief.

Kit held her in silence while the sorrow racked her. He felt her hot tears soaking into his collar. He stroked her cropped head, oddly moving in its nakedness under his hand, like a small child's.

'It's all right,' he said at last. 'It's all right to cry. Poor little Benson.'

She gave a convulsive sob, as though she had tried to answer and been waylaid by it.

'Poor little dog,' Kit said. 'Poor little Emma.'

When the weeping slowed, he manoeuvred her to the sofa, sat down with her, produced a handkerchief and gently mopped her face. At last she said, 'I'm sorry.'

'There's nothing to be sorry for.'

'Crying like that over a dog, when there were all those – in the war – everyone—'

'I understand,' he said.

She stared at the floor with swollen eyes. 'I have no-one, now,' she said. 'No-one at all.'

'You have me,' he said. He was holding one of her hands, and squeezed it to get her attention.

She looked at him, a mask of tragedy. 'Yes,' she said.

He lifted her hand to his lips. 'Marry me,' he said. He hadn't known he was going to say it until he heard the words on the air. But then it seemed like a good idea. A very good idea. He warmed to it by the second. She was looking bewildered, or disbelieving. 'I mean it. Marry me, Emma. We're good together. I have no-one either. We'll make each other happy.'

Slowly she nodded.

'Was that a "yes"?' he asked.

'Yes,' she said. She sounded dazed.

'Yes, you will marry me?'

'Yes, I will marry you.'

There didn't seem to be anything more to say then, so he drew her head onto his shoulder and held her like that for a long time.

The restaurant in Coptic Street was family-owned, and the proprietor, a small, brisk, bald Polish man, obviously knew Blake very well.

'Dorcas Overstreet's offices are in Russell Square,' he said, as they were shown to their table with beaming smiles and some flourish, 'so we tend to know all the eating places within a certain radius.'

The house had been in considerable excitement about Molly's 'assignation' as Popovka called it. They had conferred on her sole use of the bathroom; Ingrid, the potter from the basement, had pressed a small cake of her most precious verbena-scented soap into her hand; Nina had offered to lend a glorious silk scarf, which she said could be flung over the shoulder in a dramatic way that would draw all eyes to her; the students had promised to avenge her should the man attempt to take advantage of her in any way; and Popovka had come to her door with a tiny glass of vodka 'to stiffen your nerve', which he promised left no odour on the breath. Molly accepted the interference with good humour, but the accumulated effect was to make her nervous about the whole thing, and when she and Vivian Blake were finally seated facing each other across a small, white-clothed table, she felt a spasm of awkwardness and expected a difficult silence.

But he seemed perfectly at ease, and since his first question was, 'Tell me about the house where you live,' she was able to talk naturally and even, as she saw her descriptions amused him, make her neighbours' helpful interventions into a sort of comic monologue.

'They sound marvellous,' he said, laughing over the vodka. 'I should love to meet them all.'

'Oh, you must – especially Popovka. He lived through the Russian Revolution, so he has a thousand tales to tell.' She said it because by now she felt easy with him, but at the last minute heard herself and blushed. Had she really just asked a strange man to her house? What would he think of her?

But he didn't seem embarrassed. He continued to look at her with that eager, slightly curious air, as though he just wanted to know what she was really like, and said, 'I wonder

if he has a book in him? Excuse me for intruding a professional note, but of course I'm always looking for new books.
I have to impress my uncle somehow.'

'I'm not sure he would want to write a book, though he
loves to talk if you ask him the right questions. But I've
never actually seen him write anything, even a note for the
milkman; and his English is somewhat fractured.'

'It could always be ghosted, of course,' said Blake. 'In fact,
you might do it.'

'Me?' she exclaimed inelegantly.

'Don't sound so surprised. You have a wonderful way with
words. You bring Mr Popovka alive for me. And it's obvious
you're fond of him – that always works better in these
cases. You should think of turning your talents to writing
something more permanent than newspaper copy.'

'But I have. I've had some short stories published, and
now I'm writing a book,' Molly said, and confounded herself
again. Now she was boasting! Oh, what would this man think
of her?

But he looked interested. 'Where were your stories
published?'

She told him. 'They weren't literary stories, you know.
Just detective stories.'

His eyes crinkled with amusement. '*Just* detective stories?
Just some work in which the greatest powers of the mind
are displayed, the most thorough knowledge of human
nature, the happiest delineation of its varieties, et cetera, et
cetera.'

'Jane Austen,' Molly said delightedly. '*Northanger Abbey.*'

'I yield to no-one in my admiration of detective stories,' he
said. 'And, come to think of it, I'd wager I could make a guess
at which were yours – at least, one of them. The *kokoshnik*
with the poisoned pins?'

'You're right! How amazing that you saw it.'

'I read all the time, and that one made me laugh. I like

to laugh. I don't remember your name, though,' he said, seeming puzzled.

'I was still working for the civil service at that point, so I had to use a pseudonym.'

'I see. And which was the other story? Wait, wait – the arsenic in the sugar bowl? No, not *outré* enough. Don't tell me – the poisoned banana?'

She nodded, laughing. 'How did you remember that?'

'I told you, I'm hopelessly addicted to the genre. Who is your favourite writer? Agatha Christie?'

'I like Agatha Christie, but I read one called *Whose Body*, by Dorothy L. Sayers. I liked that even better. It had a certain quality . . . I wish she'd write some more.'

'She *has* written another,' Blake said. '*Clouds of Witness*. It comes out next month I believe.'

Molly smiled. 'Of course, you would know the publishing gossip.'

'I'd have liked to publish it myself, but it went to a rival, Harcourt. Unfortunately, my uncle and the board are rather high-minded about 'tec novels – they think they're too low and vulgar for a dignified old firm like Dorcas Overstreet.'

'Well, presumably that's something you can change when you inherit the company.'

'I like your frankness,' he said. 'But I doubt if I shall ever be in that happy position. Even if I do rise to be chairman, there's still the board; and the Overstreet element is represented by Jonathon Overstreet, who is absolutely with my uncle on the subject of dignity. And he's younger than me,' he added, in a final wry aside, 'so I can't even outlive him.'

'Perhaps he'll leave and start his own company,' she said, trying to offer him some comfort.

'No, I think it may be for me to do that. I have a great many ideas I'd like to try out, and I can't imagine a life of fighting for scraps with the board. We are on the brink of a great age for books. The Education Acts are having an effect at last – mass literacy takes twenty or thirty years to get going, but now more people are buying newspapers than ever before, and we have an absolute profusion of magazines, not just literary reviews but the *Strand, Grand, Argosy, Passing Show, Nash's, Pearson's Weekly, Britannia* and so on and so on – the railway kiosks are groaning with good things. There's never been a better time to be a short-story writer, and we have the best in the world in this country—'

'Thank you kindly,' Molly said, trying to dimple.

He laughed. 'Sorry, am I ranting? It's rather a passion of mine.'

'So I see – and please don't apologise. It's admirable.'

'Thank you. But why should we stop at magazines? Imagine a country in which everyone from the highest High Court judge to the lowliest kitchen-maid reads books for their daily pleasure – and good books, not just penny-dreadfuls and romantic trash!'

'That would be something indeed,' Molly said; although, shameful to admit, what she was thinking as she said it was how marvellously blue his eyes were when he was enthusiastic about something.

On Tuesday, the 11th of May, the eighth day of the strike, there were more troops to be seen on the streets in all the major cities. The talk going round was that support for the action was crumbling, strikers were drifting back to work, and the strike could not last much longer. There was not much evidence for it. There were more local newspapers available, but some shops were staying shut, certain goods were in short supply, and the transport situation was as bad as ever. There was more violence at picket lines, much of it concerned with attempts to get buses and trams moving again.

Behind the scenes, meetings were going on all day between TUC and miners' leaders, and with Sir Herbert Samuel, trying to find a way to make his settlement palatable, suggesting refinements to the pay structure, trying to ensure the lowest-paid would not suffer, specifying help to miners who needed to move to find work, in the form of subsidised housing or home improvements.

But even as they struggled to reconcile their differences, a severe blow was struck to the trade unions. The general secretary to the National Sailors' and Firemen's Union, who had been against the strike from the beginning, had resented his members being called out over his head, and sought an injunction, saying it was against his union's rules to strike without a ballot. In the Chancery Division of the High Court, the judge, Sir John Astbury, granted the injunction, and declared the whole General Strike to be illegal. He said it was not an industrial dispute at all: *that* was a disagreement between employees and employer. But, apart from the miners, there was no cause between any of the strikers and their employers. The General Strike did not therefore fall within the Trades Disputes Act of 1906, which gave unions immunity from damages.

The Astbury ruling left the unions vulnerable to litigation from employers for breach of contract, and even from their own members for breach of union rules. Damages could prove colossal, and union coffers were already drained by providing strike pay. Bankruptcy and the end of the whole union movement might follow.

Molly met Vivian Blake for supper again on Tuesday night, and in the course of their wide-ranging conversation, he raised the subject of the British Broadcasting Company. 'I think John Reith has rather overplayed his hand. He ought to have let himself be commandeered as Churchill wanted.'

'Surely he was right to want to maintain independence?' Molly said. 'Popovka says the first thing the Bolsheviks did in the revolution was to seize the means of communication.'

'But what sort of independence has he got? The last thing the cabinet wants from the BBC is true impartiality, and since Reith will soon have to negotiate with that same cabinet for his licence, he obviously has to support the government side. If he'd been commandeered, he could have said it wasn't his choice.'

'But I suppose he would have sided with the government anyway, wouldn't he?' Molly said.

'Probably, but he might have given the TUC side more airwaves had he not been looking over his shoulder.'

'Well, I don't suppose it's done much harm,' Molly said.

'No harm to the people, perhaps, but to the BBC – he'll never be able to convince anyone now that it's genuinely independent.'

'Do you think the strike will end soon?'

'It's hard to say. I think a lot of the strikers are sick of the whole thing, and the loss of wages must be hurting them. On the other hand, if they capitulate without getting any concessions, the unions will lose membership hand over fist. They'll want to stick it out, but I don't think they can win. The government's given nothing so far, and most of the country hasn't suffered at all.'

On Wednesday, the 12th of May, the ninth day of the strike, something was in the air. The tone of the newspapers had changed. The *Daily Express* headline was 'The Strike with a Broken Back', and the article wrote of TUC committee members who admitted the tide was turning against them. The *Daily Mirror* said that the strikers were not, after all, Red revolutionaries, but ordinary men and women anxious to get back to work. The *British Gazette* said order and quiet reigned throughout the land.

'If they don't feel the need to throw vitriol at the strikers,' Molly commented to Popovka, 'it must mean they think the strike is nearly over.'

'Only in England could this happen,' he said, with a reverent air. 'In my country, you celebrated victory by crushing your opponents all the more fiercely.'

'Oh, we like to be magnanimous towards the defeated,' she said, laughing, 'in the hope that they'll return the compliment.'

Meetings between the TUC and Samuel continued, polishing the details of the agreement, on the understanding that the strike would have to be called off before the government would talk to the strikers, but that the subsidy to the miners would be renewed and the lock-out notices would be withdrawn. But the miners refused to be part of the meetings, and when the General Council sent details of the settlement to the miners' leaders, prior to going to Downing Street, they refused to have anything to do with it. The TUC, they said, had been the Prime Minister's doormat from the beginning, and had never had any enthusiasm for the strike. They would not come to Downing Street. They would not give up the strike.

BOOK TWO

Signposts

But happy now, though no nearer each other,
We see the farms lighted all along the valley;
Down at the mill-shed the hammering stops
And men go home.

Noises at dawn will bring
Freedom for some, but not this peace
No bird can contradict: passing, but is sufficient now
For something fulfilled this hour, loved or endured.

W. H. Auden: 'Taller Today'

CHAPTER TEN

Felix and Pooley sprang from a car, came rushing up to the tea stall, hopped up and down until Molly had finished serving her customer, and broke into a confused chorus.

'It's over!'

'It's all over!'

'They've gone to Downing Street.'

'Pugh and Thomas of the General Council. We're going too.'

'Come on! You must come.'

'See the fun!'

'I can't come,' Molly said, looking nervously sideways at Lady D'Aubeny and Mrs Potter, who were chatting together and ignoring a patient soldier clutching a sixpence. Felix looked too. 'What – Gog and Magog? What can they do to you?'

'They can't sack you,' Pooley pointed out. 'You're a volunteer.'

'I can't leave my post.'

'Don't we tell you the war's over? It doesn't need three of you, anyway.'

This was true. It was a quiet time. The car at the kerb hooted.

'Come on, they're waiting,' Pooley said. 'You can't tell your grandchildren you missed the moment when the General Strike ended.'

'Those grandchildren again!' Molly put down her tea-towel and stripped off her apron. 'I'm going out for a time,' she called to Lady D'Aubeny. 'I'll be back later.'

'That's the ticket,' Felix said, grabbed her hand and ran. Gog and Magog were so overcome with outrage they could not find their voices, which was just as well.

The might that was lined up against the strikers was obvious when the car full of excited young people went past Wellington Barracks, and they saw troops drilling, being paraded in gas masks, practising with machine-guns, over-hauling tanks. It gave Molly a shiver down her spine to think that such things might ever have been thought to be needed. Popovka would have had a different view: in Russia, shooting your opponents had been commonplace. But this was England, and thank God for it! The strike was over and not a shot had been fired.

They pulled in to the kerb in Whitehall and ran the last few yards into Downing Street, where a growing crowd had gathered, together with a pack of press photographers. As they jostled themselves into position, those around them told them the news.

'We saw Pugh and Thomas.'

'They looked glum as twopence.'

'Baldwin won't even see 'em unless they call the strike off, but that's what they've come to do. "Forthwith", they say.'

'But the miners aren't going back. It was in a leaflet this morning.'

A functionary came out from the door of number ten and walked away, threading through the crowds. More words were passed back.

'Baldwin's rung Lord Reith. There's going to be an announcement on the wireless.'

'They're talking about how to get everyone back to work without confusion. There's no guarantees for the miners. It's unconditional surrender.'

Molly looked at Pooley and Felix. 'It's rather an anticlimax, isn't it? All that sacrifice and struggle on both sides, and for what?'

Felix looked at her in amazement. 'But we *won*!'

There was a surge of movement, and the photographers, now numbering around a hundred, elbowed their way to a clear view. The door had opened, and the policeman on duty was looking back expectantly. An official motor-car drew up at the kerb.

'He's coming!' someone called.

Then the Prime Minister stepped out, looking tired but otherwise as if nothing momentous had happened in his whole life, let alone the last nine days. The crowd burst into cheers, and 'Good old Baldwin!' and the battery of flash guns exploded. Baldwin seemed taken aback. He stopped, and said, 'I say!' And while he was hesitating, Mrs Churchill came running out of number eleven towards him, beaming and waving in congratulation. He shook hands with her – she looked as though she might well have kissed him in her excitement – and another salvo went off, capturing the moment for posterity. The Prime Minister looked round and gave a bemused smile to the crowd. Someone shouted, 'Three cheers for Baldwin!' and they were given with gusto. Then he got into his car and it moved away down Downing Street, with the excited crowd running behind it, waving and cheering all the way to the House.

All over the country, there was celebration on Wednesday night. Perhaps because of the large number of extra students in London, the revelry there took on the aspect of Boat Race night, and there was a great deal of broken glass in the gutters and a number of sore heads by the morning.

Emma and Kit went to dinner at the Vibarts' house, and they sat down a large number at the table, which saved her from having to pretend to be jolly. The Yorks were there, and

213

the Prince of Wales, his equerry Joey Legh with his wife Sarah, Fruity and Baba Metcalfe, the Holkams, and Oliver and Verena. Emma had asked Kit not to tell anyone yet about their engagement, and he had made no fuss about it, seeming to understand how upset she was about losing Benson, for which she was grateful. Afterwards everyone went on to the Café de Paris for dancing, but the Yorks left early, which allowed Emma to claim a headache and go home.

In Mecklenburgh Square, there was a party for the whole house in the basement, but as there were parties in a great many other flats around the square, they tended to migrate and merge and the fun went on so long that Felix and Pooley, who had gone to a student spree, found plenty still to join in with when they staggered home. Molly started the evening well, but went through a low stage. She found herself sitting with Popovka, crammed into a corner of the artists' basement, which was so full of people it had become as hot as a furnace. A gramophone was blaring, and despite there being only standing room, two couples were attempting to Charleston, which was resulting in some well-distributed bruising.

She was clutching a jam-jar full of beer – glasses had run out long since – and half a Scotch egg, and had been perfectly happy until suddenly a melancholy overcame her.

'It seems awfully flat, somehow,' she said, putting her mouth near Popovka's ear so he could hear her. 'Now the strike's over, I keep wondering, what was it all for?'

He gave her a considering look and said, 'You don't want to go back to work.'

'Well – no, not really. But I don't think that's to do with the strike.'

'I think it is. You liked your job before. Now you have seen a glimpse of a wider life.'

'Perhaps. But I can't have it. And what has anyone gained? That's what I keep asking.'

'*You*, at least, have gained a new friend,' he said with a significant nod.

'Have I?' she said. 'But we just met and talked for two evenings, because he had time to spare and his usual friends were busy. Now things are back to normal, I don't suppose I'll ever see him again.'

'*That* is why you are not happy,' Popovka said, with his Socratic air, as though he had led her to conclude this for herself.

And Molly, who hadn't thought of it, realised it was. He hadn't come to her stall today, and she hadn't heard from him. 'I suppose he's out celebrating with his own people tonight,' she said. 'I so enjoyed talking to him.'

'Then he must have enjoyed talking to you. It is a thing that cannot work in one direction only. You will see him again.'

'He doesn't know where I live. And I don't know where he lives. I know where he works, but I can't go and ask for him.'

'No, no, that would not do. But a man will always find a way, if he wishes.'

If he wishes. And why would he? she asked herself. She thought of his eager face and bright eyes. A man in his position must have his pick of all the women in London. She imagined fascinating beauties of the Bloomsbury Set, rich, titled, intellectual, draped in their William Morris silks and long, ensnaring hair, discussing books and quoting poetry at him, and thought, *What would he want with a brisk, tweed-skirted ex-civil servant who is nearing thirty and has never been a beauty?*

One of the Charlestoners did a high kick and sent someone's glass flying. It smashed on the wall, showering the people sitting beneath, and everyone erupted into laughter. Molly only managed a sigh.

But then someone changed the record, the Charlestoners

retired, red-faced, and a young man in a sleeveless Fair Isle pullover appeared in front of Molly, and yelled, 'Come and dance!'

'In this space?' she yelled back.

But she gave her jam-jar and Scotch egg to Popovka and allowed herself to be yanked to her feet. In a few moments the ridiculousness of the exercise had her laughing, her partner was telling her funny stories, and the melancholy had passed. She had friends, an agreeable place to live, and a job to go to that one day might be fulfilling. She had nothing to feel sad about.

The nation did not spring back into shape on Thursday morning like a rubber ball. The strike had been called off by the TUC, but it was not only the miners who defied them. Many workers did not immediately go back to work, and many who did, and were faced with new terms of employment, turned around and went away again. In Hull there were thirty thousand railwaymen, dockers, printers and engineers still on strike in support of tram employees who had been sacked. There were riots in Doncaster and Darlington, and at several docks, and violent resistance in many places to attempts to get trams and buses running again. In Eastbourne, all trades were protesting about victimisation of tramwaymen. A march of thirty thousand railwaymen took place in Manchester, and a defiant afternoon march of miners through York.

Transport was worse than ever, for the volunteers had not come in, but the transport workers were mostly still out. There were Communist pamphlets everywhere on the streets, talking about betrayal and treachery, saying that the fight was no longer for the miners, but for the whole British working class, and calling for action; and in nervous reaction, there were more troops and police visible than ever, fearing a Red backlash.

Molly went in to work, but found she was not needed. Mr Churchill had wanted to keep the *Gazette* running as long as the crisis lasted, but though the proprietors had reacted with horror to the idea, the normal paper would not be produced that day. The printing trades were all still out and, being faced with the necessity of negotiating the terms on which they might get their jobs back, looked likely to be out a few days more.

She went back to Hyde Park, but the tea stall was unaccountably missing. A policeman said it had been dismantled by soldiers early that morning but he didn't know why. After some hesitation she went along to the offices of *The Times*. Blake was not there – she supposed he did his own work during the day – but she discovered a more enlightened attitude to women, and a group led by Lady Diana Cooper was folding newspapers.

'We've enough on folding,' the supervisor said. 'Can you work a switchboard?'

Molly, eager for something to do, said yes, privately telling herself that it could not really be hard. There were two other women already there, one of whom, with scarlet lipstick, painted nails and her hair tied up turban-style in a silk scarf, immediately said, 'Thank God!' abandoned her position and went out. The other, a rather meeker and dowdier sort, gestured to a third seat in front of the machine, which seemed at first glance to Molly a Medusa head of twisting cords. 'She's just gone to the lav, and for a smoke,' she said and, glancing at Molly's face, 'You've done this before?'

Molly shook her head, and it was an intense learning period, involving a great many flashing lights and irate people who had been cut off, but in fifteen minutes she had got the hang of it, and was rather enjoying herself. It was just as well, as the other woman did not come back.

'Can you come again tomorrow?' the supervisor asked, at the end of the day, and Molly agreed. It was always good to learn a new skill; and she liked to be useful. She looked around sharply as she left the premises, but it was not his time to be there, of course; and on the way home she had a wild thought that perhaps he would somehow have found out where she lived and there would be a note from him. But there wasn't. She sighed, shook herself by the scruff of the neck, and folded away the memory of those two suppers in a drawer marked 'Agreeable moments from the past'.

On Friday, May the 14th, the government made a determined attempt to settle the miners' grievances. It published proposals to amalgamate and reorganise pits, to restrict recruitment to unemployed miners, to set up a national wages board, and to initiate a levy on pit profits to provide for miners' welfare. It also restored the subsidy, but only for six weeks, not the three months set out in Samuel's report, after which there would be wage reductions.

The TUC felt this was close enough for them to put their support behind it, and still to claim they had won a victory. But the miners were having none of it, and stuck to their original demand of not a penny off the pay, not a minute on the day. The mine owners, meanwhile, objected indignantly that it was their business to deal with the miners, not the government's, and demanded the same freedom from political interference as other industries. So the lock-out notices remained and the miners stayed out.

In York, Henrietta arranged relief for the miners' wives – food and children's clothes. She had to do it quietly, for the mine owners were important men in York. The Morlands had had family connections with the Ansteys in times past, and Lord Anstey would have considered it a slight to have anyone from Morland Place 'siding with' the pitmen.

'But it's not a case of "siding with them",' she said to Amy, who had discovered her sorting through cast-off clothes and wormed it out of her. 'The women and children can't help themselves. Why should they suffer?'

'You know what the men would say,' said Amy. 'That it's for the miners to support their own families.'

'It's everyone's business to relieve suffering,' Henrietta said, with a stubborn look.

'And they'd say helping the families takes the pressure off the miners and encourages them to stay out.'

'Are you going to tell Teddy?' Henrietta asked. It wouldn't stop her, but she didn't want trouble in the house.

'No,' said Amy. 'I'm going to come with you.'

Henrietta was alarmed. 'You shouldn't do that. Teddy might not like it – it would put him in a difficult position in York if it came out, and there's already so much bad feeling. It's different for me – I'm just his sister – but you're his wife, and it would reflect on him.'

'I've been poor. I know what it is to miss meals because the rent has to be paid. I want to help. Don't worry. No-one will ever know.'

The women were grateful for the help, but were equally anxious for their husbands not to find out they'd taken anything. 'There's a lot o' bad feeling, ma'am,' one miner's wife explained. 'They feel they've been let down, and just now anyone from the upper class is their enemy – begging your pardon, but it's how they feel.'

'How are things, in general?' Henrietta asked, looking round the bare, scrubbed room which was kitchen, living room and bedroom all in one.

'Not so bad, ma'am, thank 'ee,' the woman said unconvincingly. She had two small children with her, a girl of about four and a boy of two, who stood just behind her, holding on to her skirt and staring up at the strangers. They were pale, and Henrietta knew from the way they had looked at her basket and then away again that they were hungry. 'It's a good job it's May and noan so cold,' she added, in a burst of confidence, 'because they've stopped us takin' our bit o'coal up at t' pit.' The miners were allowed so much per family, and in the past the quantity had been fairly elastic. 'I've had me elder ones out fetchin' wood for the cooking, but with everyone at it, it's getting hard to find. If it were winter now . . .'

'It won't last until winter,' Henrietta said firmly. 'They'll come to an agreement in a few more days – a week at the most. Meanwhile, you must let me know if there's anything you need particularly.'

'Thank 'ee, ma'am, but this bit o' bacon will do us nicely, and the shirt for our Billy. I'm right grateful. But there's plenty worse off than us, so I won't be greedy.'

'And how is your man?'

The woman smiled, transforming her tired face. 'It's a queer thing, is that, ma'am, but things are so bad down t' pit, he's better in himself for the fortneet out of it – aye, though food's been short. He's coughin' much less, and he says his back's not grievin' him so much.'

'I'm glad to hear something good has come of it,' said Henrietta.

Outside, Amy said, 'Are conditions really so terrible down the mines that the men are better off not working?'

'Only in that respect,' said Henrietta. 'And the women will starve themselves to feed the men. As long as they stay out, I shall have to do what I can. But you really mustn't get involved.'

'Oh, I'll be careful,' Amy said, looking thoughtful.

William Pennyfather had enjoyed the strike so much that he felt almost bereft without it. On Sunday, everyone went to church; then there was dinner; but after that he felt at a loss. His restlessness communicated itself even to Jessie, who had been distracted so far by the need to help prepare the dinner, since their last cook had left on Friday. 'Not that she was any great loss. How anyone can take good ingredients and spoil them like that . . . If I didn't know, I'd think she was trying to poison us.'

'If you want a recommendation,' Bertie said, 'I'll write you one myself, and you can have the job. That meal was delicious.'

'A little rough round the edges,' Jessie said, 'but at least it was edible.' She sighed. 'I suppose we can carry on as we are for a bit, with Tomlinson and me sharing the cooking, but really—'

'I was joking,' Bertie said, alarmed. 'I didn't marry you to make a skivvy of you. Advertise for another cook immediately.'

'It's Sunday.'

'Immediately on Monday.'

'Advertising's the easy part,' Jessie grumbled, and then her eye was drawn to William. 'What *is* the matter with you? You're like a bee in a bottle.'

'Sorry,' he said; and then, 'I wish I had something to do.'

Jessie and Bertie exchanged a look, and Jessie said kindly, 'You might go down to the stables.'

William brightened immediately. 'Really?'

'Yes, there is one job, which is best done on Sunday, when it's quiet.'

Half an hour later, he was lungeing Flying Colours in the paddock at Twelvetrees. The stallion was full of himself, and bucked, shied, and kicked out, but William was patient and firm and eventually he settled down and trotted and cantered more or less steadily on either rein. After a good hour, when he had tired him out, William called him in to the centre to make much of him and give him some pieces of chopped carrot.

A voice called, 'What are you doing?' making Flying Colours jerk in surprise.

William looked round. A small figure was sitting on the

221

top rail of the paddock, twiddling a stick and watching with solemn eyes. It was Laura – thin as a twig herself, six and rather small for her age, with soft brown hair and brown eyes, but a surprisingly well-developed mind. She was the quiet one in the nursery at Morland Place, preferring her own company, or that of a book, friendly only with her half-brother Martin, and not very close even to him. William had heard the nursery-maids calling her 'a queer one' and 'changeling'. They had a prejudice for pretty, smiling children, so there was little about Laura to recommend her.

He looked at her with interest. 'What are you doing here?'

'I asked first,' she said.

'I'm lungeing him.'

'Why?'

'Because it's good for a stallion to be handled. At Twelvetrees, they don't believe in letting the stallion go wild.'

'Why?'

'It makes it difficult if you have to do anything with him – move him from one place to another, or treat him for anything.' The grooms also said it made for better-tempered foals, but he didn't really believe that. Temperament, he thought, was bred into a horse, though it could be improved or spoilt by handling.

'Why don't you ride him, then?' Laura asked.

'He doesn't get ridden. He's not broken to saddle,' William said. 'Now it's your turn. What are you doing here?'

'I got bored,' she said.

'Couldn't you play with the others?'

'They don't want me,' she said indifferently. 'Can I come and see him?'

'Yes,' he said, 'if you move quietly and don't startle him.' He was rather taken with her. She didn't speak like a child, and he had the odd image of a tiny adult stuck inside a child's body. They said she looked like her mother, but

William had never seen Maria, of course – nor her father, the tragic Father Palgrave.

Laura climbed down from the fence and walked across, moving lightly, like a blown leaf, he thought, so that she hardly seemed to bend the grass. He felt full of pity for her, poor little orphan, outsider in the nursery. He was close enough to childhood to bet that the other children made sure she knew she was no relative of theirs, and 'did not belong' in the house.

The stallion watched her, his ears pricked with interest, then snorted and pawed the ground warningly with a fore-foot. But she did not falter, and when she reached them, Colours lowered his head and touched her hair, then blew sharply out through his nostrils. She accepted the greeting, looked up at William and said, 'Can I stroke him?'

'Give him this first,' he said, and reached in his pocket for some carrot. She seemed absolutely fearless, though the horse towered over her. Colours took the carrot and crunched noisily, and then since he seemed quiet, William said she might stroke him. She reached up and laid her small hand against the big black neck, and ran it down and over his shoulder a few times. The stallion stood quietly, flicking an ear against an annoying fly.

'He's lovely,' she said seriously. 'I wish he was mine.'

'What would you do with him?' William asked, amused.

She didn't smile. 'I'd ride away on him, and gallop and gallop until we got to the end of the earth.'

'Stallions aren't for riding,' he said.

'I could ride him,' she said with quiet certainty. And at that moment, Colours lowered his head and looked at her, snorted, touched her arm with his muzzle, and looked away again. He had merely been checking on her, William knew, but it looked strangely as though he had been agreeing.

'Well, don't you ever try it,' he said sternly. 'In fact, you mustn't even go near him unless a grown-up is with

223

you. He's a lovely horse, but he could kill you with one blow of his hoof.'

'Like a swan,' she said. He was puzzled. Flying Colours was coal black, nothing like a swan. 'Nanny Emma says a swan could kill me with one blow of its wing,' she explained patiently. He could see she didn't believe either statement. 'Are you going to circle him some more?'

On an impulse, he said, 'No, I'm going to take him for a walk.' He was quiet enough now, and being led was good practice. Just up to the top paddock and back. 'Would you like to come with us?'

She nodded. She opened the gate for him, and they set off up the track together, the stallion's unshod hoofs making a soft sound on the packed earth, his head nodding, his ears pricked with interest at the new surroundings.

Laura walked in silence for a bit, and then said, 'When I grow up, I shall ride a horse like him. We'll gallop and gallop and no-one will stop us.'

'Is that what you want to do when you grow up? Work with horses?'

'That's not work. That's what I shall *do*,' she said, as though he were wearyingly slow to understand. 'I'm going to be a writer, like my father. He went away to the north, and wrote a book.'

'Will you go to the north?'

'That's what you do,' she explained, 'if you write a book. But *I* shall come back. Not like him.'

'What will your book be about?' he asked.

She thought about it for a long time, keeping pace with the big horse as he thub-dubbed along the track between the creamy may hedges. The little breeze blew some whiskered florets to settle in his mane, and in Laura's hair.

Finally she answered, 'About the world.'

She was so serious, he did not feel inclined to laugh at her, though he was at the age when it was almost compulsory to laugh at the things children said, to show you were no longer one of them.

'That will be a good book,' he said. 'I shall like to read it one day.'

She looked up at him, brown-eyed and solemn. 'I shall let you,' she pronounced.

The London newspaper workers accepted an agreement on Sunday, the 16th, though it was less generous than the terms on which they had been working before the strike, and on Monday all the papers were back to full production. Molly returned to work, and found proceedings disturbingly flat. All around her, her male colleagues chattered about what they had done during the past fortnight, while getting on with much more interesting jobs than her. She fetched and carried, filed cuttings, went down to the basement for back-numbers, looked things up in the morgue and, if she was very good, was allowed to work up the Hatches, Matches and Despatches – the birth, marriage and death notices sent in by readers for the announcements columns. She corrected spelling and rewrote particularly clumsy ones, though it was customary to let the In Memoriam notices stand exactly as sent in, mistakes and all, which sometimes distressed her. She thought how sad it would be to be remembered with a grammatical solecism that could so easily have been put right.

She went to work and came home every day, and felt as lacking in the vital spark as a machine. She was beginning to think journalism was not for her. Would she ever progress in the all-male world of the newspaper, or would she always be held back? 'Don't let the girls play, they spoil everything.' But what else could she do? She had burned her boats in the civil service, and being a secretary anywhere else would hardly be better than here: filing, typing up other people's dull words and making the tea – forever making the tea. On one level she was shocked with herself for being so lethargic and spiritless, and a good deal of scruff-of-the-neck-taking went on in the evenings, but it didn't seem to make much difference. She just felt that the *excitement* had gone out of life.

On Saturday afternoon she arrived home from work, having spent much of the morning among the back-numbers, and being consequently grimy as well as tired and fed up. All she wanted was to take a long, deep bath, and to curl up with a book on the sofa. As she reached her landing, Popovka stuck his head over the banisters from above and said, 'Ah, there you are. To my room, please, would you come? At once, please.' She looked up at him, wondering how to refuse, and he smiled and said, 'Please. There is tea.'

'I'll just take my hat and coat off,' she called back. She loved Pop dearly, but she was grubby and cross and she really just wanted to be alone. But friendship had its duties as well as pleasures – you couldn't turn it on and off to suit yourself.

She trudged up the stairs a few minutes later and, nearing Popovka's door, heard Nina, within, saying, 'Now Kschessinskaya used to do it like this . . .' *Thump*. 'But Karsavina did it like *this*.' *Thump*. 'She had good feet but no wrists, poor girl.'

If Nina was reminiscing about her Maryinsky days, Molly thought, there would be tea all right, but it would be *à la russe*. Yes, there in the angle through the open door she could see the samovar gently steaming. There were cakes, too, on a plate beside it. Cakes! Popovka really was *en fête*.

'And Simonova does it like *this*,' came Nina's triumphant voice. A thump, and then, rather breathlessly, 'Ah, but Kschessinskaya – her *port de bras* was exquisite. Sometimes when she danced one could only look at her arms. Only the arms.'

Enough, Molly thought. Once she got onto Kschessinskaya's

arms, it was but a short step to *Swan Lake*, and then to the thirty-two *fouettés*, her anathema, on which she could rant furiously for half an hour at a time, almost without drawing breath. 'It may be clever, my friend, but is it *art*?'

She hurried the last few steps, ready to burst in with a bright comment to turn the subject, but as she put her hand to the door another voice spoke from within – and it wasn't Popovka's.

'How interesting. I never knew there were such variations of style within ballet. And as to the arms, I've often thought that some dancers don't seem to know what to do with them.'

She pushed it wide and stepped in. Nina was on the far side, in a small cleared space, standing with her ballet-slippered feet in fifth position. Popovka was deep in his favourite armchair, as though keeping out of the way of flying feet, and in the chair to the left of the door, looking extremely comfortable with a glass of tea in his hand, a plate with a cake on it resting on the chair arm, was—

'You!'

Blake stood up. 'That is a very unpromising monosyllable. I can't pretend it isn't me, but I hoped it would give you more pleasure than it seems to be doing.'

Popovka had stood up too, and was beaming at her across the room. 'A nice surprise? It is, is it not, *doushka*? He came looking for you, and I asked him in to wait.'

Nina tutted and took over the introductions. 'It is your friend, *galubchik*, of whom you spoke. How can you stand there so stupidly? We have kept him entertained for you, Pop and I. I have been showing him how I danced Odette-Odile. Ah – when I was young!'

She waited for someone to protest that she was still young, but two-thirds of the other people in the room had something else on their minds.

'I think Miss Ormerod is surprised to see me here, after

such a long silence on my part,' Blake said, and hung his head in mock shame. 'It is very wrong of me to assume I should be welcome after so shamefully neglecting you, but the truth of the matter is that I couldn't help it.'

'Not at *all*,' Nina put in helpfully.

'Not at all?' Molly said, a gleam of humour returning.

'Not the least bit,' he said. 'My uncle sent me to Scotland first thing on Wednesday, and I only got back this morning. Like a fool I hadn't asked you for your address so I couldn't write to you and tell you where I was.'

'Oh,' said Molly. Astonishingly, all her crossness and tiredness seemed to have dissolved away, likewise her desire to spend the evening alone – though the wish for a bath had gone up a notch. 'How *did* you find my address? I mean – here you are.'

'I took a taxi round to Hutchinson's as soon as my uncle let me go, and persuaded them to let me have it. I can reassure you that they were reluctant to part with it, but I can be very persuasive in a good cause.'

She smiled. She knew that already. 'Am I a good cause?'

'Can't think of a better one.'

Nina said authoritatively, 'You must go out to dinner together tonight. But first you shall have tea, and we shall talk. Then you shall go and bathe and prepare yourself, *galubchik*, for it must be said you are *un peu mal soigné*, and while you prepare, Pop and I will entertain Mr Blake for you.'

Molly read Blake's face, which fortunately was not visible to Popovka and Nina, and said, 'But I don't want tea, Nina dear. No tea, thank you. I shall go and un-*mal-soigné* myself right this minute, and then perhaps Mr Blake and I will go and see that exhibition at the Royal Academy he was talking about the other day. We could fit it in before dinner, perhaps.'

'*What* a good idea,' he said. 'Yes, I should like to catch it before it closes. I'm told it's *very good*.'

'Too much egg,' Molly murmured reprovingly. Now they would want to know what the exhibition was.

She left him to his fate and sped away, grinning to herself as she heard behind her Nina's injured tones rising. 'But what exhibition is this? Should I like it? Should we all go?'

Emma and Kit were walking in St James's Park on a rare sunny day. The summer had been disappointing so far – mainly dry, but cloudy and cool – and a lot of people had taken advantage of the unexpected glimpse of the sun to do the same. Pigeons waddling back and forth across the paths were having to scurry to get out of the way of the feet, and there were a lot of dogs about. A lady went past with a fox-terrier on a lead, and Emma's eyes followed it.

'You still miss him, don't you?' Kit said, breaking what had become a five-minute silence.

Emma started and looked at him guiltily. 'I'm sorry. I know he was only a dog—'

'You don't need to apologise to me. I know the little chap meant a lot to you.'

'But it's been almost three weeks and I ought to pull myself together.'

'I didn't say that.'

'I know. I'm saying it to myself. You've been awfully patient with me. Dear Kit.'

'Think nothing of it, old girl.'

'No, I think it bodes well. If you can be patient when I'm being tiresome now, perhaps you will prove a kind husband.'

'I wasn't planning on being any other sort,' he said, and looked at her sidelong. 'So you *are* still thinking of marrying me?'

'Of course. Oh dear, did you think I'd changed my mind?'

'Well, it did strike me that I'd caught you at a bad moment. Probably unfair. And you didn't want anyone to be told.'

'I was so miserable about Benson, I didn't think I could

show anyone the right sort of happy face. But it wasn't fair on you. I'm officially pulling myself together, as of now. We'll announce it tomorrow – if *you* haven't changed your mind?'

'Oh, no. I still think it's a good idea. I mean, I have a title and you're rich – it makes perfect sense.'

'Aren't you rich?'

'Well, I'd say only middling to fairish. But you are very rich, aren't you?'

'I think so. You'd have to speak to my man of business, but the last time I asked, he said I was. Of course, you have the estate.'

'Yes. Not a bad old pile, and it's in pretty country. Needs a bit doing to it, I dare say. Of course, we needn't go there much, unless you like.'

'I think it would be rather nice to have a house and land and so on that you really belong to. I've never belonged anywhere. We could go there in the summer, couldn't we? And have an annual garden party for the neighbours and villagers.'

'We could,' he said cautiously.

'We'd be the lord and lady of the manor.'

'No denyin' it.'

'And we could have people down to hunt in the winter. Lutterworth is good hunting country, isn't it?'

'The best,' he said. 'But look here, you don't want to live in the country all the time, do you?'

'Oh, no. I'd like to have a place in Town as well. I'm a Londoner born – I can't get on without the old place.'

'Well, thank heaven for that,' he said, with theatrical relief. 'I was close to calling the whole thing off.'

'We could keep my flat as our London place,' she suggested.

'No. If you're really rich, we'd better have a proper house. Needn't be too big, but we might want to entertain in it now and then.'

They walked on, talking about houses for a while. Then

230

he said, 'So when shall we tie the knot? I suppose you'll need time to get everything organised. I know weddings are like major military campaigns. Is next year too soon?'

Emma looked at him with faint dismay. 'I don't want a big, fussy wedding,' she said. 'Something small and quiet, with just a few close friends.'

He considered. 'Not getting cold feet? Because if you've changed your mind—'

'It isn't that. It's – well, I've already gone through it all once. The preparations and the big fuss and so on. With Peter. And look how that turned out.'

Kit had been the one to bring her the news that her fiancé had shot himself on the eve of their wedding. 'That was rotten bad luck. But Peter was a mess, poor chap. Sort of shell shock, only delayed. We all realised it afterwards. You can't think it could happen again. You *know* me.'

'But I feel – superstitious, I suppose. That something bad will happen. Not the same thing, of course, but – something.'

He shook his head. 'The thing is, you've had shocking luck, engaged twice and never had a wedding, and that's all down to the war. Now you've a chance to do it properly. I want you to have a decent show. If you don't, you'll look back one day and regret it. Feel you were cheated.'

'I won't.'

'I think you will. And what about me?'

'*You* want a big wedding?'

'I *am* an earl. People will expect it. Otherwise, it will look as though you're not keen. Too shame-making.' He squeezed her hand. 'I want you to have the sort of show that you'll remember all your life – put all those other chaps out of your head.'

'*All*? There were only two,' she said sharply.

He looked at her. 'What about the fellow who gave you Benson?' he said quietly.

Her eyes filled with tears, a helpless reaction. 'No-one knew about that.'

'I guessed,' he said. 'I'm very fond of you, Emma. I want you to be happy. And I think we will be happy together. So let's have a proper wedding and show everyone *you* believe it too.'

She smiled. 'You are very good to me. All right, we'll have a big wedding. Though that may mean putting it off for a while because it will take a lot of organisation.'

'I'm in no hurry. We're all right as we are, aren't we?'

'I suppose so.'

'We'll announce the engagement tomorrow, and I'll take you to this chap I know in Hatton Garden for an engagement ring. *And . . .*' he began, with an air of having just thought of something.

'Yes?' she encouraged.

'No, I'll keep that a secret. It will be a nice surprise for you.'

CHAPTER ELEVEN

With retrospect, it seemed foolish to have thought the General Strike was the opening movement in a Red revolution, and yet Venetia knew very well that was what many in government had feared, along with those in social and political circles who had the most to lose. She had wondered about it herself, though perhaps with more justification than most, since her elder son had disappeared in the Russian Revolution, and she had consequently read more about it than any of her acquaintance.

But the British people, she reflected afterwards, were inherently conservative. They disliked change, and what they craved most of all from governments and politicians and thinkers of all sorts was to be left alone. It was not the right sort of material for those who wanted upheaval and anarchy, the tearing down of institutions, guillotines, firing squads and gutters running with blood. As the war had shown, the response of the average British man to swaggering militaristic causes was to snigger and make up a rude rhyme.

One consequence of the whole business for her, however, was to bring Thomas once more to the forefront of her mind, when she had spent two months patiently trying to send him to the back of it. In March, the seven years since he had gone missing in Russia was up, and his death was made official. She had grown used in that time to accepting his loss, and the faint, frail hope that he might still be alive somewhere had died down to an ember and then gone out. If he had escaped, she believed he would have sent her word. She had received a message in March 1919, a few pencilled words on a grubby piece of paper, but she doubted now whether that had really been from him. It was not even in his handwriting, and had said nothing that anyone might not have written. Since then, no word or whisper had ever reached her. He, and the woman he loved, were dead, she was sure – shot by Reds and tumbled into some shallow, unmarked grave in the wilds of Russia. She mourned him, her lovely son, her smiling, genial Thomas. But she was seventy-six, and her heart was not so strong any more. One day soon she would be leaving, and on the other side she would be with Beauty, her husband, and Thomas would be there, too. It was something to look forward to.

In the mean time, the law had declared Thomas dead and in consequence, her second son Oliver was now the Earl of Overton and Chelmsford, and the machinery had ground into action to pass the title and the fortune entirely into his hands. He had received his living expenses from the estate for the last seven years; now he would have it all. Next month he would go to the Palace, and he would take his seat in the House of Lords next session.

What Venetia didn't know was how Oliver himself felt about it. Her usually talkative son, who was always happy to sit up late into the night chatting to her about everything under the sun, had remained silent and elusive on this topic. As far as she knew, he had not used the title, and he was still carrying on with his professional duties as though nothing had happened. Would he continue to be a plastic surgeon, or would he give it up and devote himself to politics? Or to Court life? Or buy an estate and take up farming? She didn't know – and neither, she suspected, did Verena.

She had fallen into a reverie, her mind drifting over these questions, from which she was aroused by Ardworth opening the door, coughing gently (did he think she was dozing, damn his impudence? She wasn't that old yet!) and announcing, 'Miss Weston, my lady, and Lord Westhoven.'

Emma came in, looking very pretty in a dress of grey and white crêpe-de-Chine with a pleated skirt and a black and white printed overjacket sewn into the dropped waist-band. There was a little colour in her cheeks, and her eyes were bright. Behind her Kit looked as he always did, tall, slender, handsome, and tailored to swooning-point in pale grey, with a white gardenia in his buttonhole.

Venetia struggled to her feet. 'Emma, how very nice to see you. It seems a long while since you were last here. Kit, my dear.' She offered her cheek for his kiss. 'Ardworth, some refreshments. What will you take, my dears? Tea? It's a little early for cocktails.'

'We've something to tell you,' Kit said.

'Good news, I hope?'

'The very best,' Kit said, and took Emma's hand.

Venetia gave them both a sharp examination, then smiled, and said, 'In that case, I know exactly what we'll have. Champagne, Ardworth. My dears,' she said, when he had gone, 'it's what I've been hoping for for years and years. Tell me how it happened.'

Emma explained. 'So we've put a notice in the paper,' she concluded. 'it will appear tomorrow—'

'But we wanted you to be the first to know,' Kit broke in, 'because you're the nearest thing I have to a mother.'

'I couldn't be more pleased,' Venetia said. 'I think you will suit admirably. So, tell me, when will the wedding be?'

'We're thinking of April or May next year,' Emma said. 'There's such a lot to do, and only me to do it.'

'And I'd like to make refurbishments to Walcote House. We'd like to entertain there next summer. Emma's going to do the state rooms herself—'

'But I have contracts in hand right up to Christmas,'

Emma finished, 'so I wouldn't be able to concentrate on the work.'

'Of course, you are dreadfully without family,' Venetia said thoughtfully. 'At a time like this, your parents – your mother in particular – would be making all the arrangements. Would you like me to help you? It's quite a task to be undertaking on your own.'

'Do you mean it?' Emma said. 'I really would like help from someone who knows how these things are done. I don't mind hard work, but I'm rather in terror of getting something wrong and offending someone.'

'I should be delighted,' Venetia said. 'It will make me feel young again to be planning a wedding. Have you told your uncle and aunt?'

'I don't think they'd be much help,' Emma said. 'They're rather old and frail.'

Venetia was pleased with this reply, since the Abradales were younger than her, but she said, 'I didn't mean that, dear, only that they're your nearest relatives and ought to be told before they see it in the paper.'

'Oh – I see. You're quite right. I'll send them a telegram today. I hope they'll come for the wedding. At least they'll have to approve of Kit – he's just the sort of person they always wanted for me.'

'So *that*'s why you accepted me,' Kit said, and she laughed. Venetia was glad to see them playful together.

'And will it be a large wedding, or a quiet one?' she asked.

'Kit wanted large and I wanted quiet,' Emma said.

'So we're compromising and having a large one,' Kit said. 'St Margaret's and then, I suppose, the Savoy. And Walcote for the honeymoon.'

'Wouldn't it be nicer to have the wedding breakfast in a private house?' Venetia said. 'Hotels are rather *impersonal*, don't you think?'

'I suppose it would,' Emma said doubtfully, 'but it would

have to be a large place, you see. We mean to have several hundred guests.'

Venetia smiled. 'I was thinking of Chelmsford House. Lady Denver is giving up the lease at Christmas, and I've told the agent to leave it empty for six months because I didn't know whether Oliver and Verena might want to move in there. But whether they do or not, I know they'd be delighted to lend it to you. It was all redecorated about five years ago, for Lady Denver's granddaughter's wedding, so it will be quite fresh, and there's a ballroom, of course, and the dining-saloon is enormous.'

Venetia's expression was without guile, but Emma couldn't help wondering whether she was thinking of her background, which wouldn't stand inspection beyond one generation. The solid respectability of being married from Chelmsford House, and under the aegis of the Chelmsford and Overton families, would give her a better start in society than a rackety, fashionable 'reception' at an hotel.

Emma wasn't sure whether she wanted to get into society, even though she would be a countess. But on the other hand, it would be nice to have the choice; and Kit might like it; and there were their future children to think about. She wasn't a headstrong girl any more, and thought twice these days before slamming doors closed.

She looked at Kit, who gave her a nod of encouragement. 'I think that would be wonderful,' she said. 'Thank you so very much. As long as Oliver agrees.'

'How could he do less for his best friend?' Venetia said.

'Especially as he will be my groomsman as well,' Kit said.

Emma had expected to be taken to a jeweller's shop where she would choose from among a number of rings. But instead she was taken to an obscure little place in Hatton Garden where, in a back room, unset stones were brought out by a little gnome of a man, and laid reverently on a cloth of black velvet for inspection.

The little man was Igor Nemetsky, a Russian *émigré* – Russians, Kit told her, understood stones better than anyone in the world. Having shown them a number of diamonds, he looked at Emma with his head on one side for a while, and then said, 'I wonder if my lady would prefer a coloured stone. With her colouring she has the happy ability to wear anything – sapphires, emeralds, even rubies.'

'It's whatever you like, Emma,' Kit said. 'You're the one who'll be wearing it.'

Nemetsky said, 'If you will allow me, I have something very special which I think would suit my lady perfectly.'

He got up and went to the safe, talking as he went. 'After the melancholy events of 1917, my people fled with the only wealth they could carry, their jewels. Then, finding themselves without home or help, they had to sell those jewels to survive. There are still pieces coming on to the market. Sometimes they are too beautiful to break up, though it can be hard to find anyone these days who wishes to buy a complete parure.' He turned back to them with a large box, which he put on the table. 'But in this case, there has been considerable damage, and the setting is heavy and old. I have been thinking for a while that it would do the stones more justice if it were all broken up. I have here, you see, the Goloshchevsky Rubies.'

He said it with capital letters, as though they ought to recognise the name, so Emma smiled politely. 'Indeed!'

He drew out a black cloth bag, from which he extracted a necklace of heavy gold, set with oddly rough-looking stones of various colours – unpolished gems, she supposed. There were ugly holes here and there where stones were obviously missing. But at the centre of the necklace hung a cameo-frame of gold wires, in which was set a large ruby.

'The missing stones were yellow diamonds,' he said. 'Prised out and sold during the escape. It is a matter of luck, I suppose, that the most important stone remains. Now, my lord, what do you think? Would not this remaining ruby look far more magnificent in a simple setting upon my lady's lovely hand?

'Is it really a ruby?' Emma wondered. 'It's so dark!' It looked almost black, but Nemetsky lifted it to the light and turned it back and forth. In its heart the light flashed and showed the rich colour, like a candle illuminating the finest port. 'It's beautiful,' she said.

'The Goloshchevsky Rubies were famous in Petersburg,' said Nemetsky. 'As well as this ceremonial collar, there were earrings, bracelets, brooches, another necklace, a jewelled belt, a *kokoshnik*. I have in this box only a small part of the collection. They were supposed to have belonged to Empress Maria Feodorovna, wife of Emperor Paul, brought from Siberia for her wedding. I don't know if it is true.' He shrugged, looking at Emma from the side of his eyes.

Emma looked up at Kit. 'Do you like it?' he said. 'I must say, I do think rubies are absolutely *you*.'

'I adore it,' she said. 'It's so dark and rich. But—'

'No "buts" about it,' Kit said. 'If you like it, you shall have it.'

Nemetsky seemed pleased. They discussed settings, and he drew a sketch, which they approved. As they were about to leave, he said, 'I have one more thing to show you.' He rummaged around in the box, and drew out a bag from which he carefully extracted a tiara. It was a half-hoop, light and delicate, made of upright spikes of square stones, each column of diamonds alternating with a column of rubies.

'This,' he said, 'I shall not break up. There will be times, my lady, when you will need a tiara, and when those times come, I shall be happy for you to hire this piece from me. Try it on.'

Emma laughed nervously, but she removed her hat and let the little man set it on her hair.

'Nadya Goloshchevskaya wore it to the Imperial Ball at the Winter Palace in February 1903,' he said. 'The last Imperial Ball that was ever given.' He turned his face away, cleared his throat, and applied the back of a finger to his eyes.

There was a mirror at the end of the table. Emma turned her head, and saw a dark beauty crowned with stars. She wondered if Nadya Goloshchevskaya had been dark, whether she had survived the terror. She felt her eyes fill, and hastily took off the tiara and gave it back. 'Thank you,' she said, in a subdued voice. The romance of these Russian jewels was almost too much to bear.

Shortly afterwards, when they were out in the street, she said to Kit, 'You do have the best ideas! It was so much more fun than choosing something at Asprey's. But I must say I feel rather peculiar – as though I'd been time-travelling. I'm not sure if I'm really back yet. What an odd little man.'

'I couldn't think him funnier, could you?' Kit was cheerful. 'I'm perfectly sure all that was humbug. But he does give value for money, doesn't he? Not just the jewels, but the stories.'

'Humbug?' Emma queried.

'The Imperial Ball in February 1903 was a costume ball. Everyone went dressed in seventeenth-century costumes. Oliver told me, and Thomas told him. I've even seen photographs. That tiara wouldn't have done at all. It was probably hocked by some penurious baronet's wife from Bedfordshire.'

Emma felt weak with relief. 'I'm so glad. I was wondering whether the stones might be unlucky.'

Kit laughed. 'The Curse of the Russian Rubies? What a title for a 'tec novel! I never knew you were so superstitious. Old Nemetsky just piles it on to improve the price. But you do look a bit shaken, poor girl. What's the time? Oh, good, just about time for cockers. A stiff gin will buck you up.

Where shall we go? It's too early for Ciro's. Shall we drop in on Eddie and Sarah?'

Emma and Kit's engagement seemed to bring pleasure to everyone. They were both popular and handsome, and had for so long been going round together that they were assumed not to be available on the market, so there were no disappointed lovers to spread any gall. And Emma was much pitied for having lost Peter Gresham in that tragic way, so everyone was glad for her to be happy at last.

The Vibarts gave an engagement party for them, which was quite a sober affair with royalty present, so they gave another for themselves, at the Savoy, for the Bright Young People, with a jazz band and cocktails and dancing and a lot of noise. Everyone admired Emma's ring, and asked all the usual questions.

'They tell me you're not getting married until next year,' Padua yelled into Emma's ear over the wall of noise. 'How can you bear to wait so long?'

'There's a lot to do,' Emma said. Out of the corner of her eye she could see Kit dancing an exaggerated Charleston with Stephen Tennant; everyone was roaring with laughter. 'The time will soon pass.'

Padua shook her head, but whether to indicate she hadn't heard or didn't agree Emma couldn't tell. She leaned closer again, the White Lady in her glass lipping perilously close to the edge. 'You're too, too lucky!' she bellowed. 'Kit is heaven, that's all. He's the cat's pyjamas. I couldn't fancy him more, could you?'

'I'm marrying him,' Emma pointed out, but Padua was beyond understanding anything she said. That child drinks altogether too much gin, she thought.

The following morning, Kit called, carrying a large hat-box very carefully.

'Hello, my sweet. I have an engagement present for you.

241

I was going to give it to you at the party last night, but then I thought, no, what on earth would you do with it at the Savoy? So I saved it for today, but today it has to be, or my man will give notice. He's been looking after it for two days already and he says it isn't his place, my lord, with the particular look that tells me I'm in trouble. So happy engagement, Emma dear, and I hope you like it.'

He handed her the box, which was unexpectedly heavy, and shifted in a peculiar way in her grasp. She put it on the table and lifted the lid, and inside was a small, curly-coated black dog, which sat up and licked her wrist, wriggling its hind end in an ecstasy of wagging.

'You can't think how much trouble I went to, to get a mongrel,' Kit said, watching her anxiously. 'Pedigreed dogs are two a penny – well, not in price, obviously – but nobody seems to sell mongrels. But there he is. I hope you like him.'

The miners remained on strike throughout the summer, and by the time of the TUC conference in September there had been several attempts to resolve the dispute, but the owners would accept nothing but complete surrender, and the miners would not accept longer hours or lower pay, so the deadlock continued.

Teddy came looking for Henrietta one day and found her at last in the housekeeper's room tying up bunches of herbs. 'Can I have a word with you?' he said. A glance at his face sent Mrs Tapworth, who had been filling lavender bags alongside her, scurrying out.

'What is it, Ted?' Henrietta asked, when they were alone – though she was afraid she knew. She sighed inwardly. She was very tired and didn't want an argument.

'Look here, Hen, it won't do, you know. I've just had a fearful row with John Anstey at the club. He says you've been taking food and what-not to the miners out on strike.'

'Not to them – to their wives and children.'

'But it's the same thing! It's tantamount to taking up sides against Anstey and the others. He was furious, and so was Maitland from Riccall. It was a dashed awkward situation. They don't like bad feeling at the club – makes things uncomfortable for everybody.'

'I can't help it, Ted. Those poor creatures need the things I take them.' She sighed. 'I only wish I could do more, but there's a limit to how far I can travel by pony-trap. If only I had a car – but I knew you wouldn't like it if I took yours.'

'I'm glad you had that much sense,' Teddy said crossly. 'Think of the fuss if anyone had seen my own motor out on business like that. They would never have believed I didn't initiate it. Now, Hen, it has to stop. I promised Anstey it would stop.'

'You shouldn't have done that,' she said quietly.

Teddy looked uneasy. 'You're not going to defy me, are you? You aren't really helping them, you know. The more you give them, the longer their men can stay out on strike. They need to get back to work, for everyone's sake.'

'That part of it's not my business,' she said. 'Although it seems to me you and Lord Anstey and Sir George and the rest are just intending to starve them into submission.'

'Oh, rubbish,' Teddy began.

'But that's what you've just said. The quicker they starve the quicker they'll give in.'

'It isn't like that. You don't understand these things. But you really will have to stop openly helping the miners. I can't afford to get on the wrong side of the local business people.'

She had spotted the loophole. 'So if I get someone else to help them on my behalf – if I don't do it myself – that will be all right?'

He knew he had been cornered. 'As long as it doesn't come back to me, I suppose . . . But I really feel you'd do better to let them alone. The sooner the men get back to work, the sooner the women will have wages coming in again.'

243

'I have to do my conscience,' she said. 'But I won't go myself any more, if that will content you. I've been feeling, actually – well, lately it's got a bit much for me.'

Teddy looked at her more carefully, and said, 'I say, Hen, you don't look very well. You aren't sick, are you?'

'I'm never sick,' she said automatically, but her voice was dull. 'I have a headache, that's all.'

'You never get headaches,' Teddy said, alarmed. 'And you look as though you have a fever.' He touched her forehead. 'Good God, you're burning up!'

Henrietta sighed. 'Well, if you *must* know – I do feel a little unwell.' She tried to stand, swayed, and sat down again.

'You've caught something,' Teddy accused. 'Down at the miners' houses – some fever.'

'Mrs Black's two little girls weren't well,' Henrietta murmured. 'I didn't really think about it at the time . . .'

Teddy strode to the door and called for help.

Dr Hasty came into the drawing-room where Teddy was waiting. 'It's measles.'

'*Measles?*'

'No doubt about it. The papules in the mouth are quite distinctive. I suppose she didn't have it as a child?'

'Neither of us did,' Teddy said, feeling bewildered. 'Chicken pox, but not measles.'

'Well, it's quite serious in adults, so you must stay away from her. Indeed, you must find out which of your staff have never had it, and keep them well away, too, or we shall have it spreading like wildfire. It's very infectious, through the air as well as by contact, so you must keep everyone out of her room. And let me know at once if you or anyone else has any symptoms – fever, cough, runny nose, and especially spots. I wonder where she picked it up,' he mused. 'I haven't had any other cases.'

Amy, who had been standing silently behind Teddy until then, said, 'Mrs Black's children were sick.'

'Which Mrs Black is that?' Hasty asked.

'At Kelfield.'

'Kelfield? That's way out of my area. What was Mrs Compton doing—' He pulled himself up. That was not his business. 'I shall have to make enquiries, find out which physician covers the area, see if he knows about it. An outbreak must be stopped, if possible.'

Teddy was staring at Amy with shocked eyes. 'You went too,' he said. She looked at him unhappily, and nodded.

Hasty did not catch the import. 'You were exposed to it as well? How are you feeling, Mrs Morland?'

'I'm all right,' Amy said. 'I had it as a child.' She looked pleadingly at Teddy. 'Let me nurse her. She has been so good to me. Let me do it.'

Teddy shook his head in bewilderment, but he said to Hasty, 'Would it be safe for my wife to nurse her?'

'Catching the disease in childhood confers immunity. As long as Mrs Morland's general health is good—'

'It is,' she said.

'And she is not – *ahem* – with child?'

'I'm not,' Amy said quietly, not meeting the eyes of either man.

'Then there should be no danger. But you and Mr Morland will have to keep apart until the infectious period is over. I would advise that you did that anyway, as you have been exposed.'

'Then I might as well nurse her,' said Amy.

'What is the treatment?' Teddy asked.

'Good nursing, that's all. We have no specifics against this kind of disease.' Hasty looked at their drawn faces. 'Try not to worry too much. It *is* serious in adults, and unpleasant for the sufferer, but it is rarely fatal.'

'Fatal?' Teddy had not got as far as thinking about that.

'Rarely, as I said. With good nursing she should pull through all right. The important thing is to keep it from spreading.'

When Jessie came into the bedchamber, Henrietta tried to struggle up. 'You shouldn't be here! Don't come near – it's very catching.'

'Oh, hush!' Jessie smiled. 'I had it when I was little – don't you remember?'

'No, I don't.'

'Well, Bertie does. He said I was a monster while I had it, always wanting to get up and go out. So I shan't catch anything.'

'But you'll take it back to the children!'

'No, I won't. I'm not leaving here until you are up and about again, so just lie down and rest. Amy can't care for you all on her own – she must rest some time. And you know I wouldn't have a moment's peace, so I might as well be useful here, as at home driving everyone mad.'

Henrietta subsided onto the pillows, looking very small and lost in the big bed. She was back in the Blue Room, which she had shared with Jerome during their married life. 'I feel very foolish, catching measles. It seems such a silly thing to do.'

'Well, I wouldn't recommend it,' Jessie said cheerfully. 'How are you feeling?'

'Hot. Thirsty. And my head does ache so.'

'That's enough to be going on with,' Jessie said. 'First let me sit you up a little, then I'll give you a drink. Mrs Stark made you some wonderful lemonade. And then I'll bathe your poor head.'

'Thank you, darling,' Henrietta said when these things were done. 'I'm more comfortable now. You are such a good nurse.'

'I learned from the best person,' Jessie said, leaning over and kissing her forehead. 'Some more lemonade?'

'No, thank you. Later, perhaps.'

'I'll tell Mrs Stark you liked it. She's in a spin, trying to conjure up every kind of invalid food at once. She's making ice cream for your supper.' Henrietta smiled faintly. 'Is there anything else you want now?'

'No, thank you. I think I might sleep a bit. Could you draw the curtains a little? The light hurts my eyes.'

Jessie did as she was asked, and said, 'I'll leave you to rest, then, but I'll keep looking in. Ring if you want anything.' She made sure the bell pull was within reach, smiled at her mother and walked softly out. Outside, she paused to compose herself. She knew her mother well, and the fact that she had mentioned the headache must mean it was very bad. And Jessie didn't like the sensitivity to light. Dr Hasty hadn't mentioned that.

She and Amy moved into the Red Room next door, and set up a rota with Nanny Emma, who had had every ailment in her childhood in rural Norfolk – fortunate, as she couldn't have been kept away from her mistress anyway. She had a truckle bed put into the Blue Room and slept there. Contact with the rest of the staff was avoided. It was hardest on Teddy, who would come and stand at the end of the corridor several times a day, waiting for someone to come out and call a bulletin to him.

Henrietta had a restless night, and slept much of the next day, which Hasty said was just as well. When Jessie looked in at suppertime, her mother was awake, but seemed low, not trying to sit up, not even looking at her.

'How are you now?' Jessie asked. Henrietta didn't answer. 'I looked in before but you were asleep. Do you think you could manage something to eat?'

'The children,' Henrietta said indistinctly. 'Are they all right? Hasty must look at them every day. If they show any symptoms . . .'

247

'They're fine, all of them. Don't worry.'

'I was with them,' Henrietta said. 'I came home from the Blacks' and I was with them. I shouldn't have . . .' Her voice trailed away, and she frowned. 'What day is it?'

'Thursday,' Jessie said. She was alarmed. Her mother was speaking in a mumbling sort of voice, not like her own; and she was not looking at Jessie, but staring at nothing in an unconnected way. Jessie went and laid a hand over her forehead, and she moaned and tried to move away. The skin was scorching. 'You're feverish,' Jessie said, feeling some relief. Fever would cause that disconnection, and fever was understandable. 'I'll get a cold cloth.'

Amy came in while she was bathing Henrietta's head. 'How is she?' she whispered.

'The fever's rising again,' Jessie replied. 'When's Dr Hasty's next visit?'

'He'll be here in ten minutes.' She stared at Henrietta, and bit her lip. 'It's my fault. I should have stopped her.'

Jessie stood up and moved Amy away from the bed. 'It's not your fault,' she said, low but stern. 'My mother has been sick-visiting all her life, and never caught anything. You couldn't have stopped her, anyway. She'd have gone without you. Now, pull yourself together, or you'll upset her, and be no use to me. She's going to be all right. As soon as the fever breaks she'll be fine.'

'I'm sorry,' Amy said, her eyes filling with tears. 'I keep thinking . . .'

'Well, go away and think, then,' Jessie said. 'I can't have you bothering her.'

The tears spilled over, and Amy hurried from the room. After that, Jessie and Nanny Emma nursed her. Teddy was glad to have Amy out of the sickroom, unable to believe there was no danger to her there. Amy, longing to be useful, constituted herself the messenger, passing between Jessie and the household and keeping a distance from both. It

248

suited her desire for self-castigation just then to be an outcast.

Henrietta seemed a bit better the next morning, not quite as hot, though still admitting to a headache. She wouldn't eat, so Jessie did her best to get nourishment into her with cold drinks. 'There's nothing of her anyway,' she complained to Nanny Emma. 'Just skin and bone.' She had been worrying for a long time that her mother was too thin, and did too much. Mrs Stark beat eggs and honey and nutmeg into milk from the coldest part of the dairy, pulped soft fruit and made it into ice cream. Henrietta ate a little – not enough. She smiled at Jessie, and said, 'You are a good daughter. I'm sorry I'm such a worry to you.'

'I'm enjoying having you to myself,' Jessie said. 'These last few years we haven't had enough time together.'

'It's the war,' Henrietta said.

Jessie wasn't sure if that was a slip of the tongue, or a moment of confusion, and said nothing. She bathed her mother's face and Henrietta grew drowsy. The fever mounted again, but she slept, though restlessly.

Jessie fell asleep in the chair in the corner for a while. She woke hearing her mother's voice. She got up and went to her, but couldn't understand what she was saying. She took her hand, and Henrietta seemed to look at her. She said, 'Darling.' Jessie smiled. 'Don't worry, we'll manage somehow. Teddy will help.'

'Manage what, Mother?'

'It's not your fault.' She mumbled something, of which Jessie only caught the word 'money'. Then she said, 'Bankrupt. Can't be helped.'

She thinks I'm Papa, Jessie thought. It was because he had gone bankrupt that they had come back to Morland Place to live, on Uncle Teddy's charity, all those years ago when Jessie was a child. Her mother was confused, or hallucinating. And she was burning up. Jessie wrung out a cold cloth and put it on Henrietta's forehead, but she moaned and turned her head from side to side on the pillow, as if trying to escape the touch. 'My head hurts. My head hurts,' she moaned. Jessie went to the door to tell Amy to get Dr Hasty back. He was due to call again in an hour or so, but Jessie did not like this new turn of events.

'Encephalitis,' said Hasty, out in the corridor, to Jessie and Amy, and to Teddy, standing at the other end of the passage, looking as miserable as it was possible for a man to be. 'It's a known complication of measles, I'm afraid.'

'But what is it?' Amy asked. Jessie could see she was trembling all over like a frightened horse.

'Swelling of the brain. The headache and the confusion are being caused by it.'

'What can we do?' Jessie asked, keeping a tight hold on herself.

'Just try to bring the fever down. Bathe her head. Aspirin, crushed up in water so she can swallow it, should help.'

Jessie met his eyes, and read in them for the first time what she had not at any point expected to see. It was not just bad, it was very bad. She felt a hollow sensation of sickness in her stomach. She had nursed in France during the war – but this was her *mother*.

The bedroom door opened and Nanny Emma appeared. 'Doctor!'

Henrietta was shaking and jerking in the bed, her head jittering on the pillow.

Hasty hurried over. 'A mild seizure,' he said, ten minutes later, when Henrietta was still again. 'You must prepare yourselves for more of them until the fever comes down.'

Hasty didn't leave after that, but he was relentlessly cheerful – his stock in trade and the reason he was such a good doctor with children. He insisted that Jessie and Nanny Emma went down in turn to take some supper – 'You won't be any help if you starve yourselves' – and then Jessie told him to go and eat for the same reason.

'Ten minutes, then,' he said, seeing the patient was quiet for the moment, the fever a little lower. 'But call me if anything happens.'

Shortly after he left the room, Henrietta opened her eyes, looking round in an unfocused way. Jessie hurried to her and took her hand. 'How are you, Mama?' she said. Henrietta tried to wet her lips with a dry tongue, and Jessie carefully lifted her head and helped her drink some water. When she laid her back down, Henrietta sighed.

'Good to me,' she said. Jessie squeezed her hand. 'You must be mistress now,' Henrietta went on, her voice faint, but quite clear. 'Take over. Everything. You can do it.'

'Of course, if you want,' Jessie said, puzzled. 'Just until you're better.'

'Glad you married Teddy.'

She thinks I'm Amy, Jessie thought, and felt a pang of jealousy. The eyes were not focused on her, but moved about as if following someone around the room, and Jessie wondered suddenly if she could see at all. Henrietta smiled. 'Will he go in side-saddle?' she said. Then she closed her eyes and slept.

Hasty came back. The fever climbed again, and she became restless, moaning and turning her head back and forth. She opened her eyes once and looked at Jessie, and seemed to know her, and Jessie was filled with hope, thinking she was getting better. Hasty said it was a good sign.

Just before ten o'clock she had another convulsion, a major one this time, arcing her head back so that the cords of her neck stood out, her body lifting from the bed, her feet jittering. Jessie watched with her heart in her mouth, while Hasty tried to prevent her biting her tongue. Then the iron hand that seemed to be wrenching her about released her. She relaxed slowly, subsiding onto the bed, with a long, sighing breath, and was gone.

251

CHAPTER TWELVE

Teddy was inconsolable. He had lost two wives, but Henrietta had always been there. As children they had been closer than the others, huddling together in the shadow when all the sunlight fell on their elder brother. They had been a large family; now Teddy was the last one left.

Amy was still racked with guilt, and Jessie took her aside and told her fiercely to pull herself together. 'Uncle Teddy needs you. And you have to take over the household. I can't do it. I have my own house to run.'

'I can't,' Amy said, her eyes filling with helpless tears.

'Oh, don't be foolish,' Jessie said.

'She was born to it. I worked in a flower shop. I don't know the first thing about it.'

'That's not true. Mother's been training you ever since you first came here. All you have to do is follow her routine, and it's all written down in the Household Book. That's in the housekeeper's room. Mrs Tapworth will show you. The servants know what to do – most of them. You just have to show them you're in charge.'

Amy shrank from the thought. 'I can't be mistress. I'm not fit to take over from her.'

'*She* thought you were,' Jessie said. 'She told me so. So, no more nonsense, please. Whether you like it or not, you are mistress of Morland Place, and there are responsibilities as well as pleasures. Uncle Teddy needs you, the servants need you, everybody needs you. There'll be plenty of people to help you, so don't worry.'

'Will *you* help me?' Amy said timidly.

Jessie smiled. 'Of course I will. I'm only a mile away, and we have the telephone. Ask anything you want. But you won't need me. You'll do finely.'

And Amy, pulling herself together, suddenly realised what this must be costing Jessie. 'You've lost your mother. I'm so sorry – I've been thinking of nothing but myself.'

Jessie's throat tightened. 'No sympathy, please, or I shan't be able to get by.' She hated to cry.

Jack and Helen came for the funeral, bringing the children with them, because they didn't want to leave them with the servants when they were upset. Basil had looked forward to playing with his cousins again and was disappointed to find them in black and their activities severely restricted by the servants, who had firm ideas about what was proper in a house of mourning.

'Why didn't you tell me?' Jack said to Jessie, walking round the moat. 'I'd have come. I never had the chance to say goodbye.'

'It was so quick,' Jessie said. 'There just wasn't time. We didn't know it was serious until the last minute, and then it all happened so quickly you couldn't have got here. I'm sorry, Jackie. I know how you must feel. I'm just glad that I was nearby.'

They stopped, and put their arms round each other. It was a minute before he could speak, and then she heard from his voice that he had been crying. 'I know – it was hard for you,' he said. 'But at least – you could help.'

'Not much,' Jessie said, trying not to cry herself.

'Did she – did she suffer much?'

Jessie watched the swans drifting up, dabbing idly here and there at a strand of floating weed. It was a sweet, mild autumn day, golden and soft, with the smell of grass and woodsmoke on the air. But her mother would not see it. 'I don't think so,' she said, through the pain in her throat. 'She was so feverish I don't think she knew where she was. At one time she was talking to Papa. She's with him now, Jackie. She's with Papa and Frank and Robbie. You must think of that.'

They walked on. Jack looked at the old house, almost five hundred years old. His mother had been born here, had gone away to marry as women did, but had come back. She had been happier here than anywhere else. It exerted such a powerful influence on them, the Morlands. He felt it too. It called to him, and when he was here, he felt at home, no matter that his life was now hundreds of miles away, in a different county, with different people. He suddenly thought that when he died, he would like to be buried here, among his mother's people – his people.

Venetia came to the funeral, accompanied by Oliver – Verena, who was pregnant again and not feeling well, remained at home. Violet came, accompanied by her eldest son, Robert, a tall, solemn boy of almost seventeen, proud to be entrusted with looking after his mother. James was back from school on an exeat, looking troubled, his usual boisterousness quieted. Ethel and her husband came, Ethel unexpectedly distressed, showing how much she had cared for Henrietta, though she had never showed it much while she lived at Morland Place.

Jessie thought of her half-sister Lizzie, her mother's eldest child, in America and unable to come back to say goodbye. And of Polly, to whom Henrietta had been all she had ever known of a mother. Her own mother had died at her birth, and Teddy's second wife, Alice, had been an amiable cipher. It was Henrietta who had guided her and cared for her, and she would mourn her like a daughter.

The chapel was so full on the day of the funeral, with family, servants, tenants, friends and neighbours, that late-comers had to stand in the aisles, and the doors were left open so that more of the overspill could stand out in the hall. There were people there Jessie didn't recognise, people she supposed her mother had done good to at some time over her long life. She was glad to see such a crowd, to know how many lives her mother had touched. Henrietta, so small and quiet and modest, had been a great lady in her way, and the multitude that gathered to see her off showed it.

Julian discovered the depths of his own sadness, and his voice failed several times during the service. Most of the servants and many of the women and children were in tears. It was as it should be, Jessie thought. The end of a good life should be attended with great emotion. It was right that her mother should be launched into her new life on a flood-tide of tears. With Ottilie on her lap, she looked down the row of grandchildren lined up along the front pew, all the way down to little Laura at the end, who was weeping dreadfully. She was no relation, of course, but she had been Henrietta's as much as any of them, and she had lost a champion and defender. Poor child, she was truly an orphan now.

After the service, the committal, for the family only. The vault was opened, and the coffin was lowered in, to rest beside that of her husband. Two of her sons, gone before her, lay far away, in foreign lands. Jessie found herself thinking, as Jack had earlier, that she hoped she would rest here when her turn came. The coffin looked very small down there, and Jessie suddenly, achingly missed her mother beside her. *Oh, Mother*, she thought. Had she loved her enough, told her so enough, pleased her enough while she'd had the chance?

After the committal, the celebration: of life's race well run, life's work well done. In the Great Hall everyone had gathered, high and low together, and friends and family members helped the servants bring out the food and drink, and everyone handed round and saw to it their neighbours were served. Before death all were equal. Ham sandwiches and cakes, sherry and beer and lemonade; everyone mingled and talked, at first in low voices, still gripped by the emotion of the service, but later more cheerfully, remembering and sharing their memories, being glad they had known her, through the ache of losing her.

Teddy stood at the end of the room, receiving as people came up one after the other to talk to him about his sister. Several times he found himself looking round, wondering where she was and whether she had noticed that old Colonel Hound needed a chair or that the patties were running low. And several times he saw that Amy had gone to see to whatever the minor problem was. In between times she stood at his side, and people talked to her almost as much as to him. He could see in the subtle change of their demeanour towards her that something had happened. She was no longer Teddy Morland's scandalously young wife. She was Mrs Edward Morland, mistress of Morland Place.

The measles outbreak spread among the miners' families, but with quarantine imposed and the schools locally closed, it was contained, and overall only two villages and a few outlying cottages suffered. Many physicians were of the opinion that it was no bad thing for children to catch it, saving them from a worse infection later in life, though it could be serious even in childhood, with deafness and epilepsy possible side-effects. But there were only three fatalities: an old man, a former miner, in Kelfield, a very young baby in Riccall, and a boy from Moor End who succumbed to secondary pneumonia.

The miners began to drift back to work in October, those in Yorkshire accepting a seven-and-a-half-hour day. In the north-east, Scotland and South Wales a longer day and lower wages were imposed, but as the cold weather set in in November and hardships increased, the last of the strike crumbled, and by December all the coalfields were working again. And in the new parliamentary session, in January 1927, the government introduced a Trade Dispute Bill, which would make general strikes and sympathetic strikes illegal. They were determined the country would not be held to ransom again.

'I've been thinking,' Emma said to Kit.

'Oho,' said Kit. 'I thought that was what our entire lives were dedicated to avoiding.'

They were sitting one at either end of a deep sofa in the hall of Endercott Place, the Northamptonshire mansion of Lord and Lady Endercott, who were hosting a hunting weekend. Endercott was an Elizabethan pile and the hall was a vast, vaulted affair, but their hosts were generous with fires, and in one of the high-backed settles, drawn up in a hollow square around the inglenook, with what looked like an entire tree burning under the chimney, it was possible to feel quite comfortable, even in February. The room was full of people, chatting, laughing, relating their day's experiences. The sofas were much in demand, and it was thanks to Kit, who hadn't hunted and had secured one before the rush, that they had the whole of one to themselves.

Their hosts were also generous in the matter of tea, and there were five kinds of sandwich and four kinds of cake, to say nothing of toast with jam or gentleman's relish, and dish after dish of hot buttered muffins. Emma had been out on a borrowed horse, and had given herself a good appetite. She had eaten so lavishly of the muffins she was afraid she would spoil her dinner, but when the footman came past again with a plate of Battenberg cake, of which she was particularly fond, she could not resist.

'We must have Battenberg cake at Walcote House,' she

diverted herself. 'It will have to be the defining question when hiring a cook.'

Kit eyed her with interest. 'Are you fattening yourself up for the wedding? I only ask because if I'm to carry you over the threshold I need to know what I'm in for.'

Emma gave him a cold look. 'I notice that you ate a great deal of tea yourself, despite not having hunted today. Incidentally, on that subject, I thought one of the things you wanted to do after we were married was to entertain at Walcote House. I'm sure hunting was specifically mentioned.'

'I saw the nag Jimmy Endercott was proposing to lend me, and didn't care to risk my neck on it,' Kit said. 'I suppose it had four legs, but I wouldn't swear they were all the same length. I shall hunt all right, when I have horses of my own.'

'Oh, well that's all right, then,' Emma said. 'I was worried that you were having second thoughts.'

'You look magnificent on a horse, by the way,' Kit said.

'I learned to ride at Morland Place.'

There was a moment of silence as she thought of Henrietta. Morland Place would not be the same without her.

'You were saying that you'd been thinking,' Kit prompted her, after a moment.

'Oh, yes. It's something I've been considering for a while – ever since the General Strike, really. You remember when we went to rescue that lorry driver in the East End? It was the first time I'd seen how those people really lived. Of course, one knows there are poor people, but until one sees for oneself . . . The conditions were simply appalling. I haven't been able to get it out of my mind. The houses were like rotting carcasses – and the smell . . .' She shuddered. 'Anyway, I've decided I'd like to do something about it.'

'There are charities, I believe,' Kit said diffidently.

She shook her head. 'Since the war ended, I've just gone along doing empty things and simply trying not to think.'

'We've all done that,' he said kindly.

'I know; and perhaps we had to, for a bit. But ever since we became engaged, I've been asking myself, what was it all *for*? I remember someone saying we were fighting to make a land fit for heroes, but during the strike I drove through streets of houses that weren't fit for animals. Well, I have money, and the thing I know about is houses. I buy them and make them modern and smart for rich Americans. Why can't I buy up horrible slums and make them into decent flats for poor people? What do you think?'

Kit did not want to be made to feel uncomfortable. There had been so many times that Oliver had twitted him about giving up surgery and wasting his life on frivolity, but he had taken a vow when the war ended that he would never think seriously about anything ever again. And his life rested in any case on such fragile supports that he didn't want to contemplate the future or risk changing the past.

But he had asked Emma to marry him and, as his wife, she deserved his support, even if it disturbed his comfort. So he thought about it seriously, and said, 'I think it will use up an awful lot of money. Remember, there won't be any profit at the other end of the process.'

'I don't want to do it for profit,' she said.

'I know, old thing, but if there's no profit, it means the money you lay out isn't being replaced. Your fortune will get used up and then you won't be able to carry on.'

'Of course, the financial side of it will have to be gone over very carefully,' she said.

'You'll have to speak to Bracey. That will be fun,' said Kit. He and Emma by chance had the same man of business, so of course Kit knew him well. 'I can imagine how pleased he will be that you want to throw away your fortune on paupers.'

'But I shan't,' Emma said. 'To begin with, these houses won't be for paupers, but for the working poor. They won't be almshouses – the tenants will pay a rent, so there will be some money coming in, and the buildings themselves will have value. So it isn't throwing money away. And I won't use all my fortune that way, only a bit of it.'

Kit nodded. 'Well, if it's what you want to do, I wouldn't try to stop you. You shall do as you please with your own money, and if Bracey comes the ugly, I shall sit on him. I shall miss our little venture, though – I've enjoyed working on the apartments with you. Somehow I think Weston's Rents, earnest and worthy though they may be, won't be half as enjoyable.'

'Oh, but I shall still do the other sort,' Emma said. 'It's fun, and they make a nice profit that I can put into the new scheme. It might even turn out that the one finances the other.'

'Clever girl,' said Kit.

'And you know,' she said, 'I think you'll get quite wrapped up in the other thing once you start. Designing economical and rational housing for the poor will be quite an exercise. I shall want your brain. You're so good at seeing how to fit things into spaces.'

'You shall have my brain, future Countess Westhoven. Well, we must talk to Bracey and see what's the best way to go about it. I imagine he will recommend setting up a trust – I believe there are tax advantages to be had from that.'

She smiled. 'You pretend to be such an ass, but you understand an awful lot more about this sort of thing than you let on.'

'Playing the giddy goat is my hobby. It doesn't mean I am one. What shall you call it?'

'The trust? Well, if you are going to help me, perhaps it should be the Westhoven Foundation.'

He wrinkled his nose. 'Too cumbersome. It's your money, so it should be the Weston whatever, anyway.'

'I suppose, since my money came from my father, that would be fair. The Weston Trust. If you're sure you don't mind?'

He reached out and took her hand. 'You know, just talking about this has given you colour in your cheeks. It really matters to you, doesn't it?'

She nodded. 'I shall feel better about everything if I am helping someone else, not just frittering my life away.'

'And yet you fritter so prettily. Prettily and wittily. That will be much missed by all.'

'Oh, but I still mean to fritter as well. I still want to see our friends and have fun and dance and—'

'And frivol,' he concluded for her. 'Then you certainly have my full approval. Frivolity and good works – a heady brew. I feel drunk just thinking about it.'

'Ass!' she said affectionately.

Teddy summoned Julian and Miss Husthwaite to the steward's room one evening. They attended, found him seated behind the big desk, and stood before him, Miss Husthwaite feeling absurdly as though they had been called up before the headmaster for ragging in the dorm. This impression was increased because, after his opening words, 'I've finished reading Father Palgrave's book', he lapsed into silence, and stared at them across the desk with a thoughtful frown.

They had finished everything they wanted to do by the end of January, and Miss Husthwaite had handed the neatly typed manuscript to her employer for his approval, after which it had disappeared from her sight and nothing more had been said. Now it was mid-March: outside, the bare trees were being swayed by bitter north winds, and there had been another shower of snow last night, dappling the earth brown and white. Miss Husthwaite was a chilly creature, and found it hard to get warm enough to sleep at night. But the sudden cold might at least kill the flu outbreak, which had struck the north in the unusually mild and damp weather of early March. And the farmers said it was good for the fruit trees.

Miss Husthwaite had time for all these thoughts as

261

Mr Morland stared blankly into space. She ought not to have been surprised that it had taken him six weeks to read the book. She had worked with him for several years now and she knew he was a slow reader. But she had invested so much of herself in the book that she was naturally nervous. She felt, she amended, as if she were a parent called before the headmaster on account of some grave misdemeanour of a cherished child.

There was a fine big fire under the chimney, and a tangle of five dogs had settled themselves there, migrating from the Great Hall where they usually lay, because there were fewer draughts in the steward's room. Every now and then the living blanket heaved about and fell into a new pattern as one dog or another got too hot or wanted to be hotter. One of these convulsions took place now, accompanied by some sighing and one enormous yawn that ended in a whine, and the sound seemed to wake Teddy from his reverie. He met their eyes solemnly. 'I don't know what to say,' he said.

It didn't sound promising. Miss Husthwaite and Julian exchanged a nervous glance. 'I hope you don't think we compromised the integrity of the original,' she said.

'We felt the extra material helped to create a context,' Julian chipped in. 'But it can, of course, easily be removed if you think it wrong.' Not easily, thought Miss Husthwaite. 'The immense power of the original writing,' Julian went on, 'moved us so profoundly that—'

Teddy realised at last that they thought he was disapproving. His eyes widened and he started to smile. 'Good heavens! Don't take me wrongly. I think the book is ripping! I've never read anything like it. I can tell you, there were times when I was in tears – and the maps and historical stuff are nothing but a help. I can see you've worked damned hard on all that, and it certainly made my mind clearer about certain things. I wouldn't have understood it half so well

262

without your extra bits. As it is – well, I think it ought to be read by every schoolchild in the land!'

Miss Husthwaite felt weak with relief. Her child, approved by the head! Julian threw her a delighted look.

'What we have to decide now is what to do about it,' Teddy said. He stood up and came from behind the desk. A dog's head raised itself from the jumble by the fire, assessed the likelihood of a walk, and subsided again. Teddy paced up and down a bit, which always helped him think. 'I do believe the book ought to be published – not just for poor Father Palgrave's sake, but because it's damned good. The whole nation ought to have a chance to read it. Oh, please, sit, sit.'

Julian and Miss Husthwaite sat down, which gave Teddy more room to pace. 'I was prepared to have it privately printed,' he said, 'as a memorial, and for poor little Laura's sake, since she has nothing else of her father's. But it occurs to me – I don't know a great deal about these things but if it were published in the regular way, by a proper publisher, it might make some money, which could be set aside for her. What do you think? *Do* books make money? I suppose publishers must make a profit somewhere or they wouldn't exist.'

'Yes, indeed,' Julian answered for them both. 'Books can make quite a pleasant amount of money, if they sell enough copies. Some writers make a decent living, and some, I believe, are even well-to-do.'

'The writers, eh?' Teddy said, another snag occurring to him. 'Well, in this case, that's you two – at least as far as the extra bits go.'

Julian lifted his hands. 'Please – you mustn't think of it. Miss Husthwaite and I would not wish to profit in any way. This has been a work of love, and a tribute to Palgrave's talent and his suffering. If the book were published, we should only wish our names to appear somewhere, as appropriate. Any financial benefit ought to go to the child.'

'I agree,' said Miss Husthwaite. 'We have enjoyed doing it so much, but the original does not belong to us and our work wouldn't have existed without it.'

Teddy looked pleased. 'It's very good of you to put it like that. And it clears the way nicely for me to find a publisher. I suppose London is the place for that. Julian, you must know a publisher or two?'

'Those I know are academic and scholarly publishers. I think to reach as many people as possible, this book should be looked at by a general publisher, who will put it onto a wider market.'

Teddy nodded. 'Yes, I see. Then perhaps I should take it to London, and consult with our friends there. If Cousin Venetia and Oliver don't know, they will know who to ask.' He seemed pleased with his decision. 'Yes, I think I should go myself and see what I can do.'

To Amy, afterwards, he said, 'March is a good month to go to London, not too crowded. Wouldn't you like to have a little trip, spend a few weeks there?'

Amy looked pleased. She was enjoying her new role as mistress of Morland Place, but there was no doubt it had been a strain. A few weeks away would be just the thing to restore her. 'I should like it very much,' she said. 'But we have engagements for the next couple of weeks, and the party coming to stay on the twenty-sixth and twenty-seventh.'

'Well, April's just as good as March,' Teddy said cheerfully. 'Nicer, in fact. The new shows will be on. And there's little Emma Weston's wedding. We might go for the whole month, or a bit more if we're enjoying it.'

'But can we leave everything here?'

'Of course,' Teddy said blithely. When he had a plan he could never bear any objections to it. 'Jessie and Bertie will keep an eye on things. What a good thing it's turned out that they settled near us.'

*   *   *

Molly and Vivian Blake had settled into a pleasant routine of seeing each other on Saturday evenings and Sunday afternoons, and occasionally on a weekday evening as well. Sometimes he had to go to literary dinners, or dine with board members or other important people, or take a writer or agent out to dinner on the Saturday; sometimes he was called to spend the Saturday-to-Monday at his uncle's country house; and sometimes he had to go to Edinburgh to Dorcas Overstreet's Scottish headquarters there. And once a month Molly went to see Helen and Jack on a Sunday. These disruptions to the routine happened just often enough to make Molly realise how much she missed seeing him

Usually on a Saturday night they would go out to supper at one of the little places that were springing up everywhere in Bloomsbury or Soho or in the streets behind Oxford Street. Molly did not mind that he did not suggest taking her to expensive restaurants, though he was obviously well-to-do. She hadn't the clothes for expensive places; besides, she enjoyed the intimacy of the little restaurants, which generally had a candle stuck in a bottle on the table, an illumination she felt did more for her looks than bright lights. Sometimes they went to the theatre or a concert instead; and now and then there would be a gathering in her house, and they would spend the evening in the basement wrangling over art and politics with the always voluble members of the household. She knew Blake had a flat of his own in Belgravia – in Wilton Row – but she had never been there, of course. That would have been quite improper.

On Sundays they would generally go to a museum, or the zoo, or an exhibition or, if the weather was fine, for a walk in one of the parks. Whatever they did on a Sunday, it was merely the means to a conversation. She loved talking to him, and they never seemed to come to an end of things to say.

One Sunday at Helen and Jack's she mentioned missing

her Sunday with him, and Helen said, 'Why not bring him here, then? We'd love to meet him.'

Molly was grateful for the kindness, but it was a long while before she got up the courage to ask him. It seemed something too intimate; an imposition. She loved her sister, and Jack, and the children, but there was no reason to suppose he would feel the same. He worked hard and long hours, and might think his free time was too precious to waste on other people's relatives.

But when her Sunday in March was looming, and she reminded him that she would not be able to see him at the weekend, he looked disappointed and said, 'I'd forgotten it was this Sunday. I haven't anything else planned. I shall feel very much at a loss – I do so enjoy our Sundays.'

And so, very cautiously, she said, 'Of course, you could come with me, but I expect you'd find it rather a bore.'

'From what you've told me of your sister and her husband, I can't believe they could be boring if they tried. But it's a family occasion. I should be intruding.'

'No, no,' Molly said eagerly. 'Helen's often said how much she'd like to meet you.' And then, feeling that was probably too eager, she added, 'They love company. They're very sociable. And I know you'd find Jack interesting. There aren't so many flyers who served all through the war.'

Blake laughed. 'Trying to find me a new author, eh? Thank you for that. But I'd like to meet your family anyway, with or without a book attached.'

So it was arranged. They met at the station on Sunday morning and travelled down by electric train, and Jack met them at the station in his motor-car, with Basil bouncing on the back seat.

'I made Daddy bring me. I knew you'd want to see me first,' he said confidently. 'I've made a Fokker Dr.1 out of balsawood. I'll show it to you when we get home. It's a triplane like the Red Baron's in the war. I'm going to paint it red when I get my pocket money to buy the paint. Daddy flew a Camel in the war. We have a gardener, Mr Orris, with a wooden leg. He takes it off when he has his tea in the potting shed. You can see through the little window if you stand on the wheelbarrow. He's at home now, but if you come on Saturday next time I'll show you. He smokes Wild Woodbines. Daddy smokes Ogden's so I can have the cards. They're doing Association Football team captains. There's forty-four in the set and I've got thirty-nine so far. If you smoke Player's, could I have the card? They're doing warships and I can swap them at school. There's a boy at school has two white mice and he's teaching them to dance. If you sit in the back with me I can show you my school – we go right past it.'

'*I'll* go in the back,' Molly said. 'Mr Blake didn't come here for your benefit.'

'I bet he'd sooner talk to me,' Basil said. 'Grown-ups are such dull talkers. Except you, a bit,' he said generously, 'because you say funny things sometimes. But you aren't a proper grown-up, not really, because you're not married like Mummy and Daddy and everyone.'

Jack was holding his head in his hands, but Vivian Blake was laughing as he took the front seat next to him. Molly did her best to keep Basil occupied in the back to allow Jack and Blake to get to know each other. They seemed to get on straight away, and Molly thought afterwards it was probably as much Basil's doing, in breaking the ice, as anything, and felt he deserved a tip for it when she left.

The whole day went very well. Blake seemed to like Helen, and was impressed when he learned that she had been a flyer too. Conversation ran smoothly between the adults, Blake approved of the sherry, and didn't seem put out when the children came downstairs again for luncheon. Barbara was shy, and would only give her name with eyes firmly downcast, but Michael was quite equal to taking the attention away from Basil, and secured a promise that the visitor would look at his kite after lunch.

The meal went well – the roast beef was rare and the Yorkshire pudding crisp, and the plum pie made with bottled plums produced a row of stones for which Blake proved to have a more enterprising rhyme than the usual 'Tinker, Tailor'. His was 'Banker, lawyer, general, admiral, publisher, scientist, archbishop, MP.' He said it was made up of the things he had understood as a child it would be acceptable for him to do.

Helen laughed. 'Nothing like instilling ambition in children!'

'In truth,' he said, 'there was never much chance I should escape "publisher". It's a good job it turned out to be what I wanted to do anyway.'

Basil liked the rhyme, but insisted that airman ought to be in there somewhere, and since he hadn't much idea what an archbishop was, he substituted airman for that. Molly said it worked better that way. 'More euphonious.'

After lunch, as it was fine, Helen suggested a walk. Michael ran for his kite, and they went to the common to try it out. The male half of the party being thus happily occupied, with Barbara as usual standing near and watching Basil with hero-worshipping eyes, Helen was able to link arms with Molly and say, 'I like your friend very much. I'm glad you brought him. It took you long enough.'

'I was a bit worried about asking him. It seemed like too much intimacy being thrust on him too soon.'

'He could always have said no.'

'Far too polite.'

'I suppose so. But you've been going out together for – what – almost a year now?'

'Ten months.'

'That's almost a year in my book. It isn't so soon, really, is it?'

'I don't know.' Molly sighed. 'I do like him awfully, and we have such nice times together. I never tire of talking to him. But I can't tell if he likes me or not – you know what I mean.'

'I know.'

'If we're just going to be friends for ever, well, I'll accept that, but I would like to know.'

'Because you like him a bit more than that?'

'Yes,' Molly said. 'You know I always used to say the person I was supposed to marry got killed in the war? When I met him I thought I was wrong, but now I'm wondering whether I was right after all.'

Helen squeezed her arm. 'Give him time. Men are like that – awfully slow to see what's under their own noses. Look how long it was before Jack realised he was in love with me.'

'Was it?'

'Years and years. In the end I had to tell him so myself. He *would* run about after these silly, frilly, empty-headed things that clucked like chickens and made big eyes at him and called him a hero. I was just sensible Miss Ormerod, his *friend*.'

'Oh dear. That sounds like me again. What did you do?'

'Made him see what it would be like not to have a rational woman for a wife.' She smiled. 'And then I told him I never wanted to see him again. What you might call a beneficial shock.'

'So you won him by threats,' Molly said.

'Yes. But it wouldn't have worked any earlier. I knew that was the moment. You'll have to choose yours just as carefully. Be patient, dear. Important things can't be rushed.'

On the train going back to London, an unusual silence fell between them. It was not awkward or unfriendly – just that each of them was thinking about something at the same moment. Finally, Blake said, 'Do you mind if I smoke?'

'Don't forget to save the card for Basil,' Molly said.

He smiled. 'I'll bet that youngster is a handful. And yet they're the ones who often go furthest. Wouldn't it be interesting to wind the clock on fifteen or twenty years and see how people turn out?'

'*Very* interesting,' Molly said. In ten years she'd be nearly forty. Ah, me, how fleeting is life.

'I did enjoy meeting your family,' he said. 'Helen's lovely, and Jack is so interesting. There must be a book in him somewhere, with all he experienced during the war.'

'Did you ask him?'

'I did, while we were looking at the garden. He laughed. But I shall keep it in mind. People sometimes come round to it. And the nicest thing, I think,' he concluded, 'was to see how well suited they are – Helen and Jack. They are obviously in such harmony with each other.'

'Similarity of interests,' Molly said.

'I expect that helps a lot,' he said, lighting his cigarette. They had the compartment to themselves. Outside it was almost dark, and the suburban terraces of identical Edwardian villas dashed past, showing their modest lights. Inside, the fire would be bright, men would be lighting their pipes and women getting out their knitting, the children lying on the floor, Mary with her book and Tom with his Meccano, and perhaps the wireless would be on, while the ghost of the roast beef and cabbage faded gently from the air. Domestic bliss seemed so easily attainable for some, so difficult and distant for others.

'There is something I've been meaning to ask you,' Blake said, and a slight diffidence in his voice made Molly look up with a suddenly accelerating heart. 'Before I go on,' he said, 'I have to tell you that it's rather a delicate question, so I want you to promise that you'll say no if you want to, without being afraid you'll upset me. I *hope* I haven't mistaken your feelings, but in case I have, I don't want it to spoil our friendship. So will you be quite honest with me about it?'

'Yes, of course,' Molly said. She couldn't help thinking this was a very odd way of going about making love.

'Thank you,' he said. 'Well, the fact of the matter is that I have felt for some time that you aren't really enjoying your job at the newspaper – that it isn't giving you the chance to use your abilities. It happens that one of our junior editors is leaving at the end of April. So my question is, would you like to have his job? Would you like to change careers and come and join us at Dorcas Overstreet?'

'As a junior editor?' Even to her, Molly's voice sounded faint. She hoped it did not sound disappointed.

'Book editing is different from what you've been doing at the newspaper, but I think – I'm sure – you'll find it more interesting. And if you have a talent for it – which I believe you have – you could make a satisfying career of it. Naturally you'll have to learn the ropes at first, but I can promise you promotion in time, with the prospect of a stable of your own authors and the freedom to develop them as you think fit. *And*,' he concluded, as though it were the clinching argument, 'there'll be nothing to stop you carrying on with your writing, and when you do complete your first novel, you'll be in the ideal position to get it published.'

Molly laughed. 'And that's what you wanted to ask me?'

He looked puzzled. 'Yes. Was I wrong to bring it up? If you are happy in journalism, you have only to say. I haven't offended you?'

'No – how could you? I was only surprised you thought it a delicate question, or that I might say no. Of *course* I'd like to join your firm. From hearing you talk, I'm convinced I'll be happier in the world of books.'

'Then – shall we shake hands on it?' he said. 'I must tell you that by bringing you in, I'm hoping to shake things up just a little. You will be the first female editor Dorcas Overstreet has ever had. I expect to have a little trouble getting the appointment past the board – but don't worry,

I shall prevail. I know two of them will be on my side from the start, and my uncle will trust my judgement. He's not a bad old boy. You'll have to meet him at some point.'

'Well, you've met my family.'

'Mine's a little less lively,' he admitted. 'But to the job: you may have to go quietly at first, until they get over the shock of having a female about the place, but once you're settled in I expect you to start bringing in your own writers, creating your own list, helping me to take the firm in new directions. You have just the sort of lively brain we need.'

So that's what you wanted me for, she thought. My brain. Ah, well. She shook herself sternly and told herself not to be foolish. Here she was on the brink of a new career – which she was certain would be much more interesting. And she still had his friendship. She had lost nothing, so there was absolutely no reason for her to feel disappointed. Long ago she had decided marriage would not be for her, so all she had to do was to go back to that way of thinking, count her blessings, and be happy in her lot.

'I'm flattered that you asked me,' she said. 'And I can't tell you how much I'm looking forward to it.'

'I'm so pleased you said yes,' he said, his blue eyes alight with eagerness. 'And, by the way, what did you think of that collection of poems I left with you last week? We're thinking of publishing them, but I'm not entirely convinced. I'd like your opinion.'

The new Molly kept herself firmly from thinking about the blue eyes, and gave her opinion dispassionately.

CHAPTER THIRTEEN

Venetia was having a busy time in the early months of 1927, which was just as well, for losing her oldest and dearest friend, Henrietta, affected her deeply. So she was glad to help Emma arrange her wedding. She had been left as one of Emma's guardians when Tommy Weston died, and had brought her out. And Kit – who was a distant cousin of her brother-in-law Charlie Du Cane – had come under her wing during the war, staying with her whenever he was on leave, and becoming such a close friend to Oliver they were like brothers. Kit's mother had died when he was fourteen and he had never got on with his stepmother. His father had died just before the war began and his brother was killed at Armentières in 1916, so Kit was as much an orphan as Emma, and Venetia had played a role in both their lives.

'It seems you are to be mother and mother-in-law simultaneously to both bride and groom,' Oliver said. 'I hope you won't buckle under the weight of contradictions.'

'I'm fond of them both, and they're very well suited,' Venetia retorted. 'I see no contradictions in that.'

Kit was determined to invite 'everyone' to the wedding, which meant not only all their friends but as many relatives as could be rounded up. His expansive generosity was not only motivated by a liking of crowds, but by the desire that Emma should not be seen as an orphan without attachments to the world. In fact, though her parents were dead, she had

had five half-brothers and -sisters, the product of her father's first marriage. The eldest, Fanny, with whom Emma had often stayed in childhood, had died of appendicitis in 1917, and Alfred had been killed in Palestine, while the other brother, Thomas, had emigrated to South Africa. But Ada and Octavia were still alive, and there were plenty of nephews and nieces to call in.

And, of course, there were the Morlands. Some of the happiest times in her life had been her holidays at Morland Place, and the fact that her great-grandmother had been sister to Jessie's great-grandfather meant they were cousins of a sort. With Teddy and Amy, Jessie and Bertie, Jack and Helen and Molly on her side of the church, as well as her half-sisters and nephews and nieces, she would be adequately covered. She insisted, therefore, that Kit should have Venetia, Oliver and Verena, Violet and Holkam and Eddie and Sarah on his 'side', otherwise he would have no relatives at all.

'Holkam won't like it,' Oliver said to his mother. 'He won't think it proper to swap relatives like cigarette cards – and it's only Uncle Charlie who's a blood relative of any degree.'

'Holkam may sit where he likes,' Venetia said sternly. 'Violet shall sit with us. This is *my* wedding, and I shall decide the seating plan.'

Oliver grinned. '*Your* wedding, is it? Well, you're still as lovely as a bride to me.'

'You talk such nonsense! Go away and stop bothering me.'

The wedding was not the only thing that took her away from her research. Emma's desire to do something about the housing for the poor naturally brought her to Venetia for help and advice. Venetia had long been interested in the connection between housing and ill-health in the poor, and had been involved in similar work years before with Octavia Hill. She was delighted that Emma's interests had taken this new turn, praised her for wanting to do good with her father's money. At the moment the main business was setting up the trust, which was lawyers' work, but it did not stop Emma and Venetia from discussing living spaces and essential fitments when they were not discussing the wedding breakfast and seating plans.

There was another demand on Venetia's time. The Prime Minister, Stanley Baldwin, had announced in January that he intended to bring a Representation of the People Bill, which would give the vote to women on equal terms with men, reducing their voting age to twenty-one. Her indefatigable friend Millicent Fawcett at once launched a new campaign. The Bill would come before Parliament in 1928, which gave them a year to ensure that the vote would go the right way. She came to Venetia to enlist her help in winning over the members of the House of Lords. So Venetia had to find time to visit various peers, present the arguments, confirm those in favour, steady the waverers and attack the antis. It was rather weary work – she had done it all so many times before – but in the face of Millie's fresh determination and apparently endless energy, she could not refuse to do her part.

And then there was Verena's pregnancy. She was due to deliver in May – one of the reasons Emma and Kit had decided on April for the wedding. Her early discomfort had passed, and everything seemed to be going well, but Venetia was never complacent, and kept a close eye on her daughter-in-law. She found she was looking forward to the new baby to an absurd degree. She was very fond of Oliver's first-born, named John after his grandfather, and now bearing his grandfather's cadet title. Venetia as often referred to the two-year-old as Hazelmere as by his given name. 'I can't get used to "John",' she told Oliver. 'I never called your father that – and I must say little Hazelmere is the image of him.'

With the new baby coming, one question arose that Venetia did not want to ask: would Oliver and Verena want to move? At the moment, Oliver was continuing with his surgical work and not behaving very like an earl, but with two children, and having settled into his title, might he not want something bigger, more suited to entertaining? Venetia had no wish to hold him back, but she would miss them terribly if they moved out.

It had been a happy arrangement, and not just for the pleasure of having another doctor to talk to: he made such fun for her. He was interested in all the new ideas, and it kept her young. He had taken lately to having 'talking dinners', where he invited a select group of friends around to discuss the topics of the day.

They discussed Dr Serge Voronoff's work in treating senescence with 'monkey glands' – actually thin slices of testicular tissue from chimpanzees and baboons implanted inside the patient's scrotum. In his book, Voronoff claimed the treatment improved the sex drive, the memory and concentration, and through strengthening the muscles around the eye could relieve the patient of the need to wear glasses. He speculated that it could benefit sufferers from dementia praecox, and even prolong life. Oliver's gathering discussed not only whether prolongation of life was likely, but if it was desirable. If it were possible for man to live to a hundred and fifty, what would be the consequences?

They discussed the nature of the atom, and relativity, and whether the universe was governed by abstract mathematics or whether there was an intelligence behind it. Was it finite or unbounded? If space was curved, was time also curved? What were stars actually made of?

They discussed the new fad for banting and diets: the lettuce diet, the lemon-juice diet, the red and white diet, the carbohydrate diet. Was there any scientific value in any of it? To what degree was health governed by food – not just having enough of it, but the kind of food that was eaten? The current fashions made young women want to be svelte, but was that a good thing or a bad thing? Did cigarettes keep you slim? Did they relieve constipation?

His medical gatherings discussed the work done in Toronto in treating diabetes with laboratory-prepared insulin; and the current theory that disease was caused by 'septic foci' within the body, so that removing the adenoids and tonsils from children and the caecum and appendix from adults while they were still healthy could pre-empt infections.

It was all fascinating to Venetia, and she was grateful to Oliver. The only point on which she disagreed with him was over the wireless. When Oliver had brought his first crystal set home, Venetia had banished it to his own quarters because of the hideous noises he could make with it – howlings and shriekings he seemed to enjoy more than the proper broadcasts. But things had become more serious. All-electric radios, which worked from the mains electricity, had just come out, making 'tuning' a simpler matter. The new sets coincided with the change of the British Broadcasting Company to the British Broadcasting Corporation by Royal Charter on the 1st of January – a move designed to ensure its independence from government coercion. John Reith had learned an important lesson during the General Strike. And the previous summer, the BBC had moved its technical operation from Chelmsford to a new transmitter at Daventry, with which it could reach almost every part of the kingdom. The wireless was now becoming an important part of every Briton's life.

In honour of this dawn of a new age in broadcasting, Oliver had splashed out on a new set, the Brunswick-Panatrope electric radiogramophone, which not only received radio broadcasts but played gramophone records. It was large and solid as a sideboard, set into a mahogany cabinet, and emitted its sounds by loudspeaker, so that you did not have to put on earphones. Oliver was thrilled with it, especially with how loudly it could be made to play: at full volume it made the chandeliers tinkle.

Venetia hated it, and absolutely refused to have it in the

drawing-room. 'Too, too horrid and vulgar! You can't, you simply can't have it anywhere anyone might see it.'

'But, Mum, look how handsome!' he protested. 'Nice mahogany veneer, brass hinges on the lid, all this curlicue nonsense over the loudspeaker bit.'

'It looks like pokerwork!'

'No, no, like filigree! Perfectly rococo.'

'It cannot stay in this room. If you must have it, you will have to take it upstairs to your own room.'

'You can't think how much it cost,' Oliver complained, 'and to have it banished like a naughty child . . . I was going to buy all the new recordings, too – dance bands and crooners – Al Bowlly and Gene Austin, "When my sugar walks down the street",' he sang.

Venetia put her hands to her ears. 'Stop that! I tell you once for all, Oliver, I will not have that thing in my drawing-room.'

He sighed. 'Then I suppose I shall just have to buy a house of my own to keep it in.'

Venetia whitened. 'You must, of course, do as you wish,' she said quietly, with a feeling of doom in her heart. 'You are quite old enough not to want to live with your mother – especially now you're a family man.'

He saw what he had done, and was contrite. 'No, no, I was only joking. Don't look like that, please! I like living here – Verena and I are perfectly happy. We don't want to leave.'

Venetia sighed. 'My dear boy, the last thing in the world I want to do is blackmail you. I've been thinking for some time that this house isn't really suitable for you, with a growing family.'

'It was all right for you and Papa when we were growing,' he said. 'And it's very convenient for Harley Street and the hospitals – for everything, really. Please don't give it another thought.'

'But I must,' Venetia said. 'You're the earl now, and you have a certain position to keep up. Sooner or later you will want something that reflects your status. In fact, getting Chelmsford House ready for Emma has made me think that it would be a good idea for you and Verena to take it over, rather than letting it again.'

She saw the idea did not immediately repulse him. 'Well, perhaps one day,' he began. 'It's not something to hurry into. And in any case,' he concluded briskly, 'if we did ever move somewhere else, you would come with us. You wouldn't want to stay here all alone; and we couldn't have little John growing up without your influence.' She was looking at him carefully, evidently believing he was only being kind. It hurt him to think she could believe she was not wanted, and as was his way when he was hurt, he made a joke of it. 'Chelmsford House is big enough to have a separate room entirely for the Brunswick. In fact, given the power of the loudspeakers, it might be as well for it to have an entire wing to itself.'

Now she smiled, though it still seemed a troubled smile. 'You foolish boy.'

He became serious. 'I enjoy living with you as much as I think you enjoy living with me. So that's settled, isn't it?'

'Very well,' she said. 'But now please ring and have that thing taken upstairs.'

'You're implacable. Very well, I'll comply – if you will just listen to one record. I won't make you listen to jazz,' he said, seeing her expression. 'I have a recording of Caruso singing "Vesti la giubba" from *Pagliacci*. Will you let me play you that?'

Venetia could only agree. She sat down, composed herself, and listened. At the end of it, Oliver looked at her earnestly and said, 'Well? Wasn't that magnificent? He's thought to be the greatest tenor the world has ever known, and you would never otherwise have had a chance to hear him.'

Venetia still thought the machine an abomination, and she

was sure that Caruso in life had not sounded like the hollow, disembodied voice coming from the box, as if he were singing upstairs in the bathroom. But she could see Oliver was genuinely enthused, and she loved her son, so she said, 'Quite remarkable.' And, trying really hard, 'It is a piece of history come to life.'

Which proved to be enough for Oliver, who meekly removed the offending machine, leaving Venetia to enjoy her drawing-room unsullied.

'I'm so pleased for you,' said Emma, when Molly had finished telling her about her new job. 'It sounds like just the thing.'

They were dining together in a small restaurant in Orchard Street – Emma reflected that it was one of the biggest changes since the war that single women could eat alone in restaurants without becoming *déclassé*. It still gave her a sense of freedom, remembering how things had been.

'And I'm very pleased about your new housing trust,' Molly said. 'Do you remember, towards the end of the war, how we talked about what we could do afterwards?'

'Yes, – you said we should do good together, with my money.'

'I was shameless about spending someone else's fortune, wasn't I? Golly, how impertinent! But I'm so glad it has come to fruition at last. With your position in society, as well as your fortune, you can do so much.'

'I hope you will help me,' Emma said. 'It would be fun to work on some designs together. You have a good eye, and you know what it is to live in a small space. I do think it's important to get as much in as possible, but without its feeling cramped and horrid.'

'I'd love to help,' Molly said, 'but I don't suppose our paths will cross very much once you're married.'

'Do you mean to drop me?'

'Not at all, but you and I will move in such different circles—'

'Now please don't begin that again. We lost touch once – and I know that was my fault, but I'm a changed person. I don't mean to lose touch with you again. I don't have so many real friends that I can afford to forget them.'

'Well, you know where to find me,' Molly said. 'And it was very nice of you to invite me to your wedding. I've never been to such a grand "do" before. Pop and Nina are in ecstasies over it, and Nina is already worrying about what I shall wear.'

'Isn't there anyone you would like to bring?' Emma said, fishing. 'Anyone you've brought to Mr Popovka for his approval?'

'No,' Molly said. 'That sort of thing is not for me. I leave it to you to do the romantic stuff.'

Emma was so busy, with setting up the trust, arranging the wedding, and dashing up to Lutterworth with Kit to oversee the renovations to Walcote House, that the time fled away in a blink, and she had no leisure to be nervous. In no time, she was having the final fitting for her wedding dress. She asked Violet to come with her, as being the one among her friends who knew the most about clothes.

Hemlines had gone up again that year, and even brides were wearing short dresses, but Emma felt that at thirty-one she ought to aim for a little more dignity. Bare legs in a wedding photograph, she thought, would strike an odd note in years to come. Her gown was simple, of cream silk, falling straight from the shoulder to hip level, where the dropped waistline was marked by a band of pearls and crystal beads. From that the softly fluted overskirt of chiffon hung into handkerchief points to just below the calf. The sleeves were bloused, and also of chiffon, with cuffs to match the waistband. The headdress was mitre-shaped, of stiffened organdie sewn all over with pearls, and from it hung the veil of silk illusion.

281

Violet sat holding Emma's dog, which she had called Alfie, and her own poodle Fifi, given to her at Christmas by the Prince of Wales, and watched wistfully, thinking of her own wedding so long ago. How differently marriage had turned out from what she had expected. But her wedding had been lovely . . .

'What will you do about jewels?' she asked, as the seamstress made one or two last tiny adjustments.

'I'm not going to wear any for the ceremony,' Emma said. 'The dress is too simple for that. But at the wedding breakfast I shall wear the sapphires your mother gave me, and Kit is giving me earrings to match as a bride-gift.'

Violet nodded approval, and as the seamstress stepped away, she stood up, putting the dogs down on the floor, reached into her handbag, and came across to place something in Emma's hand. 'When I got married,' she said, 'Jessie gave me a dear little brooch in the shape of a hand. I have it still.'

'I've seen you wear it,' Emma remembered.

'So I'd like you to have this, Emma, dear, and I shall wish, as Jessie wished for me, that you will be always happy.'

Emma unwrapped the black cloth from around a small brooch in the shape of a purple pansy, enamel set on gold, with a diamond stem.

'Pansies are for thoughts,' Violet said, 'and I hope it will make you think of me.'

Emma leaned over and kissed Violet's cheek. 'I don't need anything to remind me of you. But it's beautiful, and I shall cherish it always. Thank you.'

When all the fitting was done, they went out into the street where a car was waiting for them, to take them to lunch with the Prince of Wales at the Savoy. He admired the brooch, enquired in great and surprisingly informed detail about the wedding dress, and insisted on ordering champagne. He had brought his little white West Highland terrier with him, and the three dogs each had a bowl of chopped-up chicken in the corner behind the table.

The happy couple had departed, and most of the guests had gone. Oliver and Verena were to host an informal supper party for family members that evening. Violet had taken Verena home to rest before it; Holkam had gone to the House; Teddy and Amy had gone to their hotel to rest; Jessie and Bertie had taken Helen, Jack and Molly to their hotel to spend a little time together catching up on news. The latter three would go to their own homes that night, and Jessie and Bertie would go home first thing the next morning.

Which left Oliver and Venetia at Chelmsford House taking a last look around before going home to change. 'It was a nice wedding,' Oliver said. 'How did you like being "mother of the bride"? I've never seen Emma look better.'

'She was always a pretty girl,' Venetia said, 'but today she looked beautiful.'

'Sentimental!' Oliver teased. He looked around the great hall, with its black and white marble floor. 'You know, the old place isn't half bad. I expected it to be much more fusty, but I could imagine a person living here.'

'It was designed to be lived in,' Venetia said, 'unlike some old houses that were designed for show. It's seen its share of happiness and sadness over the years. My mother was born here, and practically imprisoned by her father, after he cast her mother out. He was terribly injured in a duel, poor thing, and went mad with pain, we think. But there were lots of happy times too. I wanted to have Violet's come-out here – the ballroom is so pretty – but there were tenants in at the time. I'm glad we could have Emma's wedding here.'

'It was nice of the Prince of Wales to look in,' Oliver said. 'Give Emma and Kit the royal seal of approval.'

Venetia glanced at him, not sure if he was being ironic or not. The royal cachet would have been conferred by the

Duke and Duchess of York, who were much closer acquaintances, but they were abroad on a long tour of Australasia. 'He was invited to the ceremony,' she said, 'but I suppose he was busy. Shall we go? We're getting in the way of the servants. And I must rest before this evening's party. I'm not used to standing for so long.'

Oliver linked arms with her and turned towards the door. 'Come along then, dear old thing. You know, your idea about living here isn't half bad. We'd all fit in nicely without tripping over each other, and I could play my radiogram in the ballroom to my heart's content.'

Venetia ignored the tease, and said, 'If you're really serious about moving, I think I would quite like the opportunity to live here, just once. I never have, though it's been my house since my mother died. And no-one's building these great houses any more. I'm afraid their day is passing.'

'Yes . . . Emma and her like are turning them all into apartments as fast as they can. We should catch hold of history's tail before it disappears,' Oliver said. 'I'll talk to Verena about it. And we should all come over one day and look at the place properly. I dare say there will be lots to do to make it quite comfortable. Should you like that?'

'Yes, indeed,' she said, and then, remembering, 'but don't call me "dear old thing".'

The motor-car fled up the road, which lately, with the passion for classification of the modern age, had been allocated the number A5, and even, here and there, bore a sign showing it. But the Romans had called it Watling Street, and had laid it die-straight across a forested and uncertain land, from the great beacon light at Richborough through London and St Albans and north-westwards all the way to the wild marches and the tribal lands of the Ordovices at Wroxeter.

Where tunics had swung and sandalled feet had beaten the causeway with their weirdly unrelenting rhythm, Kit and

Emma rolled in comfort on pneumatic tyres. They stopped in Stony Stratford for a rustic supper of bread and beef and beer at the Cock, an old coaching inn whose rivalry with its neighbour the Bull had led to such unrestrained boasting about their competing merits as to give rise to a figure of speech, cock and bull stories.

After Towcester there were no more towns, only scattered little villages to either side of the road. The landscape emptied, there was no moon, and Emma, who had taken over, drove through blackness under the starry wheel of the universe, her world reduced to the yellow pinpricks of lamps marking the windows of unseen cottages, and the little pool of light cast ahead on the road by her headlights. Here a great tree at the roadside would jump into being and dislimn again; there a cottage wall, a barn, an empty hay-wagon resting on its shafts. Kit, who had chatted until Stony Stratford and since then had lapsed into silence, roused himself from his torpor to point out the new transmitter at Daventry, an unlikely skeletal Eiffel Tower rearing against the background of stars; and then again to say, 'It's not far now. Better stop and let me take the wheel.'

They turned off down a narrow country road between hedges, and crept through a tightly sleeping village and a network of interconnecting, identical and unsignposted lanes, and at last came to a pair of gateposts, one of them missing its crowning stone ball, with the gates hospitably open. 'This is it,' said Kit. He sounded subdued. Emma was feeling very tired. For all its glory, it had been a long and draining day. The drive ran straight between tall trees. 'Chestnuts,' Kit said. 'Some of them want felling and replacing – they're too close to the road.'

'You know about trees,' she noted, sleepily amused.

'I grew up here,' he said. The house appeared, a very plain Georgian front faintly gleaming in the starlight, with a

285

muddle of outbuildings and chimneys behind it. 'Here at last,' he said.

As he pulled up before the steps, the door opened, a rectangle of yellow light, and the servants trooped down to line up and receive them: a small staff – extra would be hired as needed. In line stood butler, housekeeper, footman and two housemaids. The butler and housekeeper were survivors from Kit's father's day, the others were new, but Emma had met them all on previous visits. Emma's maid and Kit's man were also there, having come down by train with the luggage.

'Welcome, my lady, my lord,' said the butler, Wilson.

My lady, Emma thought. So it really was true.

'And, if I may be permitted,' Wilson went on, 'congratulations, my lord, and felicitations, my lady, on behalf of us all.'

'Thank you, Wilson,' Kit said.

'There are sandwiches in the library, my lady. Mrs Peatling has gone to bed, but if you should care for something hot—'

'Sandwiches will do very well,' Emma said. The wedding breakfast had been lavish, and the bread and beef had filled the gap. Besides, it was late.

'Very well, my lady. Your rooms are ready, and the water is hot if you should wish for it.' It was unnecessary for Wilson to add the last part, but he was clearly fascinated by the idea. One of the changes she and Kit had wrought at Walcote since his proposal was to improve the central-heating system and pipe hot water upstairs into two new bathrooms. Before that, hot water had been brought up in cans to wash-stands in the bedrooms, and baths were taken before the fire in the old manner for ladies, while gentlemen had the use of a bathroom at the end of a corridor where only cold water was available.

'How could you live like that?' Emma had asked.

Kit had shrugged. 'Remember, I haven't lived there for thirteen years. And not a great deal before that, what with school. Anyway, I don't think anyone who has been to an

286

English boarding school can ever be disconcerted by primitive living conditions. It's probably the prime reason we won the war.'

In the library – still shabby, but at least clean now – there was a fire lit (central heating could do only so much in these big rooms) and *foie gras* sandwiches, coffee and the drinks tray. Kit went straight to the latter and poured himself a large brandy and soda. 'Would you like something? Sherry? Or I can have wine brought up if you don't care for spirits.'

'No, thank you. Just coffee, to warm me up.' It was not very good – too weak and not hot enough. Emma could see Kit would have to school the staff in the art of coffee-making. They talked a little about the day, but Emma was sleepy – the coffee was too weak to change that – and Kit seemed either tired or out of sorts. When she had eaten enough, she said, 'I think I'll go up.'

'Oh. Very well,' Kit said. 'I'll – er – I'll be up in a while.'

Emma felt herself blushing with the implication. This was the point at which things got serious. She and Kit had been friends for years, but they had never so much as kissed in a romantic way. He was very easy about putting his arm round her or linking it with hers, holding her hand, or putting his head in her lap while lying on the grass at a picnic, and he was free with kisses, but they always landed on the cheek – just as he kissed the other females of their acquaintance.

Now all that was to change, and they were to engage in an intimacy that she knew about only in theory. She was afraid it would be embarrassing to begin with; she supposed that might account for Kit's descent into monosyllables. He was probably nervous too, and the thought comforted her, and gave her a fond, warm feeling for him. She would have liked to say, 'Don't worry, we'll work it out between us,' but it simply wasn't possible.

He stood up when she did, and as she hesitated, leaned forward and kissed her lightly on the lips, and smiled. 'Well,' he said, but the sentence didn't seem to be leading anywhere, so she smiled back, and retired.

Spencer woke her, rattling back the curtains. Emma stirred, squinted, put her arm over her eyes. She had a slight head-ache. 'What time is it?' she asked.

'Almost nine, my lady.' Well done, Spencer, Emma thought, getting the title right first time. 'Will you be going down for breakfast, or having it here?'

Emma sat up. 'Where is his lordship?'

'In his room, my lady, but I gather he is going down for breakfast.'

'Then I will too,' Emma said. 'Have we any aspirin?'

Kit was in the dining-room when she entered, reading the paper. He looked up, smiled, and said, 'I recommend the tea, if you can bear it. We really will have to do something about the coffee – it's like dishwater.'

'It's first on my list of things to attend to,' Emma said, and went to the sideboard. She was puzzled. She had expected him to make some comment about last night – about the fact that she had fallen asleep before he came up. She supposed he had been too gallant to wake her and had simply gone to sleep in his own room. Should she say anything? She served herself with tea, and then, discovering that she was hungry, eggs and bacon. She carried it to the table and sat cater-corner to him. He had sausages on his plate, and had gone back to the newspaper.

'I had a bit of a headache this morning,' she said, to get things going.

'Bad luck, old thing,' he said kindly. 'Would you like an aspirin?'

'Spencer had some. It's gone now. How do you feel?'

'Pretty well, considering what a long day we had yesterday.'

'I'm fine too, now the headache has gone.'

He put the paper aside and addressed his sausages, dabbing

them carefully with mustard. Our first breakfast together, she thought, and it felt odd – unreal. 'What would you like to do today?' he asked. 'I thought, if you cared for it, we might go to the farm and look it over. We could have lunch afterwards in Lutterworth, and then perhaps have a drive around the villages, show you the lie of the land. And tomorrow I thought we might go and have a look at some horses. The sooner we get ourselves mounted the better. There are a couple of point-to-points next month that it might be fun to enter. We'll do ourselves no end of good with the local people if we show an interest in the hunt.'

'Yes,' said Emma. 'That sounds good. I'd love to see the farm.' She felt she had to address the issue, however shy she felt about it. 'Um – Kit – about last night,' she began, feeling her cheeks instantly grow warm.

He looked at her and then away. 'Yes, I'm sorry,' he said. 'Funked it. Can't explain why. Sorry, old girl. Do better tonight.'

Emma was silent, knocked off balance. She was apologising for having fallen asleep – but it seemed he hadn't actually arrived.

He looked at her nervously. 'Friends?' he asked.

She didn't want him to feel bad about it. 'Of course,' she said. 'As a matter of fact, I think I was too tired to have – I mean, I was very tired.'

'It was a full day for both of us,' he said, sounding relieved. 'First time I've got married, as a matter of fact.'

'Me too,' Emma said. And then, because it was getting too awkward, 'Tell me about the farm. You only have the one, now, don't you?'

'No, there is another out at Kimcote, but most of the estate's income is from property.' He went into an explanation, and though Emma had heard most of it before, she listened willingly, glad to have got away from the awkward subject.

★　★　★

They dined that evening with neighbours, the Curtis-Bennets, in Kibworth. 'We just asked a few people,' Mrs Curtis-Bennet said. 'All neighbours and good friends of ours, and I'm sure of yours, too, very soon. I didn't want to overwhelm you on your first day, but of course everyone is *dying* to meet you, dear Lady Westhoven. We're all thrilled that you are opening up the house again. Things were very sad just after the war – so many dear people gone, houses closed, estates being sold. It seemed then as if the good old times were gone for ever. But things do seem to be getting back to normal, slowly. You and Kit will be *very* popular in the neighbourhood if you mean to entertain much, because we've all been quite dull these past few years.'

It was a dull evening, Emma thought – though perhaps she was suffering from a sense of anticlimax. They were all perfectly nice people, but she didn't feel she wanted to talk to them, or listen to their parochial chat. They did their best to include her, but inevitably they could only ask her questions about herself, which made it feel like an interrogation. Kit jumped in and rescued her from time to time, but he was engaged in conversations of his own. Most of these people had known him since childhood, and had known his parents and brother, so much of what they said was incomprehensible to her.

On their way home, Kit said, 'I'm sorry about that. I don't think you were enjoying yourself very much.'

'No, it's my fault. I should have made more of an effort – they are our neighbours, after all. It's just that I feel rather flat. Reaction, I suppose.'

'Oh, we'll soon remedy that,' he said.

When they got to the house he sent Wilson for champagne, had the carpet in the small sitting-room rolled up and the gramophone brought in, and put on dance-band records. Emma laughed a protest, but he bowed, offered his hand, and insisted that she danced. It was very nice, very soothing in a way, because it reminded her of their previous life together. She drank champagne and grew a little dizzy. They danced, and Kit clowned and joked until she ached with laughing. It was a lovely end to a disappointing evening. She went upstairs, with Kit saying he would follow shortly, but the champagne and dancing did their work and she fell asleep almost as soon as her head touched the pillow.

When she went down the next morning, Wilson told her his lordship had got up early and gone out, but would be back at ten to take her to see the horses that were for sale. So she breakfasted alone, wondering when they would, in fact, get to the embarrassing intimacy she had worried about. Kit came back cheerful, his usual self, and took her off to look at horses, and then to luncheon at a country inn, and then to look at Leicester Castle. In the evening they dined with hunting friends at Melton Mowbray and were back very late. Kit said he'd have one last drink in the library, and this time Emma stayed awake, but he did not come.

A pattern established itself. Emma was not unhappy. During the day Kit was his old self – affectionate, amusing, always good company – and they did interesting things, exploring the country, visiting, making plans. They didn't find horses to their liking, but he said there would be more available in May, when the hunters were let down, and people decided what they wanted to sell. 'We can come down again and pick up something then. It's important to get it right.'

She did wonder when they would finally get to the consummation, but she was not worried about it. She thought he was just a great deal more shy than she had supposed. His nervy, quicksilver clowning might well conceal a deeply sensitive and reserved nature.

On the Saturday they entertained, giving a dinner for neighbours and friends, with more young people coming later for dancing to gramophone records. It was a very jolly evening and went on very late, the young people dancing and drinking into the early hours, long after the more steady folk had gone home. It was rather like old times in London. When Emma finally admitted defeat and went to bed, there were still half a dozen young men who had settled in with Kit to drink and talk in the library until the sun came up. She did not even expect to see him that night.

But the next day, after church, when they were walking back in some very grateful sunshine, that cool, damp spring, she felt she ought to say something. Being in church again reminded her that, strictly speaking, they were no more married now than they had been on the morning of the wedding. It might be embarrassing – it certainly *would* be embarrassing – but as man and wife they ought to be able to talk to each other, surely, even about something as difficult as this. And perhaps it was making him unhappy, and she ought to show him she was interested in his well-being. So, as they reached the chestnut walk (yes, one or two of those trees really ought to come down) she slipped her hand through his arm, and said, 'Kit, I want to talk to you.'

'I thought you had been, all the way home,' he said. 'Someone who sounded very much like you, anyway.'

'Don't joke,' she said. 'I really think we ought to talk about what's happening – or, rather, I suppose I should say what's not happening.'

He groaned and pulled away from her, and went to swipe at the long grass with a stick he had picked up, boy-like, on the walk. 'Oh, Lord! I knew it was going to come up. I suppose we have to have it out. I'm sorry. I know I've let you down.'

'No, no, it's not that. But I do wonder – well, I'm bound to wonder, really . . . Is it something I've done? Or not done? If there's anything I can change . . .'

'No, no, it's not you. You're perfect,' he said, still with his back turned. 'It's me. I can't. I just can't.'

'I don't understand,' she said hesitantly. 'I thought you loved me.'

'I do. You can't think how much I love you. Goodness!'

'Then – can't we work it out together? I mean, I know it's new to both of us, and it might be difficult at first. Lord knows I worried about it before we married. But we're sensible people, and if we love each other we can solve any problem, can't we? Don't you think?'

He turned to face her, and met her eyes with a desperate, goaded look. 'You don't understand. I just can't do it. I thought I would be able to, but I can't.' He turned away again, put his hands over his face, rubbed his eyes miserably. Emma stood dumbfounded, not knowing what to think, what to say. 'If you want to leave me,' he said, muffled by his hands, 'I'll understand.'

She thought he meant now, to go back to the house alone. Then she caught his meaning. 'Divorce?' she said, shocked.

'No, not that – the other thing. Annulment. If the marriage isn't – you know – you can get an annulment. I won't oppose you. And there'd be no shame on you.'

But there would be on him, she thought. And it would be too horrible, exposing them to probing eyes and malicious tongues. 'Is that what you want? Do you want us to part?'

'God, no!' he said, turning to her again. His face looked drawn and old with misery. 'I do love you, Emma. I'm happy with you. I *want* to be married to you. But I can't expect you to put up with me if I – disappoint you.'

'But you don't,' she said hastily, unable to bear hurting him. 'I love being with you. And we're going to do so much together – this place, the trust, the apartments. I don't want to give all that up.'

'Then – do you mean – will you stay?'

'We're married,' she said firmly, taking his hands, 'and nothing's going to change that. I'm not going to leave you, unless you make me.'

'I'd never do that. I couldn't get on without you now.'

'Then that's settled,' she said.

'Friends?' he said.

'Friends,' she confirmed.

And they were – that was the best of it. Friendship was the best basis for marriage, a solid foundation, and everything else would follow in time. She turned him, put her hand through his arm, and resumed walking. His head was down, his gait was brittle; she felt his strain through her hand.

She squeezed his arm and said, 'Don't worry, it will all work out in the end. It's not a big thing, and I can wait. As long as we love each other, everything will be all right.'

CHAPTER FOURTEEN

At the end of May, Jack received a letter from someone at the Air Ministry, asking him to come and see him.

'It's signed W. S. Borthwick,' he said to Helen. 'Could that possibly be old Curly Borthwick? I probably mentioned him to you – we were in the same mess when I was stationed near Amiens.' He looked at the letter again, and handed it to Helen. 'If it is him, he probably just wants a chinwag.'

'It can't be that,' she said. 'Look, he says he has a proposition to put to you.'

'If it's Curly Borthwick, the proposition will only be that we slip out for a pint or two,' Jack said.

It was said humorously enough, but Helen knew he was still smarting a little. Just the previous week the newspapers had been full of the exploits of the winner of the Orteig Prize. The magnificent $25,000 had originally been offered by a New York hotelier in 1919 for the first non-stop flight in either direction between New York and Paris within five years; but though it had not been won in that time, Orteig had extended the offer in 1924, in view of the continuing improvement in aircraft design.

There had been an unhappy history of attempts: in 1926 in America two men had burned to death when their landing-gear collapsed on take-off and the aeroplane caught fire; earlier in 1927 two more were killed in a take-off accident, and two French aviators setting off from Paris disappeared over the Atlantic and had not been heard of since.

So when in the early morning of Friday, the 20th of May, a twenty-five-year-old former 'circus' flyer took off alone, in a single-engine, single-seater Wright Whirlwind monoplane from Roosevelt Field on Long Island, a similar fate had been feared for him.

It was not an auspicious start. The aeroplane was heavy with all the fuel needed for the 3,600-mile journey, and taking off downwind and in driving rain it only just cleared the trees and telephone wires at the end of the field. And flying solo for that distance was hugely hazardous: no-one to help keep you awake, no-one to crawl out onto the wings to free them from ice, no-one to navigate and keep a look-out for hazards. But at twenty past ten in the evening of Saturday, the 21st of May, the tiny monoplane appeared out of the Parisian fog and landed safely at Le Bourget.

Like everyone else, Jack had avidly consumed the details of Charles Lindbergh's amazing thirty-three-and-a-half-hour flight, alone over the limitless wastes of the Atlantic. Lindbergh had had no radio, no map and no parachute, and his monoplane was not fitted with floats. His only equipment was a compass, an inflatable raft in case of ditching, two pints of water and five sandwiches. At times he had had to climb to ten thousand feet to get above storm clouds; at others he had skimmed the wave tops at ten feet and seen a school of dolphins at close quarters; at others again, fog had closed in and he had had to fly blind for several hours. He had had to contend with icing – not just outside but inside, too, because he had left the cockpit window open to keep himself awake. He had navigated by the Pole Star, and at one time was puzzled by the position of the moon, until he realised he hadn't taken into account the rotation of the earth. When the stars weren't visible, he had had to rely on dead-reckoning, but it was well known that compasses were never accurate in aeroplanes.

Jack could appreciate the courage of the venture, the loneliness and sometimes stark fear that must have attended the effort, the weariness of holding the little aeroplane steady hour after endless hour, all the while wondering whether you were heading in the right direction, or would run out of fuel and plummet into the unmarked sea without ever knowing where you were. Lindbergh's great dread had been of falling asleep – he had not dared eat his sandwiches for fear they would make him sleepy – and at one point he had realised he had drunk half his water during the night without having the slightest recollection of it.

After twenty-eight hours he had spotted some seagulls and then a group of fishing boats, and he dropped down and circled them, and shouted to a man who looked up at him, 'Which way is Ireland?' But the man either didn't hear or didn't understand. Finally he saw a stretch of rocky coastline and crossed it with relief; but the fog had come down again, so he had only dead-reckoning by which to guess where Paris was. He rumbled on in what he hoped was the right direction, with no real idea where he was.

But in the Place de l'Opéra in Paris an electric sign had flashed out the news that he was on this side of the water, and a hundred thousand people clambered into their cars and streamed out to Le Bourget field, where they left on their headlights to help guide him. The airfield switched on its beacon and sent up rockets and star shells; people even ran out from their houses with torches and lanterns and waved them – anything to bring him in.

As soon as the aeroplane was down, Lindbergh opened the cockpit and called out, 'Where am I?'

A joyful shout went up: 'Paris!'

The handsome young man was literally dragged from the cockpit by the huge crowd hysterical with delight, and pieces were hacked out of his aeroplane's linen outer skin for souvenirs before a force of soldiers and police could intervene to save them both from the mob, and escort them to the safety of a hangar. Charles – or, as he had been dubbed, with some reason, 'Lucky' Lindbergh – was now famous, his face and name as well known as those of Monsieur Blériot, and a great deal better known than those of Alcock and Brown: people always preferred a solo hero to a team. His place in history was assured. He was embarking on a series of celebratory flights within Europe before returning to America, where adulation, money and honours would no doubt await him.

Jack was wholeheartedly pleased for the young man, but though he didn't say anything, Helen knew he couldn't help reflecting on his own achievements. He had been a pioneer flyer, had won prizes and had enjoyed some fame as a test and exhibition pilot at Hendon and Brooklands before the war – and, yes, the war! He had been flying in wartorn skies over France when young Lindbergh had still been a schoolboy with a passion for motor-cars. But who had heard of Jack Compton now? He would not go down in history for achievements in flying, his lifelong passion.

Helen, his other lifelong passion, knew all this, and knew that, because he was a decent person, he would fight off such unworthy feelings and be back to normal in a day or two. She was glad the letter had come from the Air Ministry, for it would at least distract him during the adjustment period. He was her adored husband and father of her three fine children, and that was achievement enough for her, but she was too wise to say so until he had got over his sorrow for his lost youth.

It *was* 'Curly' Borthwick. He stepped out from behind his desk beaming in welcome, his bald head shining, complete with the scar across his forehead from a bad landing when half his tail had been shot away by German Archie, and the broken nose, which was a souvenir of a very rough and drunken game of mess polo.

'Uncle!' he exclaimed, grasping Jack's hand. 'By all that's holy, I swear you haven't aged a bit! Of course, you were so old to begin with . . .'

'You haven't changed a bit either,' Jack said, grinning with pleasure. 'Still as ugly as a bedstead. How you always managed to get the women chasing after you beats me. I remember a certain night in Amiens when they were fighting over you.'

'Tsh! None of that. I'm a respectable married man, these days. Lord! I can't tell you how we young things back then envied you your wife and nippers at home.'

'I would never have guessed.'

'Oh, we made a lot of noise and chased a lot of mamzelles, but seeing you sitting there every night writing to the memsahib made us realise that there was no-one like that who would care when we bought our piece of earth. Remember Sheridan and his bloody Beethoven sonatas?'

'He was a fine player,' Jack said, 'but I think you know we all preferred your tuneless ivory-bashing. You played things we could sing to.'

'Ah, the dear old tuskers. Happy days.' He was serious suddenly. 'Sheridan bought it at Yprcs.'

'Yes, I heard,' Jack said.

'Burned up,' Borthwick said starkly. 'And Hodgson went down in 1918 somewhere near Paris. And White lost a leg.'

They mourned their old colleagues, and asked after those who had survived – not so many of them.

'But here *we* are, anyway, Uncle,' Borthwick concluded. 'All merry and bright. And at least you're still flying.' He slapped his desk with the palm of his hand. 'This old crate never takes off. You're lucky.'

'Well, it keeps my hand in, I suppose.'

'Ready to fight the next war?'

'God, I hope not.'

'We'd be up a gum tree all right, with the way they've run down the RAF,' Borthwick complained. 'That review after the war said we needed fifty-two squadrons to match the air power of France, and what have we got? A skeleton force.'

'Yes, but no-one takes France seriously, these days, do they?' Jack said. 'And, besides, you know, it might turn out to be a good thing.'

'How so?'

'Well, ships become obsolete after twenty years, rifles after fifty years, but aeroplane design is developing so fast I reckon they're becoming obsolete in ten, even five. The French and Italians are just lumbering themselves with a great fleet of useless old buses, whereas if there is another war – which God forbid – we'll have a clean slate. We'll be able to arm ourselves with the very latest.'

'Now, you see,' Borthwick said admiringly, 'that's exactly why we need you, Uncle. You've got a thinker between your ears. You think of things that pass the rest of us by.'

Jack was about to disclaim the compliment, but was arrested by the words 'we need you'. 'What do you mean, you need me? Who is we? And for what?'

'Steady on, Uncle. One question at a time. I'm not a jolly old brainbox like you. All I can do to remember my own name. I say, look here, it's getting on for lunchtime. What say we stagger off? Absorb a spot and talk in comfort. They do a decentish claret at the club.'

Jack could see that he would have be patient and abide by Borthwick's timetable, so he agreed. The two men assumed their hats and went out to get a taxi to the RAF Club in Piccadilly, and there was no talk of anything but old times, and friends and families, until the soup and chop were vanquished, and Borthwick had sent for a second bottle and a 'bit of mousetrap to chase it down'.

Then at last he came to the point. 'Now, you've heard of the Imperial Airship Scheme?'

'Yes, of course,' said Jack. 'It's been going on for long enough. It used to be the Burney Scheme, didn't it?'

'Yes, but it changed in 1924 with the MacDonald government. Dennis Burney's was a commercial scheme. Now it's official.'

'I thought it was the Admiralty's baby?'

'It's everyone's baby. Have to have some means of transporting chaps and letters to the distant outposts of the Empire without all that fooling about changing trains and dealing with frisky natives. And aeroplanes can't go the distance. Of course,' he admitted, 'we didn't have old Lindbergh flying across the Atlantic when we started but, realistically, it's going to be a very long time before passenger flights to Canada, India, Australia and so on are practicable, if they ever are. Carrying enough fuel for a decent payload looks likely to remain impossible.'

'That's what people said about heavier-than-air flight when I was a lad – impossible. I didn't believe them.'

'Fair enough. But for the moment aeroplanes can't cut the mustard, so it has to be airships – they might be slower, but they're much safer, and they can take the weight. We're aiming for something that can carry a hundred and fifty passengers with all their luggage, plus the mail, plus a crew of about forty. And if there *is* another war, they'd carry two hundred soldiers or five fighter aircraft. No aeroplane is ever going to be able to provide that sort of capacity.'

'No airship can provide it, either,' Jack pointed out. 'You'd need something like – what? Ten million cubic feet? That's well beyond present designs.'

'Eight million, by our calculations,' Borthwick said. 'I'm impressed. You obviously know something about it.'

'Oh, I read. Airships aren't my first love, but if it flies, I'm interested.'

301

'It's that brainbox again. I can't think of more than one thing at a time. Had to forget everything about our sort of flying when I got this job. Now I spout all sorts of figures, but between you and me, I don't understand half of 'em.'

Jack laughed. 'You don't fool me. You wouldn't have your own office and desk at the Air Ministry if you weren't bright upstairs.'

'Lord! If you think that, you don't know the civil service. More claret? Not too bad, is it? Now, let's get down to it. If you know about the scheme, you know we are currently building two airships, not quite up to the eight million mark, but both of five million cubic feet. We're looking for a passenger capacity of a hundred to start with. Vickers are building one in Yorkshire, at the old RNAS base at Howden. That's Dennis Burney's mob. And we've got a team drawn from all sorts, building the other one at Cardington under Air Ministry supervision. Someone thought a bit of healthy competition might throw up some good ideas.' He grinned. 'We call ours the socialist airship, and the Yorkshire one the capitalist airship.'

'And how are they both getting on?' Jack asked.

'Oh, the going's a bit bumpy,' said Borthwick, cutting a sliver of cheese. 'Throwing up all sorts of problems. We've a fancy the Howden set might be getting on better. Dennis Burney's got a frightfully bright cove for a designer – chap called Barnes Wallis, Yorkshireman like you.'

'Oh, yes – I've come across him. He was a marine engineer – I started that way, too. When I was at Rankin's in Southampton, he was just across the water at White's in Cowes. We met once or twice at regattas and competitions. Awfully nice fellow. I wondered what had become of him.'

'He left White's in 1913 and went straight into airships.'

'And I went into aeroplanes. So I'm wondering what I can do for you. Airship design is not my field.'

'Oh, quite, quite. But you are an engineer, and I know

you've designed aircraft engines. The engines are one of the problems we have. And you have experience – probably no-one has better – of the passenger side of the business. We need some thoughts on how to arrange all that, and what people are likely to need on a long flight.'

'You must surely have people on your team with experience just as useful.'

'Yes, we have people on our team,' Borthwick said with a hint of bitterness. 'All too many of 'em. A committee might sound like the perfect way to build something to a civil servant – they do everything by committees – but to chaps like you and me it's a bad dream. Everything gets talked about and nothing gets done. So I had a word with my minister, Sir Samuel Hoare, and he had a word with Winston. He holds the purse strings – and he has to be kept up with everything, especially if it involves flying.'

'Yes, I remember he always was air-minded.'

'Quite, and of course he's very keen that this airship scheme should succeed. Flying and the colonies, two of his pet subjects. He remembered you, by the way – it seems you took him up for a flight once, in his palmy days.'

'That's right. Our paths crossed once or twice.'

'And there's someone else who remembers you – the Director of Civil Aviation.'

'Sefton Brancker?' said Jack. 'He took his aviation certificate with me.'

'So he says.'

Sefton Brancker was a few years older than Jack, a lean and handsome man from an old military family, who had been in the Royal Artillery before taking his Aero Club certificate in 1913 and switching to the Royal Flying Corps. He had held important RFC administrative posts during the war, was knighted and promoted to air vice marshal in 1919, became chairman of the Royal Aero Club in 1921, and Director of Civil Aviation in 1922, in which position he was doing a great deal to open up flying and persuade other cities to create airfields.

'Yes, he remembers you all right,' Borthwick went on, 'and says you're just the sort of bright spark we need. So here's the griffin: Hoare, Churchill and Brancker all agree that what's needed is an outsider with the right sort of knowledge to come in and look the thing over, bring a fresh perspective, see if he can spot any obvious flaws we've missed, or come up with bright suggestions for the problems we've encountered. We're trying to create something new and modern, not just plod along tried and trusted lines. And *that's* where you come in. You've got the sort of brain that sees round things and past things and to one side of things. Will you do it? Take a squint? Give us the once-over? Have a look at the Howden mob, make comparisons, cross-fertilise? It needn't take up too much of your time – a couple of days a month, perhaps. We wouldn't expect you to be there all the time with your sleeves rolled up and a spanner in your hand. You'd be suitably remunerated, of course.' He named a figure that surprised Jack. 'Official car to take you to and from. Secretary to type up your notes if you want, and a desk here at the ministry to work on. All the facilities.'

'It's very generous,' Jack said. 'There is just one thing.'

'Name it,' said Borthwick. 'We're desperate to get this thing moving, so I think I can promise you anything within reason.'

'Oh, it isn't more rhino or anything. I just need to know how the rest of the team would feel about an outsider coming in. There'd be no point if I was just going to put people's backs up.'

'Oh, quite, quite, grasp your point entirely – but don't worry, the whole thing is pukka. The chaps want to get this right as much as we do; and everyone likes you, Uncle. Always did. Likeable chap. Which brings me to another little favour I want to ask you.'

'Another?' Jack said, with heavy irony. 'After forcing me to accept a small fortune in exchange for a few hours' enjoying myself poking about an airship works?'

'I'm a cad,' Borthwick said solemnly. 'It's this: the government's put a lot into this scheme, and it wants a big fuss made of it. Lots of publicity and good stories. Difficulty is in getting anything so technical across in a way that the public can grasp. What we need is a jolly good chap to stand up there and blab in a charming sort of way. Someone attractive whom everyone likes.'

'You aren't still talking about me? You need Charles Lindbergh.'

'No *bon*. He's American. No, it's you again. As aforementioned, everyone likes you, old horse. And you're a genuine, dyed-in-the-wool war hero. Medals and everything. Red Baron, watch out! You're the bee's knees, that's all. So will you do it? It only means talking to the press now and then, showing selected chappies round the works, feeding them sugar and being photographed leaning in heroic manner against some suitable lump of machinery. Be the stick man for the whole project. What do you say? It might make you famous, but I can't see any other serious disadvantages.'

Jack laughed. Was this what he was to go down in the history books for? He wasn't sure how he felt about it, or how Helen would feel about it either. But she would certainly like the extra money – the children weren't getting any cheaper to feed and keep – and he would *love* (he suddenly discovered) to be on the inside and get to see everything and find out everything, poke about and ask questions and perhaps even get his hands dirty. He had never been passionate about airships, but a project of this size and importance almost had his mouth watering. 'What do I say? I say yes – and thank you for thinking of me, Curly old man.'

'Thinking of you? Who else? You popped straight into my mind, Uncle, even before Sir Sefton named you, and I couldn't get you out. Lucky my mind's largely empty so there was plenty of room! Now, what do you say to a cup of coffee and a spot of brandy to go with it? Waiter! The coffee's filthy here, but they've got a very nice old brandy they keep for chaps like us who know the difference.'

Verena went into labour one sunny May morning, and Venetia was made aware of the blessing of the telephone, as she had Ardworth put through calls to Dr Hepplewhite and to Oliver at his office, rather than having to send servants with notes. The consequence of this speed of communication was that both men arrived in plenty of time. Venetia could have delivered the baby herself, of course – she had delivered more than she could count in her time – but she had rather not have to. She had been feeling very old and very tired of late, and all that bending over would have been a misery to her back.

The labour was straightforward and remarkably quick, and Venetia had hardly had to think about occupying Oliver's mind when Hepplewhite came in with a small, wrapped bundle and said, 'A girl, my lord. Mother and child doing finely.'

'A girl!' said Oliver. It was what he had hoped for. As Hepplewhite approached him, he directed him to take the baby to Venetia first.

With a quick glance of gratitude at her son, Venetia opened her arms to the tiny thing. As always, she marvelled at how light it was – one forgot so quickly how small newborn babies were. The squashed red face and the slick of damp black hair meant nothing: soon enough the creased butterfly wings would unfurl, and you would be able to see what she looked like. She felt the divine, trusting warmth and inhaled the incomparable smell of a new baby, and ridiculous tears rose to her eyes. *Oh, little one, what lies ahead of you?*

Oliver, watching, saw the tears, and felt them like a needle into the heart. His mother *never* cried. She looked up, saw his expression and composed her own. 'She's lovely,' she said. 'New life is all of hope.' She looked down into the tiny face again and murmured, 'Nothing is ever lost.'

Oliver could guess what was in the back of her mind. Losing her best friend was still too close. 'Would you like it if we called her Henrietta?'

Venetia smiled. 'No, darling. That would be a terrible burden to place on a child. But thank you for the thought. Here, you must hold her.'

She passed the child to him, and watched almost greedily the expression of wonder and love on his face. 'I must go and see Verena,' he said, unable to take his eyes from his daughter's face.

'Then take the baby back to her. She'll be longing for you both.'

They decided to call the new baby Amabel, a name Verena had a fancy for. Lady Amabel Winchmore. 'It has a good sound to it,' Venetia conceded.

Little John Winchmore, two and a half, was brought down later to see his new sister and to wonder what all the fuss was about. Afterwards he wandered disconsolately into the drawing-room where Venetia was sitting. His world had been turned upside down, no-one was in their right place, and his mother was ill in bed. When grown-ups were ill in bed, it was so serious that you had to be afraid they might die. And everyone was making such a fuss of the new baby they had forgotten to give him any tea.

Grandmama, usually so fierce about people following the routine and obeying the rules, did not scold him for coming into the drawing-room uninvited. She saw the droop of his lip and the set of his shoulders and said, 'What's the matter?' in such a kind voice that he dared to answer. Out of all his grievances, the only one he could find words for was 'I haven't had any tea.'

'That will never do,' she said. 'I haven't had any, either. Should you like to share mine?' To his incredulous gaze and nod, she added, 'Ring the bell, then.'

He had never been allowed to touch the brass handle beside the chimney-piece, and with a tremendous sense of importance he did as she asked, imagining the bell ringing downstairs in the kitchen and wondering if they could tell it was him who rang it. He must be sure to tell them – and to tell Nanny, who was always saying little boys should be seen and not heard, though it seemed to him often enough she didn't want him to be seen, either.

'Come and sit by me,' Grandmama said, as he stood staring in a bemused fashion at the bell handle. He obeyed, and hitched himself with difficulty up onto the slippery brocade of the sofa. She caught him as he was about to slip off and settled him further back, so that his legs stuck out in front of him. He was grateful to be touched. He had felt no hands on him since early that morning.

'Well, Hazelmere,' said Grandmama – it was her special name for him. She called him Hazelmere, never John, and said he was her boy, as Daddy had been her boy when he was little. 'What do you think of your new sister?'

A strict nanny was the best education for teaching a boy to be tactful, even at two and a half. He considered his words carefully. 'She isn't very pretty,' he said at last. 'And she sleeps all the time.'

'She's had a hard day,' said Venetia. 'She'll wake up by and by. And she'll get prettier. In a few years, I dare say she'll be as pretty as a kitten.'

'I like puppies better,' John said wistfully. 'I wish we had a dog, like Aunt Violet and Uncle Prince.'

Venetia winced at this casual coupling of her daughter's name with that of the Prince of Wales. But the prince was very fond of children, and made a point of talking to them and bringing them presents whenever he could.

'You won't need a dog now you have a new sister,' she said. She looked at his furrowed brow. 'What's the matter? Out with it. I won't be cross, I promise.'

He felt around in his mind for his troubles, finally bringing out the worst one. 'Will Mummy be well again soon?'

'Yes, very soon,' Venetia said. 'She's not ill, only tired. It was hard work for her as well as your sister. But she'll be her old self, and out of bed in no time.'

He nodded, relieved, but she saw there was still more. 'What else?'

This one was even harder to articulate. He felt close to tears. He tried hard to be a man, but his lip trembled despite himself as he said, 'Now we have a new baby, will I still be your boy?'

Venetia was almost undone. She saw the world suddenly from his small, overwhelmed viewpoint: the giant, inexplicable grown-ups who ordered his universe, the fear of things changing, the terror of being lost down the cracks and forgotten now a new star was born. She put her arm round his narrow shoulders and felt, after an instant of surprise, his grateful yielding into her warmth. 'I solemnly swear,' she said, 'that you will always, always be my boy. No matter what.'

He nodded, and she saw his thumb try to creep to his mouth before it was sternly ordered down again. Luckily, tea came at that moment; and since it had been intended for her, it included what were to John almost unimaginable luxuries of toasted teacakes, strawberry jam and cake. He tucked in and soon was lifted far out of himself on a tide of well-being, chattering to her so hard between mouthfuls that he didn't even notice when his flustered and red-faced nanny opened the door and looked in, and was sent away with a scowl and a sharp shake of the head by his grandmother.

★   ★   ★

Teddy and Amy's first action, on the day after arriving in London, had been to arrange a visit to Helen and Jack, in the course of which they had naturally mentioned Father Palgrave's book, and Helen and Jack had naturally mentioned Molly's new job with a publishing firm. Since Teddy had heard of Dorcas Overstreet, whose reputation was as an old-established and traditional company, and since he knew nothing about publishing or how to start to get a book into print, it was natural for him to follow the path of least resistance and ask if Molly would help in the quest.

A meeting was set up at Teddy and Amy's hotel, Brown's. Molly was invited for luncheon there, and Helen came up for it too, to ease any possible awkwardness, since Teddy and Molly hardly knew each other and were of very different generations. But it all went well, despite the fact that Molly had, of course, to get back to work and consequently needed to hurry matters along faster than Teddy's more stately manners would have liked. She agreed to read the book and advise, as far as her limited knowledge of book-publishing allowed, on the next step to take, and took the manuscript away with her.

She had been a little anxious about it, expecting the worst of the book and not wanting to hurt anyone's feelings. She started to read it that evening when she got back from work, and had to force herself to stop and go to bed. Over the next two evenings she finished it at a gallop. It could have been a very awkward amalgam, but there had been scholarly skill involved in framing the vivid and passionate voice of the army chaplain with the dispassionate commentary that made the context clear. The coolly factual side made a setting for the wild and moving song of suffering, as effective as plain gold to glittering diamond. Palgrave's account of his war sent shivers down Molly's spine.

It did not take her much thought to decide to show it to Vivian Blake. She knew Dorcas Overstreet to be a good and conscientious publisher; and if the book turned out to be a success, she naturally wanted Blake's firm to reap the benefit.

Blake took the manuscript away, and spent so long reading it that Molly feared she had done wrong in asking him, or that he hated it and now questioned her judgement, or probably both. The time delay was hard for Teddy, too, who sent a poignant letter enquiring politely if she had any news for him, and she was forced to write back that she hadn't, but that the matter was in hand. But on the last Saturday in May, Blake invited her out to dinner, and this time it was not at a little Bloomsbury restaurant but at the Ritz, where he met her with heart-melting smiles and champagne.

'I salute you,' he said, doing just that with his glass. 'I knew I was doing the firm good by bringing you in, but to bring you in with this manuscript is beyond anything I could have expected. You are going to be getting off on a very strong footing – and that reflects well on me, too, for which I thank you.'

'You liked it, then?'

He laughed. '*Liked* it? It is a brilliant piece of work! I have to admit it had me in tears once or twice.'

'Oh, I'm glad it wasn't just me,' Molly said.

'But it's more than just a voice from the trenches, exciting though that is. The other work makes it an important account of the war in the academic sense, and yet it is so accessible it will appeal to the general public. I can see it becoming a bestseller.'

Molly was thrilled. 'Really?'

'Really.' He smiled and reached across the table to squeeze her hand. 'I knew I was right to trust my instinct about you. You knew this book was good and you brought it in. Keep doing that and you will be the star of the company in a few years.'

Molly was, for once, without words. The pressure of his

hand lingered in her nerve-endings, though that hand was back on his side of the table again.

'There's just one thing,' Blake said. 'The title won't do. We don't want it to sound like a scholarly tome. It must have a title that will attract the ordinary man and woman in the street. Something more immediate – more romantic.'

She thought for only a moment, before saying, 'Didn't you just say it was a voice from the trenches?'

He tried it over in his mind, and then smiled at her again. 'That's it. *A Voice from the Trenches.* Perfect! You've done it again.'

'You said it,' she pointed out.

'But you noted it. I don't mean to take anything away from you. This is *your* book, first and last. And it will endear you to my uncle no end,' he concluded, with an impish look.

'Ah,' she teased, 'he's been twitting you about hiring me, has he?'

'He did have reservations about a woman being able to do the work,' he admitted. 'Now he'll have to eat his hat. Think what a blow you've struck for equality and women's rights.'

'Oh, yes,' she said drily, 'that was foremost in my mind the whole time.'

He refilled her glass. 'We must get down to brass tacks. We shall have to talk advances and prints runs and decide on a publishing date, and have everything clear in our minds before we talk to the authors. It will be an interesting problem,' he went on, 'to work out a contract with three authors involved.'

'And one of them dead,' Molly said.

'Not always a bad thing,' he said. 'On the whole, dead authors are easier to deal with. It's the living ones who can be awkward, as you'll find out.'

★   ★   ★

Raymond Romano was back in England, this time in the company of the beautiful film actress Veda Lamarr, with whom he had starred the previous year in *Compassionate Hearts* – a romantic film about the doomed love of a doctor and a nurse in wartorn France. They had come to England for the shooting of their new moving picture, *Bess of Hatfield*. It was based on the little-known historical episode where Good Queen Bess was besieged in Hatfield Castle by the forces of the Evil Queen Mary, until heroically rescued by Lord Robert Dudley, who smuggled her out dressed as a man and galloped away with her on his saddle to Scotland where they celebrated a secret and forbidden marriage over the anvil at Gretna Green. It was never precisely explained why it was forbidden, but it accounted for the fact that for the rest of her life she turned down all offers of marriage and remained a virgin. 'Thou cannot be king, Robert, but none other shall ever reign beside me. Thou shall always be king in my heart.'

Raymond was playing Robert Dudley with a Vandyke moustache and beard that were going to make his female fans go weak at the knees, and Veda Lamarr was Good Queen Bess with a good deal of kohl around her eyes, and much looking forward to the scenes in which she put on tight breeches and showed off her legs.

'It's a good thing movies are silent,' Raymond told Oliver, when he called in first thing to see him at his consulting rooms, 'because darling Veda has a Bronx accent you could cut with a knife. She sounds like a foghorn with adenoids. But she looks wonderful in the crown and ruff. I'm just pleased to be back in costume,' he went on. 'Lord Robert Dudley has long hair that Bess toys with in various scenes, so I can keep covered. I had to have a military haircut in *Hearts*.'

'But there's no need to be nervous any more,' Oliver said, getting up and coming round his desk. 'Your new ear is perfect. Let me see.' He lifted the curls away from it and inspected it closely. 'Beautiful. Really, no-one would ever know it wasn't always like that.'

Raymond sighed. 'It's just hard to get used to *not* hiding it. I've been conscious of it for so long – it's like something you see out of the corner of your eye even when it's not there.'

'I know what you mean,' Oliver said. 'But you will get used to it in time. Try showing it off on the beach next time you're on holiday.'

'Oh, who has time for a vacation?' Raymond said. 'Honestly, I'm so much in demand after *Hearts*, I hardly have time to go and see my mother, let alone go to the beach. Veda and I are here until September, then it's straight back to Hollywood for me to start on *The Dancing Years*. That's about Vernon and Irene Castle. I play Vernon, of course, and they're getting Coraleen Benbrook for Irene, which is amusing because she can't dance a step, poor darling, but she's popular after *Once Upon Manhattan* last year, and it's the name that makes the box office. There's talk that Irene herself might do the dancing, long-shot, but I don't know. She's a star in her own right, these days. And then right after *Dancing Years* Veda and I get together again for a Mexican bandit movie, *The Cactus and the Rose*. Guess which of us is which! So, you see? Busy, busy, busy.'

'Well, now you are here,' Oliver said, 'you must come to dinner. My wife would love to meet you both. We both loved *Compassionate Hearts* – though your surgical technique had me in stitches, if you'll pardon the joke.'

'Oh, my dear, don't talk of it!' he said. 'I hadn't the least idea what I was doing. All those pretend wounds. Too ill-making. And they kept making me dip my hands in some horrible fake blood. I *hate* having sticky hands. It was ghastly.'

'And Nurse Angelus – wonderful name, by the way – wouldn't have died so prettily if she really *had* had typhus.'

'They were going to make it Spanish flu,' Raymond confessed, 'but they thought it didn't sound dramatic enough and, besides, too many people would have known someone who had really died of the flu, so it might have been upsetting. But she did die beautifully, didn't she? You can't beat Veda on a deathbed. The scriptwriters are putting in an extra scene at the end of *Bess* just for her. The story really ends with her becoming queen and explaining that I can't be king and me riding off to my death in the Spanish wars, but they've added a postscript showing the end of her life. As she lies dying, she whispers my name, and I come in as a ghost, and she croaks trying to hold my hand. Terrific stuff!'

'I can't wait,' Oliver said, his eyes dancing with merriment. 'So you will come to dinner? In fact, you must let me throw a dinner party for you. I know my sister will want to see you, and my cousin Eddie – Lord Vibart – and his wife.'

'Veda will like that. She can't get enough of real lords. The nearest she's got at home is Earl Butler, the railroad man who keeps asking her to marry him, but Earl's only his Christian name. And what about your friend Kit? Will you be asking him? He's a lord, too, isn't he?'

'Oh, of course. Yes, he's an earl – the real sort – and he's even more of a cinema-*devoté* than me. I'll definitely ask him.'

'Then I think I can promise you Veda. She'll love it. Besides, if I go out in the evening without her she'll be trapped in the hotel. She's scared to go out on her own.'

Oliver was a little surprised at the casual way Raymond talked about Veda, because ever since *Compassionate Hearts*, the more excitable elements of the press had been talking about the big off-screen romance between them. It had started in America, of course, but by the time *Hearts* had come out in England, the talk had spread to the English popular papers and magazines. On their journey across on the *Berengaria*, they had been photographed dancing cheek to cheek, and on arrival leaning over the taffrail waving with an arm around each other. The English press were now having a wonderful time chasing the stars about London, photographing them going into and coming out of glamorous places, clamouring for interviews, and writing speculative pieces with a great many rhetorical questions in place of definite facts.

They were certainly seen everywhere together and seemed on terms of the greatest affection, and anyone who claimed any more intimate knowledge of them, be it only a hairdresser or chambermaid, could be sure of a hearing from one or other of the less particular papers. Everyone liked a romance, and a romance between big Hollywood stars had that extra element of glamour that made the story irresistible: it was Pickford and Fairbanks all over again. So even had Oliver been inclined to tell someone on the *Daily Muck* that Romano had described his co-star as 'a foghorn with adenoids', they would have given it no credence – or not yet. Such destructive stories would have to wait until Miss Lamarr's star began to wane.

In the middle of the excitement of starting her new job, with the added element of being interviewed by Blake's uncle, Mr Dorcas, and praised for bring the company *A Voice from the Trenches*, and being told she would be allowed to work on it, albeit with the oversight of a more experienced editor, Molly still had time to be pleased that Simon Baron, the actor in the attic, was no longer out-of-work. He had secured employment on the set of the film *Bess of Hatfield*.

'They have a lot of walk-on parts,' he told the house at an impromptu interview on the landing. 'They call them "supers" in the film business – courtiers, servants, soldiers and so on. I think it's short for "supernumerary". The pay's very good compared with stage work, and there's always the chance that you might be picked out for a small named part, and that's the way to catch the director's eye. It could be the start of something very big for me. At least,' he added, coming back to earth, 'it's money in the pocket – and for acting, not teaching elocution to horrible people's horrible children.'

'Talk about biting the hand that feeds you,' said Megs, one of the artists from the basement. 'I shall tell what you said next time I see one of them.'

'You won't be seeing any of them for a while, because I've cancelled most of my classes until the shooting's over, and you'll have forgotten by then.' Which was too true for Megs to argue about.

At the end of his first fortnight of filming, everyone gathered in the basement for a late supper to hear how he had got on. He celebrated his sudden access of wages by treating the gathering to several bottles of wine.

'So, how was it?' Megs asked.

'Well, to begin with, we aren't shooting anywhere near Hatfield House. Actually, I don't think Hatfield comes into the story at all – I think they just liked the name. Or they may have confused Queen Elizabeth with Bess of Hardwicke. It's really hard to tell with American filmmakers – history doesn't seem to be their strong point. At the moment they're using a frightfully bogus mock-Tudor house in Chorleywood. It's only about twenty years old, but it's got large grounds for filming in, and it's right by the main road, which means the film company can get all its equipment in easily. And it means the stars can stay in London, which they prefer, and come out each day by motor-car. We supers have to take the Metropolitan Line, and a motor-bus picks us up from the station.'

'And what's the filming actually like?' Ingrid, the potter, asked.

'There's quite a lot of standing around, waiting for the

light to be right, for instance, or for an aeroplane to pass. It would look rather odd for Queen Mary to be riding up to a house in a ruff and farthingale and have a plane pottering over the trees in the background.'

'Goodness, yes. I wouldn't have thought of that,' said Ida, the other artist.

'But then when everyone's in position and the director and the cameramen are happy, you have a wonderful surge of action for a few minutes, and then it all stops again. It's quite exhilarating, suddenly acting like mad, dashing about or shouting blue murder at the drop of a hat. Takes one back to drama school, when they used to shout at you to register despair, then fury, then happiness all in quick succession. I remember once ricking my neck quite badly going from menace to supplication too quickly.'

'So who are you playing?' Molly asked.

'Oh, everyone. I'm a courtier a lot of the time, but I've also been a soldier, a groom and a monk. You have to be ready to dash up to Wardrobe any moment for a quick change.'

'What was a monk doing in the story?' Felix demanded. 'Elizabeth was *after* the Dissolution.'

'I don't know. There are quite a lot of them hanging around on the edges,' Baron said vaguely. 'I think the producer had a lot of monk costumes left over from another film that he wanted to use. And they're supposed to add an air of menace. One of the director's assistants told me there would be sinister music every time they appeared and it would "give people the shivers", to quote his phrase. But I must tell you – my career is already looking up. I happened to mention in the hearing of the producer that I can fence – it's always worth making sure they know that sort of thing – and he got quite excited. You see, they'd brought in a fencing instructor from a gym in Aylesbury to teach two of the stars how to do it, for the scene where Robert Dudley and Philip of Spain fight a duel on the lawn in front of the house—'

318

'*What?*' said everyone, simultaneously.

He grinned. 'My dears, you have to put history out of your minds for the duration of this story. They nobly agree to fight a duel to decide the outcome of the conflict, in order to save innocent lives, but it ends in a draw so they have to go back to the siege. Anyway, said stars couldn't get the hang of it at all, so now it's been decided that the duel will take place mostly long-shot, with the instructor and my jolly old self taking the parts. And then they'll cut in one or two close-ups of the stars when they get to those bits where we're breast to breast and straining against each other. So, you see, I've already been promoted, and the director now actually knows my name. I'm "You, what'syourname, Baron" instead of just "You".'

'That's tremendous,' Molly said. 'I'm so pleased for you.'

'Thank you. It really does make a big difference, you know. If anything like a small part comes up, he's much more likely to say, "Give it to that fellow, what'shisname, Baron", than to pick out someone at random.'

'Tell us about the stars,' Ingrid said. 'Do you get to talk to them?'

Simon Baron held centre stage for most of the evening, as was fitting; but then other topics drifted in and the conversation broke up into separate camps. Baron went round with the last of the wine, filling glasses and, on reaching Molly, flopped down beside her on the sofa and said, in a low voice, 'There was something I wanted to talk to you about, but I didn't want to do it in front of the others.' There was enough noise now in the rest of the room to cover anything that was said quietly. Apart from the conversations, someone had put on the gramophone, and Ben Bernie and his orchestra were enquiring 'Ain't She Sweet?' at considerable volume.

'What is it?' Molly asked. He looked rather troubled.

'When I was telling about the stars, and how they have their own dressing-rooms in the house, there was something

I didn't mention. I'd gone in to get changed myself, and the director's assistant told me to knock on Raymond Romano's door and tell him they'd want him in five minutes. I'd just got to the end of the corridor when his door opened. It's at the far end of the corridor from the stairs. The first person to come out was someone whose photograph I've seen often enough in the papers, particularly this year, to recognise him. It was Lord Westhoven.'

'Oh, really?' Molly said, not seeing where this was going. 'I knew that he knew Raymond Romano. He met him when he was over here last year. I suppose Mr Romano invited him to come and watch the shooting.'

Baron looked uncomfortable. 'I've wondered whether to tell you this at all,' he said, 'but I know you're friendly with Lady Westhoven.'

'She's an old friend,' Molly said. 'I went to her wedding.'

'I know. And that's rather the point. I've thought and thought about it, but – well, I decided in the end I ought to tell you.'

'Tell me *what*?' Molly was growing impatient, and straining to hear against the noise was tiring.

Baron seemed to make up his mind. 'Lord Westhoven stepped out of the room, and Romano came to the door behind him, saying goodbye, I suppose. It's quite dark by the stairs, and they didn't see me. Westhoven turned back and kissed him.'

'Well,' said Molly doubtfully, 'I suppose actors are rather more—'

'On the lips.'

There was a silence – at least, Molly fell silent, and for a moment she ceased to hear the noise around her. She said, 'What are you suggesting?'

He shrugged. 'It isn't just that – though it confirmed it for me. But he's been to the set several times this week. I've seen them together.'

'What are you *saying*? That they're – they're—' It was not something a well-brought-up girl had vocabulary for, though as a modern, cosmopolitan young woman she knew such things existed. 'They're *pansies*?' He nodded. 'You *must* be mistaken,' she said. 'Kit married my friend. And Mr Romano is having a romance with Veda Lamarr.'

'As to the romance, I'm pretty sure it's something cooked up by the studio for publicity purposes. They do that sort of thing all the time. Romano and Lamarr don't seem particularly attached to each other when they're away from the public eye.'

'Even so – Kit? You must be mistaken.'

'I'm not. They say it takes one to know one,' he said even more quietly.

She caught his meaning. '*You*'re one?'

'I don't talk about it – and I hope you won't either. But there's quite a lot of it in the acting profession. In the arts in general. I have a friend at the Royal Ballet Company. I hope you won't tell anyone. I've put myself in your power by telling you this, but I wanted you to know I'm telling you the truth. And so that you can tell your friend if she doesn't know. I won't say a word to anyone else. I leave it to you.'

Molly was too bemused to know what to think, but she saw his anxious expression and said, 'I won't betray you. Of course I won't. As to Emma – I'll have to think carefully whether to say anything. But I'll be discreet. You can be sure of that.'

'I knew I could trust you.'

She gave him a bitter look. 'I wish you hadn't. I'd much sooner not know. It's a burden I'd be happy to be without.'

CHAPTER FIFTEEN

Emma and Kit had spent only two weeks at Walcote before coming back to London. They did not want to miss the rest of the Season, and would have time in the summer to carry on with reshaping their country home. Once back in London, things seemed to settle down into the old groove. They had not yet got a house, so they were living in Emma's apartment in Queen's Walk, and their old circle welcomed them back with enthusiasm. Except that Kit was sleeping in her second bedroom, and was there at breakfast time, Emma found little difference in her life between being single and being married. Spencer called her 'my lady' instead of 'miss', and she was receiving invitations from a whole new swathe of people, but otherwise nothing seemed to have changed.

Kit was just as Kit always had been, amusing, affectionate, interested in what she did. There were perhaps more light kisses on her cheek or brow, more pats on the shoulder as he passed, more compliments on her looks (though he was just as critical if he did not like any of her outfits). He was an attentive husband, liked to bring her flowers and little presents – generally something novel or ridiculous intended to make her laugh – and seemed comfortable with the way things were between them.

And because she was so busy, Emma forgot the missing element in their marriage for most of the time. When she remembered, it tended to be in the middle of the night when he was not there anyway, and by the time Spencer was waking her with her tea and the increasingly large morning post, she had forgotten it. She supposed at some time they *ought* to talk about it again, but it would be such an embarrassing conversation she was only too glad to put it off. She hoped and expected that the thing would sort itself out naturally. Once Kit got used to their being husband and wife and got over his nervousness, the time would come. Perhaps one night after a delightful dinner *à deux* at home, with cocktails and then wine and a brandy or two and a lot of laughter, he would just slip quietly into her room and it would all go smoothly and nothing would need ever to be said. She loved him and he loved her so everything would be all right in the end. How could it not be?

So it was a happy Emma who met Molly one day in late July. Molly had been so busy with her new job that they had not been able to have luncheon, and Emma was so busy in the evenings they had not been able to have supper together. They met eventually one Saturday. Emma was looking at houses for her and Kit, and picked Molly up in the motor to go with her. They had plenty of time to talk, both between and in the houses, 'because this is just a preliminary glance, to get the idea of the space and location. Whatever we take, we'll want to change everything inside anyway.'

'How is Kit?' Molly asked, a little nervously, since she wasn't sure she wanted to know the answer.

'He's very well. Just the same old Kit, you know,' Emma said. 'He never changes.'

'*Doesn't* he?' Molly said. 'I would have thought getting married would have to change a person a *bit*, anyway.'

'Do you think I've changed?'

'Not that I can notice.'

'There you are, then.'

Molly felt there was a flaw somewhere that she couldn't put her finger on, but she asked the main thing she wanted to know. 'But are you happy? I mean, being married – is it what you expected?'

'Well, no, I don't think it is,' Emma said, with a slight frown. 'To be truthful, I always believed it would be a huge change and that one would feel quite different afterwards, but in fact, I've known Kit for so long and we're such good friends, it doesn't feel any different at all. It's been very easy. And I couldn't be happier.'

Molly was relieved. Emma said she was happy, and she seemed happy, so either what Simon Baron had said wasn't true or – well, no, she couldn't think of another alternative. He must have been mistaken. So she certainly wouldn't say anything to Emma about it. If Emma had been unhappy or confided that something was wrong, it might have been a different matter – though quite how she would have broached the subject she couldn't think.

'What about you?' Emma was asking 'How is the new job?'

It was a relief to change the subject, and Molly told her in detail about the job, the other people at Dorcas Overstreet, the books she was working on, and the authors she had met.

'You sound as though you are enjoying it,' Emma said.

'I am. I think it's exactly the right job for me, though it's taken me a while to find it. What about your slum clearance? How are you getting on with that?'

'It's a slow start, naturally, but we're getting the legal and financial sides sorted out, and I've started to look out for the right buildings. I have an agent who goes with me, because it can be rough in the East End – though most of them are good people, really.'

'I'd love to come with you some time,' Molly said.

'Would you? Then you shall. I should like to have your opinion. But it's very harrowing sometimes – well, all the time, if I'm honest. The conditions these people live in, the squalor, the derelict houses. They somehow get by – and some of the men have been getting by that way ever since they came back from the war. It breaks your heart.'

'But you're doing something about it. That's the important thing.'

Emma sighed. 'When I see the scale of the problem, when we drive through street after street like that, I start to think that one person, even a rich person, can't really hope to make any difference.'

'Nonsense,' Molly said robustly. 'To change the fortunes of even *one* family by giving them a decent home is worth while. You mustn't let it get you down.'

'I shan't. To be honest, I'm so busy most of the time there isn't room to think at all. Kit is always having to go to things without me, these days.'

'Poor Kit. I'm sure he wants to show off his new countess to everyone.'

'He's all right without me. He has a new interest – the film business. You've heard of Raymond Romano, the film star? Well, he's over here making a film, and he takes Kit to the set now and then. Kit finds it all very interesting.' She smiled. 'I think he's half longing to be a film actor himself.'

'He certainly has the looks,' Molly said.

'I won't tell him you said so. He's vain enough as it is. They're shooting in Hertfordshire at the moment, but next month they'll be going off on a sort of tour to other places, to film castles and so on, so I suppose I shall have him to myself again.'

'So Kit knows Raymond Romano?' Molly asked.

'They're great friends. They're out on the town together whenever I can't make it.'

'And you don't mind?'

'Why should I? I'm glad he has a new chum. Though I'm afraid Raymond is rather a snob. He's longing to be intro-duced to the Prince of Wales, and I suspect he thinks Kit is his best way in. Not that the Pragga Wagga would object to having a film star introduced to him, I'm sure.' It was what their circle called the Prince of Wales. 'He likes to be modern-minded.'

That could well be the whole reason Raymond Romano was interested in Kit, Molly thought. And she only had Simon's word for it that there had been a kiss at all – he'd said it had been dark in the corridor. One had to allow for an actor's temperament and tendency to exaggerate. She was going to put the whole thing out of her mind, and it was a great relief to do so.

It was quite a coup for Teddy and Amy to come home not only with a large parcel of news about the family to share around (the wedding, Verena's baby, Molly's new job, Jack's new position, genuine sightings of famous Hollywood film stars) but the exciting information that Father Palgrave's book was to be published in the spring of 1928.

Teddy broached the delicate matter of the contract, but Miss Husthwaite was quick to protest: 'Oh, but we've already said we don't expect any payment for it. Good heavens, no! It was quite a labour of love – and a privilege to work on something so rare and important.'

Julian added his disclaimer: 'Just so. The work was not done with any expectation of reward.'

Teddy was pleased, but felt obliged to introduce a note of caution. 'The publisher believes it could be a bestseller,' he said. 'It might make a considerable sum of money – perhaps several hundred pounds.'

'Anything that does accrue from the book's publication must go to the poor little girl,' Miss Husthwaite said. 'I am quite prepared at any point to sign a document, if that is required, to settle the matter.'

'I agree,' said Julian.

'Well,' said Teddy, delighted, 'I do applaud your spirit. Extremely noble and unselfish.'

'If it is a bestseller,' Amy said, 'that could furnish a dowry for Laura, for she won't have anything else, poor child.'

'Hm,' said Teddy. 'But, you know, I think we ought not to get her hopes up too much. In fact, I don't think we should mention the book to her at all until it is actually published, and we have a copy to place in her hands. Disappointment is very hard for little children to bear, and many things could happen between now and next spring.'

Later that evening on their way up to bed, Miss Husthwaite said to Julian, 'I hope you didn't mind what I said about not taking any pecuniary benefit from the book?'

'No, indeed. We had already agreed on that. But I think we ought to ask to have our names on the cover – perhaps in smaller type than Palgrave's, but still . . .'

'Oh, yes – that would be *most* agreeable,' she said. 'I'm sure Mr Morland can't object to that. He is very fair-minded.'

'I feel rather at a loss without the book, if truth be told,' said Julian, pausing as they reached the branch of the corridor where their ways parted. 'It has been a part of our lives for so long.'

'Yes, it does leave a gap,' Miss Husthwaite said wistfully.

'I have my academic work to take up again, of course,' he said, 'and yet that prospect does not excite as it once did. I wish you and I had another project on which we could work together.

'Do you really feel that?' Miss Husthwaite said eagerly. 'Because there is something I have been thinking of for some weeks now, ever since Mr Morland took the book away to London. I don't know if you have come across the Household Book?'

'No, I don't think so. What is it?'

'It is a series of ledgers that have been kept by the mistresses of Morland Place for hundreds of years, recording events, detailing household routines, recipes, methods for cleaning, sicknesses and their cures and so on. The whole history of Morland Place is there. Quite fascinating. I have been borrowing it from Mrs Tapworth for bedtime reading.'

Julian was looking at her keenly. 'And you thought we might do the same as with Palgrave's book? Transcribe, edit it, and –'

'– add the historical context,' Miss Husthwaite completed. 'It would be a very different kind of historical research, of course – and perhaps not the sort to appeal to a man . . .'

'But not at all!' Julian exclaimed. 'Tudor domestic economy is my subject. Nothing could be more suitable – I shall be able to suggest the right references for a large part of it. Oh, this is exciting!'

He spoke with such fervour that Rusty, sitting on his tail waiting to go to bed, jumped up and barked.

Miss Husthwaite laughed, and put her finger to her lips. 'We'll wake the household. Shall we talk about it tomorrow?'

'We shall,' he said. 'How pleased I am that you thought of it! A good piece of work that will keep us busy for many, many months.'

'We shall have to ask Mr Morland's permission.'

'I can't think it will not be forthcoming. For now, good-night, Miss Husthwaite, and thank you.' He held out his hand.

'Pleasant dreams,' she said, shaking it. She watched him walk away for a moment with a small smile playing on her lips, then pulled herself together. She called, quietly but sharply, 'Rusty! This way!' and made her way to her own room, reluctant dog at heel.

In the summer of 1927 President Coolidge took his vacation in the Black Hills of Dakota, staying in the Custer State Park and enjoying himself riding, fly-fishing and attending rodeos. His choice of destination, and the news coverage of it, brought a surge of tourists to the area, which greatly pleased the local businessmen and the state authorities. It was from the Black Hills that he set off his bombshell, in the form of the short statement: 'I do not choose to run for president in 1928.'

He had been vice-president in 1923 when Warren Harding died suddenly in August in the middle of his term of office; a further four-year term as president would mean he had been at the White House for ten years. Ten years, he explained, was longer than any other man had had in Washington, and it was too long. The presidential office took a heavy toll of those who held it.

The news galvanised Ren. His friend and patron Herbert Hoover, the commerce secretary, was popular with the people and the obvious choice for the Republican nomination. 'We must get busy right away,' he told Polly.

'But the election isn't until November next year,' she said. 'Even the convention is a year away.'

'A year is nothing. Coolidge doesn't really want Hoover nominated. He doesn't like him much.' Polly knew this – Coolidge rather looked down on Hoover's thrusting ambition and called him 'Wonder Boy'. 'I don't think he'll openly oppose him, because that might split the party. But there are other less loyal Republicans out there who might make Coolidge's reluctance their excuse. We have to start working right away to make sure our man takes the nomination on the first ballot.'

'But who will run against him?' Polly asked.

'I can't imagine – unless they drag out poor old Frank Lowden again. But he's done nothing since he quit the governorship of Illinois. All the same, we can't take any chances. The campaign starts right now.'

It was literally true: he had hardly stopped speaking when a call came through from Hoover's office, and he had to hurry away. On his return he told Polly she must give up her fashion house and dedicate herself full-time to the Party's business.

It was a complete surprise to Polly, who could only repeat, 'Give it up?'

'I think you should sell it,' he said. 'I know you are proud of it, but it's served its purpose, and there are more important things at stake. It's my chance to show up well and make a name with the Party. Get its backing for a governorship or a seat. Hoover will have his two terms, and then it will be my turn – president in 'thirty-seven.'

'Nineteen thirty-seven?' Polly repeated, a little bemused. Suddenly it didn't seem so far away.

'I'll be at my peak. America's a young country, and it's ready for a young president. But there's a heck of a lot of work to do, Polly. So you must give up the business. You ought to get a good price for it if you sell it now, with the fall fashions coming up. And I'll invest the money for you.'

Polly found she wasn't too upset by the idea. She had been spending less and less time on the business as Ren's political concerns made more demands of her. Fashion needed close personal attention, and she knew some of the flair had gone from Maison Polly since she had not been able to give it her whole mind.

She spoke to Lennie about it, when he called on her at the Alexanders' summer house on Long Island. He agreed with Ren. 'It wouldn't be a bad idea to realise your profit while you can. The fashion trade is too uncertain unless you're very big,' he said. 'And a good businessman knows when to get out. The best way to lose everything is to hang on too long.'

'I suppose you're right,' she said, with only a hint of a sigh. It had been her own invention from the start – her baby.

'What will you do with the money?' Lennie asked.

'Ren said he'd invest it for me.'

'Well, you've got the right man there. He knows everything

there is to know about speculation. He put me onto a very nice little bond – in General Motors – which made me twenty thousand just when I needed it to put into my business.'

'Twenty thousand? How is that possible? No, don't tell me. I don't understand the stock market. Ren talks to me sometimes, but it might as well be Dutch he's speaking.'

'There's no reason you ever should understand the stock market,' Lennie said. 'Let your husband do that for you. He knows what's what.'

Polly wrinkled her nose. 'I've seen bonds – just a piece of paper with writing on it. Nothing to compare with a real, solid shop on Fifth Avenue. Well, just *off* Fifth Avenue,' she added honestly.

'You do *want* to sell, don't you? He isn't forcing your hand?'

'No, no. I want to sell. It's just that – well, it was Granny Ruth's gift to me.' She had died last winter, and they both still missed her.

'Granny was never a piker,' Lennie said. 'She wasn't one to come looking to see if the vase she gave you was still on the mantelpiece.'

'You have a nice way of putting things.'

'It comes of working with artistic types. Some of it's bound to rub off.'

'Artistic types,' Polly said, with a teasing smile. 'Like Veronica Starr, perhaps?' This was a musical-comedy actress he had been seen squiring about New York that spring.

He shook his head indulgently. 'I haven't seen Veronica for months. You're woefully out of date. There have been two others since then – an opera singer and a socialite.'

'Which is the current flame?'

'Neither of them. I'm on my summer break – unless someone on the beach catches my eye. There are an awful lot of pretty young things displaying their limbs in Oyster Bay, some of them in Polly bathing costumes.'

'Lennie Manning, you are perfectly heartless,' she scolded him.

'Yes, I am,' he said. 'I gave my heart away a long time ago and never got it back.'

Polly lowered her eyes and turned her face away. 'Don't,' she said quietly. 'I'm a married woman.'

'I know. And as long as you're happy . . .'

'We'll be going back to the city soon,' Polly said. 'Ren's leaving tomorrow morning.'

'New York in August? Impossible.'

'Oh, I shan't go until the end of the month. Ren has a lot of business to clear up before we start the Party's work, but he says there's no point in opening up the house when we'll be off travelling right away. He's going to stay at the club and send for me when he's ready.'

'Then you'll need an escort for the Van Plessets' party tomorrow night.'

'Are you going?'

'I *wasn't* – they invited me, but those things are so deadly.'

'Deadly? How can you say so? It's the biggest party of the summer, the one everyone wants to go to.'

'With you on my arm, perhaps I would see it in that light too.'

'Then you may escort me. You're the best dancer on Long Island – when Ren's away.'

Lennie bowed. 'The pleasure will be all mine.'

It was one of the many cuts he had to endure, that Ren thought him a perfectly safe escort for Polly when he was unavailable. He had settled into his role as dull, safe friend, since that was the best way of keeping close to Polly. He looked at her now, talking about the party and the arrangements, her profile cut out against the summer light from the window. She was twenty-seven, no longer a girl but a beautiful woman, cool, poised and capable. In New York, stylishly dressed, her close-cropped hair showing off the lovely shape of her head and long neck, her slender body (too thin to his mind) enhancing the straight, androgyne shapes of current fashion, her long legs in flesh-coloured stockings that made them look bare – in New York she was as polished, brittle and untouchable as any other young society matron. But at the holiday home, when there was no-one to see her, as now, she took off her makeup, and her sleek hair curled in the warm, salty air, and her limbs really were bare, ending in bare feet; and then he could see the little girl Polly, like a luminous ghost overprinting the rich man's wife, the political hostess. Then he loved her more than ever.

She was not for him, he accepted that: she was happy with Ren, and they were going grand places, perhaps to the White House. She would make a wonderful First Lady. And he would love her as much then as now. He would love her all the way to the grave. But he understood that he would only be allowed to stay near her if he did not make that too obvious – hence Veronica Starr and the other young ladies. He was a wealthy man, his first million behind him, and attractive enough to females to make it easy to fill the place on his arm during the social season. He didn't keep any of them long – he had no wish to raise false hopes – and he was afraid he was getting a reputation as heartless. That did not spoil his attractions, of course; girls always wanted to be the one to 'tame' the heartless man. But he was afraid Granny Ruth in Heaven was shaking her head and thinking he was turning into a cad. He tried not to be, to give the girls a good time and never let them think he cared for them. That was partly why he travelled so much, to give him the excuse to get away from all entanglements.

Having no romantic distractions was very good for business. Manning's Radios was thriving, expanding rapidly on both coasts, and his name was becoming known in high places. It helped to have a president who was radio-minded. Coolidge frequently made use of the wireless and just that year had signed the Radio Act, which assigned regulation of broadcasting to a newly created Federal Radio Commission. That Lennie had been asked to be a member of the commission was a tremendous feather in his cap. He supposed he owed his advancement in part to Herbert Hoover, with whom he was tolerably well acquainted; he only hoped Ren had had nothing to do with it.

In August London emptied, and Society went to the country, the seaside and abroad. Violet and Holkam went to the South of France where various friends had taken adjoining villas and the Prince of Wales was expected if he could 'get out of' Balmoral. Oliver, Verena and the children had gone to Wolvercote to stay with the Aylesburys. Venetia, with Violet's two younger children, went to Shawes – the elder two were visiting school friends. Helen rented a small house in Hove and took the children, Jack came down whenever he wasn't working, and Molly came to stay for a week. And the Bright Young Things went on a circuit of each other's and their parents' country houses, meeting each other over and over with every appearance of pleasure and novelty.

Emma and Kit went first to Wolvercote – the Aylesburys were distant cousins of the Winchmores and therefore of hers too, and the present earl's heir was of their age so there were enough of their friends there for comfort. Kit was besieged with requests, by those who hadn't heard it yet, to describe exactly what went on on a film set, and had they really allowed him to take part in a scene, and was Veda Lamarr as beautiful as she appeared on the screen, and Raymond Romano as charming? He told with great good humour, embellishing where he saw the audience was agape for it, until Emma slapped his hand, laughing, and told him not to exaggerate. The August weather was rather cool and cloudy, but that at least made it suitable for more energetic pursuits. Emma enjoyed riding round the extensive park, Kit showed his prowess on the river with both oars and pole, and there was plenty of tennis, and dancing every evening.

After a fortnight Emma and Kit went to Scotland for the grouse, and fitted in a quick visit to her uncle and aunt, then came south again and migrated between various house-parties before returning to Walcote to host their own in the latter part of September. It was a happy summer. Kit acquired a tall and elegant dog, an Arabian greyhound called Sulfi, because he said it was bad for Alfie to be an only-dog, Emma learned how to play billiards one extremely wet weekend, and their harmony together seemed only to grow. Emma had thought that, because in most houses they would be expected to share a room, the thing that hadn't happened might happen, but it didn't. Kit usually liked to stay up later than her, so often she was asleep when he came to bed. When they did go to bed at the same time, he changed in the bathroom and put the light out before getting into bed. The first time she had reached out and touched him, he had flinched, but then he had rolled over and taken her in his arms. Nothing had developed, but it was very pleasant lying like that. They sometimes fell asleep nestled together like puppies in a basket.

When they got back to Walcote where he had his own bedroom and bathroom, she missed the warmth and companionship, and said so.

'Won't you come and sleep with me?' He looked at her, she thought, suspiciously, which hurt. 'I like it very much when we sleep with our arms round each other.' And, she thought privately, he was never likely to overcome his strange barrier if they were never closer than down the corridor from each other.

'Well,' he said, smiling, 'I will sometimes, but not every night – I don't want to spoil you.'

'It won't spoil me.'

'But I must keep my mystique. It's part of my charm.'

335

'You have altogether too much charm for one person,' Emma assured him.

He looked pleased. 'Do you think so?'

'*And* mystery. It's a mystery to me how a person who trained as a doctor can be satisfied with living a life of idleness.'

'Now you've hurt my feelings. Besides, I shan't be idle when we go back to Town. I'm going to help you with your slums. You'll need my expert knowledge. The medical training includes a lot about drains and ventilation and suchlike, didn't you know that?'

Emma laughed. 'You never cease to surprise me.'

Their house-party was a great success, and everyone said it was the best they had been to in years. Emma had drawn on her experiences and tried to make sure that all the things she had wished differently in other people's houses were addressed in hers, which Kit said meant she was going to be a great and famous hostess. October brought pheasant shooting and cub hunting, and at the end of the month it was back to Town for the opening of Parliament and the Little Season.

'I feel as if I haven't sat down for a moment all summer,' Emma said, as they entered their apartment again, where a heap of mail was already waiting for them on the table in the vestibule.

'That's the best sort of summer,' Kit said. 'No time to think.'

She looked at him with slight concern. He seemed tired and, unusually for Kit, there was a droop to his lips. 'Darling, the war's been over nine years now. We ought to be able just not to think about it, without having to drive it out of our heads.'

'Can you?'

'Most of the time,' she said. 'Being happy helps.'

'*Are* you happy?'

'You know I am. Married to you, lots of friends, plenty of money, and something useful to do – what more could anyone ask?'

'You are absolutely and completely right,' he said, catching her face in his hands and kissing her briefly and lightly on the lips. 'I'm happy too. I don't know what came over me – *fin de siècle*, perhaps. But when one season ends another begins – new plays, new books, new exhibitions, new films.'

'Ah, that's why you're feeling let down,' Emma said teasingly. 'No Hollywood film stars around, flattering you and making you feel famous.'

He clapped his hand dramatically to his chest. 'Ah, right through the heart! How well you know me, my princess. But you don't know the half of it. My brief contact with the world of the silver screen has corrupted me utterly. The truth is, I hoped I had caught the director's eye and would be whisked away to become the next Rudolph Valentino. But I can see from here there's no overblown movie-studio invitation in my pile.'

'Well, there's always another year,' she said comfortingly. 'I don't suppose that's the only time a film will be shot in England.'

'For that,' he said, 'I shall make you a cocktail.'

'I must change.'

'No, let's have a drink first. Take off your hat and fling yourself on the sofa, darling, in an abandoned attitude. And light me a cigarette while I shake up the doings. I shall do it in the style of the Sheik of Araby, so hold onto Sulfi or she might be overcome with passion and ravish me.'

That was the wonderful thing about being married to Kit, Emma thought: he made such fun for her.

A fortnight later she was coming back from the East End in the car, alone, having dropped off Beeseley, her agent, at a tube station. She was feeling tired and rather grubby after spending the day looking over some very bad houses in Whitechapel. She was a little depressed, too, for there were people living in several of them, and despite the conditions, they had seemed upset at the prospect of moving. The landlord was willing to sell, and Beeseley had told her the tenants had no rights over the properties and could simply be moved out – the threat of the police would be enough to make them go. But that was not why she was embarking on this work – to make people homeless. She could see that she was going to have to have some kind of interim plan, some just-less-than-derelict houses into which she could move people temporarily. But supposing they didn't want to go? It was all a lot more complicated than she had imagined when she had had her bright idea that day during the General Strike.

The traffic in Oxford Street was heavy, as usual, and she was glad that she was not driving as they stopped and started and inched their way along. They had stopped for a particularly intractable jam when she realised they were outside Selfridges, and she had been meaning for some time to get Alfie a new collar, so she told the chauffeur she was getting out, and would take a taxi home. She tucked Alfie under her arm and hopped out, judged her moment carefully to dash through the human traffic to the shop, and was just smiling at the doorman, who was touching his hat and reaching for the door, when a voice behind her said, 'Emma, is that you?'

She turned, and saw, with a sinking of the heart, that it was Vera Polk. She was not looking well: her face was pale and drawn, her hair quite grey now under an unfashionable beret, and she limped heavily as she came towards her. She looked ten years older since they had last met.

'How are you, Vera?' she asked, expecting a tirade.

But Vera reached out to pat Alfie's head. 'Who's this little fellow? I suppose Benson's dead, is he? He must have been an old dog. You'd had him since the war.'

Emma winced at her directness, but said, 'Yes, he's dead. This is Alfie.'

Vera examined her. 'You're looking well.'

'Thank you. I am. And you . . . ?' She couldn't finish the sentence honestly, so she made it a question.

Vera shrugged. 'Having trouble with the leg. Some kind of infection in the bone. Hurts a bit.'

Emma was shocked. Her time at the Front told her how serious that was – and how painful. She was about to speak when the doorman, still holding open the door, coughed politely. They were causing a traffic jam. In a moment of compassion Emma said, 'We can't stand here blocking the path. Will you come and have a cup of tea with me?'

Under the artificial light in the tea room, Emma thought Vera looked even worse, almost like an old woman. She ordered tea and toast, and braced herself for the usual embarrassment. But Vera seemed pleased to see her, and chatted pleasantly about the doings of the FANY and news of their common acquaintances. Then, to deflect the subject from herself, Emma told her about Molly's new job, and Vera seemed genuinely interested, and said some intelligent things about publishing and books in general.

'By the way,' she said suddenly, 'isn't there an actor called Simon Baron living in the same house as Molly?'

'Yes, I believe so,' Emma said. 'I've never met him but I think that was the name Molly mentioned. How did you know?'

'He's a friend of one of my lodgers, Richard Vanbrugh – he's an actor, too. You might know his brother – Edward?'

'Edward Vanbrugh? *Lord* Vanbrugh?' Vera nodded. 'I didn't know Van had a brother.'

'I'm not surprised. Richard is the black sheep of the family. They cast him off.'

'For being an actor?' Emma said. 'That's awfully Gothic, these days.'

'Oh, not only for being an actor. By the way, congratulations on your marriage. I must say, I couldn't have been more surprised that Kit Westhoven married you.'

Emma bristled. 'I *beg* your pardon?'

'I suppose I should have said, that *you* married *him*.'

'Why on earth shouldn't I?' Emma asked, with a sinking feeling that she had been lulled into a false sense of security. Vera was going to be embarrassing after all. 'We'd been seeing each other for ages.'

'Oh yes, *seeing* each other. I hear he's wonderful company. Naturally one never expected you'd actually get married.'

Emma's nostrils flared. She said quietly, 'I don't care for innuendo. You had better say what it is you want to say and get it over with.'

Vera cocked her head. 'You don't mean you don't *know* about Kit? Surely you must do by now. It was never really much of a secret. I mean, before the war there was Tim Beaufort – he was killed at Cambrai. Then there was Rommie Worseley. I know you know the Worseley girls, because I've seen your picture quite recently with Padua.'

'I know Rommie,' Emma said, puzzled. Romulus Worseley came between Amalfia and Padua in age, so he was a couple of years younger than her, but he had hung about on the fringes of their group for years. 'What's he got to do with Tim Beaufort?'

Vera didn't answer that. 'And then Kit's been running about all over London with Raymond Romano – you must know about that because that's *since* you were married. It's very broad-minded of you, and I salute you, really.'

'What are you *saying*?' Emma said, frustrated, but with dread knocking at the door of understanding. 'Why shouldn't Kit be friends with a film star?'

'It's a bit more than friends, isn't it?' Vera said, in a small, deadly voice. 'That's why one was surprised he got married, because he was never one for the ladies. And don't give me that look, because you know exactly what I mean.'

Emma was stunned. She couldn't speak for a long moment, and Vera took her chance to continue twisting the knife.

'Funny how it's always the artistic ones, isn't it? I mean, Oscar Wilde, obviously, actors like Richard and Simon B, poets like Siegfried Sassoon, ballet dancers – lots of *them*. They're always hanging around my house, the poor Russian boys, lost and lonely. And, of course, that sort always know about each other, which was how I knew about Kit years ago. *Years* ago, long before Richard came to lodge. People in your circle must have been whispering, even if it wasn't openly talked about—'

Emma found her voice. 'You utterly poisonous, horrible woman,' she said, in a low hiss. 'All you ever want to do is spread misery around. How dare you talk about my husband like that? We're happily married – *happily* married, I tell you! He's the best man in the world, worth a hundred of you!'

She reached into her handbag, fumbled out a pound note and threw it down on the table as she stood up, reaching for her fur. 'You can pay the waitress. I'm going now, and I never want to speak to you again.'

Vera waited until the last moment before saying, in a low voice that Emma only just caught, 'They think I may have to lose the leg.'

Emma froze, and turned back – oh, so reluctantly! – as though she were being dragged round by hooks. 'Oh, God, I'm sorry,' she said. Vera's face was a mask of misery, and she was, she really was sorry. She wouldn't wish that on anyone.

'I don't care,' Vera said. 'I'd sooner lose it, if it gets rid of the pain. I can't bear it any more.'

'I'm sorry,' Emma said again, and for a moment, they looked at each other awkwardly. But there was nothing more to say, and she still never wanted to see Vera again. Her lips rehearsed a few words, but in the end she turned and walked away without speaking.

Vera watched her go, and her expression changed into one of satisfaction. Revenge at last! Not on the people she hated most – Venetia and Violet – but at least on one who was dear to them. And then coals of fire on top of that. How Emma would writhe!

She picked up the pound note. The tea wouldn't come to two shillings, and the rest would pay for a very nice supper in Soho for her and her two best friends. She finished her tea, paid the waitress and walked out, her limp miraculously improved.

Kit came in, and Sulfi came rushing to him, her long, fringed tail beating the air like one of those verandah fans, he thought. Alfie came skittering after, his nails slithering on the parquet, and Emma appeared in the doorway to the drawing-room.

'Something wrong?' he asked, seeing her tense expression.

'I need to talk to you,' she said.

'In that case, cockers first,' he said, making for the drinks tray.

'It's serious, Kit,' Emma said.

'All the more reason. Gin soothes the spirit, softens the tongue, and acts as a topical anaesthetic for whatever bit you're about to slice into. No, no, I insist, sweetheart. One cocktail, and I'll sit and listen quietly like a good boy to whatever you have to say.'

He mixed a White Lady, poured, handed one glass to her, and flung himself down on a sofa in one of his most flexible attitudes. Sulfi immediately jumped up and draped herself across him.

'You know I don't like the dogs on the furniture,' Emma said sharply.

Kit pushed the dog off, smiled and said, 'Phew! Well, that wasn't so bad. What shall we talk about now?'

'Kit, please be serious,' Emma said miserably. 'This is hard enough as it is.'

'All right,' he said, sitting up and eyeing her apprehensively. 'But before you say anything else, please think about whether it's really necessary. Bad things are always best put off until they don't matter any more. Like the jolly old unopened letter.'

'It's no use. Something was said to me today, and I can't rest until I know whether it's true or not.'

'Oh dear, what a bore! That's the worst kind of something. Hearsay poisons the air, even when there's nothing in it.' Suddenly he was subdued. 'Well, go on, then,' he said, almost sulkily. 'Out with it.'

'It's about . . .' Oh, God, this was so difficult. 'It made me wonder about our not – you know – consummating the marriage.' He looked at her with a mute pain that seemed suddenly the match of her own. 'Is it because—' She cleared her throat and tried again. 'Someone said to me today – that – that you don't like women.'

'Of course I like women,' he said. 'Women are darlings.' But he was looking at her like a condemned prisoner.

'Don't make this harder for me,' she pleaded. 'You know what I mean. They said you were . . .' She knew the various words, 'cissy', 'nancy-boy', 'faggot', 'fairy', but had never thought any of them would actually pass her lips. With a blush of deep shame, she finished the sentence. '. . . that you were a pansy.'

There, it was out. She wished it wasn't. He flinched, actually flinched, as though she had hit him.

'Well,' he said, in a small, toneless voice, 'that lets Felix out of the jolly old haversack, doesn't it?'

Emma discovered now that, all along, she had expected him to deny it indignantly. She felt sick, as though she had been punched in the stomach. At last she said, 'How long?'

'As long as I can remember,' he said, looking at his hands, not at her.

'At school?'

'God, yes! That's where it began, I suppose. My mother had just died. I was miserable and lonely. I hated school. My fag-master was kind to me. I'd have died for him. Then I went into medical training. Women's bodies – gynae-cology, obstetrics – the suffering, the things that could go wrong. They terrified me. But men's bodies seemed so simple, so noble. And then in the war they were being blown to bits.' He rubbed at his face, not knowing he was doing it.

'I don't understand,' she said unhappily. 'Do you love men the way – the way other men love women?'

'How do I know?' he said abjectly. 'There was a time, when I was in the sixth form, a bunch of us went on the spree. They picked up some girls – common girls. They pushed one at me. She was drunk and her hair smelt dirty and she stuck her beery mouth over mine and I couldn't breathe . . .'

Emma was crying now, trying not to, but the tears were unstoppable. 'Is that how you think of me?'

'God, Emma, no! No!' He was off the sofa and across the room, kneeling beside her, catching her hands. 'How can you think it? You're lovely. I love you. That's why I married you. I couldn't love you more. You must believe me.'

'I love you,' Emma said, 'only—'

'No "only". Darling Emma, aren't we happy together? I can't do that one thing, but is it so important, when we have so much else?'

'Won't you want to – to go with men? Like Raymond Romano.'

He looked startled. 'Is that what you think?'

'He's one too, isn't he?'

'Yes, he is. And I like Ray, I like his company. But we're

344

just friends. Emma, I swear I'll never be unfaithful to you. I can do without that – little thing. I don't have to do it with anyone.' She said nothing, only looked at him with wet, troubled eyes. He sighed. 'Then I suppose you will want the annulment, after all. I won't contest it, even though it will ruin me.'

'No,' she said, alarmed. 'If we got an annulment, it might come out – what – what that person said about you. You could go to prison.'

'I haven't done anything to be imprisoned for,' he said quietly. 'I told you – not now I'm married. I wouldn't do that to you.'

'But they'd dig up your past, they wouldn't believe you. If it got in the papers . . . No, no. We can't risk it. And besides,' she pulled herself up suddenly, 'I don't want you to leave me. I like being married to you.' *Who knows?* she was thinking. *One day you may change your mind.*

'You aren't thinking that one day I may change, are you?' he said.

She laughed, shocking herself as much as him. And laughing made her cry. 'You see?' she said, through the muddle. 'You see how perfect we are together? You're like my very, very best friend.'

'I *am* your best friend.'

'Then let's stay together.'

'Are you sure?'

'Absolutely sure. We have so much. We're happy. The rest of the world can go hang.'

He was so touched by her fortitude, he wanted to cry himself. He folded her hands together in his and kissed them. 'Darling Emma, so brave. I wish I was a better man. I wish I could be the husband you deserve. But I do love you, and I'll always be true to you. I just want you to be sure that this is what you really want. Because it may seem all right now, but in years to come, you may feel I've cheated you out of the life you ought to have had, and then you'd hate me, and that would break my heart.'

She looked at him levelly. 'I can't tell how I will feel in years to come. Except that by then you'll have become a habit, and habits are hard to break. But if I change my mind, we'll just have to find a way through it.'

He looked at her, thinking. 'Emma,' he said hesitantly, 'if you wanted children, I shouldn't mind terribly much if you—'

She flattened her fingers over his lips. 'Don't say it. We'll be true to each other. Who cares about children, anyway, when we have dogs?'

He didn't want to laugh, but he had to. 'You are a most remarkable woman.'

'I know,' she said. She drank off the cocktail in one gulp, gasped at its strength, and said, 'Make me another of these. And then I must have a bath. I'm all over East End. And then we'll get dressed and go out and paint the town red.'

'Well, pinkish,' he temporised. 'It *is* only the Little Season. There's no-one up.'

After the second cocktail, when she got up to go to her room, he said quietly, 'You didn't say who it was told you. It must have been someone you trusted for you to believe it.'

She looked blank for a moment, and then said, '*Not* someone I trusted. And I *didn't* believe it. But it's better that we've had it out, now.'

'Will this person tell other people?'

She saw, despite his air of calm, that he was frightened. 'She's nobody,' she said. 'And she won't talk.'

Oddly, she believed this last to be true.

CHAPTER SIXTEEN

Being without the shop and the business was an odd sort of relief to Polly. She had thought it was important to her, because it was something that she had done herself, with her own talent; but she discovered that she had less need now to prove herself. She was Ren Alexander's wife, which was a source of envy to most people. He was rich and handsome, and he was 'going places': in this thrusting, ambitious country that was something to admire, whereas at home, she thought, you were more admired for *being* somewhere and *staying* there.

The extent of the envy was illustrated to her when at a literary luncheon in January 1928 she met Olga Graham, who gripped her shoulder with a claw-like hand and said, 'My God, it's little Mrs Renfrew H. Alexander! I can't believe you've managed to hang on to that dangerous man for – how long is it?'

'We've been married nearly three years, Mrs Graham.'

'Oh, my child, it's not Mrs Graham any more! I divorced Benny last fall. I'm on my third, now. I'm Mrs William J. Culver.'

Polly didn't know whether to congratulate or commiserate, and made a neutral murmur.

Olga divined her difficulty and said, 'Nobody stays married to number one any more. Fidelity is such a bore! That's why I can't get over the fact that I haven't heard *any* rumours about the glorious Mr A – not *one*! What on earth is your secret? You look as though butter wouldn't melt in your mouth, but you must be as hard as nails underneath to hang on to him. I hear you've sold your business.' She laughed in a glittering sort of way. 'What a shame! No more special gowns for me at cut prices!'

Polly had never given her a cut price, but did not point this out. 'I hadn't time for it, with all our other commitments.'

'Oh, don't tell *me*! Herbert Hoover's making his big play, and Ren's quite his blue-eyed boy. You'll find it mighty expensive funding Hoover's campaign for him. Ren may be a millionaire, but a million doesn't go far in a presidential campaign.'

'Ren isn't paying for the campaign,' Polly said, slightly shocked by the implication that it was for his money that Hoover patronised her husband.

Olga swiftly changed stance. 'Of course not, dear. I'm just saying it comes expensive. Not that it isn't an investment, in a way. But if anyone can lay his hands on the money, it's your hubby. If there's a banker he doesn't know, *I*'ve never heard about it. Unless that's why he made you sell your baby? Maison Polly, I mean.' Her eyes raked Polly up and down. 'Skinny as ever, my dear. No sign of any other sort of baby. But I suppose you don't have time. It can't be through any lack of devotion from Mr A, because I know I would have heard about it if he was straying. Still, there's always time. The White House has its own allure, and you'll have a harder job keeping him once he's in there all day without you. Just let me know when he's on the loose so I can try my luck.' And she laughed, like ice tongs being dropped on a tin tray.

Polly managed to make an excuse and move away, feeling as if she had been put through a mangle. But she comforted herself that Olga wouldn't have given her such harsh treatment if she wasn't eaten up with envy.

It wasn't only on Hoover's behalf that Ren was busy. He had told Polly one day that Hoover had been talking to him quite openly about succeeding him in the presidency.

'He thinks it's of vital importance that the president should always be someone who understands business. And understands that the government's job is to keep out of the way and let businessmen make money. But Lamont and Mitchell and some of the others say I ought to have some kind of public office under my belt before trying for the nomination. They say I must have a record to show.'

'Is that true?' Polly asked.

'It is unusual to stand for president without having ever held an elected position, although Hoover did it.'

'Well, perhaps it would be wise to be prepared,' Polly said. 'Have you got something in mind?'

'Governor of Massachusetts would suit me. It's a two-year term, so there wouldn't be any difficulty in co-ordinating with the presidential term, and it carries a great deal of prestige. Boston is an agreeable place to have a house for a couple of years. You wouldn't mind that, will you?'

'No, of course not. I like Boston.'

'It's only four hours by rail, so we could keep the house here. I should have to spend time here anyway, for business, so I wouldn't want to be too far away. The next term for governor begins in January 1929, but that's too close. Once the November elections are over, the fact that Hoover is in the White House will be to my credit, and if the Party backs me I could go for it in January 'thirty-one.'

He talked on about his plans, but Polly found herself drifting a little. She did not really understand the complex system of relationships, pressures, alliances and debts of obligation that seemed to keep the political universe spinning. It was an arcane – and a dark – art; and even thinking about not understanding it made her sleepy. The words 'White House' naturally came up frequently, and against her will she kept finding herself thinking of Olga Culver's words about having difficulty in 'keeping' Ren once he was there. But Olga was only making trouble, of course; and she hadn't been talking about the presidency. Even if Ren had been inclined that way – and she did not believe for a moment that he was – it was impossible to imagine any President of the United States sullying that great office with tawdry *affaires*.

In England it had been a hard winter, beginning in November 1927 with a total eclipse that the less educated took as a bad omen. There seemed some justification. In December sixteen hundred people hurt themselves badly enough to have to go to hospital after slipping on icy pavements. The flu epidemic came back and at one point a hundred people a week were dying. There was heavy snow throughout December, and in January a sudden thaw combined with heavy rain caused the Thames to flood, killing fourteen people and refilling the Tower of London's moat with a freak tidal wave. The freeze returned, and in February eleven people were killed by violent hailstorms.

So, it was a relief when at the end of April the weather turned mild, with gleams of sunshine and soft, southerly winds. If Molly had believed in omens, she might have taken that as a good one for the publication of *A Voice from the Trenches*, which was to come out in the last week of April.

'I don't know why I'm so nervous,' Molly said to Popovka on the eve. '*I* didn't write it.'

'Still, it is your first child, sent out into the world to face the storms alone, to sink or swim by his own strength,' Popovka said sagely.

Molly gave him an old-fashioned look. 'It's no use using motherhood metaphors with me. I'm an old maid.'

'Oh, so very old!' he laughed. 'Wait until you need to use

your hands to get out of a chair, instead of leaping up the way you do.'

'I shall never be *that* old,' Molly said. 'But really, Pop – you've read it.' She had brought home a set of galley proofs at his earnest request. 'Is it good?'

'It is good,' he said, and she was satisfied.

She smiled and hugged herself. 'Vivian says it could be a very important book. And he says the time is just right. Even a few years ago people wanted to forget the war. But now there's a curiosity, especially among people in their twenties who were too young to fight. He says there will be a spate of war *mémoires* in the next few years, and we will do well to get in first. And do you know what I've been thinking?' Popovka looked receptive. 'Perhaps if the book does well, they might even make a film of it.'

'Why not? People like to be harrowed when they go to the cinema.'

'Well, they do!' she laughed. 'Everyone likes a good cry from time to time.'

'But first, to concentrate on the book?'

'Gosh, yes. I'm so nervous about tomorrow. You will come, won't you?' There was to be an official launching of the book at Foyles next day, with reporters and literary figures invited, and refreshments provided.

'We shall all be there,' he reassured her, 'though you will hardly see us for the throng of eager customers. Now, Nina instructs me to ask you a most important question – what shall you wear?'

The launch the next day was a great success, thanks in no small measure to the presence of the Duchess of York. It was a great coup to have her there, photographed buying a copy. She had lost one brother during the war, killed at Loos, while another had been posted missing in 1917 and had spent the rest of the war as a prisoner in Germany. She was extremely interested in this first-hand account of what it was like for a sensitive, educated man to face the horrors of the trenches, especially as Palgrave had also been at Loos. The duchess's presence had been secured by Emma and Kit, who had persuaded Eddie to work on the duke. Eddie, Emma and Kit were also at the event, as were Oliver, and Jack and Helen, all eager to make it a success for Molly, and all of them bought copies.

The presence of the duchess brought Vivian Blake's uncle, Mr Dorcas, out of his lair, and he put himself in the forefront, all smiles and with a gardenia in his buttonhole, so that even Vivian was pushed into the background, and Molly found her fears of being in the public gaze had been groundless. She need not have bought a new suit, she reflected – a little glumly, because it had been more expensive than she liked and she wondered when she would have the chance to wear it again. She didn't even get to meet the duchess. But there would be good coverage in the papers, and some nice pictures for the illustrateds. And the book itself looked very fine, handsome binding and a sober but elegant dust-jacket, with just the title and 'by Denis Palgrave' on it. On the inside title page, underneath these words, it said, 'Edited, and with extra material, by H. H. Husthwaite and J. K. Julian, MA, PhD, D. Litt, FRHS.'

There had been some polite but emphatic argument at Morland Place when it came to this attribution. Both Miss Husthwaite and Mr Julian agreed the cover should belong to Denis Palgrave alone, and Dorcas Overstreet had said it was quite appropriate for their names to appear inside in this manner. The argument was over whose name went first. Miss Husthwaite felt it should be Julian's: 'You are the real scholar.'

He felt it should be hers. 'You did twice the work that I did, not just research but the actual transcribing and deciphering the handwriting. And easily as much actual writing as I did.'

'But you have all those letters after your name. It will do the book so much more good than my name, which is nothing.'

'My letters will still be there. Your name should go first because the whole thing was your idea.'

'You are the senior.'

'Ladies first.'

In the end, Teddy had to step in and adjudicate, and unwilling to upset either of them, ruled that it was logical for the names to be presented alphabetically, which allowed them both to retire from the argument with dignity.

When the arrangements for publication day were being set out, it had been thought that a Morland Place party should be there, with Teddy as the prime mover, the two editors, and Laura Palgrave as the owner of the copyright and representing the author. Miss Husthwaite and Mr Julian declined, neither of them wanting the publicity and not wishing to detract from the importance of the author. On learning that the Duchess of York would be there, Mr Dorcas immediately conceived what a pretty picture it would make to have little Laura present her with a bouquet and perhaps a specially bound copy. But Teddy, who had been toying with the idea of taking Laura to the launch, realised then what a strain the whole thing would be on a very small girl not yet eight years old, vetoed the idea and said that he himself would not be attending either. Let the book stand or fail on its own merits.

So Morland Place was not represented; but Vivian Blake had secured a copy from the printers and posted it to Teddy the day before so that it arrived actually on publication day; and Teddy himself placed it in the hands of a rather bewildered little girl at breakfast, and told her she could be very proud.

After the business at the bookshop, Mr Dorcas whisked Vivian away for a grand luncheon with leading literary critics, booksellers and press barons, and he went with a half-humorous, half-apologetic look at Molly over his shoulder. Molly shrugged to herself – this was business, and she quite understood – and then went off for a celebration of her own with her friends at the Lamb and Flag in Rose Street.

Within a very few days, it was known that the book was going to be a success. Blake was proved right that it was just the time for such *mémoires*, and the additional material made it easy for a new generation to understand the context, while Denis Palgrave's powerful words conveyed an unforgettable impression of his experiences. The literary critics were impressed; the popular critics were in raptures; Foyles reported record sales; other bookshops were clamouring for copies faster than they could be printed; men in their clubs said it was very true, very accurate; academics said it should be required reading. John Julian received an invitation from his own college to give the memorial lecture, and the Royal Historical Society asked him to address them. And Dorcas Overstreet received letters from all over the country praising the book.

It was as well that Molly had the pleasure of that success to bolster her confidence, for once the fuss had died down, Vivian Blake came back to her about her own book, which she had finished at Christmas and asked him, rather tentatively, to read. In an interview that seemed to be almost as embarrassing to him as to her, he told her that, while it was not without merit, he didn't feel he could publish it.

'Because it's a detective story?' She remembered he had told her his uncle didn't approve of them.

'That's part of the reason,' he said. 'It is a good detective story. The plot is competent, the writing is accomplished, it's marvellously witty in places. But . . .' He walked to the window so that he did not have to look at her embarrassed face. '. . . it feels to me as though you were holding yourself back – as if there is another, much more powerful book underneath this one, trying to get out, and for some reason you won't let it.' He turned back to her. 'Am I right?'

She didn't know what to say. She had had such high hopes that this book would see her in print. 'I don't know,' she said at last, and cursed herself for intellectual feebleness.

'It feels a little hurried at times,' he said, trying to help her along. 'Did you rush it?'

She *had* written it quickly, but that was the way it had come. Trying to agree with his criticism – for he *must* know better than her – she said, 'I wanted to get it ready for you to see. And – there was another book I wanted to start.'

'But that's wonderful! That means you are a real writer – always with another book coming up behind.'

She smiled uncertainly, glad of the compliment, but still embarrassed that he hadn't liked her first. 'So – *Death's Acres* . . . ?'

'I don't want to ask you to revisit this manuscript when you've already started on the next. Every writer has early works where they try out their strengths, find out what they can do, discover the tools of their trade. It would be fatal to lose the impetus by fiddling around with the last book instead of getting on with the next.'

'I see your point,' she said. She so wanted to agree with his analysis, but the fact was that she had been happy with *Death's Acres*. It had come out pretty much the way she had conceived it; and as far as she had got with the second, it looked like being in the same vein, which would mean it was also too light for him. It was worrying to think that she might be betraying her destiny as the writer of serious literary masterpieces; but even more worrying that Vivian Blake might have got it wrong, and that she really wasn't that person, but just the light and cheerful writer of light and cheerful fiction. She desperately didn't want to disappoint him.

'I'll just put *Death's Acres* aside, then,' she said diffidently. In her bottom drawer – that was the phrase they used.

Blake hesitated. 'I don't know if I should say this to you, but while it won't do for us, it might well do for another publisher. I don't know whether it would do you good to have the experience of being published, or whether it would distract you from your more serious work. And there's the question of your name. If you were to become known for writing light fiction, your later works might not be given the same respect.'

'I could always use a pen name,' she said, feeling more cheerful. 'D. H. Montagu doesn't have a reputation to lose. Do you really think another house would take it?'

He nodded. 'It's a good 'tec story. I could give you a list of the likeliest, if you promise not to tell my uncle.'

'Not *me* – Mr Montagu. And I'm sure he won't spill the beans. I don't think he even knows your uncle.'

'And, meanwhile, you'll press on with the new book?'

'Yes, every spare minute.'

'Don't hold yourself back. And don't rush. Let it develop as it wants to, in its own time and space.'

'I will,' she said.

He paused again, and said, 'Perhaps I shouldn't ask, since it would be taking you away from your work . . . You did say "every spare minute"?'

'That was a literary device,' she said. 'Hyperbole, if I'm not mistaken.'

'Oh, good. In that case – would you care to waste a little time this evening, and favour me with your company at supper?'

The fine weather carried over into May, when the Representation of the People Bill was going through the Upper House. It had passed in the Commons in March by 387 votes to 10, meaning that a large number had not voted at all. 'Presumably,' Venetia said to Oliver, 'the "antis" don't want to antagonise half their future constituents if the

Bill *should* go through, so they took the coward's way out and abstained.'

Ten years had passed since the first stage of votes for women had come into being, and no great catastrophe had befallen the country. But the newspapers were still full of letters and articles suggesting that while women of thirty seemed to have been safe after all, women of twenty-one were infinitely dangerous, and enfranchising them would be a national disaster. Look at their hair, their hats, their skirts, their smoking, their jazzing, their parading about on beaches in bathing costumes that *left their arms and legs bare!*

Venetia and her friend Millicent Fawcett – whose eightieth birthday party she had attended the previous June – increased the pace of their campaign, and wrote letters, gave interviews, addressed meetings and cornered individuals in drawing-rooms with the opposing view. Young women, they said, led a new sort of life nowadays, which was much healthier, and gave them independence of mind. They were frank and outspoken, and this led to better manners and more thoughtfulness than the old repression and formality. They were as sincere as they were charming.

'Old age has its drawbacks,' Venetia said. 'We all value the wisdom and experience of age, but we do not disenfranchise those who are not wise, or whose experience makes them bitter, stubborn or slow to learn.'

'Let us give the young a chance,' said Millie. 'They will grow old soon enough. Let us benefit from their youth as long as it lasts.'

'We have great problems before us,' Venetia said. 'The young will inherit them: let them contribute to the solution.'

Late in May, the two old friends sat side by side in the gallery for the two days of the debate, as they had listened so many times before while their masters decided their fate. In the body of the House, Venetia could see Oliver, with

Eddie and Kit, all ready to add their weight where necessary, and to vote 'content' when the time came. So many friends there now; still some implacable enemies; and at her age it was not hard to see the ghosts of those who had passed into the other world in the course of the long, long struggle. She thought of her cousin, Anne Farraline, and young Emily Davison, the two best-known martyrs to the cause; of her dear husband, and Millie's Henry, who had supported them through all difficulties; of so many friends whom the ever-rolling stream had borne away.

Down below in the chamber the old, old arguments were brought out again, dusty and rusty now, but still stubbornly thrust forward. A woman's place was in the home; women could not and indeed should not understand politics. Enfranchising women would destroy marriage and the sanctity of the home, would lead to bad governance and the ruin of the country. The voices sounded hollow to Venetia, grey and thin; their arguments were the bare sticks of scarecrows in a frozen winter field, dressed in rags, with a turnip for a head. How was it possible for anyone still to believe such things? Venetia looked at Millie, and she felt the look and turned her head, and smiled serenely. She had no doubt any more. The issue would be theirs.

The Leader of the House stood up to make the concluding speech – not Lord Curzon this time, but an equally implacable 'anti', Lord Birkenhead. He was opposed, he said, and would always be opposed to the enfranchisement of women – and he rehearsed once more the grim, tired arguments that had condemned women to be, not half the human race but a separate and inferior species, like rabbits or mice. But, he concluded, the will of the Other Place had been made clear; the majority there was too strong; their lordships could do nothing about it. He urged them, therefore, 'in a spirit of resignation', to vote for the Bill. Thus, with a final insult, the champion of wrong left the field.

It was all over. The Bill was passed, and the vote would be given to women 'on the same terms as it is, or may be, granted to men'. They stepped out into the warm evening, and paused to savour the moment before a crowd of well-wishers engulfed them. 'Sixty-one years,' said Millie. 'Do you realise it's almost exactly sixty-one years since I heard John Stuart Mill introduce the suffrage amendment to the Reform Bill?'

Venetia nodded. 'The twentieth of May 1867,' she said. It was a date engraved on every suffragist's heart. 'You saw the beginning and now you've seen the end. Such a long and winding road. We've all come so far, and given so much.'

'And gained so much,' Millie said. 'Including so many good friends. Bless you, Venetia, dear.'

'And you, Millie. None of it would have happened without you.'

Across the street, two young women hurried by, arm in arm, their silhouettes in cloche hat, draped coat, stockinged legs and high-heeled shoes seeming the very essence of the age. They had their heads together, talking, as they tip-tapped along the pavement on their way to some pleasant engagement, unaccompanied by any man.

'It's for them,' Venetia said.

'Yes,' said Millie, knowing exactly what she meant. 'They will take up their freedoms and do wonderful things. The best is yet to come.'

'And their daughters won't know how much we suffered for it,' Venetia said. 'They'll take it for granted.'

'Which is the greatest freedom of all,' Millie concluded comfortably. 'Come, my dear. I think there are reporters who want to talk to us.'

The Act was given Royal Assent on the 2nd of July, and that summer was marked with many and joyful occasions, services of thanksgiving in St Martin's and Westminster Cathedral, victory breakfasts, rallies, private parties and dinners. There were pictures and interviews in the newspapers, a newsreel at the cinema, and on the 8th of July, Nancy Astor, the first ever woman Member of Parliament, gave a magnificent garden-party at Cliveden on the banks of the Thames in celebration.

A few days later Venetia left her old home at Manchester Square for the last time. Oliver and Verena had taken back Chelmsford House and had been making improvements all that year, with the advice of Emma, who squeezed time to help from her own work on putting up the first Weston Trust building. Venetia was going to Chelmsford House with them and the children, and would have her own suite there, with all her furniture and belongings about her, and a laboratory to carry on with her work. Still, it was hard to leave the old house, where she had been happy for so many years, where she had brought up her children, where Thomas had come on his last leave, where Beauty had last said goodbye to her before leaving to catch the train for Scotland and the doomed HMS *Hampshire*.

It was nice that Emma and Kit were taking over the lease. They had not found a house exactly to their taste, and were still living in Queen's Walk; and it had been Kit who had suddenly said, at a family dinner one evening, 'But we're all fools! Why let this house go to a stranger? Emma and I shall live here. What do you think, wife?'

Though taken by surprise, Emma liked the idea. The house was large enough, conveniently placed, and it would be fun to 'do it up' completely. She had not seen anything in all the months of searching that had seized her imagination, which she supposed must mean that one house was going to be much the same as another to her; but if Kit was attached to this one, as she saw he was, it would mean at least one of them loved the place as more than merely somewhere to live.

'And it means you won't have to quite give it up,' she said to Venetia, when it was all settled. 'You can come here and visit any time you like.'

Venetia was glad that people she loved would be taking care of the place of her memories; but she couldn't imagine herself 'dropping in' for a little nostalgia. She had far too much to do. Apart from her own research and all the reading she had to do to keep up with medical advances, she was involved in the new campaign that Millicent Fawcett had started, to change the law that said boys of fifteen and girls of twelve could contract legal marriage – which was simply a disgrace. It seemed to her that whenever you thought you had finished, there was always one more thing to do.

For Lennie, 1928 was the year of television – the hybrid name had somehow stuck, and passed into common parlance. To begin with there had not been much 'tele' and very little 'vision' to the business but, as with radio, Lennie had been convinced that the new medium would succeed and have a great future. Just as people wanted the entertainment that radio could bring into their own homes, so they would be even more delighted if the sound had pictures with it.

Since John Logie Baird had first shown his device in Selfridges, things had moved along a little. In January 1926, Baird had demonstrated thirty-line images, scanned mechanically with a disc with a spiral of lenses, at twelve and a half images per second. Almost a year later, a Japanese experimenter had improved that to a forty-line image, with a photoelectric tube attached to the transmitter and receiver to improve the speed.

In May of 1927, Lennie himself had been present at a demonstration of television in the Bell Telephone Building in New York, before an audience of six hundred, drawn from the American Institute of Electrical Engineers and the Institute of Radio Engineers. The images were blurred, the movements jerky, but it was television, all the same. The first steps of an infant, he reasoned, whether human or industrial, would always be shaky.

In January of 1928 the 'tele' part of the word received a little more attention, when Dr Alexanderson actually transmitted pictures of forty-eight lines and sixteen frames per second from his laboratory to the homes of four General Electric executives in Schenectady, where they received them on screens one and a half inches square. The following month Logie Baird sent a television picture across the Atlantic by telephone cable from London to Hartsdale, New York.

In July 1928 Charles Francis Jenkins founded the Jenkins Television Corporation, took out the first commercial television licence in the United States, and from his laboratories in Washington began broadcasting three times a week, calling his station W3XK. The images were only silhouettes, but they moved, and they were certainly broadcast. At the same time, in London, Logie Baird demonstrated a colour television system using a scanning disc with spirals of red, green and blue at the transmitting and receiving ends.

Lennie felt he had been rather left behind in the exciting new world, and set his mind to doing something about it. His early plans to open his own radio station had fallen by the wayside when he had given the money to Polly instead, secretly via Granny Ruth, to start up Maison Polly. But since then his radio sets had earned him a large fortune, and he had no shortage of funds. Polly disappeared into the world of the electoral campaign, and was hardly in New York that year, so he had nothing to distract him.

By the beginning of August, his wireless station, W2XKX, had begun regular broadcasts of news and recorded music, and he was throwing himself wholeheartedly into expanding the output. The advertising for his own products that he was able to put out with his programmes had had an immediate effect on sales.

That month, Hugo Gernsback, the radio pioneer, used his WRNY radio station, which lived on the eighteenth floor of the Roosevelt Hotel in New York, to transmit regular television pictures, using mechanical forty-eight-line images and seven and a half frames per second. The Pilot Electric Manufacturing Company, which provided the equipment, was also prepared to sell the receivers to the public. There were more than fifty radio stations and one and a half million radio sets in the New York Metropolitan area; and the enthusiasm for anything to do with radio or television was so great that, even though the image was still only one and a half inches square, there were plenty who were eager to buy the receivers, and plenty more ready to build their own, using the instructions published in the accompanying magazine.

Lennie observed this development with interest, even while he was fully occupied with his own station. He could see that the mechanical disc system had serious limitations, and that in time there had to be a clearer picture and larger receiving screens if television was to catch the imagination of the general public. The mechanical scanning system could hardly go much further, but he was already too far behind to begin the research for himself. Instead he bought shares in an experimental electronics company in Bridgport, which was working on an all-electronic method of scanning for television. That, he believed, was where the future lay.

In the mean time, his radio station was his new baby, and was growing with satisfying rapidity.

'I've never seen you so happy,' Polly said, when she came to New York for a fleeting visit in September. 'I'm sure there must be a woman in it somewhere. Are you in love, Lennie?'

'With a lady called W2XKX. What a shame no-one can pronounce her name!'

'I heard you were broadcasting sports now?'

'I've done some boxing matches – they're comparatively easy. It's too late for the baseball, but I'm hoping to get some football matches. There's a big demand for sport and the sponsors are always looking for new stations. The most exciting new development is that next month I'm beginning a weekly drama. Kelly's Cocoa is sponsoring it. It's going to be called *Kellytime Theatre*. They'll all be new plays written by talented young writers who are finding it difficult to break into Broadway.'

'And talented young actors?' Polly said.

'Yes – I'm looking forward to being able to advance their careers.'

'And actresses?'

He gave her a stern look. 'Acting in plays on the radio is different from acting in a theatre. It's a special skill, and the old stagers will find it hard to learn it. And when television really takes off, my stars will fit right in.'

'Lennie the Kingmaker.'

'I hope so.'

'It's a very worthy ambition,' she said, 'and I salute you.'

'But that's not all. I've got some serious talks lined up – Potter's Canned Meats are going to sponsor a series of lectures on popular scientific subjects.'

'Pressed ham and science? I don't see the connection,' Polly said.

'They're going in for a new line of canned fish, and the linking idea is that fish is good for the brain,' he explained. 'It's a little tenuous at the moment, but they'll have worked out their angle by the time we start broadcasting. And I'm going to try for a series of live classical concerts, which I'll pay for myself so they'll be the Manning Concerts. Then there's politics . . .'

'You'll be employing half of New York before you're finished.'

'Yes, it is turning out to be rather a kingdom.' He made some gestures with his hands. 'I shall be pulling a great many people's strings. The power is tremendous! I don't know why

I didn't get into it before. I hope it doesn't corrupt me. You know what the old saying is.'

'Not you,' Polly said. 'Not my dear old Lennie.'

'You look tired,' he said abruptly.

'Oh, the campaigning never stops. There's so much to do. It's a kind of madness.'

'But your man is doing well?'

'Yes, very well. Ren says it will be a landslide victory.'

'I expect he's right. I don't think Al Smith has much of a chance. Standing up against the Volstead Act hasn't done him any good.'

Polly nodded. 'The silly thing is that Hoover really hates Prohibition too – he says all it achieved was to make him get rid of his wonderful wine cellar – but of course he doesn't say that in public.'

'No, I've heard him: "an experiment noble in purpose", he called it.'

'Yes, and supporting it in public gives him the backing of so many temperance groups, and Christian groups, and women's groups – especially the women's groups, because the temperance ladies are terribly fierce, and their husbands won't dare go against their wishes.'

'And after the election, what next for Ren?' Lennie asked. 'Is he going to run for office?'

'We don't know yet. Hoover won't let him down – there'll be something for him, but whether a secretaryship, or a seat somewhere, we don't know. Ren's hoping for the latter. He's not sure a secretaryship will be enough if he's to be president in eight years.'

'Well, he has the first qualification, all right – I hear he's a very rich man.'

'Yes, and it's nice that that's thought admirable in this country. Everybody wants to get rich – and it seems to me that practically everybody is, these days.'

'Don't I know it. Buying bonds used to be the preserve

of the few, a cosy club of bankers and their friends in Wall Street. Now everybody's buying them.'

Polly laughed. 'Even my maid has bonds. She checks in the newspaper every day to see what they're worth. It's too funny.'

'The doorman at my club told me he's made six thousand dollars so far this year, buying on margin. Six thousand!'

'Ren said something about that the other day – buying on margin. What does it mean?'

'It's a way of investing when you don't have the capital. You go to a broker, and put up ten per cent of the share price, and he borrows the rest for you. So if you have a hundred dollars, you can buy a thousand dollars' worth of shares. Then when the price goes up you sell them, pay back what you owe, and keep the profit.'

'That must be what my maid did, because I can't think she ever had much in the way of savings. It sounds like a very good scheme.'

He frowned. 'It's not without risk. What happens if the shares don't go up?'

'But they always do,' Polly said. 'The market goes up and up all the time. It never has gone down, has it?'

'Not since the war.'

'There you are, then. You have to speculate to accumulate.' It was the cant of the age. 'And *you* buy shares – I know you do, because I know Ren gives you tips.'

'He does. Good ones. But I can afford it.'

'You mean, only those who have a lot of money should be allowed to make more?'

She gave him an innocent look, and he laughed. 'I know when you're teasing me. Now, are you busy today?'

'I have a few hours. I'm meeting Ren later – there's a dinner at the Whitneys' we have to go to, with a congressman and some industrialists who might be useful.' She sighed. 'Remember when we judged people by whether they were interesting or not?'

366

'Never mind. Let me entertain you for those few hours. How would you like to have a look round my radio station?'

'I'd love it,' she said, her face lighting. 'As long as you don't try to explain to me how anything works. I was cornered by an automobile man last week who tried to tell me how the internal combustion engine works. I thought I'd crack my jaw trying not to yawn.'

'Poor Polly! I shan't explain a thing, just let you watch them rehearse a *Kellytime* play, and introduce the actors to you. We'll watch the news broadcast going out, and then we'll snatch some lunch. I'll take you to Sardi's, if you like.'

'Lovely! Maybe they'll think I'm an actress and do my caricature for the wall. I'm sure when you go in you're usually with an actress.'

'Still harping on Veronica Starr?'

'Are you?'

'No, there's someone else now. She'll be at the studio today. I'll introduce her to you.'

Polly wasn't sure she liked the idea of that, but though she quizzed Lennie all the way over to the studio he wouldn't tell her anything about the actress, only that it would be a surprise. To which she retorted that surprises weren't necessarily pleasant.

But this turned out to be both, for the actress was Rose – grown tall and beautiful now at nineteen, finishing her third year of drama school and starting out in the tough world of acting. Lennie had been glad to be able to give her a start on *Kellytime*, though he said it was a waste of her prettiness for her to be on a purely sound medium. 'But, then, if she was in the movies, we'd be missing her lovely voice,' he added.

Rose and Polly embraced each other and asked and answered questions. Since she had sold the fashion house, Polly had hardly seen Rose, for she had been so busy, and away from New York so much with the campaign, that she had not had time to visit Lizzie and Ashley. Polly watched a little of the rehearsal and marvelled at how Rose had grown up, and how well she acted.

They left the actors to it while Lennie showed her round the premises – the top two floors of a small office block in West 45th – and they watched the news being read, after which they picked up Rose and the three of them went off for a very jolly lunch.

They talked and laughed and revived old jokes and remembered family history, and Polly felt ten years younger. She couldn't remember when she had last had such fun. It was only spoiled when, as they were leaving the restaurant, a press photographer let off his flash gun in her face and his companion shouted, 'Mrs Alexander! Any tips for the election?' and she was forced to stop and pose and say something appropriate before she could shake them off and get into the cab Lennie had waiting.

CHAPTER SEVENTEEN

Teddy's son James had struck up quite a friendship with William Pennyfather during the summer. They were of an age – there was only a few weeks between them – and were both well-brought-up, good-natured boys. William was by far the sharper of the two, more intelligent and with ambition and drive. James resembled his father in *his* youth – easy-going to the point of indolence, and with no ambition but to enjoy himself.

'Not much point in *my* having ambition,' he said to William, as they rode side by side along a baked and dusty track under the summer sun. 'I know where I'm going to end up – right back here, whether I like it or not.'

'*Don't* you like it?'

'Oh, Lord, yes! I like it all right, which is just as well. I mean, Dad's really ripping, but if I wanted to do something else he'd have a fit, that's all.' He looked around at the green fields and the peacefully grazing animals with contented eyes, sitting his horse with the easy grace of one who had been put into the saddle at the age of two and spent his childhood scrambling about on ponies. 'I couldn't love the old place more,' he said simply.

Years of expensive education had not rubbed the delicate bloom off his native ignorance: he could not have put into words, as William could have, all that Morland Place meant to him. It was his home. But the duty of care was greater even than the bonds of love. He could not express these things, only feel them. He admired William for being such a brainy cove, and for not despising such a dimwit as he was.

William truly loved James for the straightforwardness, generosity and sweetness of his nature. James could not add two numbers together the same way twice, and had never read a book to the end, but he could ride any horse, and sick or injured animals placed themselves trustingly in his hands. He could look at a field and know instinctively how many acres it was, and what it was good for growing. He knew when it would rain, and when snow was coming. He could measure out exactly the right feed for a horse without the use of scales. Children loved him, he was courteous to women and respectful to old people, and he had almost never met a person he didn't like.

James had come home from Eton for the final time in June, having gone first as a pink faced boy and returned at last a tall, strong, deep-voiced man. He had been a prefect, head of rugger, cricket all-rounder, rowed stroke for his house, and little boys had practically fought each other to be his fag, because his demands were so few, he never thrashed, and his casual generosity was legendary. Despite his popularity, he was very glad to get away from college with the prospect of never going back. Academic work irked him, he hated frowsting indoors so much of the time, and being baffled by mental activities that he saw other boys coping with easily was almost the only thing that could make him angry. The worst beating he had received (being high-spirited, he had had his share over the years) had been for throwing a Latin book onto the fire in a fit of fury because he simply *could not* understand it, no matter how many times it was explained. Old Podger – Mr Podmore – had laid it on thick and rare because disrespect for books was the root of all evil, or something like that.

So he arrived at Morland Place in a state of happiness close to ecstasy. He dashed around the house, romped with the children, played with the dogs until they were almost hysterical, ate hugely, and settled down to enjoy the summer. William had to work, of course, but Jessie thoroughly approved of their friendship, which she thought could only benefit them both, and tipped the wink to the head man to facilitate it. So, they spent many long summer days riding – there were always horses to exercise or school – and if the boundary between work and leisure grew blurred, who was to notice?

William's special job that summer was the training of Rocket and his brother Dark Stranger, two promising colts out of Elegy by Flying Colours. It involved long sessions of lungeing, but also cross-country rides to develop balance and suppleness, and gallops against each other to develop speed. It was work ideally suited to two young friends whose greatest pleasure in life was to get away from everyone and enjoy each other's company.

They talked endlessly, about everything under the sun. James had his own sort of shrewdness, and despite his indolence was a noticing sort of person. And he found he could say an awful lot more things to William than to anyone else, because William *got* things so quickly, and could help him out with words when he was stuck. In William's company, James felt almost clever. And William found James the most receptive companion anyone could want, interested in everything he had to say, and knowing a great deal about the natural world, animals and farming and the countryside, that he was too modest to think important.

The other great pleasure they had came from James's birthday present. His birthday had been in April, and he had been very disappointed when the thing he had longed for most did not materialise – though being a nice boy he thanked his father heartily for the new fountain pen and the hunting

371

whip he had given him. But when he got home in June, his father had taken him to one side and said, 'There's something particular I want to show you, my boy. It's out in the stables. Will you come?'

James had gone with him, expecting to see a new horse or a litter of puppies – perhaps Dad was going to give him a dog of his own, he thought, blushing with excitement. The reality was beyond his wildest dreams. There in the stall opposite the stable door, propped on its foot rest, was a brand-new, shiny motor-bicycle. He turned to his father, his heart in his face, struck completely dumb.

Teddy smiled with pleasure at his reaction. 'I know it's what you wanted on your birthday, but you couldn't have got any use out of it at school, so I thought I would wait until the summer holidays, when you could be out and about on it. Happy birthday, my dear boy, though it is two months late.'

James was so lost for words that he flung his arms round his father's neck and hugged him, something he had not done for years, not since a fellow at school told him only girls kissed while proper men shook hands. Teddy patted his shoulder awkwardly, his heart full to bursting. He loved to give – but to give to his dear boy, and know it gave him so much pleasure, brought him almost to tears.

Now James was hanging over the machine, a Sunbeam Model 90, examining every detail with a lover's eyes. 'She's *beautiful*!' he said at last.

So she was, neat, sturdy and elegant, gleaming with chrome and black paint, with the signature gold line edging the name panel under the crossbar. Sunbeams had such an untouchable reputation for quality, finish and reliability that the roadster models were often dubbed 'the gentleman's motorcycle'; but the Model 90 was also fast, the most sporting of any roadster, capable of holding its own against all-comers.

'It's the best present I ever had,' he said. 'Thank you, Dad.'

'Well,' said Teddy, pleased, 'let's see you ride her. Wheel her out and you can take her up and down the track and show me.'

James obliged, and continued to ride up and down the track long after Teddy had had enough of admiring the new mount and had gone inside for tea. Since then, riding the Sunbeam, cleaning the Sunbeam, oiling and polishing the Sunbeam, and standing gazing at the Sunbeam like a lovesick swain, had competed with all the other activities of a busy summer.

William was his natural ally, the one person who could truly appreciate the fabulous nature of the gift. They spent many a happy evening cleaning it together, examining and discussing the engine, and James was generous about offering 'turns', which only convinced William that his life would not be fulfilled until he, too, owned a motor-bicycle, and that he must start saving at once.

The Sunbeam only had a saddle for one, but the luggage carrier over the back wheel could take the weight of a 'shrimp' like William (who was as tall as James, but much lighter in build), and they often went off together, with William riding pillion, his long legs dangling to either side, his feet held up off the road. It was wonderful, James found, to have such a freedom to get about, particularly in the evening when a fellow might want to go into York, or to the Have Another, as everyone called the Hare and Heather. He and William went to the cinema together, and to one or two dances and tennis parties, where they met nice young ladies who were very impressed by the Sunbeam – although they always, always asked what her name was, as though she were a pet or a doll. James had secretly named her Black Beauty, but he hadn't told anyone that, not even William, because he had a suspicion that Black Beauty had actually been a gelding – and besides, it was a little silly to give a motorbike a *name*. So when the young ladies asked, he would laugh in manly fashion.

Towards the end of August, however, a shadow fell over James's charmed life. He and William were out on Rocket and Dark Stranger. They had been on a long cross-country run, and 'taken the fizz out of' the two blacks, so they now walked quietly on loose reins. They came to a favourite stopping place of theirs – a big, lone oak tree on a slight mound – and William said, 'We should let them rest and graze a bit before we go home. They're still youngsters.'

'Suits me,' James said. They dismounted, loosened the girths, and sat down in the outer shade of the tree, holding the reins at the buckle so the horses could graze. 'Gasper?' he offered, taking out his cigarettes. They lit up, and the gentle smoke drifted up into the branches. They sat with their arms around their knees, the dappled shade moving gently over their heads, gazing out at the heat dithering over the green country. The horses ripped at the grass with steady crunches, the bit rings jingling pleasantly like small music; the oak leaves rustled like a conversation just too low to distinguish; far overhead a pack of swifts tore down the sky shrieking in bliss.

James sighed, and when William glanced at him, he saw it was not a contented sigh, something so unusual he was almost startled. He didn't like to poke his nose into a fellow's business, but James looked practically glum, so after a moment he said, 'Is there something wrong?' A horrid thought came to him. It was unlikely, but less unlikely than that James was unhappy. 'You're not ill?'

'I'm never ill,' James said, with simple truth. 'No, it's the pater. He was on again this morning about sending me to Oxford. I keep trying to put him off, but he's absolutely bally determined, and once the old man makes up his mind, you can't shift him.'

'Don't you want to go to university?'

'I can't see the point of it. I'm no scholar, like you. Now if *you* went, it would probably suit you no end.'

'I'm afraid there's no chance of that,' William said sadly.

'There you are, you see,' said James. 'You ought to go. You're cleverer than a whole pack of foxes. What's the point of filling up the place with dunces like me? I'll give the beaks a fit, that's all.'

'Have you said that to your father?'

'Oh, he knows I'm a dimwit, but he says it doesn't matter. He went to Oxford when he was my age, so *I* have to go. It's not for learning stuff, he says, and only swots and trades-men's sons take the degree. But you have to go to meet the right sort of people, learn how to behave and dress and so on, and make friends for the rest of your life. He says just being there is part of a gentleman's education.'

William thought. 'Don't you think you might enjoy it, if you don't have to study too much?'

James sighed again. 'I suppose some of it might be all right – I've heard the men there cut up some larks. And there's the rowing, and the cricket, and the rugger in the winter. Oh, Lord, winter – the hunting season. I'll miss it all again!'

'Can't you hunt in Oxford?'

'One could go out with the Bicester, I suppose. But I don't imagine Dad will let me set up my stable there, which would mean hunting on a hireling. Too shame-making! It's just not fair! All I want to do is stay at home, get to know the estate and Dad's other businesses – get on with my life, not start it three years late.' He looked gloomy. 'Another three years stuck in the middle of a town, miles from home, no horses, no dogs, no freedom.'

William said, 'If you have to go, you'll just have to make the best of it, and try and get something out of it. You might make some good friends, like your father says.'

'I've got friends here,' said James. 'Don't need any more. I'd sooner have you any day than some Oxford chap with a Town accent who's never been on a horse in his life.'

To distract him, William said, 'I may not be here for much longer.'

James looked at him sharply. Above them, the tree rustled suddenly as though taking a breath of surprise. 'How's that? You're not leaving? Don't you like it here?'

'Oh, yes, I love it. It's a fine place. But I was never meant to spend the rest of my life here. I'm very grateful to have been given a start, and I've learned an awful lot, but what I really want to do is manage a racing stable. I can't do that unless I get some experience. And, fine though it is here, this isn't my own country. Eventually I'd like to settle nearer my own home. Be near my mother, now she's getting on a bit, and my brother.'

'So you want to go home?' James said, feeling a little bleak inside. He had never thought of not having William around.

'The racing at Wincanton is up and running again, and I'm pretty sure, with my granddad's influence and all I've learned here, Lord Stalbridge would take me on. I want to try, anyway. If there isn't an opening for me there – well, there are lots of other racing stables.' He looked at James apologetically. 'Like you, I feel I want to get on with my life. I'm eighteen – I'm not a kid any more.'

'Well, I can't say I blame you,' James said, 'but I shall miss you frightfully. When were you thinking of going?'

'Oh, I haven't said anything to anyone yet. And you won't, either, will you? I don't want Sir Bertie and Lady Parke to think me ungrateful – I mean, they've treated me like a member of their family. What I want to do is have a talk with the people at some of the racing stables hereabouts, see if they can give me any hints or advice. And then I don't suppose anything would come up for months. I expect it would be next spring before I'd move.'

James felt better. Next spring was a long way away. Anything might happen before then. And William's plan was vague enough never to come to anything. There was still his own problem, though. He knew his father well enough to know he wouldn't change his mind. They finished their cigarettes, and stood up to get moving again. 'How long is the university term, do you know?' he asked.

Teddy didn't change his mind, but two factors softened the blow for James and made it less of a wrench to leave home when the time came: first, that he could take Black Beauty with him. Teddy said he would arrange for it to go down on the train, and find a garage in the town where he could keep it, for it wouldn't be allowed in college. And second, he could take his horses with him because Teddy had an old friend ('You see how useful it is to go to Oxford and make friends?') who had a large house and park out on Headington Hill and would be glad to stable them for him. 'You can pop out there on your motor-bicycle any time, and his groom will show you the best places to ride. Oh, and Cosgrove – my friend – hunts, too, and he's willing to introduce you to the master, so you won't miss any of the season.'

James was duly grateful, and though he still thought the whole thing was a ridiculous waste of three years of a man's life, he resigned himself to his fate, and even found himself thinking he might manage to have some fun, if the other fellows were decentish. He would be going to the House – Dad had been at Christ Church, of course – would have a good set and plenty of money, and he knew without conceit that he would make friends. There would be the sports that he would excel at, and riding, thank God, and hunting; and with Black Beauty he could buzz about, all right, and he knew from experience that a man with a motorbike was attractive to girls. He didn't quite know why, but happily it was a fact.

He kept his word and did not speak of William's plans – in

truth, he was so preoccupied with his own fate that he pretty much forgot them. William also kept his counsel, but he discovered that someone else knew his secret. He was at Twelvetrees, had just brought one of the youngsters in after schooling, and had tied it up in a stall to groom it. He had just picked up the body-brush, when there was a rustling sound from above, and the horse pulled back on its halter and rumbled in surprise. There was a small square hatch in the wooden ceiling over the manger, leading to the hay loft: there was one over each stall, a cunning piece of planning so that all the haynets could be filled at once, then lowered into position. William craned up. 'Is someone there?' he called.

Another rustle, and a small face appeared in the gap, a narrow face with dark eyes framed by rough brown hair with bits of hay in it. It was Laura.

'What are you doing up there?'

'Waiting for you. I saw you coming in. That's Fieldfare, isn't it?'

He nodded. 'Do you know all the horses?'

'Mostly. Can I come down?' The face disappeared, and two bare brown legs appeared, dangling through the hatch. The horse blew in affront, tossing his head back. The grubby toes felt for the edge of the manger, and the rest of Laura lowered itself carefully down. With her feet on the rim of the manger she sat on the shelf that ran along the back of the stable wall above it, where grooms set down their tools while working.

'You could have caused a panic, coming out of the loft like that,' William said sternly. 'You're not supposed to play up there.'

'I wasn't *playing*,' she said scornfully. 'Anyway, he doesn't mind me.' The horse reached out with cautious lips and mumbled at Laura's toes. Having assured himself that they weren't either edible or likely to eat him, he sighed and settled down. 'You see. He knows me.' She straightened Fieldfare's forelock and scratched him behind the ears. He closed his eyes contentedly. 'Go on,' she said. 'You can groom him while I watch.'

William shrugged, took up the brush again, and started on Fieldfare's neck. 'Why were you waiting for me?' he asked after a moment.

'To speak to you. I *heard*.'

'Heard what?'

'Heard what you said.' There was an intensity in her tone that made him look up. She was burning with some emotion. 'I was in the tree. Why did you tell him and not me?' She spoke quietly, because of the horse, but there was no doubting the anguish in her voice.

'What tree? Told who? What are you talking about?' William was confused.

'I was in the *oak* tree when you and *James* came and sat underneath, with Rocket and Stranger, and you told him you were going to *leave*. You told *him* but you didn't tell me. You were just going to go and never say anything. How *could* you?'

He was disconcerted, and for want of anything to say, said feebly, 'Eavesdropping is not a nice thing to do.'

'I *wasn't*!' she said, so hotly that Fieldfare opened his eyes again in surprise. She caressed him quiet, her small, thin fingers operating quite separately from her voice or emotions. 'I was in the tree before you came. I often sit up there. I was there first and you came afterwards so I wasn't eaves-dropping – and, besides, it's a good job I heard because you wouldn't have told me otherwise, would you? How could you leave?'

'Nothing's been arranged yet,' he said. 'Even if I do go, it won't be until next year. But I can't stay here for ever.'

'*Why* can't you?'

He was at a loss. 'You'll understand when you're older.'

379

'People always say that when they don't want to tell you something.'

'All right, why don't you want me to leave?' he countered.

She fiddled unhappily with the stiff black forelock. 'I thought you were my friend.'

'I am your friend. But friends don't try to stop people doing things they have to do. And you'll go away one day.'

'I won't.'

'You said you would go to the north and write a book, like your father.'

'Oh,' she said.

Laura was very proud of her father's book. She kept the copy Uncle Teddy had given her beside her bed. She hadn't read it – Aunt Amy had said it was too difficult for her just yet, but that one day she would be glad to read about her father's great courage – but sometimes before she went to sleep she would stroke the name on the cover and think of what it would be like to have a father. She imagined him tucking her into bed and kissing her goodnight, and in her imaginings he looked an awful lot like William, though she didn't really think about it that way. They had told her that the book was doing very well, and earning money which was being put away for her, for when she was grown-up. She liked the idea that her father was providing her with money through his book, though she wished she could have it now and not have to wait, so that she could use it to run away if she needed to. She didn't need to just yet, but she could see if William went she might have to go too.

'But *why* do you have to go?' she asked at last.

'To seek my fortune,' he said, trying to pick words she would understand. 'Being here has been like being at school. But when school ends you have to go out into the world and seek your fortune. Everyone has to.'

'James doesn't want to go out in the world. He just wants to stay here for ever.'

'But Morland Place belongs to James. There's nothing here that belongs to me.'

She tried to follow. 'So you want to find a place that will be yours, like Morland Place is James's?'

'I suppose so.'

'And when you find it, will you stay there for ever?'

'That's the idea of it,' he said, smiling to himself as he brushed down Fieldfare's foreleg.

'Take me with you,' she said suddenly.

He straightened up. 'I can't,' he said. He saw her eyes narrow with disbelief. 'You have to stay here and finish school. They wouldn't let me, anyway.'

'Then I'll run away,' she pronounced.

He tried to look judicious. 'No, I wouldn't do that,' he said seriously. 'Running away never works. They'd just bring you back and then you'd be in trouble with everyone and things would be worse than ever. Much better wait until you're grown-up.'

'But you'll be gone,' she said starkly. 'I'd never find you.'

'Why would you want to find me?'

'To *marry* you,' she said, as though that were a given.

'Oh,' he said. He saw that she cared passionately about what she was saying, and he was not inclined to laugh at her. Poor little girl, living in her lonely world of imaginings. 'Well, you mustn't run away,' was all he could think of to say.

'Then take me with you, and we can get married right away.'

'You can't get married now. You're too young. It's the law,' he added hastily. 'I'm not making it up. Ask anyone. You can't get married for years and years.'

She was close to tears now. 'Then promise me you'll come back and marry me when it's the right time. *Promise* me!'

He felt such fondness for her, along with the pity, that he didn't want to tell her lies, even to comfort her. 'I can't promise that. I'm a lot older than you. By the time you're grown-up, it'll be ten years on. I might have married someone else. I probably will have, in fact.'

Her lip trembled, and her dirty fingers plaited themselves together. 'But you *might* not. And if you haven't – oh, *please.*'

He *had* to give her something. 'Look here,' he said. 'If you promise not to run away, then in ten years' time, *if* I haven't married someone else by then—'

'You'll come back for me.'

'I'll come back,' he said, 'and then we'll see.'

She looked at him intently, digging for the truth behind the words. 'In ten years' time. You promise? You'll come for me?'

'I'll come and find you. But you'll probably have forgotten me by then. You'll be marrying someone else.'

'Oh, no,' she said simply. She smiled, her doubts gone. She looked almost pretty when she smiled. 'And then we'll go and see the world, and I'll write my book.' She thought a moment. 'That will be 1938. I'm going to write it down, so we won't forget.' She took out from her pocket a bent, rusty nail, the sort of thing every child carries about in its pocket, along with a piece of string and a lump of putty, in case of need, and carefully, neatly, while he groomed, she scratched the numbers into the wooden wall just beside the manger.

On the 27th of September 1928, the London premiere took place in the Piccadilly Theatre of *The Jazz Singer*, the first full-length moving picture with Vitaphone effects. It had been eagerly awaited since the news of its American première a year ago, and Oliver, who loved the cinema, made sure he got tickets.

Venetia could not be persuaded to go. 'I despise blackface,' she said. The film starred the popular performer Al Jolson, who played a Jewish boy who defied his cantor father and ran away from home to become a jazz singer.

'But you actually hear him sing,' Oliver urged her.

'I can go to the opera house to hear people sing.'

'Really, Mum! You hear him talk, too. You see him and hear him at the same time!' he said beguilingly.

She gave him a withering look. 'I have that with you every day at breakfast. Really, Oliver, if you are so gullible as to waste your money on such fripperies, I can't stop you, but to expect me to sit in the dark and listen to caterwauling, crammed in with a crowd of strangers all sniffing and coughing and spraying their germs about . . .'

Oliver held up his hands. '*Pax! Pax!* I promise never to ask you again. I thought you might like to witness another new dawn, that's all. It's been months since women got the vote, and I thought life would be getting rather flat for you.'

He had made her laugh. 'You foolish boy!'

'You are happy, aren't you?' he asked her suddenly.

'Of course I am. I have you and Verena and the children, my work, and a friend or two. What more could anyone ask?'

'You don't miss Manchester Square?'

'Yes, a little, but it isn't as though it was our ancestral home. This house has been in our family for generations. Are *you* happy?' she counter-attacked. 'I must say I have been surprised that you have carried on with your practice since you came into the title.'

'I'm like you, Mother, dear – I need something to do. And I was never cut out to be the earl – that was always Thomas's job. Mind you,' he added, 'the patients are flocking to my door since I became Lord Overton instead of plain Mr Winchmore. Going under the knife is apparently much more exciting when it's wielded by a peer of the realm. If I had eight arms like an octopus, I'd still have to turn patients away.'

It was his way to make a joke to turn away pain. She laid a hand on his arm and said, 'God knows what He's doing. It's hard sometimes to see it . . .'

'I can't see what purpose taking Thomas answered,' he said abruptly. 'But I can't believe it was done to stop me mending cleft lips and grafting burns.'

'No, darling, it wasn't,' she said. 'Do you prefer that sort of work to the other?'

'Oh, I like both. There's a fascination to sculpting a new nose, especially when the original is a real horror, like that one I had the other week – I showed you the photographs.'

'I remember.'

'Poor girl could have sheltered small children under it. However, I'm not sure it's wise to bring God into the argument when talking to a plastic surgeon. A pedant might argue that God gives people these afflictions to improve their characters, and that we oughtn't to interfere in the struggle.'

'I have no difficulty with that argument at all,' Venetia said robustly. 'It was made by the priesthood about anaesthetics, and about asepsis. It could be made about any medical intervention whatever. We are not cattle, to die helpless of a broken leg that could be mended. God gave us minds and abilities to *use* them.'

'Thank you. The perfect argument. And since God obviously intended someone to invent moving pictures with sound added, don't you think you ought to come along and see it for yourself?'

'Not even if it was *La Traviata* or the entire *Ring* cycle,' Venetia said.

So Oliver and Verena went on their own. The film didn't begin very differently, although there was an excited feeling of anticipation in the theatre. There was a background musical score, and the early dialogue was silent, with intertitles giving the words on caption cards as with all films. But fifteen minutes into the film, Jolson performed his first song, and both his voice and the orchestra were in synchronised sound. At the end of the song, the cinema audience burst into spontaneous applause. Then the movie Al Jolson ran back onto the movie stage and said, 'Wait a minute, wait a minute, you ain't heard nothin' yet!' – his famous catch-phrase – and his voice was right there with his moving lips. The cinema audience shrieked with excitement and the renewed applause drowned out the rest of the words before he started singing his next song, 'Toot-toot-tootsie'.

Altogether he performed six songs in synchronised sound, and after each one there was wild and escalating applause, so that Oliver began to wonder whether the audience had forgotten this was not a live performance and Al couldn't hear them. The synchronised dialogue amounted to less than five minutes overall, but it was fascinating actually to hear a voice, when you had got so used to seeing actors and public figures mouthing silently like goldfish on the cinema screen.

As they emerged with the excited, chattering crowd into Denman Street, Oliver said, 'I'm not sure if we've just witnessed a birth or a death. Look at these people! They'll never be satisfied with silent films again.' He took Verena's arm and eased her through the press. 'Where shall we have supper?'

'Let's go home,' she said. 'I'm a little tired after all that shrieking.'

'Just as you like, my love. Shall we get a taxi, if you're tired?'

'You'll never get one here, with all these people. It's only a step. Let's walk. The fresh air will do me good.'

She had meant to tell him when they were back home, but walking arm in arm through the familiar streets made her feel so comfortable and close to him that she couldn't wait. So it was actually on the corner of Carlton House Terrace that she told him she was expecting another child.

★　　★　　★

385

A Voice from the Trenches continued to do extremely well. It had been reprinted twice, there had been a book-club edition, and a special edition was being planned for the tenth anniversary of Armistice Day in November. It was provoking discussion and continued to be mentioned in the press – Molly's old habit of gathering cuttings for the morgue was hard to break, and she collected an impressive file on Denis Palgrave's book. It pleased her to note that, even after a few months, it was settling into a place in the public consciousness that suggested it would become a classic. Perhaps the critic who had said it should be required reading was not far off track – she knew of several university libraries that had purchased copies.

Exciting though it was to watch the progress of *Voice*, she had other matters on her mind that autumn, for back in April she had submitted *Death's Acres* to the publishing firm Horace Greenstock, and with flattering speed they had written to her asking her to come in to the office and discuss a possible contract.

Everyone in the house had been excited about *Voice*, but they were even more so now. 'Because this is your *own* work,' said Pooley.

'They're going to take it, I know they are,' said Ingrid. 'I can feel it in my bones.'

'Oh, your bones! The most overworked skeleton in London,' said Megs.

'Let me read your palm,' Ida said.

'No, no, do her cards,' said Simon Baron, who liked the tarot pictures. He was cheery, these days – his appearance in *Bess of Hatfield* had made him suddenly visible among the throng of actors, and he had landed a small part in a West End play starring Tallulah Bankhead. 'The cards never lie.'

'I don't believe in any of that nonsense,' Molly said. 'Just as long as you wish me luck and cross your fingers for me, I'll be fine.'

'I shall tie a knot in the corner of my handkerchief,' said Nina, who hadn't got the joke. 'That always works for me.'

'When you are a famous author,' Popovka mourned, 'you will not wish to live here any more, and I shall lose my most promising chess partner. But I shall wish you luck all the same.'

'It's only the first book, and they haven't taken it yet,' Molly said, the verbal equivalent of crossing her fingers.

'You will not forget us,' Nina decreed. 'True friendship endures all divisions.'

'But shall you tell your gentleman friend?' Popovka asked.

Afterwards, in private, Simon advised *not*. There had been some awkwardness between Molly and Simon at first, after his 'revelations' about Kit, when she had gone back to him to tell him, rather angrily, that he must have been mistaken. But he had accepted it quietly, apologised, and told her he had not spoken to make mischief but because he had been sure he was right and had wanted to save her friend from an unhappy situation. Molly, relieved only that Emma and Kit were obviously happy, forgave him, and since then they had become as friendly to each other as any of the other tenants.

Now he said she ought not to tell Vivian Blake. 'It might place him in an awkward position, if you go to another publishing house.'

'He was the one who told me to.'

'Probably because he didn't think you'd succeed. Think how awkward he'll feel if the book he turned down is taken by a rival. He'd be laughed at.'

'But I'd have to tell him – he'd know anyway, if the book did come out. He knows my pen name is D. H. Montagu.'

'Use a different one.'

In the end, Molly thought that Simon's advice had not been so sound before so there was no reason to follow it now. She decided to tell Vivian, if the book was accepted.

She went to the interview at Horace Greenstock secretly in her lunchtime one day. The offices were not far away, in

Red Lion Street, at the top of a very dusty, shabby, narrow Georgian terrace house, the bottom floors of which were taken up with some kind of packing and despatching business. She toiled up the steep, cramped stairs, her feet loud on the uncovered wood, and thought of housemaids of yore carrying cans of hot water up and slops down. Thank God for modern life and modern plumbing!

At the head of the stairs an elderly woman with crimped grey hair was bashing away at a typewriter in a tiny office so full of papers there was no inch of floor or furniture to be seen. She gave Molly a very sceptical look over the top of her glasses and directed her to Mr Barnes's office, which was hardly any bigger, but had a large mahogany desk, and shelves and shelves of books all round the walls, all with the Horace Greenstock cartouche on the spine. It made Molly swallow in excitement. Books! Her own might become one of these, and have its place on a shelf!

Behind the desk was a very untidy man in a rumpled suit with cigarette ash all down the front, strands of hair plastered carefully over his bald top, a very blue chin and very shrewd grey eyes behind his glasses. He stood up, reached over to shake her hand, told her to sit down, reached into his drawer and held out something to her.

'Lollipop?' It was a child's sugar sweet – bright green – on a stick.

'No, thank you,' Molly said, confused.

Without comment he stuck it into his own mouth and sucked on it for a bit, while reading and turning the pages of what she recognised, with a pang, was her own manuscript, lying on the desk in front of him. Finally, he removed the lollipop and said, 'So, Miss Montagu. No, Miss Ormerod. It is Miss, I take it?'

'Yes,' said Molly, feeling it was an admission rather than a statement of fact. He had that effect on her.

'So, you want us to publish your book.'

It seemed to be a question, and she had no idea what to say. *Yes, please?* Should she give him reasons – praise the book? Be modest and deprecatory? He had appeared still to be reading, but suddenly he looked up, shooting her a sharp glance across the desk, and she realised this was all a game to unnerve her. He must have decided already whether to take it or not. He didn't need her opinion.

'I assumed that was why I was here,' she said, trying to sound cool and efficient. 'If you hadn't liked it, you could have sent it back by post.'

He laughed, and seemed suddenly much nicer. 'Quite right! It's a good piece of writing. And I didn't guess who did it until nearly the last page. Any more where that came from?'

'I'm working on the next one. I started it straight away.'

He nodded. 'I like that. No use brooding over your work if you want to make a profession of it. Get the words down and get 'em down quick. Now,' he said, slapping his hand on the manuscript, 'putting my cards on the table. I like the book. The plot's good, and it's got class. 'Tec stories are in demand – everyone wants 'em – can't get enough of 'em – especially classy ones like this. Agatha Christie, Dorothy Sayers – well-heeled folk read 'em, don't mind being seen with 'em. This one of yours – it's got a rough edge or two, but I'm willing to take it as it is. No time to fiddle about with it. I want to get it out there, let the public make the judgement. They're the ones who count, am I right?'

'Yes,' said Molly, feeling overwhelmed.

'Get it out there, get your second on its way, and the third. That's business. *But!*' He said the word so suddenly and forcefully Molly flinched. He leaned forward and fixed her with a gimlet eye. 'You're new. Nobody knows you. *I* don't know you. Who can say if you'll take? If I publish you, I have to take a chance that the readers'll cotton on to you. That's a financial risk. It could go well, it could go badly. I could lose money. Now.' He sat back. 'I'm willing to take the chance, because I like the book. But I can't pay you like I'd pay a well-known author.'

'I wouldn't expect it,' she said.

He seemed relieved. 'All right. As long as you understand that. Don't want any tears or tantrums. I'll take this book, and the next on the same terms, and sign you for an option on the next two after that, and we'll see how it goes. How's that?'

Soon afterwards Molly had found herself out on the street in a very dazed condition, and had to go back to work and try to concentrate when her mind was jigging up and down like an excited child.

Mr Barnes did not waste time: Molly was informed her book would be out with the autumn list, in October, and when could they expect delivery of the second manuscript? It was at that moment – if not sooner – that she should have told Vivian Blake, but somehow she couldn't find the right words. It was the second book that was really bothering her. It was turning out to be pretty much like the first, and the deep, meaningful, powerful book he had sensed struggling to get out did not seem to be making its presence felt to her. He thought she was going to be a 'literary' writer, of the sort that Dorcas Overstreet could make its own, but she had a nagging feeling that she was just writing books that she enjoyed writing and hoped other people would enjoy reading – and, worse, *that that was really what she wanted to do!* She so very much didn't want to disappoint him; and the longer she left it without telling him, the less she could bring herself to do it.

The day came when she found a parcel waiting for her when she got home from work, a nice, heavy, square sort of parcel, neatly tied in brown paper and string. She bore it upstairs and had only just got her door open when Popovka, Felix and Pooley all arrived like magic behind her, breathing down her neck and saying, 'Is that it? Is that your book? Let us see! Open it, open it! Do you need scissors?'

There were her six author copies, pristine and beautiful, breathing out that delicious smell of new book from their brown-paper nest. *Death's Acres* by D. H. Montagu. Oh, it looked so nice! The divine weight of it in her hand was like a living thing. The others had taken up copies and were exclaiming and congratulating but she heard them only distantly. Her firstborn! And soon it would be joined by *Stone Angels*, which she had posted to Mr Barnes just two days ago. She was a real writer!

Popovka was saying something that was intruding into her delicious reverie, and she came back to earth with a slightly cross frown at being disturbed. 'Hmm?'

'I said, now you will have to tell him.'

She didn't tell him the next day. Stone Angels was heavy on her conscience. She didn't tell him on Saturday morning, either. They were going to the theatre on Saturday evening, and were having a pre-theatre supper together at Bertorelli's, and knowing it could not be put off – he would see it in the lists, sooner or later: he looked at all the publishers' lists – she forced a copy into the pocket of her overcoat before she went to meet him at Aldwych Station. She thought how she would do it: bring it out when they were sitting down, give it to him lightly – 'A present for you!' – offer jokingly to sign it, perhaps.

But when the moment came, when she came out from the Underground and saw him waiting there for her, his hands dug into his pockets and his breath joining the thin fog around his head on this chilly autumn evening, all plans fled. She met his eyes with the pleading look of an uncertain puppy, and put the book straight into his hands without explanation.

He looked at it. She could not read the expression on his face.

'I wanted to tell you,' she said, 'but somehow I just couldn't.' He went to speak, but she stopped him. 'There's worse. I've finished the second book. I've given that to Horace Greenstock as well. I didn't try to rush it, it just came out quickly and, oh, Vivian, it isn't deep and powerful and all those other things you wanted! It's just another detective story, pretty much like this one. I'm sorry.'

He looked up from the book in his hands and, wonderfully, he laughed. He caught her by the upper arms and shook her a little, his eyes shining with amusement. 'Don't apologise! You have nothing to be sorry for!'

'But I didn't show you the second book,' she said miserably, unable yet to believe she hadn't upset him. 'And I don't think I'm going to be the sort of writer you want. Just another 'tec author. I'm so sorry.'

'No! I said you mustn't apologise! It's for me to say sorry. Which I do, with all my heart.'

She was bewildered. 'For what?'

'For being such a pompous ass that you felt you couldn't confide in me. And more than that, for being such a fool about your first book. There was nothing wrong with it! It was a good book! It was my uncle speaking, not me – I've been spending too much time with him so I've been corrupted by his ridiculous, snobbish strictures, dividing books into "proper" literature and popular fiction, and "We at Dorcas Overstreet do not handle that kind of book."' He imitated his uncle's tones.

'But—'

He was still holding her arms, and gave her another affectionate little shake. 'No "but". How dare you let me tell you what sort of writer to be? My darling girl, there's nothing wrong with detective stories. I love detective stories. Everyone loves detective stories, and why not? Promise me that you'll always write just whatever you want to, and will never let anyone else tell you to be different.'

She was smiling now, still rather bemused, but glad at the way things were going. Glad of the feeling of his hands on her arms. Glad – extra glad – he had called her his darling girl. She didn't want to feel too happy yet, though, in case of tempting Fate. A little more self-flagellation might be prudent. She said, 'I should have told you, though.'

He positively grinned. 'I've known all along. Yes! Barnes telephoned me to make sure I didn't mind. He knows you work here. I didn't say anything to you. I was just waiting, and hoping you would tell me of your own accord – and you did, of course. I knew you would. You're too honest to keep secrets. That's one of the things I love about you.'

'L-love about me?'

He tucked the book under his arm so that he could take hold of her hands. 'I've been more sorts of an idiot than I can possibly tell you about. I think I knew it when I read *Death's Acres*, except I wouldn't admit it to myself. I've always been so proud of my intellect, and I knew underneath that I couldn't give you a proper, impartial criticism, feeling about you the way I did. I dreaded having you give me your second book, and it took me weeks to realise that the real reason was that when I read your words, it's like having you talk to me, and having you talk to me is—'

'Heaven!' she interrupted.

He gazed into her face. 'Do you feel it too? I didn't believe you really could. You're so cool and independent and capable, I couldn't see what you would want me for, what use I could be to you. Especially when I couldn't even advise you properly about publishing.' He groaned and clapped a hand to his head. 'And you went to Barnes alone! Talk about Daniel in the den of lions! Please tell me he didn't sign you up to a really terrible contract. Knowing Barnes he will have tried to, but you're so clever you'll have seen through him.'

'Clever?' Molly cried. 'I was so overwhelmed that he liked the book, I'd have signed anything.'

393

She told him the terms of the contract and he groaned again. 'Options? You didn't sign options?' She nodded. A determined look came over his face. 'No, I shan't let that happen. *Death's Acres* is going to be a success. I know, and *he* knew it, the old devil. That was why he checked that I didn't mind. He must have been amazed that I let you go. You'll have to let him have the second, I suppose, but we'll get you out of that option. I can make him see reason. He won't try it on with me.'

'My hero!' she laughed.

'A hero too late – can you forgive me for being such a fool?'

'I can forgive you anything if we can get out of this cold and have something to eat. I'm starved.'

'Of course! What am I thinking?' He drew her hand through his arm and they walked away along the road, her book under his other arm. 'I can't wait to read the second book, now I don't have to be snobbish about it. What's it called?' She told him. 'Good title. And number three is on its way?'

'I haven't started it, but I have a sort of idea,' she confessed.

'Glorious! I knew it. You're a real writer. It's a pity, in a way, because I think you'd have made a good editor, but you won't want to be bothered with that when you've all this wonderful stuff going on in your head.' He stopped dead, causing a man walking behind them to swerve and tut, and turned to her, scanning her face with a harrowed look. 'Oh dear, I hope I haven't assumed wrongly? That is, I did understand, didn't I? You will marry me? I seem to have been taking it for granted but I love you so dearly. These months we've been seeing each other have been the happiest in my life.'

'Mine too,' Molly said, feeling as if her heart might burst out of her chest. 'Yes, I will marry you.'

He smiled, the best smile she had ever seen, anywhere. 'If we weren't in such a public place, I'd kiss you.'

Everything inside her seemed to go hot and shaky; but she had a reputation to keep up now. 'Perhaps later,' she said coolly, but she saw from his eyes she hadn't fooled him.

They forgot about the theatre until it was too late. Molly felt bad about the wasted tickets, but not for long.

CHAPTER EIGHTEEN

In the election of November 1928, Herbert Hoover won handsomely, even taking traditionally Democratic states such as Florida, North Carolina, Virginia and Texas. It was the first time a Republican had ever carried Texas. Hoover was known as a businessman, and as one commentator put it, 'People knew they'd make more money with Hoover.'

There was a period of euphoria within the Party, tremendous celebrations, excitement among those who expected their hard work to be rewarded. Polly enjoyed the parties, and Ren's buoyancy made him an even more exciting lover than usual, which compensated a little for the fact that he was absent from her more than ever, seeming always to be in meetings, closeted with the President-elect, taking press conferences, or pursuing congressmen to secure their support. What little time he had left over he devoted to financial business. Polly hardly saw him except in bed; but there, however long his day had been, he always seemed to have excess energy to expend.

But it was all very exciting, and she enjoyed the sensation of being caught up in the whirlwind, as the policies and strategies were hammered out. It all reached a peak on Inauguration Day in March; yet even before that, in the first months of 1929, she had begun to be aware of something being not quite right. It was as if, in a huge and complicated orchestral chord, there was just one note slightly out of tune:

such a minor discord it was not possible to isolate its source, and it was easy enough to dismiss the whole thing as imagination. But little by little she began to associate it with the question of what job Ren was to have within the new administration – for when she asked, he would never give her an answer, and his scowl grew increasingly marked when the subject was raised.

Then came the day mid-way through March when Ren arrived home at their rented house in Washington in a black mood, pushed past her greeting with a muttered 'Leave me alone, Polly. I don't want to talk right now,' and disappeared upstairs into his study. He did not come down to dinner, and Polly did not see him before she went to bed. She lay nervously awake most of the night, half afraid that he would erupt into the bedroom like a thunderstorm and ravish her, and half afraid he would not.

She woke early, unrested and with a slight headache, and lay for a moment listening to the silent house. She knew somehow that Ren was not asleep: she could almost feel his wakefulness, as a horse smells thunder. She got up, put on her dressing-gown, paused a moment to dash cold water on her face and brush her hair, and went to find him.

He was in his study, but the door was ajar, and she pushed it a little further open and looked in enquiringly. Ren was behind his desk, writing fast, with the short, hard, black strokes she had become accustomed to seeing on his notes. He was dressed, but unshaven and red-eyed: he looked as though he had not been to bed at all; but when he looked up from the page, there was no scowl. He regarded her calmly.

'I was worried about you,' she said. 'What happened?'

'Politics,' he said.

She was puzzled. 'Politics happened?'

'I should have expected it,' he said. 'I thought friendship and gratitude would have a part in it. That was naïve of me.'

She shook her head. She hated this sort of talk. She wanted facts. 'But what *happened*? What made you so angry last night?'

'Hoover is not giving me a secretaryship.'

Her eyes widened. 'Why not?'

'He says I'm too useful to him where I am.' He seemed to consider, his eyes moving away from her, regarding the wall with a slight frown. 'Which is probably true.'

Polly was angry for him. 'But he *promised*!'

'That was before the election.' His stare returned to her, and she saw that the anger was still there, only controlled. It glinted deep in the dark eyes, a furious spark being held down by an iron will. 'After all I did for him – practically funding the campaign . . .'

Polly remembered what Lennie had said. 'You gave him a lot of money?'

'Of *course* I did. And raised most of the rest. There wouldn't have been a campaign without me.'

'But – but the *ingratitude*!'

He shrugged, a gesture she would not have associated with him. 'It's politics,' he said again. 'Gratitude has nothing to do with it. I of all people should have known that.'

'You must hate him,' she said.

'Don't be childish. He and I are still working for the same things. I have my influential place in the administration.'

'But what about your career? A secretaryship, and then a seat in Congress, or governor of Massachusetts?'

'That won't happen.' Now she saw she had struck the source of that black humour. 'I'm not deemed suitable material. I have an enemy who has told Hoover certain things about me.'

'Enemy? Who?'

'He wouldn't say.'

'But "things" – what things?'

'Things which, if they became public, would cause a reaction against me. Hoover's not willing to risk it.'

'I don't understand,' Polly cried in frustration. 'What can anyone possibly say about you? You haven't done anything wrong.'

'It's not what I've done, but what I am. Hoover's been told I am of Indian blood.'

Polly looked bewildered. 'But lots of people have said that about you, and it never mattered. You've said it yourself. You've *joked* about it.'

'It's all right to have a small drop of Indian blood, far back in one's history. It's another thing to be half Apache and be brought up on a reservation.' Polly could only stare. His eyes seemed to drill into her, and she realised belatedly that he was scanning her to see if she had known. She felt a pain deep inside her that she could not at that moment account for.

'I thought,' she managed to say after a long moment, 'that your father—'

'My adoptive father.'

'Oh,' she said. 'You never told me.'

'I've never told anyone.' The hardness of his stare faltered. 'I'm sorry. I kept the secret for so long, I couldn't let it go, not even to you. I'll tell you the whole story some time. Not now. There's not much to tell, anyway. My mother left the reservation when I was about ten, she got sick, Dad and Mom took her in, she died and they adopted me.'

Polly's thoughts and feelings were in a turmoil. She had woken up in an unknown land where the person closest to her was suddenly a stranger. But, no, he was the same Ren, wasn't he? She did not know where to fit this new piece of information into the jigsaw of their lives. She tried to get a grip, and said at last, 'I don't see why it matters – being half Indian instead of just a bit.'

She could not miss the little movement of relief in his shoulders. 'I'm glad you think like that,' he said, 'but there's still a lot of hatred out there, and the Party won't take the risk of losing a seat, so they won't back me for one, or a governorship. I can't be put into the spotlight in case it comes out. Hoover believes I can remain effective in the background.'

'Oh, Ren. Ren, I'm sorry.' Polly found her fists were clenched with vicarious frustration, and loosened them consciously. 'I see why you were angry last night. But you seem so calm now.'

'Anger interferes with thinking. I have a lot of planning to do.'

'For Hoover?'

He looked at her curiously. 'I promised you the White House.'

'I don't care about that,' she began.

'Well, you should,' he interrupted, his voice hard. 'I don't want you to be kind and understanding. You should have more faith in me. I'm young, and Hoover is not the only way forward. What I want I *will* have. Do you believe that?'

'Yes,' she said. But she didn't, quite. She had come to know enough about politics to understand that it was not a one-man game. You did nothing without supporters. If Ren was so much of an outsider, how was he ever to get *in*side?

'I will be president one day,' he said, 'and you will be First Lady. I have said it. Now leave me alone, please. I have a great deal to do.'

She left him, went back to her room, mechanically beginning the business of the day. Inside she felt sore, bruised – for him, for his disappointment, for the betrayal he had suffered, for what he must be feeling about having an enemy somewhere who wanted to bring him down. But under that she was aware that there were other feelings, disappointments on her own behalf. *He had not told her the truth. He had not trusted her. She still did not know anything about his childhood.*

400

She shoved the thoughts furiously away from her, unwilling just then to examine them in depth. She was afraid of what she might discover.

Jack's association with the airship scheme naturally prompted an interest in air services to the Empire, since it was assumed that airships would be the long-distance carriers of the future. It would never be possible to carry enough passengers and cargo in aeroplanes over those long distances to cover the expense. Aeroplanes must remain fast, short-hop carriers, like the 'Silver Wing' service to Paris, which he now flew. For the first time, meals and drinks were served to the passengers on board his Armstrong Whitworth Argosy, but that was about the limit of the comforts that could be offered. On an airship, of course, there could be separate restaurants, viewing decks, promenades and even sleeping cabins, necessary to such long journeys.

But until the airships were ready, they had to do the best they could, and he took an interest in every detail of the new Imperial Airways service to Karachi, which began on Saturday, the 30th of March 1929.

The whole journey was to take seven days – a marked improvement on the weeks it took to journey to India by ship. The first leg was a flight from Croydon via Paris to Basle on the AW Argosy *City of Glasgow*. Passengers then took the overnight train – the Alps were in the way, and aeroplanes could not fly over mountains – from Basle to Genoa, where on Sunday, the 31st, they boarded the Short Calcutta flying-boat *City of Athens* to fly via Rome to Naples. On Monday they hopped from Naples to Corfu to Athens. On Tuesday they flew from Athens via Suda Bay in Crete to the seaport of Tobruk, where on Wednesday they transferred to a DH66 Hercules, *City of Jerusalem*, to fly to Alexandria.

Then followed the most intriguing part of the flight. To get to Basra on the Persian Gulf, the Hercules had to cross hundreds of miles of desert. There was no way for a pilot to navigate except from landmark to landmark, and in the desert there were no roads, rivers or buildings, just trackless wastes of sand. So to guide them, a gigantic furrow had been ploughed all the way from Palestine to Baghdad, hundreds of miles long, probably the longest furrow that had ever been ploughed anywhere in history. Following this, the DH66 reached Baghdad on Thursday, but there was delayed by a sandstorm before taking off again for Basra. On the Friday it followed the coast of the Gulf via Bushire, Lingeh and Jask, and on the Saturday completed the coastwise journey via Gwadar to Karachi.

'Remarkable,' Jack said to Helen. 'What a feat!'

'Something of a feat of endurance to the passengers, I should think,' Helen said. 'All that getting on and off and changing aeroplanes. Luggage packed and unpacked, things getting left behind. I think I'd sooner go by boat and be able to settle down.'

'That's all very well if you have the time,' said Jack. 'But supposing you had to get there by a certain date?'

'Then I should set off sooner,' said Helen, with inexorable logic.

Jack laughed. 'Woman's thinking!'

'I am a woman. You men are always so obsessed by speed. You won't be happy until you can arrive in India the same day you set off.'

'The airships won't be fast. We're only looking for a cruising speed of fifty miles an hour, though the top speed ought to be quite a bit more.'

'How are things coming along at Cardington?' Helen asked. 'Any new problems?'

He looked at her helplessly. 'Do you really want to know, or are you just being polite? Because I hardly know where to start.'

'I was just being polite, darling,' Helen said comfortably.

'I have even less interest in airships than you. Planes are my passion.'

'Pity,' said Jack, 'because I had been toying with the idea of our taking a trip on the Imperial airship, in a few years' time, when the service has settled down and the wrinkles have been ironed out. A special holiday, just the two of us. I've never been to India.'

'Ah, well, that's different,' Helen said. 'That sounds marvellous. I'll be as passionate as you like about the wretched gasbags, if it means seeing all those exotic places: Rome, Athens, Alexandria, Baghdad . . . Goodness, it's like something out of a history lesson! The Colosseum, the Acropolis, Knossos. Would we get to see a Pyramid?'

'Any number of 'em. And camels,' he assured her solemnly.

She wrinkled her nose. 'I can see camels any day, just by going to Regent's Park. What do they have in India?'

'Sacred cows.'

She slapped his hand. 'Monuments, I mean. The Taj Mahal? Oh, Jack, could we really do something like that?'

'I think we could. You deserve a holiday.'

She had been a little low recently – which he knew was simply reaction to all the excitement of Molly's wedding two weeks before, but all the same . . . And Molly and her Vivian were even now travelling in Italy for their honeymoon, and Helen had never been to Italy – or anywhere, really. Loving her as he did, he wanted to give her things, heap riches in her lap. He was not wealthy by any means, but they had been saving a little, steadily, for the last few years, and his new extra job was putting very welcome funds into the pot. He couldn't think of a better way of spending it than giving Helen a holiday she would never forget – and he would surely be able to secure a discount on the airship he had helped bring into being . . .

'We could do it for our wedding anniversary,' he said on a sudden, happy thought. 'Our sixteenth – January 1931. Nice to get away from the winter weather, don't you think?'

'You even remember our wedding anniversary?' Helen said. 'You're a very remarkable man, Jack Compton.'

'I couldn't forget the day that gave me the most precious thing in my life, could I?' he said. 'Oh, now, don't get teary. You're upsetting Stalky – look, he thinks you're hurt.'

William Pennyfather went home to Somerset for Christmas with Jessie's and Bertie's permission – he had seemed rather down of late, withdrawn and thoughtful.

'I expect he's missing James,' Jessie said to Bertie. 'They were such friends in the summer, and now James has gone away he must feel it.'

James had gone to Oxford in October 1928, taking with him quite a retinue, not only Black Beauty but two hunters, a road horse and a groom, Cobbey, to take care of them. Teddy had entered into an arrangement with his old friend Cosgrove (who was finding times rather hard and struggling to keep up his estate) whereby Cosgrove agreed to allow Teddy to pay him generously for keeping the horses and putting up Cobbey, and not to tell James about it. When James rather diffidently first visited Headington Grange to see his horses and meet their host, he was reassured by the warmth of his welcome, and felt comfortable thereafter visiting as often as he wanted, believing Mr Cosgrove loved him for himself alone. It was a happy arrangement on both sides. Cosgrove, indeed, liked James at first sight – he was a likeable young man – and was happy not just to send his own groom to show James the country but to take him himself. When the hunting started, Cosgrove introduced James to the master, and his first day out rekindled his love of hunting so much that he was out twice a week thereafter, as often as James, and something like a friendship grew up between them, as between an uncle and nephew.

So, come Christmas, James had written to say he did not

think it worth going to all the trouble of moving his stables for such a short time, and announced his intention of staying in Oxford until Easter. Teddy was disappointed but, on the other hand, glad the boy had settled in so well: he wrote of friends he had made who lived near the town and had invited him to stay during the break.

But William was obviously disappointed that James had not come home for Christmas. Having regard for his loneliness, Jessie did not wait for him to ask, but suggested herself that he might like to go and see his family. Given that the journey was so long, she gave him leave of absence of ten days, so he remained in Somerset until after the New Year.

He returned in the early days of 1929 with the news – startling to Jessie and Bertie – that he would be leaving them. He had the grace to look embarrassed, and spoke at length of the debt he owed them, and how much he appreciated all their kindness to him.

'But the fact of the matter is that Lord Stalbridge has offered me an opening in his racing stable. It's a good position to start from, and I hope that I shall be able to work my way up to trainer. You know it's what I always wanted – and I'd be near my mother, too, and my brother, and Grandpa.' He looked at them anxiously.

'Yes,' said Bertie. 'I can see how you couldn't resist. But, tell me, does this come as a complete surprise to you?'

William blushed. 'Well, sir – I didn't *know* but – that is to say . . .'

'A little bird told me you were interested in leaving us,' Bertie said, smiling to show there was no resentment. 'I don't know how these things get about.'

'I asked Mother to ask Grandpa to see if there was any chance of an opening,' William said. 'And then when you said I could go home for Christmas . . .'

'You thought you'd follow it up with a personal appeal?'

'I just went to the stables on Boxing Day – I thought I

might offer to help with the grooming or something, as I was there – and Lord Stalbridge said that Grandpa had spoken to him and asked if I'd like to take one of the horses out, so of course I said yes. And I rode every day after that, and at the end of the week he said he'd watched me around the horses and asked if I'd like a job.'

'Well,' said Jessie, looking at her husband, 'I'm glad somebody knew what was going on.'

William looked wretched. 'I hope you don't think it was wrong of me. Honestly, I couldn't be more grateful for everything you've done for me – you've been more good to me than I could ever—'

Jessie smiled and patted his hand. 'You haven't done anything wrong. I know racing is where your heart lies, and I'm delighted for you. We shall all miss you very much, but I hope this opportunity leads to the success you deserve.'

And Bertie shook his hand and said, 'You'll leave a gap, there's no doubt, but I wish you all the luck in the world.'

Alone together afterwards, Jessie said, 'The children will be heartbroken. He's their big brother – and they've already lost James.'

'You don't *really* mind, though, do you?' Bertie asked.

'No, he must follow his own star. And I never expected him to stay for ever.' Which, however, was not quite true. Lately she had forgotten to remember he was not really a fixture. 'I hope *you*'re happy with this outcome?' she went on. 'You were assuaging your guilt over poor Pennyfather. Do you feel you've done enough? Can your conscience rest?'

He smiled and slipped his arm through hers. 'Yes, darling one, I am happy. I've helped him on his way to an honest living, supporting himself by his own talents and hard work. That's all any father could want.'

In February, Jessie and Bertie took a couple of days off to go down to a horse sale in Leicester. The entire stud belonging to the Prince of Wales was being sold at the

Repository – the prince 'is not hunting any more, or riding in any point-to-point races this season', as the sale notice helpfully told them – and they thought they might pick up something interesting. They took William with them, thinking the experience of a horse auction might be good for him. It was a sort of farewell treat, for he was set to leave them at the end of the month.

At the sale the prices were high, probably as much because of the royal connection as the quality of the horses, but they did pick up one nice hunter mare that Jessie thought they could breed from. That evening they took William to dinner at the Grand, where they were staying, and there was rather a lot of wine drunk, and some close-to-tearful exchanges at the end of the evening.

A week later he was gone, and a chapter of their lives closed. He promised, of course, to come back and visit often, but Jessie did not expect it – his fate would move another way now. The children were very upset at first, particularly Thomas, and for some time afterwards Jessie kept finding Laura hanging miserably around the stables. Jessie guessed that she was missing William – she had noticed her hero-worship of the boy – so she took her home with her to play with her own children. Laura was between Thomas and Catherine in age and seemed to get on better with them than with the Morland Place children, who, Jessie suspected, were sometimes unkind to her. Nobody at Morland Place minded where Laura spent her time, so after William's departure, she was at Twelvetrees as often as not, and the number round the table stayed the same.

James was rather peeved that William had gone before he came home. Easter was at the end of March and he had been a month gone before James and his horses reappeared.

'Well, never mind,' he said, when he had had his grumble, 'we can always write to each other.'

'Of course you can,' Teddy said cheerfully.

Given that James was as ardent and frequent a correspondent as Teddy had been at his age, Jessie thought privately that the friendship was pretty much over.

'What is it, Mother, dear?' Oliver asked, coming into Venetia's living room one bright spring morning. 'You're tutting away like a woodpecker.'

She was reading a journal, sitting in a chair by the window to get the best light, and she whipped off her glasses as she heard his voice. She hated wearing those wretched 'specs' and didn't like anyone to see her in them, though such vanity was absurd in a woman of her age, as she very well knew.

She deflected attention from herself by looking him up and down with a satirical eye. 'That is a very bright suit,' she said.

'Cheery, isn't it?' he said, striking a pose. 'It's new. It'll impress the clients no end, don't you think?'

'Only if they are mountebanks,' Venetia said severely.

'Well, some of 'em are, if that's what you call Hollywood film stars,' said Oliver, irrepressibly. His acquaintance with Raymond Romano had brought other movie actors to him with minor blemishes to correct and even desired reshapings in mind. He was busier than ever. 'Have to put on a bit of a show, you know.'

'Why a *yellow* rosebud? And the pale grey is too pale. And that Glenurquhart check, Oliver – really!'

'Glen plaid, if you please,' said Oliver. 'Also known as Prince of Wales check, since it is the favourite tartan of our beloved leader. You can't object to anything the Heir to the Throne wears.'

'I object to almost everything he wears,' Venetia said. 'He dresses like someone from Captain Grimes's Riding Academy, but there's no reason for you to follow suit. You *are*—'

'An earl, yes, I know. Ancient blood runs in my veins and

the Windsors are mere parvenus. I like this business between him and Violet as little as you do,' he went on, suddenly serious, 'though perhaps for different reasons.'

'I'm so glad she's going away this summer,' Venetia said. 'Perhaps getting away from him for a bit will open her eyes.'

'I don't think it's her eyes that need opening, but I take your point,' said Oliver.

The Metropolitan Museum of Art was having an exhibition of Great War paintings and drawings, and one of the directors had written to Violet asking if she would lend Laidislaw's work for it. Violet had been eager that he should be fêted in this way, though she had confided to Oliver that she was nervous about approaching Holkam, and had asked his help. Oliver had agreed to put the request to Holkam himself, but had found his brother-in-law unexpectedly amenable. Holkam appeared both preoccupied and in a good mood, and had seemed not to care much what happened in a place as remote and unimportant to him as New York. He was not even difficult to persuade on the point of Violet's going along with the pictures – in fact, he had seemed to brighten at the thought of her absence abroad for several months.

So, things had been arranged. Violet's friends Dickie and Phyllis Damerel were going over to New York for a trip and Violet would travel with them for company. She was to take her daughter Charlotte with her: Charlotte would be seventeen in May, and Violet felt a little exposure to New York society and fashion would do her good in advance of her come-out next year. And with Robert at Oxford and Richard at Eton, it left little Henry Octavian rather alone, so she got Holkam's permission to take him with her as well. Holkam, for reasons of his own, had as soon not be left with the responsibility of him, and Violet secretly wanted her boy to be there for the exhibition of his real father's work.

So everything was nicely settled, except that Violet had

not yet told David that she was going, and would be away for several months. He did not even like her to be absent for a few days, and she didn't quite know how to break it to him. Oliver knew that his mother was hoping a prolonged separation would end the prince's infatuation with her daughter, and he was inclined to agree. If he were Violet, however, he felt he wouldn't tell David until the last minute, leaving him as little time to complain as possible. The Pragga Wagga, he had learned, was rather a harper-on when it came to grievances.

A random beam of sunlight, escaping between the fleeting clouds, lit his mother's face in passing, and just for a moment he saw how tired and old she had become in the past year. Henrietta's death had hit her hard – and she was, after all, seventy-nine now, a good age. She did not go out very much any more, and had given up her research work, though she still kept up with her reading, and there was nothing wrong with her mind. But he had been used all his life to thinking of her as the energetic, powerful, active surgeon and political hostess, and the habit was too strong to break easily. She couldn't be *old* – not his mother.

He said, 'You still haven't told me what you were tutting about. What's that you're reading?' He reached over and turned the cover back. 'The *British Journal of Experimental Pathology*? That must have been near the bottom of your pile.'

'I have time, these days, to get through them all,' she said. 'The one advantage of having retired.'

'Not much advantage if it annoys you so.'

'It's good to be annoyed. Keeps the brain active. Though, really, *this* does rile one.' She poked the page with a finger. 'The impudence of the man.'

'Which man is that?'

'Fleming of St Mary's. Professor of bacteriology, if you please, though he's just an ex-army doctor to me.'

410

'I think I met him once,' Oliver said. 'Had an article in the *Lancet* during the war – said antiseptics were killing more soldiers than infection was.'

'I remember it.'

'What's he writing about now?'

'The silly man claims he's discovered that *Penicillium notatum* kills staphylococci – as if we didn't know that already! Says he accidentally dropped some mould into a culture dish and the next day discovered a ring of destroyed colonies around it.'

Oliver shrugged. 'Not much of a discovery. As you've so often told me, Lister was there years ago.'

'And plenty of others since. Duchesne, and all that work at the Pasteur. And Gratia and Dath had *exactly* the same "accident", oh, ten years ago, it must be – and they wrote a paper on it. If this Fleming creature had done his reading . . .' She paused. 'Or perhaps he has. That's a more sinister thought.'

Oliver interrupted hastily: 'Quite, quite, but never mind that – what I wanted to ask you was whether you've seen my wife. I seem to have mislaid her.'

'She's taken John and Amabel over to the Vibarts' to play with Edward. He's rather lonely, with Georgie at school all day.'

Oliver frowned. 'She shouldn't be exerting herself like that,' he said. Verena was in the last stages of pregnancy. 'Surely one of the maids could have taken them.'

'I expect she wanted to see Sarah. Really, dear, you don't need to fuss. She's not a primigravida any more. She knows what she's doing.'

'It's in a man's nature to want to wrap his wife in cotton wool when she's expecting,' Oliver excused himself.

'"Expecting"?' Venetia said. 'My dear Oliver, what a terrible expression to hear from your lips. I think mixing with all these film stars, and such people, is having a bad effect on you.'

'Well, you should approve of my first appointment today, then,' he said. 'It's an operatic soprano with forceps scars on her jawline.'

'Maria Vilanova?'

'How did you know?'

'I've met her. But you can't see them from the auditorium, under her stage makeup.'

'She's been offered a part in a moving picture. She's to play herself in a film about her life and she's afraid the camera will see the scars all too clearly.'

'Vanity, vanity,' Venetia said. 'And what else do you have on today?'

'A burns list at the Sick Children's Hospital. Does that redeem me in your eyes?'

'Not in that suit.'

'The children will like it. It will cheer them up.'

'I haven't a doubt of it,' Venetia said unkindly. 'Children love clowns.'

He had just finished the penultimate operation on his list when a nurse came in and handed a note to the theatre sister, who came over to him and said, 'A message from home, my lord.'

It was from Venetia, to say that Verena had started labour soon after returning from the Vibarts' house. The midwife and the obstetrician had been called – Oliver had insisted on the latter, not wishing his mother to be placed under any strain at her venerable age, though she had snorted at the time and said it would be more of a strain watching someone else bungling about at something she could do with her eyes closed.

There was nothing for Oliver to do, anyway, but finish his list. He went to the surgeons' room to wash and change, and stepped out into a glorious spring evening in Bloomsbury to hail a taxi. When he reached home, the smile on the face of the footman, Edward, who opened the door to him, told him all was well.

'It's over?' he asked.

'An hour ago, my lord. Her ladyship has presented you with another daughter, my lord. Her ladyship and the baby are both doing well. May I offer my congratulations, my lord?'

The obstetrician had already left, no doubt driven out by Venetia, who was presiding happily over the whole business, confinement chamber, nursery and all. Sarah Vibart had kept the other children, so it was a peaceful household, even including the latest member, who was lying well-wrapped, red-faced and squinty-eyed in her mother's arms.

'A very easy delivery,' Venetia told Oliver as he came in. 'Hardly took any time at all. Absurd to pay Sir Horace's inflated fee for standing and watching. If he hadn't snipped the cord himself he wouldn't even have had to wash his hands.'

'Never mind, Mum,' Oliver said. 'I'd sooner have it that way than have him wanted and not here.'

He bent over his wife and kissed her, and pulled back the edge of the shawl to look at the baby's face. She squinted at him and pursed her lips from under an amazing thatch of black hair. 'She looks like a tomato in a wig,' he said.

The midwife tutted in professional outrage, but Verena met his smile with one of her own that spoke of complete understanding.

'How are you feeling?' he asked.

'Tired. Otherwise, very well.'

'Well enough to have some champagne tonight, to wet the baby's head?'

'I've already discussed it with your mother – you're both going to take your supper here, in my room.'

'Champagne is good for nursing mothers,' Venetia decreed, and she and her daughter-in-law exchanged an affectionate look. 'Now I'm going to leave you two – you three, I should say – alone for a while. I'm going to my room to rest a little. I've been on my feet for longer than I'm accustomed to, these days.' She went to the door, and turned back to summon the nurse. 'Let's leave them in peace,' she said. It sounded like a polite suggestion, but from her it was a command.

Later, Oliver was changing for supper – though it was only to be an informal meal in Verena's bedroom, he knew his mother would expect him to be wearing something other than the despised Glen plaid suit – when he heard a distant and muted commotion in the house. He exchanged a look with Hipkiss, his man, and said, 'I can tie my tie. Go and find out what's wrong.'

He didn't anticipate anything more than a dropped soup tureen, but when Hipkiss came back a few minutes later, he was trembling. 'My lord,' he said. 'My lord, it's your lordship's mother, my lord.'

At the door of Venetia's room a frightened-looking housemaid moved hastily out of his way, and Carless, her maid, came to him. Over her shoulder he could see the midwife at the bedside, leaning over his mother. She would never have allowed that had she been well.

Carless's eyes were full of tears. 'She said she'd have a little sleep, my lord, until suppertime, and I helped her off with her shoes and dress and left her. But when I came to wake her, my lord, she was gone.'

'Gone?' he said stupidly. He went past them, pushed the midwife away from the bed, stooped to look. Venetia was in her dressing-gown, lying composed on her back, her hands folded neatly, her eyes closed. He knew the look of death without needing to touch her. She had gone quietly, he thought, her heart worn out at last; had lain down to sleep and had slept. He was glad she looked seemly in death – she would not have liked to make a spectacle of herself.

Behind him the midwife said, 'I saw she was gone, my lord. Her eyes and mouth was just a little bit open and I closed them properly, my lord, just to be decent-like, but that's all. There was nothing else to do.'

He could hear someone weeping – Carless or the house-maid, he didn't know – and sensed the presence of others gathering at the door. *She's with Papa and Thomas now*, he thought, and was surprised how little the thought meant to him just then. He would be glad to think that one day, but not now. Just now, he only felt that she had gone away and left him. *One in, one out*, was what the servants said, the superstition that a birth required the departure of someone else to make room. But it had been a seemly ending, and without fear – *that* he could and must be glad of.

'Does my lady know?' he said, and his voice surprised him. He had not known he was going to speak the thought aloud.

Hipkiss answered after a brief pause. 'No, my lord. Her ladyship's maid is here, just come to see what's amiss.'

'We heard something, my lord,' came the voice of Walters, Verena's maid. 'Her ladyship asked me to see what it was.'

He turned and met the wall of eyes and faces and mouths, looking to him to tell them what to do. There was no authority above him now. He was the ultimate word in the house. That more than anything brought it home to him that his mother was gone.

'I'll tell her. Carless, stay with your mistress. I'll ring when I want someone.'

Of all of them, only Carless was crying. But she had her job to think of.

They decided to call the new baby Venetia, after his mother. There was nothing shocking, or greatly to mourn, in a quiet death in the fullness of years. Verena was cushioned from feelings by her new baby; it was Violet who felt it most, not having seen as much of her mother lately as she now wished, and knowing that she had disapproved so much of the relationship with the prince. And, before that, there had been Laidislaw. She had disappointed her mother on too many occasions to be able to accept her death with equanimity.

There was a funeral to arrange – a grand affair, for Venetia had known so many people from all walks of life, and from the highest in the land they wanted to pay their last respects: royalty, nobility, military men, politicians, the medical fraternity, suffragettes and campaigners, friends and acquaintances, former colleagues and former patients, and the legions of the humble she had treated and helped.

'She was a great lady,' Oliver said to Verena, and thought that perhaps she was the last of a generation, the last of such great ladies, who had had to be so much more than other women, in order to be anything at all.

Violet cancelled her trip, and the Damerels sailed without her. The Prince of Wales was glad, and hinted that she might give the whole thing up after all. But after three weeks, Oliver went to see Violet and told her she ought to go. 'There's still time, as far as the Metropolitan Museum is concerned. And Mother wouldn't have wanted you to mope about in deep mourning. You know how commonsensical she was about death. It will be good for Charlotte, and you know you were looking forward to it. There's bound to be someone else of your acquaintance going, if you're worried about being escorted.'

Violet considered, and said, 'I suppose I owe it to Laidislaw.'

Oliver didn't point out that she could have sent the pictures rather than taken them. He just wanted her to have a little pleasure and widen her horizons.

'It's what Mother would have wanted,' he urged, and that seemed to be the clincher.

Just when Polly had been brought to an almost unbearable peak of passion, Ren stopped and drew away. She knew why.

It was always the same. He was reaching for one of those wretched Trojans. She hated the things. She slid her arms around his smooth back and pulled at him. 'Don't stop,' she whispered urgently.

He resisted. 'What?'

'Let me feel you,' she whispered, greatly daring. 'Let me feel you properly, just this once. Darling!'

But he pulled himself free and went on with what he was doing, and suddenly all the fire had gone from her as though doused with a bucket of water. She was as cold and flat as if she had been dropped in a field. She rolled to her side of the bed and thrust her legs out, sat on the edge, feet dangling, hands clasped between her knees.

She could almost hear him thinking, calculating. At last he said, 'What's the matter?'

'I hate those things,' she said, with emphasis.

'They're necessary,' was his cool reply.

'Just for once I wanted to feel *you*, to be natural, to let love flow as it should.'

He didn't answer, but after a moment she felt the movement of the mattress. He was sitting as she was, on the edge of the bed, his back to her. She knew instinctively he would not want her to look at him at a moment like this. In their relations with each other he was curiously shy.

'Why did you stop?' she asked, and heard her voice sounding petulant, which was not what she had meant, but talking about such things was foreign to her, too.

'You know why,' came his voice, almost a grunt.

'I want a baby,' she said, and it sounded even more petulant. God, this thing was so difficult!

'Not now,' he said. 'We can't have one now. It would take up too much of your time, and I need you to concentrate on other things. When the time is right—'

'And who's to decide when the time is right? You, of course.'

'Of course,' he said calmly. 'You are my wife.'

She swung round and looked angrily at his back. His head was bent. 'I'm your wife. Does that make me your property? Your puppet, to be pulled this way and pushed that way?'

'Oh, don't be silly,' he said, as though argument wearied him. 'You can't have a baby yet, and that's that. I thought you wanted to help me in my career. That's what wives do. Good wives.'

He stood up, and for an instant the sight of his muscled back and firm buttocks, and the smooth light-brown skin over them, reawoke a little clench of desire in her. But he picked up his dressing-gown and slipped it on, and was gone, through the door into his dressing-room, where she might not follow. They had never quarrelled before, and the upset of it, combined with the unsatisfied desire that was still swirling round her body, made her feel fidgety, irritable and slightly queasy. She wanted to shout and throw things, but there was no-one to shout and throw at. She got up and walked about the room, naked as she was, clenching and unclenching her hands, until she started to feel cold. Then she put on her dressing-gown and went to sit down at her little writing-desk in the corner.

Calmness came over her, and with calmness a cold and clear reasoning. It was as if clouds had been rolled away, and from the eminence where she stood, instead of seeing only the billowing grey of hill fog, she could now see the whole landscape below her in sparkling detail. He did not want her to have a baby because she was too useful to him as she was. And the decision had to be his because he had to control everything, every single detail, not just in his life but in hers, too. He had come east to make his fortune, and everything that had happened had been by his will, until now. Loss of control maddened him. That was the worst thing for him about Hoover's going back on his promise, the whole people-talking-against-him thing: that it was out of his control

But that was not all. She looked at nothing, frowning a little as she saw in her mind things that the cloud had hidden. He did not want her to have a baby at all, because that would mean losing control over her. Her physiological processes would be outside his power, and the baby, when it came, would make demands that he could neither foresee nor limit. She had a cold certainty that there would never be a 'right time'.

And was there something else? She worried away at it, like a dog tugging at something half hidden under the carpet. It was coming now. Yes, here it was. He did not want her to have a baby because *she was not like him*. His Indian half had great power in his mind, though he might not know it himself. He was proud, and defensive. He had taken her as a prize, a hostage – the white princess he had carried away on his horse. But a hostage was not a soul-mate. He would never want her to have a baby because he was afraid of what it might be – not like him: that it might never really be his. And she might love it more than him.

She shook these thoughts away. They were night-thoughts, and she knew that in daylight things always seemed different. And yet she was certain that something had happened, some watershed had been passed. Then she knew with dull certainty what it was. She was not in love with him any more. She still had passion for him – thinking about his tall, smooth brown body even then gave her a frisson of desire – but to love someone in the other way you had to be like them. Perhaps it had always been just a physical love. She had never really been close to him, never known his thoughts or felt able to entrust him with hers. The excitement of being in love and in passion had blotted out the realisation of that fact.

Well, they were married. And their passion for each other was very great. Would it be enough? She didn't know. She yawned. She was tired and cold and wanted to sleep, to escape this troubled place her mind was in. In the morning, she told herself, she would worry about the future. She hurried to sleep as to a lover – a true lover of body, mind and heart, if such a thing existed.

BOOK THREE

Destinations

My eager feet shall find you again,
Though the sullen years and the mark of pain
Have changed you wholly; for I shall know
(How could I forget having loved you so?),
In the sad half-light of evening,
The face that was all my sunrising.

Rupert Brooke: 'The Beginning'

CHAPTER NINETEEN

The inauguration of Herbert Hoover on the 4th of March 1929 had been recorded by sound newsreels, the first time the ceremony had been broadcast to the nation. It was fitting, Lennie thought, for such a radio-minded president. He himself had immediately begun to benefit, for Hoover was ready and willing to take his advice on matters of radio and television, appointed him to a special White House committee, and set him to research various aspects of the new media and how they could be used for governmental good. Lennie was in a favoured position to get all sorts of information before the generality of press and radio stations. His own W2XKX soon had a reputation for being 'first with the news' – his own tag – which in turn brought in more advertising.

His finances were more than sound, and he was interested now in expanding his influence along with his empire. He increased his news coverage and hired more journalists; he bought more shares in television development – when that came of age he wanted to be in the forefront – and he was more often to be found in the company of politicians and opinion-makers, these days, than nubile starlets.

His interest in media extended to movies, for he could see what a large influence they might one day have. Since *The Jazz Singer* everyone was avid for talking pictures. The problem was that sound and picture had developed separately, and when they were delivered separately in a theatre, it was difficult to synchronise the two; difficult, too, to amplify the sound sufficiently for mass screenings. Sound-on-film was in the process of being developed, but so far the quality was poor. Warner Brothers had experimented with sound-on-disc movies, but that had its own problems – discs were almost impossible to edit, and expensive to distribute. Even Warner had now gone over to Vitaphone.

Through 1928 talking pictures had advanced very slowly and in fits and starts, with part-talking features among the silent majority, and many people, including studio magnates, believing talkies were a 'fad' that would soon pass. But Lennie had learned that in May 1929 Warner were to release their first all-colour, all-talking feature, *On with the Show*. Most movie theatres, especially outside urban centres, were still not equipped for sound, and *On with the Show* was to be issued in a silent version as well; but Warner expected to make a huge profit with it.

Lennie was convinced talkies were no fad and, being one always to back his own judgement, in March of 1929 he bought a share in a talking picture. It was to be produced in Hollywood by the American Box Office Corporation. ABO Pictures, as it was known, had been making silent movies for years, mainly Westerns, romances and comedic shorts, the staple of small-town American cinema; but now, with the help of a group of financiers, it was to make its own first all-colour talkie.

Lennie had been put on to it by an acquaintance, Joseph P. Kennedy, a Boston-born businessman who had made a fortune in whisky, commodities and real-estate, and had recently started taking an interest in the movie business. They had met through Ren, who had put Kennedy on to some good things in the past and vice versa.

Lennie had another reason for investing in it, besides the expectation of profit. He had seen a preliminary script for the movie – *Siren Song* was its working title – and it had an excellent small part for an attractive young actress. He was certain that his financial backing would give him enough leverage at least to see that Rose was tried out for the part, and in his view she was so talented she ought certainly to get it.

So in May he was to go over to Hollywood to sign all the papers and see what he could do to advance Rose's career. He had been invited to a ceremony on the 16th at the Hollywood Roosevelt Hotel, at which for the first time the American Academy of Motion Pictures, Arts and Sciences would make awards to leaders of the movie industry. Fifteen statuettes would be presented to actors, directors and other essential people who were deemed to have made the most significant contribution to the medium over the previous two years. The winners in various categories had been announced in February. Emil Jannings had won the category of Best Actor, while *Wings*, a silent movie set in the Great War and starring Clara Bow, had won the Best Film category. The awards were to be made at a private brunch before invited guests, followed by a party in the evening at the Mayfair Hotel. Lennie thought it would be a great deal of fun, and a suitable introduction for him to the inside world of motion pictures.

Shortly before his departure he went to see Polly to tell her about it and say goodbye. Since the election she and Ren had been spending more time in New York, but he still did not see enough of her to satisfy him, and he was glad of the excuse to call in. He found her rather preoccupied and, he thought, looking thinner in the face, less blooming.

But she listened to him with interest and commended him for his efforts on Rose's behalf. 'It sounds like just the thing to get her started, and I know it's what she's always wanted. But how will Lizzie and Ashley like it?'

'Well, they didn't at first, of course – California is a long

425

way – but they wouldn't stand in the way of her career. Ashley said that if Rose did get the part, Lizzie would have to go with her to Hollywood to take care of her, and Lizzie promptly said that she wouldn't go without him, so they would both have to move to California.'

'How did Ashley like that?'

'Oh, he was all for it. In fact, I rather think he manoeuvred Lizzie into suggesting it. He's suffering increasingly from bronchitis, and he's said on several occasions that he thinks the climate in New York is no good for him. I think he was pondering moving back to Arizona, only he was afraid Lizzie wouldn't like to go so far from the boys. But California will do just as well, besides being more fun for Lizzie, and it's obvious that Rose needs her more than Mart and Rupert, so it's the perfect excuse to get her to move. If she suggests it herself, so much the better.'

'I can't believe Ashley is so manipulative,' Polly said, amused.

'He's a businessman,' Lennie said. 'He's used to getting what he wants, one way or another.' He saw a shadow cross her face at the words, and leaning forward took her hand and pressed it in quick sympathy. 'Polly, what is it? Something's up, I know.'

'Nothing's up,' she said. 'You're imagining things.'

'I'm not. I can see you're unhappy. Won't you tell me what it is? Maybe I can help.'

Since she couldn't tell him about her feelings for Ren, she turned to the other thing, which was, after all, perhaps the source of the trouble. 'Ren's career has had a setback. Things have been said about him.'

'Things?'

She sighed. 'I can tell you – I know I can trust you not to repeat it. Though I don't really understand why it's so bad. But it seems that he's not just part-Indian, the way I always thought. His mother was Apache and he grew up on

426

a reservation. It was rather a shock to me – he'd never told me before – but I don't understand why it changes things. It won't change the way you think of him, will it?'

He met her limpid gaze with difficulty. 'I've known about it for a long time,' he said.

She stared. 'How is that possible? He didn't even tell me until recently.'

He looked down at his hands. 'Before you married, I was worried because no-one knew anything about him before he came to New York, so I – I consulted a private detective.'

'You did *what*?' Her voice was icy.

'I just needed to know he was all right. He was taking you away – you're so precious to me, Polly. I—'

'You had no right!'

He looked up. 'Only the right of loving you, and caring what happened to you.'

She brushed that aside. 'How *dare* you? How dare you set someone to snoop on my husband like that? What business was it of yours? If he wanted to keep his past hidden it was his affair. He hadn't committed a crime, or done anything wrong. Now, thanks to you, his entire career is ruined!'

'No, I promise you, it was all done very discreetly. The man I used would never have told anyone what he'd found out. Client confidentiality is everything to these people. He'd never work again if he couldn't keep his mouth shut. I *swear* it couldn't have come from him.'

She was looking at him with such thin hatred he could hardly bear it. 'Then it was you,' she said in a deadly voice. 'You're in and out of Hoover's office. *You* told him.'

'No!' he protested. 'I wouldn't do that.'

'You're the very person who *would* do it. You're jealous of Ren – crazy jealous because I married him, not you. You admit you snooped on him, pried into his past. Why would you do that and not use what you knew against him?'

'Because you loved him.'

'I don't believe you.'

'It's true. By the time I found out, you were married and happy. I wouldn't do anything to hurt you. So I just – left it alone.'

'Then if it wasn't you, who was it?'

Lennie shook his head. 'What I could find out, other people could as well. A man on the way up always has enemies. Ren's the kind of man other men are jealous of anyway – handsome, popular with women. And he was Hoover's pet. Anyone who wanted his job would be his enemy and look for some way to hurt him.'

She gave him a piercing look, then turned her head away. 'I don't believe you. It all fits too well. You knew, now Hoover knows, and Ren's hope is ruined.'

'Polly, I swear to you,' he began desperately.

'Oh, don't swear,' she said wearily.

'Have I ever lied to you?' he said quietly. 'Do you really think I would lie to you about something as important as this?'

But she wouldn't look at him. 'I don't know,' she said. 'I can't think now, Lennie. Please go. It's all too horrible. Just leave me alone, please. I don't know what to think about anything any more.'

He saw there was nothing more he could say. He got up and left her, feeling bruised and shocked. Life without her – without what little he had of her, her friendship and trust – would be intolerable. He could only hope that she would get over it, see that it was impossible for him to betray her in that way, take him back.

Left alone, Polly continued to stare at nothing, her mind almost blank. What came eventually was the memory of when Ren had told her about the trouble, and how he had looked at her to see if it had been her who had betrayed him. He had not trusted her. And now Lennie, the other person she had trusted wholeheartedly – now there was a question mark over him. She felt very alone.

In May, the Age of Marriage Act was passed, which raised the age at which girls could be married from twelve, and boys from fourteen, to sixteen in both cases. It was something that had been dear to Venetia's heart: she had worked with previous commissions on the age of sexual consent and the evils of sex with very young girls. Oliver was sorry his mother had not survived to see the Act go through. And at the end of May there was a general election, which was afterwards dubbed the Flapper Election, because it was the first one in which women under thirty were qualified to vote. He thought she would have liked to witness that, too, after fifty years of struggle.

It was an unusual election, because there was no particular cause for any side to exploit. In fact, the parliament elected in 1924 had been the first in forty years to run anything like its natural term, and there was no reason other than statutory requirement why there should be an election now at all. The government still had a large majority and there was no burning issue to excite the electors, or scandal to enrage them. The result was a very dull election and a very dull result: almost a draw between Labour and the Conservatives, with the Liberals a very poor third.

Labour with 288 seats had the largest share, but with the Conservatives on 260 and the Liberals 19, they did not have an overall majority. Baldwin, however, resigned at once, telling the King it would look 'unsporting' to hold on, and Ramsay MacDonald became prime minister for the second time. Without a majority, there was no danger of their imposing a socialist policy, and with the country prosperous and unemployment low there was no need for any great upheaval. Attention was turned instead to improving international stability, with plans to be put forward at a conference in The Hague for settling German reparations, withdrawing troops from the Rhineland, limiting naval expansion and boosting the League of Nations, so that any future international dispute could never again escalate into war.

The election and change of government passed Violet by entirely. The grief over her mother's death and the resumption of her New York plan were all she could hold in her mind, especially as the latter involved so much agitation on the part of the prince. As she had lost the Damerels as travelling companions, he was hopeful she would drop the trip altogether, so it was more than ever necessary for a suitable companion to be found.

It was Eddie Vibart who solved the problem. Avis Fellowes, an old acquaintance of his from Court, was escorting his American cousin Lorena back home to the wedding of her sister in New York. He was a man of Violet's own age (though like her he looked considerably younger) with a good war record – he had won a Military Cross with his regiment before being taken on to Headquarters staff, where he had been known as one of 'Haig's boys', and had finished the war as a colonel. Violet had met Fellowes once or twice before, and had been taken by his gentle manners. She didn't know him well, but she was aware of his sad history: he had been married at the outbreak of the war to a girl he had known all his life, but she had died in childbirth in 1917, and the baby had died too.

But he was not without liveliness: Violet met him and his cousin at a farewell dinner party given by the Bertie Yorks – Fellowes was an occasional equerry to the duke – and he and the duchess had some sparkling conversations. Lorena seemed pleasant but quiet – Eddie whispered to Violet that she was rather overawed in the presence of royalty but was amusing company elsewhere. In the drawing-room after dinner she told Violet in a rather subdued voice that she was looking forward to travelling with her; Fellowes made himself pleasant and said he was entirely at her service, and Violet felt quite comfortable with the arrangement.

She had a man from Bonham's in to pack up the paintings and drawings and send them to the ship. She had plenty to do with her own shopping and packing, and dealing with the fluctuating moods of David, who was by turns tearful, cross and clinging. He told her he envied her the trip, that he loved New York and the American people, advised her of places to go and things to see. 'I'll be stuck here with all my wretched "princing", and you won't think of me at all.' Assuring him over and over that she would took up a lot of time.

He gave her a lovely dressing-case as a going-away present, and his dog gave Fifi a smart jacket in Prince of Wales check 'to wear on deck in case of bad weather'. He insisted on taking them to Southampton himself, an offer Holkam seized on quickly. 'I'll say goodbye to you here, then, dear,' he said, before disappearing into whatever it was that was occupying him, these days.

The prince's presence at the docks caused excitement to the public, and gratification to the press and photographers, who were always on hand. It was not what Violet would have liked, but she had become resigned in recent years to having flash guns go off in her face. David handed her over to Fellowes in Lorena's stateroom, but not before pressing her hand and giving her a most tearful look, with a whispered entreaty to write to him 'every single day'.

But then he was all brave smiles, chatted sensibly to Fellowes, and was kind and charming to the children. He was especially fond of Henry Octavian, and gave him a very handsome parting gift of a wrist-watch. It was still thought caddish to wear them in London, but he assured the boy it was quite acceptable in America and he would find it very useful. Henry was thrilled and swore he would never take it off. Champagne was served. The prince laughed, smoked endlessly, teased the dog, chatted lightly about boats and his many previous trips, and when at last he departed, Violet was left feeling rather flat.

When she went back to her own cabin, she found it full of flowers, most of them from David, and on the table an expensively wrapped box. Inside was a small brooch in the shape of a dog, of diamonds with sapphire eyes, and a note hoping she would wear it while she was away to remind her of him. There was little chance of forgetting him, as he sent her three or four cables a day, to which she replied; but otherwise, she was finding an unexpected sense of freedom on the ship. It was a relief to be away from David, for though she was fond of him, his demands on her time and attention were incessant.

It was exhilarating to be away from London, heading for an unknown destination, and transplanted into a very different and much freer society. For no matter who made up the passengers on the great ocean liners, there was always a transatlantic flavour to the proceedings. The ostentatious luxury, the casual manners, the vivacity, the cocktails and dancing and flirting: it was New York in little. The few old-fashioned English upper-class passengers who did not care for this style of living kept themselves apart and were hardly seen, except taking their constitutionals round the deck either very early or very late. In between and elsewhere, the ship belonged to the jazz-agers.

Violet found Lorena a pleasant companion. It transpired that, at the Yorks', she had thought the Prince of Wales would be travelling with them, which accounted for her shyness with Violet. Now among her own sort of people she was lively and amusing, and since she knew most of their fellow travellers, they were never short of company. Under her urging Violet had her hair 'done' at the salon – shocking her maid who thought it unladylike – and for the first time ever submitted to a massage, though she found the process

432

so embarrassing she had only just begun to understand why it was enjoyable when it was over. Lorena was particularly kind to Charlotte, and did a great deal to draw her out of herself, for she was a very shy girl, and had hardly been in company before.

Avis took great pains with Henry, arranging for them to be shown round the ship, playing deck quoits with him, talking to him about the war, teaching him the principles of navigation. In the evenings Violet was glad of Avis's company and protection, for she sometimes found the gatherings noisy, and she did not care to dance with strangers, which he quickly understood. He kept unwanted attention away from her, partnered her when she wanted to dance, fetched her wrap, walked her to her cabin. He danced with Charlotte, too, and though Violet was not particularly noticing about her daughter, even she soon perceived that the girl had got a severe crush on him.

Lorena mentioned it to her one day when they were walking Fifi on the deck, and passed Avis giving a lesson to Henry in shooting the sun, to which Charlotte had attached herself.

'It's painful at that age,' she remarked. 'I remember it well.'

'I beg your pardon?' Violet said, though she realised what Lorena was referring to even as she said it.

Lorena gave her an amused look. 'Don't worry,' she said. 'Avis is the safest person in the world for a girl's first crush. He's quite aware of it, and he'll be just as gentle as can be. It's not the first time, I can tell you. He has those particular looks that young girls fall for – kind of fatherly, but young. A bit like the prince, I suppose, not that he's fatherly, really, but a young girl would see him that way as he'd be so much older than her. It was sweet to see how he was with Henry – the prince, I mean. He *is* fond of your children, isn't he?'

'Yes,' said Violet, stiffly. She was afraid Lorena was about to be impertinent.

But Lorena noticed the ice. 'I beg your pardon,' she said. 'I have a terrible habit of saying whatever comes into my head. My American directness, Avis calls it. I hope you won't find New York too much of a shock. I expect you'll be bumping into quite a few Bohemian types in the art world.'

Polly didn't know Violet very well, being of a different generation – Violet had always been Jessie's friend – but she was close enough to family to make it natural for her to offer to meet Violet and the children at the boat, to see them to their hotel, and to show them around if they required it. Violet had accepted the offer gratefully. The Felloweses had their own commitments, and though she hoped to see them again during her stay, they would not be around to help settle her in.

Polly was glad of the distraction of Violet's visit. Since the Inauguration she was more or less permanently in New York again. Ren went to Washington fairly often but he did not always take her; indeed, he had taken to flying there and either coming back the same day or staying only one night. But though he was in New York more often than not, she did not benefit from his company. He worked very long hours, and the time they spent together was usually in the company of others, at social events that were as much business to him as the time spent in his office.

He was different, since his 'betrayal' by the Party: more serious, inward-looking, even more driven. When they were in company together she saw the old Ren, amusing, lively, charming, but she knew this was an act he put on to win people over and keep them on his side. He did it brilliantly, and she wouldn't have known, if she didn't know, that it was not real. But alone with her, he did not bother to dissemble. He was unsmiling, even grim, always tired, unavailable for conversation that did not directly concern his business.

She resented at first that he did not make an effort for

her, and one evening when they were dining alone and in silence, she had said, 'I see you busily charming all those congressmen and tycoons and their wives, but when you're with me you don't even try.'

And he had looked up at her in surprise, obviously coming back from a long way away, and said, 'I don't need to try with you. You're my wife.'

She gave a tight, ironic smile. 'Some might say I'm the person you should try most with.'

He only looked weary. 'I come to you for peace and quiet. Don't pick a fight with me, Polly. I thought we were on the same side.'

So she had felt guilty, and after that did not trouble him when he was at home. But it left her lonely. They still made love, perhaps more frequently than before – it seemed a release to him – and in the throes of passion Polly could revive the old feelings she had had for him. But since that night of revelation she had become aware of a gap in her life. Now she was not *in love* with him any more, his self-absorption made her feel she was not really important to him.

She missed Lennie, too. She still felt sore from their last meeting, but still half believed it had been him who had derailed the Alexander train, despite his protestations. She did not trust him; but she missed trusting him, missed having someone for whom she was the most important person in the world. She wanted to be loved, and she wanted to love; she wished she could have a baby, because that might fulfil both of those needs; she was in a dangerous state of mind.

So Violet, Charlotte and Henry were a welcome distraction. Polly hadn't seen Violet for something like eight years, and could see the difference in her: at thirty she had still had the looks of a girl, despite having had four children; now she was a matron nearing forty. But she was still extremely beautiful, with that beauty of perfect bones and skin, of poise and serenity, that never fails. Charlotte had been a child when Polly left England. Now, at just seventeen, she had grown tall and seemed all joints and knuckles and uncontrolled movements, like a foal. Polly found her unexpectedly plain, considering the good looks of both her parents, and was sorry for her. It must be hard growing up the only girl in the shadow of so lovely a mother. She was very dark, so that had she been a boy, one might almost have called her swarthy, her nose was too big for her face and her forehead too narrow.

She was also very ill-dressed, and Polly was surprised, until she realised that Violet was one of that generation of mothers who left their children to others to dress until they entered the public realm. Polly longed to take Charlotte in hand, and a few appraising glances told her there was much she could do for the girl. She hesitated to raise the subject with Violet, but on the second day, when they had unpacked and settled into their suite at the Waldorf-Astoria, Violet herself mentioned it.

'I don't wish to impose on you, Polly, but I would like to consult you about clothes for Charlotte. You are in touch with the fashions over here, and you are nearer to her age. Of course, she is not "out" yet, but I understand these things are more flexible here than at home, and you will know how to tread the line between schoolroom and young-ladyhood. Would you consider helping us?'

'I'd like nothing better,' Polly said happily, smiling at Charlotte, who looked as though she had just woken up and found Christmas had come again. 'Girls' fashions are very pretty this year, and the longer hems will suit her height.'

Having reached almost mid-thigh the year before, hemlines in the Paris collections that spring had come right back down to below the knee: it was said that patrons watching the shows had been tugging uncomfortably at their skirts before the end, already feeling *demodé* and embarrassed by their own bare legs.

It was a matter of sadness to her that Violet would not let her get Charlotte's hair cut, which she felt would have been a great improvement, but she did at least take her to her own hairdresser, who gave her a rinse to bring out the 'dark lights', as he called them, and devised a style more becoming for her, to deal with the forehead and nose issues. Charlotte, who had been crushed by the schoolroom and fierce nannies all her life, began to emerge and bloom in all the attention.

Henry, at thirteen, was at the least difficult age for entertaining, being interested in everything, though Polly wished heartily that Lennie had been in New York to show him around. Violet was meanwhile wishing for Avis Fellowes for the same reason. The problem was solved when Lennie's father, Patrick, came to pay his respects on the third day. He immediately divined the problem and made a surprising offer of himself to take the boy off the ladies' hands and show him around. Henry's look of profound gratitude was thanks enough: he had been imagining himself dawdling about dress shops and kicking his heels in the hotel through endless fittings. Patrick, he saw, was an old fellow, but at least he was a fellow, and promised to take Henry out of doors.

It turned out to be a match made in heaven. Patrick had a young mind, and he knew everything that Henry so badly wanted to know: the height and weight and method of construction and speed and history and future of everything man-made in Manhattan. Patrick, meanwhile, enjoyed himself immensely, rediscovering why he loved the city so much. He had not had a vacation in years, and felt no qualms about taking one now to show his home town to Henry. He took him on buses, explored the subway, crossed on the Staten Island ferry, and discovered a pleasure-boat that went all the way round the island. They paid a reverential visit to the great temple of steam, Grand Central Station, with its gilding and marble and different levels, and the huge, sighing monster locomotives lurking like dragons in their caves. They went to the Statue of Liberty and the zoo in Central Park, to the Wall Street canyon, and up every tall building that had public access, and to quite a few that didn't: no sense in being an architect if you couldn't call in a few favours.

In between, when Patrick was in need of a rest, Henry was introduced to the delights of coffee shops and automats, for deli sandwiches and pickles, hot dogs, hamburgers, pretzels, malted milks, doughnuts and pistachio ice cream, none of which had come his way before. He couldn't imagine being happier, and was only afraid that the rest of his life was going to be an anticlimax by comparison.

The opening of the exhibition in the Metropolitan Museum was a hiatus in this rule of pleasure, when he had to be dressed in his best suit and be solemn and accompany his mother to stand reverently in front of the works of the man he had been told was his father. Some of them he thought jolly good, for he was naturally interested in soldiers: his favourite was a large canvas called *The Match at the Front*, which showed two teams of soldiers playing a game of football and was full of colour and movement. He thought it was ripping.

But he felt awkward about the whole father thing because he had never met the painter Octavian Laidislaw and, as far as he was concerned, his father was Lord Holkam; moreover, he was aware that the painter-father complication was meant to be kept a secret. He rather wished his mother had never told him about it: it would have made things much easier. He wasn't sure whether anyone in New York was meant to know, and therefore kept his mouth firmly shut and avoided meeting anyone's eyes, in case they should ask him questions he would not know how to answer.

There was a tremendous crowd of people, all old like his mother, or even older like Patrick (but not as jolly as him), and lots of reporters from the papers. There was champagne – they gave him lemonade instead, but he saw his sister Charley get a glass, which he bet his mother didn't know about – and little bits of food on silver trays which he had a lot of and which was topping, especially the little sausages and the pastry things with different fillings. So there were compensations, but on the whole it was very yawn-making, and his mother got tears in her eyes at one point, which was embarrassing – he was afraid she might start talking to him about the Laidislaw man, and call him Octavian, which she had practically stopped doing back home since the prince had been around. His name was Henry and he hated being called that other thing.

He was glad when it was all over, and he could resume his happy wandering with Patrick, who was a jolly decent cove, and knew everything, but was not a bit stuffy like the beaks at home. He had even half promised to take him to the Yankee Stadium to see a baseball match one day, though when he described baseball to Henry, it seemed to be pretty much like rounders, which was rather a kids' game, and not as exciting as cricket. Still, it would be a new thing, and Henry was all for new things, especially if they involved food, which it appeared baseball did – hot dogs seemed to be practically compulsory.

In a tiny, dark flat somewhere to the back of Baker Street Station, Lord Holkam was kneeling down, removing the artificial silk stocking from the right leg of a young woman called Mabel. The fact that the silk was artificial was somehow as stimulating to him as the bouquet of a fine claret to a wine connoisseur. He kissed her knee, then ran his hand down her leg and picked up her foot, kissed her toes and pressed them to his nose, inhaling the scent deeply.

'Oh, give over, Bob,' Mabel said playfully but with a hint of unease. 'Don't be so daft.'

That she called him 'Bob', and said things like 'Give over', gave him intense pleasure. She had been one of the waitresses at his club (female servants were an innovation since the war, much deplored by older members) where she had called him 'my lord' and never dared raise her eyes to his; but from the first he had been fascinated by the salmon-coloured rayon stockings emerging from the hem of her black uniform dress, under the absurd frilly apron.

Since their liaison had begun he had insisted she leave the club, since he could not have been sure that she would not talk to the other servants about him. He gave her money to replace her wages and visited her in her little flat. It was the first time he had had a girl 'in keeping', and there were advantages and disadvantages to the arrangement. On the one hand, it was good to know that he could have her whenever he wanted; and there was something deliciously lower-middle about this place and its appurtenances. On the other, it lacked the excitement of adventure that he got by taking girls off the street; he could foresee that he would tire of Mabel fairly soon, and then what would he do with her?

Also he had intercepted unfriendly looks from one of the longer-established servants at the club, Harold, and suspected he knew that Mabel's sudden resignation had something to do with him. Had Mabel confided in Harold in the scullery one day? Harold wouldn't dare say anything, not about the Earl of Holkam, who could get him the sack at the lift of a finger. All the same, one could not be too careful. Thus he thought, even while realising that his behaviour since Violet had left for New York had been not just verging on but beyond the reckless.

He didn't know what had come over him. He had always had certain appetites, but they had been in the background and, intermittently satisfied, had not bothered him. It had been as small and unimportant a part of his life as cleaning his teeth – something one did but never thought about. But from the time Violet had said she was going, and had made it clear she expected to go without him, he had been consumed by a strange holiday spirit. It was the sort of euphoria he used to feel when boarding the train home at the end of a half at Eton. The sense of being let out of durance vile, of sudden freedom . . . He had hated Eton; hated being at home almost as much. His father (though he loved him and longed to please him) had been an ogre and a tyrant. Holkam had been brought up to be seen and not heard – and not too much of the former either. There had been terrible lectures on his shortcomings, translated into savage beatings. He had always thought of that, involuntarily, when he heard the padre at church talk about the word being made flesh: his father's words, his own sorry flesh.

But for an hour or two, on the train home, between two states of persecution, he had known freedom. Violet was hardly a tyrant – in fact, she was a very accommodating wife, with her own peccadilloes to be held against her if ever she became unreasonable – but her removal from the scene had filled him with a wild desire to do outrageous things, to let go of all restraint, to 'let his hair down', as the saying was. He had not been free in that way since the war – and, oh, how he missed the war! What a picnic that had been! And the Paris Conference – oh, the waitresses and showgirls and those little sluts from the *banlieue*! It had been a feast, and he had gorged himself. But that was nearly ten years ago.

And there were his other troubles now, from which he desperately needed to escape – things he hardly dared think about. Though the new man had given him hope. Meyer was an American financier and Holkam didn't care much for Americans, but he was sharp, and he had ideas – yes, if he could make good his promises, there might be light at the end of the tunnel . . .

Meanwhile, in Violet's absence, he had been indulging himself, to the extent that he was hardly doing anything else, neglecting his duties, cancelling meetings and simply not arriving at committees. Only meetings with Meyer were sacrosanct. He slept, when he slept at all, by day, for his real life took place at night.

Mabel was only a part of it. It was restful here, but by the same token, it was not exciting. One night – actually, it was before Violet had left – he had dressed as shabbily as he could, making sure to empty his pockets of any valuables, and with only a sufficient wad of money and a door key to get back in, he had left his house and walked through the quieter streets to Soho. He was known to one or two of the more discreet houses there, but he had been after stronger meat. He had picked up a girl on a street corner and, in a transaction thrilling in its directness, had gone with her to a room, given her money and had her.

Later, wandering in a state of exaltation, he had been beckoned by a girl in a doorway and had done the same again. Twice in one night! He had felt an obscure sense of pride, as well as the excitement of degradation. Sin was so much saltier when it was low like that. It had been the beginning of a new era for him. He could not wait for Violet to leave. Coming to see Mabel was almost like a cleansing, like going to church. He was amazed at his stamina as much as his appetite. Vaguely he wondered if there was something wrong with him, some medical condition, but he dismissed the idea, because he did not care. He was having a holiday, and as it would not last for ever, he meant to enjoy it to the full.

He dropped Mabel's foot and ran his hands up her other thigh to start on the other stocking.

*   *   *

At a race meeting at Belmont Park on Long Island, Violet looked round at the elegantly dressed crowds with approval. Belmont was always the occasion for dressing-up for New Yorkers. Thoroughbred owners and breeders took their horses very seriously, and since they were far richer than their English counterparts, there was a gloss on the occasion only rivalled by Royal Ascot.

She was watching Charlotte, who was talking to a group of girls and young men about her own age. The child had come out of her shell, and with Polly's help in dressing her, she now passed muster among the American young people, though they still seemed older and more sophisticated than her. But, of course, the nursery system was quite different over here.

She was standing alone for the moment, and was glad to do so, for she had been rather put out by a number of people who seemed to be scraping acquaintance with her for the purpose of asking her questions about David, and even in one case hoping to be presented when they came to England. Her liaison with the Prince of Wales was not discussed in society in England, and it was a shock to have it openly spoken of here.

She thought wistfully of her old friend and escort Freddie Copthall. Though appearing to be the amiable ass, he had had a wonderful way of dispatching anyone who annoyed her. But she never saw Freddie now. Since his marriage to the banker's daughter he had dropped out of their circle, had bought a small place in Hampshire near his wife's family, and was living a life of quiet domestication. He was farming his own land and, if the stories were true, he had taken up pig-breeding and was doing well at it, even winning prizes with his sows.

The idea of her elegant, fastidious Freddie having anything to do with those smelliest of farm animals defeated Violet's imagination. She half believed it was an elaborate joke on

443

the part of the gossips, made up to tease her. The Copthalls had two children now – a girl born in 1926, and the son-and-heir Adrian born in 1928. There had been the usual announcements in the papers and Violet had sent congratulations and received a polite reply from Cordelia, but that was the only contact she had had. Freddie was completely out of her life, as if he had never been. The only hint that he had ever felt anything for her was that the daughter had been named Mary Violet Adelaide. She wondered rather what Cordelia felt about that.

She was thinking these less than ecstatic thoughts when an English voice at her elbow said, 'In a brown study, Lady Holkam? I hope you haven't been disappointed by a horse.'

She turned to find Avis Fellowes standing there, looking at her enquiringly, as though not sure of his welcome. 'Not at all,' she said. 'In fact, I've only bet on one race so far. And you?'

'I've only just arrived,' he said. 'Have you anything on for the next race?'

She looked at the race card in her hand, having entirely forgotten it was there. 'Cherry Ripe,' she said, reading a name at random. 'Such a pretty name, don't you think?'

'Hmm. Handsome is as handsome does. He's never won over this distance before. I was thinking of Invictus. Won or placed on every one of his last six outings.'

'Oh, don't talk to me about form,' she said. 'I've heard too much of it from our hosts today. I'm here with the Whitney party – Ren and Polly are friends of theirs – and they take it all very seriously. Besides, I shan't be betting on anything now all the men seem to have deserted me. I don't like to do it myself.'

He had resumed his hat, and now raised it again, with a very English sort of half-bow. 'Then will you allow me to assist you?' He offered his arm, and she took it gladly.

'How come you are here?' she thought at last to ask. 'I

444

thought you were in . . .' she racked her brain '. . . Bridgeport.'

'So I was. But the wedding is over, and Lorena has embarked on a series of visits to relatives and old school friends. She doesn't need me, so I thought I'd come back to New York for a while.'

'I expect you have many friends here,' she said politely.

'Not really. But I'd rather be at a loose end in New York than in Bridgeport.' He paused. 'Is there any way in which I can be of service to you while I'm here?'

He looked down at her hesitantly, and she was aware of the warmth of his arm under her hand and the strength of his body beside her. It was good to have a man to lean on again.

'I expect it would be a dreadful bore for you,' she said, 'but I do have a number of engagements coming up and no-one to escort me. And while Henry has seen all the sights of New York, I haven't seen any.'

She was afraid she had asked too much, but he looked pleased at the idea. 'My time is completely at your disposal,' he said. 'You must let me know which sights interest you, and I'll take you to them.'

'No, you must tell me which ones I *ought* to visit. I'm sure you know far better than I what there is to see.'

'Well,' he said, 'if it's a matter of advising you, let me persuade you away from Cherry Ripe, to begin with.'

She laughed. 'No, I shall bet my way and you shall bet yours. And to prove I have faith in my choice, you shall put twenty dollars on him.'

Cherry Ripe came in first at five to one. The favourite scratched at the last minute and Invictus, who had been second favourite, pulled up in the final furlong. Violet was more pleased with her hundred dollars of winnings than any money she had ever had in her life. Her large dowry had gone straight from her father's bank to her husband's, and almost everything she bought was put on an account and settled monthly. Actually having a hundred dollars in bills in her hand was an amusing and novel sensation.

She enjoyed teasing Fellowes about their disparate fortunes. He insisted it was a fluke, and as she didn't care to test the theory by betting again that day, he took that to be an admission on her part and he teased her in his turn. It was amazing, Violet thought, how quickly they had become at ease with each other.

CHAPTER TWENTY

Polly enjoyed the race meeting, too. She loved the horses, and Ren for once seemed almost relaxed, happier than she had known him for some time. He seemed to have taken a holiday just for once from his relentless canvassing, and he strolled about with her on his arm, looking at the horses and studying the race card, talking pleasantly with her about nothing but the present moment.

The only time he referred to his career was when he remarked, on seeing Violet at a little distance, talking to a group of people, 'Your friend Lady Holkam is the hit of the season. It's a pity she's not staying for longer – we might have made use of her.'

Polly was annoyed enough by the suggestion to say, 'I don't think that was her purpose in coming here.'

He did not seem to notice the sarcasm. Still looking at Violet, he said, 'It won't do any harm for you to cultivate her, at any rate. Be seen with her. And we should give a dinner while she's still here.'

'I don't *need* to cultivate her,' Polly said. 'She's my cousin.'

'Just so,' Ren said, unaffected.

He changed the subject, and Polly tried not to let the brief exchange spoil her day.

She was spending a lot of time with Violet and Charlotte anyway, and was glad to see Charlotte finding her feet. The opening gala at the Metropolitan Museum gave rise to lots

447

more invitations of the same sort – Polly had discovered before that in the New York season, one party led to another, and the trick was to catch the right one. It was like jumping on to a moving train, and the train she found herself on was the arts train, which she had ridden in the days before her marriage, thanks to Julie Margesson, but not so much lately. It was rather nice, she discovered, being back in that circle: she had lots of acquaintances, and they all seemed glad to see her again.

At one party she met Olga Culver – someone whose acquaintance she would have been happy not to renew – who immediately buttonholed her and wanted to know all about Violet and the Prince of Wales. Polly fobbed her off as best she could, and advised her not to ask Violet questions of that sort, as she didn't like the prince mentioned.

'Oh, my dear, as if I would! I know a stiff neck when I meet one. It's a marvel what he sees in her, because I know for a fact he's the least stuffy person in the world – my oldest friend Mipsy Oglander met him in San Diego when he inspected the naval base there, and said he was the dearest little man and just full of fun. But, of course, she *is* very beautiful – Lady Holkam, I mean. That very English beauty, icy, you know, but men do seem to like it.' She sighed, and then looked sharply at Polly. 'And what about you, dear? Still holding your own with that heavenly Ren? Let me know when you're finished with him because I mean to try him out some day. Culver is a good husband but every woman needs a lover as well. I wonder what the prince is like in that department. I suppose just the fact of his being a prince would give you a thrill.'

Polly broke away from her as soon as she could, and felt a curious desire to wash her hands. She hastened to attach herself to Julie Margesson, who was talking to Freda Holland.

Freda looked at Polly with amusement as she joined them, and said, 'Escaped at last, Polly, dear? I wish we didn't have to have that dreadful Culver woman in tow, but she is very generous to the arts.'

'She used to be much nicer,' Julie said. 'She seems to get brasher as she gets richer. It's a shame.'

'Oh, my dear,' Freda said, 'she was always like that – coarse fibres, you know. She's from a naval family in Baltimore. I met her at school in Washington, and the only reason she was quiet was that she didn't have any money so she couldn't throw her weight about. She married Jack Philips straight from school and they hadn't a bean. But her uncle was an admiral, and when he died unexpectedly at sea her father inherited his fortune, and from that moment her true nature started to emerge. She dropped Philips and married Al Graham for his money, but he wasn't rich enough so she swapped him for Bill Culver. I wouldn't like to bet on how long Culver will stand the course. But let's not talk about her any more. Polly, I was telling Julie about my new young man, but you didn't hear, so let me talk about him some more. He's an absolute find, a brilliant painter, and European, which is even better, because they're so much more romantic for the clients than the home-grown article.'

'European?' Polly asked with inward amusement. It always tickled her that Americans could lump together such disparate people and countries as if they were all of a kind.

'He's English, actually,' Freda said. 'Eric Chapel – I don't suppose you know him? No. Well, he studied and worked in Paris for some years, then came over here. Settled in Boston. Married a local girl. He was working in a bar to finance his painting, and a friend of mine, an art dealer who looks out for new talent for me, was approached by him with some pictures to sell. Arnold – my friend – saw the potential at once and wrote to me and, well, here we are. You will come to the launch, won't you, Polly, you and Ren? I'm dying for you to meet him. You'll love him!'

Polly remembered what Mrs Culver had hinted at one

time about Freda Holland – that she only ever discovered handsome young male artists, and that their ability to draw or paint was not their prime attraction in her eyes. But that was the sort of thing Mrs Culver said – and what *she* would probably have done if she had been in Freda's position. Anyway, a Holland launch was always worth attending – glittering occasions, with everyone important there, lots of champagne and delicious food.

'Thank you, I'd love to come. I can't speak for Ren, but I'm sure he'll be there if he's free.'

Freda beamed. 'And bring Violet Holkam, if you can,' she said, spoiling the effect.

As it happened, Ren wasn't free, but the arts circle was much more hers than his, and she was happy to go alone – Violet was otherwise engaged on the evening, but said she would look in later if she could, which was enough for Polly to be able to satisfy Freda.

The gallery was on Fifth Avenue, a very modern-looking building with lots of glass, and grand with gilding, marble and electric chandeliers inside. In London, galleries were usually small, dark places with wood panelling, pictures crowded together on the walls, and very limited floor space, but the Philip J. Holland gallery had a wide frontage and went back an enormous distance, so there was plenty of room for parties. Paradoxically, with so much wall available, there always seemed to be very few pictures, each one artfully spotlighted and surrounded by acres of empty space.

There was a red carpet outside and three uniformed porters, opening car doors, keeping back the crowds and ushering guests into the brilliantly lit room. A black-uniformed maid relieved Polly of her summer fur, a waitress appeared in front of her with a tray of champagne glasses, and as she took one, Freda came up to her with her husband – a small, very dark man with heavy-rimmed glasses, considerably older than her, who had made his money in steel and was now using it to amass an enviable collection of *objets d'art*.

'Polly, dear! So glad you could make it. I think it's going to be a success, don't you?' She looked around happily at the glamorous throng. 'I'm glad, because Eric's a perfect pet, and he has such a talent – hasn't he, Philip?'

'Remarkable,' said her husband. He was a man of few words.

'I must introduce him to you,' Freda said, 'but he's giving a press conference at the moment. Have a look at the paintings, and I'll bring him over to you later. Hilda, darling! What a pleasure!'

She was off. Philip Holland stood for a polite moment, and then was drawn away by the hooked fingers of an elderly dowager, so weighted with diamonds it was a wonder she could stand upright. Polly was happy to be alone to look at the pictures, and she wandered slowly from one to another, exchanging nods and greetings with acquaintances as she went. The pictures did not greatly enthuse her. They were large, with great expanses of colour – abstracts with concentrations of shapes in different parts of the canvas. She tried to make sense of them, but then supposed if they were abstracts they were not meant to make sense. If viewed simply as patterns and colours they were quite attractive in their way. She was glad for Freda's sake, and that of the unknown artist, that several were sporting 'sold' stickers.

As she was staring at one vast, mainly red expanse with heavy black lines like a portcullis in the centre over squares of dull green and blue, she was startled and rather annoyed to be suddenly accosted by Olga Culver, who had her husband with her for once – a large, perspiring man, with the soft chin and disappearing hair of the sedentary businessman, and a number of fobs and seals on his watch chain, which Polly guessed were the symbols of various men's associations.

'Well, what do you think?' she demanded of Polly.

'I'm not a great expert on abstract paintings,' Polly said. 'I can see they are powerful, and I'm sure they'll be a great success.' 'Powerful' was always a safe word to apply in these cases. Nobody ever praised a painting for being 'weak'.

Olga laughed. 'Oh my dear, not the paintings – though they are fine, I must admit. I'm trying to persuade Bill to buy one for me.'

'Persuade away, my dear,' said Culver, good-naturedly. 'As long as I don't have to look at the darned thing when you get it home.'

'I'm talking about the artist, dear,' Olga went on, as if he had not spoken. 'What do you think about the divine Mr Chapel? Freda's got herself a good one there. I never liked that Spaniard she got her claws into last year – shifty little eyes, and I don't believe he washed enough. This one has the looks of a Greek god, nice manners and that oh-so-English accent! I die for it!'

'I haven't met him yet,' Polly said.

'Well, you must, dear. I tell you, if it weren't obvious that he owes everything to Freda, I'd make a play for him myself.'

'Now, dear,' said Culver. 'Come come.'

She ignored him. 'As a matter of fact, I'm not sure friendship stretches as far as respecting her property, so I might try anyway. You'd better meet him while you can!' She laughed. Polly was turning away with a strained smile when Olga's hand shot out and gripped her arm. '*There* he is! Now, isn't he a work of art? Don't tell me you've seen anything prettier this evening. There, look, talking to Helen Passmore and Philip Holland.'

Polly looked in the direction indicated, saw Holland and the elegant Mrs Passmore talking to someone whose face was blocked for her by the intervening bodies – she could only see the top of his head. Then someone moved, a gap appeared, the artist turned his head slightly, and Polly felt her stomach drop away as though she were in a fast elevator. The lean face was older, and much less brown; the fair hair that had been sun-bleached almost white when last she saw it was slicked down for the evening and politely mouse-coloured from the oil; but she'd have known him in a crowd of a hundred thousand. He seemed to feel someone looking at him, and the blue, blue eyes left his two companions and swung round, finding her instantly through the throng as though he had known she would be there. He looked straight into her eyes, and for Polly, the whole world seemed to stop, the din was hushed, and in a frightening, pulsing silence she looked back at the man who had been dead for ten years, the man who had taken the fresh first love of her girlhood to the grave with him.

The brightness in which he stood was edged with black, and she dragged her eyes away and shook her head, feeling dizzy. She bent her head and pressed her fingers to her temples. There was a ringing in her ears. She concentrated on breathing deeply, hoping she would not either faint or be sick. Gradually the moment passed and the voice of Olga faded back in like a radio being tuned, still talking about Freda and her new artist. But Culver had noticed that something was wrong and he placed a kind, fat hand on her arm and said, 'Are you feeling faint, Mrs Alexander? You look quite pale.'

'It's nothing, just the heat,' she managed to mutter. 'If you'll excuse me, I think I'll just . . .'

She glanced to where he had been standing, but the configuration of the crowd had changed and he was not in sight.

'Do you want me to go with you, dear?' Olga asked with scant sympathy, and the obvious desire of hearing 'no, thank you'.

'No, thank you. I'm quite all right. I'll just splash a little water on my face,' Polly said, and made her escape.

The powder-room was right at the back, in a separate corridor that also, she guessed, led to the offices and storage rooms. She shut herself into a cubicle and sat on the closed seat, her face in her hands. It was not him, of course. He was dead. But the man had looked so like him. And then there was the name. Obviously, that must be what had started the chain of connections in her mind. Eric Chapel – Erich Küppel. The name had triggered the memories, and probably this Chapel had a faint resemblance, which her imagination had exaggerated. When she met him, she would see he really looked nothing like Erich. Strange, that similarity of the name. She had not noticed it when Freda first mentioned it to her. Probably her American accent had neutralised it for Polly's ears. And she hadn't thought about Erich in a long time.

She was feeling better now, having rationalised her fainting fit to her satisfaction. The dizziness and queasiness had passed. She stood up, flushed the cistern for form's sake, and went out into the powder-room. She washed her hands, damped a paper towel and pressed it to her cheeks and forehead, reapplied her lipstick, examined her back view in the mirror, touched a wave of her hair back into place, and went out into the corridor.

He was there, waiting for her. There was no-one else in sight. They were only a foot apart, looking into each other's faces. She saw the lines of intervening years, the marks of experience and loss; but the blue eyes burned into hers with the old intensity, the lips she had dreamed of so often were smiling – smiling for her.

'It *is* you,' he said. Surely that should have been her line. 'I thought I could not be mistaken. But what are you doing here?' She could not speak. He reached out and caught her hands, and she felt the living flesh, warm, hard, strong – no

454

ghost, no imagination. 'Such cold hands! I was surprised, but you look shocked. What is it?'

'They told me you were dead,' she said.

He seemed disconcerted by her words, and looked at her searchingly, the smile fading away, but he kept hold of her hands, as though afraid she might somehow escape him. He said at last, 'But I'm not, you see.' Then he seemed to understand. 'Did you think you'd seen a ghost?'

'They told me you were dead,' she said again, tears rising, hurting her throat.

He pressed her hands gently, and said, in a voice that stepped past all barriers and straight into her heart, 'I thought I'd never see you again.'

They faced each other across a small table in the darkest corner of a little Italian restaurant in the Village. Where to go that they could talk? That had been the single problem occupying their minds for two weeks. Polly had been to two more 'arty' events at which he had been present, but they had been able to exchange only a few snatched words: Freda kept close to his side, and there were always too many people nearby. Then, at a party given by the Waldo Channings, they had found themselves alone for a moment in a corner, and had been able at least to articulate the problem.

'We must meet.'

'Yes, but where?'

'I'll find somewhere. I'll send you a note – where and when.'

'What if I can't get there?'

'I'll wait, and if you don't come I'll try again.'

The message came in a bunch of flowers, scribbled on the back of the florist's card. It was lucky she had been looking out for it, for Plummer would probably have thrown it away. It looked so casual, as if the florist's girl had used the card to jot down a hurried note when she couldn't find a piece of paper, and then forgotten about it. For Plummer's sake, she said, 'There's no message with the flowers, to say who they're from. I'll telephone the florist later and find out.'

At the designated time she was actually at a charity luncheon, and she feigned a fainting fit to excuse herself and leave. Her emotions were in such turmoil that it was practically true. She took a cab to Mulberry Street, and got out a block away, feeling like a conspirator. It was a restaurant she didn't know and had never been to before, and it was so small and cheap and obscure it was unlikely anyone she knew would come in there, but all the same she felt very nervous, and stalked in like a cat, nostrils wide and eyes everywhere, wondering what to say to the waiter. But as soon as he saw her, he gave a conspiratorial smile and, without a word, beckoned her into the darkest depths away from the windows.

There was Erich, rising to his feet, looking at her with such gladness her heart came crowding up into her throat.

'How did he know?' she asked him, when the waiter had left them alone. 'I didn't have to say anything.'

'I described you,' Erich said. 'And a hint was enough for him to understand we wanted privacy. The Italians are great ones for romance.'

'Romance?' she queried doubtfully. Was that what this was?

'It is the best excuse to keep him on our side,' he said – a neutral answer. She was glad of it.

Wine came, and menus. She could not read the words, was too distracted to choose. She pushed the card away and, understanding, he ordered rapidly and in Italian for them both. Other people came in – working men, office girls, elderly couples – all from the local Italian community: middling sorts, neatly but cheaply dressed, not the sort of people likely to know Polly. They were seated at the front near the windows, and did not give the couple in the dark corner a single glance. Erich had chosen well.

456

And once they had started talking, the place and the time and all other thoughts melted away. She told her story first: how she had been told the prisoners of war had been attacked by a mob at the docks, and he had been killed. 'I dreamed it so often afterwards,' she said. 'I saw you again and again, always in a line, all of you shuffling forward towards someone who was going to kill you, and I couldn't get to you, I couldn't cry out. It was awful.'

He told his story. 'There *was* such an attack. Dockers, warehousemen, sailors – strong men armed with iron bars and staves of wood. They hated all Germans. I heard some shout that their father, or brother, or son had not come back from the war, so why should we be allowed to go home? The police tried to keep them back, but there were so few of them, and so many of the angry. They broke through and attacked us. The man in front of me – he was hardly more than a boy – was struck down, fell to the ground. A docker had hit him with a great heavy spanner. He was bending down to hit him again, so I grabbed his arm, wrestled with him. I was strong from my farm work, but he was bigger than me, and stronger. He pulled his arm free and struck me.' He leaned forward, parting the hair above his temple with his fingers. 'You see the scar.'

She saw. The hair grew differently around it. Her throat closed up at the thought of him hurt. She wanted to touch him, but dared not.

He let the hair fall back. 'I was knocked unconscious, and carried on board with the boy I had tried to help. He died a little while later. Perhaps that was how the story came about. Lots of us were injured, but I think only two of us were carried away. It may have been thought I was dead.' He looked into her eyes tenderly. 'I'm sorry you were made to suffer. Poor gentle Polly, so young as you were then. I hate to think of you crying.'

'I did,' she said. 'For a long time it was my only comfort.

I had to do it when I was alone, because I could never tell anyone what I was crying for.' It was too hard to meet his gaze. She lowered her eyes, fiddled with a piece of bread, and asked, 'What happened when you got home?'

'There were processes when we arrived in Germany. Long processes. But at last we were released and I made my way home. It was a long journey and I did most of it on foot. Transport in Germany then . . .' He shrugged. 'When I got there, I found the Communists had taken over the village and our house. In the confusion after the war, they seized what they wanted, and there was no-one to stop them. I learned that my father had resisted and he and some loyal servants had been killed, so I had to be careful. They'd have killed me too if they'd known who I was. I couldn't go right up to the house, but I looked at it from a distance. There had been a fire and the roof of one part had burned through, but the rest was intact, though it looked neglected. I saw broken windows, pieces of plaster missing, and the grounds were churned up and full of rubbish and broken furniture and crockery. There was a Red guard on the gate and he started to look at me suspiciously, so I went away. And that was the last time I saw it.'

'Oh, Erich, I'm sorry,' Polly said.

He shrugged. 'It was just a house – stones and wood. Once my father was dead it meant nothing to me any more.' She didn't believe that was true. He went on, 'But I wish I knew what happened to my father's old dog. And the horses . . .' He sipped his wine.

She said, 'What did you do?'

'I wandered for a while. I had to get out of the area for fear of being taken up. I thought of heading for the coast and trying to get work on a ship, but Hamburg was in Red hands and I didn't want to go in that direction. I had heard bad things of Berlin, too, so I made my way towards Frankfurt instead. I got a day's work here and there, not for wages – nobody had any money – just for food and a night's shelter in a barn. But the more I travelled, the more I saw that Germany was finished. Everywhere people were starving. There were riots, gangs of armed men setting up their own little dictatorships, Reds and anti-Communists fighting it out like stray dogs over a picked-clean bone. No, it was all over for Germany, and there was nothing to keep me there any more. So I crossed by night into France near Saarbrücken and made my way to Paris.'

'Why Paris?'

'The Peace Conference was going on there, so I knew there would be no riots or Reds, and plenty of money pouring in, and work for those who wanted it. A lot of British soldiers, too. I didn't want to be German in such a place, so I made a new identity for myself. I became French. From my lessons as a boy I spoke French like a native—'

'And English, and Italian,' she noted. His English was so perfect that only an English person would have thought it was not his native tongue. He had no accent, which was what would betray him to an Englishman – but only to one who was really listening.

'It was lucky,' he said, with a faint smile. 'My father had made sure I had good tutors. French seemed to me the safest thing. If I had been English I would have interested the soldiers too much. Eric is a French name, and Chapelle was close enough to Küppel – I was vain enough to want to keep something of my old self from the wreck. I found work easily as a waiter, rented a little room, and settled down to wait – for what? I did not know.'

'For life to begin again?' she hazarded.

'Perhaps. I was in a state of shock, I think. Perhaps we all were. It hardly seemed as though the war was over. It had been going on so long it was hard to alter the landscape of one's mind all at once. Then one day the conference was over and the British soldiers left.'

459

'Was that when you became English?'

He made a gesture, not quite a shrug, almost a shrinking. 'I did not like the French. I am ashamed to say so, since they took me in and were kind to me, but I could not help despising them. It was how we were trained as soldiers. When I realised it was safe to be English again, I changed my lodgings and my job and my name, became Eric Chapel. I worked as a waiter in a restaurant in Montmartre, and many of my customers were artists of one sort or another. I was surrounded by galleries and shops selling paintings, there were people selling them on the street, and it came to me suddenly that here was something I could do. I had been taught drawing as a boy and had been good at it. I bought some paints and canvas and began.'

She was amused. 'Just like that.'

He smiled. 'The Americans were beginning to flood into Paris. There were other tourists, but the Americans were the ones with the money. I painted views of Montmartre, of the Seine, of Notre Dame, of the Eiffel Tower, and sold them in the Tuileries and on the South Bank as souvenirs. Then an American woman, Sadie Leigh Crosby, who had come to live in Paris with her husband and had a shop in the Rue de Rivoli where she sold local art, saw my paintings and took me up. On her advice I did sentimental pieces – wet cobbled streets, "colourful" cafés, spring gardens with blossom drifting down, the Seine by lamplight.' He snorted with amusement. 'They were popular. I earned money. I began to save. And I began to think that perhaps America was where I should go and make my home. I longed so much for a country untouched by war.' Polly nodded. She understood the feeling. 'So in 1922 I came to Boston.'

'How did you get a passport?'

'Sadie helped me. I made up a suitable story for the lack of any documents – there were many then who had lost everything so it caused no surprise. And in Paris, as in most cities, money irons out any little difficulties.'

'Why did you choose Boston?'

'Sadie recommended it. She said it would feel more English to me. The people were very cultured, and I'd find it easy to get a foothold. She was right. I worked in a bar by day and painted by night and made a reasonable living.'

She was looking down again. She had food in front of her – some kind of breaded cutlet with spaghetti – but she had no recollection of its arriving. 'And you got married.'

He looked at her bent head a moment, then answered neutrally. 'I was lonely. I had no family, no friends, no-one to care for me. Eva lived in a tenement at the end of my street. I used to see her going out and coming home, waiting for the bus, doing the marketing. She worked in her father's shop – he was a cobbler. Her parents were Russian refugees from the revolution. She was pretty and quiet and sad, and it suited how I felt in those days. I asked if I could paint her. She was very dark, with very white skin. I painted her draped in deep blue velvet. *Eva in Blue* was my first public success – it won a prize. A hundred dollars. Soon I wanted to paint her nude – for artistic reasons, not lascivious ones.' Polly looked up at that – a quick glance of blue, and then down again. 'But one thing led to another. Through history painters have married their models. It's a matter of propinquity rather than emotion.'

'Do you love her?' Polly was shocked to hear herself ask that, and was not surprised that Erich didn't answer. When the silence had gone on too long she looked up, to see how angry or embarrassed he was. But he was neither. He was looking at her with a faint smile and an expression in his eyes that seemed to say, *I understand every thought that passes through your mind, and there is nothing you can do or say to shock me.* A look of such *acceptance* that she felt almost faint, and was aware of her pulse beating in her ears.

461

'Did I love her? I suppose I must have done at the time, in a way,' he said. 'As one loves a puppy or a kitten or some other small, pretty animal. Do I love her? No. She is a part of the life I lived then, but my life is different now. I have grown out of her, I suppose. It is unfortunate.' He paused, as though searching for words. 'I regret now that I married her. I would not wish to cause her pain. If my success here continues I shall have to move to New York, and I suppose I must bring her to live with me. But she will not be happy. She likes to be near her parents, and she does not care for the art world, the big parties, all that – fuss. She is a simple country girl. She likes the simple family life of her forebears.'

The waiter came and took away their almost untouched plates with a sigh, and returned with cheese and fruit and another bottle of wine.

There was not much more to tell. Erich related how he had seen the limitations of the market for what he was painting. The abstract was where the big money and fame lay, so he had changed his style.

'Is it so easy to do?' Polly had asked, with a small frown.

He laughed. 'I am an artisan, not an artist. Did you think I painted from the heart all this time? I am a journeyman, a mimic. I can paint anything in any style, and if what is wanted is slabs of colour and meaningless strokes, then so be it. You have seen my paintings, Polly – what did you think of them?' She met his eyes, but couldn't think what to say. 'Yes, exactly,' he said cheerfully. 'They are as meaningless and sentimental as the rain-washed cobbles and foggy lamplit Seine. They have this merit for me – that they are far easier to produce! I prepared half a dozen canvases and took them to an art dealer who I knew traded in such things. He introduced me to Freda, and—' He shrugged again. '*Nous voici*,' he said, but there was a trace of bitterness in his voice. 'I am the *succès fou* of the season. I shall become famous and make a great deal of money. But for everything there is a price. Perhaps if I had known what a Faustian bargain I was making, I might not have done it. But then I would not have met you again.'

Faust, Polly thought. Hadn't he sold his soul to the devil? She had to know. 'Are you Freda's lover?'

'No. She is mine,' he said. 'But you are right. It was part of the bargain. I don't know how far my independence stretches. She is a powerful voice in the world of art. If I upset her, she may be able to take a revenge. And you,' he changed the subject abruptly, 'are married.'

Perhaps it wasn't a change of subject. She nodded, looking unhappily into his eyes.

He reached across the table and took her hands. Something jumped deep inside her – a feeling she understood now. His hands were warm, and hers were very cold. 'I know your husband by reputation. He is a powerful man. Is he unkind to you, Polly?' he asked gently.

'No,' she said, with a frown, looking down at their linked hands. How strong and lean and beautiful his were! 'It isn't that. I suppose, like you, I loved him at the time, but—' She couldn't think how to express it.

'Love can only be love between equals, between people who are alike,' he said. She looked up with quick relief. He understood! 'I sometimes wonder how a man and a woman can ever really love. Just being man and woman can be too much difference. And yet with some people you do feel . . . You feel as though you are on the same island, and the vast expanse of water separates you, not from each other, but from the rest of the world.'

She looked at him for a long moment. So alone! They were all so alone, and yet, as he said, sometimes you feel it might just be possible . . .

'What are we to do?' she asked at last, in a small voice.

His hands and his voice were warm and strong. 'We have

a little time. I believe we have a little time before it must end. We are owed that.'

'Is it right?' she asked uneasily.

'Such a long and winding road has led us here,' he said. 'Such a small chance it was that we would ever have met again, if things had not fallen out just so. So it becomes not a matter of right and wrong, but of necessity.' He released her hands and drew his own away. 'But you are free to go, Polly. Nothing has happened yet. You may go home with a clear mind. It must be as you wish.'

She wanted his hands back. She hated the cold emptiness. She wanted more than anything in the world to be touching him, to have him touch her. It seemed to her that she was not a complete thing, as if his body was the other half of hers. This place where they were was like a place out of time – the island he had spoken of, where only he and she existed, and the rest of the world was far away and out of reach. She didn't want to leave the island. She *never* wanted to leave it.

'Erich,' she said.

He smiled, dazzling her. 'Only you call me that,' he said, and her hands were in his again.

It seemed she had given him her answer.

Violet had had a most enjoyable visit. She had seen Laidislaw's work respectfully received and favourably reviewed – in fact, she had received so many offers to buy from delighted patrons she could have sold the whole collection if she had had a mind to. Polly's friend Freda Holland had been most urgent that she should consider selling. 'The excitement caused by the exhibition has improved the market tremendously, and if you don't sell now, I doubt you'll get the same prices in six months' time. Now, Laidislaw's work is not in my area, but I can recommend a dealer to you who specialises in that sort of thing – someone I know will treat you fairly.'

But Violet, faintly affronted, only repeated that she had no intention of selling. The *oeuvre* was Henry Octavian's inheritance – all he would have from his father. When he was grown-up, he could sell it if he wished, though she hoped he would not.

However, when the head curator of the Metropolitan approached her, it was a different matter. Laidislaw had died before the American troops had ever landed, but the war was an important part of American history just the same, and the curator believed it would be in the national interest to purchase an example of such an important war artist for the collection. Violet longed more than anything to see Laidislaw recognised as he should be. On those terms, she was willing to let a painting go. She sold the museum one of the larger canvases at an impressive price; and at the last minute yielded to urging by Ren and Polly to allow Gertrude Vanderbilt Whitney – wife of Harry Payne Whitney – also to buy a picture. She was tremendously rich in her own right, as well as the wife of a multi-millionaire, and a serious patron of the arts with an important collection. Polly told Violet that the collection was bound to be given to the nation in the long run, which swayed Violet more than the large sum being offered. The money, she determined, would be put aside for Henry.

She had had a lovely time; she had seen Charlotte improve, make friends with some nice American girls, and conduct herself more confidently with the American boys; and she knew Henry had had a most wonderful holiday that he would never forget. But it was time to go home. New York was growing unpleasantly hot, and soon the city would empty as the *ton* went to their summer homes. Several of them, with American generosity, invited Violet and her children to spend the summer with them, but she had had enough of travelling and was ready to depart. She wondered how things were going back in London, how her other two boys were faring, and Holkam.

She wondered about the prince. David had bombarded her with cables for the first few days; then they had slowed to one a day, then one every few days. But for the past week or ten days there had been nothing from him at all. She knew she would have heard if he had been ill, and she wondered whether her absence had had the opposite of the aphoristic effect, and made his heart grow less fond. If he had tired of her, indeed, it would not be surprising – he had tired of Freda Dudley Ward before her, and her own reign had been respectably long. If he had left her, she would be sorry, of course – she was fond of him, and there had been enjoyment in being at the heart of things – but in another way she would be glad to have more time to herself. He had been dreadfully demanding.

On the eve of departure, Ren and Polly gave an embarkation party for them, and invited all the family, and Violet's and the children's new friends, so there was an impressive number of guests filling the reception rooms of their large Fifth Avenue house. Violet found Polly rather distracted, and wondered if she was unwell, for she seemed pale. But Polly said it was just the heat, and that she would be better when she had got out of town. It was poignant to say goodbye to new friends, but Violet felt that, really, she would miss none of them except Polly, who had been kindness itself, and Avis Fellowes, who had devoted himself to them since he had come back to town. He was going back up-state when they had departed, to stay with his cousin for a few more days until it was time to escort her back to England.

'I wish we had been going back on the same boat,' he told Violet. 'Then I could have offered you my services again.'

'You're very kind,' Violet said, 'but I'm sure we shall be all right. I've looked at the passenger list, and there are several people with whom I have an acquaintance, so it will be comfortable enough.'

He nodded and changed the subject; but later, when they

were side by side again for a moment, he said how much he had enjoyed her company, and hoped, wistfully, that they might bump into each other in London. The thought that this might *not* happen had not occurred to Violet, and she felt an unexpected small pang; but he was a friend of Eddie's, after all, so they were bound to come across each other, weren't they? Besides, the value of a personable bachelor to a London hostess was legendary, and she said, with confidence, 'I'm sure we shall. And you must come and see us whenever you are up. Indeed, you must dine when Holkam and I are back in Town.'

He bowed and thanked her, but the wistful look, which had dissipated during the first two sentences, returned during the third.

The *Aquitania* was full, and everyone was predicting it would be a most amusing crossing. As soon as she was on board Violet sent two cables, one to her home to advise the servants, and Holkam if he was there, that she was on her way, and one to the prince to tell him when she would land. As the day advanced she rather expected a reply from David, saying how glad he was that she was coming back and promising to send a car to meet her. But by the time she and the children went down to dinner, there had been nothing.

The first night at sea was always rather informal, as everyone settled in, sought out friends and acquaintances, and lamented that their maids had not finished the unpacking so they had nothing to wear. As they stood in the entrance to the dining-saloon, wondering where they were to sit, Violet was accosted by a smart, well-dressed American woman who looked vaguely familiar.

'It's Lady Holkam, isn't it? I saw you at the Whitney party last week, but didn't have a chance to make your acquaintance,' she said, in a pleasant, well-modulated voice. 'I'm Gloria Morgan Vanderbilt – sister-in-law of your friend

Gertrude Whitney, who bought one of your lovely pictures. I must say I envied her that.'

Violet shook the extended hand, and noticed that the young woman was surveying her with keen interest, which she couldn't quite account for. 'How do you do?' she said. 'Mrs Whitney is really more an acquaintance – she's the friend of my cousin, Polly Alexander.'

'Oh, goodness, yes, I know Polly and Ren. My brother-in-law Harry always says he wouldn't invest a dime without Ren's say-so. You've been over quite a while, I believe?'

'Since May,' Violet said.

'And you've had a good time?'

'Yes, but I shall be glad to get home.'

'I expect you'll find a lot of things changed,' said Mrs Vanderbilt. She hesitated. 'I wonder—' Violet raised an enquiring eyebrow. Mrs Vanderbilt looked awkward, and said, 'Oh, nothing. Really. And this must be your daughter. How do you do, my dear? You are so lucky to have her travelling with you. I left my little girl with my mother and I miss her so much.'

Just then a steward approached and called them to their table, and Violet said goodbye and walked off, wondering what it was that Mrs Vanderbilt had not wanted to tell her.

After dinner, Charlotte was eager to dance, so Violet took her to the saloon where they joined a table of acquaintances, and Charlotte was soon asked to dance by an American boy she had met several times before. Violet watched her a moment in contentment; and then turned her head to find Gloria Vanderbilt had appeared beside her and was looking at her with the same hesitant expression.

'May I speak with you a moment, Lady Holkam?'

Violet nodded. 'Won't you sit down?'

'It's – rather delicate. Would you favour me with a moment aside?'

Violet was not a gossip and had no patience with secrets,

but Mrs Vanderbilt was looking anxious rather than sly, and she wondered suddenly if it had something to do with the boy who was dancing with Charlotte. If there was something she should know that affected her daughter, she must hear it. She stood up and walked with Mrs Vanderbilt to a small table behind, which was empty. A waiter drifted up as they settled themselves and Violet waved him away. 'Well,' she said, 'what is it you have to say?'

'It's a matter of some delicacy,' Mrs Vanderbilt said, 'and I don't know really whether I should mention it at all.'

'Then please don't,' Violet said, making to rise.

'Now, don't frost me, Lady Holkam. I mean it in all kindness. It's something concerning you which you might not have heard, since you've been away so long, and I feel you ought to hear it before you get back to England and it trips you up, so to speak.'

'Mrs Vanderbilt, I don't see why my welfare is any of your concern.'

'You will when I tell you. It concerns the prince, you see. And my sister.'

Violet became still. 'I have no interest in gossip,' she said, but she didn't rise. There had been that unusual silence from David, who previously could not go more than a few hours without speaking to her.

'Please,' said Mrs Vanderbilt, 'hear me out, because I feel uncomfortable about it. I don't know if you are acquainted with my sister Thelma.' She pronounced it without the *h*. 'She's married to Viscount Furness – do you know him? Duke's in shipping.'

Violet was aware of the existence of Marmaduke Furness, chairman of the Furness Shipping Company, but she had never met him. He was an elderly man, reputed to be rather uncouth and irascible, and was not in their circle. It was known to her as a distant fact that he had married a much younger woman, an American socialite, a very pretty divorcée, but she had never met her either, and had not even known her name. Suddenly these people on the fringe of society seemed about to leap into her ken, whether she wanted it or not.

'Well, Thelma was staying with people in Leicestershire this summer, and back in June, when I guess you were over here, she met the prince at a cattle show of some kind – he was handing out the prizes. They kind of clicked, and he asked her to dinner and, well, they've been going great guns ever since. When I saw you were on board I felt I had to make sure you weren't taken unawares. It didn't seem fair. Thelma and the prince are practically inseparable and – well – he might not have told you, seeing you were out of the country. It's not an easy thing to do by letter.'

Violet had felt a number of emotions during this speech, from indignation at the impertinence, suspicion about the motives, shock at the content, and a kind of burning humiliation that she had been ousted by this woman's sister, and was now, presumably, the subject of talk and pity. But she kept her cool demeanour and unflinching face, and would not give Mrs Vanderbilt any reaction she might speak of later. When the words stopped, she stood up with her customary grace, gave Mrs Vanderbilt a pleasant, distant smile of the sort she used at public functions, and said, 'Thank you for telling me. Now, if you will excuse me, I must return to my friends.'

Mrs Vanderbilt stood, too. 'I hope you're not offended. I meant it kindly, you know. I didn't mean to hurt your feelings.'

'I assure you, you have not offended me. Good evening.' She made her escape. Had David dropped her – and for an American, a mere industrialist's wife? There was the indisputable fact that he had not contacted her for almost two weeks. But to drop her so abruptly, without a word? Could he be so cruel?

With a sigh she acknowledged that throughout their relationship he had never consulted her convenience, only his own. She had always known, despite his many gifts and loving words, that he was a profoundly selfish man, but she had never expected anything else of the Prince of Wales, the Heir Apparent. It was the way kings were. And she had always known that one day her reign would end. She had even hoped her absence might weaken their ties. But to be thrown aside like this was hurtful in the extreme.

She sat down again, aware of some curious looks from the women of the party, and realised with a sick feeling that she was trapped on this boat, in this company, for the next five days. She had no faith that Mrs Vanderbilt would not share her news with others. Was she to suffer being talked about, and given pitying looks, wherever she went, until they docked at Southampton and she was able to escape?

She came back from a frenzy of speculation to discover that her neighbour, Mrs Graves Herschel, a comfortable and very respectable American hostess from the diplomatic circle, was speaking to her.

'I beg your pardon,' she said. 'I'm afraid I was wool-gathering.'

'No matter, Lady Holkam,' said Mrs Herschel, with a kindly look. 'I said that I hoped you were not being subjected to any familiarity by that young woman. Those three Morgan girls might be pretty and good-natured, but they had a shockingly bad upbringing, despite their father being a consul. Gloria and Thelma – they're twins, you know – and Connie, the other sister, had too much freedom too early, and they've made one bad marriage after another. It's a great pity, because they're decent girls at bottom, but got into bad ways. I shouldn't give any mind to anything Gloria says, Lady Holkam. I wouldn't mention it, but you looked a little uncomfortable when you sat down.' Before Violet was obliged to think of a reply, Mrs Herschel tactfully changed the subject.

471

'How graceful your daughter looks, dancing with young Perry Hopper. I expect she's going to have a most enjoyable crossing – there are a lot of respectable young men on board, which isn't always the case. When I brought my own daughter across, there seemed to be nothing but old men, and the poor thing had a very dull time of it. But we made it up to her in London. London society is the best in the world. I'm sure you must be longing to be back home.'

'Yes,' said Violet.

CHAPTER TWENTY-ONE

One of the pleasant things about Jack's extra job, monitoring the airships, was that when inspecting the R100 works at Howden, he found himself only fifteen miles from York, and was able to call in at Morland Place and see the family.

At the end of July 1929, when Molly's first baby was born, Jack took the children to holiday at Morland Place while Helen went to stay with Molly for the lying-in. It was a protracted labour, which the midwife said was only to be expected at the age of thirty-one, but there were no complications. When, at the end of it, a very small, very red baby boy was placed in Molly's arms, she said, 'It doesn't seem much to show for such a lot of hard work.'

'He'll improve with time,' Helen said.

'But he's so blotchy. And squashed – he looks like a bulldog pup, and I've never really liked bulldogs. Do you think I could have accidentally looked at one when I was pregnant?'

The midwife tutted, but Helen smiled. 'You're talking nonsense – that's the euphoria.'

'Yes, I feel euphoric. Realisation that it's all over,' said Molly. 'Vivian will have to be very persuasive to make me do it again. How could you have *three*, Helen?'

'I guarantee you'll have forgotten the labour in a few weeks' time. Do you know what you're going to call him?'

'We decided on Esmond if it was a boy, and Veronica for

a girl.' She inspected the baby in her arms. 'I must say, he doesn't look much like an Esmond. More like a Towser.'

'You need a sleep,' Helen said wisely, 'before Vivian comes home. Remember this brat is going to cost him dear in school fees and the rest of it, so he'll need to be persuaded that it's worth it.'

'Yes, Mother needs a sleep,' the midwife said, bustling in with a disapproving look for both of them. '*I*'ll take Baby.' The lack of proper feeling in this house, said her expression, was a scandal.

Helen stayed with Molly for two weeks, until she was up and about. The first visitor was Emma, looking happy and prosperous, bringing a wonderful set of silver spoons, two bottles of champagne and a large bunch of luscious purple grapes.

'Hamburgs,' she said. 'I know grapes are for sick people, and you're not sick, but they are simply too delicious. I couldn't resist.'

Kit had sent a bottle of perfume for the mother and an aeroplane construction kit for the child. 'I told him it was too old for a baby, but he said you might like something to do while you're confined to bed.'

Molly laughed. 'Just like Kit. Do you want to see the baby?'

'Of course. Isn't he the main attraction?'

'Don't think you're about to see a movie star,' Molly warned. 'He's pretty grim, poor soul. Kinder, really, not to look.'

But when he was placed in Emma's arms, she said, 'He's enchanting,' as if she meant it. 'His skin's so soft. And what long eyelashes he has. And those tiny fingers, complete with fingernails . . .'

Helen looked at her speculatively. Emma and Kit had been married over two years now . . . but she wouldn't ask.

Unfortunately, Molly hadn't 'an ounce of tack', as she

474

said of herself. 'If you like him so much, why not have one of your own?'

Emma reddened slightly, but she said smoothly enough, 'Oh, I simply haven't time, not at the moment, with all my schemes. Perhaps one day.'

When Molly was able to do without her, Helen went on to Morland Place to join the children. She felt a little guilty, since Jack was at home on his own, being cared for only by the servants – usually she took the children to the south coast, where he could easily reach them on his days off. But he did have two days at Howden before the end of the school holidays.

The R100 was nearing completion. The differences between the two airships were many, and Jack said it was going to be interesting to see how they both performed. For instance, early on it had been judged that the R100 could be steered without servo assistance. When Jack had told Vickers that the R101 was to have servo motors fitted, he almost caused a panic – servos meant a considerable cost not only in money but in weight, so the Howden team reckoned the R101 committee must have felt the huge ship needed them. They hastily did their calculations again, and then again, but came up with the same conclusion, that servos weren't needed. A single helmsman could steer her, they were convinced.

Jack had been particularly interested in the engines: R100 was to have had a new type of engine fuelled by kerosene and hydrogen, but after a year's work it was realised there was no chance of developing the engines in time, so the plan was dropped. The next idea was to have the same diesel engines as the R101, but Vickers decided they were excessively heavy, and eventually settled on six Rolls-Royce petrol engines. There were those who pointed out that petrol had a lower flash-point than diesel, so there could be a fire hazard, but as Barnes Wallis said, aeroplanes had been using petrol for years without bursting into flames every flight. Jack carried the comment to Cardington, but though there were some who favoured petrol engines for the sake of the weight reduction, the Air Ministry vetoed the idea, saying that the diesel engines had been developed specially for the R101 and so had to be used.

It was one of the main differences, Jack saw, between the capitalist airship and the socialist airship: at Vickers, talented men like Barnes Wallis were allowed to run with their ideas; at Cardington, everything had to be passed through the committee and got bogged down.

At the end of the summer, the R100's gasbags were inflated for the first time, and her outer covering of linen was doped with aluminium paint. The vast ship had a tare weight of 102 tons, leaving 54 tons for passengers, crew, cargo, fuel and ballast. The team was growing excited now the finishing line was in sight. It was thought she should be ready for her first flight in November or early December. Then she would be flown down to Cardington so the two airships could be compared.

It was true. She was dropped. Violet found no messages from David when she got home. After a couple of days she telephoned him at York House. She had to ring several times before she was put through to him, and then, though he chatted lightly to her, there was nothing of the lover in it. Like any common acquaintance, he asked about her trip, enquired whether she had visited his 'favourite restaurant in New York', whom she had met in Manhattan, and how the crossing had been, but never once said he had missed her. He talked in the usual way about his own concerns, golf he had played and tennis sets he had won, complained as usual about his official duties and the lack of consideration he received from everyone about him, and then, quite suddenly, said goodbye and hung up. He had not suggested meeting again, or even said that he would telephone her. It was an abrupt ending to their relationship, when only two months ago he had been in despair at her leaving.

As she hung up in her turn, she wondered what would have happened if she had mentioned meeting Gloria Vanderbilt on the ship. But he could be quite harsh with anyone who embarrassed him. Better she make her dismissal easy for him and remain on friendly terms, for the children's sake if nothing else.

London was hot and disagreeable and the weather was humid and thundery. Violet longed for the country, particularly after a visit from Phyllis Damerel: ostensibly a *congé* call to say she and Dickie were going to the South of France, but really an excuse to hint at the Wales situation, which she had heard rumours about. It was an uncomfortable fifteen minutes. Suddenly Violet wanted to get away from everyone, particularly those who knew about her and David. She had been intending to go to Shawes, but there would be too many kindly, curious people there. She decided instead to go to Brancaster. It was a draughty house in the Fens that was only tolerable in summer, but the thought of its cool airiness appealed now, as did its remoteness.

Holkam said that he had business and must stay in Town, though he might join her later. To give the servants a holiday they would close up the house, and Holkam would stay at whichever of his clubs was open at the time – all the clubs took it in turns to close so as to offer a refuge to those who found themselves temporarily homeless. The elder boys were unhappy at the choice of Brancaster – no interesting neighbours, and the nearest town, Lincoln, a sleepy and bucolic cathedral city. Fortunately, both had had invitations from college friends, and they hastened to confirm them in such a way as to spend as little time as possible in purdah.

It was rather hard on Charlotte, for she had no choice but to remain with her mother. Violet felt she had had enough fun in New York to last her through the summer and, when Charlotte sighed, told her she ought to spend the time practising her music. 'I'll be bringing you out next year, and you'll need *some* accomplishments if you are to attract a husband. It wouldn't hurt you to read the newspaper every day, too – the social columns – so that you know who everyone is and what they've been doing. You need to develop your conversational skills – the young men don't want a girl with *nothing* to say for herself.'

'Yes, Mama,' Charlotte said. It was all she ever said to her mother, whom she found even more intimidating, on account of her great beauty and elegance, than her father. *Him* she had had little to do with, and his habit of giving her a distant smile as he passed briskly on his way to somewhere important was much easier to cope with than actual conversation. She was looking forward to her Season, in a vague sort of way. The clothes and the parties would be fun, though she was worried about the balls, in case no-one asked her to dance. With her mother's example always before her eyes, she thought herself plain and clumsy. How would she get a husband? She knew that it was the purpose of the come-out, and though the idea of marriage itself rather frightened her, she felt it would be far worse not to be asked – to *fail* in the one thing she had to do in her life. *Too* shame-making! She resolved suddenly that she *would* use the time at Brancaster to improve herself.

Henry also had no choice about Brancaster, but he didn't mind in the least. He loved the freedom of roaming about the estate and, being a cheerful, friendly boy, he could always find someone to chum with – stable lad, gardener's boy, vicar's son. And if there was no boy about, he was not averse from enticing Charley into his games; and she, being young for her age and fond of him, did not usually resist. He had overheard some of his mother's recommendations to Charley about reading and practising, but he knew his sister better than that. Charley could not read two pages without yawning, and in a choice between sitting at the keyboard doing scales and romping about in the wilderness at the far end of the estate building a tree-house with him, he knew the piano had no chance.

Violet did not make any *congé* visits herself, and was at home to few of the people who called in the short time between her return and her departure for the country, but she did receive a visit from Avis Fellowes. For a moment she thought of denying him, afraid it would be uncomfortable, but after a hesitation she had him admitted, and at the first sight of his pleasant face she was glad she had. They seemed to fall straight back into the easy friendship they had enjoyed in America, and she was only sorry that a strict sense of propriety had him on his feet to leave after only a quarter of an hour. She persuaded him to sit down again, and asked what his plans were for the summer.

He told her that he was going down to his family home – he was the second son of the Earl of Belmont, who had an estate in Derbyshire.

'I'm going to another wedding,' he said. 'Wonderful to say, Reggie is getting married at last.'

'Indeed!' Violet said, trying not to sound surprised. Avis's older brother Reginald, Lord Tunstead, was a rake-helly member of a fast set whom Violet had met once or twice, as he was rather admired by the Prince of Wales and had been on sprees with him and Fruity Metcalfe in the days before Violet's time.

'Yes, really,' he said. 'The bride is an American girl, Mary Deacon, though she calls herself Minnie. Her father owns a chain of hotels. The whole thing was arranged by Lady Paget.'

Lady Paget was an American socialite turned matchmaker, who found American heiresses for impoverished English peers.

'I hope you're pleased?' Violet asked uncertainly. She had

heard Eddie Vibart describe Tunstead as a confirmed bachelor whose wild habits would lead him to an early grave; and he had added that he'd wager Belmont would be glad to have the quiet second son inherit, because Tunstead would surely ruin the estate within a twelvemonth. However nice Fellowes was, it must have crossed his mind once or twice that he might one day inherit. But with his brother marrying, that chance went away.

But Fellowes smiled. 'I'm delighted. Minnie is a very sweet girl, and I believe Reggie's truly smitten. It might quiet him down a bit,' he added, with a twinkle. Then he leaned a little closer and lowered his voice. 'I won't pretend not to understand you, Lady Holkam, but I never wanted to inherit. I'm dashed fond of Reggie, and he'll do the thing very well once he settles down. I think Minnie is the girl to tame him. Under that shy exterior there's a core of steel. Reggie doesn't know what he's let himself in for.'

At the end of another quarter-hour he rose again and this time was firm about leaving. More than half an hour would be too particular, and he would never do anything to make a lady uncomfortable. Violet said goodbye to him with regret. Such consideration was something she had never had from Holkam. Fellowes was a friend worth having.

Oliver walked into the club's library and saw Holkam at the far end, in the armchair before the fire, looking over some papers. As he moved down the room he looked into each of the bays and found them all empty. He had chosen the library for this meeting because even in the Season it was little used, and now, in August, almost everyone was out of Town anyway.

It was odd that Holkam was still here – the House was in recess and Violet, he knew, had gone down to Lincolnshire. Only Oliver's professional responsibilities had kept him up. Verena and the children were at Wolvercote, and then were going on to Emma and Kit's house-party at Walcote House, where Oliver hoped to join them for at least two weeks, and preferably more. Fitzjames House was shut up – he had walked past it the other day – so why was Holkam in Town, stewing in a club not even his own?

Holkam looked up with a frown as he approached, hastily shuffled the papers together and turned them face down on the table. Oliver caught a glimpse of columns of figures before they were hidden from view, and wondered . . . And then stopped himself. Inquisitiveness was a nasty habit, and it was bad enough having to interfere in the way he was about to, without poking sticks down other holes.

Holkam threw one leg over the other and drummed his fingers on the table with an impatient air. 'Well, Overton? What's all this cloak-and-dagger business about?'

'Not cloak-and-dagger. I simply wanted to be sure of speaking to you in confidence.'

'What in deuce's name can you have to say that's so damned private?' Holkam asked, with an irritation only just held in check.

Oliver was a little surprised at the irascibility: he and Holkam usually managed to get on politely on the occasions when they met. But perhaps he had an inkling of what was coming. Uninvited, he took the chair opposite, and decided the only way to get over the fence was to go straight at it. 'This isn't pleasant to me, Holkam, but I have to speak to you about your behaviour.'

'My behaviour? What the—'

'Please, hear me out. I have no more wish to say this than I imagine you have to hear it, but now that Violet is home I must insist on your moderating your private life. I had thought you would do so anyway when she came back from America, but it seems that—'

'You impudent dog! What the deuce do you mean, private life?'

481

'I think you know. I'm talking about your – well, for want of a better description, night prowlings.'

Holkam's face suffused with rage. 'How dare you? What right have you to question anything I do?'

'Violet is my sister – that is my right. I am your brother-in-law, and what you do reflects on me and my family. I have no desire to pry into any man's private affairs, but when they cease to remain private it becomes a different matter.'

The bluster dropped and was replaced by an alert stillness. In a dead voice, Holkam said, 'You had better explain yourself.'

Oliver shrugged. 'I have known for a long time about your visits to various . . . houses of pleasure, shall we call them? But they were the sort of discreet, semi-respectable places where I know many men of rank go, and it was not my business to object. But lately the places you have been frequenting have not been discreet or respectable. In short, Holkam, you have been picking up girls on the street, and it has got to stop. Your conduct has become a matter of gossip – not generally spread as yet, but it's only a matter of time. When a club servant gives you a hint, you know it's the tip of the iceberg.'

'Which club servant? By God, I'll have him flayed!'

'I shan't tell you his name. It is someone I trust, that's all. But, good God, man, did you think you were invisible? Doing your business in the open street where anyone could see you – you were bound to be recognised. The servant who spoke to me – it's not the first murmur I've heard about you. It has to stop.'

For once in his life, Holkam had nothing to say. He glared at Oliver, and his hands clenched and unclenched on his knees, but he seemed unable to deny the charge, or summon up enough of the old indignation to tell Oliver to mind his own business.

Oliver went on: 'I don't know how things are between you

and Violet. I've been glad of recent years to see you apparently reconciled. But I know you had separate lives at one time, and there was that Laidislaw business.' Holkam moved his head slightly as if avoiding a blow. 'And I know of other men who – who seek satisfaction away from home. None of that's my business. But you can't go on openly consorting with prostitutes in the middle of London – a man of your standing. You will bring yourself and your family to ruin.'

'You damned impudent swine,' Holkam growled. 'You jumped-up beauty doctor! You self-satisfied prig!'

'Call me all the names you like,' Oliver said indifferently. 'It doesn't alter the facts.' He looked at him more closely. 'You don't look well, Holkam. Are you feeling quite the thing?'

'How do you think I'm feeling? You make me sick!'

But the retort was without depth. Oliver noted that Holkam seemed to have lost weight. His eyes were poached, his face was pasty, and there was a sheen of sweat on it despite the fact that the library, on the north side of the building, was quite cool. 'You look as if you're coming down with something,' he said. 'Have you got a fever?'

'Don't presume to quack me, you charlatan. I wouldn't trust you to cut my dog's nails.'

'I wouldn't dream of treating you. But I recommend you go and see your own doctor. You look as if you're starting an influenza or something of the sort.' He stood up. 'Meanwhile, have I your word that you will stop this insane behaviour?'

'I shall do as I please! You have nothing to threaten me with.'

'Only what you risk already – exposure.'

Holkam stared at him, his mind evidently working. But he said only, 'Go to the devil!'

'I probably will, with or without your exhortation. But give me your word that you will not go on this way. Think of your children, if you care for nothing else.'

483

'Oh, go away and leave me alone. You have my word, if that's what it takes – now leave me alone!'

Oliver went. He glanced back at the door, and saw Holkam sitting with his face buried in his hands. He disliked the man, and yet he felt a pang of pity. Whatever demons drove Holkam to consort with such women, they were harrying him hard, or he would not have behaved so indiscreetly. It worried Oliver. He had often thought his brother-in-law mad, but he wondered now if he were on the brink of real insanity.

What troubles there were in St James's Square! The Prince of Wales had dropped Violet and started a new affair. It was not common knowledge yet, and he suspected Violet might not mind too much in the long run (though she must be hurt), but he knew Holkam had been pinning various hopes on the connection. Was it the realisation of his plans going awry that had made him desperate?

He shook his head, treading down the broad stairs and heading for the door. He had been going to have a drink or two in the bar with anyone he found there, but he couldn't relish the idea now, with Holkam brooding above in the library, like Mrs Rochester in the attic. He belonged to several other clubs, so he collected his hat and stick from the porter and left to seek one out.

It was at the end of a rough, sandy track, which led off the narrow lane that ran parallel to the sea. A home-made wooden sign, hanging crookedly from the post, told her where to turn, and she bumped carefully between the high dunes, shaggy with marram grass, and came out suddenly beside the house. She parked beside his car and got out, feeling the good breeze move her hair, smelling salt and seaweed, hearing the pounding of the waves and the mew of a gull.

It was a simple place, a single-storey wooden square, like a child's drawing, with a shingle roof and a verandah round three sides. It had been painted blue, but sun and wind had faded it to the delicate silvery shade of a harebell. He came out and walked to where she stood, and paused in front of her. He was dressed in shorts and a shirt open at the neck and rolled at the sleeve. His face and forearms were very brown, and his hair, muddled by the breeze, was very fair – he looked again as she had known him all those years ago.

He reached out and took both her hands. 'You came,' he said. 'I hoped you would.'

Polly had spent the summer in a kind of trance, as though she were viewing the world from behind glass. She had managed to see him alone only twice more – once in the dark depths of a cocktail bar, where she was terrified of being seen by someone she knew, and once walking in an obscure East Side neighbourhood park among the girls pushing perambulators and the elderly Jewish couples sitting on benches feeding the birds. For the rest, it was only glances exchanged at social events.

Ren had been so busy she had hardly seen him, for which she was grateful. He seemed more cheerful, sometimes almost elated, and when she roused herself to observe him, she discovered that it was financial not political matters that were mostly occupying him. She supposed he felt more at ease with them. He seemed to spend every hour in meetings with bankers and financiers and other speculators, to rush from one appointment to another with an air of great urgency. There were constant telephone calls. He had had a ticker-tape installed in his study, and was often up all night with sheets of figures spread around him, across his desk and spilling over onto the floor.

He slept when he could, and rarely came to her bedroom, and she was glad of it. When she looked at him now, she saw a man who seemed to have nothing to do with her: a giant of a man, too tall, too strong, dark and unapproachable, unfathomable, a member of an alien race. What was he to her? She could not find inside her any connection to him. And what was she to him? Just his trophy, the hostage he had taken in his war against the white man. She knew that was not fair, yet at some level it seemed true. He had wanted her and he had taken her, but now he had her, it seemed the conquest was all that mattered. He did not need to understand her or have her understand him, as long as she remained in his possession.

They attended some occasions together, but even then he seemed distracted, and would excuse himself from time to time and hurry out to find a telephone. And she drifted in a world of her own. If Erich was not present, nothing else mattered to her. Acquaintances sometimes said, 'What is it, Polly? You're miles away,' and she would smile and answer automatically, without being aware of them at all.

Rose's studio test had been successful and she had got her part in the movie, with the promise of a career ahead of her if she did well. Lizzie and Ashley made their final arrangements to uproot themselves and go with their daughter to Los Angeles. Patrick held a farewell party for them, and all the family was there. Ren could not come, so Polly went without him. She tried to make herself feel something – they had been good to her since she came to New York – but the glass barrier was down between them.

Lennie was there, too – he was to escort them on the journey. It was the first time he had been back from California since they had had their quarrel, and he looked at her painfully, wanting to be forgiven. She smiled and chatted to him, seeing him as if at the other end of a telescope, uninterested in what had passed between them.

He said, 'I'm thinking about possibly making my base in Los Angeles – settling over there and visiting New York rather than the other way round. What do you think?'

She missed the wistful tone. 'It sounds like a wonderful idea,' she said cheerfully, hardly knowing what he had asked.

486

'I see,' he said unhappily, and then, looking at her closely, asked, 'Polly, are you all right? You seem – absent tonight. Have you had bad news? You aren't ill?'

'I'm perfectly well,' she said. 'There's nothing wrong.'

She went to see them all off at the station, and the next day met Erich at a party at the Stuyvesants'. They managed a snatched conversation, shielded from notice by the sheer crush of bodies and the noise of New York society voices. He told her he was going back to Boston for a while – he had been away a long time and he had family duties. And he wanted to get away from Freda.

She told him Ren would expect her to go to Long Island and open the house there – no-one stayed in New York in the middle of summer.

'But I must see you,' he said urgently.

'I don't know if I could get away,' she said miserably. Though it seemed unlikely Ren would spend much time there, he would come and go, and entertain business friends, so she would be expected to be there.

'Listen,' he said. 'I shall be renting a cottage by the sea. It's understood that I have to get away from time to time to paint, and that I must be alone, so no-one will come there. I shall be there for the whole of September. Come if you can.'

And he pressed a small square of paper into her palm before Freda appeared through the throng and hooked him away. When Polly unfolded the paper later, she found it was the address of the cottage and directions of how to get there, written very small in his neat, foreign-looking hand. And at the bottom he had written, *Please come!*

She had not seen how it would be possible, but in the middle of September Ren announced he would be going to Washington for a week. He was to have important talks with President Hoover and Andrew Mellon, the Treasury secretary, about the economy – Hoover was worried that it was running too hot. Polly gave her maid the week off, inventing an invitation to a house-party in Westport and saying she would share a maid with a friend. As long as Ren didn't come home suddenly she was safe. If he did, she would make something up. She didn't think he'd care.

He lifted her bag from the car. Carrying her jacket and hat, she followed him into the house. Inside, one long room took up the whole front half: one end of it for sitting, with armchairs and a sofa arranged around a log-stove, and shelves of books in the alcoves; the other end the kitchen, with green-painted cupboards and a wooden table and chairs. The walls were bare wood, smelling sweetly of pine, the furniture simple: rustic wood upholstered in cheerful primary colours.

Behind, through the central door, was a small lobby, from which led a large bedroom – a white blind drawn down over the window to keep it cool, pale green counterpane on the bed, native rug on the wooden floor, a wicker chair with a white cushion, a green jug full of white rambler roses, spitting their petals, on the pine dresser. On the other side of the lobby was a small bedroom, filled with artist's equipment and paintings, a bathroom and a separate lavatory. The bathroom had a shower as well as a bath and basin. 'You see we're not without comforts,' he said.

In the bedroom he put down her bag on the floor, she dropped her hat and jacket on the chair, and they stood staring at each other. His face seemed so familiar, it was like looking in the mirror; and so dear she felt a strange tearfulness. He stepped close, reached out and pushed a stray strand of her hair away from her brow, smiled at the brightness of her eyes. What could he read in her face? Only that she wanted to be closer to him. Quietly he began unbuttoning her blouse. They did not speak. There was no need for words, and no hurry. All was gentle and easy. They undressed each other. His body was hard and brown, all but a white band round his loins where he had worn shorts. Hers was creamy-white by contrast, subtly curved. Yet they were the same flesh.

They lay down together on the bed, facing each other, gazing and gazing as if they could never have enough of it. He rested his lips lightly against hers and she closed her eyes. She breathed his breath, tasted his mouth. He stroked her cheek and neck, caressed her small breast. She touched him too. It was wonderful that she could – she felt no inhibition. She stroked his smooth chest, his long flank; she closed her fingers around the hard silk of his penis. With him she could do whatever she wanted, touch him any way that pleased her. There was no embarrassment.

And when she was ready for him, it was she who drew him over and into her, arching upwards for him, longing for him; and when he sank into her, she sighed with accomplishment. It was beautiful beyond expressing. He hung over her as he moved, and they looked into each other's eyes, moving together in harmony, as if they had done this a thousand times.

With Ren it was all drive and fierceness and conquering: love was something he did to her. This with Erich was something they did together, by consent, between equals. This was the way it should be. When the moment approached she almost didn't want it to come, because she didn't want this joy to end; but like a great comber it curved up and up and crashed over, and they were flung, spent and breathless, clinging to each other like two swimmers tumbled in the surf.

Afterwards they lay again on their sides, facing each other. He smiled at her in a kind of wonder; then drew her against him. His skin smelt of salt, but under that was the true smell of him, which she felt as if she had known all her life. She pushed her head into the hollow of his shoulder, and slept.

* * *

When they woke the sun was going down. He gave her towels, and she went into the bathroom and showered. She came out refreshed, dressed herself in a simple cotton frock and followed the sound of his voice. He was in the kitchen preparing food, singing under his breath. He turned as she came in, put down his knife and came to her with such gladness in his face, as if they had been apart for months. He kissed her, and said, 'I am making you dinner.' He opened a bottle of wine, poured two glasses, and said, 'Sit there and talk to me while I finish.'

She loved to watch him moving about. Everything he did was with the same strong, sure movements she remembered from home, from when she had watched him hedging and ditching, building dry stone walls, helping with a lambing. His movements were like poetry to her, everything harmonious and lyrical.

He cooked scallops, fried with some green herb she didn't know, and boiled potatoes, and made a salad – simple food, which they ate with the good, clean appetite that follows physical exertion. Afterwards there was a crumbly white cheese with a pungent taste – goat's, he told her – small white peaches and sweet grapes. They talked as they ate like old friends. Sometimes she felt they could have conversed without even speaking.

Afterwards they went out into the soft dusk. From the front of the verandah wide steps led down straight onto the sand, and fifty feet away the ocean thundered and crashed onto the shore in a torrent of white foam. The sky was darkling, with fingers of muted pink stretching from the landward, and beyond the surf the sea was pewter-coloured and quiet. The first stars were out, fiercely bright in the velvet sky. They linked hands and walked along the sand. There was not a soul about – the few houses along the shore were holiday homes, empty now, and set a mile, two miles apart. They walked without talking for an hour, and then by mutual consent turned and went back.

As they neared the house their footsteps quickened. Inside, it was quiet, warm, woodscented, safe. They pulled off their clothes and flew together, and made love on top of the bed. Afterwards it grew chilly, and they got under the sheet and counterpane, and curled into each other. They lay listening to the beat of the ocean, heard through the open doors.

He kissed her brow, and pulled her closer, and said, 'How long have you got?'

'A week,' she said. Those were the only words they spoke.

They slept lightly and woke often, and made love many times through the night. Every time she woke and reached out, hungry for him, he was marvellously close, and ready. She could not have enough him. Their bodies knew each other as if they had been united in another life.

When it grew light, he got up and left her, and she slept a little, rolling into the hollow of the bed that held his scent. When she got up, she found him on the verandah, dressed in shorts and an old blue shirt, painting. He looked up and smiled at her, so that she would understand this was not work but pleasure – he had felt the need to do it. She went back in and made coffee and brought it out in two mugs, and sat on the edge of the verandah, swinging her legs, sipping, and watching the sun come up, pale gold and round and flat, like a coin, emerging smoothly as though from a slot behind the horizon.

He looked at her. 'Are you happy?' he asked, and she told him, 'Yes.' But neither of them had spoken a word.

So the week passed. They slept together and ate together, made love a great deal, walked along the shore, sat talking and talking as if they would never stop. One day they drove into the village for supplies. It was a sleepy place, one street of clapboard buildings, with a row of shops along a board-walk: a grocery, a bakery, two cafés, a hardware store. There was a two-pump garage at one end and a bar and general store combined at the other, where the village ceased and the country began again. In a place that catered to visitors every summer, strange faces were neither unusual nor the occasion of interest. They were served politely but without even a curious look. Polly felt so free it bubbled in her.

He did all the cooking. He caught fish on a long line cast out to sea and pegged down to the shore. He bought shellfish from a local man who had a hut behind the garage, and meat and eggs and fruit from a farm a couple of miles the other way. Every day, at varying times to catch the light he wanted, he painted – the sea, mostly, but the dunes and the cottage too, and her, once, sitting on the edge of the verandah in what had become her accustomed pose. It was a different style of painting either from his harsh abstracts or the sentimental tourist pieces. The strokes were wide and free and the image emerged in the end almost from between them, the light and mood captured as if by divine accident. She marvelled at his skill. A few quick lines, almost carelessly wrought, and there she was, shoulders hunched because her hands were under her thighs, the sun and shadow and salt breeze implicit, so that she could almost smell the warmed wood of the verandah.

'I like it much better than your other kind of painting,' she said. 'There's so much feeling in it. Everything is so real and alive.'

'This is the way *I* want to paint,' he said. 'The rest was for money.'

On the penultimate day the wind changed, and there was a sense of autumn in the air. In the evening it was chilly enough to be worth lighting the stove, and she stood behind him as he laid it with paper and driftwood, thinking there seemed to be nothing he didn't know how to do. It blazed up beautifully and left a scent of woodsmoke before the door was closed, which reminded her of England.

Fall in New York meant new fashions in the shops, new

plays in the theatres, new menus in the restaurants and new faces at the parties. But woodsmoke drifting up into a soft sky, oaks and beeches and sycamores getting their bright colours, berries in the hedgerows, shiny red and black, birds flocking on the stubble fields, horses growing their winter coats – that was autumn at home.

While they ate she asked him if it was the same for him, and they talked about their respective homelands. 'Doesn't it make you sad that you'll never go back?' she asked.

'Yes, of course. But Germany is finished now. The land of my childhood is gone for ever, more truly shattered even than the part of France that was under the guns. Those fields will regrow in time, the scars will heal. But something else has grown up over the ruins of Germany, something ugly and monstrous. So there is nothing to go back to, and I must make the best of it, make a new life here.'

After dinner they stretched out together on the sofa in front of the stove, holding each other close and watching the flames, hearing only the tick and crack of the burning logs and the distant, muted murmur of the ocean. And it was then that he told her he was leaving Boston. He had had an approach from the head of a movie studio who was planning a series of religious epic movies, and wanted a 'real artist' to paint magnificent sets.

'He's a funny little man with grand ideas, but he has a way of making things work. And he is truly dedicated to his "art", as he calls it. One cannot but be moved by his enthusiasm. So I said yes.' Her head was on his shoulder, and he stroked her hair. 'He has offered me a long contract, which means security. It will make me lots of money, and probably it will make me famous, too. I shall be able to name my price for my paintings after that. I shall never have to worry about money again.'

'So you are going to Los Angeles?' Polly asked, in a dead voice.

'Yes. Eva and her parents will come too, and we will settle there. I don't suppose we shall come back.'

'You will be on the other side of the continent from me,' she said. Her voice sounded strange, because her throat hurt so much. 'I'll never see you again.'

'No, my Polly.' There was a silence – perhaps he found it hard to speak as well. He said at last, 'We knew from the beginning that we could not be together. You're married. Your life is here, with Ren. And – I did not tell you before, but there is a child. I have a son.' He felt her draw a breath, like a sigh.

So this was all they had, Polly thought. Just this one week, to say everything, to live the whole of their lives together. Just one week – and it was almost over.

As if he had heard her, he said, 'It was more than we ever thought we'd have. And we still have tomorrow. A whole day.' He kissed her head again. 'Let us not waste it with being sad.'

They did not talk much, that last day. It was cool and breezy under a faint grey sky, and the sea growled busily, beating at the shoreline as though it were a job to get done. They walked for miles along the beach, arms wrapped round each other. In the face of the long goodbye, there didn't seem to be anything much to say that they could not say with their bodies. Gulls wheeled around fretfully above them, hanging against the wind and mewing their complaint. Erich found a round stone and threw it flat onto the waves, making it skip; Polly picked up a shell, iridescent with nacre, and put it absently into her pocket; and for the rest they trudged, like refugees walking to a new country, holding on to each other, deliberately not thinking what their new lives would be like.

That night they made love, slow, tender love, touching each other's faces, breathing each other's breath. They had so little time left. Polly thought they would stay awake to

494

make the most of every second, but when they had finished they fell asleep, easily like children, curled up together, her head in the hollow of his shoulder, her nose pressed to the scent of his skin.

The wind dropped in the night, and in the morning they woke to find the world wrapped in a thick fog. She stood with him at the door to the verandah, and it was chill on her face, and smelt faintly of iodine. There was nothing before them but a featureless whiteness, no movement anywhere, no sound: even the sea's voice had been quieted to a murmur she had to strain to hear. It was as though the rest of the world had been obliterated and they were alone. They ate breakfast on the verandah, sitting close so their shoulders and thighs were touching, but not speaking. As the sun came up, the fog was flooded with illumination from within, glowing like a pearl; then it began to thin and shred, and quite suddenly it was gone, replaced in an astonishing instant with a day of blue and gold glory: the sun glinting in a creamy blue sky on a sparkling dark blue sea. A day to be happy in, you would have thought.

It was time to go. He carried her bag to the car, and then they faced each other, holding hands for the last time, memorising each other's faces.

'You were dead to me once before,' she said. 'Now you will be dead to me again.'

'Not that. Never that,' he said. 'I shall never be far from you, just – out of sight. Think of me as being in the next room. Always near you.'

He reached up and moved a thread of her hair from her forehead, as he had done so often that week, cupped her cheek in his hand for a moment, then let her go.

As she turned away, she heard him say softly, 'I will love you always.'

She didn't look back. She got into the car and drove away, bumping carefully up the track between the sand dunes.

CHAPTER TWENTY-TWO

The little flat was stifling, with a smell of dusty carpets and tinned soup, and the atmosphere was heavy with the cigarettes Holkam had been smoking one after another all afternoon. The windows were wide open but it made little difference. The sultry September day was declining but no breath of air stirred outside. As the sunset barred the western sky purple and crimson like a bruise, and the first lights came on, it only seemed to get muggier.

Mabel, her Chinese viscose silk dressing-gown bound primly about her, turned from the open window and looked at her lover, sprawled on the bed, another cigarette hanging from his lips. The bed was rumpled, the room untidy, with clothes, bottles, glasses and brimming ashtrays strewn about; there was a smell of sex and, now she came to notice it, sweat as well – man sweat. Mabel was in her way quite fastidious, and she had come to realise only lately, as he spent more and more of his time here, that Bob was not. In fact, he seemed to relish the frowstiness they created on these occasions, and if she tried to tidy up he snapped at her to 'leave things alone' or 'stop fussing'. It was only because it was so hot today that he had even let her open the windows.

He was turning into a right Grumpy Gus lately, she thought; she was starting to wonder whether the game was worth the candle. She had been thrilled and flattered at the start to get a lord, and a rich one at that. But now he was spending so much time here, she couldn't get out to do anything or go anywhere, and she was bored. To be honest, a little of his company went a long way. There seemed no pleasing him, these days, which got a girl down, and it wasn't as if he was ever chatty or amusing. She hadn't seen any of her other gentlemen friends in months, and wondered, wistfully, if it was going to be like this for ever. A girl might as well get married as live like this!

She sidled closer to the bed. 'Bob?' she said. He stared up at the ceiling, smoked and didn't look at her. 'Bobby? Can't we go out somewhere?'

He grunted, but it was not an encouraging sound.

'Please, Bobby, dear. I'm fed up staying in all the time. Can't we go out and have some fun?'

'No,' he said.

She flumped down in the little brocade chair in the corner. 'You might take a girl up West once in a while. To a show, or a restaurant or *something*. Even a pub'd be better than nothing.'

'Stop your whining,' Holkam growled.

'I'm sick of this room,' she said crossly.

'It's your room,' he pointed out.

'It's beginning to smell,' she said. '*You*'re beginning to smell.'

The movement was so swift she didn't see it coming. His hand whipped out and the ashtray, which had been lying on his chest, flew across the room. It missed her, but it hit the wall with a solid *thunk*, and ash and cigarette ends were scattered over the floor and over her. She was shocked – he had never offered violence before – and the shock roused her temper.

'Now look what you've done! Look at the mess! Who's going to clear that up? Because I'm not!'

'I pay you to clean it up. I pay for your services, such as

they are, and most of all for you to shut up and do as you're told.'

'Such as they are?' She picked on the insult. 'Well, if I'm not good enough for you, you know what you can do. I'll soon find someone else, I promise you. A lot of very nice gentlemen have been interested in me, I can tell you.'

He gave her a threatening glare, and she fell silent.

Holkam went back to thinking about his own wretchedness. In the wake of Overton's visit he had thought about what exposure would mean. He had given up his street adventures, and even the more expensive brothels, which left only Mabel; and with his house shut up and Violet away, he had nowhere to go from the club but this flat. Mabel and the flat. That was all very well, but he had discovered a great difference between visiting Mabel once in a while, among others, and spending hours with Mabel only. She really was a dreadful creature. And yet – and yet the degradation of being forced to discover what this tawdry woman was really like, and even making her worse, was a spice of a kind. He didn't have any other spice in his life now, thanks to that swine Overton.

He finished the cigarette and had to sit up and reach out for an ashtray.

She tried again. 'Come on, Bobby,' she said, wheedling. 'Don't get mad. Let's you and me go out and have a bit of fun. Let's go up West and look at the shops. You can buy me a little present. You've not bought me nothing for ages.'

He could not be bothered to explain to her that *not* going 'up West' was the whole point of his being here. 'You think you deserve a present, do you?' he said instead.

'I should think I just about do!' she said, with emphasis. '*Nice* gentlemen buy a girl a present now and then. They don't have to be told.'

'Maybe I'm not a nice gentleman,' he said, with an air of closing the subject.

She stuck out her lip. 'You said it, not me,' she muttered under her breath.

'What did you say?' His voice was sharp.

It needled her. 'I'm about sick of this,' she said. 'If you don't start treating me better, I'll—'

'You'll what?' he sneered.

She tried to think of a powerful retort to shake him out of his complacency. 'You'd better not rile me,' she said, 'or I'll tell about you. I bet there's lots of them posh lords and ladies'd stretch their eyes if they knew what you got up to, Mister Bobby Lord Bleeding Holkam!'

He got off the bed and crossed the room, thinking he should not have used his real name; and yet having her know who he was had been part of the thrill. Mr Freeman and Mabel did not work the same way as did Robert Fitzjames Howard, Earl of Holkam, Viscount Brancaster, KG, DSO, and Mabel.

He put his hands round her startled throat. 'If you tell,' he said, squeezing a little, 'I will kill you.'

Her face began to go red, and her eyes became frightened, which satisfied him. He let her go.

She watched him with a mixture of fury and fear, massaging her neck where he had gripped it. As he straightened up and turned away, he suddenly staggered, gasped, and fell to his knees against the edge of the bed, clutching the foot rail, his head hanging.

She went to him, putting a nervous hand on his shoulder. 'Bobby? Are you all right?'

His face was pale, almost dusky and sheened with sweat, and he was clutching at his chest with his free hand as though trying to force it to drag in breath.

'What is it? Are you sick?'

He pushed her feebly away, and managed to turn himself so that he was sitting with his back to the bed. He moaned and put his head between his knees. His fists were clenched and his shoulders heaved as he hauled in each breath.

She stood watching him anxiously. When at last he looked up, she said, 'You look dretful. Should I call a doctor?'

He shook his head. 'Get me some brandy.'

There was no brandy in the house. She brought a glass of port, the only thing left. 'I could go out and get you brandy,' she said hopefully.

He drank the wine, and said, 'Help me into bed.' Once there, he seemed to recover a little. His breathing grew easier and the blueness around his lips passed away, but he still looked ill.

'Let me call for a doctor,' she said. 'Next door's boy can go.'

'I'm all right now,' he said.

'But—'

'No going out! Sit down and be quiet. I'm going to sleep a little. You stay there till I wake.'

She sat as she was bade, but sulkily: sat in the chair in the corner and watched him as he drifted into a troubled sleep, his face twitching. Cheesy, he looked, she thought. And that much sweat! He wasn't well, but what could you do? She hoped it wasn't nothing catching, that was all. It occurred to her that if he upped and died in her flat, there'd be the devil to pay. She sat quietly and wondered what she could do about the situation.

Violet enjoyed her time in Lincolnshire. She walked about the park with Fifi, renewed her acquaintance with her garden, supervised Charlotte's piano practice, almost read a book. There was healing in the country, she decided. Who needed London and Society?

When it was known who was in residence, Charlotte was invited to the house of a neighbour twenty miles away, where the young lady was coming out in the next Season, and her mother had arranged for a dancing master to come in and brush up her skills. To make it more interesting, Lady

Bradleigh invited all the young ladies of the appropriate age within a reasonable radius to come for two days. They would have the dancing master on the first day and a charabanc ride and a picnic on the Sunday.

Violet guessed that Lady Bradleigh was dealing with a severe case of boredom in her daughter Rosemary and was trying to put a good face on it. She was happy for Charlotte to have the treat, and had her driven over. However, as soon as she was gone, Violet discovered how empty the house was, how desolate the unpeopled silence of Lincolnshire. After two days she was beginning to crave the bright lights again, even if it meant facing some unpleasantness from one or two of the sharper-tongued ladies. She resolved to go back up at the beginning of October.

Almost as soon as she arrived, the butler, Deeping, sought her out with a look of pain on his well-trained face and said, 'I beg your pardon, my lady, I am sorry to trouble you, but I have not received the money for the servants' wages.'

Violet looked at him in surprise. 'You must apply to his lordship for that. Why are you bothering me with it?'

He looked even more pained. 'I have not seen his lordship for some weeks, my lady. I believe he *has* been in, once or twice, but not long enough for me to speak to him. And I would *not* trouble your ladyship, except that it has been two months now, and it does give a bad impression – if any of the lower servants should talk, my lady . . .'

Violet waved him away. 'I will speak to his lordship when I see him.'

She dismissed the matter from her mind, but the next day she heard Holkam come in when she was halfway up the stairs to dress to go out to luncheon. She changed direction and went back down, following the sound of his footsteps to his business-room at the back of the house. He was standing with his back to her, pouring himself a brandy from the decanter on the table by the fireplace, and when she said, 'I wish to speak to you, Holkam,' he turned so abruptly he spilled the brandy and Fifi, in her arms, barked in alarm.

'Good God!' he said. 'Why did you creep up on me like that?'

'I didn't creep up. I heard you come in and came to see you,' Violet said, puzzled. What on earth was wrong with him? She looked at him in concern. His face was pale but blotchy, his eyes pouched, and there was a slick sweat on his brow. He really seemed to have been startled by her: he was breathing heavily, and there was a grey tinge to his lips. 'Are you quite well, Holkam?'

He threw back the brandy, poured another, and sat or, rather, collapsed onto the chair at his desk before he answered. Then he said, in a more normal voice, 'Of course I'm well. You startled me, that's all.' He regarded her without expression. 'You're back, then,' he said flatly. 'What was it you wanted?'

'Decping came to me yesterday to say the servants' wages hadn't been paid.'

'Did he? Damn his impudence! He should have come to me.'

'He said he hadn't seen you. You'll attend to it, will you? He said they're owed two months.'

Holkam swung his chair round so he was facing the desk, away from her, and he began to leaf through the papers lying there in a purposeless sort of way. 'I'll see to it,' he said. 'He shouldn't have come to you.'

Violet stood looking at him in a puzzled way. 'Is everything all right? It isn't like you to forget.'

'I've been very busy,' he said. 'While you've been enjoying yourself on two continents I have had a great deal of very pressing business.' He seemed to wind himself up through that sentence, and the next was delivered with a snap. 'There are too many damned servants in this house anyway. Half of them never do a hand's turn, just eat their heads off at my expense.' He swung back to her, angry now. 'You'll have to get rid of some of them, Violet. Make some economies. You don't need all these people.'

'It's a large house,' she said. 'And when we entertain—'

'When we entertain you can hire people in. It's absurd to keep a full household doing nothing just in case you might entertain one day.'

'I really don't see—'

'Don't you? I'll show you the way, then. I'm getting rid of Dawson, and selling the Rolls.'

'Getting rid of Dawson? Then who will drive me?'

'No-one. I'm selling the Rover as well. You can call a cab when you want to go out. It makes much more sense.'

She had never known Holkam to worry about expenditure. As far as she knew, he never even asked the price of anything, any more than she did. She glanced at the papers on his desk, but they didn't mean anything to her. 'Holkam, is something wrong?' she asked tentatively. 'Is there – money trouble?'

He swung round on her as if exasperated. 'There's no money trouble. This new man of mine, Meyer, when his schemes come in we shall be very well set. The point is, you've been too extravagant for too long, and it's got to stop. There have to be economies. I don't mind your having what you want, but I can't bear pointless waste. We don't need two footmen as well as Deeping. I see housemaids all over the place, far more than we need. And why is Nanny still here, when Henry's at school?'

'She does mending. She's quite useful. I don't like to turn her off, poor thing, when—'

'Get rid of her. And one of the footmen. And at least one housemaid.'

'Very well,' she said. 'If it is your wish.'

'It is. Money doesn't grow on trees, you know.'

Violet nodded and left him, thinking that was a very coarse phrase. All the money in their marriage was hers, as it happened – he had been near penniless when he married her – but it would have been too vulgar to mention it.

The next day when she passed Deeping in the hall she said, 'By the way, Deeping, that small matter you came to me about. Has it been resolved?'

'Yes, my lady, thank you. His lordship saw me last night. All is well, my lady.'

She was looking, rather absently, over his shoulder into the ante-room, and saw the hind end of a long pair of steps, something unusual enough to pique her interest. 'What's happening in there?' she asked.

She walked to the door, and saw round the corner that one of the maids was up the stepladder, carefully cleaning the wallpaper with bread. It was something that was done during spring cleaning, not at this time of year.

Deeping, who had followed her, said, 'Doris is trying to soften the mark. Not that it's possible to remove it entirely, without cleaning the whole room.'

Only then did Violet realise that there was a large rectangle of paler paper where something had evidently been removed. What was missing? She did not often come into the ante-room – they used it only during the biggest, most formal parties – and had to think for a moment.

'Where is the Caravaggio?' she asked at last, turning to Deeping. She had never liked it – very brown and overblown, she thought, showing a crowd gathered round St Sebastian, shot full of arrows and obviously dying. Too gloomy and horrid! It was one of their more valuable paintings, though: an important work.

'His lordship sent it for cleaning, my lady, so I thought it was a good opportunity to try—'

'But if it's coming back to the same space, there's no need,' Violet said. 'Really, Deeping, what a waste of effort.'

'Yes, my lady.'

There was something rigid about Deeping's expression. Violet supposed he did not like being told off in front of a maid. She shook her head at him and walked away. And, she thought, how dared Holkam send a painting for cleaning when he'd only just been telling her off for extravagance? No-one ever looked at that horrid Caravaggio anyway, and if they did, the dirtier it was the better, in her view. Then you'd see less of the detail.

The R101 left her shed for the first time on the 12th of October and, two days later, made her first trial flight to London and back. Though beautiful and elegant, and with many ingenious and innovative features, she had some problems. One was that the engines, developed from locomotive engines, were underpowered for their considerable weight, which reduced useful lift. Another was the cover: the head of the design committee was Lieutenant Colonel V. C. 'Dope' Richmond, who had earned his nickname by developing a technique for doping linen before stretching it over the airframe – normally it was fitted first, then doped to shrink it. The method worked well on small aeroplanes, but the R101 had six acres of linen, and it was plain from the time of the test flight that the method hadn't worked and the whole cover would have to be replaced. And the gasbag valves were of a novel design and placement and tended to open slightly as the ship rolled, causing a continual leaking of gas.

'Still, they are both amazing machines,' Jack said to Helen. 'I can't wait to see them undergoing trials side by side. It will be a new dawn for air travel.'

'Are you becoming smitten?' Helen asked, amused.

'Oh, I shall never love airships the way I love aeroplanes, and I can't see any pleasure in piloting them. But there's no doubt that for long journeys they are far more practical and comfortable. You could fly in one of these all the way to Australia in the greatest comfort. That will never be possible by aeroplane – the lift-to-weight ratio will always be unfavourable.'

'Are they going to fly to Australia?'

'Eventually,' Jack said. 'To begin with, once they've done their safety trials, the R100 will fly to Canada and the R101 to India. That will be their long-distance test. It was going to be the other way round, but they decided the R100 with her petrol engines ought to have the cooler destination, and the R101 the India run because diesel's not so flammable.'

'But surely they shouldn't fly at all if there's any chance of fire,' Helen said.

'There isn't. All the committee can think is India equals heat, heat plus petrol equals fire. It's no use telling them there are petrol engines working happily all over India – and hotter places too, I don't doubt.' He bent to rub the head of Stalky, who was urgently and silently suggesting a walk might be a jolly good idea. 'I'd really like to work on developing a hydrogen engine – that's the obvious next step. The Germans' *Graf Zeppelin* operates on some new sort of gas – blue gas, they call it. The benefits of not having to carry heavy fuel along with you are obvious, and if we don't get moving, the Germans will snaffle all the long-distance trade.'

Emma and Kit came back to Town at about the same time as Violet, for the completion of the first Weston Trust building. They went to look it over the day before the grand opening, while it was still empty. It was a plain oblong facing onto the street, with a small courtyard behind for hanging out washing and for children to play in. The building was five storeys high with three flats on each floor, neatly built in London brick with a white stone coping under the roof line and a narrower one under the third-floor windows for decoration. The windows were steel-framed Crittall windows, which Kit had said would require less maintenance than wooden ones; Emma thought them pleasingly neat and modern-looking.

Inside, the flats were a miracle of clever design, making the best use possible of the limited space. She, Kit and the architect, John Douglas, had pored long over the plans, altering and improving until no inch was wasted. Each flat had a decent-sized living-room, twelve feet by fifteen, with a fireplace and a large window; the main bedroom also had a fireplace, which would be unthinkable luxury to most new tenants. On each floor there were two two-bedroom flats and one three-bedroom, and each had, besides, a small kitchen, fitted with a sink, a larder, a crockery cupboard and shelves for pots and pans, a bathroom containing a bath and basin, and a separate lavatory. They were supplied with gas and electricity on shilling meters, and there was a gas geyser in each kitchen to provide instant hot water.

Emma and Kit looked round two of the flats, strolling arm in arm and admiring the many built-in features and the light and airy feeling of them, with their large windows and decently high ceilings. The dogs ran about, sniffing interestedly at the smells of wood, new plaster and paint and the ghostly traces of workmen who had passed through. Emma now had two dogs – she had acquired a black-and-white terrier-type mongrel she had called Buster, as a companion for Alfie – and Kit had lately bought a handsome black greyhound bitch with a white star on her breast, which he had named Eos, after Prince Albert's famous pet. Emma thought wryly that the dogs were like their owners – Eos and Sulfi beautiful, elegant and languid, Alfie and Buster tough and bustling.

They went outside to where the architect was waiting. On the outside of the building, just above first-floor level, a stone panel, on which was carved WESTON TRUST 1929, was sunk into the brickwork. They looked at it admiringly, and Douglas said, 'The first of many, perhaps.'

'I hope so,' Emma said. She held out her hand to him. 'I'm very pleased with it. You have done a fine job.' She looked around. 'We have been considering that parcel of land behind the flats,' she said. There were some run-down houses and a small factory, now empty. 'If we could acquire those buildings, there would be room to build another block, making a square round the courtyard, with access into it from both sides. What do you think?'

Douglas had a look. 'It sounds like a good idea – presents certain advantages over starting with a completely new site.'

'That's what we thought,' Emma said happily. 'We'll look into it. Goodbye, Mr Douglas, and thank you again. We'll see you tomorrow at the opening ceremony.'

As they walked back to the motor, Kit said, 'Another Weston Trust right away – and a bigger one than this, by the sound of it?'

'Yes – why not? We talked about it.'

'We talk about many things. I didn't know you wanted to do it right now. Are you sure it won't be too much? You have that luxury block in Marylebone in hand.'

She stopped and faced him. 'Are you worried about my health or my finances?'

He hesitated. 'I thought you might want to wait and see how the finances of the first one worked out before taking on more.'

'Crawford Place will pay for a lot of it, and Bracey says the markets have done so well this year, I am twenty per cent richer than I was last year. As to my health,' she looked up at him, 'I have to have something to do, Kit. Now I've started, I like being busy. I believe you do, too. You're a different person these days – it's months since you've stayed in bed until noon.'

'I must say it is agreeable to be bustling about,' he admitted. 'I'd forgotten that part of surgery, the feeling afterwards of having earned one's leisure.'

They looked at each other for a long moment. Emma said, 'It has worked well, hasn't it – our being married?'

'I couldn't be happier,' he said. 'To spend all the time one wants with one's best friend . . . But, Emma darling, are you *quite* happy? I do wonder sometimes – whether you wouldn't like to have a child.'

Her eyes flickered away for one telling moment, but she smiled and said, 'What do I need with a child when I have the doggies? And I'm far too busy for babies.'

She stepped away to the car, and he opened the door for her, then the back door for the dogs, and went around to the driving-seat. As they pulled away into the traffic, he thought the leather-scented, womb-like privacy of the motor-car was peculiarly suited to confidences (and to quarrels – they had had plenty of both in motors over the years), and after a pause he said, 'I've been thinking, myself, lately about a child. The title, you know, and the estate. And – it might be rather nice, just for the thing itself. What do you think?'

Emma thought that she would be thirty-four in January and time was running out, and that her recent urge to add another dog to their pack might well represent a need to have little creatures running about her. On the other hand, many, many couples had perfectly happy and contented lives without children. And there was the undoubted problem, in their case, of – well – the mechanics of the thing. She glanced sideways under her lashes at her husband. Was this just a passing fancy of his? He had so many. Or was he worried that she really wanted a child and was trying to humour her? He liked to be kind to her, and she knew he was bothered by conscience from time to time about his limitations as a husband.

'Emma?' he urged, as the silence had gone on too long. 'What *do* you think?'

'I wonder how serious these thoughts of yours are,' she said lightly. 'You do have odd urges from time to time, but they don't last. That plaid waistcoat, for instance, and your idea of growing pineapples for profit.'

He was hurt. 'This is a different order of thing.'

'I know,' she conceded. 'But how much do you mean it? Because it's not a thing to be trifled with. You can't put a child in a drawer if you change your mind, like that waistcoat. And it's a lot of fuss and bother having one around.'

'Oh, what trouble could it be? Once it's arrived, I mean. That's what nannies and nurseries are for. And if it turns out we don't like it much, we can always send it off to school. But I've a notion that any child of yours will be utterly adorable, like its mother. I've been thinking about it a lot just lately, and I keep getting keener on the idea. Like having a dog, only better.'

He had a way of stepping into her thoughts, and in the face of his sympathy, her defences crumbled. 'I would like a child,' she confessed. 'I know I said it didn't matter, but seemingly it does.'

'And I said that if you wanted children in the end, I wouldn't mind if you found a nice fellow, as long as it was discreet.'

She looked at him, shocked. 'I don't want just any children, I want yours.'

He gave a wry smile. 'Dear Emma, how nice you are!'

He didn't say any more, and after a moment she said in a small voice, 'Is it out of the question?' He shrugged, looking at the road ahead. 'You know,' she went on carefully, 'we haven't tried. Not since – well, not for years. Don't you think, given that we do love each other – and for a good cause . . . ?'

He was silent until the traffic light in Piccadilly brought him to a halt. 'That policeman in his horrid little box – he always does it to me. I swear he waits for me to come along deliberately. Too boring!'

'Kit!' said Emma

510

He looked at her, seeming suddenly very young and shy, like a boy back from school facing the first girl of the summer. 'If you can bear it – if you want me to – yes, we can try. I'd like to.'

She laid a hand on his leg. 'Thank you. I'd like it, too.'

'Be careful,' he said. 'The policeman's watching. We'll get taken up for public indecency.'

It was like him to change the subject with a joke, but she had read many things in his face in the brief moment his guard was down.

Ren did not arrive for cocktails at Mrs Wensum's, and Polly had to make an excuse. 'It'll be the market again, just heed my words,' Mrs Wensum said lightly. 'It's been up and down this last month like I don't know what. Walter's been like a cat on a griddle, wondering whether to sell or buy. I say to him, "You men spend so much time worrying about that darned old market, you'd be better off taking all the money out and putting it under your bed. At least that way you'd get a good night's sleep!"'

Polly laughed, glad she was taking Ren's absence so well. Walter Wensum only said, 'Now, Martha. You ladies don't understand these things,' but he looked at Polly rather thoughtfully.

'You wouldn't believe the people who are buying stocks, these days,' said Claude Ansell. 'I went to my barber the other day, and as he took off the sheet he whispered in my ear, "Buy Standard Gas. I've doubled. It's good for another double."' He looked round, laughing. 'I had no idea he liked me that much! I'm glad to know it. When a man wields a sharp knife close to your throat, you need to be able to trust him.'

'Oh, goodness, my maid gave me a tip the other day,' Mrs Farebrother broke in. 'Can't remember what it was – but, my dear, my *maid*!'

But Mrs Wensum had had enough. 'Let's not talk money matters. Mrs Alexander, that's a darling little frock you have on. So simple. I always say better to be underdressed than overdressed. Where *did* you get it?'

Polly considered the weight of sequins and jewellery on Mrs Wensum's capacious bosom and swallowed the implied insult. 'I designed it myself and had it made up.'

'How clever! It's too charming. Tell me . . .'

The conversation cantered off in another direction.

Polly took a cab to their next engagement and arrived at the restaurant just as Ren was climbing out of another cab. He came across to her, and stooped to kiss her cheek. 'I'm sorry, darling. I couldn't get away sooner. There was a sudden drop in the market in the last hour – automobile stocks. So many shares sold, the ticker-tape fell an hour behind.'

She tried to guess from his expression whether he was worried or not, but his lean dark face showed nothing. 'But it will go up again, won't it? As it has before.'

'Of course,' he said. 'Don't say anything about it in there. Mustn't alarm anyone.'

She understood by now that the market ran on confidence and the worst thing would be to make any of the ordinary investors worried. The market had dropped in September, risen again, dropped earlier this month and risen again. Volatility, it was called. It was not a good thing, but nothing to worry about in the long run.

'Why automobiles?' she asked, as they walked towards the entrance.

'The companies have just posted poor results. I guess a lot of people have decided it's a good time to get out.'

The next morning, the 24th of October, when Polly left her room she heard the chatter of the ticker-tape from Ren's room, where he had left the door open, and walked along to look in. He was there, the telephone tucked between his jaw and shoulder – he had one of the new sort, with the transmitter and receiver joined together at either end of a common bar. He was running the tape through his hands, its entrails winding rapidly into a pile on the floor. He looked at her, raising his eyebrows as he listened to the telephone and made a few terse comments. Then he replaced the handset abruptly in the cradle and said, 'I'm afraid there's trouble. The market's dropping like a stone. I shall have to go to Wall Street.'

'People are still selling?'

'Yes, and not just automobiles. This has the feeling of a panic. That was Lamont on the line. He wants me to meet him and some other bankers to see what can be done.'

He grabbed his jacket from the back of the chair and brushed past her without another word.

By the time Polly went out, rumours had begun to spring up like mushrooms. The doorman touched his cap as he opened the street door for her, but his face was drawn. 'Is it true what they're saying, Mrs Alexander, that the market's crashing? You'd know if anyone did. I saw Mr Alexander leave in a hurry.'

Mindful of Ren's warnings, she smiled and said, 'Oh, it's just an adjustment. The market does it all the time. Nothing to worry about.'

He didn't look convinced. 'I got all my life savings in stocks. Me and the missus—'

'Would you get me a cab, please? I'm in rather a hurry.'

She was lunching with Julie Margesson and her friend Maggie Prentiss, a clever woman with her own antique-furniture business, and by the time she sat down she could hear by the volume of talk around the restaurant that the news was spreading. Some people were reading newspapers at the table – unheard of.

Julie stood up and kissed her. 'I didn't think you'd be here. Good for you. We have to carry on.'

'What does Ren say?' Maggie asked. 'They're calling it Black Thursday in the papers.'

'I haven't seen a paper,' Polly said, sitting down.

'The market's dropped thirty-three points. Everybody's selling,' said Julie. 'I don't know what to do. Frank deals with all that sort of thing, of course, but I have shares in my own name, too.'

'I nearly sold last time there was a dip,' Maggie said, 'but everyone said hang on, it will come up again, and it did. But if everyone sells . . .'

Polly knew the principle of it. If a lot of people sold, prices dropped, and that upset others, who would then sell in their turn. In the end, it turned into a sort of panic, with everyone trying to offload their holdings at once. The problem for each individual was deciding when to join the panic.

'Ren's gone to Wall Street to meet Thomas Lamont and some others. They'll figure out what to do,' Polly said, as confidently as she could. There was something about the background murmur and the looks on some faces around the room that worried her. And, though she didn't mention it, her cab driver had told her that hundreds of people, ordinary investors, were converging on Wall Street. 'Honest to God,' he had said, 'I never seen such a crowd. Couldn't get through any ways. They got cops on horses tryna keep the road clear but I hadda drop my fare at the corner. An' you shoulda seen the look on their faces, ma'am, all those folk standin' around kinda bewildered, like they'd just woke up and found 'emselves there, like sleepwalkers.'

She thought of what Lennie had told her about 'buying on margin'. If you had borrowed ninety per cent of the money you invested, and the stock price fell, and the lender wanted their money back, you would have to pay back more than you actually possessed, wouldn't you? Judging from what she had heard over the past six months or so, that would be thousands, maybe millions of people. What would happen to them all if the market didn't go back up?

★   ★   ★

514

Wall Street was packed from side to side with people of all marks and from all walks of life: everyone, from senior managers to shoeshine boys, had been riding the carousel of share ownership that year as it whirled faster and faster, intoxicated by the bright lights and jangling music. Up, up, up goes the market – you can't lose! And it was the patriotic thing to do. You had to believe in America, invest in America; you had to dream the American dream, or what sort of American were you?

Now they waited with an air of stunned disbelief as news filtered back every moment of more falls. There were by now four hundred mounted police on hand to keep the crowds in order, but the crowds were not in a frame of mind to give trouble. Some were simply curious onlookers, but the majority were staring ruin in the face, wondering if they would wake up tomorrow possessed of anything but their own skins. There was no shouting, very little movement, just an eerie, muted murmur of voices, like the distant sound of the sea.

At one o'clock, a man in shirtsleeves pushed his way through the crowds to cross the street to number 23 Wall Street, the J. P. Morgan building. Word was quickly passed back that he was Charles E. Mitchell, the president of the National City Bank, and they had already seen Richard Whitney, the vice president of the Stock Exchange, go in. Lamont, head of J. P. Morgan, was already there, with Mitchell and Whitney, and Wiggin of the Chase National, and Ren Alexander, the famous speculator, and John D. Rockefeller, the oil magnate. A little surge of hope went around. These important people, bankers and financiers, were meeting to sort things out. Maybe it would be all right, after all.

Lamont had been at the meeting Ren had attended with Hoover and Mellon when the volatility of the market had been discussed. Hoover had been worried, and asked if something should be done: he had warned President Coolidge

515

as far back as 1925 about the dangers of excessive stock-market speculation. But Lamont had said there was no need for any action. The market would always correct itself. 'The future looks brilliant,' he said. Since Mellon believed it was not the government's business to interfere in private financial transactions, Ren's words of warning had had no effect.

Now all were of the opinion that something must be done. Something like twelve million shares had been sold in one day; it could not go on. Between them, the men gathered in that room represented some six billion dollars of wealth. It was decided that an ostentatious purchase of shares – two hundred and fifty million dollars' worth, with some steadying statements to the press, should cool things down. Rockefeller and Whitney together walked across the road to the Stock Exchange and, while traders watched, they bought twenty-five thousand United States Steel shares, and other blue-chip holdings.

Whitney gave a calming statement to the press. Rockefeller's read, 'Believing that fundamental conditions of the country are sound and that there is nothing in the business situation to warrant the destruction of values that has taken place on the exchanges during the past week, my son and I have for some days been purchasing sound common stocks.'

President Hoover issued a statement that there was no need to panic.

And Ren, standing at the edge of the trading floor, his dark face impassive as always, saw things begin to steady, the storm of selling abate, the calm sunshine of buying spread its balm over the wounded bear of the market. Prices firmed, and by the end of trading the Dow Jones was only six points down on the day.

Friday and Saturday were quiet, but newspapers and journals took the news of Black Thursday out across the country to people who had not yet heard it. Sunday, the day of rest, gave them time to digest and be alarmed by it. And on

Monday, when the market opened, the selling began in earnest.

Everyone wanted to get out of their shares. There was wave after wave of selling. It was unstoppable. The ticker-tapes couldn't keep up with the sheer volume, and the lack of information drove investors to a frenzy. The phone lines to New York were jammed. Men stood out in the street trying to sell stocks to passers-by. Ten thousand people gathered in a great, despairing mass, blocking the Lower Manhattan streets from Broadway to the East River. Paper boys ran out with two-cent extra editions, the ink still wet, and they were snatched from their hands faster than they could take the money. Sixteen and a half million sales were recorded in the Stock Exchange, the greatest number ever in one day; the ticker was three and a half hours behind. When the market closed the Dow was down thirty-eight points, having lost thirteen per cent of its value.

And on Tuesday – Black Tuesday – things only got worse. Now the big-name important stocks – steel, radio, General Motors – plummeted. The Dow Jones lost another thirty points, and by Tuesday evening all stocks had lost twenty-two per cent of their Monday opening value. Fourteen billion dollars of private wealth disappeared on that day; over the five days, the loss was thirty billion – a sum ten times greater than the annual budget of the federal government.

New York lay stunned under the blow. Rich men had gone from hundreds of thousands to a handful of dollars in five days. Barbers, dressmakers, waiters, maids, doormen, taxi drivers had lost all their life's savings. But there was worse. There were half a million 'margin accounts' on the books of New York stockbrokers, one and a half million through the country, and those people had lost more than everything. They were ruined, facing an impossible debt. The first stories of suicide began to circulate. It was said a financier had thrown himself out of the window of a Wall Street skyscraper to his death; another was said to have shot himself in Central Park.

Polly sat by the telephone all day, taking calls from distraught friends, receiving and passing on rumours and information, listening to the wireless and the ceaseless chatter of the ticker-tape in Ren's room. He had gone out before dawn and had not returned. The building supervisor called on a transparent excuse about a dripping tap that did not exist, really to tell her that he had lost everything. 'What shall I do? What shall I do?' he asked, wringing his hands, his eyes staring blankly over her shoulder. She had had to answer the door herself. Plummer was in floods of tears, sobbing in her room, having lost all her savings.

The disaster had roused her from the glassy torpor of the past few weeks. She had determined not to think about Erich, and she managed pretty well. She was not a girl any more, to indulge herself in weeping and repining. She was a woman with a husband and responsibilities, and she tried to get on with her life. But there was a shocked emptiness inside, and it was difficult to be interested in anything, though she tried. Only in bed at night, alone, staring into the darkness, did she yield to thoughts of him, and long for his dear, warm presence, ache for the touch of him.

The stock-market crash threw her forcefully into the present, as she tried to grasp the desperate misfortune that had come upon so many around her. It was only when the stories of the suicides began to circulate ('They say dozens of them are jumping out of the buildings in Wall Street!') that she began to wonder about herself. Were they ruined, too? Had they lost everything? And what of Ren? He was a proud man. He would not easily bear failure. And she hadn't seen him or heard from him all day. What if he killed himself, what then? *Oh, dear God, what would become of them all? Ren, Ren, where are you?*

It was after ten when he finally came home, dog tired,

smelling of sweat and a thousand cigarettes, his eyes raw, his hands shaking slightly.

She ran to him. 'I was so worried! Where have you been?'

He shook her off. 'Trying to stop this thing. But it was hopeless. Now there's a hell of a mess.'

'Why didn't you call? I was afraid you might have—'

'What?'

'They say men are committing suicide.'

He stared a moment in surprise, and said shortly, 'Ridiculous.'

She stared, too, trying to read his face. How bad was it? She had to know. 'You can tell me. Are we ruined?'

He shook his head slowly, like a goaded bull. 'Don't ask stupid questions.'

'But—'

'Leave me alone, now. I'm tired.' He pushed past her without another word, but he didn't go to his bedroom. He went into his business-room and closed the door.

CHAPTER TWENTY-THREE

Like the aftermath of an earthquake or a bomb blast, people wandered the streets in a state of shock. No-one could talk of anything else. Everyone was affected, one way or another, everyone wanted to tell their story; no-one wanted to listen. Those who were not ruined did not like to spend ostentatiously, and the expensive restaurants had thin pickings, though the cheaper bars were full of men drowning their sorrows. Theatres were empty; cinemas, where you could forget everything in the darkness for an hour or two, were full. The society ladies met in each other's houses to talk in muted tones and ask the question to which no-one had an answer: what will happen next?

Polly was very much in demand, had more invitations than she could accommodate. She accepted enough to keep her busy for, though all anyone wanted to know was what Ren thought about it – something she couldn't answer – it was better than staying at home alone. Ren was out from dawn to the early hours, and she hadn't seen him to speak to in a week. She had no story of her own to tell, being still ignorant of whether they were ruined or not. Was he out desperately trying to save something from the wreck? It was not just his money, it was hers, too. She had given him the proceeds of the sale of her business to invest, and he had invested the money her father had given her from the beginning. If it was gone, it was all gone. And what would they do then?

The first signs of what was to come were seen around the city already: the businesses that had 'closed' signs on the door, the men sodden with drink leaning on walls or sitting on the kerb, the suicides. Stories were exaggerated, but there were several very public ones – in a city of skyscrapers the means to death were readily available – and no doubt many more private executions. Most shocking in Polly's circle was that of Olga Culver's husband, William J. Culver: he had shot himself in the library of their Central Park West town house with his old army revolver. He had been speculating on margin – no doubt, the less charitable whispered, to satisfy Olga's social cravings.

Polly took a moment to be glad Erich had gone to California. Somehow she felt he would be safe there. She had no idea if he had ever speculated, but she doubted it – his fame and fortune had come so lately; and he was too sensible, surely, to have risked it. And he would have his large income from the movie studio. He had a good future ahead of him, with his wife and son. It was better to think of him like that than wickedly done to death in a dockyard as an outcast. She hoped he would be happy.

She came home one day, dog tired, from a round of morning engagements that had occupied her but given her no pleasure, to find Ren in his business-room, gathering papers together and putting them into an attaché case. He looked up as she came in, and she was glad to see he seemed less tense – or, rather, tense in a different way. There was almost something hopeful in his bearing and the swift movements of his hands.

'What is it?' she asked.

He didn't smile, but the scowl was gone. 'I'm going to Washington. Hoover has called me to a series of emergency meetings to decide what can be done. I shall be gone about a week – perhaps more. If it looks like being a long session, I shall send for you.'

She studied his expression, trying to guess what it meant. Would he look so almost-cheerful if he had lost everything? Or was he hoping to recoup a lost fortune in Washington?

'This is good for me, Polly. Good for us. I warned Hoover and Mellon back in the summer that the bubble would burst. I've been proved right. Now they'll listen to me. Hoover telephoned me himself to ask me to come. He's asking *me* what to do next. I've got plenty of ideas. This is when I prove myself, become so valuable to them that the other thing – being Indian – won't matter. I shall be respected now. And if I can help them through this crisis, I can have any job I want. We're back on track, Polly. This is my chance.'

'I'm glad for you,' she said. 'You deserve it. But you still haven't told me – what about us? Did we lose everything? Are we ruined?'

The near-smile faded. 'Is that all the faith you have in me?' he asked quietly.

She was wrong-footed. 'I didn't mean – I know you are clever. But you've never said a word to me. I didn't know what to think.'

He studied her for a moment and said, 'I'm sorry. It was wrong of me not to set your mind at rest. But I thought you would know – that you'd have faith in my abilities. Of course we're not ruined. Would I be so careless as to put *you* at risk – the most important thing in my life? I love you, Polly. I will always take care of you.'

She felt herself blushing, and could not find any words, any at all.

'I got out of the market back in the summer, before the September fall,' he said. 'There were plenty of us who knew it wouldn't last. Paul Warburg saved his bank; Joe Kennedy got out intact. Those people I advise have shifted their wealth elsewhere. Apart from what I put up on Black Thursday to try to calm the market – that's a dead loss – it's all safe, for now.'

'For now?'

'It doesn't end with the stock market,' he said, and now his face was grave. 'This is a national disaster, and the repercussions are only just beginning. People borrowed to speculate. Now the banks will want their money back. When they default, the banks will lose heavily, and some of the smaller ones will fail. If one bank fails, people will start to worry about their own, and there'll be a run on the banks as they try to withdraw their savings. And there'll be a shortage of credit, so a lot of businesses will go under. This isn't over, Polly, by a long way.'

'But – we're all right? Where did you put our money?'

'Mostly into gold. It's permanent and portable. I have large deposits here and in London. And property. I bought a house in London and another in Paris, and we have this one, of course. But property prices will fall – we would have difficulty in selling this for anything like what I paid for it.'

'Sell it? Why would we sell it?'

'Only as a last resort, if we had to leave the country. But it won't come to that. I'm going to Washington, and I *will* end up in the White House.'

She looked at him curiously, glad to see the old light of ambition back in his eyes. 'Yes, I believe you will,' she said.

He took her hands and his clasp was almost painful. 'I *will*,' he said again. 'And you will be the most beautiful and accomplished First Lady the country has ever known. We'll have glittering *soirées* and dinners, entertain heads of state from all over the world, encourage artists and musicians, go down in history as the most cultured occupants the White House has ever known.'

'History,' she repeated, with a faint smile.

He smiled too, now, and she felt a small pang in her stomach, remembering how his smile had devastated her when they first met. 'Are you ready to take your place in history?' he said. 'Because I wouldn't do this if I didn't have you beside me. Success would be dust and ashes without you.'

I had no idea you loved me so much, she thought. Fortunately she didn't say it aloud. But another part of her mind, sadder, lonely and unmoved, said, *Yes, but I'm still the hostage, the prize, part of what he has to have to prove himself*. It was not love as she thought of it, as now she knew it could be.

But she was his wife, for good or ill; he was her life now and for always. She said, 'Wherever you go, I shall be there at your side.'

He pressed her hands in response, and dropped them. 'I must get ready. Hoover has arranged an aeroplane to take me to Washington. I must hurry – I have to get out to Roosevelt Field.'

'I'll help you pack,' said Polly.

On the 28th of October the London Stock Exchange fell sharply in response to the Wall Street crash, but though the newspapers were full of the American disaster, few people in England were directly affected. Speculation was the hobby of a small group of society, not a national sport as it had been across the pond. And there had been nothing like the Wall Street Bubble, just a series of small booms and a few defaults spectacular enough to make it into the newspapers. Those who had American shares lost, some of them badly. The actress Evelyn Laye told Oliver at a dinner party at Emma and Kit's that she had dropped ten thousand dollars.

Kit had not lost his taste for the theatre and the movies, and there were always actors and directors and such people at his parties. Tallulah Bankhead was a regular; Noël Coward was a frequent guest, as were Ivor Novello, the Welsh actor and playwright, and his friend the actor Bobbie Andrews. Oliver found these evenings fun, though Verena was a little reserved around the theatricals and said she often didn't understand their jokes and their slang. But whatever play was the current hit of the West End, you would be likely to meet its leading lights at Emma's. And the illustrateds always carried pictures, for their parties were becoming famous. Oliver almost choked with laughter over their Safari Party, where the guests all came as animals. Emma and Kit presided, dressed as big-game hunters, and halfway through the evening Kit disappeared, to come back dressed as a tiger, whereupon Emma pretended to shoot him, and he ended up flat on the floor with her boot on his back, shouting, 'Where's Elinor Glyn?'

Oliver was glad to see Violet out and about again, though usually without Holkam – he seemed to be keeping a low profile, these days. Violet seemed a little quieter than usual, though that was perhaps not surprising, given that the Prince of Wales was being seen everywhere with Lady Furness. Those in the know avoided asking Violet on the same occasions with the prince and his new friend. It was inevitable they should meet sometimes – when they did, the prince treated her with commonplace friendliness, as he might any casual acquaintance.

But Lady Furness seemed to be leading him into a different stratum of society, one that Violet did not inhabit. Oliver had no spleen against Thelma Furness: she was a very pretty, slight, smart young woman – rather like Violet in physical type, if that meant anything – always friendly, good-natured and easy-going, without any apparent ambition or jealousy concerning the prince. But she was light-minded and relentlessly frivolous, having no interest in anything but fun: jazz, parties, cocktails, clothes and more parties. She knew little of protocol and cared less, and under her influence the prince began to slide back into his natural tendencies of idleness and selfishness – avoiding responsibilities, dressing carelessly, missing appointments, keeping people waiting, treating dignitaries without due respect.

Eddie and the other equerries believed that Lady Furness

was a bad influence. 'Joey Legh says she's ruining him. She never reminds him of his duty. Anything that doesn't relate to her own comfort she has no interest in. Freda and Violet at least kept him straight, and stopped him drinking so much. And the people he mixes with! Chips Channon says he's getting downright common, these days, and I agree with him. The King's furious – says the Pragga's been Americanised.'

That year, the King had given the Prince of Wales a house at the edge of Windsor Great Park – a castellated folly called Fort Belvedere. It was rather dilapidated and the grounds were a jungle, but the prince threw himself into renovation, modernisation and ground-clearing with an enthusiasm he gave to nothing else.

'It's his first real home,' Eddie said. 'He's having everything done up in modern taste – putting in a swimming-pool and tennis court. And he's suddenly mad about gardening. He ropes everybody in. Jack Aird spent the entire weekend digging. Find an excuse if you get invited down. He'll shove a billhook in your hand and make you hack down the rhodo-dendrons. I've still got blisters from my last duty.'

'A home of his own will be a good thing, though, won't it?' Oliver said. 'Settle him down?'

Eddie rolled his eyes. 'You know him better than that, old thing. It'll be his excuse to behave as he pleases – jazz and cockers and soft collars all round. You wait and see. Once he moves his "weekends" down there, there'll be no influencing him.'

Oliver didn't think he would be high on the visiting-list, since he and Verena were considered rather staid company, but Kit and Emma were likely to be asked, on account of their show-business connections. Perhaps they could interest the prince in their housing scheme. Oliver had been to the opening of the Weston Trust, when the first tenants, looking bewildered and almost tearfully grateful, carefully dressed in their best with their over-scrubbed children drooping behind, had ceremonially received the keys. He thought the flats themselves very well designed.

His current interest outside his work was the Road Traffic Bill, which was brought in the Lords on the 28th of November by Earl Russell. The impetus for the Bill lay back in 1926 when there had been a shocking number of road accidents – 124,000 crashes and 4,886 deaths in a single year. A Royal Commission had been set up to see whether there should be more regulation of cars and their drivers.

The previous Motor Car Act of 1903 had provided that all motor-cars should be registered with the county council in which the owner was resident, and be given a unique registration number, which was to be affixed and displayed on the car in a manner prescribed. The Act had also provided that all drivers must have a licence, which was purchased from the council on presentation of the sum of five shillings. Drivers had to be over the age of seventeen, or fourteen for motor-cycles. And the speed limit of fourteen miles per hour, which had been set by the Locomotives on Highways Act of 1896, was raised to twenty miles per hour.

The fact of the matter was that there was virtually no regulation of the over two hundred thousand cars now registered – and the number was going up rapidly every year. Anyone could obtain a licence, without any test of competency, and drive at furious speeds on roads designed for horse traffic and frequently unrepaired. Blind humps, sharp bends, multiple junctions, obstructions like ancient trees and war memorials in the middle of the road, ruts and potholes, wagons and horses and flocks of sheep encountered suddenly blocking the way: it was no wonder there were accidents. The Bright Young People in particular were given to piling into motor-cars and roaring about the country, often the worse for drink, and knowing much less about the skills of driving than they thought they did. The speed limit was never enforced, since there was no-one to do it. A policeman on foot or on a bicycle could not give pursuit, and had no way of telling what speed the offender was doing, other than believing it was 'too fast by half'.

Oliver was frequently faced with the end results of the accidents, having to reconstruct faces and hands on which the effects of a speeding car were not dissimilar to that of a speeding shell. He was therefore very keen that something should be done and attended all the debates, adding his own expert testimony in what he hoped was a clinching argument.

The result, however, was a disappointment. There was agreement that the 20 m.p.h. speed limit should be abolished, but no agreement on a higher limit to be introduced. Their lordships were of the opinion that a law that could not be enforced only brought the law into disrepute. Besides, the roads were mostly in too poor a condition to allow fast driving, and the taxation of motor vehicles, which was calibrated by horsepower, ensured that most new cars being bought now were small and underpowered and not capable of doing much damage.

As to the introduction of a driving test, their lordships, like the majority in the Commons, could not see the point of it. Driving itself was easy enough: a child could do it. The rest was common sense, experience and judgement, and it was not possible to test for those. It was agreed, however, that all motor vehicles should carry third-party insurance to cover the innocent victims of crashes. Sympathy for them was frequently lacking: it was the driver who was called unlucky, while the victim was castigated for having got in the way.

There was also agreement on the introduction of driving offences: three categories of dangerous, reckless and careless driving, and driving under the influence of drink or drugs, with penalties of increasing severity; and for the formulation and publication of a Highway Code. This would embody the

528

rules and customs of safe driving and bring some kind of homogeneity to such things as hand signals.

The Bill, its wings clipped, went back for its third reading – it had been first introduced in the Commons in February by Herbert Morrison, the minister for transport – and Oliver was left with the feeling that these were probably the golden days of driving, the roads open and the driver unfettered by any rules. As long as you didn't meet some idiot coming the other way at high speed on the crown of the road.

In the evening after Ren's departure, Polly was dressing to go to dinner with the Margessons when the telephone rang. Plummer was trying to untangle a gold chain that had somehow made itself into a knot, so Polly said, 'I'll get it.'

The operator told her it was a long-distance call from Washington, and she thought it must be Ren, perhaps telling her to pack and join him. But a very formal woman's voice came on, and said, 'Mrs Alexander? I have the President for you, ma'am. Hold the line, please.'

A moment of crackling, and then Herbert Hoover's familiar voice: 'Polly, is that you?'

'Yes, I'm here. What can I do for you, Mr President?'

A pause. And then, 'Polly, my dear, you must brace yourself for a shock. Ren's airplane hasn't arrived.'

'Hasn't arrived? I don't understand.'

'We know it took off all right, because we've checked with the airfield. But it's been very foggy here—'

'Yes, it was foggy here this morning, but it cleared up by lunchtime.'

'There was a brief clear spell here, but the fog closed down again. The airplane didn't come in when it was expected. Now, you mustn't think the worst yet, because it's more than likely they put down somewhere when it got too thick to go on, and we'll hear something just as soon as they manage to find a telephone. But I thought you ought to be warned. It's only fair.'

'Yes,' she said. 'Thank you.' An awkward pause. 'You'll let me know if you hear anything?'

'The very instant. And I'd be obliged if you'd let me know, too, if he contacts you first. Ren is one of our finest young men. We can't afford to lose him. *I* can't afford to.'

She put the telephone back on its hook, and stood, staring at nothing. She saw the little aeroplane, the thickening air, the pilot dropping lower, looking for a level place to land. More than likely it would be in a field a long way from any building, so getting to a telephone would be difficult. Most farms, anyway, didn't have them. Probably they would stay with the machine and wait through the night hoping they could take off again at dawn. So there would be no message yet. But she had better stay by the telephone, just in case.

'I've done it now, madam,' came Plummer's voice. 'Did you want to wear it tonight?'

'I shan't be going out after all,' Polly said. 'Put the box away, and then get Mrs Margesson on the telephone.'

'Is something wrong, madam?'

'No, nothing. Get Mrs Margesson right away, please.'

When she heard Julie's voice, she couldn't tell her what had happened: Julie would exclaim and sympathise as though the worst had already happened, and it felt to her that talking about it might make it real. So she said that she suddenly felt unwell and was going to bed with an aspirin, endured Julie's kind injunctions to take care of herself, hung up and sat down to wait for news.

It was a long night. She couldn't bring herself to undress fully, but sat up on the bed, wrapped in her dressing-gown, the telephone, stubbornly silent, at her elbow. Plummer knew something was wrong, of course, and kept trying to bring her things – drinks, sandwiches, the paper – but eventually she went off to bed and Polly was left in peace.

There was no peace in her thoughts. The unearthly feeling of being awake and alone in the small hours drove her off the bed, and she prowled along to Ren's business-room, and stood at the door a moment, looking in. The ticker-tape was silent; his telephone, too. The room carried the smell of him, the hair oil he used, and the faint ghost of his cologne. She walked in and stood by his desk, looking down at the papers spread there, as if he might have left something behind that would give her information. She looked at a paper or two, but did not understand the words, let alone the numbers. Was there good news in them, or bad, or no news at all? He told her so little about what he did. His chair was cocked at an angle where he had pushed it out to get up. There seemed something terribly sad in that, like a dog waiting for its master to come back. She saw the impatient movement of his big body, the way he thrust down on the chair arms and rose up, up so fast, like a new skyscraper. She saw the shape of his large, lean hands, the skin always brown, the fingernails meticulously cared for, and she shivered.

Then she saw there was a book under the top sheets, and pulled it out gently. It was an old, rather fine, leather-bound edition of Shakespeare's *The Tempest*. It was open, offering her what he had been reading.

She put on his reading lamp, sat down and leaned over it, and a sentence leaped out at her.

Our revels now are ended.

Yes, she thought that was apt. The revels of the whole country this last year – indeed, this whole decade – had come to a sudden end. America had danced and played, growing richer almost by the day. Golf, tennis, sea bathing and beach picnics, the cinema, the theatres, the restaurants, ever-fancier automobiles, sassy clothes, jazz, cocktails – it had been quite a revel. And now the party was over.

She read on:

> Our revels now are ended. These our actors
> As I foretold you, were all spirits and
> Are melted into air, into thin air:
> And, like the baseless fabric of this vision,
> The cloud-capp'd towers, the gorgeous palaces,
> The solemn temples, the great globe itself,
> Yea, all which it inherit, shall dissolve
> And, like this insubstantial pageant faded,
> Leave not a rack behind.

She swallowed painfully. An insubstantial pageant, indeed, it had been. *The gorgeous palaces* – yes, they had known plenty of those. And *the solemn temples* – the financial institutions, grave and powerful as churches in the old order: even their buildings were raised up like temples while America worshipped the almighty dollar. *As I foretold you.* Oh, dear Lord, he had told them, hadn't he? Why was the book here, why open? Had he thought of it just recently, and found the book to check the words? He was a great reader, knew more Shakespeare than ever did she, an Englander.

Just a few more words to the end.

> We are such stuff
> As dreams are made on, and our little life
> Is rounded with a sleep.

She put her head down on her arms and wept, but whether she was weeping for herself, for America, or for their whole generation, she couldn't have said.

★　★　★

About mid-morning the next day she had a call from Tad Wilson of the Department of Commerce, Ren's closest colleague and probably only real friend in Washington. But it was only to tell her there was no news. 'We're doing all we can, I promise you. We've put the word out everywhere, and we've got a small airplane out looking for them. The fog's mostly cleared now – it's just a bit misty – but it was pretty bad while it lasted. They might have had to put down and got stuck somewhere, or gone miles off course. He'll turn up, don't worry. Are you bearing up?'

'Yes,' she said.

'Is there anything I can do for you?'

'You Tad, when there *is* news, will you be the one to telephone me?'

'Yes, of course, if you want me to. But he'll be able to call you himself, I'm sure. Try not to worry. He'll turn up.'

It was a long, weary day and night. The following day, in the afternoon, Tad called, a very different Tad, and she knew from his voice before he had said more than 'Hello, Polly,' that the revels were all ended.

The aeroplane had been found. It had come down on the east bank of Chesapeake Bay, south of Tolchester Beach, well off course. Probably it had tried to land, but the pilot had misjudged the height in the fog and crashed: the nose was buried in the ground as if he had not levelled off at all.

Tolchester Beach itself was a popular resort for Baltimoreans, but at this time of year it was empty, and the aeroplane had gone down twenty miles to the south of it, a deserted area of marsh, reed, bog, little inlets and none but birdlife. A fisherman had found it, and he had had to sail a long way to find a telephone.

There were no survivors.

'Polly, I'm so sorry,' Tad said. 'I don't know what to say. If there's anything I can do, you must tell me. I'm just broken up about this . . . Polly, are you there? Are you all right?'

'"Our little life is rounded with a sleep,"' she said, but not out loud. When it was over, every life was little. She had never felt so tired.

Violet was about to go upstairs to dress when she happened to glance at the ante-room door, and wondered how the Caravaggio looked now it was cleaned. You couldn't see that wall from this angle – you actually had to go into the room. She changed course, and with Fifi pattering ahead of her, looking back curiously over her shoulder to check the direction, she went to the door. The bare space looked back at her. The Caravaggio was stubbornly absent. And with surprise she saw two more empty spaces, paler against the weathered colour of the wallpaper. Frowning with effort, she recalled they were the Murillo – a particularly ugly picture, she had always thought, of two urchin boys eating grapes – and the portrait of Charles I on a horse.

What on earth was Holkam doing, sending out paintings to be cleaned – paintings that were never looked at, from a room that was rarely used? As she turned to leave, it occurred to her that all three had been taken from a position where she would never notice their absence unless her attention were drawn to it. She paused in puzzled thought, then returned to the hall and, seeing the butler appear from the passage, looking harassed (they had let one of the footmen go), asked, 'Deeping, where is his lordship?'

'I believe,' he said, 'that he is in the business-room, my lady.'

He oughtn't to be there, Violet thought. He should be upstairs getting changed. She directed her quick steps to the back of the house, found the door, unusually, closed, and went in.

Holkam had been sitting with his head in his hands, and jerked it up as she appeared.

'What the—! Oh, it's you,' he said. He rubbed his face

with his hands, a gesture she had never seen him make before, not so much as though he were tired but as if to rub away something. She had seen the boys when young rub at their faces like that after a grimy day, hoping to avoid a wash. 'What do you want?' he asked. It was not exactly rude, but it was unwelcoming.

'Why is the Caravaggio not back? Why have you sent two more paintings to be cleaned? I never knew you to do such a thing – and paintings no-one looks at, while the drawing-room ones aren't touched.' He had taken down his hands now, and she studied his face. He looked really unwell – a bad colour, his once-handsome face drawn, pouched under the eyes, and with one or two blemishes visible on the skin. 'Holkam, what is going on?' she asked quietly.

He groaned, an extraordinary sound that made the back of her neck prickle. 'Why must you ask? Can't you just leave things to me?'

She grew alarmed at the tone of his voice – it sounded like desperation. 'I know there's something wrong,' she said, 'and I have a right to know what it is. I am your wife and the mother of your children.'

'That's exactly why,' he muttered.

'Why what?'

'Why I've tried to save you from it. Well,' he straightened slightly in the chair and gave a great sigh, 'if you *won't* be saved, if you *must* know – I'm ruined.'

The stark words didn't mean anything to her. 'What on earth do you mean?'

'Listen carefully and you'll understand,' he said, with what she supposed was sarcasm. 'I've lost all my money. I have no more. I am in debt and can't repay it. I'm ruined. Do you understand now?'

She tried, really hard. 'But – but what about my money?' He had brought the title and property – heavily mortgaged – to the marriage and she had brought the money.

535

He gave an unpleasant smile. 'Oh, I spent that, long ago. We've been in debt for years, my dear. While you've been living your high life, I've been struggling to keep our heads above water. That was why your relationship with the Prince of Wales was so important. I was relying on his putting some useful sinecures my way. But now that's over. We are flat, stony broke.'

The slang startled her. 'But, Holkam, we can't be! We have so much – the houses, to begin with—'

'Mortgaged,' he said shortly. 'Don't look at me like that. I know your dowry was supposed to pay them off, but we lead an expensive style of life, my love, the two of us, and the boys at school and now university – raising a boy is an expensive business – three houses to keep up, servants' wages sky high, the entertaining. One would need to be a sultan to keep up with it all.'

She reached behind her for a chair, and sat rather hard. Fifi at once jumped up onto her lap and she caressed the little dog absently.

'And then,' Holkam went on, 'I met a fellow through Chips Channon who I thought could help me. Not an American, but married to an American woman, lives half the time over there, fellow by the name of Meyer.'

'I've heard you mention him,' Violet remembered. 'Meyer.'

'Henry Meyer, but everyone knows him as Fox.' He waved away the question he saw rise to her lips. 'Doesn't matter. Fox Meyer put me on to some sure things on the American Stock Exchange. He promised enormous returns, and he was right – some stocks doubled, all of them went up by at least fifty per cent. I saw a way out – keeping us going and paying off the debts. There was no reason not to trust him. He'd steered me right for a year.'

Violet stared at him, smelling doom in the air. 'How did you find the money to invest, if you were "stony broke"?'

The words sounded peculiar in her clipped, cultured tones.

He swallowed visibly, staring straight at her, like a man facing a firing squad. 'I borrowed from the bank. A large amount. A very large amount. Well, I needed large returns.'

Now she understood. She said, almost in a whisper, 'The American business – the Wall Street crash.'

He made that groaning sound again, and rubbed at his face. 'Everything's gone. The stocks are worthless. The bank is going to want its money back, and I haven't got it.'

'The Caravaggio?'

'I sold it, and two more, to make the interest payments, so the bank wouldn't foreclose. But sooner or later . . .'

Violet stared past him at the booklined wall. She couldn't take it in. How could they have nothing when they had so much? 'But Holkam, the houses, the furniture – paintings, silver – my jewellery . . .'

'My dear, you need to understand. Everything we have, down to the last teaspoon, is owed. Your money went years ago. We were in debt long before Meyer came on the scene. Now there's no way out. *Everything* will have to be sold to pay off the debts. Even then—' He stopped himself. She was a woman – why burden her with the full horror of it?

'But what shall we do?' she asked. Fifi had curled up in her lap and gone to sleep, and her hands were clasped over the dog's back – beautiful hands, pale and well kept, with a diamond ring on one and a sapphire on the other. He didn't like to look at those rings.

'We must keep going as we are for a while longer,' he said. 'There's Charlotte to think of. She must have her Season, and the chance to get a husband. If we can get her married off, at least she will be safe. So you must not speak about this to anyone, do you understand?'

'I wouldn't think of it,' she said.

'I mean, not even to Oliver,' he said.

She was shocked. 'Oliver would not betray us.'

'Perhaps not,' he said, reserving judgement. He had no

illusions about how little Overton liked him. 'But what you tell him, he tells Verena, and she tells Sarah Vibart, and Sarah Vibart tells Baba Metcalfe, which is the equivalent of taking out an advertisement in *The Times*. So tell no-one – and don't let anyone guess from anything you do or say. Be your normal self, for Charlotte's sake. I can keep us going for a time by selling things – though I have to be careful. Any hint that we were in trouble would bring the whole house of cards crashing down.'

'That's why you wanted me to economise,' she said.

'I think I know where I can borrow a little more, if need be.' A short-term loan at extortionate rates, of course – but what was the difference now? The only thing that mattered was to keep up appearances until Charlotte was taken care of. Then the ground could open and swallow him. 'We must make a good show for Charlotte and get her off our hands. That's the most important thing.'

'And what about the boys?'

He shrugged. 'They'll have to take care of themselves. Robert will finish at Oxford. Richard will have to leave at the end of his first year. They'll have to find jobs.'

'Jobs!' she said, in a little gasp.

He gave her a wry smile. 'You have a brother who became a common doctor. Don't be so shocked. The professions cost money. Many men nowadays have to take jobs.'

'And Henry?'

'Ah, Henry,' said Holkam, and his face softened. Against all the odds, he loved Henry best of the children, and it tore at his heart that he wasn't his. 'I'm sorry that Henry won't even have Eton. We must find a less expensive school for him, or a bursary. But that can wait. For now, we must concentrate on bringing Charlotte out in the best style.'

Violet put Fifi down and got up, distressed to find her legs trembling. It was all too much to take in at once. When she got to the door, she turned and said, 'Thank you for telling me.' It must have been hard for him to acknowledge such failure. 'For trusting me. And if I can help, there's a lot of my jewellery I hardly wear.'

'I have already taken account of it,' he said, but he was touched that she had offered.

'Oh,' she said. And then, 'Charlotte's clothes – I have many things I've only worn once. They could be made over for her. It can be done,' she added, as she saw the objection in his eyes, 'so that no-one will know.'

He was trying not to cry. He wouldn't do that in front of her. 'My dear,' he said, in a strained voice, 'our debt is so huge that amounts so small are not worth saving. Let her have new clothes.'

Violet nodded, and left. She needed to be alone to try to come to terms with what he had told her. She felt as though someone had blown a hole through the middle of her mind so she hadn't enough left to think with. This could not be her life. It was all a mistake. A dream – she would wake up and laugh with relief. She watched her feet taking her along the passage, across the hall to the stairs. They didn't feel like her feet. And, she suddenly realised with horror, she would have to go out and face people tonight – probably alone, for she couldn't imagine Holkam could be ready in time. Thank God she had never been a talker. Perhaps no-one would notice that she had nothing to say for herself this evening.

Suddenly Lennie was there – dear, familiar Lennie, the only person, she realised, she could have borne to have near her. He didn't speak at first, just enfolded her in his arms and drew her to him. His coat was cold and smelt of outdoors; the shoulders and fur collar were damp.

'Is it still snowing?' she asked, against his chest. It was so comfortable there, she felt as though she might sleep. She had slept very little since the aeroplane went missing.

'A little,' he said. 'It's almost stopped.'

Oh, thank heaven, he wasn't going to say, 'You poor, poor thing', or 'I'm so sorry', or any of the other useless things. But she should have known she could trust him. She freed herself from his arms, and Plummer, red-eyed and haggard (*She has really let herself go*, Polly thought, with a frown), came forward to take his coat.

'Can I trouble you to feed me?' he asked lightly. 'I'm starved – missed dinner last night and haven't had a moment for breakfast yet.'

'Yes, of course,' she said. 'Plummer – omelettes will do. With some ham, whatever there is. Come into the parlour,' she said to Lennie. She sat on the sofa and he sat beside her and took her hands. It felt good, like warming them at the fire after a day's hunting. 'How did you get here so fast?' she asked.

'I got in last night – I had to come home on business anyway. And it was in the papers this morning. Have you seen them?' She shook her head. She didn't want to read anything about it. 'It spoke very well of him. A promising career cut short, that sort of thing. That must have come from the President's office. You'll be glad of that, one day. Do you know how it happened?'

'No-one knows. It was foggy. There was no-one around.' Oddly, speaking in this way didn't hurt. It was the sympathy she couldn't bear. 'He was on his way to talk to the President and Andrew Mellon – what to do about the crash. They arranged an aeroplane for him.' She had to stop then as her throat closed up.

Lennie nodded. 'I know he warned them back in the summer that the bubble was going to burst. He told me, and I got out of most of my shares. He was a good friend.' He hesitated. 'Polly, that business – about the private detective . . .'

She waved it away. It didn't matter in the context of the recent disasters. She didn't know any more why she had been so angry. 'Don't talk about it now. I suppose you meant well.'

'I swear I never said a word to a single soul.'

'I know. Someone else must have found out. There were a lot of people in the White House who didn't like him.'

'A lot of second-rate people don't like talented men who threaten to leapfrog them to the top.'

She looked at him. 'Was that what it was? I thought they hated him because he was half Indian.'

'No, darling, that was the excuse. Everyone could see he was the coming man, and he had the President's ear. He was bound to have enemies.'

She considered. 'That does make it better. Was he really admired?'

'Tremendously,' Lennie said. 'And he really cared for you, Polly.'

She looked away. 'I know.'

Time to be practical, he thought. 'I've come to offer my services,' he said. 'There will be a lot to do, sorting through papers, dealing with attorneys and bankers and all the rest of it. You can't do it, and you won't want a stranger, so let me. I'm a businessman and I've dealt with him. I can do everything, if you'll let me.'

She felt a wave of relief come over her, and realised that, without knowing, she had been dreading dealing with the practical and financial aspects of what had happened. She wouldn't have had the first idea of what to do. 'Would you really do that?' she said, her voice rising with gladness.

'Of course. You shouldn't be alone at a time like this.'

'I don't want people around me.'

'I know that, but I'm not people. I'll keep them all away.'

'Thank you,' she said. Something occurred to her, and she looked at him, suddenly drawn. 'What will happen about – about a funeral?' She didn't even know what had happened to his body. A momentary flash of thought wondered what state the body was in and she flung it from her with a shudder.

He saw the shudder and pressed her hands. 'I'll deal with it. Didn't I tell you I'll deal with everything? You're cold. I bet you haven't eaten since I don't know when. When did you last eat anything?'

'I don't remember.'

'Well, go and put on a cardigan or a sweater or something of the sort. And then we'll have breakfast, lunch or dinner, whichever it is.'

She obeyed, and when she came out, Plummer had laid the table and there were cheese omelettes and ham waiting. 'The bread was stale, madam, so I toasted it,' she said nasally. She had been weeping again, though Polly couldn't guess whether it was for Ren or for her lost savings. Both, perhaps.

'Toast is good,' she said. 'More like breakfast.' The smell of coffee reached her, and she was suddenly ravenously hungry.

They ate, she in silence, Lennie slipping in bits of news from California, about Rose and Lizzie and Ashley – all settling in well, Ashley like a new man in the warmer climate, Lizzie missing her boys, Rose a terrific success in her first role, the studio wanting to sign her up for five years. 'The next part could even be a second lead. But she's young, she has time to take it steady.'

He had seen her eyelids begin to droop. He moved with her to the sofa, and talked on inconsequentially until, after quite a short time, she slid into sleep, her head rolling sideways onto his shoulder. He picked her up and carried her into the bedroom, laid her on the bed, and folded the other half of the comforter over her. He looked down for a moment at her face, tired and marked with suffering, but relaxing now into the beauty of sleep, and his heart ached with the old, old longing. He bent and laid his lips lightly to her forehead, and thought that he would die for her, if it would make her happy. Ren had been a lucky man.

He straightened and went out, closing the door behind him, and headed for Ren's business-room to start the mammoth task of sorting out.

CHAPTER TWENTY-FOUR

They received the news at Morland Place by a cable from Lennie, followed by a letter enclosing a newspaper cutting, but no further information had come forward about how the accident happened. Any form of travel was dangerous, and accidents happened, that was all. Teddy was horrified that his lovely Polly had been widowed so young, and tried hard to resist the small voice that whispered in his ear that now there was no reason for her not to come home. He wrote a letter of condolence and, after long thought, wrote that they all longed to see her and that her old room was waiting for her if she wanted to come. He hoped that much would not sound tactless when it was read at the other end. There was no reply from Polly, but another letter from Lennie saying that she had been touched by the offer but was still too upset to write herself. There was no hint that she might, indeed, come home.

Amy, who was the only one who observed him closely now that Henrietta was gone and Jessie lived at Twelvetrees, thought that as well as a natural desire to see his daughter, he was feeling restless, wanting change. He had been troubled lately by bronchitis, which he put down to the cold, damp weather, but otherwise at seventy-nine he was very healthy and retirement did not suit him. He had given up his day-to-day running of his businesses, and spent more time going around the estate, but Amy thought he missed the urgency of commerce and its decisions.

The stock-market fall had lost him money, but he was not exposed to American stocks. The question was, what would the wider implications be? At present, no-one knew, but if there were a heavy fall in demand in America, his manufacturing business would suffer. There was nothing to do but wait and see, which did not suit his mood. He went out hunting two days a week, and wore himself out. Amy worried about accidents, but he said blithely, 'Good riders don't get killed out hunting. It's the novices that take the falls.' Knowing she couldn't keep him from the saddle, she had to be satisfied with that.

She had settled fully into her role now as mistress of the house, though she still caught herself thinking of Henrietta when she overheard anyone refer to 't' mistress'. After three years the servants had got used to coming to her with questions and for orders, and she enjoyed the increase of her powers. But she didn't involve herself as actively as Henrietta had. The one household task she relished and undertook herself was the arranging of the flowers – the one thing her previous life had fitted her for – and there was always some display in the Great Hall and on the round table in the drawing-room. She did the flowers for the bedrooms when they had guests and for the chapel on the great occasions; and she always put a small nosegay on the Lady's altar, as Henrietta had.

For the rest, she had her own interests. She had established a group of friends in and around York whom she visited and who visited her. She had taken up watercolour painting, and had got quite good at it. She started by painting her vases of flowers, then other still-life arrangements, then graduated to the outdoors, where she found endless fascination in trying to capture landscapes. She had tried some portraits but had no facility in human faces, though she managed one or two nice representations of the dogs when they were asleep. Teddy particularly prized a painting she had done recently of his Jack Russell, Bigelot, and his new spaniel, Blossom (Gossamer had died back in the spring), sleeping together in a patch of sunlight in the hall. He had had it framed and it now hung in his dressing-room.

She liked to go to the cinema from time to time. Usually she went with Roberta or Jeremy, or one of her friends: Teddy didn't care for it much, and tended to ask loud and plaintive questions – 'What on earth's the silly fella doing *that* for? Can't she see he's up to no good? *That*'s not the way to go about serving at table.' He did enjoy Charlie Chaplin, although he had got it into his head that he was French, and often said he wouldn't be so inept at everything if he was English.

Amy was very fond of Teddy, and eternally grateful to him for having rescued her and given her a comfortable home and secure future. He was affectionate to her and liked to give her little gifts, and his pleasure sometimes was to have her sit on his knee in the evening and listen together to some music on the gramophone she had urged him to buy. But they did not have intimate relations any more. They had stopped when Edward died.

Roberta was her closest companion at home. She was eighteen, a pleasant-looking girl, though not striking in any way, and rather young for her age. Her mother Ethel had been talking for the past year about 'bringing her out', but always balked at the expense, which also stopped her having Roberta to live with her. Roberta visited her mother regularly, but had no wish to exchange Morland Place, with all its freedoms and possibilities, for the confines of River House, in Knaresborough, and her mother's narrow interests.

She also – she told Amy in a burst of confidence one day when they were folding linens together – didn't want to 'come out'. She didn't like 'silliness and boys' and had no wish to get married. Amy worried that as her most immediate experience of marriages consisted of her mother's to Donald

Broadbent and Amy's to Teddy, she might have got hold of the wrong end of the stick. But Roberta asserted that she hated boys, and that horses were much more sensible and lovable. It was true, Amy reflected, that she was horse-mad. When she was not helping Amy in the house she was out and about all day long, riding whatever horse was available. She exercised Teddy's horses when he didn't want them, and was down at Twelvetrees helping Jessie with the schooling and exercise, and when there was nothing to ride she would groom and muck out with great willingness. And when she was not in the stables she was messing around in the kennels, for she loved dogs almost as much as horses.

Amy thought it a shame she should not have a horse of her own. But it did not seem to have occurred to Teddy, and Amy did not like to ask him direct. He already did so much for his dead nephews' children, and they were an undoubted expense to him. Roberta had managed to acquire a dog of her own: the farmer at Prospect had given her a collie that he said hadn't taken to training. The alternative would have been knocking it on the head, since a sheepdog that wouldn't work was no use to anyone, so Roberta accepted the gift of Sweep before even asking Uncle Teddy. But when she brought it home on the end of a piece of string, Teddy had at once fallen for the dog's charm and said she could keep it. It was the usual black-and-white, but had a black patch over one eye and a white one over the other, which gave it a clownish look, enhanced by one 'flying ear', which stood up instead of folding over properly as a collie's should. Sweep had erupted into the Great Hall and stirred up the house pack, being young and wanting to play all the time, but a few tussles and one or two sharp nips had shown him his place; and being out of doors all day long with Roberta took the edge off his energy, so he soon settled in.

With her own dog, horses to ride, and all the wide estate to ride in, Roberta was perfectly happy, and her only fear was that she would be wrenched away from Morland Place, either by having to go and live with her mother, or by being married, something she seemed to regard as a disease one could catch, rather than any rational decision. She did meet boys from time to time, at tennis parties and tea parties and in York, but she treated them with a gruff suspicion, which so far had kept off their unwelcome interest.

Her brother Jeremy was seventeen and had started as a junior clerk in the same bank where his father had worked – something Teddy had arranged with the owner. Harriet, at fourteen, had finished compulsory schooling, but as she was the only one of Robert's children with any kind of academic bent, Teddy had allowed her to stay on into the senior part of St Edward's. John, at thirteen, thought she was mad, and couldn't wait to be fourteen himself so he could leave school for ever.

Martin, Frank's boy, just thirteen, was showing something of his father's scholarly traits. He was quiet and 'bookish', and Teddy was already calculating how to ensure the boy went on with his studies, perhaps grammar school first, and then the university. Frank had been cut off in the spring of his brilliant promise. If Martin had Frank's brain, he should not suffer the same way.

Laura no-one really bothered about. She was only nine, so the time when Teddy might have to wonder what to do with her was a long way off. Though he loved all children, and took his responsibilities seriously, he didn't find it easy to care about her. She was always withdrawn, often sullen and awkward, and without the winning smiles and little wiles that warmed his heart. She liked nothing better than to hang around Twelvetrees, and help there as long as no-one looked at her or spoke to her much. The only person she opened up to was Jessie, whom she had come to trust through Jessie's giving her jobs in an offhand way and letting her alone to get on with them. She had come to spend as much time at

Twelvetrees House as at Morland Place, and it was rare anyone at the latter asked after her or even noticed she was missing. If she didn't turn up at mealtime or bedtime, it was assumed Miss Jessie had her.

She did not display the academic bent of her parents, and frequently played truant from school in order to roam the countryside or go to the stables. Her one intellectual pursuit was reading – she liked to take a book and hide with it up a tree or in a hayloft, somewhere no-one would disturb her. She also wrote stories, though no-one but Jessie knew that, for it was only to Jessie she showed them. Jessie found them rather disturbing. They were always about an orphan – understandable enough – who ran away from miserable circumstances and managed to get through some magic portal into another world. It was the other worlds Jessie found unsettling. Laura's imagination stretched far beyond Jessie's and often she could not understand or picture them.

John Julian and Miss Husthwaite were still working on the Household Book. It was a much vaster topic than Palgrave's manuscript, and Miss Husthwaite had often thought happily that it would keep them occupied for many years to come. Julian agreed, but it gave him less cause for rejoicing because he was worried about his job. He presided over daily prayers and a twice-weekly celebration, but he wondered whether that custom would survive Mr Morland: the new 'jazz' generation did not seem dedicated to organised religion. He was afraid his days at Morland Place might be numbered.

Indeed, he thought, when Mr Morland died, Miss Husthwaite's position would probably go too. He had a small private income, and he had been saving hard since he came here – he had few expenses. He found her company congenial, and it occurred to him that if they did suddenly find themselves cast out from Paradise, they might join forces and set up somewhere together. If they could afford a small place in York, perhaps they would still be allowed to come to Morland Place on a daily basis and continue the work on the Household Book. They would have to get married, of course. He was waiting for the right moment to discuss the plan with Miss Husthwaite, though when they were working, heads bent close together over a manuscript, exchanging ideas with the freedom of true scholars, he felt sure she would not dislike it.

Lennie had taken over everything, even the filtering of phone calls and visitors, so Polly was allowed to fall into a lethargy of shock and grief. She did not want to speak to anyone, see any of her friends, go anywhere or do anything. Social life was making a tentative return among those who hadn't suffered great losses, though for reasons of tact it was a quieter, less flamboyant life than before. But Polly wanted no part of it. She wouldn't look at any of the hundreds of letters of condolence, had flowers sent straight to the hospital. She lay on the sofa and read – Lennie was astonished to see that she was working her way through the plays of Shakespeare, and assumed she found them distracting – and listened to the gramophone for hour after hour. She wouldn't have the radio on – she hated the bright, brash voices and the advertisements – so she had no idea how things were developing since the crash. She didn't want to know. Her own crash had superseded that of the stock market.

Lennie had been living at the house since the day he had arrived, sleeping in one of the guest bedrooms. He supposed eyebrows might be raised but he couldn't help that. He had to rely on the presence of Plummer, his own man Orton and the other servants to guarantee respectability. There was a great deal to do in sorting out the estate and other problems left by Ren's sudden death. It was fortunate at least that Estate Duty – often referred to scathingly as Death Tax – was not levied when the estate passed to the spouse; and Ren had made a will leaving everything to Polly.

For the first week he tried to leave her alone at home as little as possible, doing everything he could by telephone and cable, but after that he had to go out from time to time, not only to see to her affairs but to look after his own businesses. Radio shares had taken a severe hit, but his shops and manufacturing were sound, and he expected them to hold on. If people were short of money they would stay home more, and that meant more radio sales. But there were delicate decisions to be made about what to transmit from his radio station: too cheerful might sound callous, too gloomy seem un-American. And he had already lost advertisers. Times, he thought, were going to get tough.

His father, at least, was happily preoccupied and unlikely to be affected by the outfall of the crash. He had been asked, because of his experience in the field, to join a committee designing and building a new skyscraper, which was intended to be the highest in America The race to build taller and taller towers had been going on ever since the Eiffel Tower at 984 feet had opened in Paris in 1889. America could not let that challenge pass. Currently there were two attempts, the Bank of Manhattan building at 40 Wall Street, and the Chrysler building at 42nd and Lexington.

The new building Patrick was working on was to exceed both of them. The committee was headed by Al Smith, former governor of New York and presidential candidate. John Jacob Raskob, a former vice president of General Motors, together with a number of other investors, had acquired a two-acre plot of land at Fifth and West 34th for $16 million. On the plot was the Waldorf-Astoria Hotel, whose owners had decided to sell and build a new hotel on Park Avenue. The main difficulty was that Walter Chrysler was refusing to reveal how high his finished building would be. The design of the Fifth Avenue tower would have to be flexible enough to be added to if necessary, as the Chrysler building went up and could be observed.

The demolition and clearing were complete, and excavation was due to start in January 1930, and Patrick was very excited about the whole scheme. The design was elegant and simple – the story was that Raskob had held up a pencil and asked the chief architect, 'How tall can you make that so it won't fall down?' The plan had been decided upon: a compact space at the centre would hold the vertical air shafts, the elevator shafts, mail chutes, lavatories and corridors. Surrounding this would be a twenty-eight-foot-deep perimeter of office space. For stability the tower was stepped at certain points and the floor space became smaller, compensated for by having fewer elevators. And there was to be a viewing deck near the top which would give spectacular outlooks over Manhattan.

As Christmas approached, Lennie was determined to get Polly away from the house, at least for a time. His first thought was to take her with him to California to have Christmas with Lizzie and Ashley. But it soon became clear that he would not be able to move her that far so soon. His second idea was that Patrick should host a Christmas Day dinner at his apartment, with Lennie and Polly, and perhaps Martial, Mimi and the children, the only guests. It would be a first safe step back into society.

The approach of Christmas, with Lennie insisting that she couldn't stay at home alone while he went to his father's, roused Polly enough from her torpor to become suddenly aware that something which ought to have happened had not. The crash in October and Ren's death in November had prevented her thinking about it or noticing it, but now the idea had come into her head, she could not get it out.

Finally she could not bear it any longer. Heavily veiled, she went to the doctor, the first time she had left the house since Ren had died. Just being outside made her tremble, and there seemed too many people and too much noise. But she had to know. They had a new test now, involving rabbits – she didn't care to know the details, but made a urine sample and went home again to wait. A few days later, on the 23rd of December, the result came from Dr Stutzman: she was pregnant. He asked her in for a physical examination, and told her he thought she was three months on.

At home, later, she went to take a bath to rid herself of the intrusive stickiness of the examination and, when she had undressed, paused for a moment and looked at herself in the mirror. She had not been eating properly and had lost some weight, so her collar-bones stuck out and her ribs were visible. But below them there was a definite roundness that had not been there before. She laid her hand over it tentatively, then snatched it back. There was something unsettling, almost unpleasant, about the thought of something alive in there.

What would she have said to Ren? He had not wanted a child – not yet, so he said, but she had got the feeling he meant never. Trojans were not completely safe, everyone knew that; it could be his child. Would he have been pleased? She didn't know. And how would she have felt as the child grew, wondering whether it would display traits or features of one man or the other? To deceive Ren once was bad enough, but to engage in a lifetime of deceit . . . As it was, things were simpler. She shuddered. She did not want any part of her to be glad about Ren's death.

Things were simpler, but harder. She slipped into the warm water and thought, for the first time in weeks, about Erich. The old ache of longing came back. But painful though it was to realise, this pregnancy did not make any difference. He was still married, with a child, and he had made his life far away on the other side of the continent. As far as the world was concerned, this would be Ren's child, and she would be accorded all the more sympathy because of it.

Tears seeped out of her eyes and ran down her cheeks, sorrow for the Polly who was outside her. She was almost thirty years old and nothing had ever gone right for her. She felt her throat tighten and tried not to sob, but in the end she put her hands over her face and let it come.

He had not offered to throw away the world for her, nor asked her to do it for him. She remembered the lines of suffering in his face, the tiredness behind the animation, the melancholy behind the love. He had lost too much to be careless, suffered too much to be carefree. He had put love aside for practicality, for them both. Hold on to what you have: the world is a cold and dangerous place, too hard for us to be like young lovers and risk all, dare all, for the beloved's touch. *Oh, Erich! Why aren't you here?* Would she have thrown it all away and gone with him, had he asked? She didn't know. Would they have been happy? She didn't know that either. At seventeen she'd have known the answer to both questions. But she was not seventeen any more. She had been out in the world too long.

And now there was this new person. Poor baby. She laid her hands over the curve more kindly. Poor little baby. It would be fatherless; fatherless either way. She knew then that she could not tell Erich. Loving her, she believed, as much as man could love woman, he had made his choice; and she hers. No, the poor baby would be Ren Alexander's child. And its mother would have to do for both.

At the thought something stirred in her that she had not expected – a strange little spurt of determination that this poor fatherless baby should not suffer, should be protected by her, should be safe and happy. She washed the tears from her face and under her fingers felt her mouth smiling.

It was only a momentary thing. It passed, and she was left with the familiar weariness of loss and trouble and foreboding. But it had happened. Perhaps it would come again.

*   *   *

Lennie gently but firmly removed with Polly to his father's apartment on the morning of Christmas Eve, having extracted a promise from her that they would stay at least three nights. Patrick was welcoming, sympathy in his look but with no unnecessary words for her to have to respond to. She had forgotten how comfortable he was to be with. He told her he had invited Martial, with his wife and children, for Christmas Day. 'The children will keep us merry,' he said.

St Thomas's on Fifth Avenue – a very English-looking, Gothic-style church – was famous for its men's and boys' choirs and its choral performances, and in the evening Patrick took her and Lennie to their carol concert. It had been snowing: there was a white strip along the edge of every sidewalk, and the city trees were delicately outlined, sparkling white on black. The shops were full of lights and glitter, fabulous caves of treasure, and in front of them children bounced beside their parents, tugging their hands excitedly.

In the massive church, lit with hundreds of pinprick candles like a captive galaxy, the choirboys in their red cassocks and white surplices and ruffs looked like angels, and when they sang the crystal sweetness of their voices seemed like a sound from outside the world. Polly listened to the sublime music, the soaring voices lifting with the organ's grandeur to fill the vaulted spaces, making her scalp tingle and her heart ache with the sheer beauty of it. It seemed the very essence of Christmas. She cried a little, but for the first time in months there was healing in it.

Afterwards they drove home, and when he had let them into the vestibule, Patrick said he proposed to make a special Christmas Eve drink for them all, and hurried away. Lennie helped Polly out of her coat, folded it over his arm, took her hat and gloves, then, his eyes twinkling, bowed with a solemn, butlerish look, and said, 'Thank you, modom.'

It was the mildest of jokes, but it was too much for Polly.

She put her hand to her mouth to hide the twisting of her lips, but he could see her eyes.

'Oh, Polly, I'm sorry! I didn't mean to make you cry. I guess you're not ready for fun. I'm so stupid.'

She shook her head to say it wasn't his fault, and turned her face away for a moment until she had control. Then looking at him again, with the sight and sound of those choirboys still close in her mind, she said, 'It isn't that. There's something – I have to tell you. There's going to be a child. I'm going to have a child.'

The first reaction in his face – just for a moment before the usual concern took over – was of wonder and joy, and for that same moment she was aware of a curious thought that flickered through her mind: *I wish it was yours. A baby ought to have a father who looks like that when he's told.*

Before he could speak, she said, 'Please don't say you're sorry.'

'No,' he said, understanding. 'Babies ought to be greeted as good news. When – when will it—'

'June, the doctor says.'

'June is a good month. I'm . . .' He was finding it hard to select the right words. He couldn't say, 'I'm so happy for you,' though that was how he felt. He tried, 'It must be a comfort – isn't it? That he left something behind? And if it has his good qualities, it will be a fine youngster.'

She let out her breath – she hadn't been aware she was holding it – in a trembling rush, and said, half smiling, half tearful, 'Oh, Lennie!'

Then she was gathered into his arms, and leaning against the bastion of his shoulder, she felt him gulp down tears of his own. He said, 'You needn't be afraid. You and the baby won't be alone. I will always be here. I'll always look after you. You know that, don't you?'

She didn't answer. She was thinking of the enigma that was Lennie, the ordinary, quiet, not-specially-anything but nice and kind Lennie – who yet had fought bravely in the war, won a medal for rescuing a wounded colleague and bringing him back from behind enemy lines, who to escape the Germans had taken a flying leap right over an occupied German trench and become a legend in his own regiment. He had set up his own business and succeeded and become rich, and you had to be tough to do that, even in America. Yet with her he was as gentle as a woman; and still shy and tongue-tied on occasion. She had known him half her life, but still did not really have a single image of him in her mind; and if she went away and never saw him again, she knew she would quickly find it difficult to picture his face.

She shuddered slightly at the thought of never seeing him again, and his arms tightened a fraction in response. But she didn't need to worry about that. Dependable Lennie would always be there for her to turn to on dark days, and forget when the sun shone, as she had always done.

Lennie, holding her, was staring over her head at the wall opposite while in a rapid succession all the problems and requirements of the situation tumbled through his brain: what would have to be done and how he would do it, and what would happen in the long run to mother and child. He frowned as he thought out present stratagems and future plans. Then Polly said something, muffled by his chest. He eased her away from him just a little and asked, 'What was that, dearest?'

She didn't look at him, but she said, 'I just said thank you. I don't think I could cope without you.' Then she laid her head back against him, as if that was the most comfortable place to be.

It was enough.

Sir Thomas Freeling looked stern. 'You should have come to me a long time ago.' He didn't call Holkam 'my lord'. He might only be a knight, and a medical practitioner, but in present circumstances he was the earl's equal.

Holkam looked at him with dislike. He despised doctors in the first place, and in the second, he hated being forced into this degrading intimacy. Freeling had insisted on a thorough examination, which he thought quite unnecessary. He supposed the old quack wanted to see him squirm. 'What's the verdict?' he asked tersely.

'I'm afraid the heart is considerably damaged.' Freeling thought for a moment. 'You were in Paris for quite a while, I believe?'

'For the Peace Conference,' Holkam said. 'What of it?'

'Her ladyship, if I remember, did not accompany you?'

'Be damned to your impertinent questions!'

Freeling looked unmoved, steely. 'I ask no questions that do not need to be asked. I am interested in your medical condition, nothing else. Did you, in that time, have resort to the professional services of any of the young women of Paris?'

'Damn you, Freeling!'

'I'll take that as a "yes". Very well. Did you, some time afterwards – perhaps eighteen months, two years later – suffer an episode of fever? Headache, sweat, aching joints, et cetera? Perhaps accompanied by a rash?'

Holkam stopped swearing at him, thinking now. 'I did have a feverish attack – I suppose it would be in 'twenty-three or 'twenty-four – but it passed off in the usual way. It was just PUO, trench fever. I had a touch of it in 1918 and they said it was likely to recur. It was nothing serious.'

'And did it recur a second time after that?'

'No. That was the end of it.'

'Hmph,' said Freeling. He looked at Holkam consideringly for a moment. 'You will not like to hear what I am to say, so I ask you to listen for your own good. I believe you have tertiary – that is, third-stage – syphilis.'

'What the—'

'Please. Hear me out. The disease was very rife in Paris at the end of the war. The initial chancre, being painless, is easy to overlook at the time, but it leaves a scar, which you have. The second stage is an attack of fever similar to the one you have described. The disease then generally becomes dormant and may remain so for many years. In the third stage it attacks the internal organs, most commonly the heart, though it may also affect the liver, the lungs, the joints, the skin – indeed, any part, even the brain.' Holkam was looking at him, white-lipped, but it was no longer with fury. Freeling divined the question he wanted to ask. 'There is no cure at this stage. At earlier stages, arsenic can be effective.'

'Then give me arsenic.'

'It would be ineffective at this stage. I'm sorry.'

'You're sorry, are you? You damned useless quack! Give me something!'

Freeling looked at him with interest, as though he were a laboratory specimen. 'When the disease begins to involve the brain, it is often the case that the subject becomes irascible, given to fits of rage.'

'Don't stand there pontificating at me, you charlatan! Do something!'

'For the present, I can give you something to improve the operation of the heart, and something for the headaches.'

'I don't—' Holkam began – but he did have headaches, quite dreadful ones.

'Apart from that, I'm afraid there is nothing I can do for you. As I told you, there is no cure.'

Holkam had to think and compose himself for a noticeable time before he could ask the next question. 'How long have I got?'

Freeling looked more kindly. 'As I said, the heart is severely compromised. It could fail at any time. I would advise you to avoid strenuous exercise or anything that might put a strain on it. The medicine will make you feel a little better and make your breathing easier, but it's only a matter of time. A few months at best. I'm sorry.'

As he was leaving, a while later, Freeling said, 'Oh, by the way. The disease may still be infectious in the third stage. I advise you to urge anyone with whom you have had physical intimacy to consult a physician at once.'

Holkam's eyes bulged with horror at the idea. Did this damned quack know something? 'Damn you,' he said, and though it was not with his usual fury, it was heartfelt.

In January 1930 Basil was fourteen, and started his first half at public school. Funds didn't run to one of the grander foundations, but Jack asked around his fellow airmen and was told there was a decentish place in Surrey where a boy might learn to be a gentleman while getting a useful education. He was glad to find the school was strong on mathematics and science, not just the classics; and Helen thought the daily walks would be good for him. Though well knit and, in her estimation, a handsome boy, he was not terribly devoted to the outdoor life and seemed to prefer skulking indoors, reading, and teasing his siblings.

When he was told about it, Basil said he didn't want to go, surprising Jack: for a boy to go away to school was a part of the natural order. As well object to the sun coming up in the morning. In his puzzlement he asked why, but Basil had no answer, only said he didn't *want* to. He complained vociferously for several days until Helen told him quite shortly that he was going, and that was that, in the tone of voice that even he never disputed. Thereafter he became angelic whenever the subject was mentioned, with a sweetness that roused Helen's suspicions, and even offered to help with the packing of his trunk.

Barbara, his shadow, had demanded to be allowed to go to school with him, and when she was told it was for boys only, had wept bitterly, and threatened to cut off her hair and run away. The packing went on over several days, and it took a while for any of the grown-ups to notice that as fast as things were being put in the trunk, Barbara was sneaking into the room and removing them. She was so inconsolable over her brother's departure – they had never been separated before – that Jack (rather unwisely, in Helen's view) brought her home a puppy to cheer her up. She called it Captain Midnight, which was one of the names Basil had given himself in their games. He was supposed to be a bold adventurer and daring spy, but the new Captain Midnight kept the house awake all night crying for his mother.

So Basil went to school. In his second week he broke a window in the dormitory. In February he knocked over a candle in chapel and set fire to a pile of hymn books. In March, at rugger, running head down with the ball under his arm, he overshot the touchline and hit the deputy head-master full in the bread-basket. Later that month he spilled a large amount of jam under the table at breakfast and managed to tread it extensively through the dining hall and corridor before it was noticed. In April he caused a minor explosion in a chemistry lesson, damaging a table and breaking a window.

All these things were accidents, he claimed with innocent indignation, when his delinquencies were mentioned in a letter sent home with him at Easter. The letter said he was high-spirited but ought to keep his energies for his studies and the sports field. Jack did not take it seriously, and simply said boys would be boys and it was a fuss about nothing. Helen looked at her son thoughtfully, and when she got him alone said, 'If you're trying to get out of school with these pranks, it won't work.'

Basil gave her the look of innocence she had most come to distrust, and said, 'Get out of school? But I love it there, Mum. I can't wait to get back after the hols.'

And in case she should have any fears that her firstborn had undergone a conversion, he went off with Stalky, Captain Midnight and next door's terriers to the nearest farm and, in the process of ratting in a barn with the farmer's son, managed to let out half a dozen bullocks it had taken all morning to get in for the vet to examine.

As the world turned and the year waxed, Polly grew with it. Held in the protective cocoon of motherhood, she ignored most of what was going on around her. She had no interest in newspapers and saw few people, only those who could be trusted not to gush over her or talk to her about anything but trivialities. She read a great deal – Shakespeare plays, the poetry of John Donne, novels by Dickens – having a vague feeling that these classics would somehow be absorbed by the baby. Patrick had an extensive library, and one of the few times she stirred outside the house was to go to his apartment and choose a new book. The staff had been primed to let her in whenever she arrived, offer her tea and otherwise leave her alone. Patrick would have been happy to bring her books, but Lennie thought it a good thing for her to leave her house occasionally.

Beyond the door of her home, the aftermath of the stock-market crash unfolded. First, brokers called in their loans from those who had invested on margin, and who, unable to repay them, went bankrupt. Businesses failed, employees lost their jobs, master and man both became unemployed. The banks, growing nervous, called in their loans, and as borrowers defaulted, the banks failed. Failing banks meant less credit, and otherwise viable businesses struggled for lack of working capital. And savers grew nervous in their turn and tried to withdraw their assets, causing bank runs and more failures.

Though widespread, the effects were not universally felt, and for many life went on as normal, though the boarded-up premises, the 'going out of business sale' notices, the unemployed queuing at the labour exchanges were chilly reminders. The country had entered a spiral of decline, which was slow as yet, but the financially wise could see that the process was bound to accelerate. The virtuous circle of supply and demand had swelled into a bubble and burst, and things could only get worse. Men everywhere were worried, and their wives watched them anxiously, quietly substituted meatloaf for prime rib and sponged their husbands' suits themselves instead of sending them to be cleaned.

Lennie, in between worrying about his own businesses – Philco had just put out a new model in a domed, cathedral-shaped walnut case, nicknamed the 'baby grand', and he had to get a new model out himself to challenge it – tackled the winding up of Ren's estate on Polly's behalf. He got rid of the house in Alexandria, which was only rented, and managed to offload the lease of the Long Island property at a reasonable rate while there were still rich people prepared to buy. Property prices, he guessed, would fall rapidly later in the year. He wished he could persuade Polly to sell the Fifth Avenue house while she had the chance. His father's apartment was plenty large enough to house her as well as Lennie, and Patrick was more than willing, but whereas she had shrugged indifferently over the other properties, she said quite firmly that she wanted to stay where she was until the baby was born. Lennie was unwilling to upset her by being more forceful.

Ren's will left everything to Polly, and as he had no other relatives, that side of things was simple, to Lennie's relief. And he was able to tell Polly that she had been left very well off. Polly received the news with a nod. 'Yes, Ren told me,' she said, without enthusiasm. 'He said he'd put it all into gold. And there's a house in London and another in Paris.'

'Yes, I came across the documents. Probably it would be better to sell those, too. There's no knowing how our troubles will affect world trade, and Europe already has a headache from paying for the war.'

Polly shrugged. 'Sell them if you like. I can't see I'd ever use them. If I went to England it would be to Yorkshire.'

'Do you think you might go?' he asked, his heart in his mouth.

'No,' she said. 'My life is here now. Maybe one day, just to show the child.' She sighed wearily. 'I don't want to think about the future. Don't ask me, Lennie.'

'I understand,' he said, hiding his gladness. She didn't want to go 'home'. As long as she stayed, he could make sure he was near her.

Patrick was busy with his record-breaking skyscraper, which they were calling the Empire State building – the Empire State being the nickname for New York State. Everyone involved was keeping a close eye on the Chrysler building, which was nearing completion. The Empire State building was set to be eighty floors high, but when the Chrysler passed eighty, they quickly added another five to keep ahead.

But that still only made it four feet taller than the Chrysler. 'It's not enough of a margin,' Patrick said, when he discussed it with Lennie. 'Mr Raskob is worried that Walter Chrysler will pull a stunt at the last minute, like hiding a rod inside the spire and then pushing it out on opening day, just to pip us by a couple of feet.'

At a planning meeting, they were all contemplating the scale model of the tower as it was now proposed – elegant, handsome and square. The Chrysler was to have a terraced crown of radiating arches in stainless steel, ribbed so as to create a sunburst pattern, and this terracing was what made possible the putative last-minute erecting of a spire.

'You couldn't put a spire onto a flat roof,' Patrick said. 'Unless we added some kind of tapering structure—'

That's it,' said Raskob. 'It needs a hat. Then we can go as high as we like.'

Patrick drew a piece of paper towards him and quickly sketched a stepped pedestal and then a slim tower with a rounded cap, which came to his mind from the salt pot that had sat on his breakfast table that morning.

'Not bad,' Raskob said. 'Something along those lines. But with a spike on top – I don't want to take any chances. How much height would that give us?'

'Twelve hundred feet, perhaps – twelve-fifty with a spike,' Patrick said. 'Chrysler can't go much over a thousand, whatever kind of spire they put up. We'd be well clear.'

Shreve, the chief architect, had taken over the drawing and was sketching rapidly, refining the shape, giving the tower a waisted look, adding another dome on top of the cap and erecting a spike on that. 'An idea has just come to me, sir. Rather than just a decoration, why don't we make the spike an airship mooring mast? Think of the impact that would have. Airships docking right in the heart of New York – travellers from all over the world would come to us. Other cities you have to dock way outside in some empty field and take transport in. It would give us the edge over Washington, Boston, Chicago . . .'

'Elevators inside the tower,' Patrick said, seeing it instantly. 'A special reception area on the observation deck.'

'Rich people with money to spend,' said one of the others. 'Restaurants, shops.'

'Do it,' said Raskob. 'I like that thinking.'

At home, to Lennie, Patrick said, 'It's going to be a fine building, and New York is going to be proud of it.' He hesitated.

'What is it, Dad?'

'I just have one worry. By the time we complete it, next year, will there be enough demand left for new offices?'

CHAPTER TWENTY-FIVE

Neither Emma nor Kit found it as difficult or as embarrassing as they had expected. Emma wisely did not press him, or talk about it; in the dark, in bed – which they had often shared in mere affection – and with a common purpose, Kit found he was able to do what was necessary. He surprised himself the first time, but he had not been particularly thinking about it, which was perhaps the best way. He had been holding Emma, thinking how sweet and warm she was and how much he loved her, and suddenly it happened.

They didn't talk about it afterwards, which was a relief to him. Buoyed with success, he found he got into the habit, and by the end of November they were hopeful of success. By the middle of December Emma was fairly sure, and they went down to Walcote in a state of muted excitement to celebrate Christmas with a multitude of parties. In January Emma was sure, and consulted a doctor, who confirmed the happy diagnosis and said she might expect to see the child in July. Kit was so happy with the news that she was touched, and put aside any notion that he welcomed it only for proving to the world that he was a normal husband. He would make a wonderful father, she thought, and hoped that the success of their first attempt would make it possible to provide the firstborn with a sibling.

Kit, meanwhile, was galvanised into action, first setting up the nursery at Walcote, in a frenzy of remodelling, plumbing, wiring and decoration, to create a suite that was modern, hygienic and yet aesthetically pleasing. 'Never too early to introduce a child to beauty,' he decreed. Emma was pleased to note that the night-nursery was large enough for more than one child. There were bedrooms for nanny and nursery-maids, two bathrooms, and a day nursery of splendid size with lovely big windows, which was to be equipped with such variety of books and toys, no child would ever want to leave it.

The Manchester Square nurseries also needed refurbishing, for Oliver and Verena had done very little to them, and they were much as they had been when Violet was a child. Kit insisted Emma was not to exert herself. 'I will do everything,' he said.

Emma objected. 'Did you really think I would let you undertake it alone? No, my friend, we will do it all together.'

'But, Emma, your condition!'

'I'm not made of glass. I'm a modern young woman. We make nothing of such things any more.'

Kit forbore to point out she was over thirty and that the doctor had said she must not overtax herself at her age. 'All right,' he said, 'you can design and choose colours. But you must let me handle the contractors and all that sort of thing. Doesn't that sound agreeable?'

'It sounds patronising.'

He managed to look hurt. 'Now look here, you're doing all the work about this child we're having – how do you think that makes me feel?'

'Oh, you've done your part.'

'Exactly. As far as I can see, I'm not wanted again until it's weaned and walking. So you must let me do the house. That's only fair.'

'If you put it like that,' she said, laughing. 'But I promise I'll let you hold it as much as you like when it's here.'

⋆ ⋆ ⋆

Charlotte's coming-out ball was held at the end of April, just after Easter. It had been a hard time for Violet, trying to conceal the true state of things from society, friends, family and her own household. She was terrified all the time that someone would find out, and became so silent in company for fear of eliciting the wrong question that company concluded she was still mourning the Prince of Wales. Earlier that year, Lady Furness had accompanied him on a safari to East Africa – with her husband discreetly in the background – and since their return in April she had been seen everywhere with him, and had been invited every weekend to stay at Fort Belvedere.

Violet was worried about Holkam, who seemed very unwell, and was increasingly irascible if she asked any questions. He had ceased to accompany her to social events, and she was glad to find it was quite often Avis Fellowes who was invited for her. He was always kind and conversable, and never curious about the wrong things. Indeed, he avoided the painful spots so consistently that, although she hadn't much imagination, it did cross her mind to wonder if he knew the truth. But he had such a nice knack of introducing topics she could find interesting, and then doing most of the talking himself, that she ceased to care whether he knew or not. She felt she could trust him with the secret.

She invited him to Charlotte's ball, not because she thought he might offer for her daughter but because a ball with too many girls and not enough men was deathly. Despite what was hanging over her, she had her pride: she did not want to preside over an evening people would rather forget. Holkam had done something about the finances – she did not want to know what – to keep them going this far, and told her not to stint anything. 'We're in so much trouble now it can't matter what you spend,' he said. 'It's our only chance of getting Charlotte off.'

It was for that reason she held the ball so unfashionably early. There was an adage – either the first ball of the season or the last – but anything before May was too early. However, an invitation from Lady Holkam was still a prize, and those who had not meant to come up until May made the move after Easter rather than turn it down. Nobody refused, for all the mamas wanted to see how the only daughter of the beautiful Lady Holkam had turned out, especially as there was a rumour she was not particularly pretty. The young men on the whole didn't care how soon the Season started, since the hunting was virtually over anyway, and put their efforts into telephoning around to see who they could dine with beforehand.

Violet had taken great care with Charlotte's gown, and was glad that the new styles were more feminine, fitting at the waist and flaring out from the knee to the hem. Charlotte was not a beauty, but she had a nice figure with a neat waist. Violet decided to go for something a little unusual, to give her the edge over prettier girls, and, in consultation with her dressmaker, chose a fitted peach lace overdress with puffed sleeves and a scalloped collar. It was slit open at the front from the waist down to reveal a paler peach silk underdress. The underdress had a broad band of aquamarine beading at the waist and a narrow one at the hem to give it weight and movement, and there was a large peach silk rose at the back. Coupled with a simple pearl necklace and pearl earrings, it made Charlotte look elegantly grown-up, yet still innocent and unspoilt.

Watching her daughter talking to the arrivals before the dancing started, Violet felt the trip to New York had been worth while. She was a little shy, which was pretty and natural, but not at all awkward, and she spoke to girls and men and the older people with equal ease. Tonight, Violet thought, she really looked pretty, with the colour in her cheeks and the sparkle in her eyes, and her hair freshly cut and waved by an expert. It was hard to think of the cloud that hung over her unknowing head.

Holkam, standing beside her to receive, managed to look every inch the earl, and surprisingly much like his old self, though he perhaps held himself a little cautiously. He had always looked good in evening clothes, and he was smiling and affable tonight, exerting the charm she had first been seduced by, and which she hadn't seen in a long while. Robert and Richard were both there, looking extremely handsome in evening black and white, doing their duty but privately eyeing the girls to choose their partners for later.

The dancing started, and Charlotte was led out by a young scion of a noble house, and everyone smiled and said they made a lovely couple, though Violet knew his inheritance had all gone, so he would not do for Charlotte.

Avis Fellowes appeared at her side and said, 'I suppose it won't do to ask you to dance?'

'At my own daughter's come-out? I don't wish to make myself ridiculous. But if you will take one of those girls left without a partner . . .'

'If it pleases you, I will,' he said, 'though I'd far rather stay and talk to you. But I know my duty. By the way, Charlotte looks lovely this evening. You can be very proud.'

Violet was far happier with that than she would have been with a compliment to herself; but as Avis walked off to rescue a girl, the thought came to her that perhaps he had known that, and the idea gave her pleasure.

The Holkam ball was such a good one that people stopped thinking it had been too early, and instead told each other how clever Violet Holkam had been to grab the first ball of the season. It launched the usual rush of lunches, teas, dinners and dances, and Violet carefully scrutinised and compared the invitations that flooded in so as to give Charlotte as much exposure as possible to the best candidates. The programme involved meticulous timing to fit as many events into one day as possible, and Violet regretted the loss of her chauffeur even more than the motor-car. She could not have done it with taxis, and Holkam understood that sufficiently to authorise the hiring of a motor-car with driver.

The first offer came within a week, but as it was from the penniless scion, Violet refused without even telling Charlotte. She was not aiming so high. She wanted a nice young man of decent family with enough money to take Charlotte without a dowry. She had quietly sold as much of her jewellery as she could without attracting attention, a pretty little Watteau Holkam had bought her for a birthday long ago, and all her winter furs, and kept the money in cash in a box in her dressing-table. It amounted to some thousands and would provide Charlotte with at least the semblance of a dowry – enough for a match without a title, she hoped, if the boy cared for her. It was a matter of holding on, and of luck – lots of that.

Teddy's winter bronchitis had left him with a troublesome cough, which sometimes kept him awake. He often slept in his dressing-room, so as not to disturb Amy. She could have told him it didn't matter – she could hear him through the closed door, coughing and coughing in the middle of the night – but she knew it comforted him to think she was getting her sleep.

Dr Hasty recommended he give up cigarettes. Teddy was unconvinced, saying it was well known that smoking strengthened the lungs, but he compromised, gave up the gaspers and went over solely to cigars. His cough did improve, and he put it down to his own wisdom, and told Hasty so.

Amy thought it was more likely the advent of spring and warmer, drier weather that had done the trick. She had noticed that he got breathless going up the stairs, and he took a long time reading the newspapers and sometimes nodded off over them. *The Times* had started printing a new kind of puzzle, called a crossword, which he enjoyed trying to solve, though he was often reduced to throwing the paper across the room in frustration. He was nearly eighty, and though he said stoutly that his family was long-lived, and eighty was nothing, it was not surprising that he was slowing down.

Amy was planning a special birthday party for his eightieth in August. It was supposed to be a surprise, but he knew all about it, thanks to Sawry, who didn't think it right for any secrets to be kept from the master.

The news of Polly's pregnancy brought great joy. Lennie wrote – Polly, he said, was still too upset to put pen to paper. Teddy believed the child must bring her comfort: when it was born, she would come out of her mourning and start a new life. It would be his first grandchild, a matter for celebration since he had lots of great-nephews and -nieces but nothing in his own line. He longed to see her, and in the first excitement of the news spoke about taking a trip over to New York; but when he thought about it more, the prospect became daunting. However luxurious the ship, it would not be like his own room and his own bed, with his things around him, and servants he knew and trusted. And if he went, he would have to be away six or eight weeks – it was not worth going for less – and the idea of being from home for so long made him nervous.

Instead, he pinned his hopes on Polly's being enough recovered by August to come over for his birthday, and he hoped Amy would think of it and ask her. In case she didn't, he mentioned it to Sawry, knowing that he would tell Mrs Stark and that she would find a tactful way of hinting to Amy.

Teddy's textile business so far was holding up, for most of his production was on contract for settled customers, like Cunard and the War Office. What would happen when those contracts came to an end he didn't know. There was a fall-off of trade in his stores, and credit was shrinking, which would make everything more difficult. And the fall in demand was bound to affect agriculture in the long run. Bertie and Jessie had already had orders for horses cancelled.

But York was at the centre of a prosperous part of the country, and as yet there was not much unemployment. When it came, he thought, it was likely to hit the heavy industries first – coal, steel and heavy manufacturing – because export prices were continuing to fall, and if America stopped buying they would be losing their biggest customer.

It was all very tiresome to have to worry about these things at this time of his life. He distracted himself with thoughts of Polly and her baby and the chance of seeing her again; and James's return from Oxford at the end of June. They would have parties all summer, he thought, to keep James amused. Amy would like that – he must get her to start making lists and issuing invitations. Morland Place should be full of activity and pleasure this summer, even if Polly didn't come.

Charlotte's Season seemed to be going well. She was proving a popular débutante, and had attracted the interest of several young men. Violet had her eye on one in particular, Rupert Amesbury, a nice boy with good manners and a decent blood-line, who had a promising career in the Diplomatic Corps, which ought to be enough to support a wife. He obviously liked Charlotte a great deal, always asked her to dance, and tried to sit next to her during supper and at other social occasions. Charlotte, for her part, seemed to look favourably on him. Violet spoke to him on several occasions and found him intelligent, with a vein of humour and a pleasing lack of conceit – he seemed to think he had no chance with Charlotte because she was an earl's daughter. Violet was not a person of cunning, but even she could see

573

that this circumstance would play in her favour. She needed someone who would want Charlotte for herself and be grateful.

More than that, she needed him to make an offer before the Season ended, before the truth about Holkam's situation became known. Violet engineered things so that they met as often as possible and encouraged him as much as she dared without frightening the poor thing off. She quizzed Charlotte as to her feelings, and whether Amesbury had said anything that hinted at thoughts of matrimony. Charlotte was rather embarrassed by these questions. She liked him very much, but she had no idea that there was any hurry about it.

The end came with devastating suddenness. Holkam was like a juggler, adding one plate and then another to his performance. The essence of success was that the plates must stay in the air, because there was not room in the hands to hold them all, so there could be no possibility of catching them. But one day in June one of the banks from whom he had borrowed grew nervous and asked for its money back. Then, one after another, the plates all came crashing down.

'Isn't there any possibility of borrowing some more somewhere?' Violet asked, her hands twisting together in anxiety. 'If we could only keep going a little longer – Charlotte's young man hasn't come to the point yet. Just a few more weeks, Holkam.'

'Not even a few more minutes,' he said heavily. 'It's over, Violet. We're finished. It's all coming out now. In a day or two everyone will know. As it is, I couldn't borrow sixpence from any financial house in the land. They all want their money back, and I haven't got it.'

'So – what, then?' she asked, feeling very cold and rather shaky. Holkam looked really ill, old and tired, ten years more than his age. It was the deadness of his eyes that killed her last hope.

'Everything will be sold to go towards the debts. This

house and Brancaster, and all their contents – furniture, pictures, silver, everything. The land at Holkam – not that it will fetch much. Shawes.'

'Shawes?' Violet queried. Her mother had left it to her personally.

'Mortgaged,' he said shortly. 'Don't you remember signing the papers?'

'I – I don't know. I don't really worry when you ask me to sign things.'

'Everything will be sold, and it won't be enough. The debts are huge.'

'What will happen to us?' She couldn't grasp the concept of having nothing. What did that *mean*?

'I'll be lucky if I don't end up in gaol,' he said, and she couldn't tell if it was a ghastly joke or not. 'You and Henry and Charlotte will have to find a place to stay – God knows how. The boys will have to find jobs. I don't know how you'll live. I don't know what's going to happen.' He rubbed at his face with his hands. 'I wish you would leave me alone for a while. I can't bear to talk any more now.'

The boys' terms were virtually over anyway, and summoned home by telegram they arrived the next day, afraid someone was ill, to be faced with the news. Robert was inclined to be indignant and angry – 'My friends will hear about it! I'll be disgraced! And a *job*? I'm Lord Brancaster – I can't take a *job*.'

Richard, who was closer to his mother, saw her wretchedness, and said, 'Shut up, Bobbie. We'll manage all right – won't we, Mater? I don't mind getting a job. It will be jolly. I didn't care much for Oxford anyway – didn't see the point of it. I've always fancied selling motor-cars. Driving about demonstrating 'em – the freedom of the road and so on. Don't look so blue, Mama. We'll manage – eh, Bobbie?'

'Oh – er – yes. Right-ho it is!'

'You're the brainy one, and you're always scribbling. You

could get a job on a newspaper or in a publishing house, I'm sure of it.'

Violet felt a small surge of hope. 'Yes, what about Cousin Helen's sister, Molly? She married a publisher. I'm sure she could help you find something.'

'There you are,' Richard said. 'Couldn't be righter. You mustn't worry about us, Mama. We'll be fine.'

Henry, when he got home from school later that day, was similarly robust. 'Won't I be going to school at all? Whizzo! I could be a butcher's boy. They have tremendous fun, tearing about in a pony and trap. There's one who dashes through Eton every morning – the fellows make bets on how fast he can get from one end of the street to the other.'

'Of course you'll go to school,' Violet said hastily. 'It won't be Eton, that's all – just . . . just an ordinary school.'

'But what about Charley?' he asked, putting his finger on the sore point with a thirteen-year-old's devastating accuracy.

Charlotte, looking pale and on the brink of tears, rallied herself. 'I'll stay with you, Mother, and help about the house. I expect we'll have to let some of the servants go.'

Violet hadn't the heart to tell her that not only would they have to let all the servants go but that there would be no house, either.

It was a horrible time: bills and bailiffs, assessors and attorneys, the servants in tears, the children miserable, Fifi, sensing the atmosphere, wanting to be picked up all the time. Everyone and everything was out of place, and the sound of strange voices and over-heavy boots made the house feel already like someone else's. After a couple of days Holkam said to Violet, 'There's no need for you to subject yourself to this. Why don't you ask your brother if you and the children can stay there for a while?'

'I thought you didn't want me to speak to him about it,' she said.

He gave a grimace. 'My dear, we are long past that point. If he doesn't know it already I should be surprised.'

'But what about – our things?'

'You can take your clothes and personal items, like hairbrushes and pins and so on. Go and see Oliver. If he says you can stay, you can pack everything this afternoon and be there tonight. It will be miserable here for you.'

'And you?' she asked timidly.

'I shall be miserable anyway,' he said. 'I have to stay.' He couldn't imagine Oliver would be happy to have him. He'd be glad to be alone, without the reproach of the presence of his wife and children, whom he had so utterly failed. 'Go to Oliver, my dear. There's nothing for you to do here.'

It turned out that Oliver did know, and had only hesitated as long as he had out of tact, not knowing the full extent of the breakdown and not wanting to tread on Holkam's toes. But Violet's story made him blanch. 'Everything? Are you sure he said everything?'

Violet nodded unhappily. 'Nothing left but our clothes, he said.'

'Oh, Vi!' He took her hands and chafed them. He felt he should have known, should have done something. But what? 'I was going to come and see you tomorrow anyway,' he said. 'Perhaps a small loan . . .'

'It's gone too far for that,' Violet said dolefully. 'What I wanted to ask was, could the children and I come to stay for a while, until it's all finished? It's so horrid there, with little men going around writing down all the furniture.'

'Of course. There's plenty of room. You and Charlotte can have Mother's old suite, and the boys can have bachelor rooms. But what about Holkam?'

'He has to stay,' she said, and tried not to notice her brother's relief.

'Where will you live when it's all over?' he asked. 'I suppose the house will have to go?'

'All of them,' she said. 'Shawes too.'

'But that's yours,' he objected. Since the Married Women's Property Act, a wife's possessions could not be sequestrated for a husband's debts.

'We took out a mortgage on it,' she said. 'We can't pay it back.' And then she cried. She had been holding it in for a long time, and he took her in his arms and let her cry, patting her back vaguely as he thought. Fifi whined and clawed at his leg. His mind darted back and forth. There must be something . . . The prince? No, it would never do to involve him, even if he were willing, which was doubtful. How could Holkam be such a fool? But many people had invested in the American bull run. And Violet had said they were deep in debt even before that. The classic case of a gambler gambling on to try to recoup his position.

Holkam would have to go abroad when it was all wound up. He couldn't very well get a position here. The King would not countenance a bankrupt at Court, and the government would not trust him even with a sinecure. His knowledge and experience might find him a post in France – he must have contacts there. Would he take Violet with him? Poor little Charlotte, what an end to her come-out! Holkam must try to find billets for the older boys before he left. And Henry – what would become of him?

Violet had stopped crying, and freed herself to wipe her eyes. He said, 'Well, you must come here for as long as you need. And after that – we'll see. Don't be afraid, little sister – I won't let you starve.'

'You're very good to me,' she said. But she thought of a life of dependency for her and Charlotte, helping round the house in return for their keep. It was not what she had imagined that day so long ago when she walked down the aisle in Westminster Abbey.

And Oliver was thinking, *Mother was right – she always felt there was something unsatisfactory about Holkam.*

Violet's maid, Sanders, wept dreadfully when she was told she had to go. She had been with Violet a very long time. 'Can't I stay with you, my lady? Who will take care of your things?'

'I hardly have any things now,' Violet said gently. 'Not worth a maid's time. And I can't pay your wages.' It took her a great deal to admit this to her lady's maid, and Sanders knew it. It made her cry all the more. She was holding Fifi, who, at a loss, did her best by licking the tears as they overflowed.

'I'll work for nothing, my lady – just my keep.'

'I shall never be in a position to pay you,' Violet explained. 'I shan't be keeping a maid any more. I'm so sorry, Sanders, I wish it were otherwise. I – I shall miss you.'

It was an unheard-of admission, and proof of how shaken Violet was. Sanders pulled herself together. 'I understand, my lady.'

'I will give you a good reference. I'm sure you'll find a position.'

'Yes, my lady. Thank you, my lady. But it won't be the same. I'll take Fifi outside, now, for her run, my lady.'

But at the door she couldn't help turning, and seeing Violet just standing there, as if she didn't know what to do next, she said, 'It's the times, my lady. Nothing's been right since the war. I just don't know what's going to become of us all.'

Violet only nodded, dismissing her. But she stood a long time after Sanders had gone, thinking of the war and everything that had happened since. It was like a twisting path through a wood: you couldn't see where you had come from, or where you were going. You just had to keep going on.

*   *   *

Helen and Jack heard the shocking news of Holkam's break-down, and were glad to learn that Violet and the children had taken sanctuary with Oliver. Jack wrote a letter of sympathy to Violet – he had seen very little of her in recent years, but they were cousins and had played together as children. 'Everything's changing,' he said to Helen, with a sigh. 'There's Mother gone, and Cousin Venetia, Polly in America and never coming back as far as we know, and now Violet in trouble. The world seems to be falling apart. Thank heaven Jessie's all right, at least.'

'Yes, she sailed into a safe haven,' Helen said. 'And Molly, too. And there's Emma's happy news. And what about Jack Compton? He's all right, isn't he?'

Jack smiled apologetically. 'Of course – I'd forgotten him. Married to the love of his life, with a job he enjoys and three fine children.'

'I notice the children came after the job.'

'I've been a pilot longer than a father.'

'Very witty. And thank you for saying "three fine children" when one of them is a little less than fine at the moment.'

Basil had gone back to school with an angelic expression that filled Helen with dread, and had spent his second term behaving worse than he had in his first. He let loose a white rat, bought from a local boy, in chapel, and several frogs in the dormitory. He climbed the clock tower and got stuck, requiring the services of the fire brigade with their long ladder to get him down. He was caught with monotonous regularity smoking in the latrines. In cricket he seemed to have an uncanny knack of hitting the ball through windows and, when on the further square, into the cold-frame or the greenhouse in the headmaster's garden.

His one redeeming feature was that he came in first week after week from the cross-country run; but then a concerned citizen reported that as soon as he was out of sight of the school, he cut across a field to the village and sat in the café there, eating buns, until the first runner hove into view at the far end of the high street, when he rejoined the race at the front with a very long lead.

'Don't you like it there? Is that what this is all about?' Helen asked him, when he arrived home with a trunk full of dirty clothes and a very terse letter from the headmaster.

'I love it, Mum,' he said, with the angelic look. 'I can't wait to go back next term. I've thought of lots of really interesting things I can do.'

'What sort of things?' she asked suspiciously.

'Oh, just . . . things,' he said dreamily, gazing into space.

But his father had read the letter, and said later to Helen, 'The little blighter's been sacked. The headmaster thinks he's a bad influence on the other boys, and suggests he might be happier somewhere else.'

'For goodness' sake, don't tell Basil he's been sacked. If I know him he'll think it a great lark.'

'Good Lord, no,' Jack said. 'But what got into the young devil? What was he up to?'

'He always was a devil,' Helen said. 'You wouldn't know, being out at work all the time, but I've always kept my eye on him and kept him from his worst excesses.'

'Worst excesses? You make him sound like a criminal, not a child.'

'Oh, there's no harm in him. He's just high-spirited, and plainly they let him get out of hand.'

'Well, we have the problem now of finding him another place. Fortunately, the school isn't going to put it on record he was sacked, as long as we withdraw him. So we can just say he wasn't happy there.'

'What about our second choice from last time?' Helen said. 'That place on the Sussex Downs.'

'By Jove, you're right. That would be just the thing. All that bracing sea air, cold baths, lots of sports. Rugger season coming up – take the fizz out of him, wear him out, and he'll be good as gold.'

Helen looked slightly doubtful, given Basil's lack of interest in sport until now, but they had rejected the school in the first place for being too tough. Now it looked as though a little more toughness would be a good thing. One could only hope. 'Well, bags you be the one to tell him,' she said.

'We have to get him in, first,' Jack reminded her.

Apart from Basil, the foremost thing in his life was the completion of the tests and adjustments to the R100, and the approach of her maiden flight. During the last trial flight her tail fairing had started to come away under the aero-dynamic pressure, and the tail had had to be redesigned, shortening it by fifteen feet and giving it a more rounded shape. But the job was done now, and she was ready for her long-distance trial to Canada in July.

Jack revealed to Helen that he had been offered a seat on the flight. 'But it's not a good time for me. I've a lot on at work. Besides, I've rather set my heart on the other flight, on the R101. India will be much more interesting than Toronto. I think I shall say no thank you, but yes please to R101 in October.'

Helen looked relieved. 'I wish you would. With the children all home from school – and Nanny's going to her sister for two weeks in July – I'd really like to have you coming home every day.'

'Right you are. And there's the new school to sort out,' Jack remembered. 'R100 will have to fly without me.'

James came home from Oxford, preceded by his trunks and the horses. Teddy gladly sent not just a cart for the luggage but a groom to help Cobbey with the horses, and it was as well he had: James had gone back to Oxford after Easter with two road horses, and had come back with three.

'I went to a horse sale in Woodstock with some of the

fellows a couple of days ago, just for a lark, and you never saw such topping animals. It was some fellow's breakdown sale, and he must have had a ripping stables, Dad. And when I saw this one, I couldn't resist.' He glanced anxiously sideways at his father. The old man seemed to be taking it pretty well so far, but you never knew. 'Isn't he a beauty? And he was a bargain price. I've called him Firefly.'

Teddy walked round the horse, being held by Eddoes. It was a red chestnut of a particularly rich shade, with a blond streak in its tail, only about fifteen hands. Very handsome, and it had a fine head but was light in the bone, too light, he would have thought, for James; and despite the long journey, it was fidgeting about, tossing its head, and when Teddy put his hand on its rump it lifted a hind foot warningly.

But he loved his son, and said neutrally, 'What's he like to ride?'

James now fidgeted in his turn. 'Well, that's the thing, really, you see, Pater. When I got him home, and tried riding him, he was all over the place. Mr Cosgrove came out and watched me struggling. He called me over and gave the horse a thorough look over, and said . . . well, he said he's only a two-year-old and probably unbroken.'

'I was just about to say, sir,' said Eddoes, 'that he looks like a youngster to me.'

'Didn't you think to look at his teeth?'

James was embarrassed. 'I know I should have, but it was an auction, and everything was happening so quickly, and I didn't want to lose him. So I just bid. You see what a beauty he is. And he was such a bargain . . .'

Teddy said, 'Well, you seem to have fallen on your feet, though you don't deserve to. I can't see anything wrong with him. If you break him carefully and school him on, you'll probably have a very nice horse in a few years. But I hope it will be a lesson to you never, ever, to buy a pig in a poke, especially when it comes to horses.'

James was beaming in relief. 'I shan't, I promise. I've had my scare. When he kept walking backwards and shaking his head . . .'

'Lucky he didn't throw you off. He must have a good temperament.'

'Oh, he's gentle as a lamb. Ask Cobbey.' Cobbey, standing well back as if dissociating himself from the whole business, only rolled his eyes at Eddoes.

And then Teddy asked the question James had hoped he'd avoided. 'Where did you get the money to buy him?'

James felt himself blushing, to his own annoyance. 'He was a frightful bargain.' His father looked at him steadily. 'Well, the fact is, Dad, that I had to leave one or two bills unpaid in the town.' He was prepared for his father to be angry, to shout at him, but what he wasn't prepared for was the way he seemed to go pale, and turned away, gasping for breath. 'Dad! Dad! Are you all right? I'm sorry, really I am. I'll never do such a thing again. But don't be ill. Please don't. The traders don't mind – really they don't. They're used to giving credit. I'll pay them first thing out of my next allowance.'

Eddoes shoved the horse at Cobbey and helped his master a few steps to sit on the mounting block, warning James off with a stern look. Teddy hung his head, chest heaving, for a few minutes, until his breathing slowed and his colour started to come back. Cobbey led Firefly away into the stables, while Eddoes went to the kitchen door and came back with a glass of water. When he had drunk it, Teddy was recovered enough to fumble out his case and light one of his small cigars.

James watched it all, humbled and contrite. 'I'm sorry, Dad,' he said again. 'Don't be angry.'

'I'm all right,' Teddy said. 'Shortness of breath. Comes over me now and then.' He stood up, and placed a hand on James's shoulder, noticing with a pang that the boy was taller than him now. His fair, handsome face and thick toffee-coloured hair, sun-streaked, made him a nice-looking lad. He had a look of his mother about him. He was twenty now – not really a boy any more. Teddy supposed he was lucky it was horses he was making a fool of himself over, rather than women. All the same . . . 'These are hard times, my boy. The stock market's down, exports are down, prices are down. We can't afford to throw money away.'

James had never heard his father talk about money before. There had never been any question that he could have anything he wanted – never any suggestion of 'not affording' things. 'Is it really bad, Dad?' he asked, in a small voice.

Teddy hated to see his fine lad looking chastened, even though that was what he had set out to do. 'No, no, don't you worry. We're not in the poorhouse yet. But I don't like to see you leaving debts behind you. It ain't gentlemanly. Come to the business-room before tea and tell me everything you owe and I'll make out cheques for you to send. Tradesmen shouldn't be kept waiting – the money means more to them than to us.'

The session in the business-room was galling for James, and he felt like a cad. But at teatime his former nursery companions were there, and delighted to see him. Jessie and Bertie brought their children, and they climbed all over James and made a fuss of him, so he soon got over his chagrin and felt like the returning hero, especially as he had thought to bring small gifts for the younger ones.

Jessie and Bertie were to dine, while the children had the excitement of staying the night with their cousins. When the tea had been cleared away, James enjoyed a real, grown-up conversation with Bertie on the subject of farming, with a detailed discussion of Bertie's prize dairy Shorthorns and his plans for improving the land; and then he talked to Jessie about horse-breeding. The consequence was that he was not only rehabilitated by dinnertime, but positively primed, and when Amy mentioned something about 'next term at Oxford' it was the equivalent of a match to the fuse, and he went off.

'I don't want to go back. Dad, really, please don't make me go. It's such a waste of time. I'm not a scholar, I never was – and Aunt Hen used to tell me you weren't, either, when you were my age, so you must understand. What's the point of my spending three years grinding away at a lot of nonsense when I could be here at home helping you, and learning about the estate?' He drew breath and thought of another argument, which the exchange in the stableyard brought to mind. 'And it's a waste of money, too. It must cost a lot to keep me at the House, when I don't want to be there and it's not doing me any good.'

Teddy frowned, not liking the mention of money at the table. 'When I can't afford to keep you at Oxford, I'll tell you,' he said shortly. Amy looked at him anxiously. The terse voice usually meant a fit of coughing or breathlessness was coming. It always attacked him when he got tense or annoyed.

'But what's the *point* of it?' James wailed.

'The *point*,' Teddy snapped, 'is to make you a gentleman, which is plainly necessary or you wouldn't have brought up this subject at the dinner table.' He gave a preliminary cough, suppressed and low in his throat, and Amy tensed, making herself not watch him. He coughed two or three times, and then took a draught of wine, which seemed to do the trick.

Jessie stepped into the breach with what she hoped was a diversion to a happier subject. 'I wonder when we'll hear about Polly's baby,' she said. 'It must be due to appear any time now. And then there's Emma's, due next month. I'm so happy for her – she deserves some good luck at last. And Helen writes that she thinks Molly might be going to have another. Babies are always the best and happiest of news, aren't they?'

It was a sentiment worthy of her mother, and looking at

her across the table, Teddy thought that she looked a little like Henrietta just then. She'd had her share of bad luck, too, but all was well now. His face softened into a smile, and without his knowing it, all the other people round the table relaxed in relief.

CHAPTER TWENTY-SIX

The loveliness of a New York May passed into the steady heat of June, and the weekend exoduses to Long Island began. Polly suffered from the heat, but she was uncomfortably big, and moving around defeated her, let alone travelling for hours by motor or train just to be by the sea. She stayed put.

Lennie tried to persuade her to go into a nursing-home for the last weeks and give birth there. 'We'll find a nice one, out of town. Just the one journey, and I'll do everything I can to make it comfortable. Then you can be away from the heat and noise, in the fresh green of the countryside, or overlooking the ocean, with those fresh ocean breezes.'

Polly turned her face away. The sea shore now belonged for ever to Erich; and the fresh green, if it wasn't the fresh green of England, Yorkshire, home, meant nothing to her. She wanted just to be left alone. Lennie had moved back into his father's apartment at her request after Christmas, and though she saw him every day, she spent much of her time on her own. She was like a dog who had made her nest in a dark cupboard and retired there to have her whelps. She was safe here, and she wasn't coming out until it was over.

Lennie, thwarted of his plan, did the obvious thing, and appealed to Lizzie, and Lizzie, understanding instantly, abandoned her husband, daughter and full social life and took the train east. She arrived on Polly's doorstep with a small suitcase. Plummer recognised the cavalry coming over the hill when she saw it, and let her in with a 'thank Heavens' eye-roll. Polly accepted Lizzie without a word and, despite herself, with inward relief. Lizzie was calm and quiet and unfussy; she didn't talk much, though when she did it was worth listening to. Best of all, she didn't look at Polly with a mixture of adoration and panic as Lennie did.

Lizzie discovered that no preparations had been made for the baby's arrival, and quietly remedied the situation. She went out shopping, and soon afterwards things started to arrive – two dozen diapers, six belly bands, a cot and mattress, a tiny bath on folding legs, white cotton baby shirts. The things disappeared into one of the spare bedrooms. Polly was indifferent at first, but when Lizzie set to work on the room, had a man in to paper it afresh and put down hygienic linoleum on the floor instead of carpet, bought pretty new curtains for the window and a child-sized chest of drawers, she grew interested in spite of herself. Having the room prepared made the baby suddenly seem real. Soon he or she would be here. Polly took to spending time in the 'nursery', looking into the drawers, folding and refolding things, sitting on the window-seat and staring at the cot, empty now but soon to be filled, wondering what the baby would be like.

She had been lonely, she realised now – in spite of poor Lennie's efforts – and afraid. She had shut herself off from the idea of the birth because it terrified her. Now Lizzie was here, and was lifting the burden off her shoulders, so she didn't need to be afraid any more. Lizzie would take care of things, the way Aunt Hen always had. And she made it seem all right to be a mother, not a terrifying responsibility. 'Don't worry,' Lizzie said calmly. 'You'll be fine when the time comes. It's what we do – what we've always done.'

And Polly thought, She's right. Women have been becoming mothers for thousands of years. It can't be so very hard.

Lizzie booked the midwife and the month-nurse and a nursemaid for the baby, and then just settled in to wait. She had forgotten, in the short time she had been away, how impossible New York was under the glaring light of summer, and missed California, the green hills and the nearness of the sea. She knitted and read, wrote copious letters home, chatted when Polly seemed to want it, and kept Lennie from fretting her when he visited.

The baby came on the last day of June. Polly woke in the early hours with the first pains, and whimpered quietly, not wanting to wake anyone so early; but Lizzie had a mother's ear and heard her anyway. It turned out another hot day, and for hours Lizzie sat by Polly, fanning her as the sweat ran down her struggling body. It was a hard labour, but straightforward, and as the ravines of Manhattan threw their sharp shadows over the going-home traffic, a long, red, wailing baby came sliding into the world.

'It's a boy,' said the midwife.

'He looks just like his father,' Lizzie said.

When he was finally placed in her arms, wrapped up in clean cotton, like a bundle from the laundry, Polly looked at the squashed red face under the astonishing thatch of black hair, and wondered how anyone could say he looked like anything but just another baby. But he wasn't just another baby – he was hers, and she felt her heart lurch almost painfully, as if it were being wrenched open. She had not known she could feel anything so intense as she felt that first instant when the living thing that had been inside her was placed in her arms. She wanted to cry and laugh and put back her head and howl. She wanted to be utterly silent and do nothing but stare at him for ever and ever. *My baby.*

Appealed to by Helen on Violet's behalf, Molly consulted Vivian, and he managed to find Robert a position without too much trouble. He was a clever young man, well educated, despite not finishing his degree, and desperate: just the right qualifications for an assistant to an editor, a job that was undefined but flexible in scope, and very ill-paid.

Richard found a job all on his own. He was the one with the personality – devil-may-care, energetic and charming – which made Oliver look at the boy's parents and wonder where he got it from. He was rather like Oliver's own father in character, though not particularly in looks, and he wondered if such things could be passed down two generations. At all events, Richard went out one morning without saying where he was going, and came back in the afternoon having got himself a job with a motor-car showroom in Kensington, demonstrating and selling the most luxurious motor-cars. 'They seemed to think I'll be good at it,' he said, beaming, and Oliver felt that was probably true. He had even charmed a small salary out of the owner, though such jobs were usually on a commission-only basis.

Richard got Robert to one side, talked to him vigorously until he had worn him down, and when they came down they announced that, with all due gratitude to Oliver and Verena, they were going to find some diggings to live in on their own. Oliver had no objection, and Verena was glad – she had not liked the thought of Oliver's being dragged into supporting Lord Holkam's entire family for God-knew-how long – though Violet was anxious and unhappy, fearing it was the first step to losing them. Richard petted her and told her they would only be a couple of miles away at most and would see her very often.

He had known from the first moment they arrived at Chelmsford House that he could not stay there. Robert was more fearful, anxious about giving up the security, but he wanted to go, too, as long as Richard could assure him it would be all right. Chelmsford House was just another such as Fitzjames House, an ancient family seat full of gloom and antiques and the patina of dead ancestors on every surface.

It reminded him too much of home and what had happened, the poor old pater and so on, and he could not wait to get out from under its clammy grasp.

Out there, he had told Robert that evening, was a whole new world – a modern age, the jazz age, full of wonders and inventions, lights, noise and fun, machinery, cars and cock-tails, and doing what you liked, not what had been laid down five hundred years ago.

'But I'm Lord Brancaster,' Robert had said anxiously. 'I have a dignity to maintain.'

Richard had slapped him on the back with a broad grin. 'My dear old thing, there's not going to be much dignity left to the Brancaster name by the time all this is over. If I were you I'd drop it and be plain Robert Fitzjames Howard – or even just Bobbie Howard. Let go, old chap, and have some jolly old fun! Agreed?'

And Robert had said, after a pause, 'Agreed.'

'Good. Then let's totter down and tell the old folk, and see if Uncle Olly's mixing the cockers.'

Violet had been back to the house a few times, when requested by Holkam, to mark or remove things that belonged to her rather than the estate. Laidislaw's pictures, fortunately, were still packed up from the New York trip, which made them easy to have removed to safety into one of Oliver's attics. Otherwise, she did not go out much. The story had gone all over London by now, and she imagined how people must be talking about them. Laughing. Despising. She had sympathetic letters from one or two friends, but she did not trust them, wrote very short replies and made no effort to keep up the acquaintance. Eddie and Sarah kindly offered to have Henry to stay, and to take him with them when they went down to the country, and Violet accepted on his behalf. Though George and Edward were rather young for him, they were better company than none, and it would give him more freedom of movement, for there were still journalists hanging around Chelmsford House, and he soon got tired of the garden.

That left only herself and Charlotte to worry about. Charlotte was very low in spirits, having had her Season cut short and all her hopes dashed. She had also been fonder of her father than her elder brothers were, and worried about him. She had the same anxieties about the future as her mother, but they were worse for her, for her life was only just beginning, and if marriage was now an impossibility, as the penniless daughter of a disgraced father, what was left for her? She had had such hopes of a certain young man . . . She cried a lot in the privacy of her bed. She saw her mother's looks of concern in the morning when she was pale and red-eyed, but couldn't seem to help it. *Jane Eyre* and *Agnes Grey* had long been two of her favourite books, and she had the notion that poor girls from good families had no choice but to become governesses, and be badly treated.

It would not have comforted her much if she had known that her mother was worrying about her along very similar lines. Violet was glad, now, that the boys had gone. It was the first step to their being independent and having lives of their own. But what would happen to Henry in September, when it was time to go to school? There were free schools, where poor children went, but she was afraid he would be bullied by them. And after that, what?

As for her and Holkam, she couldn't begin to think. With no money at all, how could they live? She had a vague idea that people in their circumstances went abroad, though she didn't understand how that worked. Wherever you were, you needed *some* money to live on, didn't you? She thought a little guiltily of the money in the box in the dressing-table, and of Laddie's paintings. But she was determined to keep the former for Charlotte, and the latter was all there was left for Henry from his father – the money from the sales in America Holkam had lost. She would not sell them.

She was alone at home one day in July, sitting in the garden on a bench under the shade of a tree, sewing. She had always been good at sewing, though since she married she had not used the talent much, having always had a maid who could undertake small repairs. Now there was no Sanders, and no money. She sat mending stockings, with a blouse of Charlotte's to follow, where the sleeve had pulled away at the shoulder seam. She was hardly aware that for the moment she felt content. The birds were chirping and trilling in the trees, the gentle breeze was sending shadows pattering over the grass from the tree above her, and Fifi, having explored to her nose's content, had come back and flung herself flat out on her side in the grass to cool off. Violet stitched away, and thought, comfortably, of nothing.

The happy interlude was broken by the squeak of the garden-room door – it needed oiling – and the sound of approaching footsteps. One of the servants bringing tea, she supposed. She would welcome a cup – it was warm even in the shade. Someone loomed up beside her. She looked up, and jumped so hard she ran the needle into her finger.

'Oh!' she said, and quickly dropped the stocking so as not to get blood on it, thrusting her wounded finger into her mouth.

'I'm sorry,' said Avis Fellowes. 'I didn't mean to startle you. I hope you're not hurt?'

She removed the finger and looked at it doubtfully. Another ruby jewel was forming. Before she could do anything, his handkerchief appeared, and he quickly wrapped it around, and folded the ends into her palm.

'What are you doing here?' she managed to ask at last, which was to the point, though hardly elegant.

'I'm so sorry. There was only a young footman in the hall, and he told me to come straight out. I suppose I should have questioned whether he knew his job,' he added, with a faint, disarming smile, 'but I was rather afraid if I made him come and ask, you might refuse me. They tell me you never go anywhere now.'

Violet could not keep looking up at him – there was something about his face that was so comforting – and looked instead at her hugely swaddled finger. 'Won't you sit down?' she said shyly.

He lifted the sewing basket off the iron garden chair in front of her, put it on the grass, and sat down. Fifi came mincing and prancing up to be noticed, and he caressed her curly head automatically, his eyes on Violet. 'I hope you are well?' he said.

'Quite well,' she said, still not looking at him. Now he would sympathise, talk about the terrible news and so on, and she couldn't bear that.

'I hope you don't mind my calling,' he said. 'I met your brother in Harley Street and he said I should.'

So it was Oliver's doing. 'I'm glad to see you,' she said, and discovered it was true.

'It's very pleasant here,' he went on, looking around. 'Actually, I think it's cooler than in the country. I've just been in Derbyshire, and it's unbearably hot there.'

'You've been visiting your father?'

'Yes. He's rather unwell, and Reggie and Minnie are in Italy for the summer so it falls to me.'

'I hope – not very unwell?' Violet ventured.

'I'm afraid so. I don't think it will be *very* long – a matter of weeks.'

'Oh. I'm sorry,' Violet said. The door squeaked again as the delinquent footman appeared with the tea tray. He had only been at Chelmsford House a week and, judging by his chastened look, some more senior member of staff had shown him the error of his ways before sending him out with the tea. Avis jumped up and moved the wrought-iron table to a convenient spot between them, and the footman placed the tray down over-gently and made his escape.

'Shall I pour?' Violet said, for something to say into the silence he had left behind. She put out her hand, and the vastly swaddled digit appeared, hanging in the air between them like a dirigible. They caught each other's eye and laughed, and the ice was broken.

'Allow me,' he said, unwound the handkerchief, and held her hand a moment while he examined the finger. 'I think it's stopped,' he said.

'I'm sorry about your handkerchief. I'll have it laundered.'

'It doesn't matter in the least,' he said, stuffing it carelessly into his pocket. 'By the way,' he said, as he watched her pour, 'I heard some good news the other day, about your – cousin, is it? The one you were staying with in New York. Mrs Alexander?'

'Oh, yes, Polly – she is a sort of cousin.'

'It seems she had a baby – a boy, which must be a comfort after the loss of her husband. Mother and child both doing well.'

'I'm glad,' said Violet.

'And how are your children?'

'Very well,' she said automatically. To tell him about Robert and Richard getting 'jobs' was impossible. She offered him the plate of bread-and-butter instead.

'How is my friend Henry? A most ingenious boy. I enjoyed talking to him.

'He's away for the summer,' she said, pleased with his comment. 'Lord and Lady Vibart have taken him with their children, to the sea first, and then to Gloucestershire.'

'And Lady Charlotte?' he asked. 'She looked so pretty at her ball. This must be harder on her than anyone, I imagine.'

It was his first mention of the matter, and done so nicely and naturally that the barriers she had erected crumbled, and she found herself talking to him as she had done on the ship, as though she had known him all her life and had no secrets from him. She told him about her earlier hopes for Charlotte, and how she had modified them by the time she brought her out, and nice Rupert Amesbury, and how every hope was now dashed. 'I don't know what's to become of her if she doesn't marry,' she concluded miserably. 'I can't bear to think that she'll just moulder away at home with me and become an old maid. I put a little money aside for her, for a dowry – it isn't much, just a few thousands, but enough if a man really loved her. But if she can't even go out and meet young men, how will anyone have the chance to fall in love with her? And she's such a good, sweet girl, she deserves a chance at life.'

'Everyone does,' he said. He hesitated, wondering how far confidences would go.

She filled the pause by handing him the plate of macaroons and offering him more tea. When she had refilled his cup, the atmosphere between them felt so warm and easy, he dared to ask, 'What about you? Where will you go when all this is over?'

'I don't know. I suppose we will have to go abroad,' she said. She sighed. 'It will be bad enough for us, but poor Charlotte . . . Do you suppose she'll have to marry a foreigner?'

'It may not come to that,' Fellowes said. He saw he had made her uncomfortable, and changed the subject. 'I don't know if you've read the new Evelyn Waugh novel, *Vile Bodies*.'

'I don't care for murder mysteries,' she said vaguely. 'I don't understand how all these female authors can bear to write them – like Agatha Christie and D. H. Montagu. She's a woman too. She's the sister of my cousin Jack's wife, which is how I know.'

Happy to have her talking on a neutral subject, he allowed the question of Evelyn Waugh's gender to slip away and chatted about books until the striking of a clock somewhere near reminded him that the rules of etiquette demanded he take his leave.

Emma's baby was born in the middle of July. Kit was an extremely nervous father, and paced the drawing-room floor, wincing at every sound from upstairs. Alfie, Buster, Eos and Sulfi followed him anxiously in a close pack, turning when he turned, like gulls following a plough. The house still smelt of paint. As well as preparing the nurseries they had gone ahead with the general refurbishments and alterations, which were almost finished. He tried thinking about decorating and building matters to keep his mind off what was happening upstairs. He was aware that Emma was what was known to the doctoring trade as an elderly mother, which had made him laugh when he first heard it, but didn't raise a smile now. *If anything should happen to her . . .*

The whole thing went on for more hours than he would have thought possible and, having sent away his dinner hardly touched, he was wondering how his wife was keeping up her strength in such a titanic struggle, and whether something ought to be sent up – something light, perhaps, like an omelette – when there was a different sound from above, one that had all the hairs on the back of his neck standing on tiptoe. Surely that had been a baby crying.

Some inexpressibly long time later – the clock said it was ten to nine in the evening – there were footsteps, and a housemaid came to say the doctor's compliments and would he come up now, my lord? In Emma's room there was a very steamy, not to say a somewhat butchery, smell. She was sitting up in bed, propped by many pillows (couldn't be too bad if she was sitting up, surely), looking as tired as if she had just come in from a very strenuous day's hunting, and in her arms was a small white bundle, which made Kit's heart jump as if a raw nerve had been touched. Was that it? Was that his baby? Good Lord, who would have thought a fellow could feel so discombobulated?

Emma looked up as he approached, and said apologetically, 'Oh dear, I'm awfully sorry, darling, but we seem to have got a girl.'

'A girl?' he said, stunned. He had never thought of its being anything but a boy. He shook his head to clear it. 'But it's all right? Are *you* all right?'

'Mother and baby doing very nicely, thank you,' the midwife cut in.

'No reason at all for concern,' the doctor said, giving the midwife a look that said *he* should be the one to deliver medical opinions. 'Her ladyship did very well, considering all the circumstances, and should recover very nicely in a few days. And the child is perfect.'

'I bet it is, if Emma had anything to do with it,' Kit said staunchly.

Emma smiled at that, and held out the bundle. 'Here, you hold her. Don't look like that, it's just like a puppy, only it wriggles less. You won't drop her.'

He took the baby. He looked down into her pearl-like face, held in the fastness of sleep, and her tiny nacre-tipped fingers, moving softly as though she were a pianist remembering music she had been playing just a moment ago, and he was taken, right then, on that instant, as cleanly as a netted rabbit. He was hers.

'What do you think?' Emma asked, watching him anxiously. 'Is it all right?'

He looked up and smiled blissfully. 'She's perfect. She must have a very special name. We must give it some serious thought – no half-measures will do for her.'

Emma looked relieved. 'You don't mind, then, her being a girl?'

'Mind? Why should I mind?'

599

'Only that – if you want a son, we'll have to do it all again,' Emma said cautiously.

He came and sat down on the edge of the bed, still holding his daughter, and freed one hand to take Emma's. 'Do you mind that? Having to do it again? Because, seeing what good results we seem to get, I must say I'm all for it.'

By the time Molly came to visit, they had decided to call the baby Alethea. Molly thought it a very good name. 'It means "truth",' she said. 'Did you know? Oh. Well, it's a particular Greek word for "truth", meaning "that which is not forgotten" – an interesting definition, don't you think?'

'I just thought it sounded pretty,' Emma said, laughing. 'And what about you?'

'Yes, mine has been confirmed. I'm due again at the end of February or the beginning of March. Nice to do it in the cold weather – you must have been so uncomfortable the last few months.'

'Tell me more news. I feel as if I haven't been out for ages.'

'Well, I've finished my fourth book. It's to be called *Granite Roses*, and Vivian doesn't want it to go to Horace Greenstock, even though they've offered me better terms this time. He really wants to publish it himself, but the trouble is that Dorcas Overstreet still won't take detective novels. So what do you think? He's talking about leaving his uncle and setting up a publishing house of his own.'

'Molly! How wonderful! But won't it take a lot of money?'

'He has a private income, and he's sure he can borrow enough. And lots of authors will want to come with him. It could all be up and running by next year, he thinks. It's very exciting. A new business and a new baby all at the same time.'

'And a new book,' Emma reminded her.

'Well, that's another kind of new baby. And I've got an idea for the next one already. Shall I tell you? Well, there's a solicitor with an office in Bedford Row . . .'

*   *   *

Polly's baby was a self-contained creature, rarely crying, just sleeping and taking nourishment as if he knew his business and was getting on with it. Was that more like Erich or Ren? Both had been practical and determined. Polly sat for hours gazing at her sleeping baby and wondering. She knew it was absurd to look for likenesses at so early a stage, but she couldn't help doing it. Urged by both Lennie and Lizzie, she allowed a few visitors – the faithful Julie Margesson, Martial's wife Mimi, Maggie Prentiss – and they all exclaimed how much like Ren the baby was, but she thought they were being seduced by the black hair, which the midwife said was just birth hair and meant nothing. It would all come away in a few weeks' time and his real hair would come in underneath.

Her visitors asked the baby's name, and Polly told each of them, 'I haven't decided yet.' It was not that she hadn't thought about it, but every name she tried in her mind sounded wrong, and the baby didn't seem to suit any of them. Lennie added his urgings as the allowed time for registering ran out, but on the final day, when he came in with firm jaw to insist she gave him something to take to the clerk, Polly forestalled him.

'I've been thinking,' she said, 'and I've come to a decision. I'm going to go back to being Polly Morland. I'm not going to be Polly Alexander. It doesn't feel like me any more.' Perhaps it never had, she reflected. Who had that woman been, the elegant rich-man's wife, the society dame, the political hostess, glittering and smiling at fund-raising dinners and charity balls? Whoever she had been, she had gone now. It was as though she were taking off a shell and finding the old Polly Morland had been there inside all the time.

'Are you sure?' Lennie asked, though the news pleased him. It was Polly Morland he had always loved.

'Yes, I'm sure.'

'But what about the baby? How will that affect him?'

601

'He'll be Morland too. And Alexander will be his first name.'

'Alexander Morland,' Lennie said. 'Yes, I like that. It's a name a fellow can grow into.' He tried it out in his head a few times, and then asked, 'No middle name?'

'Yes,' she said, 'I did think of one. If you have no objections, I'd like it to be Lennox. Alexander Lennox Morland.'

Lennie was unbearably touched. 'You're naming him after *me*?'

'Who has been more important to me since I came to America? Who has stood by me – and him – all this time? Is it all right? Can I use it?'

'I'd be honoured,' Lennie said. He bent over the baby to hide his face and touched its sleeping cheek. But Polly saw anyway, and was brought close to tears. She cried easily these days – something to do with giving birth, the midwife said – but it brought home to her again, as if she was in danger of forgetting, what a good man Lennie was.

At Morland Place, the news of the baby's birth and his name came in the same letter, from Lennie – who explained tactfully that Polly was still recovering from the birth and hadn't yet written to anyone herself. There was great rejoicing over the news, and Teddy had the house bell rung for his grandson – he was particularly pleased it was a boy. And he was even more pleased that Polly was reverting to her own name, and giving it to the boy as well. 'A real Morland,' he said happily. 'A Morland boy. That's the best news of all!'

Alone with Bertie after a celebration dinner at Morland Place, Jessie said, 'I hope Uncle Teddy doesn't put James's nose out of joint with all this excitement. I thought he repeated "a Morland boy" rather too often for someone who already has a Morland boy.'

'Yes, but he's always loved Polly especially,' Bertie said. 'She was his firstborn.'

'I know. But I'm worried it's a sign that he's disappointed in James in some way.'

'Oh, I don't think so,' he said, removing his cufflinks, while Jessie sat on the bed rolling down her stockings. He liked the intimacy of these moments, and was glad Jessie didn't have a proper lady's maid. He hoped he would always be the one to unhook her hooks and unbutton her buttons. 'Uncle Teddy adores James. He's just excited with his first grandchild.'

Jessie stood up. 'I wonder – would you undo my hooks, please? – what it means, changing her name back to Morland. Perhaps losing her husband like that has made her fall out of love with America.'

'It's an accident that could have happened anywhere. Aeroplanes crash all the time, particularly in fog.' He undid the last hook and kissed the back of her neck, which always made her shudder in a way that delighted him.

'Hmm. But do you think she might come home? I wonder if she would come for Uncle Teddy's birthday.'

'Why don't you write and ask her? Or, better still, cable – a letter will take a week to get there.'

'Perhaps I will.'

'I should, if I were you,' Bertie said seriously. 'If she wants to see her father – and have her father see the baby – she'd better come soon.'

Jessie turned to look at him, startled. 'What do you mean? That cough of his? It's just the old bronchitis.'

'That's what he says,' Bertie said gently, 'and probably what he wants to believe. But I've seen Hasty's face. I don't think he has very long to go, darling.'

'Oh, Bertie,' Jessie said, stricken. She put her hands in his for comfort. 'Why didn't you say something before?'

'I didn't want to upset you. I assumed, you being a nurse, that you had noticed for yourself and were simply trying not to think about it.'

'No,' she said unhappily. 'I suppose when it's someone close to you, you don't really look at them that way.' She thought a moment. 'Does Amy know?'

'I'm pretty sure she sees which way the wind is blowing.'

'And James?'

'James is at the age when he assumes everyone is immortal. I don't imagine Uncle Teddy would want him bothered with it.' He drew her against him and patted her back. 'And don't you say anything to Uncle Teddy either. Let him choose his own way to go.'

'No, I wouldn't say anything,' she said, her cheek against his shoulder. 'But I will send that cable.'

James was enjoying his holiday at home. There was so much to do. He went for spins on Black Beauty, racing through the narrow, winding country lanes to the annoyance of other road-users – harvesting farmers with overloaded carts and stockmen moving cattle and sheep from one field to another. He rode, too, every day, and lunged Firefly. Eddoes suggested he back the youngster, but advised against putting any great weight on him at this stage when he wasn't fully grown. James enlisted the help of Laura, who was always hanging around anyway, and when Firefly had got used to wearing the saddle, he put her up and led him about the field to accustom him to a living weight. Firefly took it well, put his ears back and hunched a little, but he didn't try to buck. Treated kindly, he had no reason to fear these strange sensations once he discovered they didn't hurt. James went on to the next stage of lungeing with Laura in the saddle, and praised her for her good seat, which allowed her to keep still and not unbalance the youngster. She glowed under the praise, and offered to ride Firefly alone. 'I know I can do it. I can teach him the aids while you're busy with other things.'

James thanked her but said, 'He's not ready for that. I haven't got him used to the bit yet. And it will be months before he's ready to school. You can't take a young horse too quickly – that's how they get spoilt.'

Any of the older members of his family would have been amazed and pleased to hear him advocating patience; Laura felt disappointed and frustrated, but with William Pennyfather gone, James was her new god, and she accepted his edicts.

As well as horses and motorbikes, there were tennis and boating and picnics with other local young people, among whom he had a large acquaintance. The heir of Morland Place would never have to struggle for acceptance in and around York. There were house-parties every weekend, and James enjoyed them, but what he liked even more were the impromptu parties he had in the middle of the week. There would be a rush of telephoning, and six or eight young people would pack into a couple of motor-cars and toodle out to Morland Place, where they would take over the Great Hall, which saved having to get up carpets for dancing. James would have the gramophone moved in, one footman would take charge of it, while another would serve drinks, and they would laugh and chat and, most importantly, dance all through the evening and into the small hours.

James made sure he had all the latest tunes – 'Ain't Misbehavin'', 'On The Sunny Side Of The Street', 'I Got Rhythm', and for the slower numbers, 'Georgia On My Mind' and his own favourite, Duke Ellington's 'Dreamy Blues'. Roberta and Jeremy were invited to join them, and relished this taste of fashionable society. Roberta, who had forsworn admiration for anything with fewer than four legs, suddenly found herself so in love with her handsome cousin it hurt to breathe – though some deeper part of her mind knew really that this was just a stage in growing up. Jeremy, quite unconsciously, copied James's slang and the way he smoked his cigarette, and even started parting his hair like James, though it had been brushed straight back for so long it didn't really like it.

Sometimes the younger ones, Harriet, John, Martin and Laura, would creep out of bed and crouch behind the balustrade looking down on the gay scene below, nodding to the beat of the music and speculating about the nature of the delicious morsels to eat that were brought in on wide silver trays. After a while the boys would tire of it and go back to bed, but the girls often stayed there for an hour, wondering what it would be like to be one of those ladies in their pretty, backless dresses, laughing so confidently with the men and two-stepping so elegantly, almost cheek to cheek with them. Laura looked sharply to see who James danced with, but though Harriet whispered that he was obviously 'nutty' about Nancy Tibbett, whose father owned a chain of tobacconist's shops, and who was one of the prettiest girls in the neighbourhood, Laura, who was with him much more and observed him more minutely, saw that he did not favour one over another. He danced with them all, and flirted with them all, but he did not care twopence for any of them, in her opinion, though they were all out to 'catch' him. She firmly believed that he loved horses far more than any girl, and she saluted his good taste.

Happily occupied, James did not notice his father's failing health. When Teddy did not come down to breakfast, and Amy said he was having a lie-in, he accepted it, and did not seem to register that it was every day now. And when he went to bed straight after dinner, it did not impinge on James, who was often off out, or had friends in, and so was not in the drawing-room to miss him. He did not notice that his father's appetite, always a fine specimen, had deserted him, and that he picked at his food, and was losing weight, so that his suits hung on him. James was at a time of life when frailty and sickness were the furthest things from him, and out of his ken.

One day Teddy did not get up at all, and James, coming in from riding to the luncheon table, looked round in surprise and said, 'Where's Dad?'

'He stayed in bed today,' Amy said neutrally, looking at her plate.

'Is he ill?'

'It's his bronchitis. It's bad today. He breathes more easily in bed.' It was said with the greatest casualness, not to alarm James – which was what Teddy wanted – and James was duly not much alarmed, though he had never known his father stay in bed in his whole life. He said, 'I'll go up and see him after lunch.'

'No, don't do that, dear,' Amy said. 'He's sleeping now.'

He didn't come down any more, and after the first shock of it, James got used to his father being upstairs in bed. He was constantly told there was nothing to worry about, and the doctor's visits were always when he was out of the house. But the day came when he went up to see the Old Man and discovered an oxygen apparatus in the room, and his father breathing through a mask over his nose and mouth. This, at least, they could not shrug off. He was alarmed. 'Dad! What is it? Are you ill? I thought it was just bronchitis.'

Teddy couldn't answer, and Amy did it for him. 'It's got worse lately, and it's hard for your father to breathe. The oxygen helps, that's all.'

'But he'll get better, won't he?' James asked, looking at those closed eyes above the mask, the lines in the pale face. It had not occurred to him until that moment that his father was old. Dad had always been just Dad, the master of the house and a rock of granite immutability. He had always been there, just the same, and always would be. 'He'll be better soon?'

Teddy's eyes opened and looked urgently into Amy's. 'I expect so,' she said reluctantly. She thought James ought to know the truth, but Teddy was insistent, and agitating him made him gasp and choke in the way that so distressed her. 'I hope so.'

James went to the bed and took Teddy's limp, damp hand

from the counterpane. 'Dad, you must get better soon,' he said urgently. 'Your birthday's coming and you must be well for that.' Teddy squeezed his hand, and the grasp felt full of vigour, which comforted him. If his father could only get rid of this wretched bronchitis!

When James had left, Teddy removed the mask to gasp to Amy, 'Don't worry him.'

'All right, I won't, I promise,' Amy said. 'Put the mask back on, dearest.'

Teddy held it off for long enough to ask, 'Did Polly write?'

He asked the same question every day, 'Did Polly write?' And when, in an effort to spur his father into recovery, James told him about the grand party they were planning for his birthday, he asked Amy daily, 'Is Polly coming?'

A letter finally came back in response to Jessie's cable, and in Polly's own hand, though Jessie would not have recognised it, having seen so few examples over the years. She wrote mostly about the baby and his progress – he was clearly the most remarkable infant that ever lived. She said that while it would have been nice to be at her father's special birthday party for his sake, she could not arrange the trip at such short notice, and especially not with a new baby in tow. She plainly did not believe any more than James did that her father could ever die, for she said she hoped to come home for a visit some time, when her father was in better health. It would only trouble and annoy him to have visitors around when he was not feeling quite the thing, she said, with some knowledge of her father – though it was the father she had left behind many years ago.

The oxygen went from being an occasional thing, when a bad attack came, to being in almost continuous use. Hasty recommended a night nurse so that Amy could sleep, and then a day nurse too, and the routines of the sick room took over the Great Bedchamber with their timeless, tireless hand. Teddy slept a great deal, and when he woke he looked first for Amy. She slept on the *chaise-longue* on the other side of the room to be on hand, for it troubled him if she was not there. And from time to time he would gesture for the mask to be removed, and speak a single word: 'Polly?'

Amy would answer guiltily, 'She's coming. We're not sure when she'll be here.' There seemed no harm any more in comforting him.

At last James was in no doubt that his father's life was drawing to an end, and he sat by his bedside for hours, with a patience astonishing to those who knew him. When Teddy was awake, James's was often the first face he saw, before his eyes hunted for Amy. James talked to him about the estate, the horses, the harvest, the milk yield – such things seemed to soothe him. When he slept, James often continued to sit, staring blankly at the bedhead and thinking of his father's patience with him, his many kindnesses, his goodness and generosity, and all the times he had disappointed or annoyed him. It was a totting up of accounts that he did not know always happened at such times, and it worried him terribly. He was not very good at arithmetic, and had a horrid feeling he was badly in the red. But Amy had told him sternly not to bother his father when he was awake, and all James could do was to murmur, as he saw him slip into sleep, 'Thanks, Dad, for everything.'

On the day before his birthday, Teddy hardly woke, only drifting up near the surface and then down again. He muttered a little from time to time behind the mask. In the middle of the morning, he opened his eyes, and they moved about, searching for the faces he needed to see. Amy was there, to his right. James was sitting on a chair drawn up beside her. And here on his left was Jessie, who had come to help with the nursing and to support Amy. Dear Jessie. He smiled, and though his mouth was hidden, she saw it in his eyes, and was touched. He made a sound, and his hand moved, lifting a little and falling again. She guessed what he wanted, and bent over to move the mask from his face. The escaping oxygen hissed a little, and Teddy's voice was now hardly more than a whisper. She leaned close, and he said the one word again. 'Polly?'

Her other hand was on his wrist, discreetly feeling his pulse. She said, 'She's coming, Uncle. Any day now.'

He nodded and closed his eyes with relief, and she put the mask back.

A while later she said, 'He's sleeping now.' She looked at James, who was unshaven and red-eyed and utterly despondent. 'Why don't you go out for a ride, just for an hour? Get some fresh air.'

'I'm not leaving him,' James said.

'He'll sleep for a while, now. Go on, you need to get out. You too, Amy – go and have a walk in the garden.'

They went at her urging, though Amy only took the air for ten minutes before returning. She didn't like to be away from him.

James had Cymbal, the faster of his two road horses, saddled, and rode out through the fields. His heart was sore, his head was choked, and he felt bewildered and heavy. He put Cymbal into a canter, then drove her into a gallop, crouching forward and letting the wind dry the tears on his face, kicking her on every time she slowed. Dad couldn't die, he *couldn't*! He was not ready for it, he was not ready to grow up and be master and manage the world without his father. He gave a hoarse sob and it was snatched away by the wind and drowned by the drumming of Cymbal's hoofs on the hard summer earth.

She finally slowed, too tired to be urged on any more, and he rode her up on to Cromwell's Plump to let her rest. There was a breeze: it was swaying the distant trees, bowling the clouds fast across the watery sky, lifting

Cymbal's mane, and humming against his ears in a way he found pleasantly distracting. It was only when he turned his head out of the wind that he heard a bell tolling. He thought for a moment that it was the church bell from the village, but when he turned his head this way and that, he realised the direction was wrong. It was coming from Morland Place. It was the house bell, which used to call the men in from the fields for dinner, but was now rung when there was a birth in the family; and when there was a death.

His heart gave a great painful lurch, and he caught his breath in what, had he been ten years younger, would have been a sob. Then he turned Cymbal and kicked her on as fast as she would go, towards home.

Oliver was due at a facial reconstruction – a twenty-year-old girl who had lost an ear and half her cheek in a motor accident – so he grabbed his morning post from the hall on his way out and took it with him. It was not until early afternoon when he got back to his desk in his consulting-rooms to look at some X-rays that he opened Jessie's letter. As he read, the world seemed to go quiet, the traffic outside hushed, and he sat for a moment staring ahead of him at the dust slowly filtering through a bar of sunshine from the window. It was the end of an era, he thought.

He saw Uncle Teddy in his mind always in frock coat and top hat, a thick cigar between his fingers and a watch chain across his waistcoat. He was a quintessential Edwardian, a man of careless generosity and strong moral purpose, of religion lightly worn and profoundly felt, of unshakeable loyalty, his roots deep in the land.

James, he reflected, belonged to a different world, to the post-war age of hustle-bustle, of noise and motor-cars and cocktails, of constant movement, modernity, and a yearning for change. James was chrome and glass and viscose silk.

Uncle Teddy was polished mahogany and plush red velvet, unchangeable as the hills. He was England.

Oliver sighed. They would not see his like again. He called to his secretary to make a note of the date of the funeral, put down Jessie's letter, adjusted his spectacles and reached for the first of the X-rays.

Polly held the cable for a long time, staring at it as if reading it over and over again could change the words. There are things you take for granted in the world: that the sun will come up in the morning, that a thing dropped will fall earthwards, that water will be wet and fire will burn. One could not easily accept any other state of affairs.

She had left home so long ago: physically, when she first came to New York; and then with her heart when she was so angry with her father for marrying and abandoning her. But now these barriers of distance were wiped away by the stark words on the cablegram, and she was little Polly Morland again, the one who never needed to fear anything because her father was there to take care of her, just as God was in His Heaven, so all was well with the world. Morland Place would always be there, and as long as it was, Teddy Morland would be there too, the master, the king of Polly's kingdom, *saecula saeculorum*.

She had not been there. He had not seen his grandchild. He had been the giant figure in her life, all her life, and it did not seem possible that he had just gone, so suddenly, and without saying goodbye. For a moment she wanted to rush out, buy a ticket on the next boat and go home, saw herself in an express train hurrying north through England, racing against time to get there. But a second thought asked her, *For what?* He would not be there. He was gone, and nothing she could do would get him back so that she could say sorry, and thank you, and I love you.

She mourned; and though she could not have articulated it, she felt in a wordless way, deep down, that she was mourning for more than her father. It was for a whole world that had passed away, and would never be seen again.

CHAPTER TWENTY-SEVEN

The August hush had settled over London; the traffic was slowed to a trickle, the great houses were shut up. In the prevailing quiet, the activity around Fitzjames House had become all the more painfully obvious. If there had been anyone who didn't know, they would know now.

The servants had long departed, and Holkam had been living for the last few weeks in a cheap hotel behind Victoria Station, where he had to pay cash in advance for the room. Verena and her children had gone to the seaside for six weeks, and had taken Violet, Charlotte and Henry with them. Violet had been reluctant to leave, but Holkam had persuaded her. Besides, where would she stay? Oliver was going to his club and joining his family when he could. It was not fair to ask him to keep the house open for her alone, and Holkam's room had a single bed. So she had agreed and, looking miserable, said goodbye.

Holkam oversaw the last removals, endured the last interviews with lawyers and money-men, and now, finally, the house was empty, stripped down to the bare floorboards, nothing left but dust, mice and cobwebs, and the ghosts of paintings on the walls. Everything had been removed to a warehouse, under lock. The auction would take place in October, when everyone was back from the summer break, in the hope of raising the most money possible.

He took one final walk around, while the assessor waited

at the front door to receive the keys. The house had been built in the 1670s and acquired by the Fitzjames Howards in the 1720s, so it had been in the family for two hundred years. Now it was going. These days it was hard to find a buyer for a house of this size. The assessor had hinted that it might be sold to a bank or for a gentleman's club; the worst fate would be for it to be butchered and turned into flats. Two hundred years of family history, the forty-nine years of his own history, wiped clean, like a cloth passing over a slate. His son would never be earl here, nor his son's sons. But he was too tired to feel more than a spasm of guilt. He walked down the stairs, his steps sounding like giant's clogs in the emptiness, passed the keys to the assessor and walked out into the baking street without a word, without a backward look.

He could not bear to go back to the hotel room, and instead just walked. He found his way to the river and turned along it, finding some solace from the eternal surge of the Thames and the multitude of boats, passing busily, hull-down with coal and iron going up to Brentford and the canals, coming down with goods from the Midlands and produce from the West Country. The river's life seemed to have nothing to do with the life of the city, but went on regardless, a self-contained world that moved at a different pace, more easily than the land-stricken ever could.

He walked so long and so far he had no idea where he was when at last the sun began to decline and he found himself dog-weary, with sore feet. He left the river and walked up until he found a main street, and took the first bus he saw – he had coins in his pocket, but not enough, he feared, for a taxi. It took him to Bishopsgate, which he recognised from the railway station, and from there he was able to get back to the hotel by two more buses. He thought people on the buses looked at him curiously – he supposed his suit still looked expensive, despite his generally unkempt appearance. He hoped it was no more than that.

In the hotel room he opened the windows – it was stiflingly hot – took off his jacket and shoes and lay on the bed. There was nowhere else to rest, for the only chair, an upright wooden one, had a cracked leg and would not take his weight. He propped up his head with the stale-smelling pillow and stared out at the rooftops and the changing colour of the sky behind the chimneys.

It was all over. He had been handsome and fêted in his young-manhood, had married a rich, beautiful woman, had had a good war, and a promising career afterwards. But he had thrown it all away. Why? Now, with all human passion spent, he could not remember what it had felt like to want things so much he would risk all for them. It seemed like a kind of madness.

Yet all his successes had been as nothing against the great failure of his life. His father had not loved him. He had hoped and hoped that his father might one day say he was proud of him, but the old man had died without a single word of approval. So he had been doomed from the beginning. He had never had a chance.

The sky was luminous deep blue behind the chimneys now, dark above, and the first stars were pricking the blackness. The day was almost over, and he had no desire and no reason to see another. He had half a bottle of brandy left, standing on the bedside table. It would be enough to numb the pain of his thoughts and wash down the pills. The doctor had carefully told him how many was the safe limit to take, how much of an overdose would kill him. Had he foreseen this moment? If he had, he deserved a blessing. Holkam still had his service revolver, but that was an unpleasant way out, and unpleasant for Violet, too. This way, they might well think his heart had simply failed. She would be able to live with that.

He took the pills carefully, and kept sipping at the brandy while he waited for them to take effect. The sky was completely dark now, and only a stain of light from some window out of sight lower down gave the roof and chimney definition. He stared at the chimney pots as they faded, and thought of nothing.

After the R100 had joined her sister at Cardington, and had exhibited various faults, which had had to be corrected, the R101 engineers had hinted strongly to the Air Ministry that neither ship was ready to undertake a lengthy flight, and that the developmental stage should be extended.

The R100 team, who naturally felt their ship was better than its rival, responded indignantly that she was perfectly capable of flying safely to Canada and back, and since the Air Ministry was impatient for the scheme to move forward, the R100 duly departed Cardington for Canada on the 29th of July.

The ship took what was called the Great Circle route, which covered 3,300 miles, and arrived at St Hubert airport, Montréal, seventy-eight hours later, having shown an average speed of 42 m.p.h. She docked on to the mooring mast, which had been specially erected for her, and for twelve days was the toast of Québec, attracting huge attention, a hundred thousand visitors, numerous press and magazine articles, and even a specially written song. She made short passenger flights to Ottawa, Toronto and Niagara Falls, and could have sold the tickets for them ten times over. She finally left Canada on the 13th of August and arrived home at Cardington after a flight of just fifty-seven and a half hours.

'It couldn't have gone better,' Jack said to Helen, reading the official reports and some newspaper cuttings from Canadian papers that had been sent to him. 'It's a tremendous boost to the programme. Now it's up to the Socialist team to get R101 ready. Thomson's determined to go to India in October.' Lord Thomson was the Secretary of State for Air, but he was well known to pilots of Jack's generation as, after a distinguished war career, he had become chairman of both the Royal Aeronautical Society and the Royal Aero Club. It was his enthusiasm that had got the airship programme off the ground in the first place.

The R101 was bigger and longer than her sister – in fact, she was the biggest flying craft ever built, exceeding even the *Graf Zeppelin* – but Jack was still not happy with the engines, which were so heavy they had to perform extremely well to justify their weight. One of the five was positioned astern and was designed only to be used at the start and finish of the journey, for docking manoeuvres. For the rest of the time it was just dead weight, and Jack was working with the Cardington team to enable it to run in reverse and therefore be used for propulsion as well. There were still problems with the propellors and the gasbag valves, which were of a novel design, but now that R100 had proved her worth, the Cardington team were working flat out to get their own ship ready on time.

Jack's employers, Imperial Airways, were happy to release him from his normal duties to take part in the inaugural journey. It would be the beginning of a whole new age of passenger flight, in which Britain would surpass the Germans and connect up the far-flung parts of her Empire, and Jack would be their representative for the historic occasion.

Jack was very excited to be going, and consoled Helen that they would make the flight together, as promised, for their wedding anniversary.

'You go and have fun, darling,' she told him comfortably. 'I'm quite happy to stay home, and I'd really like to be on hand to make sure Basil settles into his new school.'

'What can you do if he doesn't?'

'I see myself as the wicket keeper,' she said, 'there to catch him as he hurtles past. I just hope he doesn't set fire to the place.'

'That would be embarrassing,' Jack agreed solemnly.

★　★　★

On a fine day at the end of September, Oliver invited his sister to walk with him in the garden. Holkam's death, the inquest and then the funeral had necessitated his opening the house again and taking up residence so that Violet had somewhere to stay and someone to support her.

Holkam's doctor had been able to attest that he had been under treatment, and that his heart was damaged and could have failed at any moment, so it was brought in as natural causes, without the need for a post-mortem, to everyone's relief.

Now the physical business was over and everything else was in the hands of the lawyers and administrators. Oliver had tried to persuade her to go back to the seaside, but she didn't want to. She was too miserable to be around the children – Verena could keep them on a level course much more easily if she wasn't there – and she couldn't rest until she knew how things were going to come out and what was going to happen to her. The older boys, too, needed support. Robert was now Earl of Holkam with no estate and no money, living in lodgings with his brother, and wondering what his accession to the title would mean. Oliver was on hand to explain to him the duties of the House and the mechanism for taking his seat, but he was acutely aware of the anomaly between his style of living and his title.

Richard was shaken by his father's death, having not realised before that he had a weak heart. But of the four children he had had the least to do with him, and it could not be said he missed him in any personal sense. He was enjoying his new life, and still found it fun to cope with the little daily necessities that had never come his way before, and never would have, had there not been the breakdown.

The one thing he had not yet adjusted to – Robert was even more put out by it – was how difficult it was to keep clean.

'You have to pay Mrs Cotter extra for baths, and even

then she doesn't like it if you ask for one more than one a week. And it's so difficult to wash standing up at a basin. I understand now why the people on the tube smell the way they do.'

Oliver had responded in practical style by inviting them to come round any time they liked to take a bath; and given that their funds were limited, he had also issued a general invitation to them to come for Sunday luncheon. It was amusing and rather sad to see them tucking in to the ample meal with enthusiasm and appreciation. They also brought with them on a Sunday a package of shirts, collars and underthings, which Oliver good-naturedly directed to be laundered along with the family's wash for them to collect the following Sunday.

But these arrangements were not satisfactory in the long term, and it was clear that there was no-one but Oliver to take care of his sister and her children. Fortunately, there was a solution. As he told her that September day, the fortune he had inherited from their mother included a property portfolio, and one of the houses, in Lancaster Gate, had just come back in hand. Its lease had ended and the tenant was not renewing.

'It's a small house, but it has four bedrooms and two attic rooms, and, I believe, a decent drawing-room and dining-room with folding doors between. And it's just opposite the park, which will be pleasant in summer, and for walks.' He smiled. 'Fifi will love it – lots of other dogs to make friends with.'

'You're offering it to me?' Violet cried.

'Now don't blub, there's a dear girl. Robert and Richard can come and live with you and help support you. They aren't really comfortable in diggings. If Henry takes one of the attic rooms, you can have a bedroom each, and there are schools nearby, so we'll easily find one for him. I'll make you an allowance for yourself and Charlotte, and if you're careful you ought to be able to afford a maid-of-all-work – she can have the other attic. What do you think? It will give you a home of your own, at any rate.'

'Oh, Oliver,' was all Violet could say at first. Eventually she managed, 'You're so very good to me.'

'Nonsense. Can't have my little sister wandering the earth like a gypsy. Now, if you're happy with the idea, I'll have the place cleaned right away, and you can move in as soon as you like. It is furnished, but when you've settled in, if there's anything you need, let me know. There's bags of furniture lying about this place that's never used.'

Violet thanked him again, incoherently, and he felt the best thing was to let her alone for a bit to have her cry out, so he squeezed her hand and went indoors. It was a rum business, he thought, this whole Holkam thing. A private word with the lawyers had suggested there'd be nothing left at all when they'd finished their business and taken their fees – the whole estate would not be enough to cover the debts Holkam had run up over five or six years of living beyond his means. He thought of Violet's glittering life of new gowns, furs, jewels, motor-cars, giving magnificent dinners and attending every important function, and thought it had brought her little pleasure in the end. It would have been better if she could have married some more modest chap who'd have made a good husband in an unspectacular way. But he absolved his parents of ambition. His mother had told him that Violet had been madly in love with Brancaster, as he was then, and their father had been too tender-hearted to deny her.

Still, it was a good thing the heart did sometimes rule the head, or Verena would never have married him.

The R101 was gassed up and floated in her shed on Friday, the 26th of September. Lord Thomson had hoped to be departing for Karachi that day – he had to get to India and back in time for the Imperial Conference on the 20th of October – but the winds were not favourable, and it was not until the early morning of Wednesday, the 1st of October, that she was brought out and hitched to the mooring mast, ready to complete her trials for her certificate of air worthiness. It was a twenty-four-hour ordeal, at the end of which the captain noted to the conference – called on the evening of the 2nd – those things that had been of concern before seemed all to be cured. There was practically no movement of the outer cover, no leaks in the gas valves; the sealing strips and the padding all seemed to be secure.

Lord Thomson said they must not let his impatience affect them, but must make a decision based on their own judgement. Jack pointed out that full-speed testing of the engines hadn't been carried out, but the captain responded that it had never been intended to run the engines at full speed on the India trip. So the decision was made, with all agreeing, that the flight to India should be undertaken, leaving on Saturday.

The flight was dependent on the weather, as always, and Jack left home on the Friday evening to go to Cardington, to be on hand for a final check. The trip was expected to take five days going out, with a stopover of four days, and a flight back of six – a round trip of fifteen days. Helen packed a valise for him, and put in a couple of books, though he assured her he would be too busy observing and checking things to have time to read. 'There are always the evenings,' she said.

He grinned. 'With the magnificent dinners and cocktails and champagne receptions that will be going on all the time?'

'Hmph,' said Helen. 'I've a mind to forbid you to go.'

On the morning of Saturday, the 4th, the weather report said that over France it was becoming cloudy and with moderate winds. Two further reports suggested conditions would deteriorate, though the winds would not strengthen significantly, so it was decided to begin the trip that evening and get past the bad weather before it got any worse. The supplies and luggage were hurriedly loaded, the eminent passengers hustled on board, and the ship was ready to depart by half past six in the evening, in full darkness and a fine, misty rain.

On the morning of the 5th of October, the newspapers were full of the shocking news that the R101 had crashed in woods near Beauvais. In stormy weather with low cloud, rain and gusting winds, she had come down at two in the morning, had caught fire, and was still burning fiercely. There were not thought to be any survivors.

Helen tried to telephone the Air Ministry, but on a Sunday it was a hopeless task. If there was anyone there, they were not taking calls, and all the numbers the telephonist tried were unanswered. Then she rang the newspapers. At the *Daily Mail* the editor knew Jack's name very well, and was sympathetic. He told her that the ship had sent a routine message at midnight giving her position as fifteen miles south-west of Abbeville, and saying that the distinguished passengers had enjoyed an excellent supper and a last cigar and retired to bed.

So they would have been in bed and asleep when she came down, Helen thought. What chance had they had to get out?

The editor said the midnight message had said everything was as it should be, no hint of any trouble, and nothing more had been heard after that. But, he added, weather reports were of gale-force winds and poor visibility in the region of Beauvais. He promised to ring her if there were any further news, but the last he had heard, the wreck was still burning and was likely to burn for many hours yet.

When she rang off from the newspaper, Basil rang her from school, having been allowed to call from the headmaster's office in the particular circumstances. He was in tears, and begged to be allowed to come home.

'I don't know anything yet,' she told him. 'I can't spare the time to come and fetch you. You must just stay put.'

'Daddy's dead, isn't he?' he said, sounding suddenly very young, eight rather than fourteen.

Helen's throat closed up. She couldn't say yes. It would hurt too much. Equally she couldn't lie to him. At last he prompted, 'Mama?' in a small voice, and she managed to say, 'We must keep praying. I'll let you know as soon as I hear anything.' And she rang off only just in time to save him the sound of his mother sobbing. She didn't care now to know why the ship had failed, how it had crashed. It was irrelevant. She had lost her husband, her lover and friend, the lode-star of her life. She had gone through the war expecting daily to get the dread telegram, and now, ironically, the fatal blow had fallen in the days of peace, when they had thought there was nothing more to worry about.

It was the most horrible day. Barbara and Michael were sent home from school at lunchtime as an act of compassion, which she could have done without. Better for them to have stayed where they were and tried for a modicum of normality. As it was, one look at their mother's red, swollen eyes and tear-streaked face sent them plummeting into the most acute misery. She comforted them as best she could, gave them bread and cheese and sent them out into the garden to play with Stalky and Captain Midnight, who were drooping miserably – they had never seen the mistress cry before, and knew something bad was happening.

Helen couldn't eat. She found herself desperately thirsty and made some coffee, which helped, and smoked cigarette after cigarette, waiting for the confirmation. The first storm of weeping over, she felt dead inside, heavy and stunned with loss. The telephone rang from time to time – concerned friends and acquaintances, and she told them all she was waiting for news and asked them not to call again as the line must be kept clear. Gradually the calls died out and silence fell. The children crept in from the garden and she discovered it was teatime; she fed them, and sent them upstairs to play in the nursery.

It was the burning that was the worst thing. She knew that in the war it had been the fate flyers feared most. She knew how many of them had thrown themselves out of their burning aircraft to fall to their deaths, rather than burn. And this time they had been in bed, asleep, when it happened – no time to free themselves of their blankets before the wall of fire engulfed them. No clean, merciful death for the man who had risked his life again and again through the four years of war. She could only pray that it had been too quick for him to suffer much, but a gaping place of horror deep in her mind told her it could not have been instantaneous. *Oh, Jack, Jack!*

When the phone rang again, she knew, with some lover's instinct, it was news. The hair stood up on her scalp and her palms prickled. They were going to tell her now, tell her the worst thing she would ever hear in her life, if she lived to be a hundred. She was in a cold sweat of dread. *Don't say the words. Please don't say the words!* Let there be some kindly silence spread over the worst aspect of it.

There seemed to be a roaring in her head when she put the receiver to her ear, and she couldn't hear anything, but gradually she realised it was a poor line.

'Yes, this is Mrs Compton,' she managed to answer, to an insistent query in a woman's voice.

'This is Sister Fairchild from the Bedford Hospital,' the voice went on. 'We have your husband here.'

She thought she had misheard. 'I beg your pardon?'

'Your husband was brought in here yesterday evening,' said the voice.

Helen was bewildered. 'He can't have been. He was on the – on the airship. You must have made a mistake,' she said.

'I don't think so,' the woman said firmly, a capable woman who didn't make mistakes, never had. 'A Mr Jack Compton. He gave us this telephone number himself. He was brought in last night with a severe concussion. He has only properly recovered consciousness in the past hour.'

Helen's heart was beating so fast she was frightened by it. 'Let me speak to him!' she croaked.

'I'm afraid that is not possible. He must be kept very quiet for the time being. He was able only to give us the telephone number, and ask us to call you with the message, "Ring Kipper." I made him repeat it to be sure. I don't know if it makes sense to you.'

'Yes, yes, it does,' Helen said with a laugh that sounded like a sob. 'How is he? Can I see him?'

'His condition is stable for the moment but he has sustained a severe concussion and must remain very quiet. He's asleep again now, in any case. You can visit him tomorrow.'

When she rang off, she found her hands shaking so much she had to clasp them together for a moment before she could pick up the phone again and dial another number. 'Kipper' was one of the engineers at Cardington, a friend of Jack's, John 'Kipper' Hering, who had been working on the R101. The young man who answered, sounding audibly shaken, said he thought everyone had gone home; then said there was a light on in the shop and he would go and see if anyone was there. Helen held the line, waiting between life and death, still half sure there had been a mistake some-where, despite the telephone number and the 'Kipper' message.

And then a man's voice said, 'Hering here.'

'Kipper – it's Helen Compton.'

626

'Helen! You've heard the news. God, it's so terrible! No-one can think how it happened, why she caught fire. Airships have crashed before without catching fire. We can't understand it—'

'Kipper – about Jack,' she said desperately, speaking over him. 'I just heard from Bedford Hospital. They say – they say they've got Jack there.'

There was a brief, painful silence, as she heard her question hanging on the nothingness of the line and waited for the puzzled denial, the stroke of death to hope, to come back. And then Kipper said, 'God, Helen, I'm sorry. Have you only just heard? Someone ought to have telephoned you.'

'It's true? He's at Bedford?'

Kipper was burbling on with his apologies, not realising what she had been thinking. '*I* should have given you a ring, damn it, but I thought one of the admin bods would do it, and then there was so much else to do. The news of the crash came in just as we were going home, and since then—'

'Kipper, tell me what happened!'

'Yes, yes, of course. It was just a stupid accident. Jack was up on one of the movable ladders, taking a last look at the stern engine. He was coming down backwards, and a gust of wind shook it. It was raining a bit and the steps were wet and somehow his foot slipped and he fell, fetched his head an almighty crack on the concrete. Knocked himself clean out. So two of the fellows got him into a car and drove him to Bedford Hospital. I suppose the young idiots just dumped him there and dashed back in the hope of seeing the fun – it was only just before take-off. How is he?'

'They said he's only just regained consciousness, so I suppose they didn't know who to ring before. They said his condition is stable.'

'I'm sure he'll be all right. Those old war pilots have skulls like coconuts. You can't bust 'em. But—' Now at last he got it. 'You didn't know. God, Helen, you thought he was on the airship. I'm so sorry. Lord, have you been thinking all this time he was . . . ?'

'Yes. All day.'

'Dear God. I'm so sorry. It must have been hell for you.'

'Worse than that.'

'If only I'd thought to ring you. Poor old Jack. We were all thinking what rotten luck it was to have missed the trip. Now, of course, we're thinking—'

'Yes,' said Helen. 'Have you heard if there were any survivors?'

'Not officially, but unofficially they're saying four or five of the engineers got out, because their engine cars were outside the hull. None of the passengers escaped, as far as we know.' There was a silence between them, as they both thought of the implications of that. 'I'm glad Jack wasn't there,' Kipper said at last. 'Will you let me know how he goes on?'

'Yes, of course,' Helen said, and went to ring off, her mind already on hospital visits, what to take Jack – washing things, fruit, cigarettes, a book in case he was well enough to read. She heard Kipper's voice speak again, and put the receiver back to her ear. 'What was that?'

'I said, we didn't manage to get his kit off before the departure. His valise. I'm sorry. It will have been – you know.'

For some reason Helen thought of the two books she had packed for him. One of them had been *Gulliver's Travels*. She had meant it as a joke. He would want something to read in hospital, she thought vaguely. 'It's all right,' she said. 'I can find him another book.'

It was a remark Kipper was destined never to understand.

At Morland Place they were horrified to hear about the loss of the R101, especially the fire, which claimed the lives of almost all those on board. Five engineers, a wireless operator and two riggers survived, though one of the riggers died shortly afterwards from his injuries. The government did what it could: it arranged a memorial service for the Friday at St Paul's, was bringing home the bodies by warship, and asking permission of the bereaved for the victims to be honoured by being given a public burial in a common grave with a suitable memorial over it.

But the Morlands were spared the particular day of grief for Jack since they hadn't known he was to have flown on the airship. Until Helen telephoned to say that Jack had suffered a concussion but was recovering and ought to be completely well again in a few weeks, they hadn't even known he was hurt.

Bertie had seen the notice of Holkam's death in August in *The Times*, and told Jessie about it. It simply said 'suddenly', which could mean anything – though Bertie said it usually meant either a heart attack or a stroke. Jessie had tried to telephone Violet at Fitzjames House, and, when the telephone was not answered, assumed she had gone down to Brancaster for the summer and sent a telegram there. Holkam's breakdown had at that point not become common knowledge, outside their small circle. She followed the attempt with a letter of sympathy, and waited for Violet to get over the first shock of grief and write to her. When the letter, addressed to Fitzjames House, was returned marked 'Gone Away', she assumed it was a mistake on the part of the post office and wrote again.

And then the news filtered through from local sources that Shawes was for sale. James brought it home from York – a thinner, rather listless-looking James, harassed by business since his father had died. 'I thought it was a hum at first but it seems to be true,' he said. 'I had it from a chap who had it from the estate agent who's handling the sale. It'll be going to auction later this month.'

'But why? Why would Violet want to sell it? Cousin Venetia gave it to her for her own, and she always loved it there.'

James shrugged. 'I don't know. Perhaps she thinks it's too far from London. All I know is I wish I could buy it. It would be a jolly good property to add to the estate, though the house ain't to my taste.'

'It's said to be the finest example of Vanbrugh's work,' Jessie said, with a small smile.

'Oh, but we're in a new age now. We have to be modern. If it was mine, I'd pull it down and put up something completely new, with every modern feature there is, and all the conveniences.'

'It's a good job, then, that you can't afford it,' Jessie said.

By the time the second letter was returned, Jessie was too busy with their own catastrophe to do more than send a puzzled letter to Oliver, asking for news of her old friend. Young Mr Pobgee of Pobgee, Micklethwaite and Dashwood, who had been going into the estate in the hope of settling Teddy's will and getting it proved before they were all too much older, came to visit James with an ominously bulging briefcase and an even more ominous frown. When he had gone, James rushed out to the stables, saddled Viscount and hurtled over to Twelvetrees House, where he flung himself into one of the armchairs in an attitude of abandoned despair. Since his father had died he had come to rely on Jessie and Bertie more and more for advice and comfort, and it was natural for him to go straight to them. Fortunately, Bertie was at home and came to join them before James was more than a few disjointed sentences into his story.

'I wish Dad had never died. Well, I wish it anyway, of course, but this is too sick-making. I'm not cut out for this sort of thing, Jessie, honestly. I never was any good at maths, and business just escapes me, and now all this is going to be dumped onto my shoulders, and everybody's livelihoods, as that beast Pobgee kept on saying. He couldn't have been more gloomy!'

Jessie gave Bertie a grateful look as he came in, and Bertie settled down to get sense out of his young cousin.

'He says Dad didn't have any liquid assets. I told him he had the finest cellar in the Riding, but it seems it don't mean that. I didn't get a handle on what exactly it *did* mean, but apparently it's a big problem, because of death duties.'

Bertie and Jessie exchanged a quick glance. It was a subject they had discussed privately already, what effect death duties would have on the estate. So many of the big landlords had been ruined by them.

'Liquid assets are money you can get your hands on quickly,' Bertie said. 'Not things like land and houses that you have to sell.'

'Well, I thought that was more or less what he meant. Anyway, it seems you have to pay the dratted duties before you can have the estate. But if you haven't got any money and need to sell things to pay the duties, you can't. I don't understand it. It doesn't make any *sense*.'

'Did Pobgee give you any idea how much they're likely to be?' Bertie asked.

James slumped even more and looked miserable. 'A lot,' he said. 'He hasn't got it all worked out. Apparently it will take months of work to get it all written down – and a nice lot of fees for him and his chums, I suppose – and then it has to go through probate, whatever that is, and the long and short is it's likely to be next summer before it's all wound up. But he says in the long run I'll probably have to sell three-quarters of the estate to cover the death duties.' He looked up at Jessie, his expression wounded now. 'Why would they do that? Why would the government try to destroy us? When you think of all the people we employ, and the food we grow for the country, and the stuff Dad's factories make, why knock it all down?'

'I don't know,' Jessie said. 'Death duties are iniquitous, I've always said so. As if income tax wasn't enough.'

'Did your father not make any provision for death duties?' Bertie asked.

'Apparently, so Pobgee says, he was going to, but things got tough, with the American crash and the exports going down and suchlike, and of course he didn't expect to be dying so soon, so I suppose he thought there'd be time to get out of trouble first and make provision afterwards.'

'I'm sorry, James,' Jessie said. 'It's a terrible thing to be facing. Does he really think you'll have to sell?' She faltered. 'Not Morland Place, surely.'

'That'd be the last go, obviously,' James said, sitting up a little. 'I'll do damned well anything before I sell the old Place to a stranger. But the factories, the shops, some of the farms – maybe all but the home farm. And,' tears came to his eyes and he dashed them away impatiently, 'the horses. He said if I wanted to be left with the "core inheritance", as he put it, I'd have to cut out all unnecessary luxuries. I said horses weren't luxuries, but he didn't listen. He recommends I start straight away economising so as to cut back the running costs. Sack some of the servants, no more lavish parties, get rid of the horses . . .'

He put his arm over his face while he struggled for control.

Jessie sat on the arm of the chair and put her arm round his shoulders, which felt then very thin and young. 'I'm so sorry,' she said. 'We'll help you all we can, won't we, Bertie?'

'Of course,' he said, but with a worried look. There wasn't very much they could do, except offer moral support, and guide him towards what economies could most easily be made.

Jessie was staring at nothing, thinking that it seemed like the end of everything. All Uncle Teddy's kingdom to come crashing down? Everything going – perhaps Morland Place itself? It was a terrible prospect.

'I don't want it,' James said pitifully, from behind his arm. 'I don't want to be master. I wish there was someone else. I don't want all these decisions and people looking up to me. I wish I could just get on Black Beauty and ride away. I'd travel all over the world – Italy and Egypt and South America – and see everything. I'd be like one of those explorers in that book Father Palgrave used to read to us. I'd travel through India with three ponies and a native guide all the way to the Hindu Kush. And I'd never come back.'

'Never come back? Jessie said. 'But you love Morland Place.'

'I loved it when Dad was here and looked after everything,' James said. 'But if it's going to be torn apart and ruined I don't want to see it.'

Amy, dignified in her grief, was doing what she could by keeping the household going, and trying to cut down on the lavishness that had always been a feature of Morland Place. She had worries of her own. Her portion, which had been placed in trust at the time of her wedding, was outside the reach of the death duties, but the securities it had been invested in had been damaged by the crash and downturn. Away from Morland Place, it would provide her with a competence, no more. But James had already indicated that he did not want her to leave, that she must stay for as long as she liked, for the rest of her life. The Morland estate had no dower house, and it was what his father would have expected, he said.

'Anyway, you belong here,' he concluded.

She was touched. 'I want to stay,' she said. It had been her home with Teddy, and she wanted to remember him here. But in that case, she insisted, James must have the money from her portion towards the death duties. Pobgee told her it was a very bad time to sell and that she would not realise anything like the true value of the investments.

'In any case,' James said starkly, 'it wouldn't be anything

like enough. A drop in the ocean. No, you hang on to it. My father wouldn't want me to be sponging on you.'

So there was nothing to do but try to find economies. Jessie was drawn into the long and painful conferences over what cuts could be made in the running costs of the house. John Julian came up with the first important one. At a meeting with Jessie, Miss Husthwaite, Amy and James one evening he said, 'I think I must say, though I regret it deeply, that my time here is up.'

'Up? What do you mean?' Amy asked.

'My spiritual duties are light, and – forgive me, James – I have the feeling you are not as devoted to your religion as your father, and that you would not be upset if there was no more celebration in the chapel, or even regular prayers.'

James looked embarrassed, and muttered something about there being always so much else to do.

'I have enjoyed my time here, more than I can say, but I have not supposed that I would stay for ever. I have an income of my own, and some savings, and Miss Husthwaite and I have an understanding.' Everyone perked up at that, and Miss Husthwaite blushed. 'We decided some time ago that, when the time came, we would throw in our lot together – in short, that we would marry and find a home away from Morland Place.'

In her mind Jessie could almost hear Uncle Teddy saying, 'The devil you did!' 'I'm so pleased for you,' she said.

'Same here,' said James, 'but you don't need to rub off now.'

Julian smiled. 'Oh, I think we should. Far better to go while you still feel that way than to outstay our welcome. There is a little house in Fulton I have had my eye on. We can be ready to go in a month, and it will save you our salaries and our keep.'

They talked about it for a while, but Julian was quite determined and Miss Husthwaite seemed to like his forcefulness and agreed with everything he said.

634

'There's only one thing I regret,' he said at last, 'and that is that we have not finished the Household Book. I had no idea when we began what an enormous task it would be, and it would take another year at least, perhaps more, to do what we want to do.'

'No trouble about that,' James said. 'If you're only going to Fulford, you can take it with you – as long as you bring it back.'

So it was not until the end of October that Jessie finally wrote to Oliver, delicately enquiring if there was any reason Violet did not reply to her letters, other than the shock of bereavement. Oliver wrote back only that Violet had changed her address, and gave Jessie the new direction. He thought it better to leave it to Violet how much she wanted to tell her. Jessie wrote again to the new address, and this time had a reply from Violet, saying how glad she was to hear from her, and how she longed to see her again. She asked Jessie to come and stay with her, though her house was small and they would have to share a room. The thought of Violet reduced to having no spare bedroom was so poignant that Jessie did not hesitate. Holkam's death must have left her badly off, she thought.

And so to London, to the little house in Lancaster Gate, where Violet welcomed her with fierce hugs, quite unlike the cool, collected Violet of old; and in the course of long, long conversations, in the drawing-room, in the garden, and most of all walking hour on hour in Hyde Park, with Fifi prancing like a miniature Hackney in front of them, reminder of a different age that seemed a century ago, she told Jessie everything.

They strolled, arms linked and heads together, as they had used to do that Season long ago when they came out together, with all their dreams intact, the world untried and seeming full of hope. How differently it had all turned out.

'I never thought,' Violet said once, 'that we would end up like this. How could we have been through so much, just in our short lives?'

'We're not so young any more,' Jessie said. 'I'll be forty in December, you know.'

'The war changed everything,' Violet said. 'If only we could go back to the way things were. Everything seemed so safe.'

'Well, we can't,' Jessie said. Thinking like that could paralyse you. You had to face forwards, always. 'But there's something we *can* do.'

Violet looked up, her blue eyes reflecting the autumn sky, sad and enquiring. 'What's that?'

'The refreshment hut isn't far away,' Jessie said. 'We can go and have tea and buns and get out of this wind.'

Violet managed a faint smile. 'Yes, I'm getting quite chilly.' She slipped her hand through her friend's arm. '*Dear* Jessie!'

CHAPTER TWENTY-EIGHT

In January 1931, Oliver and Verena held a small dinner at Chelmsford House. Eddie and Sarah were invited, and Emma and Kit, who were passing through London on a migration from one hunting weekend to another. And to celebrate his miraculous escape, they asked Jack and Helen.

Jack was recovered from his concussion, but none of them had properly recovered from the shock of what might have been. 'Even Basil is behaving like an angel at the moment,' Helen confessed.

It had not yet been determined what caused the airship to go down, though theories were plentiful. Jack said that the outer covering was probably heavy with rain, which together with the gusty gale-force wind had caused the ship to be unstable. There seemed to have been no failure of the airframe – the only crack found in one longeron would have been caused by the impact with the ground. One of the survivors had testified that the ship came down so gently he was hardly rocked on his feet and kept his balance: it was the fire that had caused the fatalities. The hot diesel engine must have set fire to gas escaping from one of the envelopes.

Sarah felt it was time to change the subject from such sombre thoughts, and asked how Jack and Helen had passed Christmas. 'We went with the children to Morland Place,' Helen said. 'James was very eager to have a large party – his first as master of the house.'

'Yes, he invited us,' Oliver said, 'but we were already otherwise engaged.'

'It was very cheery,' Jack said. 'All the old traditions, lots of neighbours dropping by, and a big ball.'

'I think he was trying to make sure we didn't miss Uncle Teddy,' Helen said.

'The Boxing Day hunt?' Oliver asked. 'That was always a thing, wasn't it?'

'Yes, there was a lawn meet at Morland Place,' Helen said. 'Jack and I didn't go out – too long since we were last on a horse – but Jessie and Bertie did, looking very splendid and well mounted. All the children went out, too, and James very kindly arranged a suitable mount for Basil. I must say, there's nothing like a day's hunting for taking the devil out of a child – he was too worn out after it to misbehave.'

'I wish it took the devil out of grown-ups, too,' Sarah said, with a look at her husband.

'We've just come back from Melton Mowbray,' Eddie explained. 'Burrough Court. Hunting weekend.'

Burrough Court was the Furnesses' place. 'Oh, yes,' Oliver said, 'you were on duty, weren't you?'

'Yes, and Lady Furness kindly invited Sarah, too.'

'I do like her,' Sarah said. 'She's perfectly agreeable. But she does have some very vulgar friends.'

'And she encourages Wales to behave badly. He can be quite blisteringly rude.'

Kit said, 'We were at a weekend with them before Christmas, at the Fort, and there were some very sinister people around. There was a very strange woman wearing a monocle and a man's suit of plus fours. I didn't mind, but you never saw such dreadful material – a kind of yellow and red check.'

He shuddered, and Emma shook her head and laughed at him. 'He can be quite sensible when he wants,' she assured the company.

'Do tell about the vulgar friends, though,' Kit urged.

'Well, Connie and Bennie had been invited,' said Eddie, 'but they both had colds and chucked.' Connie was Lady Furness's sister Consuelo, who had married Benjamin Thaw, a Pittsburgh banker's son and now first secretary to the American Embassy. 'And to take their place, Thelma invited the most shocking couple, the Simpsons. I suppose he was harmless enough – a ship-broker, English father and American mother, a bit of a cit, very dull, and rather a social creeper, one gathers, frightfully pleased to meet the Pragga Wagga. But his wife! Vulgar and loud-voiced. She had a strange name – can't recall it just now.'

'I think I've met her,' Emma said. 'She's from Baltimore, isn't she?'

'I have no idea.'

'Yes, I think it must be the same person. You remember I did Mipsy Oglander's house a couple of years ago? She's from Baltimore too, and I remember she said her friend with a queer name was coming over – Wallis, I think it was.'

'Yes, that's her. You actually met her?'

'Mipsy wanted me to do some work on her flat, but it turns out the Simpsons haven't much money – certainly not enough to do what *she* wanted doing. She seemed to think I'd do it for love of Mipsy. I didn't take to her.'

'I don't think Wales thought much of her,' Eddie said. 'She said something stupid across the table to him, and he snubbed her quite rudely. I don't think she realised she'd been snubbed, though – too coarse-grained.'

'But so many of Lady Furness's friends are like that,' Sarah said. 'And now, of course, they are Wales's friends.'

'Violet's well out of it,' Oliver said, and catching his wife's look, went on, 'Darling, it's a family dinner. Everyone here knows all about it.'

'It doesn't mean we have to talk about it,' Verena said.

'Besides, it's illogical,' said Eddie. 'It's Thelma Furness

who's introducing all these people to the prince, and she wouldn't have been around if he'd stayed with Violet.'

'How *is* Violet?' Helen asked, seeing Verena didn't like the way the conversation was going.

'She's recovering, slowly,' Verena said.

'I know Jessie went to see her, but I haven't seen her in years,' Helen said.

'She's living very quietly,' Verena said. 'She still doesn't like to go into company – I asked her to this dinner this evening, even offered to send a car, but she refused. But I think she's coming to terms with it now.'

'It's Charlotte one feels sorriest for,' Sarah said. 'There's no chance of her marrying decently now.' She and Verena had talked about the possibility of giving Charlotte a second Season between them, but they had no daughter to bring out, and it was doubtful other hostesses would invite her. The stain of her father's bankruptcy would still stick to her.

'I suppose it depends,' Helen said thoughtfully, 'on what you mean by decently. If she were to meet a nice, ordinary man with a steady job who loved her—'

'But she's Lady Charlotte Fitzjames Howard,' Sarah objected. There was no answer to that.

Besides,' Verena said, after a moment, 'where would she meet such a person?'

In America, the aftermath of the Wall Street crash continued to spread. Over the course of 1930, there had been around seven hundred and fifty bank failures, with the loss of millions of dollars in assets, and no government guarantees or Federal Reserve regulations seemed to be able to halt the run. Desperate bankers called in loans that borrowers had not the means to repay; the surviving banks became reluctant to lend, building up their capital reserves instead, and inability to access credit led to more business failures and more bad debts. It was a vicious downward spiral.

The government's attempts to shore up the economy with tariffs only caused retaliatory tariffs from other countries, and world trade started to decline. The troubles were most acutely felt in agricultural areas, with the rapid fall of commodity prices, and in logging and mining areas where, as unemployment rose, there were few other jobs available. Those who kept their jobs were on the whole better off through 1930, as prices fell while wages held steady; but as the credit crisis deepened in 1931, wages began to fall too, and unemployment spread.

In New York there were as yet few obvious signs of the crisis. There was perhaps more rubbish in the gutters, as street cleaners were laid off by City Hall to save money; and the working people going back and forth in the streets looked a little shabbier. There were long queues at the labour exchanges, waiting rooms at employment agencies were full of people seeking positions, and in the newspapers there were more 'job wanted' advertisements than 'position vacant'. But still those who had jobs, and the rich who had not been caught up by the crash, managed to carry on with their lives pretty much as usual.

The areas of commerce that remained buoyant were illegal alcohol, movies and radios. People needed something to keep them cheerful. Even when pennies were pinched, many preferred a couple of hours' distraction in the dark of a movie theatre to new soles for their shoes. Lennie, occupied in two of these trades, was still doing well. The ABO Pictures' *Siren Song* had its opening in January 1931 and was a moderate success. Senior people in ABO believed it was the kind of movie that would grow support as more people saw it, and that the agreeable profit it showed immediately would eventually be handsome. Lennie had already invested in his second talkie, *When the Boys Come Home*, which was now being shot in Hollywood. It was about American wives at home during the war, waiting for their men, and Rose had third lead in it, as the youngest wife, whose husband had left for Germany on the day after their wedding and never come home. The pathos of the part was sure to get her noticed.

Lennie was in talks with ABO about another film, and there was disagreement over what the subject should be. *When the Boys* had been made following the enormous success of *All Quiet on the Western Front* in April 1930, but war films were out of favour now. The trend seemed to be towards movies that frightened: in January there had been *Little Caesar* with Edward G. Robinson, and in February *Dracula* with Béla Lugosi. *The Public Enemy*, with James Cagney, another violent gangster movie, was expected in April, and there was talk around the lots of an adaptation of Mary Shelley's book *Frankenstein* for a fall release.

'Monsters and gangsters, that's all that's selling now,' Al Feinstein, the president of ABO, told the meeting. 'Blood and screams. People wanna be taken out of themselves.'

'But romance does that too,' Lennie objected. 'Look at *City Lights*.' It had come out in January. 'A runaway success. And it was silent, too.'

Feinstein waved his cigar. 'Chaplin,' he dismissed it. 'You can judge a trend by Chaplin. He's always gonna sell.'

'A good story's always going to sell,' Lennie said, patting the script in front of him, *Hills of Autumn*.

'I've read it,' Feinstein said. 'It's not bad. Got a beginning, a middle and an end. Nice weepy closing scene.'

'Why's it *Autumn*, anyway, not *Fall*?' one of the other backers asked.

'It's from an English book,' Lennie said. 'And *Hills of Fall* sounds like a mountaineering accident.'

'But if we're going up against *Frankenstein* and *Dracula* and shoot-'em-up Capone movies,' Feinstein said, slapping his hand down on the table, 'we gotta come up with something punchier than two English kids and a bunch of leaves. We want blood, and lots of it.'

Lennie said, 'How about a movie about a vampire gangster who robs blood banks?'

'Now you're getting it,' said Feinstein, who wasn't really listening. The man next to him, Sidney Vessel, was whispering in his ear. 'Sid here has a great script. Needs a little work. About an English guy – you'll like that, Lennie – who kills hookers in Victorian London.'

'Not *Jack the Ripper*?' said Lennie.

'You've read it?' said Feinstein. 'Have to cut out the hookers, though. Make 'em decent girls, down on their luck. And let's make the Ripper guy a gangster, and set it in present-day Chicago. History's a pip. And the ending's no good: no-one knows who the guy really was? What sort of a story is that? We'll put in a handsome hero who rescues the pretty girl and catches the murderer. Part there for your kid, Lennie,' he threw out carelessly. 'Reckon Rose can scream? Audiences love a pretty girl in jeopardy.'

'But don't you think they'll want a nice romance as a change from all this gore?' Lennie asked desperately. He was pleased that Feinstein wanted to use Rose, but he was afraid screaming might be all she was asked to do, and a serious acting career would go down the drain.

'You win the race riding the horse, not throwing yourself off it,' Feinstein said. 'We're going with the Ripper. Have to change the title, though. *Jack the Ripper* – that's not going to pack 'em in. Think of something that sounds more like gangsters, Sid. Okay, you in, then, Lennie, my boy?'

It was Feinstein's way to ride roughshod over objections and get his way by simply assuming that was how it would be. But Lennie had backed two of his movies and knew him a little better now. He had seen the gleam of calculation in Feinstein's eye. And, though he was not the only backer, he was a big one, and Feinstein needed his money.

'I'm in,' he said, '*if* we make *Autumn* as well.'

There was a pause as he and the boss stared each other out. Lennie did not flinch, and eventually Feinstein shrugged. 'Sure, why not? Most of the action takes place on city streets. We can used the same sets for both and shoot 'em side by side. Like you say, the women'll go for a bit of romance for a change.'

The economy had swung it for Feinstein, Lennie thought. As they went off for lunch, he'd vowed he'd make sure Rose got the acting part, and some other starlet the screaming.

Lennie divided his time between New York and Los Angeles, and since Lizzie had gone home when the baby was a month old, no-one was keeping a day-to-day eye on Polly. She was still living in the Fifth Avenue house, which was far too big for her, but when he tried to persuade her to move into something more convenient, maybe on the Upper West Side where there were nice parks for the baby, she refused, saying it was her home and she was used to it. She was going out a little more now, seeing a few other people. She had been to the theatre with the Margessons, and had lunch with Julie quite regularly. Patrick, who was as fond of little Alexander as if he were his own grandson, visited often, sometimes taking Polly and the baby out for a walk in the park, and asked her to dinner at his apartment from time to time.

But Lennie was still concerned that her life was too confined. It was over a year since Ren's death, and surely she should be coming to terms with it by now and making plans for the future. But she seemed to move about in a dream – not seeming sad so much as absent. Even when he talked to her, her eyes seemed to be focusing on something else. He got the curious feeling she was waiting for something, though he couldn't imagine what.

She adored her child and loved doing things for him; and she would watch him sleeping, sitting by his crib in the rocking chair for hours, rocking herself slowly, her hands in her lap, just gazing at him. At ten months he was big for his age and strong, with sturdy legs. He was already pulling himself up, and chattered constantly to his mother – mostly baby gibberish, but he knew several real words: man, car, ball, drink. And 'up' – pronounced with increasing emphasis, arms lifted, straining towards his mother's shoulder. 'Up. Up. Up!' he would cry, until she lifted him onto her hip.

He would say it to Lennie, too, and with the boy on his hip, his face close to his, Lennie would study him and try to see a likeness in his features. He was fair, like Polly, and Lennie sometimes thought he saw a hint of Ren in his face, but he looked more like Polly than anyone. Perhaps that was appropriate, he thought, since the boy was to be a Morland. Alexander Lennox Morland. Lennie would use all three names ceremonially when he first arrived and said hello. But when they were playing together, he mostly called the boy Alec, and he had noticed lately that Polly was doing the same.

Patrick was planning to rent a small place on Long Island for the summer, in the hope that Polly would bring Alec and they could all have a seaside holiday together. Lennie was all for it, but he cautioned his father against pushing Polly along too quickly. Perhaps, he said, if they just kept talking about the place and gently assuming Polly would be coming, she would come to feel it had been decided and go along with it. Any attempt to get her to decide about anything seemed to result in her sticking her heels in and refusing to budge.

Patrick's work on the Empire State building would be over by summer. The building was finished, ending the Chrysler building's brief reign as tallest in the world – the Empire State at 1,250 feet was comfortably clear. It was to be opened on the 1st of May in a grand ceremony with press and bands and famous people. Al Smith's grandchildren were to cut the ribbon, and President Hoover would be switching on all the lights from Washington with a special button. The tower had already captured imaginations: there were articles galore in the papers and magazines, and everyone wanted to visit the observation deck on the eighty-sixth floor. Whether, with, the economic outlook so gloomy, anyone would want to rent the office accommodation was another matter.

'I'm afraid it's in danger of being dubbed the "Empty State building",' Patrick said to Lennie.

'Well, that's not your fault. And it is a beautiful thing. A real symbol of what man can achieve in this modern age, when he reaches for the stars.'

Patrick smiled at his enthusiasm. Lennie had been devoted to the tower ever since he had taken him for a special trip to the deck on the hundred-and-second floor. 'It lifts us a little closer to them, perhaps,' he said. 'And the outlook from the top is certainly spectacular. Maybe what we lose in rentals we can make from tourists riding up for the view.'

April brought Hyde Park to life, and the softer weather enticed Violet out often to walk there, to enjoy the new leaves unfurling, the spring flowers, the ducks crowding on to the waters. She had settled into the little house, and after one or two mismatches had got a maid-of-all-work who suited her. Mrs Drayton called herself a cook-general, which gave her a lot more dignity and a 'handle' to her name, but she could certainly cook, and did a fair amount of the other work. The first two girls had been slovens and their cooking abysmal. Violet had discovered, though, that one woman couldn't do everything. She herself had taken over the dusting and polishing the silver. The boys and Charlotte all made their own beds and kept their rooms tidy, Henry did the boots and the older boys carried up coals. They sent the heavy washing out, and Mrs Drayton was quite obliging about washing other things when she had time, but Charlotte had to help with it, and she did most of the ironing, while Violet had been forced to take up the needle again. She had never realised quite how quickly male creatures went through the heels of their socks.

It had been hard for her to adjust to the new life, and often in bed she wept over the state of her hands and, even more often, at the memory of Charlotte at the scullery sink wringing out stockings. But once she had got past the shock of it, she found there was a satisfaction in doing things about the house. When she had tidied and dusted the drawing-room, she could stand back and enjoy the result, where before she had taken it for granted, and only noticed if something was amiss.

It had been easier for the boys, having come to this from university and not from the cushioned palace of their child-hood. Now that there was enough hot water and a bath, and the meals at home were edible, Robert was content, and was enjoying the publishing world. He even had hopes of being promoted. Richard was just the same happy-go-lucky crea-ture, whether he was flush on commission or lean in the pocket from not having sold anything for a week. Whatever his finances, he was out in the evening more often than not, coming in late and shiny-eyed, having danced the night away at a variety of exciting venues in the West End. When Robert asked him how he could afford it, he only grinned and said, 'The girls are always willing to pay if you make 'em laugh.' That, Robert understood, was not for their mother's ears. She still tried to maintain strict standards in spite of every-thing, and was always berating Richard for whistling the latest popular tune.

They had found a decent school just a few streets away for Henry, who had settled in and got on well with his fellow pupils, being a friendly boy with an enquiring mind and an interest in almost everything. The one friction in his life was not being allowed to go home to tea with his friends, which

Violet forbade because she could not reciprocate. She did not want curious questions asked about their situation. Start having the boys home, and the next thing the mothers would want to call.

It was Charlotte she worried about most. On the surface, she had adapted as well as anyone, helped out around the house without complaint, went to the shops when there was something they could not get delivered – she even prided herself on getting bargains, and told her mother she could do the shopping cheaper if Violet would let her do it all, instead of having it delivered. But Violet balked at that. Bad enough having Charlotte slip out for eggs because Mrs Drayton had run out, but to have her out every day plodding from shop to shop like a drudge . . .

For entertainment Charlotte read, played games with the boys, walked with her mother, and now and then Richard would find time in his busy evening life to take her to 'the pictures' – though Violet was convinced she would pick up a flea at the cinema. When Richard quizzed her as to why Charlotte would when *he* didn't, Violet couldn't answer. It was illogical, but a bone-deep prejudice. Ladies did not frequent cinemas. But then ladies did not travel on buses or tube trains, and they had had to do both lately.

When the Season began again, Violet worried even more. Charlotte would be nineteen in May, and she ought to be going to parties and dances and meeting nice young men. All she had had was one truncated Season. They didn't get invitations any more, and Violet would not have her going to public dance halls, even if Richard accompanied her. But what would become of her? They knew now that there was no more money and never would be. They were going to have to live like this for ever. When Robert came home in the evening with a newspaper, she tried to make sure Charlotte didn't see the social pages with their reminders of a life she no longer had. She thought guiltily about Laidislaw's

648

pictures. Perhaps if she sold some of them, she would have enough money to give dinners, then if Robert and Richard had made any suitable friends they could bring them home. Perhaps someone in publishing wouldn't be too bad – it was a gentlemanly business, after all.

The resumption of the Season had disturbed Violet – she had grown used to her new life through the winter, and had felt a sort of peaceful numbness towards the future. But now spring was bringing her painfully to life. She found herself secretly scouring the newspapers for news and photographs of people she knew. There was the odd mention here and there. She had seen a notice back in November about the deaths of Lord and Lady Tunstead – Avis Fellowes's adventurous brother and sister-in-law – in a motoring accident in the Alps; at the beginning of May she saw the name of Lord Tunstead mentioned at an embassy dinner, and realised it must mean Avis, who was obviously out of mourning. She hoped he was over the loss, and wished him well.

It was only a few days later that she was crossing the hall on her way upstairs when the doorbell rang. She had just that moment left Mrs Drayton on her knees scrubbing the kitchen floor so she called down the kitchen stairs, 'I'll go, Mrs Drayton.'

She opened the door and there was Avis Fellowes himself, a motor-car at the kerb behind him. He swept off his hat, and Violet blushed violently at being caught opening her own door.

'I hope I'm not disturbing you?' he said. 'I know it's rather impertinent of me to call like this, but I was actually passing right by and felt I couldn't miss the opportunity. If it's inconvenient I'll go away again.'

'No, it's – I'm – it's quite convenient,' Violet stammered, and then managed to collect herself. 'Won't you come in?'

Once he was in, she was at a loss to know what to do with him. Visitors had always appeared in the drawing-room ready undressed, accompanied by a servant who then knew to bring the refreshments of the hour. She supposed she must take his coat and hat herself, if he was staying – and she hoped he was. Unnerved though she was to have been both discovered and caught out, she wanted him to stay.

'Will you have tea?' she asked.

'I'd like that,' he said.

'Let me – take your coat,' she said, and on her lips it sounded the oddest thing she had ever said. He took off his own coat and gave it to her with his hat, and then she realised she would have to go down to the kitchen to ask for tea, for if she rang, Mrs Drayton wouldn't know what she was ringing for. Encumbered by his coat and hat she looked around for somewhere to put them, and he saw her difficulty and took them away again, and said, 'Perhaps on this chair.'

'I won't be a moment,' she said, blushing again, whisked down the stairs to hiss an urgent entreaty to Mrs Drayton, and up again to say as graciously as she could, 'This way, please. The drawing-room is upstairs.'

Charlotte wasn't there – she must have gone to her room – and Violet was glad. She took a chair and Avis sat on the sofa, and at the same instant they both said, 'How are you?'

Avis said, 'You first. How are you, Lady Holkam? It's been such a long time.'

'I'm quite well, thank you. I was sorry to read of your brother's death in the newspaper. It must have been a shock to you.'

'It was a tragedy,' he said, 'and a terrible shock to my father. He has become quite frail since the accident. It wasn't so much of a shock to me – Reggie's been doing mad things for years now. We always said he'd kill himself one day – but, of course, one says such things lightly and doesn't expect them to happen.'

'Of course not.'

'I've been in Derbyshire all winter, trying to get everything straightened out. Reggie never really took an interest in that side of things, and Papa's agent is as old as he is, and let things get in a fine muddle.'

'I'm sure your father is glad to have you,' she said warmly.

'I don't know. He always loved Reggie best. I don't think he really noticed me much.' He shrugged. 'And you – I'm so sorry about Lord Holkam.'

'I received your letter of condolence,' she said. 'I'm sorry I was not able to reply.'

'I didn't expect a reply. Are you – coming to terms with it?'

'Yes,' she said. There didn't seem much else to say, and she didn't want to talk about Holkam. 'How did you find me here?'

'I met your cousin Overton in the House the other day – I'd gone to pick up some papers for my father – and naturally I asked after you. He told me you were settled here, and kindly said he thought you'd welcome a visit.'

'I'm glad to see you,' she said. 'Are you in Town for long?'

'I have to go back down to Derbyshire tomorrow,' he said, causing her a pang. Then he went on, 'But I shall be up again next week. I mean to stay up for the rest of the Season. So many invitations – it's nice to know one wasn't forgotten.'

'And I suppose, now you're next in line, you will be looking for a wife,' Violet said, trying for lightness. 'All the heirs seem to be marrying American millionaires' daughters these days. You'll have to be quick, before they're all gone.'

'Fortunately, there seems to be an endless supply,' he said, equally lightly. 'And I'm in no hurry.'

Mrs Drayton came in just then with a tea tray and a smut on her nose, and threw Violet into confusion again. There was no cake in the house, so she had cut bread and butter, and put on a dish of jam. The meagreness of it all shamed Violet – and the jam was boughten.

But Lord Tunstead ate bread and butter with relish, and

praised Fifi for her good manners in not begging. 'Not like Lady Paget's terrier – he has his feet in the jam before you can say knife.' He chatted to Violet about London, the Season, common acquaintances and the weather, and put her so much at her ease that she didn't notice the time pass. At the end of half an hour, he rose to take his leave.

'I was wondering,' he said. 'We're having such a spell of fine weather, might I be permitted to take you and your daughter for a spin in the motor-car tomorrow? If you are free in the afternoon, we could perhaps find somewhere agreeable by the river for tea.'

Violet accepted happily for both, glad that he had included Charlotte, and did not think it necessary to mention that she was free every afternoon – and the mornings, too.

It was the first of several outings, and Violet was glad to see Avis taking the trouble to bring Charlotte out of her shell. Of course, they had been good friends in New York, so it was not hard to revive that ease between them. Violet did have a passing and rather painful thought that perhaps he was interested in Charlotte as a potential wife; but when her head cleared she saw it was not that kind of interest. Coming back from one of these trips one day they were late enough to find Henry in the hall, idling about rather disconsolately, and his rapturous greeting of Avis produced an invitation for all four of them to go out for a spin on the Saturday to a place on the river that had a steam museum.

When she was showing him out, Violet said, 'You didn't need to trouble with the museum – he'd have been happy just for a motor-car drive.'

'Oh, I shall enjoy that myself. But, in case you ladies are bored, will you permit me to bring another gentleman along to keep you amused with conversation while Henry and I discuss pistons and valves?'

He seemed pleased with himself, and Violet knew she

could trust him to bring someone who would not embarrass her, so she assented.

At the appointed time on the Saturday, the bell rang, and Henry beat Charlotte to the door. Violet joined them, to see Avis outside on the step, chatting to the excited Henry about his motor. Charlotte seemed rather white and, surprised, Violet looked past her to see a man just getting out of Avis's car, his hand going up to his hat. It was Rupert Amesbury.

Avis and Violet strolled along the riverbank, allowing the youngsters to get further ahead. Amesbury was explaining something to Henry with expansive gestures, and presumably being very funny about it, for Charlotte was laughing helplessly. Fifi ran between the two groups trying to urge them together like a sheepdog.

'I met him at the embassy reception,' Avis said. 'He'd been abroad. It seems that he was sent to Washington just after you disappeared so suddenly in the middle of the Season. He had no idea where you'd gone and, with the sudden posting, had no chance to find out. We got chatting and he asked after you and Charlotte. He sounded so wistful, poor chap, that I felt I ought to do something about it. I had the idea last year she was quite taken with young Amesbury.'

'She was. But she thought she'd never see him again.'

He nodded. 'He was so obviously keen I thought the best thing to do was to throw them together and let nature take its course. I hope you don't think I did wrong?'

'No,' she said, though she sounded doubtful. 'As long as he's serious. I should hate her to have her heart broken.'

He didn't pretend not to understand her. 'He knows about the bankruptcy, but as he's accepted the invitation we must assume he doesn't mind about it. His parents are both dead, which makes things easier, perhaps. He's in a position, at any rate, to make up his own mind.'

They walked on. Henry had run ahead and was throwing

653

a stick for Fifi, and the young people were strolling with their heads together, deep in conversation. It looked promising. Perhaps nothing would come of it, but at least Charlotte had seen him again and had her chance to shine. She was looking happier than she had in almost a year.

Avis was watching Violet's face. 'Spring is a wonderful thing, don't you think?' he said. She looked up enquiringly. 'A time of renewal, and fresh starts and new possibilities.'

Jessie had watched with concern as James flagged under the weight of responsibility. His gay insouciance, his upright, eager walk had changed to bowed shoulders, a frown half puzzled, half dismayed, and a faint air of unkemptness. Since Christmas he had had no more large parties, and seemed genuinely to be trying to economise, but it was not in his nature, and it bent him out of shape. Jessie could see he tried conscientiously to take his father's place, but his own inabilities drove him to frustration, and his outlet was to jump on his motorbike and tear off, roaring round the narrow lanes at breakneck speed until the desperation had subsided for a time.

Jessie had done what she could to keep things going, helping Amy to run the house, trying to keep some sense of normality in place for the servants and the children. With no hostess duties to distract her, Amy was clearly feeling the uncertainty about her own future, and was growing thin and pale. If Morland Place went, where would she go? She might have enough to live on in a frugal way, but she had given her heart now to the house and its people, and would pine without them.

Miss Husthwaite had become Mrs Julian in January and they had moved out to the cottage in Fulton, but though she no longer took a salary, she came over several times a week to try to help James through the paperwork. His economies had not gone far. There were several elderly servants who did not really have a proper job but had been kept on by Teddy because they had nowhere else to go. He couldn't get rid of them, any more than he could ask his cousins to move out and look after themselves. He managed to sell some of the horses, and looked to see if there were any rents he could raise. The factories were just about profitable, though what would happen when the present contracts ran out was unsure. Makepeace's in York was breaking even, but the other two, in Leeds and Manchester, were losing money, and he did not know what to do about that. And commodity prices were falling here as well as in America. Milk and beef were bringing in less, and the next harvest would suffer from falling cereal prices.

When the probate finally went through and the bill for the death duties came in, James could think of no response but to go out and get dead drunk. It had to be paid before any part of the estate could be sold, and to pay it he would have to take out a loan, which would add further to the debts. His instinct was always to put off bad things, and there was a six-month period of grace before the bill had to be paid. He went about after that like a sleepwalker, part of him worried to death, part of him hoping against hope that something would turn up.

In desperation, her heart aching for him, Jessie wrote to Polly, explaining the situation.

I don't know if there is anything you can do for him. One always imagines that everyone in America is rich, despite the terrible crash, but I do remember Lizzie saying when you married that your husband was a very wealthy man. Even a loan could make a difference – bank rates are ruinous, these days. I know your life is over there now, but Morland Place was your home from childhood, and I know you must love it. It would be terrible if it had to be sold to strangers. My greatest fear is that, even if the old house itself and the immediate land could be kept, James may feel so broken by the whole business that he'll lose the heart to fight for it, and just let it go. For Morland Place to pass out of Morland hands after all these hundreds of years would be quite terrible.

Dear Polly, if you *can* do anything, I beg you won't delay. As I'm sure the lawyers have written to tell you, your father left you a number of things – pictures and furniture and so on – and you could make them the excuse to come over and see how things lie. We would all so love to see you again, and the dear little baby. Even if you can't help, do come, just to see us. And to see Morland Place. It might be your last chance.

Polly read the letter, sitting on the window-seat. *Morland Place to pass out of Morland hands?* No, that mustn't be. What was James thinking of? Wouldn't fight for it? If Papa had left it to *her*, she would have fought to her last drop of blood. Why was he so poor-spirited? And it might be her last chance? That made her go cold. She had missed the last chance to see her father, wrapped up as she had been in her own troubles. That had been bad enough. But Morland Place – that was more than people, more than all of them. It was home and family and history, and a piece of England that was almost holy in her mind. For it to go was more than a tragedy: it was sacrilege.

She looked up, looked around her in a sort of bewilderment, for she had been thinking about it so intensely she had felt herself there, and for a moment she didn't know where she was. *Your life is over there now.* But was it? What was she doing here, living in this too-big house all alone, drifting from day to day with nothing to do, and nothing ahead of her but more of the same? What future was there for Alec here? Money they had, all right, plenty of it, but what was money beside land? And what was any land beside your *own* land, the land your forefathers had nurtured and fought for and died for? Five hundred years of Morlands at Morland Place: their bones were buried in the crypt under the chapel, where she had always assumed, in her childhood's innocence, hers would one day lie.

'I must go home,' she said, and hearing it aloud, it seemed like the right, the obvious, thing to do. Home, to Morland Place, to the green rolling spaces of Yorkshire, which fitted into her heart as perfectly as a dove fits into its nest. She felt she had been in a strange dream, one of those enchantments of magic smoke you get in fairy tales – only in her case the smoke had been the heady glamour of New York. But even in her enchanted sleep, she had called her baby Alexander Morland, as if she had always known this moment would come.

'I'm going home,' she said. Yes, even Ren had foreknown this necessity, for why else had he deposited a large sum of gold in London? She would use it to rescue Morland Place, and if James would let her, she would live out her days there, working for the estate, taking care of the house, keeping the legacy alive, raising her child a Morland.

Now she was longing for the fields and hills and trees and the grey stones, like a thirsty man for water. She wanted to ride, ride, over Morland land, with the sweet damp wind on her face, and see the twilight mist come up from the fields, and hear the distant curlew and the sweet, plangent robin's call.

Outside, the traffic idled up Fifth Avenue, and people went by on the pavement head down, hurrying, as if every one was on urgent business. Across the road was Central Park, a green space, but on the far side of it the apartment blocks rose like concrete cliffs. New York had been good to her, and she had been happy, much of the time. But looking back, she saw that it was Erich who had broken the spell, a ghost from the Old World coming to call her home. He had been the unfinished business from which she had fled to the New World; but now the circle had been completed, the accounts were squared, and it was time to go.

She went and found pen and paper, and sitting in the window-seat, one foot tucked up under her, she wrote, 'Dear Jessie, I'm coming home . . .'

Polly took James's horse Cymbal, bridled her and, not bothering with a saddle, mounted from the block and clattered out over the drawbridge. She rode hard and fast, driven by a feeling that was half elation, half bewilderment; Cymbal, glad to be out after a whole day in the stables, went like the wind, with her tail kinked and her ears thrust forward. Polly let her go, hardly noticing where they went. Her need just now was for speed. She leaned over the neck and swayed with the movement.

The mare finally slowed and dropped into a walk, her sides heaving, and gave two or three tremendous sneezes that almost shook Polly loose. She pushed the hair from her eyes, took note of her surroundings, and guided the mare's steps along a series of paths that she knew as well as the lines on her palm, towards the higher ground, and there she stopped, between the War Memorial and what had always been called the Mares' Field. The sun was going down, big and red, and she turned Cymbal to face it, turned into the little westerly airs that brought the damp smell of sunset across the fields.

It was done. She had signed the papers, James had signed, witnesses had signed, and it was done. For weeks the lawyers had talked, argued, given their grave warnings and extensive caveats, but through it all James had not wavered. It was what he wanted; and since it was what Polly wanted too, what more was there to say?

She had hardly recognised her half-brother when she first set eyes on him, at the end of her long journey – he had been just a boy when she went away – but she would have known him anywhere. Afterwards it came to her that they looked very alike, and that was why he seemed so familiar. It was an odd thought. She wondered whether Alec would grow up to look like James. She hoped so.

James's face had lit with delight as he welcomed her, and the tired baby had gone to him with a naturalness that made her know he was good with animals. Everyone had welcomed her so warmly, she felt almost ashamed, because she had not deserved it. Jessie's hugs and the children's excitement, and dear old Sawry and Mrs Stark trying not to cry, and the dogs battering round her knees just as they always, always had when she was a girl and Papa was here and the world was young and safe . . .

It had been strange to meet Amy at last – strange and embarrassing to begin with, for she could not help thinking of this youngish woman in her father's arms. She thought she saw the same awareness in Amy's eyes, and the two of them had blushed at the same moment; and then Polly had felt ashamed of having been so cold-hearted and ungenerous about something that had given her father happiness. She saw now that this was no harpy, but an ordinary, kind, good woman, rather sad and tired, whom she could have liked if she had met her in other circumstances; and she saw, with a pang, the hungry way Amy looked at the baby, and remembered she had lost her own son. So on an impulse she had placed Alec into Amy's arms and whispered, 'I'm sorry.' And she saw tears come to Amy's eyes, and knew that it would be all right between them after that. Not easy, not yet for a while, but all right.

But it was James who had been most eager for her. Over the next few days, as he rode with her round the estate and told her his troubles, she had seen his bowed young shoulders straighten like grass when the foot is lifted. He talked and talked, and out of it all, as gently and naturally as a flower opening, the idea had grown. She had proposed somehow to lend him the money to pay the death duties, but the new idea when it finally bloomed seemed as right to her as it did to him. He wanted her to buy the estate from him.

Of course there had to be argument: it was his inheritance, he was the heir, he could not just give it away, he would part with it now only to regret it – and so on, and so on. But even while she tried to change his mind, she knew that it was right, and that he knew it too.

'I always thought about being master one day,' he said, 'but somehow it was Morland Place as it was with Dad alive. Without him . . . I don't want it, Polly. I don't want the responsibility. I'm not fit for it. The thought of facing up to it for the rest of my life . . . I want to travel. There's so much to see, and I want to see it all! I want to be free to roam where I want, and stop a little, and go on, without anyone to please but myself.'

'But one day you'll want to come home.'

'I expect so. And I hope you'll let me come and visit. Maybe settle down one day in a little cottage out on the moor. That's all. I love Morland Place, and I'll come back, but not as master.' He hesitated, and said, half ashamed of talking nonsense, 'It wants to let me go, Polly. It knows I'm not the one.'

The swollen sun had slid below the horizon now, and the furnace glow along the edge of the world was cooling, fading to pink. The blue in the sky was seeping away, leaving it greenish, shading into yellow towards the west. The mare sighed and shifted her weight from one hock to the other.

It had been a tougher job to persuade the rest of the family, and the lawyers; but now they were standing together, and of the same mind, they knew they would not be shaken.

660

Polly's wealth was more than equal to redeeming the estate without selling anything, and that brought Jessie on to her side. For the Morland estate not to be broken up . . . it was why she had written to Polly in the first place, in the hope that gold from the New World might save this little piece of the Old World.

Finally James had drawn himself up in dignity and they had seen he would have his way. And he had picked up Alec from Polly's lap and held him against his shoulder, like a king showing his heir to his people. Polly could see the same thought was in everyone's mind that was in hers. Why else had she called her boy Alexander Morland? It had been Fate, guiding her hand.

So the cautious lawyers had crept to the same conclusion that Polly and James had reached two months earlier, and at last the papers were all drawn up, bank drafts written out, signatures attached and witnessed. And Morland Place was hers.

Dusk was coming up, breathing out of the ground like smoke, and the unearthly stillness of a country twilight spread out under the fading sky. In the paddock the grazing mares had wandered to the fence and stood quietly looking at her, flicking their ears back and forth, uneasy in the strange half-light, wondering if she had come to take them home.

Morland Place was hers, and with it the lives and security of so many people, not just the servants and tenants and workers but the dependants, the cousins, Amy, the children in the nursery. She had told everyone they could stay on, and that she would not change things, and she had seen the relief in every face. No, she would not change things; though as she had signed her name, her mind had raced with plans for improvements: the house, the farms, the shops, the factories – she would make it all work, build up the estate and the fortune for Alec, who would be master one day. She had so many ideas . . .

661

But now, as the last pinkness at the rim of the world faded, and she smelt the warm, damp sweetness of the earth on the summer-night air, her mind was quiet, and she let it stretch out, spreading dark, soft wings to carry her over the fields and woods and becks she knew so well, her thoughts streaming over the place she had grown up in. She had travelled a long road, and come back, and now she would never have to leave again. Morland Place was hers; but she understood in that moment that she belonged to it far more than it would ever belong to her.

The mare stirred, wanting to be going, not standing here in the encroaching dark, wanting her stable. The trees were sharp black shapes against the last pastel of the sky, and looking down the slope, Polly saw yellow squares appear where the lamps had been lit at the great gate to guide her home. She discovered her bare legs were damp with dew, a feeling so familiar to her from her childhood it made her smile.

She turned the mare, and they jogged down the hill towards warmth, light and supper.